THE CAMBRIDGE EDITION
OF THE WORKS OF

JANE AUSTEN

MANSFIELD PARK

Cambridge University Press and the General Editor
Janet Todd wish to express their gratitude to the
University of Glasgow and the University of Aberdeen for
providing funding towards the creation of this edition.
Their generosity made possible the employment of
Antje Blank as research assistant throughout the project.

THE CAMBRIDGE EDITION
OF THE WORKS OF

JANE AUSTEN

GENERAL EDITOR: Janet Todd, University of Aberdeen

VOLUMES IN THIS SERIES:
Juvenilia edited by Peter Sabor
Northanger Abbey edited by Barbara Benedict with Deirdre Le Faye
Sense and Sensibility edited by Edward Copeland
Pride and Prejudice edited by Pat Rogers
Mansfield Park edited by John Wiltshire
Emma edited by Richard Cronin and Dorothy McMillan
Persuasion edited by Janet Todd and Antje Blank
Later Manuscripts edited by Brian Southam
Jane Austen in Context edited by Janet Todd

Frontispiece: 'Fitting out Mastr Willm Blockhead HM Ship Hellfire, West India Station' (1835). Caricature in aquatint by George Cruikshank, reproduced by permission of the National Maritime Museum, Greenwich.

JANE AUSTEN

MANSFIELD PARK

Edited by
John Wiltshire

CAMBRIDGE
UNIVERSITY PRESS

CAMBRIDGE UNIVERSITY PRESS
Cambridge, New York, Melbourne, Madrid, Cape Town, Singapore, São Paulo

Cambridge University Press
The Edinburgh Building, Cambridge CB2 2RU, UK

Published in the United States of America by
Cambridge University Press, New York

www.cambridge.org
Information on this title: www.cambridge.org/9780521827652

First published 2005

Printed in the United Kingdom at the University Press, Cambridge

A catalogue record for this book is available from the British Library

Library of Congress Cataloguing in Publication data
Austen, Jane, 1775–1817.
Mansfield Park / edited by John Wiltshire.
p.   cm. – (The Cambridge edition of the works of Jane Austen)
ISBN-13: 978-0-521-82765-2
ISBN-10: 0-521-82765-5
1. Young women – Fiction.   2. Children of the rich – Fiction.   3. Social classes –
Fiction.   4. Country homes – Fiction.   5. Adoptees – Fiction.   6. Cousins –
Fiction.   7. England – Fiction.   8. Uncles – Fiction.   I. Wiltshire, John.
II. Title.   III. Series.
PR4034.M3   2005
823′.7 – dc22   2005006336

ISBN-13   978-0-521-82765-2   hardback
ISBN-10   0-521-82765-5   hardback

CONTENTS

GENERAL EDITOR'S PREFACE

Jane Austen wrote to be read and reread. '[A]n artist cannot do anything slovenly,' she remarked to her sister Cassandra. Her subtle, crafted novels repay close and repeated attention to vocabulary, syntax and punctuation as much as to irony and allusion; yet the reader can take immediate and intense delight in their plots and characters. As a result Austen has a unique status among early English novelists – appreciated by the academy and the general public alike. What Henry Crawford remarks about Shakespeare in *Mansfield Park* has become equally true of its author: she 'is a part of an Englishman's constitution. [Her] thoughts and beauties are so spread abroad that one touches them every where, one is intimate with [her] by instinct.' This edition of the complete oeuvre of the published novels and manuscript works is testament to Austen's exceptional cultural and literary position. As well as attempting to establish an accurate and authoritative text, it provides a full contextual placing of the novels.

The editing of any canonical writer is a practice which has been guided by many conflicting ideologies. In the early twentieth century, editors, often working alone, largely agreed that they were producing definitive editions, although they used eclectic methods and often revised the text at will. Later in the century, fidelity to the author's creative intentions was paramount, and the emphasis switched to devising an edition that would as far as possible represent the final authorial wishes. By the 1980s, however, the pursuit of the single perfected text had given gave way to the recording of multiple intentions of equal interest. Authors were seen to have changed, revised or recanted, or indeed to have directed various versions of their work towards different audiences. Consequently all states had validity and the text became a process rather than a fixed entity. With this approach came emphasis on the print culture in which the text appeared as well as on the social implications of authorship. Rather than being stages in the evolution of a single work, the various versions existed in their own right, all having something to tell.

The Cambridge edition describes fully Austen's early publishing history and provides details of composition, publication and publishers as well as printers and compositors where known. It accepts that many of the decisions concerning spelling, punctuation, capitalising, italicising and paragraphing may well have been the compositors' rather than Austen's but that others may represent the author's own chosen style. For the novels published in Jane Austen's lifetime the edition takes as its copytext the latest edition to which she might plausibly have made some contribution: that is, the first editions of *Pride and Prejudice* and *Emma* and the second editions of *Sense and Sensibility* and *Mansfield Park*. Where a second edition is used, all substantive and accidental changes between editions are shown on the page so that the reader can reconstruct the first edition, and the dominance of either first or second editions is avoided. For the two novels published posthumously together, *Northanger Abbey* and *Persuasion*, the copytext is the first published edition.

Our texts as printed here remain as close to the copytexts as possible: spelling and punctuation have not been modernised and inconsistencies in presentation have not been regularised. The few corrections and emendations made to the texts – beyond replacing dropped or missing letters – occur only when an error is very obvious indeed, and/or where retention might interrupt reading or understanding: for example, missing quotation marks have been supplied, run-on words have been separated and repeated words excised. All changes to the texts, substantive and accidental, have been noted in the final apparatus. Four of the six novels appeared individually in three volumes; we have kept the volume divisions and numbering. In the case of *Persuasion*, which was first published as volumes 3 and 4 of a four-volume set including *Northanger Abbey*, the volume division has been retained but volumes 3 and 4 have been relabeled volumes 1 and 2.

For all these novels the copytext has been set against two other copies of the same edition. Where there have been any substantive differences, further copies have been examined; details of these copies are given in the initial textual notes within each volume, along with information about the printing and publishing context of this particular work. The two volumes of the edition devoted to manuscript writings divide the works between the three juvenile notebooks on the one hand and all the remaining manuscript writings on the other. The juvenile notebooks and *Lady Susan* have some resemblance to the published works, being fair copies and following some of the conventions of publishing. The other manuscript writings consist in part of fictional works in early drafts, burlesques and autograph and allograph copies of occasional verses and prayers. The possible dating of the manuscript work, as well as the method of editing, is considered in the introductions to the relevant volumes. The cancelled chapters of *Persuasion* are included in an appendix to the volume *Persuasion*; they appear both in a transliteration and in facsimile. For all the manuscript works, their features as manuscripts have been respected and all changes and erasures either reproduced or noted.

In all the volumes superscript numbers in the texts indicate endnotes. Throughout the edition we have provided full annotations to give clear and informative historical and cultural information to the modern reader while largely avoiding critical speculation; we have also indicated words which no longer have currency or have altered in meaning in some way. The introductions give information concerning the genesis and immediate public reception of the text; they also indicate the most significant stylistic and generic features. A chronology of Austen's life appears in each volume. More information about the life, Austen's reading, her relationship to publication, the print history of the novels and their critical reception through the centuries, as well as the historical, political, intellectual and religious context in which she wrote is available in the final volume of the edition: *Jane Austen in Context*.

I would like to thank Cambridge University Library for supplying the copytexts for the six novels. I am most grateful to Linda Bree at Cambridge University Press for her constant support and unflagging enthusiasm for the edition and to Maartje Scheltens and Alison Powell for their help at every stage of production. I owe the greatest debt to my research assistant Antje Blank for her rare combination of scholarly dedication, editorial skills and critical discernment.

Janet Todd
University of Aberdeen

ACKNOWLEDGEMENTS

Work on this edition of *Mansfield Park* was supported by an Australian Research Council Discovery Grant during 2003–4. I wish to thank the Council for awarding me the grant and the anonymous referees who supported my application. Research was carried out at the La Trobe University Library; the Rare Books room at Fisher Library, University of Sydney; the State Library of Victoria; the Shakespeare Memorial Trust Library, Stratford-upon-Avon; the City of Portsmouth Municipal Library; the Bodleian, Oxford; the University Library, Cambridge; the British Library, London; and at Stoneleigh Abbey, Warwickshire. I thank the staff and librarians at these institutions for their readiness to help, and especially Peggy Cochrane and Sharon Karasmanis of the Interlibrary Loans section of La Trobe University Library.

Professor Kathryn Sutherland was generous with her time and gave me some vital clues at the beginning of the whole enterprise. I also want to thank Professor Jocelyn Harris for reassurance, advice and comradeship at this stage, as well as much later. The archivist of John Murray Ltd, Mrs Vanessa Murray, kindly sent me photocopies of documents concerning *Mansfield Park* in the Murray files. In embarking on this project, I had the benefit of advice from Professor Clive Probyn and Dr Bruce Steele.

I've always known that my work was supported by the Faculty of Social Sciences and Humanities at La Trobe. I'm lucky, too, to have worked in a friendly and encouraging department and I thank my colleagues for putting up with my endless pestering for obscure pieces of information. My friends Ann Blake, Stephen Clarke, Rachel and Denis Gibbs, Ann Newton, David Rawlinson,

Judith Richards, Bryan Reid and Carl Stanyon have also been called upon, as have Jon Spence, and David Fraser of the Derby Museum and Art Gallery. I'm especially grateful to Linda Bree, my editor at Cambridge University Press, and my colleague Iain Topliss, for their comments on my Notes, and to Brian Southam for putting me onto material I would otherwise have missed. I have found in *Jane Austen and the Navy* a valuable resource.

I reported on work in progress to the Sydney-based Jane Austen Society of Australia, and to the Jane Austen Society of Melbourne. I should like to thank Susannah Fullerton, Fay Jones and Andrea Richards, the Presidents of the two societies, for arranging these meetings, and the members for their questions, as well as their willingness to act as informal research assistants. My greatest indebtedness however is to Laura Carroll and Brian Lloyd, my research associates at La Trobe University. Laura worked on the Notes with exemplary care and perceptiveness, and contributed important new information. The note on *Lovers' Vows* in this edition is her work. Dr Lloyd was in charge of the text, and collated the variants over a long period with great good-humour. I'm grateful also to my niece, Helen Moreno, who found invaluable material in the British Library.

The latter period of work on this volume has been carried out in rather difficult circumstances, and could not have been completed at all without our children, Ruth and John, and my sisters, Marie Eddy and Roseann Moreno, as well as Judy Goldberg, helping to provide time for me. During these last stages I have read the text aloud several times over with my wife Zaiga, whose memory of her earlier readings of Jane Austen is so vivid that she has raised questions and suggested connections which have decidedly improved this edition. Our collaboration on this has been a great pleasure.

Copy-editing benefited greatly from the assistance of Laura Carroll and Daniel Vuillermin in Melbourne. I thank them, and my copy-editor in Cambridge, Caroline Howlett, for the care they took over a complex task. Laura and Daniel, together with Max Richards, formed a wonderful proofreading team in Melbourne. I should also like to thank the General Editor of the Cambridge Edition of the Works of Jane Austen, Professor Jan Todd, Dr Antje Blank, her research assistant, and the Press's Editor, Dr Linda Bree, for their intellectual comradeship and encouragement over the long period we have been working together.

I cannot omit a formal acknowledgement to those previous Jane Austen scholars, foremost among them R. W. Chapman, Jan Fergus, David Gilson, Deirdre Le Faye, Brian Southam and Kathryn Sutherland, without whose work this edition could most certainly not have been undertaken or completed.

CHRONOLOGY

DEIRDRE LE FAYE

1764
26 April   Marriage of Revd George Austen, rector of
Steventon, and Cassandra Leigh; they go to live at
Deane, Hampshire, and their first three children –
James (1765), George (1766) and Edward (1767) –
are born here.

1768
Summer   The Austen family move to Steventon, Hampshire.
Five more children – Henry (1771), Cassandra
(1773), Francis (1774), Jane (1775), Charles (1779) –
are born here.

1773
23 March   Mr Austen becomes Rector of Deane as well as
Steventon, and takes pupils at Steventon from now
until 1796.

1775
16 December   Jane Austen born at Steventon.

1781
Winter   JA's cousin, Eliza Hancock, marries Jean-François
Capot de Feuillide, in France.

1782
     First mention of JA in family tradition, and the first
of the family's amateur theatrical productions takes
place.

1783
     JA's third brother, Edward, is adopted by Mr and
Mrs Thomas Knight II, and starts to spend time with

them at Godmersham in Kent.
JA, with her sister Cassandra and cousin
Jane Cooper, stays for some months in Oxford
and then Southampton, with kinswoman
Mrs Cawley.

1785
Spring   JA and Cassandra go to the Abbey House School in
              Reading.

1786
              Edward sets off for his Grand Tour of Europe, and
              does not return until autumn 1790.

April   JA's fifth brother, Francis, enters the Royal Naval
              Academy in Portsmouth.

December   JA and Cassandra have left school and are at home
              again in Steventon. Between now and 1793 JA writes
              her three volumes of *Juvenilia*.

1788
Summer   Mr and Mrs Austen take JA and Cassandra on a trip
              to Kent and London.

December   Francis leaves the RN Academy and sails to East
              Indies; does not return until winter 1793.

1791
July   JA's sixth and youngest brother, Charles, enters the
              Royal Naval Academy in Portsmouth.

27 December   Edward Austen marries Elizabeth Bridges, and they
              live at Rowling in Kent.

1792
27 March   JA's eldest brother, James, marries Anne Mathew;
              they live at Deane.

?Winter   Cassandra becomes engaged to Revd Tom Fowle.

1793

23 January	Edward Austen's first child, Fanny, is born at Rowling.
1 February	Republican France declares war on Great Britain and Holland.
8 April	JA's fourth brother, Henry, becomes a lieutenant in the Oxfordshire Militia.
15 April	James Austen's first child, Anna, born at Deane.
3 June	JA writes the last item of her *J.*

1794

22 February	M de Feuillide guillotined in Paris.
September	Charles leaves the RN Academy and goes to sea.
?Autumn	JA possibly writes the novella *Lady Susan* this year.

1795

	JA probably writes 'Elinor and Marianne' this year.
3 May	James's wife Anne dies, and infant Anna is sent to live at Steventon.
Autumn	Revd Tom Fowle joins Lord Craven as his private chaplain for the West Indian campaign.
December	Tom Lefroy visits Ashe Rectory – he and JA have a flirtation over the Christmas holiday period.

1796

October	JA starts writing 'First Impressions'.

1797

17 January	James Austen marries Mary Lloyd, and infant Anna returns to live at Deane.

February	Revd Tom Fowle dies of fever at San Domingo and is buried at sea.
August	JA finishes 'First Impressions' and Mr Austen offers it for publication to Thomas Cadell – rejected sight unseen.
November	JA starts converting 'Elinor and Marianne' into *Sense and Sensibility*. Mrs Austen takes her daughters for a visit to Bath. Edward Austen and his young family move from Rowling to Godmersham.
31 December	Henry Austen marries his cousin, the widowed Eliza de Feuillide, in London.

1798

	JA probably starts writing 'Susan' (later to become *Northanger Abbey*).
17 November	James Austen's son James Edward born at Deane.

1799

Summer	JA probably finishes 'Susan' (*NA*) about now.

1800

	Mr Austen decides to retire and move to Bath.

1801

24 January	Henry Austen resigns his commission in the Oxfordshire Militia and sets up as a banker and army agent in London.
May	The Austen family leave Steventon for Bath, and then go for a seaside holiday in the West Country. JA's traditionary West Country romance presumably occurs between now and the autumn of 1804.

1802

25 March	Peace of Amiens appears to bring the war with France to a close.

Summer	Charles Austen joins his family for a seaside holiday in Wales and the West Country.
December	JA and Cassandra visit James and Mary at Steventon; while there, Harris Bigg-Wither proposes to JA and she accepts him, only to withdraw her consent the following day.
Winter	JA revises 'Susan' (*NA*).

1803

Spring	JA sells 'Susan' (*NA*) to Benjamin Crosby; he promises to publish it by 1804, but does not do so.
18 May	Napoleon breaks the Peace of Amiens, and war with France recommences.
Summer	The Austens visit Ramsgate in Kent, and possibly also go to the West Country again.
November	The Austens visit Lyme Regis.

1804

	JA probably starts writing *The Watsons* this year, but leaves it unfinished.
Summer	The Austens visit Lyme Regis again.

1805

21 January	Mr Austen dies and is buried in Bath.
Summer	Martha Lloyd joins forces with Mrs Austen and her daughters.
18 June	James Austen's younger daughter, Caroline, born at Steventon.
21 October	Battle of Trafalgar.

1806

2 July   Mrs Austen and her daughters finally leave Bath; they visit Clifton, Adlestrop, Stoneleigh and Hamstall Ridware, before settling in Southampton in the autumn.

24 July   Francis Austen marries Mary Gibson.

1807

19 May   Charles Austen marries Fanny Palmer, in Bermuda.

1808

10 October   Edward Austen's wife Elizabeth dies at Godmersham.

1809

5 April   JA makes an unsuccessful attempt to secure the publication of 'Susan' (*NA*).

7 July   Mrs Austen and her daughters, and Martha Lloyd, move to Chawton, Hants.

1810

Winter   *S&S* is accepted for publication by Thomas Egerton.

1811

February   JA starts planning *Mansfield Park*.

30 October   *S&S* published.

?Winter   JA starts revising 'First Impressions' into *Pride and Prejudice*.

1812

17 June   America declares war on Great Britain.

14 October   Mrs Thomas Knight II dies, and Edward Austen now officially takes surname of Knight.

Autumn   JA sells copyright of *P&P* to Egerton.

1813

28 January	*P&P* published; JA half-way through *MP*.
?July	JA finishes *MP*.
?November	*MP* accepted for publication by Egerton about now.

1814

21 January	JA commences *Emma*.
5 April	Napoleon abdicates and is exiled to Elba.
9 May	*MP* published.
24 December	Treaty of Ghent officially ends war with America.

1815

March	Napoleon escapes and resumes power in France; hostilities recommence.
29 March	*E* finished.
18 June	Battle of Waterloo finally ends war with France.
8 August	JA starts *Persuasion*.
4 October	Henry Austen takes JA to London; he falls ill, and she stays longer than anticipated.
13 November	JA visits Carlton House, and receives an invitation to dedicate a future work to the Prince Regent.
December	*E* published by John Murray, dedicated to the Prince Regent (title page 1816).

1816

19 February	2nd edition of *MP* published.
Spring	JA's health starts to fail. Henry Austen buys back manuscript of 'Susan' (*NA*), which JA revises and intends to offer again for publication.

18 July	First draft of *P* finished.
6 August	*P* finally completed.

1817
27 January	JA starts *Sanditon*.
18 March	JA now too ill to work, and has to leave *S* unfinished.
24 May	Cassandra takes JA to Winchester for medical attention.
18 July	JA dies in the early morning.
24 July	JA buried in Winchester Cathedral.
December	*NA* and *P* published together, by Murray, with a 'Biographical Notice' added by Henry Austen (title page 1818).

1869
16 December	JA's nephew, the Revd James Edward Austen-Leigh (JEAL), publishes his *Memoir of Jane Austen*, from which all subsequent biographies have stemmed (title page 1870).

1871

JEAL publishes a second and enlarged edition of his *Memoir*, including in this the novella *LS*, the cancelled chapters of *P*, the unfinished *W*, a précis of *S*, and 'The Mystery' from the *J*.

1884

JA's great-nephew, Lord Brabourne, publishes *Letters of Jane Austen*, the first attempt to collect her surviving correspondence.

1922

Volume the Second of the *J* published.

1925

The manuscript of the unfinished *S* edited by R. W. Chapman and published as *Fragment of a Novel by Jane Austen*.

1932

R. W. Chapman publishes *Jane Austen's Letters to her sister Cassandra and others*, giving letters unknown to Lord Brabourne.

1933

Volume the First of the *J* published.

1951

Volume the Third of the *J* published.

1952

Second edition of R. W. Chapman's *Jane Austen's Letters* published, with additional items.

1954

R. W. Chapman publishes *Jane Austen's Minor Works*, which includes the three volumes of the *J* and other smaller items.

1980

B. C. Southam publishes *Jane Austen's 'Sir Charles Grandison'*, a small manuscript discovered in 1977.

1995

Deirdre Le Faye publishes the third (new) edition of *Jane Austen's Letters*, containing further additions to the Chapman collections.

INTRODUCTION

COMPOSITION AND PUBLICATION

Mansfield Park, the third of Jane Austen's novels to be published, appeared in three volumes in May 1814. It was the first to be written, and probably to be conceived, after Austen settled down to write at Chawton in 1809. Her first book, *Sense and Sensibility*, was accepted by the publisher, Thomas Egerton, by February 1811, and according to her note, *Mansfield Park* was 'begun somewhere about Feby 1811 – Finished soon after June 1813'.[1] Yet the approximation of these dates contrasts with the precise ones her sister Cassandra gives for the composition of *Emma* and *Persuasion*, *Emma* taking fourteen months from 21 January 1814 to 29 March 1815, and *Persuasion* the year from 8 August 1815 to 6 August 1816.[2] On this dating, *Mansfield Park* took about twenty-eight months to write, compared to the slightly longer *Emma*, which took half that time. And though the earlier novel, according to the memorandum, was more or less 'finished' in June, it was eight or nine months more before the manuscript was taken to London to be published. Why, on this evidence, *Mansfield Park* took so long to write, and why it was then held back from publication – if this indeed was the case – are significant questions. It is clear, though, that for Jane Austen this novel's publication was very important. Explicitly set in the contemporary world, and with several references to current events

---

[1] Jane Austen, *Plan of a Novel and Other Documents* (Oxford: Clarendon Press, 1926), facsimile following p. 35.

[2] R. W. Chapman (ed.), *The Novels of Jane Austen*, vol. 6: *Minor Works* (London: Oxford University Press, 1954), plate facing p. 242. Cassandra's note repeats her sister's dates for *Mansfield Park*.

and controversies, *Mansfield Park* marked the beginning of a new phase of her writing.

These memoranda may conceivably suggest that Austen was merely planning the novel in early 1811. Deirdre Le Faye comments that 'it seems unlikely that the actual writing of this work could have started at so early a date' as February 1811, since Austen was then busy with both *Sense and Sensibility* (correcting proofs) and revising *Pride and Prejudice*.[3] She conjectures that *Mansfield Park* was begun after *Pride and Prejudice* had been finished, 'probably in the spring of 1812', thus reducing the time taken in actual writing to just about the same as *Emma*. References in Austen's surviving letters during 1813 have usually been assumed to indicate the progress of the novel's composition, and might support Le Faye's suggestion, if we assume that Jane Austen's requests for information refer to a project that is at that moment on hand. Jane's letter to Cassandra at Steventon of 24 January 1813, for example, mentions that there is no Government House in Gibraltar, so that 'I must alter it to the Commissioner's'. (A speech of William Price in vol. 2, ch. 6 casually refers to the women's fashions he has seen there.) In the same letter, Austen mentions that the party at the rectory the previous night formed a 'round Table': 'I made my Mother an excuse, & came away; leaving just as many [six] for *their* round Table, as there were at Mrs Grants.–I wish they might be as agreable a set.'[4] This is a reference to the 'round game' played at the parsonage by those characters not occupied with Whist, which occurs in the next chapter of vol. 2.

But the letter assumes Cassandra's knowledge of the novel, and the tone of shared familiarity resembles Austen's references to incidents in other novels like Frances Burney's: it is therefore possible that Austen's writing has advanced well beyond this – not half-way – point at this date. The reference to 'Ordination' in the next letter of 29 January 1813, in which it appears that Jane has asked Cassandra,

---

[3] Deirdre Le Faye, *Jane Austen: A Family Record*, 2nd edn (Cambridge: Cambridge University Press, 2004), p. 197.

[4] Deirdre Le Faye (ed.), *Jane Austen's Letters*, 3rd edn (Oxford: Oxford University Press, 1995), p. 199.

at that time staying with their eldest brother James, a cleric, to confirm some information – 'I am glad to find your enquiries have ended so well. —If you c^d discover whether Northamptonshire is a Country of Hedgerows, I s^d be glad again.—'[5] – probably refers to Edmund's visit to his friend near Peterborough, where 'they were to receive ordination in the course of the Christmas week' (vol. 2, ch. 8). But it sounds, again, as if this is already written into the text, since Austen is pleased to find from Cassandra that what she has assumed is correct. The reference to hedgerows may point to a moment in vol. 2, ch. 4, when Fanny declares 'Three years ago, this was nothing but a rough hedgerow', but R. W. Chapman's speculation that Austen had some idea of using it as a device to get Fanny to overhear a conversation seems more plausible.[6] Whatever one concludes, it is notable that, on the sisters' timetable, it would have taken Austen almost two years, and on Le Faye's nine or ten months, to reach the twenty-fifth chapter out of forty-eight by this date, leaving the rest of the novel, more than half in length, to be finished within the next six months. This is not impossible, but it might well be that *Mansfield Park* has been written out by this time, having been begun nearly two years before, and that it is now being revised, or rewritten, or that the author is polishing it up.

At any rate, work on the novel must have been interrupted, and in part overshadowed, by the 'long illness' and inevitable death of Eliza, the wife of Jane Austen's brother Henry, on 25 April 1813. Jane Austen went to their London home in Henrietta Street on 22 April, coming back to Chawton on 1 May, and returning later. But by mid-year (6 July) she was able to announce – in the postscript to a letter to her brother Frank, then in Sweden – that she has made a nice profit on *Sense and Sensibility*. With the money she had from selling *Pride and Prejudice*, she writes, 'I have now . . . written myself into £250.—which only makes me long for more.— I have something in hand – which I hope on the credit of P. & P.

---

[5] Le Faye (ed.), *Letters*, p. 202.
[6] R. W. Chapman, *Jane Austen: Facts and Problems* (Oxford: Clarendon Press, 1948), p. 83.

will sell well, tho' not half so entertaining.'[7] This 'something in hand' evidently involves mentioning 'two or three' of Frank's 'old Ships' (which would be in vol. 3, ch. 7) and she asks whether he minds. So the Portsmouth chapters are certainly already written. Having something 'in hand' does not necessarily mean, though, 'completed and ready for publication'. Austen is perhaps as likely to mean something in progress, being dealt with at this moment, or in other words, in the course of being revised.

Jane Austen might then be still working over the novel at this time, and therefore 'Finished soon after June 1813' may not tell the full story of the novel's completion. Judging from the surviving manuscript of the cancelled chapters of *Persuasion*, Austen worked on her texts, revised phrasing, rewrote paragraphs (which involved pasting a new version over the original) and inserted substantial additional passages, in the process of revising a text that was itself then further revised, and then largely discarded for a new version. The manuscript of *Sanditon*, though it is evidently a first draft, also suggests that some intense revision took place as a novel was being put together and also, presumably, at later stages. This may give a clue to the long period of *Mansfield Park*'s gestation, and also perhaps to the delay, after it was said to be 'in hand', in getting the manuscript to the publisher.

Given Jane Austen's keenness to publish, and to make money, this slowness is intriguing. In September 1813 Jane was at Henry's again, but only for a brief three-day visit. Frank had evidently pointed out that if she used the genuine names of his ships in the novel her authorship would soon be out. 'I was previously aware', she writes in her letter to him of 25 September 1813, 'of what I sh^d be laying myself open to—but the truth is that the Secret has spread so far as to be scarcely the Shadow of a secret now—& that I beleive whenever the 3^d appears, I shall not even attempt to tell Lies about it.—I shall rather try to make all the Money than all the Mystery I can of it.'[8] Austen could easily have used fictional names for the ships: she is thus in this novel implicitly throwing off the

---

[7] Le Faye (ed.), *Letters*, p. 217.   [8] Le Faye (ed.), *Letters*, p. 231.

mantle of anonymity. One explanation for *Mansfield Park*'s being held back is that Egerton, Austen's publisher, may have wanted to delay it. In a postscript to her letter she told Frank 'There is to be a 2^d Edition of S. & S. Egerton advises it.'[9] She revised that novel, and it was published, together with Egerton's (unrevised) second edition of *Pride and Prejudice* at the end of October 1813.[10] The publisher, reasonably, may have wanted to make as much as possible out of the earlier novels, before their share of the market was contested by the appearance of a new novel by the same author, and Austen, who was risking money by bringing out a second edition of *Sense and Sensibility*, might have felt disinclined to risk even more on *Mansfield Park* till she saw how well the second edition of the earlier novel sold. During September and October of this year she was on a long visit to Godmersham Park, her second brother Edward's house in Kent, from whence he took her to London on 13 November. She stayed with Henry for a fortnight.[11] It might have been on this visit that Henry negotiated the acceptance of *Mansfield Park* by Egerton, or it might have been on another, in January 1814. At this stage Henry had certainly not read the new novel. Did Egerton agree to publish the book also without reading it? (He was to praise its 'Morality' and its lack of 'weak parts'.) But then, why another delay, between mid November and early March – three-and-a-half months – before the manuscript was delivered? Perhaps it was just the weather that impeded Jane Austen from taking it to London before March – it was very cold and foggy that winter – or perhaps she was not quite happy with her text.

An agreement certainly was reached with Egerton either late in 1813 or early in 1814 that this novel would be published, like *Sense and Sensibility*, 'on commission'. This meant that Egerton would undertake all the industrial side of the publishing venture – purchasing paper at the best price, arranging printers and distribution, etc; whilst Henry and Jane would see to the editorial side, and be responsible for proof-reading and corrections. For his work, and

---

[9] Le Faye (ed.), *Letters*, p. 232.   [10] Le Faye, *Family Record*, p. 207.
[11] Le Faye, *Family Record*, p. 208.

risking his initial outlay, the publisher would charge the author a commission of 10 per cent on sales.[12] Jane Austen would retain the copyright. In fact it seems likely that the Austens took a very active role in the novel's publication process. Travelling together in the carriage from Chawton to London in early March, Jane and Henry read the fair copy of the novel – the manuscript ready for the printers. Then Egerton, following the usual practice of farming copy out to different printers, sent the first and the third volumes in Jane Austen's fair copy to G. Sidney, of Northumberland Street, off the Strand, whom he had previously used for the second and third volumes of *Pride and Prejudice*, and the second volume to Charles Roworth of Bell Yard, Temple Bar.

Jane's being in London at this time, coupled with her eagerness for profit, suggest some speculations. A tantalising fragment of a letter written from Henry's address on 21 March, meaning that Jane had been in London for three weeks, a long visit, contains the phrases 'and only just time enough for what is to be done. And all this, with very few acquaintance in Town & going to no Parties & living very quietly!' With no parties, and few acquaintance, what is Miss Jane Austen (if she is speaking of herself and not of Henry) occupying herself with in town? It seems plausible that she is working on the proof sheets as they arrive from the two printers. She adds 'Perhaps before the end of April, *Mansfield Park* by the author of S & S.—P. & P. may be in the World.'[13] This estimate, not so far off the mark, contrasts with her pessimistic estimate of the progress of *Sense and Sensibility* in 1811, when on 25 April she had said 'I have scarcely a hope of its being out in June' and had actually to wait till November, despite, as she writes, Henry's hurrying the printer. It suggests that the Austens (both of them on the spot for the whole printing process this time) really now have the novel 'in hand', that they are working actively and energetically with the publisher and printers to get this one out, and possibly making up for lost time.

---

[12] Jan Fergus, *Jane Austen: A Literary Life* (London: Macmillan, 1991), pp. 16–17.
[13] Le Faye (ed.), *Letters*, p. 262.

The book was advertised as 'this day . . . published' in the *Star* on 9 May 1814, which, it seems, was correct.[14]

It still remains rather a mystery why the novel took so long to write, and why it was so long before it was handed over to the publisher. I speculate that *Mansfield Park* is a novel that has been carefully revised, and in places, perhaps, thoroughly rewritten. It is unlikely, since paper was so expensive, that Austen actually rewrote the whole novel before she copied it out for the printers; but it is likely that before she was ready to submit the volumes to the publisher, she went over her manuscript. In this period she could check details: whether ordination could take place during the Christmas week, such things as the names of ships or the distances between places, and possibly add some items to make the book more vivid. One sign of this revision process might be the double time scheme of the novel. There is no reason to dispute Chapman's correlation, in the first appendix to his 1923 edition, of the calendar of its events, beginning with the ball on 22 December, with the calendar of 1808–9. When William Price earlier declares 'This is the Assembly night' at Portsmouth, this correlation would almost certainly make that day a Thursday, which was correct. But this calendar does not fit with other references such as to the *Quarterly Review*s whose pages are supposedly turned over at Sotherton in mid-1808, since that journal was first published in February 1809. Such an oversight might suggest that Jane Austen, coming back to the first volume after several months (perhaps more than a year), has decided to ignore the dating entailed by her original mapping of the time scheme. Why should she be pedantic about it anyway? When Fanny Price, at Portsmouth, notes that Easter was 'particularly late this year', the calendar of 1809 is also disregarded. This reference, very late in the novel (vol. 3, ch. 14), might also suggest that Austen, writing, or rewriting, in 1813 when Easter was indeed very late, has forgotten, or abandoned, a scheme set out in 1811. Most writers would certainly want to return to the earlier chapters of a novel that

---

[14] David Gilson, *A Bibliography of Jane Austen*, 2nd edn (Winchester: St Paul's Bibliographies, and New Castle, Del.: Oak Knoll Press, 1997), p. 49.

is completed so long after they first put pen to paper. 'I hope when you have written a great deal more', her aunt advises Anna Austen, a few months later, on 9 September, 'you will be equal to scratching out some of the past'.[15]

Both Jane and Henry Austen must have realised that a bad bargain had been made when, probably to save Henry trouble during his wife's fatal illness, Jane Austen had sold the copyright of *Pride and Prejudice* to Egerton outright. By October 1813, *Pride and Prejudice* has been well received, and gone into a second edition. Jane Austen, as her letters to Frank suggest, is now a confident, nearly professional and successful author. This new novel will consolidate her reputation, and recover some of the money that, through circumstances, she has forfeited with *Pride and Prejudice*. Like Henry, at this time a successful banker, she is ambitious and, as she was later to say, 'greedy' for more. These assumptions would find some confirmation in details of the novel's first publication. Once with the publisher, the first edition of *Mansfield Park* was produced quickly and, it seems, cheaply. In the arrangements for publishing 'on commission', printing and paper costs were charged to the author. The paper used for *Mansfield Park* is thinner than the paper used for *Pride and Prejudice*, and because each page has twenty-five, not twenty-three lines as in the earlier novels published by Egerton and printed by the same printers, it looks as though they were under instructions to save money on paper.[16] Almost certainly the edition was of a cautious 1,250 copies.[17]

It is plausible to suggest then that Jane and Henry, who might have felt he had let her down over *Pride and Prejudice*, together determined to make *Mansfield Park* yield as much profit as possible to the author. *Sense and Sensibility* had been published at 15s. When *Pride and Prejudice* was announced, '*18ˢ*', Austen wrote indignantly to Cassandra on seeing Egerton's advertisement in January 1813, 'He shall ask £1–1– for my two next, & £1–8– for my stupidest

---

[15] Le Faye (ed.), *Letters*, p. 276.   [16] Fergus, *Literary Life*, p. 144.
[17] Chapman, *Facts and Problems*, p. 157; Fergus, *Literary Life*, p. 145.

of all.'[18] She is already regretting the decision to sell *Pride and Prejudice* outright, and determined to publish for herself from now on. In the event *Mansfield Park* was published again at 18s, but (partly because of the care taken over the printing) Austen did make money. Most calculations suggest that her profit, after paying Egerton commission, was between £310 and £350, about three times as much as the sum for which she had sold *Pride and Prejudice*. The novel was not reviewed, but Austen's surmise that 'on the credit of P. & P.' it would 'sell well' was correct. She tells her niece Fanny Knight in a letter of 18 November 1814 that 'the first Edit: of M. P. is all sold', and that Henry 'is rather wanting me to come to Town, to settle about a 2^d Edit:'.[19]

The pressure that Austen indicates in the fragment of her letter from London during the printing of *Mansfield Park* may go some way towards explaining why this first edition of *Mansfield Park* is badly printed. It is a text with many rather obvious errors. But novels were not highly regarded, and the Austens may have struggled to get the printers to do even the poor job they did. As the cheapness of the printing and the original binding in plain boards suggest, *Mansfield Park* of 1814 is a product, like Austen's earlier novels, destined in large part for the circulating library market. It is usually suggested that these, by this time established in most towns, large and small, would have taken at least three or four hundred of a new publication likely to appeal to their readers. There were many non-commercial book clubs too, and these might also order any successful new novel. Since *Pride and Prejudice* had certainly been a success (Egerton's second edition is advertised at the back of his issue of *Mansfield Park*), the advance orders for *Mansfield Park* are likely to have been on the high side. Three-volume novels were the pulp fiction of the day: their shelf-life was short, three months if you were lucky, and those unsold, then as now, were remaindered or pulped. These were objects to be consumed; read and disposed of. But at 18s, *Mansfield Park* was not cheap. As the proprietors of circulating

[18] Le Faye (ed.), *Letters*, 29 January 1813, p. 201.
[19] Le Faye (ed.), *Letters*, p. 281.

libraries advertised, one could borrow and read many volumes for less than that sum. You did not expect to reread a novel, so the ordinary gentleman or lady with a modest income – the audience to which Austen's novels are plainly addressed – rarely bought them. For the same outlay you could borrow many from the local library and return them often, as Mary Musgrove does in *Persuasion* (vol. 2, ch. 2). As Robert Southey wrote in his *Letters from England* (1807), 'In truth, the main demand for contemporary literature comes from these libraries, or from private societies instituted to supply their place . . . It is not a mere antithesis to say that they who buy books do not read them, and that they who do read them do not buy them.'[20]

Thus, having told her niece that a second edition of *Mansfield Park* is envisaged, Austen in her next letter has to decline Fanny's congratulations as premature. 'It is not settled yet whether I *do* hazard a 2^d Edition . . . People are more ready to borrow & praise, than to buy—which I cannot wonder at'.[21] But having done so well with the first edition of the novel, Austen was 'very greedy' for the increased profit that a second edition would promise, as she had written to Fanny on 18 November.[22] Publication on commission is obviously again the arrangement envisaged for another edition; a risk, as Austen intimates, even for a novel that has sold out in its first, and made the author a handsome sum. But negotiations with Egerton may have broken down; Deirdre Le Faye speaks of Egerton's 'refusal' to bring out a second edition when the Austens met with him on 30 November, but it is not clear what went on.[23] Only fragments of letters survive for the months between November 1814 and September 1815, months during which *Emma* is completed and prepared for publication.

By this time Henry has moved from Henrietta Street, Covent Garden, south-westwards to 23 Hans Place, Sloane Street, in the

[20] Robert Southey, *Letters from England* (1807), ed. Jack Simmons (London: Cresset Press, 1951), p. 349, Letter 16.
[21] Le Faye (ed.), *Letters*, 30 November 1814, p. 287.
[22] Le Faye (ed.), *Letters*, p. 281.   [23] Le Faye, *Family Record*, p. 220.

more fashionable district of Knightsbridge. During this period another publisher, John Murray of Albemarle Street in neighbouring Mayfair, becomes interested in Austen's novels, and *Emma* is offered to him. It is not clear how or why a decision was made to approach Murray, or whether perhaps Murray approached Austen. Perhaps Egerton did not refuse or decline to print another edition of *Mansfield Park*: perhaps Murray stepped in. On 17 October 1815 Austen is writing to Cassandra that 'Mr Murray's Letter is come; he is a Rogue of course, but a civil one. He offers £450 – [for *Emma*] but wants to have the Copyright of MP. & S&S included. It will end in my publishing for myself I dare say.'[24] Austen was not going to make the same mistake she had made with *Pride and Prejudice*, and held out against the selling of the copyrights. In the end Murray published *Emma* in December 1815, in an edition of 2,000 copies, but on commission, and a second edition of *Mansfield Park* on the same arrangement – Henry Austen, on Jane's behalf, having refused his original offer.

Murray (actually John Murray II) had taken over his father's business in 1803. By 1815 he was firmly established as the most prestigious of London publishers, the proprietor of the influential *Quarterly Review*, with connections in the Cabinet and a number of important writers on his books. His library and drawing room at Albemarle Street had become the centre of literary London. (There, on 9 April 1815, occurred the meeting between his two best-selling and most famous authors, Lord Byron and Walter Scott.) John Murray had published few novels, though he had floated the idea of a series of 'British Novelists', to include Richardson and Fielding, but also Burney and Charlotte Smith, in 1808.[25] After 1814, with his publication of *Waverley*, Scott's first novel, a work which is often thought to have taken the status of the genre to a new height, and a great publishing success, he may well have been particularly keen to add a new writer, a novelist whose work had been widely

---

[24] Le Faye (ed.), *Letters*, p. 291.
[25] Samuel Smiles, *A Publisher and His Friends, Memoir and Correspondence of the Late John Murray* (2 vols., London, 1891), vol. 1, pp. 86–8.

praised, to his list. And Jane Austen was a writer who, as he must have known, was read in aristocratic as well as genteel families, and whose writing was, as a surviving reference in the Longman archive confirms, already respected in the trade.[26]

Murray's chief reader (the role was unofficial at the time – and a secret) was William Gifford, the editor of the *Quarterly Review*. Perhaps as part of the negotiations that took place during 1815 Murray passed on a copy of *Pride and Prejudice* to him. (It is conceivable that Murray might have had some idea of buying the copyright from Egerton.) Extracts from two of Gifford's letters to Murray were printed for the first time in Samuel Smiles' *A Publisher and His Friends* (1891) and, though brief, they are illuminating. In the first Gifford says he has read the novel, which is 'really a very pretty thing'. On 29 September 1815 he writes 'I have read "Pride and Prejudice" <u>again</u> – 'tis very good – wretchedly printed, and so pointed as to be almost unintelligible'.[27] The underlining of 'again' in this letter is significant. After all, one does not usually read novels twice: they are not of a nature to demand rereading. Gifford may be saying, in effect: 'This is a novel people would want to have: it deserves to be printed well. We can do better than Egerton.' Jane Austen herself commented on the 'Typical errors' in the setting of *Pride and Prejudice*.[28] The reference to 'pointing' – punctuation – is also interesting: it suggests that Gifford would be personally prepared to attend to the punctuation of Austen's novels. It certainly sounds as if he is looking at *Pride and Prejudice* from the point of view of a prospective publisher, who will need to do a better job. His letter immediately goes on: 'Make no apology for sending me anything to read *or revise*' (my italics). Most of all, it is significant that Gifford's letter is written before there is any whisper on Austen's

---

[26] 'We are particularly interested for the success of the Austen and we sincerely regret that her works have not met with the encouragement we could wish', letter to Amelie Opie of October 1813, quoted in Fergus, *Literary Life*, p. 188, fn. 21.

[27] Smiles, *Publisher and His Friends*, vol. 1, p. 282.

[28] Le Faye (ed.), *Letters*, 29 January 1813, p. 202.

side of contact with Murray. On the same day as his letter was written, in fact, she writes from Chawton that she is soon 'going to London for a week or two'. It was only there, at Henry's, that she carried on those negotiations for the publication of *Emma* that were to entail the second edition of *Mansfield Park*.

John Murray, then, having published *Emma* in late December 1815, went on to publish a second edition of *Mansfield Park* on 19 February 1816. In her business letter of 11 December 1815 to Murray, in which, among other matters, she advises him of that novel's dedication to the Prince Regent, Austen adds 'I return also, Mansfield Park, as ready for a 2^d Edit: I beleive, as I can make it.—'[29] This is unlikely to have been the manuscript, which having been sent to two different printers, would be dispersed, nor a proof of the second edition, but a marked-up copy of Egerton's edition. So it is clear that Murray and his reader, if there were one, had referred the novel to the author, and were expecting to produce a better edition than the first. Each volume was printed by a different firm, presumably to speed up the work. Roworth, whose name is prominently displayed as printer in the *Quarterly Review*, took the second volume, as he had in 1814, but with the benefit of that copy beside them, the compositors spaced the text rather more elegantly. It is worth noting, in view of the poor printing of both the first and third volumes by Sidney in 1814, that Murray, though farming it out to three different firms, volume 1 to Moyes, volume 2 to Roworth, and volume 3 to Davison, made no use of him.

The second edition of *Mansfield Park*, published by John Murray, was of 750 copies. It was printed on good-quality paper, costing 35s per ream. The Austens and Murray had misjudged the market, however: even at a special price of 12s 6d per copy for advance orders by booksellers, only six firms took six copies each. Still un-reviewed, the edition sold slowly, and in December 1817 588 copies still remained. In January 1820, almost 500 of them were sold off at 2s 6d each. No wonder copies of it are rare. The loss on *Mansfield*

[29] Le Faye (ed.), *Letters*, p. 305.

Park was set against the profit on *Emma*, so that when Austen made a note on the profits of her novels, she recorded only £38. 18s for *Emma*.[30] A failure, then. Austen never lost money with Egerton, but when Murray's ambitions coincided with hers and Henry's, they overreached themselves.

Nevertheless, Murray's adoption of Austen is an important moment in the history of her novels and their reputation. His agreeing to republish *Mansfield Park* in 1816 has special and perhaps under-appreciated significance. It suggests not only Jane Austen's valuation of her novel, but the confidence that it might be sold, not just to circulating libraries, but to private buyers. The implication is that this is not a novel to be read by the volume, and returned for another, and another, but a work to be displayed on the shelves, to be reread. If this is so, one might suggest that what we have here is the gestatory moment of the literary, or – going further – the very beginnings of 'canon formation'. Austen's accession to Murray's list is a vital stage in her novels' elevation to classic or canonical status: she joins Scott, Southey, Byron and many others sharing broadly Tory political principles on the list of a man whose standing and connections were impeccable, and 'in her brief season of literary fame bask[s] in the sunshine of attention and compliment from Albemarle Street'.[31] It is probably not coincidence that during these same months Jane Austen receives the invitation to dedicate *Emma* to the Prince Regent: it is the moment when this lady author from Hampshire is received into the literary establishment. And *Mansfield Park* – ambitious, substantial, serious, wide-ranging – was her entry ticket.

THE 1814 AND 1816 EDITIONS

As already mentioned, in December 1815 Jane Austen returned a copy of the first edition of *Mansfield Park* to John Murray 'as ready

---

[30] Jane Austen, 'Profits of My Novels, over & above the £600 in the Navy Fives', in *Plan of a Novel*, facsimile following p. 35.

[31] Chapman, *Facts and Problems*, p. 155.

for a 2ᵈ Edit: I beleive, as I can make it', which would authorise
the assumption that Austen herself had a hand in (which does not
mean complete control over) the changes – slight in themselves
but cumulatively important – that mark the novel's republishing.
Austen's words however are not unambiguous. On one interpretation she is claiming complete or thorough revision; on another she
is handing over the text to the publisher, saying 'I've done my best',
with the implication that not all the work of necessary correction
might have been done.

In this matter of business dealing, we are not likely to find irony
or word-play, and it is reasonable to assume that Jane Austen means
exactly what a common-sense reading of this note would infer: that
she has corrected the text to the best of her ability. On this basis it
might be sensible to conclude that the corrections introduced into
the text in 1816 have the author's authority. These might not extend,
however, to all matters of presentation, like punctuation, which
customarily was left to the compositors, sometimes working to the
publishers' house style. (Changes in spelling of certain words –
'choose' in vol. 1, 'chuse' in vols. 2 and 3 – probably demonstrate
that the compositors followed house style, rather than the copy
before them.) What is clear is that the second edition will not
be merely a reproduction of the first, and that the author, either
at her own request, or at the bidding of the publisher, has taken
some responsibility for the correction or adjustment of the text. A
comparison of the two texts in fact suggests that some of the changes
are highly unlikely to have been made by anyone but Austen herself:
not just the revision of technical details in the first Portsmouth
chapters (the inclusion, for example, of William's phrase 'It's the
best birth at Spithead': vol. 3, ch. 7) but also some, at least, of the
adjustments to punctuation and syntax, and other additions and
amendments. It is reasonable to conclude that Austen and Murray
wished to produce a second edition of the novel which, whilst it
may not have been closer than the first to the author's original
manuscript, would be more creditable to both.

The edition of 1814, as the editor of that text, Kathryn Sutherland, has argued,[32] in its looser, less emphatic punctuation, is certainly likely, despite the carelessness of its printers, to be closer to what Jane Austen originally wrote, and, in a way entirely characteristic of this author, transcribes the rhythm and cadences of heard and imagined speech. The punctuation of Murray's 1816 edition is firmer, more disciplined according to grammatical requirements, often replacing a comma with a semi-colon. It is a text which has been 'corrected' either by the author or (more likely) by the printing houses, to accord with 'standard' practice, which therefore lends itself to a reading aloud obedient to the received indicators of emphasis. 'It was meant and done by Mrs. Grant, with perfect good humour on Mr. Rushworth's account, who was partly expected at the park that day' (vol. 1, ch. 7). This is momentarily confusing (who has the good humour, Mr Rushworth?). The comma that 1816 inserts ('good humour, on'), grammatically required, makes it clear. But it can be argued in this and many other instances that the original punctuation captures some of the natural emphasis of the voice.

Judging from the surviving manuscripts and the fair copy by Jane Austen of 'Lady Susan', probably made in 1805, the original manuscript distributed to the printers would have included many capitalisations, contractions and the characteristic Austen dash after a full stop. Because paper was expensive, Jane Austen rarely began a paragraph on a new line, and this too would be left to the compositor to implement. These so-called 'accidentals' contribute to the meaning of a text, and cannot be dismissed as incidental textual 'noise'. But there is no way of knowing whether the edition of 1814 accurately transcribes Austen's original (or, to be precise, more accurately than 1816). Most of the capitalisations are removed in 1816, but many remain in 1814, especially in chapters 11, 12 and 13 of the first volume: 'Here's what may leave all

---

[32] 'Introduction', in Kathryn Sutherland (ed.), *Mansfield Park* (Harmondsworth: Penguin, 1996); Kathryn Sutherland, 'Speaking Commas / Reading Commas: Punctuating *Mansfield Park*', *Text*, 12 (1999), pp. 101–22.

Painting and all Music behind, and what Poetry only can attempt to describe' (vol. 1, ch. 11). This suggests that the compositor of 1814 reproduces Austen's fair copy here more exactly than elsewhere, but also, of course, that some removals have taken place in the rest of the text, even in the earlier edition. There is a patch of archaic capitalisation in vol. 3, ch. 6 of the 1816 edition. Both 1814 and 1816 expand authorial contractions and probably eliminate most of the dashes.

'Accidentals' are not just commas or capitalisation, though, but features more native to Austen's personal style: the dash and italics. Italics, in particular, seem to identify something important to Austen's writing, and are plentiful in both editions of *Mansfield Park*. Both conventions were used by other contemporary authors, italics often to underline distinctions, as they are used by Edmund Bertram in the text itself ('the *manners* I speak of, might rather be called *conduct*': vol. 1, ch. 9). Austen, by contrast, often utilises italics as a means of transferring certain qualities of spoken speech to the printed page. The variation in emphasis conveyed through the convention mimics differences of tonal range and length of stress given by speakers to their words, since, by juxtaposing varying levels, energy and vivacity can be communicated: 'those indefatigable rehearsers, Agatha and Frederick. If *they* are not perfect, I *shall* be surprised' (vol. 1, ch. 18). The occurrence of italics in the narration, common to both editions, has a similar effect, as when Mrs Price's treatment of Susan is recalled: 'The blind fondness which was for ever producing evil around her, *she* had never known' (vol. 3, ch. 9). Or, three pages later, 'They sat without a fire; but *that* was a privation familiar even to Fanny.' In neither of these instances are the italics necessary to the sense; they are the transcription of a vivacious, energetic authorial voice.

The presence of italics in *Mansfield Park* is thus an indication of that 'acoustic trace' which Sutherland has identified as characterising the 1814 edition, but such instances are present in both texts. Italics are less in evidence in the narrative of *Emma*, possibly as a result of the correction of Austen's copy by Gifford, Murray's reader. Judging, too, from the surviving manuscripts of *Persuasion*, the house of Murray also removed italics from authorial narration in that text. The last chapter, in the manuscript, has twelve separate italicised, or rather underlined, words (*'she* had a *future* to look forward to, of powerful consolation'), none of which retains the italics in the 1818 printed text. If one were to take these chapters of *Persuasion* as a model (leaving aside the question of whether Jane Austen would delete all or some of the underlinings in her fair copy), one would conclude, indeed, that the printers were responsible for much more of the punctuation of the novels than we care to imagine, for there, too, the dashes in Austen's manuscript are all replaced by commas or semi-colons. The fair copy of 'Lady Susan' that Austen made in 1805 only uses dashes for parenthetical phrases. Italics were unpopular with printers, as both old-fashioned and a nuisance, since they involved reaching over to another bank of fonts. They may also have been disliked as exemplifying a peculiarly female style – the style, they may have thought, of overwrought sensibility.[33]

Italics are such a characteristic of the narrator's 'voice' in *Mansfield Park*, though, that it is significant that the 1816 text includes, in the final two chapters, three italicised words that are not in the 1814 text. (There is also one in vol. 2, ch. 8 in which Mrs Norris' partiality for the Bertram sisters is underlined.) Two of these changes are in the authorial narrative, one in the transcription or mimicking of Edmund's self-deceiving thoughts about Mary Crawford: 'considering the many counteractions of opposing habits, she had certainly been *more* attached to him than could have been expected' (vol. 3, ch. 16). Another change is quite important: Fanny's misconstruing of Edmund's feelings – 'Long, long would it be ere Miss Crawford's name passed his lips again' – is ironically pointed by the beginning of the next paragraph: 'It *was* long . . . it was not till Sunday evening that Edmund began to talk' (vol. 3, ch. 16). These changes would not have been made by a compositor

---

[33] But Isaac Disraeli's *Despotism: or the Fall of the Jesuits* (London, 1811), one of the few novels Murray published, is full of italics.

and must be ascribed to the author's intervention. Thus 1816 may certainly be regarded as restoring something lost in the 1814 edition.

DATING OF THE ACTION

The dating of the action of *Mansfield Park* is controversial, and upon it depends the interpretation of several incidents or circumstances in the novel. As already mentioned, Chapman, collating the middle of the novel with a calendar for 1808–9, showed that the occasion of Fanny Price's 'coming out' ball on Thursday 22 December coincided with the calendar of 1808, and that subsequent events and dates can all be keyed exactly to the calendar of 1809. On this dating, Sir Thomas and Tom go to Antigua in 1806; Tom returns in September 1807, after about a year, and his father in October 1808.

Other readers have proposed later dates, notably Brian Southam, who argues that 1812–13 is most likely. Southam's argument rests on 'a single reference' in vol. 1, ch. 16, to 'Crabbe's Tales', which he assumes means Crabbe's *Tales in Verse*, published in September 1812.[34] This places Sir Thomas' return, after two years away, in October 1812. It can be supported by the telling and exact reference to Easter being 'particularly late this year' (vol. 3, ch. 14), when Fanny is at Portsmouth, as it was in 1813 (18 April), and not in 1809 (2 April). Southam also suggests that the chronology of 1812–13 'provides the right slot' for Tom's reference, on his dating in September 1812, to the 'strange business this in America' (vol. 1, ch. 12), which he argues is the outbreak of war with the States, though, if set in 1808, it might more plausibly be to events following the passing of the Embargo Act of December 1807. There are several problems with the 1812–13 dating, since 22 December in 1812 was on a Tuesday, and from the date of the ball Jane Austen – like Fanny Price, 'a most accurate and honest reckoner' (vol. 3, ch. 11) – monitors subsequent events virtually by the day. Another is that it appears to take the aftermath of the main action – the

[34] Brian Southam, 'The Silence of the Bertrams: Slavery and the Chronology of *Mansfield Park*', *TLS* (17 February 1995), p. 13.

months when Crawford and Maria live together, the Rushworths' divorce, the settling of Maria with Mrs Norris, the courtship of Fanny and Edmund and Fanny's possible pregnancy – past early July 1813 when the author told Frank that it was 'in hand' and possibly even past the date of publication.[35] This is not a fatal objection, if we suppose that the final chapter is to be understood largely in the subjunctive sense, relieved of the tight time constraints of a novel constructed according to the realist mode, which have certainly been adhered to in the preceding volumes. But if the last chapter of *Persuasion* shifts into the present tense, the last of *Mansfield Park* does not.

These incompatible dating signals can be reconciled if we suppose that an extended period of the novel's preparation and composition allowed two things to happen: that, as I have argued, Jane Austen revised *Mansfield Park* extensively, and possibly more than once, and that her revision involved the inclusion of more contemporary references. This would mean dispensing with or disregarding the earlier calendar framework when it had fulfilled the purpose for which she had consulted it. (It was especially important to have a precise calendar when so much depends upon the recurrent delays in Edmund's proposing to Mary, which the novelist needs to make plausible; it was also instrumental in generating suspense.) A further resolution is to suggest that Jane Austen was not concerned with the precise dating of her novel, only that it should appear to readers as reasonably contemporary.

These issues are critical ones, since they bear upon the novel's treatment of class and slavery. Fanny's reported question about 'the slave-trade' in vol. 2, ch. 3, for instance, may read differently if one takes the view that the novel is set not long after the abolition of the trade (which passed into law in September 1807), making this incident belong to October or November 1808, or to the subsequent period in which, though officially abolished, the trade still continued, and in which slaves still worked the West Indian estates.

[35] Trevor Lloyd, 'Myths of the Indies: Jane Austen and the British Empire', *Comparative Criticism*, 21 (1999), pp. 59–71.

Southam, like many subsequent critics, bases his conception of Sir Thomas' character on the later dating of 1812–13, which makes it easier to position him as an unscrupulous, hypocritical planter; the earlier date, on the other hand, is consonant with the view that Sir Thomas, though the owner of estates, may well have been a proponent of abolition. The different dates also authorise or prompt different speculations about the reason for his and Tom's journey to Antigua.

I have taken the view that Chapman's dating is likely to be largely correct, that the action of the novel, running mainly from 1808–9, reaches its climax in March or April 1809, and that the aftermath takes place over the next year or two, bringing it up close to the date on which Jane Austen probably began planning or composing in 1811. It is certainly after the abolition of the slave trade, but I do not believe that Jane Austen meant the reader to recognise that the action took place in a precise year or years. This has critical implications, since it gives more weight to her interest in the internal consistency of the action than to its correlation with, or referencing of, external events.

CONTEXTUAL AND INTERTEXTUAL ISSUES

Many critics have thought that the name Mansfield in the novel's title refers to Lord Mansfield,[36] the great eighteenth-century judge, who gave a judgement in effect forbidding slavery on English soil in 1772. Since Austen knew Mansfield's descendants, and because Mansfield was better known for many other important decisions, this is an implausible, though tempting attribution. It is more probable, if any reference is intended, that Mansfield Park alludes to Mansfield-house in Richardson's *Sir Charles Grandison*, a novel that Jane Austen certainly knew well.[37] (*Grandison*'s presence in

---

[36] Margaret Kirkham, citing the Mansfield judgement of 1772, declared that 'the title of *Mansfield Park* is allusive and ironic'. *Jane Austen, Feminism and Fiction* (Brighton, Sussex: Harvester Press, and Totowa, N. J.: Barnes and Noble, 1983), p. 116.

[37] Samuel Richardson, *The History of Sir Charles Grandison* (7 vols., 1754), vol. 4, letter 10. 'Every circumstance narrated in Sir Charles Grandison . . . was

Mansfield Park is profound: both relate a contest between religious conviction and love, with the heroine on the sidelines, herself the hero's second choice.) More likely still, the name was chosen for its generic Englishness, as with the French novel *Amelie Mansfield* reviewed in the *Quarterly Review* of May 1809. The other name in the novel which has been thought to suggest a reference to slavery is Mrs Norris, since John Norris, formerly a slave-captain, later apologist for the slavers of Liverpool, appears in Thomas Clarkson's *History of the Abolition of the Slave-Trade*, which Austen very likely read.[38] The name may also be a pun on the French 'norrice' or nurse, since Mrs Norris is the reverse of a nurse, and instead of supplying comfort and nourishment lives through others, the servants and her three nieces.[39]

The name Fanny Price has been thought to derive from a tale in the second section, 'Marriages', of George Crabbe's *The Parish Register* (1807). Crabbe was another favourite author, and the reference, conscious or unconscious, is plausible.[40] But Fanny, like Price, was a common British name, and one found in a previous text would be unique in Austen (though perhaps Willoughby in *Sense and Sensibility*, which may allude to the rake Sir Clement Willoughby in *Evelina*, is an exception). Since 'Price' is used in fictions of the period to signify a lower-class person, there is no need to suppose a reference to the Revd Richard Price, Edmund Burke's antagonist. The name Edmund, which 'breathe[s] the spirit of chivalry and warm affections', is more interesting, since it is specifically

familiar to her; and the wedding days of Lady L. and Lady G. were as well remembered as if they had been living friends.' James Edward Austen-Leigh, *Memoir of Jane Austen* (1870), ed. R. W. Chapman (Oxford: Clarendon Press, 1926), p. 89.

[38] Thomas Clarkson, *The History of the Rise, Progress, and Accomplishment of the Abolition of the African Slave-Trade by the British Parliament* (2 vols., London: Longman, 1808), vol. 1, pp. 378, 478–81.

[39] Barbara Hardy, 'The Objects in *Mansfield Park*', in *Jane Austen: Bicentenary Essays*, ed. John Halperin (Cambridge: Cambridge University Press, 1975), p. 185.

[40] Frank W. Bradbrook, *Jane Austen and Her Predecessors* (Cambridge: Cambridge University Press, 1966), p. 77.

discussed in the novel (vol. 2, ch. 4), and suggests a broad range of associations including Spenser, Burke, and the hero, Edmund, of Clara Reeve's medieval romance, *The Old English Baron* (1778), who like Fanny is brought up in a baronet's family. Another novel whose influence may lie behind *Mansfield Park* is Charlotte Smith's *The Old Manor House* (1793). Monimia, as youthful as Fanny, lives in a remote part of the great house – in her case a turret, accessible only through a ruined chapel. Monimia's aunt berates and chides her as Mrs Norris does Fanny. Like Fanny, Monimia is a virtual unpaid servant, kept at needlework, though her quietness and willingness gradually endear her to the mistress of the house. And, like Fanny, Monimia is in love with its potential inheritor, a young man with a romantic name – Orlando: an interdicted love, like that in *Mansfield Park*. But then again, orphan-figures in big, frightening houses, with cruel aunts, like Emily, the heroine of *The Mysteries of Udolpho* (1794), are not uncommon in novels of the period.

Sotherton Court, the subject of the visit in vol. 1, ch. 10, is sometimes said to be modelled on Stoneleigh Abbey, Warwickshire, the house inherited by Mrs Austen's cousin, the Revd Thomas Leigh, and visited by Jane and her mother in 1806.[41] There are certainly features in common: it is hard to believe that the rectangular, elegant room which is the chapel, belonging to the house's eighteenth-century wing, is not in Austen's mind when she makes it feature, oddly and anomalously, in Sotherton, described as an Elizabethan house, 'a large, regular, brick building' (vol. 1, ch. 6) 'complete in its style' (vol. 1, ch. 10) with no mention of any later additions – an elision the effect of which is to heighten Fanny's disappointment. The size of Sotherton, with its many rooms and windows, also perhaps suggests a reminiscence of Stoneleigh, as do the many family portraits; the phrase 'regal visits and loyal efforts' in

---

[41] Mavis Batey, 'A Mere Nothing before Repton,' in her *Jane Austen and the English Landscape* (London: Barn Elms, 1996), pp. 79–94. See also Gaye King, 'The Jane Austen Connection', in *Stoneleigh Abbey: The House, Its Owners, Its Land*, ed. R. Bearman (Warwickshire: Stoneleigh Abbey Limited, 2004), pp. 163–177.

Mrs Rushworth's patter seems to point specifically to the Royalist traditions of the Leigh family, epitomised in the phrase 'Loyal Leighs'. Moreover, the two estates discussed in the novel for their possibilities of improvement, Compton and Sotherton, correspond more or less in size and character to the two properties, Adlestrop and Stoneleigh, that Thomas Leigh had 'improved'.

But if Stoneleigh is made use of, Austen does not intend a direct reference. The grounds were certainly redesigned by Humphry Repton, whose work is discussed in the novel, and Crawford's characteristically sardonic remark 'I see walls of great promise' might well point to Stoneleigh, which had a large walled forecourt to the west front, blocking the view, that was demolished in 1808. Sotherton also has a bowling green, and this, being quite unusually late for the period, might also suggest a reminiscence of Stoneleigh, which still had one on the north side of the house. But other details of the chapter make it unlikely that Austen is describing a specific house. There is, for example, no avenue indicated in Repton's sketch plan of Stoneleigh and its grounds in the Red Book of plans which he presented to Thomas Leigh, and no mention of an avenue in his discussion, whereas the avenue of oak runs for half a mile in the novel, and is the focus of some significant dramatic interchange.[42] The house at Stoneleigh is close to the lodge: in the novel it is nearly a mile away. Fanny's 'The house fronts the East, I perceive' (vol. 1, ch. 8) emphasises that Sotherton's orientation is the reverse of Stoneleigh's. Drayton House in Northamptonshire, remodelled early in the eighteenth century, was notable for its 'long walls of enclosure . . . pierced with gateways into which splendid iron gates were hung . . . quaint flights of steps led from one level to another'.[43] Knole Park in Kent is another possibility. Frances Burney was taken there in 1779 and reports a park

---

[42] The Red Book for Stoneleigh Abbey is held at the Shakespeare Memorial Library, Stratford-upon-Avon.

[43] J. Alfred Cotch, *The Growth of the English House*, 2nd edn (London: Batsford, 1928), p. 157.

'seven miles in circumference', with courtyards before the entrance, and that 'the general air of the place is monastic and gloomy' ('a dismal old prison', Rushworth calls Sotherton).[44] It is not certain that Austen in her dialogues about improvement intends any critique of Repton's landscaping approach, and possible in fact that she would have sympathised with many aspects of his work.[45]

Mansfield Park is often understood as a country house novel, but it is as well to notice that the isolation of Northamptonshire is specifically monitored against the racy Regency world the Crawfords know and to which the Bertram sisters long to escape. As far as is known, Jane Austen had never visited the county, but the place names Stoke and Easton, as well as 'Stanwix Lodge', mentioned in the text (vol. 1, ch. 15; vol. 2, ch. 1; vol. 2, ch. 12) suggest that she had consulted a map of the area. Stoke Bruerne and Stoke Goldington (over the county boundary in Buckinghamshire) lie within a few miles of Easton Maudit, all of which are not far from Olney. It is possible that Jane Austen set her novel in that county because of its association with authors dear to her. Northamptonshire is the home of Harriet Byron, the heroine of *Grandison*. Jane Austen would also have known that William Cowper had lived in Olney, where poems remembered by Fanny Price, 'The Task' and 'Tirocinium', were both composed. In 1786, he moved to Weston Underwood, which like Olney is not far from Northampton. In the Northamptonshire of the novel, travelling is difficult, since the roads, except in the vicinity of Sotherton, remain un-'made' – untarred, stony tracks. Mansfield village still has its common, and Sotherton, with its archaic pheasantry and bowling green, is also a survival from an earlier age.

[44] Austin Dobson (ed.), *Diary and Letters of Madame D'Arblay* (6 vols., London: Macmillan, 1904–5), vol. 1, pp. 270–1.

[45] Richard Quaintance, 'Humphry Repton, "any Mr Repton", and the "Improvement" Metonym in *Mansfield Park*', *Studies in Eighteenth-Century Culture*, 27 (1998), pp. 365–84; see also Stephen Clarke, 'What Smith Did at Compton: Landscape Gardening, Humphry Repton, and *Mansfield Park*', *Persuasions*, 21 (1999), pp. 59–67.

'I do not call Tunbridge or Cheltenham the country', says Edmund, speaking of Mary Crawford's usual winter places of residence: they are the satellite resorts of metropolitan culture. A range of names – Brighton, Ramsgate, Weymouth, Cheltenham Spa, Bath, Tunbridge Wells, Twickenham, Richmond – suggests this new leisured culture, as well as the very specific references to Mayfair, the fashionable London district, where most of the houses were built in the later eighteenth century. Mrs Rushworth's house in Wimpole Street, like Mary's references to cousins of the Bertrams who live 'near Bedford Square', denote precise calibration of the social significance of an address. Hill Street, west of Berkeley Square, the home of the adulterous Admiral Crawford, would have been recognised by Austen's readers as a fashionable one. Thus the sober and repressive morality of Sir Thomas Bertram, in a part of England associated with the piety of Cowper, is deliberately contrasted with the new age, and geography is understood in its ethical and historical dimensions.

This is still more true of Portsmouth, the other main centre of the action. As Jane Austen's first readers would most certainly have known, this was the key port for British defences during the continuing Napoleonic wars, strongly fortified by walls, patrolled ramparts and a moat, its dockyard the largest in the world, and a magnet for tourists. It was to Portsmouth that Nelson had been summoned and from where, through the 'sally-port', mentioned in the novel, he went to his decisive victory over the French fleet at Trafalgar in 1805. Austen situates the domestic sadness of Fanny's disappointment amid the quasi-comic hurry that accompanied the sudden call for a ship to sail. The reader is being invited simultaneously to sympathise with the tired, diffident and bewildered young woman and to recognise the terrific importance and global significance of the preparations for William's departure on a mission against England's enemies – an enclave of private life made the more poignant for being set in a real, famed, crucially significant place.

1

Although Jane Austen takes a serious, 'old-fashioned' and earnest milieu in a comparatively isolated part of England as her subject, *Mansfield Park* itself is influenced by the increased earnestness of English culture. By 1814, she was writing more sympathetically of Evangelicalism than she had earlier. These 'fathers of the Victorians' were successfully dictating the terms of the debate about morality and the church, in a project of national renewal that depended upon reforming the 'manners' of the leisured and governing classes. The mood of the country had shifted decisively towards Anglican seriousness. It would no longer be possible, in a novel of 1814, to have a clergyman hero like Henry Tilney in *Northanger Abbey* declare airily that he will be 'obliged to stay two or three days' at his second parish (vol. 1, ch. 11): residency of the clergy of the Established Church was now widely understood to be essential if the growing influence of Methodism, strongest in country villages and towns, were to be countered.

It is significant that two very successful novels of the years preceding *Mansfield Park*'s composition, Hannah More's *Cœlebs in Search of a Wife* (1809) and Mary Brunton's *Self-Control* (1810), are both strongly Evangelical in feeling. Austen had certainly read the second, and almost certainly the first. More was a famous name and a very active Evangelical; Brunton was the wife of a Scots clergyman. Brunton's Laura Mandlebert is the exemplary 'Christian heroine' that many critics have thought Fanny Price to be. But whereas Fanny only prays desperately for Edmund's happiness (as a psychological resource or displacement of her own unhappiness) or asks in her anger that 'God grant' Mary's influence not make Edmund 'cease to be respectable' (vol. 3, ch. 13), Laura, as the narrator remarks admiringly, has modelled her conduct on the saints and martyrs, and falls on her knees in prayer at every Burneyesque crisis the plot inflicts upon her. *Self-Control* will be among those novels referred to in Austen's side-swipe at 'unconquerable young ladies of eighteen' in vol. 2, ch. 7. Austen might have admired the crisp intelligence of some of More's writing in *Cœlebs*, but the unreality, not to speak of the tedium, of the moral and ecclesiastical debates – loosely modelled on Samuel Johnson's *Rasselas* (1759) – in this 'novel' would have earned her scorn. Maria Edgeworth, on the other hand, was certainly a novelist whom she admired, and who had made political and social affairs the mainstay of many of her novels, such as *Patronage*, published the same year as *Mansfield Park*. *Mansfield Park*'s conversations about the clergyman's vocation, on the clergy's social function, on residency, and on the delivery of sermons may suggest Jane Austen's awareness that there was an audience for such material, and certainly indicate a decision to make her book engage with contemporary debates.

The term 'principle', which is introduced in the first paragraph of the novel, is a key word in Christian thought of the period, and is especially common in Evangelical writings. Because everyone knew what 'principle' meant, precise definitions of it are hard to find, but perhaps Thomas Clarkson's 'that fundamental principle of Christianity, which says, that we shall not do that unto another, which we wish should not be done unto ourselves' comes close.[46] Other sources would suggest that the fundamental principle is the love of God, whence all virtue springs. Thus 'principle', a kind of absolute, is often used as a collective noun for a range of 'principles', all of which could be thought to stem from this original one. Jane Austen takes for granted a consensus among her readers that the conviction that one ought to put another's well-being before one's own, that one ought to command one's own desires, especially sexual desire, and that, through faith, one has (perhaps) the capacity to do so, are key indices of moral virtue. When Sir Thomas recognises that 'principle, active principle, had been wanting' in his daughters' education, though, the explication of 'principle' that follows avoids the language of religious enthusiasm, and is in fact closer to the Christianity of a John Locke or Samuel Johnson than to the rhetoric of Evangelical writers of the period. 'That they had never been properly taught to govern their inclinations and tempers, by that sense of duty which can alone suffice', 'no moral effect

[46] Clarkson, *Abolition of the Slave-Trade*, vol. 1, p. 422.

on the mind', and 'the necessity of self-denial and humility' (vol. 3, ch. 17) are phrases belonging to another register than the Evangelical, which would speak, for example, of the religion of the heart, of inner fervour, of the 'beauty' of 'all the Christian graces'.[47]

As in Evangelical writings, the person of 'principle' is often contrasted with those who live in 'the world' (fashionable London society as a metonym for personal advancement and pleasure or 'fortune and consequence, bustle and the world': vol. 2, ch. 3). Fanny, says the narrator, 'had all the heroism of principle', but – in a significant gesture towards the reader's expectations – 'let her not be wondered at', if principle – signifying her struggle to repress her own feelings – proves a fragile bulwark against her love for Edmund. In passages like these Austen uses an Evangelical vocabulary, but her novel might simultaneously be seen as commenting with some wryness on such passages in *Cœlebs* as that in ch. 12 in which Mrs Garland, loving another man but married to a rake, conquers her previous 'attachment' through 'religious principle', eventually winning her husband over to piety by an assiduous display of feminine submissiveness and tact. As the word 'serious', also reiteratively deployed, suggests, Austen's novel is coloured by the Evangelical movement, but in many respects it is a critique of Evangelicalism; in fact, it may be said to rewrite the Evangelical novel into the mainstream Anglican novel.

Hence, *Mansfield Park* picks up many phrases from the King James Bible; or, to put it more exactly, Austen's prose frequently carries a biblical allusion, though without deliberate or ostentatious reiteration of phrasing. Thus, for example, the word 'riot' in the narrator's sweeping account of Henry's lifestyle – 'all the riot of his gratifications' (vol. 1, ch. 18) has a slightly biblical ring, for the word 'riot' is used of the unrighteous – 'they that count it pleasure to riot in the daytime' in a passage which also condemns the unrighteous because 'they speak evil of the things that they understand not' (Second Epistle of Peter, ch. 2, v. 12–13), and is thus recalled in

[47] Hannah More, *Cœlebs in Search of a Wife*, 12th edn (London: Cadell and Davies, 1809), ch. 34.

Edmund's defence of Mary's not thinking evil, even if she 'speaks evil' (vol. 2, ch. 9). This latter phrase, used of Mary Crawford, though, has a more specific function, as when Edmund says that Fanny's is a 'heart which knew no guile'. The echo of the psalm's blessing of those 'in whose spirit there is no guile' is a convincing dramatic rendering of Edmund's inner mental world shaped by the phrasing of the scriptures. Occasionally one might suppose a more overt biblical allusion, as when Fanny's time in Portsmouth, counting the days till Easter, is described as a 'penance', or when she is said, like the Israelites in the wilderness, not to have a spirit of 'murmuring'. But these are far from the wholesale recital of biblical and liturgical phrasing found in Evangelical writings, and might be ascribed rather to her culture's saturation in scriptural phraseology than to a specific intention to alert the reader on Jane Austen's part. It is interesting in this more serious novel that though Fanny is subject to intense emotions, only the clergyman, Edmund, thanks 'God' (vol. 3, ch. 16). Mr Price swears 'By G—' (vol. 3, chs. 7, 15), but the text includes no equivalent of Elinor Tilney's 'Good God, what will your father and mother say!' (*Northanger Abbey*, vol. 2, ch. 8).

The work that the novel engages with most explicitly is certainly *Lovers' Vows*, an immensely successful play, adapted from Kotzebue's German original, by another distinguished woman writer, Elizabeth Inchbald. Jane Austen might have taken some familiarity with the play for granted among her readers. Mr Yates's talk of the rehearsals at Ecclesford (vol. 1, ch. 13) throws the names of the characters about almost as much as those of the aristocrats he has been staying with, but it is not necessary to be familiar with the play to enjoy his speech. On the other hand, the discussions of ranting, and the apportioning of parts, in vol. 1, ch. 16 have a general air of allusion to material one might be expected to recognise. A reader's understanding of the dispute between the Bertram sisters over the part of Agatha would be heightened by knowing how much opportunity the actress has of physical contact with Frederick, as the stage directions of the scene reveal, and as someone who had seen

the play in the theatre would remember well; Edmund's immediate reaction to the announcement that this is the play chosen
seems also to rely upon *Lovers' Vows*' reputation among conserva-
tives as controversial and risqué. Then again, it may well be argued
that a dramatic purpose is served by *Lovers' Vows* being as much
a closed book at this point to the reader as it is to Fanny Price.

Whether or not Jane Austen also draws parallels between the
characters in *Lovers' Vows* and her own characters – between Baron
Wildenhaim and the baronet Sir Thomas Bertram, for instance, or
between the fallen woman Agatha and the woman rehearsing her
part, Maria – is less certain. But the intensity of the sequence in
which Fanny, her nest of comforts broken into by Mary Crawford,
is forced to witness Mary and Edmund playing their scene together,
is certainly heightened by recognising how closely Amelia's relation to Anhalt reproduces Fanny's real relation to Edmund. Both
clergymen have 'formed' their pupil's 'mind', and both young ladies
are in love with their mentor; the difference is that Mary, in the part
of Amelia, can audaciously express a love that Fanny must smother
within. In this scene of intimate colloquy – chairs drawn together at
the front of the 'stage' – Edmund, as Anhalt, miraculously recipro-
cates his younger pupil's desires. Here as elsewhere, the play's licence
and style become simultaneously alluring and hateful to Fanny, and
Jane Austen is using it as one of the means by which she fills out the
character's inarticulable or unconscious life – carried also in Fanny's
recall of passages from Cowper and Scott.

The most memorable intertextual moment in this novel, though,
occurs when something secreted is given acute and direct expression. Its reference is not to the Bible, or Cowper, or Johnson, or
Scott, the Christian, Tory and early Romantic texts on which Fanny
feeds her inner life, but to the liberal and Whig Laurence Sterne's
A Sentimental Journey (1768). Maria's declaration 'I cannot get out,
as the starling said' in front of the locked gate at Sotherton (vol. 1,
ch. 10) is the culmination or crisis point of a sequence that can be
considered the greatest dramatic achievement of Austen's fiction.
The pleasure grounds at Sotherton draw upon many associations

which Jane Austen may not have been deliberately invoking, and have to do with the long history of garden layout itself, which has always carried a freight of symbolic, even of religious, meaning. So it is appropriate that readers should feel that the garden's wilderness and pathways of dalliance remind them of Spenser, or *Paradise Lost*, or *A Midsummer Night's Dream* or *As You Like It*, and that the gate should suggest to some the wicket gate through which Christian passes after his confrontation with Mr Worldly Wiseman in Bunyan's *Pilgrim's Progress*, or Marvell's 'iron gates of life'. Others may remember the scene in *Clarissa* in which the heroine is lured to betray herself by Lovelace, as Maria is by Henry, in front of a 'garden door'.

The allusion to *A Sentimental Journey*, though, is of a different order. The breaking into Maria's speech – 'as she spoke, and it was with eloquence' – of a quotation from Sterne is unnerving in its unexpectedness. One effect of its eruption is to require or force the reader to supply a context that the context of the novel itself seems to assume. The bird is a prisoner, that is clear; but the reference is evidently meant to recall also Yorick's resignation to his imprisonment in the Bastille. The bird's cry (as disconcerting in Sterne's text as Maria's here) reminds him that however one makes up one's mind to endure imprisonment, its suffering is intolerable. Maria's expression is all the more powerful in its effect because she is here trapped as much by Henry Crawford's innuendoes and double-meanings as she is prevented by the locked gate itself. The effect is to make her speech sound not like the outburst of a selfish and petulant woman, but like the cry of all women caught in what might be defined as patriarchal society, but might equally well here be called her fate.

The passages in this novel concerned with Maria's engagement to Rushworth are damningly and savagely precise. Her reflections on having committed herself to a loveless marriage are delivered in abrupt sentences and staccato rhythms which simultaneously convey anger, self-punishment, and her need to flee from the truth, in a mode that can only argue the influence – not direct, not apparent, not easy to pinpoint – of the Shakespearean soliloquy. It has been suggested that there is special significance in the choice of *Henry VIII* for reading aloud in *Mansfield Park*, either because of analogies between Crawford and the King, or between Katherine and Fanny, but such resemblances are not hinted at in the text. Shakespeare's influence is to be seen not in specific allusions or quotations, but much deeper, in Austen's transformation of the Shakespearean soliloquy into her mode of free indirect discourse. As generations of critics and readers have agreed, the most pervasive influence on Austen's prose (and perhaps on her thinking about the moral life) is Samuel Johnson, and his trenchant representations of the insurgent power of covert motives and desires must also have contributed to such passages as these as well as those which represent Fanny's struggles with envy and jealousy. Inspired, then, by her forebears – Shakespeare, Johnson, Richardson, Burney – in this novel Jane Austen has found distinctive means by which to convey overlapping, interloping and sabotaging impulses buried within her characters' hearts.

CRITICAL RECEPTION

The story of *Mansfield Park*'s reception over the past two hundred years resembles the story of its heroine in the house itself. Like her, it has been neglected, passed over, misunderstood, sneered at and ill-used. It has had its defenders, and a surprising number of them have been, like her cousin Edmund, men of the cloth. Gradually, however, its qualities have become impossible to overlook. Yet, even when *Mansfield Park*'s stature is acknowledged, it is with reluctance: a great, but not a favourite, novel; not the obvious heir to the Austen estate, thought to be lacking in comedy and even in irony, not 'out', but not exactly 'in', either. And just as Fanny cherishes secret, illicit desire, some critics have argued that the novel itself harbours the untoward, that behind its principled, conservative exterior lie shameful secrets. Unlike Jane Austen's other novels, then,

Mansfield Park has presented less an invitation than a challenge to its readers.

The first critic of the novel was Jane's brother Henry. Unlike *Pride and Prejudice*, *Mansfield Park* does not seem to have been read aloud to the Austen family group as it was being written; only Cassandra was privy to its contents. That is why Austen is so interested in Henry's responses as they read through the novel in the carriage to London on a cold March day in 1814. 'We did not begin reading till Bentley Green', about ten miles into their journey, Austen tells Cassandra. 'Henry's approbation hitherto is even equal to my wishes; he says it is very different from the other two, but does not appear to think it at all inferior. He has only married Mrs R. I am afraid he has gone through the most entertaining part.—He took to Lady B. & Mrs N. most kindly, & gives great praise to the drawing of the Characters. He understands them all, likes Fanny & I think foresees how it will all be.'[48] At home in Henrietta Street, three days later, Henry 'is in the 3^{d} vol.', and tells his sister that he likes the book 'better & better'. 'I beleive *now* he has changed his mind as to foreseeing the end; – he said yesterday at least, that he defied anybody to say whether H. C. would be reformed, or would forget Fanny in a fortnight.'[49] When Austen next writes to Cassandra Henry has finished the book '& his approbation has not lessened. He found the last half of the last volume *extremely interesting*.'[50] Perhaps that did not mean quite unqualified praise. It is clear that this almost professional author, keen, as she said, to make 'pewter' out of sales, wants her reader to experience both entertainment and suspense: neither she nor Henry say anything about the novel's morality.

But on publication *Mansfield Park* is met by silence. The journals that reviewed *Pride and Prejudice* do not notice it. In response to this, and to allay her authorial anxiety over its reception, Austen collects the verdicts of family and friends – perhaps amused by their

[48] Le Faye (ed.), *Letters*, 2 March 1814, p. 255.
[49] Le Faye (ed.), *Letters*, 5 March 1814, p. 258.
[50] Le Faye (ed.), *Letters*, 9 March 1814, p. 261.

variety, perhaps disconcerted by the tepid nature of their praise. The anxieties assuaged in her reporting of Henry's reactions are discernible in these 'opinions', which like those produced in response to an interviewer's questions are shaped by those questions themselves.[51] Her governess friend Anne Sharpe's response is candid and representative: 'I think it excellent – & of it's good sense & moral Tendency there can be no doubt. – Your Characters are drawn to the Life – so *very, very* natural & just – but as you beg me to be perfectly honest, I must confess I prefer P & P.' This, as it turned out, was the verdict of most readers throughout the next century. But John Plumptre's comment is reassuringly like Henry's: 'I never read a novel which interested me so very much throughout, the characters are all so remarkably well kept up & so well drawn, & the plot is so well contrived that I had not an idea till the end which of the two w^d marry Fanny, H. C. or Edm^d. Mrs Norris amused me particularly'.

Many of the 'opinions' contradict one another, and Austen puts them down so that their contradictoriness is amusingly exposed. Not unexpectedly, though, her first readers, as her first critics would do, praise the book and its characters for being 'natural', and the more staid or cautious of them praise its good principles, as would the Regent's librarian, James Stanier Clark. Their expectations heightened by Lady Catherine and Mr Collins, they often light on the novel's comedy. Cassandra '[d]elighted much in Mr Rushworth's stupidity'; Mary Cooke 'enjoyed Mr Rushworth's folly'; 'Mrs Anna Harwood delighted with Mrs Norris & the green Curtain'; 'Miss Burrel – admired it very much – particularly Mrs Norris & Dr Grant'; 'Mrs James Austen, very much pleased. Enjoyed Mrs Norris particularly, & the scene at Portsmouth.' As the novel's reputation has advanced, its comedy has seemed to recede from critical attention: in most late twentieth-century readings, it has virtually disappeared. At any rate, few modern readers could

---

[51] 'Opinions of Mansfield Park', in Austen, *Plan of a Novel*, facsimile between pages 11 and 13.

say, as Austen's mother did, that they 'enjoyed' Mrs Norris and leave it at that.

When Scott, responding to Murray's request – it was publicity for another Murray publication – reviewed *Emma* in the *Quarterly Review*, he did not mention *Mansfield Park*.[52] Nor is the novel cited, in fact, on the title page of *Emma*, which is 'by the author of *Pride and Prejudice*, etc, etc'. This may suggest that Murray, who would have canvassed what people in London thought of the preceding novel, had little faith in it, and only consented to publishing a small second edition as the price of securing *Emma*. At any rate Austen was disappointed, and made her disappointment clear in a letter to Murray.[53] The next substantial criticism of Austen's novels, however, which appeared in the *Quarterly Review* in January 1821, is clearly intended as a corrective to Scott's earlier omission.[54] Though it is formally a review of the two posthumously published novels, Richard Whately spends more time on *Mansfield Park* than on either of them. Like Scott, he notes that the novel form has recently risen in prestige, and attributes this to its greater 'naturalness'. The discussion of the natural and the improbable in recent fiction which follows is in effect an approach to questions of technique: Whately's interest is in how Austen overcomes the readers' resistance to the 'supernatural' character of the 'omniscience and omnipresence' (pp. 353, 361) of the third-person narrator's claim to delineate 'the inward workings of the human heart'.

Like Austen's relatives and friends, he praises Austen's 'fools'. But the most individual passage in his article concerns the 'inward' quality of Austen's depiction of Fanny Price's 'heart' (p. 361):

Fanny is . . . armed against Mr. Crawford by a stronger feeling than even her disapprobation; by a vehement attachment to Edmund.

[52] [Walter Scott], review, *Quarterly Review*, 14:27 (October 1815), pp. 188–201. (The review is unsigned.)

[53] Le Faye (ed.), *Letters*, 1 April 1816, p. 313.

[54] [Richard Whately], review, *Quarterly Review*, 24:48 (January 1821), pp. 352–76. Page references to this article are given in the text. (The review is unsigned.)

The silence in which this passion is cherished – the slender hopes and enjoyments by which it is fed – the restlessness and jealousy with which it fills a mind naturally active, contented and unsuspicious – the manner in which it tinges every event and every reflection, are painted with . . . vividness and . . . detail.   (p. 367)

Few later critics of the novel were so keenly to recognise Fanny's 'passion'. Whately goes on to make the identification, pre-'Victorian' in its candour, of Austen's heroines as sexual beings, or desiring subjects, and notices how *Mansfield Park* transgresses the code that barred the expression of a woman's uninvited passion. She presents women, he says, 'As liable "to fall in love first", as anxious to attract the attention of agreeable men, as much taken with a striking manner, or a handsome face, as unequally gifted with constancy and firmness, as liable to have their affections biassed by convenience or fashion, as we, on our part, will admit men to be.' This in turn means that Austen is able to depict Fanny's jealousy, happiness at others' misery, shame at her parents and anger at Edmund's obtuseness, 'feelings, all of them, which, under the influence of strong passion, must alloy the purest mind, but with which scarcely any *authoress* but Miss Austin [sic] would have ventured to temper the aetherial materials of a heroine' (p. 367). It would be a long time before the intelligence that is now partly obscured by this young churchman's overtly masculine bias was matched in the criticism of this novel.

Much of the subsequent history of Austen's novels in the nineteenth century is to be traced not in formal criticism, in fact, but in their presentation and illustrations. *Mansfield Park* was reissued as one of Bentley's Standard Novels in 1833, with an engraved title page and frontispiece. It is telling that the title page features the scene of near-farce in the makeshift 'theatre' in which Sir Thomas confronts Mr Yates in full ranting mode. Tom Bertram is seen in the background, enjoying this spectacle with his usual impudence. In the engraving opposite, Mary Crawford, grasping Fanny's hand, shows her how well the necklace (a heavy beaded affair) looks in a pier-glass mirror. Fanny is wearing a bonnet and shawl, and, as a contemporary reviewer pointed out, the depictions were anachronistic. From this date the novel was commonly issued with at least one illustration, and this is how it was circulated and presented to readers throughout the nineteenth and early twentieth centuries.

The six illustrations for the Groombridge edition of 1875, however, represent a reading of the novel that is melancholy, even Gothic in feeling. The best of them shows Fanny in shadow between two gnarled oak trees gazing over the park towards Edmund as he gives Mary her riding lesson. In another engraving, Fanny, dressed in the costume of the 1870s, waits on a rustic seat at Sotherton whilst Edmund and Mary wander off in a brightly lit tunnel of foliage. This is a grave, serious *Mansfield Park* in which, presciently perhaps, the country house and its estate are dominant features. At the end of the century editions with illustrations by the well-known artists Hugh Thomson (1897) and C. E. Brock (1898) were published, and frequently reissued over the next decades. Both illustrators tend to single out the novel's comic moments; sometimes, as with Thomson's 'A circle of admirals' extrapolating these from the text, or making comedy out of apparent crises in the narrative by their drawing of facial expressions. Several other illustrated editions appeared during the same period. The history of Austen's reception by intellectuals, novelists and critics can thus be supplemented with her reception by readers appealed to in the marketing of her novels through their pictorial elements. This decorative packaging of Austen's novels was continued in their remaking as popular films in the later twentieth century. The afterlife of *Mansfield Park* in Victorian and later fiction is a topic too broad to be discussed here, but its influence can be felt in, for example, Charlotte Brontë's *Jane Eyre* (1847) and Somerville and Ross's *An Irish Cousin* (1889) and *The Real Charlotte* (1903).

In 1917 the *Quarterly Review* published a centenary appreciation of Austen's novels by Reginald Farrer, who had some highly critical things to say about *Mansfield Park*.[55] In calling it Jane Austen's '*gran*

---

[55] Reginald Farrer, review, *Quarterly Review*, 227:552 (July 1917), pp. 1–30. Page references to this article are given in the text.

refiuto', her great denial, Farrer anticipates the reaction of many later critics, and suggests more or less the same explanation – Austen's capitulation to her 'clerical relations' (p. 20) or conventional moral values. The discussion is constructed around a series of dramatic oppositions, of antithetical structures. 'None of her books is quite so brilliant in parts, none shows a greater technical mastery, a more audacious facing of realities, a more certain touch with character', he writes. 'Yet, alone of all her books, "Mansfield Park" is vitiated throughout by a radical dishonesty' (p. 20). The author is oppressed by a 'purpose of edification' which is at 'cross purposes' with her natural gift. The Crawfords 'obviously have her artist's affection as well as her moralist's disapproval' (p. 21). '[F]iction holds no heroine more repulsive in her cast-iron self-righteousness and steely rigidity of prejudice' than Fanny. Mary, on the other hand, 'would be . . . most delightful as a wife' (p. 22), a remark which rather gives the game away. This is an early example of the male writer, cheated of the expected textual love-object, losing his critical head. Farrer's description of Fanny Price as a 'penniless dull little nobody' would be echoed even by one of Austen's great critics, D. W. Harding, who in the 1970s called her 'a dreary, debilitated, priggish goody-goody'.[56] Nevertheless Farrer ends his discussion with a perceptive account of the novel's 'technical triumphs' (p. 22), especially the management of the Sotherton and rehearsal scenes, in which a crowd is 'manoeuvred simultaneously in a complicated maze of movement, that never for an instant fails to get each person into its right prominence at the required moment'.

The next important moment in the novel's history was R. W. Chapman's Oxford Edition of 1923. This varies the tradition by rejecting 'imaginative' pictures and instead includes images 'from Contemporary Sources'. All the same, these constitute, like the earlier illustrated editions, interpretive gestures and emphases. The frontispiece shows 'before' and 'after' watercolours from Repton's

[56] D. W. Harding, 'Mansfield Park', in *Regulated Hatred and Other Essays on Jane Austen*, ed. Monica Lawlor (London and Atlantic Highlands, N. J.: Athlone Press, 1998), p. 122.

Red Book for Harleston Park, Northamptonshire, which, it was implied, but nowhere stated, might be the model for Sotherton Court, or perhaps Mansfield Park itself. This led in turn to a significant critical literature around the topic of 'improvement'. Chapman's inclusion of the full text of *Lovers' Vows* also effectively set the agenda for much of the critical work on the novel for the next decades, and throughout the 1930s and 40s several papers appeared claiming, or disputing, parallels between the characters of the novel and the figures in the play. At the same time, Chapman's edition, by giving Austen's novels the editorial treatment up to this time reserved for the Greek and Latin canon, effectively confirmed Austen's 'classic' status, and commentary in the subsequent years by Virginia Woolf, E. M. Forster, Mary Lascelles and Lord David Cecil, as well as the study of her development by Q. D. Leavis, effectively took this for granted.

In the years after the Second World War university study of English literature greatly expanded in the English-speaking world, and it was in this context that the next phase of the novel's reception was played out. Instead of the English upper- and middle-class authors who, belonging to the gentry themselves, could still effectively share many of Austen's cultural assumptions, writing on the novel for the next decades was largely the work of North American male academics, aggressively making 'cases' or explications of its argument, but within that paradigm of the 'new criticism' which severed the text from its cultural context and historical setting. In this phase of its reception it is worth noting that the two most influential articles to have been published on *Mansfield Park* are by manifest outsiders: one a New York Jew, the other a New York Palestinian, colleagues and friends at Columbia.

The American prestige of *Mansfield Park* can be traced to Edmund Wilson, whose 'A Long Talk about Jane Austen', reprinted in his *Classics and Commercials* (1950),[57] contains a telling page on

---

[57] Edmund Wilson, *Classics and Commercials, a Literary Chronicle of the Forties* (New York: Farrar Straus, 1950), pp. 196–203, originally published in *The New Yorker* (24 June 1944).

the novel. Dismissing the 'familiar' reaction of readers who repudiate Fanny Price, Wilson stresses its qualities as a work of art, the 'purely aesthetic' 'delight in the focusing of the complex group through the ingenuous eyes of Fanny, the balance and harmony of the handling of the contrasting timbres of the characters, which are now heard in combination, now set off against one another'. Wilson encouraged Vladimir Nabokov to include the novel in his course on European Fiction at Cornell in 1950. Nabokov's published lecture[58] is a leisurely exposition of the novel's recurrent 'themes' or aspects of the plot, the artist's skill in modulating from one theme to another, and style. He identifies several weaknesses in its structure, notably the devices that drag out the delay in Edmund's proposal to Mary Crawford, necessary so that time can be allowed for Henry's courtship of Fanny and seduction by Maria, until 'his slowness becomes something of a farce'.[59] Though he says 'the whole play theme in *Mansfield Park* is an extraordinary achievement', his praise of Austen's 'exquisite needlework art' is more than a little patronising.[60]

In 1948 appeared R. W. Chapman's *Jane Austen: Facts and Problems*. In a section on *Mansfield Park*, Chapman wrote that this is the work of Austen in which it is 'hardest to be sure of the writer's general intention. She wrote to her sister, at the outset, that she was going to take a new subject, ordination'.[61] Many writers up to and including Claudia L. Johnson in 1988 and Edward Said in 1991[62] cited this reference as significant, though in fact Chapman's remark is misleading. In her letter to Cassandra announcing the arrival of the first copy of *Pride and Prejudice* in January 1813, Jane Austen writes, after saying a good deal about that novel, 'Now I will

---

[58] Vladimir Nabokov, *Lectures on Literature*, ed. Fredson Bowers (London: Weidenfeld and Nicolson, 1980), pp. 9–60.

[59] Nabokov, *Lectures*, p. 50. [60] Nabokov, *Lectures*, p. 10.

[61] Chapman, *Facts and Problems*, p. 194.

[62] Claudia L. Johnson, *Jane Austen: Women, Politics, and the Novel* (Chicago: University of Chicago Press, 1988), p. 94; Edward W. Said, *Culture and Imperialism* (1993; London and New York: Vintage, 1994), pp. 73, 101. Subsequent references to both these works are given in the text.

try to write of something else; – it shall be a complete change of subject – Ordination.'[63] Chapman had printed this as 'Now I will try to write of something else, & it shall be a complete change of subject', in his edition of the letters,[64] prompting the assumption that Austen was turning her mind to a new novel. But this was not 'at the outset' of *Mansfield Park*'s composition: the novel was well on the way by that date. In a letter to the *TLS* of 19 December 1968 Hugh Brogan pointed out Chapman's error, saying that he was 'understandably perplexed by the author's apparent statement, but did not notice she had never made it'. 'Ordination' as an entry to the novel played a major interpretive role in the criticism of the next few decades, including the next important contribution, by the American Lionel Trilling.

'Nobody, I believe, has ever found it possible to like the heroine of *Mansfield Park*', declared Trilling in his essay, originally published in the *Partisan Review* in 1954, and reprinted, with one paragraph omitted, in the widely used *Pelican Guide to English Literature* in 1957.[65] Wilson, whom Trilling greatly admired, had already written that 'Fanny, with her humility, her priggishness, and her innocent and touching good faith, is a perfect picture of one kind of woman'; Nabokov had called her 'subtle and sensitive'.[66] But the sweeping, magisterial manner of Trilling's paper, the first full-dress account of the novel by an established critic, effectively set the agenda for discussion and interpretation over the decades that followed.

Unmentioned in the essay, but clearly a stimulus to it, was Marvin Mudrick's *Irony as Defense and Discovery* (1952).[67] In his unsubtle

---

[63] Le Faye (ed.), *Letters*, 29 January 1813, p. 202.

[64] R. W. Chapman (ed.), *Jane Austen's Letters to Her Sister Cassandra and Others*, 2nd edn (London: Oxford University Press, 1952), p. 298.

[65] Lionel Trilling, 'Jane Austen and *Mansfield Park*', in *The Pelican Guide to English Literature*, vol. 5: *From Blake to Byron*, ed. Boris Ford (Harmondsworth: Penguin, 1957), pp. 112–29. Subsequent references to this essay are given in the text.

[66] Wilson, *Classics and Commercials*, p. 200; Nabokov, *Lectures*, p 46.

[67] Marvin Mudrick, *Irony as Defense and Discovery* (1952; Berkeley: University of California Press, 1974).

chapter on the novel Mudrick argued, like Farrer, that in *Mansfield Park* Austen betrayed herself. Her attitude to life was ironic and playful; in this novel she attacks irony and playfulness and throws in her lot with the dreary, conventional Fanny and Edmund. Mudrick's passionate dislike of the novel gave his essay a special force. Andrew Wright's argument in *Jane Austen's Novels: A Study in Structure*, published a year later, is colourless in comparison, though he states the same position: '*Mansfield Park* provides enduring proof that Jane Austen is not always ironic . . . the two central characters are presented straightforwardly, entirely without contradictions of any kind' so that 'this work can only be contrasted to the rest of the canon'.[68] Trilling's essay begins by rehearsing the views of these two critics: 'there is one novel of Jane Austen's, *Mansfield Park*, in which the characteristic irony seems not to be at work' (p. 113). A. Walton Litz's chapter (1965), in the wake of Trilling, also declares that 'for once in Jane Austen's art the familiar tensions and qualifications are resolved into bald didacticism'[69] – not a comment on the novel's final chapters (where it might be justified) but on its pervasive attitude.

The strategy of Trilling's essay is to lead the reader to believe that those who reject *Mansfield Park* are right, and then to turn the tables on them (as he suggests the novelist does in *Northanger Abbey*). He affects to speak the voice of a contemporary consensus. In Trilling's repeated verb, the novel 'seems' to deserve the 'bitter resentment' of readers who think it betrays Jane Austen's values. 'To outward seeming, Mary Crawford . . . is another version of Elizabeth Bennet', yet Austen repudiates her. Then comes the key pronouncement, spaced for rhetorical effect as a single paragraph: 'Yet *Mansfield Park* is a great novel, its greatness being commensurate with its power to offend' (p. 116). Trilling then begins his rehabilitation of the novel, firstly seeking to explicate and historicise Austen's recommendation

[68] Andrew Wright, *Jane Austen's Novels: A Study in Structure* (London: Chatto and Windus, 1953), pp. 123–4, 134.
[69] A. Walton Litz, *Jane Austen, A Study of Her Artistic Development* (London: Chatto and Windus, 1965), p. 116.

of Fanny Price. 'Fanny is a Christian heroine', whose 'debility' is a sign of her saintliness. 'The question of ordination is of essential importance to the novel' (p. 118) since it entails a conception of professionalism and duty which looks forward to the Victorians, but which 'we' find hard to accept. 'The seemingly absurd episode of the play' (p. 121) has great 'cultural significance' as a diagnosis of the dangers of impersonation that lie at the heart of the Romantic, and thus of the modern, self. This is the style of the modern metropolis in which 'we' – Trilling and his readers – are bound, thus associating us with the fatal, condemned personalities of the Crawfords. At this point a personal, even eccentric, yearning seems to infuse Trilling's continual use of the plural pronoun. 'In our dreams of our right true selves', he writes, 'we live in the country.' And, in the final words of the essay, *Mansfield Park* speaks to 'our secret inexpressible hopes' (p. 129).

Trilling's essay was influential, not through his far-fetched and idiosyncratic readings of the novel, but through his evident seriousness and commitment. He did not undermine those critics who derided the novel for its conventionality; he simply rehabilitated that conventionality through his own argument. The novel remained a straightforwardly moral one, without inner irony, but with the values restressed or reversed. His argument is important because he gave provocative expression to a common conflict of feelings. It is its apparent conservatism that makes *Mansfield Park* confronting – and many readers cannot get past it. Not all: in Whit Stillman's film *Metropolitan* (1989) the leading characters debate Trilling's essay; the film itself, remaking or recreating the novel in terms of New York high life at the end of the twentieth century, effectively repudiates the suggestion that its morality is out of date.

In the decade after Trilling, many American critics sought to supplement his detection of 'insincerity' in the Crawfords and to explicate the novel's ethical scheme or argument, implicitly to an audience to whom it would appear alien. 'Integrity', which Trilling had used, is the key word of many critiques. The most distinguished contribution to this school of criticism is the essay by Thomas

R. Edwards, Jr, 'The Difficult Beauty of *Mansfield Park*' (1965).[70]
As Martin Price wrote in a rather later essay which explored the
deftness and subtlety of the novel's irony, 'we may have reached a
moment . . . when moral rigor has a renewed attraction, even a
romantic appeal'.[71] Such exclusively ethical readings of the novel,
however, never thought to connect it with its Evangelical context.
Evangelical campaigning in the years of the Napoleonic wars was
always linked to a project of national renewal. In the years of the
'cold war' this, in a different era, and for different ends, was the –
largely unconscious and certainly undeclared – project of this criticism too.

Tony Tanner's 'Introduction' to the Penguin edition of *Mansfield Park* (1966) first appeared in a British publication circulating in schools and colleges, and was current for many years and
widely influential. Trilling's formulations are picked up: 'the book
does seem . . . to speak for repression and negation, fixity and
enclosure'; 'in the debilitated but undeviating figure of Fanny Price
we should perceive the pain and labour involved in maintaining true
values [aka 'integrity'] in a corrosive world of dangerous energies
and selfish power-play'.[72] Vigorously written, Tanner's piece was
well-adapted to the market it served: once again the novel is seen
as without irony, and Fanny Price as 'never, ever, wrong'. *Mansfield Park*, following Trilling, is said to celebrate immobility and
rest: Fanny Price 'suffers in her stillness. For Righteousness' sake',
a characterisation of the novel's religious feeling, like the earlier
critic's, more appropriate to American Transcendentalism than to
the novel's sober Anglican tone. The ascription of stillness to the

---

[70] See for example, Joseph M. Duffy, Jr., 'Moral Integrity and Moral Anarchy
in *Mansfield Park*', *ELH*, 23 (1956), pp. 71–91: Thomas R. Edwards, Jr, 'The
Difficult Beauty of *Mansfield Park*', *Nineteenth-Century Fiction*, 20 (1965),
pp. 51–67.
[71] Martin Price, 'Austen: Manners and Morals,' in his *Forms of Life: Character
and Moral Imagination in the Novel* (New Haven and London: Yale University
Press, 1983), pp. 65–89, p. 70.
[72] Tony Tanner, 'The Quiet Thing: *Mansfield Park*', in his *Jane Austen* (London:
Macmillan, 1986), pp. 142–175, pp. 143, 171–2.

figure, as replicated in such descriptions of Fanny as Leo Bersani's 'a stable non-desiring center of judgement' (1976) effectively erases her erotic life.[73]

In the same year as Trilling's article, Q. D. Leavis' Introduction to the Macdonald Illustrated Classics edition appeared and made a clear and unembarrassed claim for the novel's greatness.[74] The weakly sentimental images in this volume – sketches of a quasi-Regency idyll, by Philip Gough – suggest the illustrative tradition at its last gasp; they contrast sharply with the tenor of Leavis' bold presentation of *Mansfield Park* as a searching and 'tragic' work, shaped by Austen's reading of Shakespeare. Trilling and Leavis concurred in finding *Mansfield Park* the work of Austen most fit to be compared with the masters of the European novel.[75] By this time, then, *Mansfield Park* was widely accepted as an authoritative, and deeply interesting, if 'problematic' text, which investigated and exposed a culture poised on the cusp of the modern world.

Alistair Duckworth's *The Improvement of the Estate* (1971)[76] began to move towards a more precise historicism than is evident, for instance, in Trilling's gestures towards Victorian conceptions of 'duty'. Framed as a reply to what he designated the 'subversive' school of Austen criticism (primarily such writers as Farrer, Mudrick and Harding), Duckworth's book claimed that the novel's moral order was fundamentally sacramental, or sanctioned by the authority of God, and linked this to what he argued was Austen's

---

[73] Leo Bersani, *A Future for Astyanax: Character and Desire in Literature* (Boston: Little Brown, 1976), p. 76.

[74] Q. D. Leavis, 'Introduction', in her edn of *Mansfield Park* (London: Macdonald, 1957), pp. vii–xviii; reprinted in her *Collected Essays* ed. G. Singh (Cambridge: Cambridge University Press, 1983), 2 vols., I, pp. 161–71.

[75] This would be taken up in, for example, Roger Gard, 'Mansfield Park, Fanny Price, Flaubert and the Modern Novel', in his *Jane Austen's Novels: The Art of Clarity* (New Haven and London: Yale University Press, 1992), pp. 121–54.

[76] Alistair Duckworth, *The Improvement of the Estate: A Study of Jane Austen's Novels* (Baltimore and London: Johns Hopkins University Press, 1971, revised paperback edition 1994).

opposition to 'improvement', meaning change and innovation. Just as Edmund Burke had attacked those who would destroy the 'fabrick of the house' (Burke's metaphor, in fact, for the whole of established society), Austen – in this version – attacks those who would destroy the existing landscape and gardens, and by implication, Duckworth argued, traditional social values. The theatricals are a similar violation of established order, which Austen utterly condemned. An account which notably elides the central section of the novel finally focuses on Fanny Price's movement from the periphery to the 'centre', to become the 'effective mistress of the Mansfield estate' and 'the true trustee of its traditions' (p. 72), notions that were to have successful careers.

1975, the bicentenary of Jane Austen's birth, was commemorated by the British post office with a set of stamps; the stamp of *Mansfield Park* (appropriately the most expensive) features the Crawfords (Henry in a gorgeous morning gown), not the hero and heroine, thus probably reflecting a popular view of the novel's interest. The year was also marked by the publication of a number of monographs and collections. Marilyn Butler's *Jane Austen and the War of Ideas* was the most important of these. Reiterating the moral or didactic reading of the novel of the previous decades, Butler gives this new life by relating it to a contemporary context: Austen's novels, as she claims, are articulations, or dramatisations, of an ideology common to writers arguing against the new social and cultural innovations associated with the French revolution. Concentrating again on the first volume, Butler demonstrates how the novel contrasts Fanny's values with the worldly materialism and amorality of the Bertrams and the cynicism of the Crawfords, paralleling such contrasts in work by other anti-Jacobin novelists of the period.

Fanny's status as a specifically Christian heroine is important to Butler's reading. She is an exemplar of scrupulous self-examination, a figure who must undergo a series of trials. 'Portsmouth is Fanny's exile in the wilderness, her grand temptation by the devil Mammon' in the person of Henry Crawford, who offers her the material establishment of his Norfolk estate.[77] Portsmouth and London are both versions of a materialist world; Fanny 'rejects' them both, and in an echo of Mudrick (who had declared that 'Fanny's only freedom is to choose among worlds')[78] 'she chooses peace': 'her third alternative, Mansfield, promises her a social life of affectionate service, together with an inner life of meditation' (pp. 242, 245). Butler's thesis, in which delineation of the inner life is associated with the Romantic narrative, entails a sweeping and extraordinary claim: 'The theme of *Mansfield Park* is the contrast of man-centred or selfish habits of mind, with a temper that is sceptical of self and that refers beyond self to objective values. Since Fanny is the representative of this orthodoxy, the individuality of her consciousness must to a large extent be denied' (p. 247).

Thus Butler finds the second and third volumes of the novel, where, as she suggests, attention shifts away from Fanny as observer to Fanny as experiencing subject, much less successful than the first, and eventually finds the figure of Fanny a 'failure' (p. 248). This is a reading which, after a first acknowledgement, omits altogether reference to Fanny's feelings for Edmund. However, 'so entangled are her "disinterested" principles in all kinds of self-interested feelings and fears', as Mary Poovey was to put it a few years later in her important section in *The Proper Lady and the Woman Writer*,[79] that the reader may find it difficult to credit Fanny with any free or morally exemplary 'choice'. 'Fanny is not torn by conflicts', Butler declares: though not as melodramatically as this implies, one could certainly argue that Austen displays Fanny as a conflicted and troubled person. Butler's reading represents the novel as, in effect, a 'skilful dramatization of the conservative case' (p. 249) in the war of ideas, which, though much more sympathetic, offers something akin to Mudrick's 'novel of uncompromising moral purpose'.[80]

[77] Marilyn Butler, *Jane Austen and the War of Ideas* (Oxford: Clarendon Press, 1975), p. 237. Subsequent references to this work are given in the text.
[78] Mudrick, *Irony*, p. 242.
[79] Mary Poovey, *The Proper Lady and the Woman Writer* (Chicago: University of Chicago Press, 1984), p. 218.
[80] Mudrick, *Irony*, p. 172.

By this time, overtly feminist readings of the novel were beginning to appear. The most important of these, in the wake of
Mary Poovey, was undoubtedly Claudia L. Johnson's in *Jane Austen:
Women, Politics, and the Novel* (1988) and what made it so com-
pelling was, in part, its direct and witty confrontation with the
previous traditions of *Mansfield Park* criticism. Her reading, like
Butler's grounded in the literature of the period, is an implicit rebut-
tal of that earlier account, as well as of Duckworth's alignment of
it with a Burkean celebration of the country estate. She argues
that the novel 'erodes rather than upholds' conservative values
(p. 114), and her own reformulations of Austen's writing certainly
bite like acid. *Mansfield Park* exhibits conservatism only to undermine and reveal the deceptions and 'bad faith' that sustain its reign
(p. 101). Fanny Price's circumstances mean that she accepts or inter-
nalises the mandates of patriarchal power with especial depth, but
she will not marry a man she does not love. Sir Thomas fancies
he is the upholder of principle and good governance, but is actually displayed as only able to sustain his self-image by processes of
self-deception. Lady Bertram is a parodic representation of the idle
decorative female postulated as the ideal woman in conservative
ideology. Throughout the novel self-interest is veiled or disguised
by tricks of speech or behaviour; and as Johnson demonstrates, the
'drapery' of self-deceptive 'decency' variously covers selfish motives
(p. 100).

The general drift of Johnson's argument about Sir Thomas
Bertram was highly persuasive. Sometimes simplified into the idea
that the figure is a tyrant and treats his womenfolk like slaves –
rather than, as Johnson suggests, enjoying the sense of his own
benevolence to those who are nevertheless in his power – this
reading of the figure was to become almost standard in criticism
over the next decades. Acknowledging the dominant tradition,
Johnson remarks on the 'ungratifying humorlessness' of the novel
(p. 194), though the percipience of her own readings reflects delight
in Austen's powers of playful exposure. Most importantly, in the
wake of Butler and Poovey, the domestic dramas of the novel were

understood as infused with politics – with issues that bore upon and could readily be related to broader social debates of the period. '[T]he novels of Jane Austen focus on the discourse rather than the representation of politics' (p. 27), so that the vocabulary of domestic life and affective relations was understood as coterminous with the language of historic conflict. Following Butler and Johnson, feminist readings in the last decade of the twentieth century tended to converge with 'new historicist' accounts which increasingly gave emphasis to Austen's affiliations with contemporary – and especially female – writers, and to her understanding of legal and economic structures as they bore upon women.

'The family fortunes [Sir Thomas] rescues depend on slave labor in the West Indies', Johnson remarked (p. 96). This premise is contestable, but was to be reiterated in the next decade's criticism of the novel.[81] During the last years of the twentieth century when a form of political radicalism became almost mandatory within academic criticism, many chapters and articles appeared which based their interpretation of *Mansfield Park* on this hitherto ignored or slighted aspect of the Bertrams' circumstances. They gave readings of the novel derogatory of the gentry estate, in effect reversing the claims of those earlier commentators who invested the country house and its grounds with a near-transcendental or 'religious' aura. The most influential, though not the first, of these readings was in Edward W. Said's *Culture and Imperialism* (1993) where a section on *Mansfield Park* forms a key part of the opening chapter. If imperialist assumptions could be shown to pervade a work of the least political, most genteel of novelists, then the way would be open to demonstrate how they informed other texts and prepared the ground for the British public's acceptance of its imperial mission. In new-historicist or Foucauldian terms Austen's novel performed this cultural 'work' (p. 85). Without being jingoistic or assertive, he argued, this 'pre-imperialist' novel is 'implicated in the rationale' for colonial expansion and exploitation (p. 100).

[81] Lloyd, 'Myths of the Indies', pp. 59–78.

As Said remarks, his reading of the novel is only possible after 'the emergence of a post-colonial consciousness' (p. 115). Avowing this position, Said approaches it with some deliberate awareness of his reading as an outsider's. His account conspicuously reverses the text's own emphasis: what in *Mansfield Park* is unstressed, peripheral, touched upon at a few moments, becomes the centre, the dominant theme of his reading. The 'comfort' – not merely material comfort, but composure and calm – which is so valued at Mansfield Park, rests, Said argues, upon an unacknowledged world beyond, which is the material precondition of its spiritual and moral principles. Moreover, in a critical move which was to be widely imitated and amplified, Said declares that Austen 'synchronizes domestic with international authority' (p. 104), arguing, in effect, that Fanny Price, a 'transported commodity' (p. 106), replicates the slave, and that Sir Thomas' efficient management of his estate on his return (which involves burning unbound copies of *Lovers' Vows*) evokes the authoritarian style of the slave-master. (An alternative reading is that he burns the scripts because the sight of them reminds him bitterly of his children's indifference.)

The premise of Said's account, that the Bertram estate is 'sustained' by the West Indian plantations, and that Sir Thomas therefore is to be identified as a member of the planter class, was taken up by many critics, notably Brian Southam in a widely reprinted piece, 'The Silence of the Bertrams' (1995), but subsequently disputed by other writers, who argued that the money from Antigua forms a lesser proportion of the estate, and that Sir Thomas plainly identifies himself as a member of the Tory landholding class or 'interest'. Much certainly suggests that Mansfield is a functional and profitable enterprise in itself. Many others, especially those reading in previously colonised domains, found the perspective on the novel offered by Said liberating, freeing them from their subaltern status in relation to Austen's texts. Still others found Said's reading of *Mansfield Park* not radical enough.

Despite his numerous caveats to the effect that Austen cannot be held responsible for imperialism, coupled with an insistence on the novel's aesthetic status and complexity, the effect of Said's argument is to give *Mansfield Park* agency, to attribute to this novel, in which patriotic and nationalistic feeling is certainly more subdued than in numerous texts by Austen's contemporaries, a power and significance in the formation of consciousness whose referent is not its contemporary audience, but the audience it has acquired as a part of the established canon. Yet the fruitful tension in Said's piece between appreciation of Austen's art and the requirements of a post-imperialist political reading was rarely sustained in later accounts in the 'post-colonial' mode. These frequently rely on the notion of a textual unconscious, and read many signs in the text as transliterations of material that Austen either sought to keep out of her novel or deliberately kept hidden. Some see Austen as a vigorous exposer of the slave trade ('figured' in the lower-class characters of William and Fanny Price, with Fanny as a trafficked commodity among men) and others view her as complicit with traditional 'aristocratic' domination.

Thus, the 'conservative' versus 'subversive' dispute that was in evidence in the discussion of her broader politics is reformulated. The anxiety which has surrounded Austen's work from its first reception – what exactly is the relation of these domestic novels to the wider political world, and hence by what criteria of 'seriousness' are these novels to be received? – reappears in this new guise. How do we justify our absorption in these novels of insular life in a world that is increasingly, in Samuel Johnson's phrase, 'bursting with sin and sorrow'? From another perspective, these responses to the tantalising 'silence' noted in relation to 'the slave-trade' are an articulation of the post-structuralist or Derridian imperative to find in the fissures of a text the locus of its meaning; in such readings post-structuralist and post-Freudian recovery of repressed significances come together.

The post-colonial versions of *Mansfield Park* readily cohabited with feminist readings, since it could be argued that imperialism itself was an expression of patriarchal values. It could be suggested, too, that the impercipience of the male characters in the novel (let alone its critics) to the emotional life and agency of Fanny Price were a form of colonialism, the easy self-deceptions identified by Johnson and others following the familiar path by which the coloniser overlooks the subjectivity of the colonised. Thus accounts in the next decade tended to amalgamate feminist and post-colonial with historicist readings and, following Said, to take the novel's preoccupation with slavery for granted. Increasingly then, interest focused on Fanny Price as an adopted, quasi-orphaned and transported figure, whose interiority became the object of critical attention partly because it bears the impress of the pressures and tensions of her uprooting.

Readings of *Mansfield Park* at the end of the twentieth century and beginning of the twenty-first commonly take its stature as Austen's most historically searching novel as understood. Most engage both with historical formations such as Evangelicalism and the emergence or consolidation of British imperial power, and with Austen's highly sophisticated renderings of her characters' psychological lives. They inspect Austen's representation of her heroine with an almost forensic intensity, exposing the conflicts, elisions and self-deceptions secreted within the syntax of Fanny's thought, and link these to the ideological critique mounted by Austen in the novel. The still, principled fulcrum of moral right, celebrated or excoriated by earlier critics, is thus understood as a trembling, unstable entity, this erotically driven and conflicted figure both victim and apostle of values inscribed within her by her history of adoption.

Mansfield Park confounds popular conceptions of 'Jane Austen' as a light and amusing novelist, as well as the expectations of readers fresh from her other books. Some of the criticism of *Mansfield Park*, indeed, might have been written by its characters themselves. Sir Thomas' attitude to the theatricals was as 'unintelligibly moral' to Lionel Trilling as to Mr Yates; and for some early feminist criticism Fanny Price was not far from being considered, as she was by Mrs Norris, 'the daemon of the piece'. Many have despised her as 'creepmouse', as did her cousin Tom. Others, taking a point of view not unlike Edmund Bertram's, studiously outlining the novel's ethical organisation, and seeing no humour or irony, are blind to all those moments when the narrator is exasperated by or pokes fun at her hero and heroine.

The critical history of this novel has been not unlike the theatrical history of Shakespeare's 'problematic' comedy *All's Well That End's Well*, whose determined heroine – also in love with a man called Bertram – met with nothing but resistance from audiences and critics for two centuries and more. Nonetheless, the years have also seen the publication of much very fine criticism of *Mansfield Park* unmentioned here. Most of this work has, in one form or another, taken the part of Fanny Price.

LITERARY SIGNIFICANCE

Elizabeth Bennet, 'as delightful a creature as ever appeared in print', is not however without her textual mothers and sisters. Plays and novels too numerous to mention had featured a forward, provocative heroine, whose wit, verging on impudence, delighted and stirred the combative and erotic instincts of men. But Fanny Price, the leading character of this novel conceived at a later phase of its author's life, has no precedent. True: submissive and dutiful young ladies abound in the novels of Austen's contemporaries. But here for the first time is a heroine whose quiet and acquiescent exterior is matched by an inner life of complex and agitating feeling, a dutiful heroine conceived with an ego, with strong convictions and emotional demands. A youthful eighteen-year-old, modest and pliable, whose disposition is shaped by an ugly and poorly nourished childhood and removal to an uncaring, even abusive, adoptive world, a figure without buoyancy and resilience, but with a powerful centre of self, was something new in fiction. What was also ground-breaking was the novelist's technique of charting that self's urgent inner life, and its relation to her outward demeanour.

In the earlier novels Jane Austen rendered her characters through dialogue and through the notation of their thoughts, which were presented as if they were a coherent unspoken speech. In this novel the heroine's private consciousness is rendered more or less as inner speech, but it is also conveyed through a range of techniques, suggestions and depositions that require more subtle inference and construing. When Edmund invites Fanny Price – six years his junior – to give her opinion on Mary's disrespectful attitude to her uncle, she says, quickly, that Mary is 'very ungrateful I think' (vol. 1, ch. 7). The accusation of ingratitude does not emerge out of the objective situation, as Edmund here points out, but expresses Fanny's own indoctrination, and reflects her own story and accommodations as much as it comments on Mary's. A similar effect occurs towards the end of the novel (vol. 3, ch. 16), when Fanny accuses Mary of cruelty – an accusation Edmund rightly rejects, but which is the trace of Fanny's stored up suffering at Mary's unconscious hands. The effect of Austen's presentation of Fanny is that such signs of anterior history, of unadmitted feeling, can be found in almost all of her utterances, not least in the fragments of verse and remembered quotations which hint at her solitary emotional life. Speaking to Edmund of the beauty of the night sky, Fanny praises the 'soothing' qualities of its space and silence, thus articulating the inner yearnings of a self that scarcely knows an interval of rest from anxiety, and is here especially anxious about Edmund's attraction to Mary. Her 'nest of comforts', the East Room, depicted with astringency and wit, is at the same time an enclave, a metaphoric representation of her psychology, evoking Fanny's need somehow to construct a form of that maternal reassurance which no-one except William has given her.

Fanny Price may outwardly model the quiet heroine, submissive to masculine authority, of Evangelical novels and conduct books, but Austen endows her through such techniques with a specific inner life. Fanny's stronger passions are known to the reader not in their expression, but through their substitutions, denials and displacements. Thus the sequence (vol. 1, ch. 7) in which Fanny, looking down the park, watches Edmund coaching Mary's riding: 'After a few minutes, they stopt entirely, Edmund was close to her, he was speaking to her, he was evidently directing her management of the bridle, he had hold of her hand; she saw it, or the imagination supplied what the eye could not reach.' The careful punctuation of the passage (identical in both editions) supplies a tempo to the rhythm that communicates the undercurrent of jealousy: Fanny 'sees', her imagination inflamed by her feelings, more than her eye actually 'reaches'. After this, early in the novel, the reader alerted to such indirect communication – here through Austen's control of syntax and emphasis – can be in no doubt that Fanny's love for Edmund is a sexual, not a sibling, passion.

Becoming aware of her feelings, she immediately disavows them to herself, deflecting them into anger against Henry Crawford and pity for the horse. (The cost of her self-suppression in rage is allowed only once, in vol. 3, ch. 13, to find words.) Such a clear-eyed representation verges on the comedic. Here, as so often in *Mansfield Park*, alertness to self-deceit, displayed in gross form in Mrs Norris and insidiously in Sir Thomas, infiltrates the rendering of even the sober, principled protagonists. Edmund and Fanny invite an amusement which is then deflected or subdued by the author's other purposes, leaving it up to the reader to notice, here and elsewhere in the novel, the hand of a writer to whom satire and mischief were second nature. Authorial amusement is often mediated through the figure of Mary Crawford, as when she remarks 'There, you have quite convinced Miss Price already', following a particularly lengthy and ponderous argument from Edmund (vol. 1, ch. 9).

Broad comedy belongs mainly to the first volume: with the disappearance of Tom Bertram early in volume 2, much of the writing in *Mansfield Park* might be characterised as comedy manqué. A better description would be the novel's: it is a comedy 'à la mortal, finely chequered', in which amusement is always potential, but – subdued by anxiety – threads through the drama, and only occasionally emerges. One enjoys, for instance, Mrs Norris' resourcefulness in draining every bit of pleasure from Fanny's invitation to the Grants' (vol. 2, ch. 5), or finds some wry entertainment in Sir Thomas' complacency about Crawford's proposal (vol. 3, ch. 1). The comedy of cross purposes, latent there, briefly surfaces when

Edmund watches Henry's indefatigable courtship: Fanny was 'trying, by every thing in the power of her modest gentle nature, to repulse Mr. Crawford, and avoid both his looks and enquiries; and he unrepulsable was persisting in both' (vol. 3, ch. 3) – a scene from farce, if we didn't care about Fanny's feelings.

In the riding scene too, Austen displays a control of spatiality that was much less in evidence in the earlier novels. The mixture of loneliness and envy in Fanny is already present in the sentence 'The sound of merriment ascended even to her'. Graphically evoking the expanse of the park, this makes Fanny's geographical separation from the group, as with the east room, a simultaneous index of her emotional isolation. This novel, most remarkably and tenaciously in the Sotherton episode, registers the precise positions and movements of its characters within space. There, as in much of the first volume, Austen is handling a group of eight or nine figures, each of which is imagined in relation to the others, each of whose position is telling, and whose movements – as for example, Mary's moving of her chair as a response to Mrs Norris' scolding of Fanny – are understood not only by the narrative, but also by the participants, as loaded with meaning.

It would be possible to claim that such choreography has a symbolic dimension. The novel generates meaning not merely through the realistic depiction of behaviour, and certainly not through the importation or imposition of symbols, but – as in the 'pleasure grounds' at Sotherton – by availing itself of the symbolism already imbued in the cultural material at its disposal. The most pointed example of this is the incident of William's 'cross': the necklace, contaminated by the ambiguous history of its bestowal, does not suit, but Edmund's chain is perfect. More subtle is the focus on whether Fanny is 'out' and the subsequent ball at Mansfield, a ritual that is always already symbolic, but which is deployed by the novel to raise questions not merely about social status, but about social caste.

Mansfield Park departs from the mode of all preceding novels in its deliberately shifting, serial, roving representation of consciousness. The anchoring focus is on Fanny Price, but from the first chapter her story is pointedly embedded within the story of the Bertrams. The divisions within this family party are displayed to the reader through the text's fluent movement between distinct inner narratives. This is an intimate group which is at the same time a congeries of independent, competing personalities and projects. Even in the first chapters the reader is made privy not only to Fanny's thoughts and emotions, but also to the inner purposes and reflections of Sir Thomas Bertram, Maria Bertram, Mary Crawford and Edmund Bertram. In the first chapter of volume 2, for comic payoff, the narrative adopts the viewpoint of the insouciant Tom. This shifting angle of vision is a structural principle of great salience. Through the adoption of distinct perspectives the novel generates a kind of structural or endemic irony: one person's project or desire immolates them, and puts them, unknowingly, at cross purposes with another's. The reader, both inside and outside the guiding consciousness of Fanny Price, participates in and is amused by the various forms of that selfishness which more or less governs them all.

The exploitation of point of view for ironic purpose is most deliberate in the scenes set at the Parsonage. There conversations take place which bear upon Fanny's fate without her being aware of them; there the fraternal love the narrator commemorates in relation to Fanny and William Price is brilliantly dramatised between Mary and Henry. Adopted, like Fanny, into an unhappy household, the Crawfords' personal styles are shaped by an analogous history. The reader is thus provided with an additional irony when Mary's conversational defences contend with Fanny's – one's social style with the other's cautious generalities – making their connection impossible. When Fanny's hopes and prospects advance with Edmund's ordination, Mary's recede, and the narrative focus shifts to give space and credence to her jealous agitation. When Fanny refuses Henry Crawford and she is left alone, unsupported even by the aunt whom she loves, the narrative swings towards Edmund's point of view, with three chapters leading with his name (vol. 3, chs. 3, 4, 5) – Edmund, who sees how the marriage would forward prospects of his own – and thereby bestows irony and pathos on Fanny's reliance on his endorsement.

Mansfield Park is premised upon a domesticity the more firmly understood for having in its background not only the sophistication of Regency 'Society', but the position of England in the world. Deeply ambitious, original, and aware of that world, it evokes imperialism and war only to disavow them as narrative material. The tales of danger and horror with which William enthrals the Bertram family are left unspecified, whilst the narrative line, carefully controlled by punctuation and syntax, focuses the reader on the comic behaviour, at once interfering and parsimonious, of Mrs Norris' search for a second-hand shirt button. Likewise, 'the slave-trade', emerging only in Fanny's question to her uncle, recedes again into obscurity. The preparations for William's sailing in the war against Napoleon are treated as comic bustle, and his actual departure, perhaps for years, is noticed only as a loss to Fanny: the narrative attends, instead, to an incident more germane to its interests, the disturbing, distressful squabble over Susan's silver knife.

Mansfield Park is a tragedy set (uncomfortably in the end) within the form of the romantic novel. The driving forces of its action are the sexual passions of two women: Maria Bertram's unappeased desire for Henry Crawford, and the unyielding tenacity of Fanny Price's need for Edmund Bertram. Sexuality is implied everywhere, most evidently by the scarcely quoted-from *Lovers' Vows*, emerging in such passages as Maria's memory of Henry pressing her hand to his heart, a moment burned into her consciousness, linking her to him for ever. Through the convincing attribution of intransigent need and uncompromising drive to her heroine, Jane Austen explodes current notions of femininity that Fanny, outwardly modest and submissive, models. And what Austen does with the Romance genre in this novel is to withstand romance. At almost every turn, her writing deflects the reader's desires for a simply satisfying, or fantasy resolution. She denies the wish to see Henry as insincere and to make Fanny's marriage to him unthinkable.

Fanny is not an ideal figure of moral righteousness, and Mary's wit is not an index of vital health; nor is either the mere victim of their circumstances and upbringing. If *Mansfield Park* does end in marriage to the man she loves, Fanny Price's final happiness is contingent, a fallout from the motives, projects and passions of the rival figures whose lives have been so tellingly intertwined with hers.

NOTE ON THE TEXT

This edition is based on the second edition of *Mansfield Park* published in three volumes by John Murray in 1816, from a copy in the University Library, Cambridge (copy 3: Syn. 7.81.70). This has been checked against a microfilm of a copy in the Library of the University of Illinois, and against two other copies in the University Library, Cambridge. Accidentals in this copy such as dropped and missing letters have been corrected in the text presented here. These accidentals and their corrections are listed at the back of the volume. Volume III, Chapter XVI is headed Chapter XIV in both editions, and this has also been corrected. Otherwise, inconsistencies of presentation and spelling have been retained. The principle has been to reproduce the text of 1816 as closely as possible, only amending distracting typographical oddities. There is a small hole in page 233/234 of the copytext, through which letters of the underlying pages are visible. The correct text has been supplied from other copies of the 1816 edition.

This edition also includes variant readings drawn from the 1814 edition of the novel, published by Thomas Egerton. These variants are taken from a microfilm copy of the novel in the University of Illinois Library which has been checked against copies held at the University Library, Cambridge, and at the Fisher Library, University of Sydney. The 1814 edition in all copies consulted is poorly printed, especially in Volume I. It is not always apparent whether the many variations from the 1816 text are to be understood as accidentals (inadvertent typographical features) or true variants, such as alternative punctuation and spelling. All variations between the texts of the 1814 and 1816 editions will be found at the foot of the page. The first reading there is the 1816 reading, reproducing the text above, followed by the 1814 reading. On the few occasions where the 1814 reading is preferred to the 1816 reading this is indicated by the direction of the square bracket.

All emendations are listed in the appendix, 'Corrections and Emendations to 1816 Edition'. Disputable readings are accorded an explanatory note, in which possible alterations to the text are discussed.

The Introduction includes a comparison of the 1814 and 1816 texts, and there is a brief additional discussion of the text of *Mansfield Park* 1816 in the Appendix.

This edition also includes Elizabeth Inchbald's *Lovers' Vows*. The Prologue and Epilogue, sometimes printed with the play, which are not mentioned in the novel and are not by Inchbald, are not here included. This text, in which printing errors have been corrected, is taken from the 1805 edition of Inchbald's plays, published under the supervision of the author, and includes 'Remarks', in which she defends the play against its critics.

MANSFIELD PARK:

A NOVEL.

IN THREE VOLUMES.

BY THE

AUTHOR OF " PRIDE AND PREJUDICE."

VOL. I.

SECOND EDITION.

London:

PRINTED FOR J. MURRAY, ALBEMARLE-STREET.

1816.

The title page of the second edition, used as copytext for this edition of *Mansfield Park*. Reproduced by permission of the Syndics of Cambridge University Library.

MANSFIELD PARK

Volume I

Chapter 1

ABOUT thirty years ago, Miss Maria Ward of Huntingdon,[1] with only seven thousand pounds, had the good luck to captivate Sir Thomas Bertram, of Mansfield Park, in the county of Northampton, and to be thereby raised to the rank of a baronet's lady,[2] with all the comforts and consequences of an handsome house and large income. All Huntingdon exclaimed on the greatness of the match, and her uncle, the lawyer, himself, allowed her to be at least three thousand pounds short of any equitable claim to it. She had two sisters to be benefited by her elevation; and such of their acquaintance as thought Miss Ward and Miss Frances quite as handsome as Miss Maria, did not scruple to predict their marrying with almost equal advantage. But there certainly are not so many men of large fortune in the world, as there are pretty women to deserve them. Miss Ward, at the end of half a dozen years, found herself obliged to be attached to the Rev. Mr. Norris, a friend of her brother-in-law, with scarcely any private fortune, and Miss Frances fared yet worse. Miss Ward's match, indeed, when it came to the point, was not contemptible, Sir Thomas being happily able to give his friend an income in the living of Mansfield,[3] and Mr. and Mrs. Norris began their career of conjugal felicity with very little less than a thousand a year. But Miss Frances married, in the common phrase, to disoblige her family, and by fixing

line 1: Ward of Huntingdon,] **1814** Ward, of Huntingdon,   //   line 10: elevation; and] **1814** elevation, and

on a Lieutenant of Marines,[4] without education, fortune, or connections,[5] did it very thoroughly. She could hardly have made a more untoward choice. Sir Thomas Bertram had interest,[6] which, from principle[7] as well as pride, from a general wish of doing right, and a desire of seeing all that were connected with him in situations of respectability, he would have been glad to exert for the advantage of Lady Bertram's sister; but her husband's profession was such as no interest could reach;[8] and before he had time to devise any other method of assisting them, an absolute breach between the sisters had taken place. It was the natural result of the conduct of each party, and such as a very imprudent marriage almost always produces. To save herself from useless remonstrance, Mrs. Price never wrote to her family on the subject till actually married. Lady Bertram, who was a woman of very tranquil feelings, and a temper remarkably easy and indolent, would have contented herself with merely giving up her sister, and thinking no more of the matter: but Mrs. Norris had a spirit of activity, which could not be satisfied till she had written a long and angry letter to Fanny, to point out the folly of her conduct, and threaten her with all its possible ill consequences. Mrs. Price in her turn was injured and angry; and an answer which comprehended each sister in its bitterness, and bestowed such very disrespectful reflections on the pride of Sir Thomas, as Mrs. Norris could not possibly keep to herself, put an end to all intercourse between them for a considerable period.

Their homes were so distant, and the circles in which they moved so distinct, as almost to preclude the means of ever hearing of each other's existence during the eleven following years, or at least to make it very wonderful to Sir Thomas,

line 18: matter: but] **1814** matter; but

that Mrs. Norris should ever have it in her power to tell them, as she now and then did in an angry voice, that Fanny had got another child. By the end of eleven years, however, Mrs. Price could no longer afford to cherish pride or resentment, or to lose one connection that might possibly assist her. A large and still increasing family, an husband disabled for active service,[9] but not the less equal to company and good liquor, and a very small income to supply their wants, made her eager to regain the friends she had so carelessly sacrificed;[10] and she addressed Lady Bertram in a letter which spoke so much contrition and despondence, such a superfluity of children, and such a want of almost every thing else, as could not but dispose them all to a reconciliation. She was preparing for her ninth lying-in,[11] and after bewailing the circumstance, and imploring their countenance as sponsors to the expected child, she could not conceal how important she felt they might be to the future maintenance of the eight already in being. Her eldest was a boy of ten years old, a fine spirited fellow who longed to be out in the world; but what could she do? Was there any chance of his being hereafter useful to Sir Thomas in the concerns of his West Indian property? No situation would be beneath him—or what did Sir Thomas think of Woolwich? or how could a boy be sent out to the East?[12]

The letter was not unproductive. It re-established peace and kindness. Sir Thomas sent friendly advice and professions,[13] Lady Bertram dispatched money and baby-linen, and Mrs. Norris wrote the letters.

Such were its immediate effects, and within a twelvemonth a more important advantage to Mrs. Price resulted from it. Mrs. Norris was often observing to the others, that she could not get her poor sister and her family out of her head, and

line 3: years, however, Mrs.] **1814** years Mrs.   //   line 13: lying-in, and] **1814** lying in and   //   line 28: twelvemonth] **1814** twelve month

that much as they had all done for her, she seemed to be
wanting to do more: and at length she could not but own it
to be her wish, that poor Mrs. Price should be relieved from
the charge and expense of one child entirely out of her great
number. "What if they were among them to undertake the
care of her eldest daughter, a girl now nine years old, of an
age to require more attention than her poor mother could
possibly give? The trouble and expense of it to them, would
be nothing compared with the benevolence of the action."[14]
Lady Bertram agreed with her instantly. "I think we cannot
do better," said she, "let us send for the child."

Sir Thomas could not give so instantaneous and unqualified a consent. He debated and hesitated;—it was a serious
charge;—a girl so brought up must be adequately provided
for, or there would be cruelty instead of kindness in taking her
from her family. He thought of his own four children—of his
two sons—of cousins in love, &c.;[15]—but no sooner had he
deliberately begun to state his objections, than Mrs. Norris
interrupted him with a reply to them all whether stated or
not.

"My dear Sir Thomas, I perfectly comprehend you, and do
justice to the generosity and delicacy of your notions, which
indeed are quite of a piece with your general conduct; and
I entirely agree with you in the main as to the propriety of
doing every thing one could by way of providing for a child
one had in a manner taken into one's own hands; and I am
sure I should be the last person in the world to withhold
my mite[16] upon such an occasion. Having no children of my
own, who should I look to in any little matter I may ever
have to bestow, but the children of my sisters?—and I am

line 4: expense] **1814** expence

sure Mr. Norris is too just—but you know I am a woman of few words and professions. Do not let us be frightened from a good deed by a trifle. Give a girl an education, and introduce her properly into the world, and ten to one but she has the means of settling well, without farther expense to any body. A niece of our's, Sir Thomas, I may say, or, at least of *your's*, would not grow up in this neighbourhood without many advantages. I don't say she would be so handsome as her cousins. I dare say she would not; but she would be introduced into the society of this country under such very favourable circumstances as, in all human probability, would get her a creditable establishment.[17] You are thinking of your sons— but do not you know that of all things upon earth *that* is the least likely to happen; brought up, as they would be, always together like brothers and sisters? It is morally[18] impossible. I never knew an instance of it. It is, in fact, the only sure way of providing against the connection. Suppose her a pretty girl, and seen by Tom or Edmund for the first time seven years hence, and I dare say there would be mischief. The very idea of her having been suffered to grow up at a distance from us all in poverty and neglect, would be enough to make either of the dear sweet-tempered boys in love with her. But breed her up with them from this time, and suppose her even to have the beauty of an angel, and she will never be more to either than a sister."

"There is a great deal of truth in what you say," replied Sir Thomas, "and far be it from me to throw any fanciful impediment in the way of a plan which would be so consistent with the relative situations of each. I only meant to observe, that it ought not to be lightly engaged in, and that to make it really serviceable to Mrs. Price, and creditable to ourselves, we must secure to the child, or consider ourselves engaged to secure to her hereafter, as circumstances may arise, the provision of a gentlewoman, if no such establishment should offer as you are so sanguine in expecting."

"I thoroughly understand you," cried Mrs. Norris; "you are every thing that is generous and considerate, and I am sure we shall never disagree on this point. Whatever I can do, as you well know, I am always ready enough to do for the good of those I love; and, though I could never feel for this little girl the hundredth part of the regard I bear your own dear children, nor consider her, in any respect, so much my own, I should hate myself if I were capable of neglecting her. Is not she a sister's child? and could I bear to see her want, while I had a bit of bread to give her? My dear Sir Thomas, with all my faults I have a warm heart: and, poor as I am, would rather deny myself the necessaries of life, than do an ungenerous thing. So, if you are not against it, I will write to my poor sister to-morrow, and make the proposal; and, as soon as matters are settled, *I* will engage to get the child to Mansfield; *you* shall have no trouble about it. My own trouble, you know, I never regard. I will send Nanny to London on purpose, and she may have a bed at her cousin, the sadler's, and the child be appointed to meet her there. They may easily get her from Portsmouth to town by the coach, under the care of any creditable person that may chance to be going. I dare say there is always some reputable tradesman's wife or other going up."

Except to the attack on Nanny's cousin, Sir Thomas no longer made any objection, and a more respectable, though less economical rendezvous being accordingly substituted, every thing was considered as settled, and the pleasures of so benevolent a scheme[19] were already enjoyed. The division

line 14: heart: and,] **1814** heart; and,

of gratifying sensations ought not, in strict justice, to have been equal; for Sir Thomas was fully resolved to be the real and consistent patron of the selected child, and Mrs. Norris had not the least intention of being at any expense whatever in her maintenance. As far as walking, talking, and contriving reached, she was thoroughly benevolent, and nobody knew better how to dictate liberality to others: but her love of money was equal to her love of directing, and she knew quite as well how to save her own as to spend that of her friends. Having married on a narrower income than she had been used to look forward to, she had, from the first, fancied a very strict line of economy necessary; and what was begun as a matter of prudence, soon grew into a matter of choice, as an object of that needful solicitude, which there were no children to supply. Had there been a family to provide for, Mrs. Norris might never have saved her money; but having no care of that kind, there was nothing to impede her frugality, or lessen the comfort of making a yearly addition to an income which they had never lived up to. Under this infatuating principle, counteracted by no real affection for her sister, it was impossible for her to aim at more than the credit of projecting and arranging so expensive a charity; though perhaps she might so little know herself, as to walk home to the Parsonage after this conversation, in the happy belief of being the most liberal-minded sister and aunt in the world.

When the subject was brought forward again, her views[20] were more fully explained; and, in reply to Lady Bertram's calm inquiry of "Where shall the child come to first, sister, to you or to us?" Sir Thomas heard, with some surprise, that it would be totally out of Mrs. Norris's power to take any share in the personal charge of her. He had been considering

line 7: others: but] **1814** others; but // line 9: friends.] **1814** friend's.
line 28: inquiry] **1814** enquiry // line 28: sister,] **1814** Sister,

her as a particularly welcome addition at the Parsonage, as a desirable companion to an aunt who had no children of her own; but he found himself wholly mistaken. Mrs. Norris was sorry to say, that the little girl's staying with them, at least as things then were, was quite out of the question. Poor Mr. Norris's indifferent state of health made it an impossibility: he could no more bear the noise of a child than he could fly; if indeed he should ever get well of his gouty complaints, it would be a different matter: she should then be glad to take her turn, and think nothing of the inconvenience; but just now, poor Mr. Norris took up every moment of her time, and the very mention of such a thing she was sure would distract him.

"Then she had better come to us?"[21] said Lady Bertram with the utmost composure. After a short pause, Sir Thomas added with dignity, "Yes, let her home be in this house. We will endeavour to do our duty by her, and she will at least have the advantage of companions of her own age, and of a regular instructress."

"Very true," cried Mrs. Norris, "which are both very important considerations: and it will be just the same to Miss Lee, whether she has three girls to teach, or only two—there can be no difference. I only wish I could be more useful; but you see I do all in my power. I am not one of those that spare their own trouble; and Nanny shall fetch her, however it may put me to inconvenience to have my chief counsellor away for three days. I suppose, sister, you will put the child in the little white attic, near the old nurseries. It will be much the

---

line 6: impossibility: he] **1814** impossibility; he   //   line 7: more bear] **1814** more bare   //   line 9: matter: she] **1814** matter; she   //   line 14: us?" said] **1814** us," said   //   line 21: considerations: and] **1814** considerations; and   //   line 27: sister,] **1814** Sister,   //   line 28: attic,] **1814** Attic,   //   line 28: nurseries.] **1814** Nurseries.

best place for her, so near Miss Lee, and not far from the girls, and close by the housemaids, who could either of them help to dress her you know, and take care of her clothes, for I suppose you would not think it fair to expect Ellis to wait on her as well as the others. Indeed, I do not see that you could possibly place her any where else."

Lady Bertram made no opposition.

"I hope she will prove a well-disposed girl," continued Mrs. Norris, "and be sensible of her uncommon good fortune in having such friends."

"Should her disposition be really bad," said Sir Thomas, "we must not, for our own children's sake, continue her in the family; but there is no reason to expect so great an evil. We shall probably see much to wish altered in her, and must prepare ourselves for gross ignorance, some meanness of opinions, and very distressing vulgarity of manner; but these are not incurable faults—nor, I trust, can they be danger-ous for her associates. Had my daughters been *younger* than herself, I should have considered the introduction of such a companion, as a matter of very serious moment; but as it is, I hope there can be nothing to fear for *them*, and every thing to hope for *her*, from the association."

"That is exactly what I think," cried Mrs. Norris, "and what I was saying to my husband this morning. It will be an education for the child said I, only being with her cousins; if Miss Lee taught her nothing, she would learn to be good and clever from *them*."

"I hope she will not tease my poor pug,"[22] said Lady Bertram; "I have but just got Julia to leave it alone."

"There will be some difficulty in our way, Mrs. Norris," observed Sir Thomas, "as to the distinction proper to be

line 3: help to dress her] **1814** help dress her // line 28: tease] **1814** teize // line 28: Lady Bertram; "I] **1814** Lady Bertram, "I made between the girls as they grow up; how to preserve in the minds of my *daughters* the consciousness of what they are, without making them think too lowly of their cousin; and how, without depressing her spirits too far, to make her remember that she is not a *Miss Bertram*. I should wish to see them very good friends, and would, on no account, authorize in my girls the smallest degree of arrogance towards their relation; but still they cannot be equals. Their rank, fortune, rights, and expectations, will always be different. It is a point of great delicacy, and you must assist us in our endeavours to choose exactly the right line of conduct."

Mrs. Norris was quite at his service; and though she perfectly agreed with him as to its being a most difficult thing, encouraged him to hope that between them it would be easily managed.

It will be readily believed that Mrs. Norris did not write to her sister in vain. Mrs. Price seemed rather surprised that a girl should be fixed on, when she had so many fine boys, but accepted the offer most thankfully, assuring them of her daughter's being a very well-disposed, good-humoured girl, and trusting they would never have cause to throw her off. She spoke of her farther as somewhat delicate and puny, but was sanguine in the hope of her being materially better for change of air. Poor woman! she probably thought change of air might agree with many of her children.

line 11: choose] **1814** chuse

Chapter 2

THE little girl performed her long journey in safety, and at Northampton was met by Mrs. Norris, who thus regaled in[1] the credit of being foremost to welcome her, and in the importance of leading her in to the others, and recommending her to their kindness.

Fanny Price was at this time just ten years old, and though there might not be much in her first appearance to captivate, there was, at least, nothing to disgust her relations. She was small of her age, with no glow of complexion, nor any other striking beauty; exceedingly timid and shy, and shrinking from notice; but her air, though awkward, was not vulgar, her voice was sweet, and when she spoke, her countenance was pretty. Sir Thomas and Lady Bertram received her very kindly, and Sir Thomas seeing how much she needed encouragement, tried to be all that was conciliating; but he had to work against a most untoward gravity of deportment—and Lady Bertram, without taking half so much trouble, or speaking one word where he spoke ten, by the mere aid of a good-humoured smile, became immediately the less awful[2] character of the two.

The young people were all at home, and sustained their share in the introduction very well, with much good humour, and no embarrassment, at least on the part of the sons, who at seventeen and sixteen, and tall of their age, had all the

line 19: awful] **1814** aweful

grandeur of men in the eyes of their little cousin. The two girls were more at a loss from being younger and in greater awe of their father, who addressed them on the occasion with rather an injudicious particularity. But they were too much used to company and praise, to have any thing like natural shyness, and their confidence increasing from their cousin's total want of it, they were soon able to take a full survey of her face and her frock in easy indifference.

They were a remarkably fine family, the sons very well-looking, the daughters decidedly handsome, and all of them well-grown and forward of their age, which produced as striking a difference between the cousins in person, as education had given to their address;[3] and no one would have supposed the girls so nearly of an age as they really were. There was in fact but two years between the youngest and Fanny. Julia Bertram was only twelve, and Maria but a year older. The little visitor meanwhile was as unhappy as possible. Afraid of every body, ashamed of herself, and longing for the home she had left, she knew not how to look up, and could scarcely speak to be heard, or without crying. Mrs. Norris had been talking to her the whole way from Northampton of her wonderful good fortune, and the extraordinary degree of gratitude and good behaviour which it ought to produce, and her consciousness of misery was therefore increased by the idea of its being a wicked thing for her not to be happy. The fatigue too, of so long a journey, became soon no trifling evil. In vain were the well-meant condescensions of Sir Thomas, and all the officious prognostications of Mrs. Norris that she would be a good girl; in vain did Lady Bertram smile and make her sit on the sofa with herself and pug, and vain was even the sight

line 17: as unhappy as] **1814** an unhappy as

of a gooseberry tart towards giving her comfort; she could scarcely swallow two mouthfuls before tears interrupted her, and sleep seeming to be her likeliest friend, she was taken to finish her sorrows in bed.

"This is not a very promising beginning," said Mrs. Norris when Fanny had left the room.—"After all that I said to her as we came along, I thought she would have behaved better; I told her how much might depend upon her acquitting herself well at first. I wish there may not be a little sulkiness of temper—her poor mother had a good deal; but we must make allowances for such a child—and I do not know that her being sorry to leave her home is really against her, for, with all its faults, it *was* her home, and she cannot as yet understand how much she has changed for the better; but then there is moderation in all things."[4]

It required a longer time, however, than Mrs. Norris was inclined to allow, to reconcile Fanny to the novelty of Mansfield Park, and the separation from every body she had been used to. Her feelings were very acute, and too little understood to be properly attended to. Nobody meant to be unkind, but nobody put themselves out of their way to secure her comfort.

The holiday allowed to the Miss Bertrams the next day on purpose to afford leisure for getting acquainted with, and entertaining their young cousin, produced little union. They could not but hold her cheap on finding that she had but two sashes, and had never learnt French; and when they perceived her to be little struck with the duet they were so good as to play, they could do no more than make her a generous present of some of their least valued toys, and leave her to herself,

line 18: every body] **1814** everybody

while they adjourned to whatever might be the favourite holiday sport of the moment, making artificial flowers or wasting gold paper.

Fanny, whether near or from her cousins, whether in the school-room, the drawing-room, or the shrubbery, was equally forlorn, finding something to fear in every person and place. She was disheartened by Lady Bertram's silence, awed by Sir Thomas's grave looks, and quite overcome by Mrs. Norris's admonitions. Her elder cousins mortified her by reflections on her size, and abashed her by noticing her shyness; Miss Lee wondered at her ignorance, and the maid-servants sneered at her clothes; and when to these sorrows was added the idea of the brothers and sisters among whom she had always been important as play-fellow, instructress, and nurse, the despondence that sunk her little heart was severe.

The grandeur of the house astonished, but could not console her. The rooms were too large for her to move in with ease; whatever she touched she expected to injure, and she crept about in constant terror of something or other; often retreating towards her own chamber to cry; and the little girl who was spoken of in the drawing-room when she left it at night, as seeming so desirably sensible of her peculiar[5] good fortune, ended every day's sorrows by sobbing herself to sleep. A week had passed in this way, and no suspicion of it conveyed by her quiet passive manner, when she was found one morning by her cousin Edmund, the youngest of the sons, sitting crying on the attic stairs.

"My dear little cousin," said he with all the gentleness of an excellent nature, "what can be the matter?" And sitting down by her, was at great pains to overcome her shame in

line 17: astonished, but] **1814** astonished but

being so surprised, and persuade her to speak openly. "Was she ill? or was any body angry with her? or had she quarrelled with Maria and Julia? or was she puzzled about any thing in her lesson that he could explain? Did she, in short, want any thing he could possibly get her, or do for her?" For a long while no answer could be obtained beyond a "no, no—not at all—no, thank you;" but he still persevered, and no sooner had he begun to revert to her own home, than her increased sobs explained to him where the grievance lay. He tried to console her.

"You are sorry to leave Mamma, my dear little Fanny," said he, "which shows you to be a very good girl; but you must remember that you are with relations and friends, who all love you, and wish to make you happy. Let us walk out in the park, and you shall tell me all about your brothers and sisters."

On pursuing the subject, he found that dear as all these brothers and sisters generally were, there was one among them who ran more in her thoughts than the rest. It was William whom she talked of most and wanted most to see. William, the eldest, a year older than herself, her constant companion and friend; her advocate with her mother (of whom he was the darling) in every distress. "William did not like she should come away—he had told her he should miss her very much indeed." "But William will write to you, I dare say." "Yes, he had promised he would, but he had told *her* to write first." "And when shall you do it?" She hung her head and answered, hesitatingly, "she did not know; she had not any paper."

"If that be all your difficulty, I will furnish you with paper and every other material, and you may write your letter

line 12: shows] **1814** shews

whenever you choose. Would it make you happy to write to William?"

"Yes, very."

"Then let it be done now. Come with me into the breakfast-room, we shall find every thing there, and be sure of having the room to ourselves."

"But, cousin—will it go to the post?"

"Yes, depend upon me it shall; it shall go with the other letters; and as your uncle will frank it,[6] it will cost William nothing."

"My uncle!" repeated Fanny with a frightened look.

"Yes, when you have written the letter, I will take it to my father to frank."

Fanny thought it a bold measure, but offered no farther resistance; and they went together into the breakfast-room, where Edmund prepared her paper, and ruled her lines with all the good will that her brother could himself have felt, and probably with somewhat more exactness. He continued with her the whole time of her writing, to assist her with his penknife or his orthography,[7] as either were wanted; and added to these attentions, which she felt very much, a kindness to her brother, which delighted her beyond all the rest. He wrote with his own hand his love to his cousin William, and sent him half a guinea under the seal.[8] Fanny's feelings on the occasion were such as she believed herself incapable of expressing; but her countenance and a few artless words fully conveyed all their gratitude and delight, and her cousin began to find her an interesting object. He talked to her more, and from all that she said, was convinced of her having an affectionate heart, and a strong desire of doing right; and he

line 1: choose.] **1814** chuse.   //   line 4: breakfast-room] **1814** breakfast room   //   line 7: "But, cousin—] **1814** "But cousin—   //   line 8: "Yes, depend] **1814** Yes, depend   //   line 13: father] **1814** Father

could perceive her to be farther entitled to attention, by great sensibility of her situation, and great timidity. He had never knowingly given her pain, but he now felt that she required more positive kindness, and with that view endeavoured, in the first place, to lessen her fears of them all, and gave her especially a great deal of good advice as to playing with Maria and Julia, and being as merry as possible.

From this day Fanny grew more comfortable. She felt that she had a friend, and the kindness of her cousin Edmund gave her better spirits with every body else. The place became less strange, and the people less formidable; and if there were some amongst them whom she could not cease to fear, she began at least to know their ways, and to catch the best manner of conforming to them. The little rusticities and awkwardnesses which had at first made grievous inroads on the tranquillity of all, and not least of herself, necessarily wore away, and she was no longer materially afraid to appear before her uncle, nor did her aunt Norris's voice make her start very much. To her cousins she became occasionally an acceptable companion. Though unworthy, from inferiority of age and strength, to be their constant associate, their pleasures and schemes were sometimes of a nature to make a third very useful, especially when that third was of an obliging, yielding temper; and they could not but own, when their aunt inquired into her faults, or their brother Edmund urged her claims to their kindness, that "Fanny was good-natured enough."

Edmund was uniformly kind himself, and she had nothing worse to endure on the part of Tom, than that sort of merriment which a young man of seventeen will always think fair with a child of ten. He was just entering into life, full of spirits, and with all the liberal dispositions of an eldest son, who feels born only for expense and enjoyment. His kindness to his little cousin was consistent with his situation and rights: he made her some very pretty presents, and laughed at her.

As her appearance and spirits improved, Sir Thomas and Mrs. Norris thought with greater satisfaction of their benevolent plan; and it was pretty soon decided between them, that though far from clever, she showed a tractable disposition, and seemed likely to give them little trouble. A mean opinion of her abilities was not confined to *them*. Fanny could read, work, and write,[9] but she had been taught nothing more; and as her cousins found her ignorant of many things with which they had been long familiar, they thought her prodigiously stupid, and for the first two or three weeks were continually bringing some fresh report of it into the drawing-room. "Dear Mamma, only think, my cousin cannot put the map of Europe together[10]—or my cousin cannot tell the principal rivers in Russia—or she never heard of Asia Minor—or she does not know the difference between water-colours and crayons!—How strange!—Did you ever hear any thing so stupid?"

"My dear," their considerate aunt would reply; "it is very bad, but you must not expect every body to be as forward and quick at learning as yourself."

"But, aunt, she is really so very ignorant!—Do you know, we asked her last night, which way she would go to get to Ireland; and she said, she should cross to the Isle of Wight.[11] She thinks of nothing but the Isle of Wight, and she calls it *the Island*, as if there were no other island in the world. I am sure I should have been ashamed of myself, if I had not known better long before I was so old as she is. I cannot remember the time when I did not know a great deal that

line 1: rights: he] **1814** rights; he // line 6: showed] **1814** shewed // line 13: drawing-room.] **1814** drawing room. // line 16: Asia Minor—or she] **1814** Asia Minor—she // line 17: between] **1814** b tween

she has not the least notion of yet. How long ago it is, aunt, since we used to repeat the chronological order of the kings of England, with the dates of their accession, and most of the principal events of their reigns!"

"Yes," added the other; "and of the Roman emperors as low as Severus; besides a great deal of the Heathen Mythology, and all the Metals, Semi-Metals, Planets, and distinguished philosophers."[12]

"Very true, indeed, my dears, but you are blessed with wonderful memories, and your poor cousin has probably none at all. There is a vast deal of difference in memories, as well as in every thing else, and therefore you must make allowance for your cousin, and pity her deficiency. And remember that, if you are ever so forward and clever yourselves, you should always be modest; for, much as you know already, there is a great deal more for you to learn."

"Yes, I know there is, till I am seventeen. But I must tell you another thing of Fanny, so odd and so stupid. Do you know, she says she does not want to learn either music or drawing."

"To be sure, my dear, that is very stupid indeed, and shows a great want of genius and emulation.[13] But, all things considered, I do not know whether it is not as well that it should be so, for, though you know (owing to me) your papa and mamma are so good as to bring her up with you, it is not at all necessary that she should be as accomplished[14] as you are;—on the contrary, it is much more desirable that there should be a difference."

Such were the counsels by which Mrs. Norris assisted to form her nieces' minds; and it is not very wonderful that with all their promising talents and early information, they should

line 1: is, aunt, since] **1814** is aunt, since // line 4: reigns!"] **1814** reigns." // line 21: shows] **1814** shews // line 22: But, all] **1814** But all

21

be entirely deficient in the less common acquirements[15] of self-knowledge, generosity, and humility. In every thing but disposition, they were admirably taught. Sir Thomas did not know what was wanting, because, though a truly anxious father, he was not outwardly affectionate, and the reserve of his manner repressed all the flow of their spirits before him.

To the education of her daughters, Lady Bertram paid not the smallest attention. She had not time for such cares. She was a woman who spent her days in sitting nicely dressed on a sofa,[16] doing some long piece of needle-work, of little use and no beauty, thinking more of her pug than her children, but very indulgent to the latter, when it did not put herself to inconvenience, guided in every thing important by Sir Thomas, and in smaller concerns by her sister. Had she possessed greater leisure for the service of her girls, she would probably have supposed it unnecessary, for they were under the care of a governess, with proper masters, and could want nothing more. As for Fanny's being stupid at learning, "she could only say it was very unlucky, but some people *were* stupid, and Fanny must take more pains; she did not know what else was to be done; and except her being so dull, she must add, she saw no harm in the poor little thing—and always found her very handy and quick in carrying messages, and fetching what she wanted."

Fanny, with all her faults of ignorance and timidity, was fixed at Mansfield Park, and learning to transfer in its favour much of her attachment to her former home, grew up there not unhappily among her cousins. There was no positive ill-nature in Maria or Julia; and though Fanny was often

line 10: needle-work,] **1814** needle work,   //   line 22: add, she] **1814** add she   //   line 25: Fanny, with] **1814** Fanny with   //   line 25: timidity, was] **1814** timidity was

mortified by their treatment of her, she thought too lowly of her own claims to feel injured by it.

From about the time of her entering the family, Lady Bertram, in consequence of a little ill-health, and a great deal of indolence, gave up the house in town, which she had been used to occupy every spring, and remained wholly in the country, leaving Sir Thomas to attend his duty in Parliament, with whatever increase or diminution of comfort might arise from her absence. In the country, therefore, the Miss Bertrams continued to exercise their memories, practise their duets, and grow tall and womanly; and their father saw them becoming in person, manner, and accomplishments, every thing that could satisfy his anxiety. His eldest son was careless and extravagant, and had already given him much uneasiness; but his other children promised him nothing but good. His daughters he felt, while they retained the name of Bertram, must be giving it new grace, and in quitting it he trusted would extend its respectable alliances; and the character of Edmund, his strong good sense and uprightness of mind, bid most fairly for utility, honour, and happiness to himself and all his connections. He was to be a clergyman.

Amid the cares and the complacency which his own children suggested, Sir Thomas did not forget to do what he could for the children of Mrs. Price; he assisted her liberally in the education and disposal of her sons as they became old enough for a determinate pursuit: and Fanny, though almost totally separated from her family, was sensible of the truest satisfaction in hearing of any kindness towards them, or of any thing at all promising in their situation or conduct. Once, and once only in the course of many years, had she

line 15: uneasiness; but] **1814** uneasiness, but   //   line 26: pursuit: and] **1814** pursuit; and   //   line 30: Once, and] **1814** Once and   //   line 30: years, had] **1814** years had

the happiness of being with William. Of the rest she saw nothing; nobody seemed to think of her ever going amongst them again, even for a visit, nobody at home seemed to want her; but William determining, soon after her removal, to be a sailor, was invited to spend a week with his sister in Northamptonshire, before he went to sea. Their eager affection in meeting, their exquisite delight in being together, their hours of happy mirth, and moments of serious conference, may be imagined; as well as the sanguine views and spirits of the boy even to the last, and the misery of the girl when he left her. Luckily the visit happened in the Christmas holidays, when she could directly look for comfort to her cousin Edmund; and he told her such charming things of what William was to do, and be hereafter, in consequence of his profession, as made her gradually admit that the separation might have some use. Edmund's friendship never failed her: his leaving Eton[17] for Oxford made no change in his kind dispositions, and only afforded more frequent opportunities of proving them. Without any display of doing more than the rest, or any fear of doing too much, he was always true to her interests, and considerate of her feelings, trying to make her good qualities understood, and to conquer the diffidence which prevented their being more apparent; giving her advice, consolation, and encouragement.

Kept back as she was by every body else, his single support could not bring her forward, but his attentions were otherwise of the highest importance in assisting the improvement of her mind, and extending its pleasures. He knew her to be clever,

---

line 4: determining, soon] **1814** determining soon   //   line 8: mirth, and] **1814** mirth and   //   line 8: conference, may] **1814** conference may   // line 13: Edmund; and] **1814** Edmund, and   //   line 17: her: his] **1814** her; his

to have a quick apprehension as well as good sense, and a fondness for reading, which, properly directed, must be an education in itself. Miss Lee taught her French, and heard her read the daily portion of History;[18] but he recommended the books which charmed her leisure hours, he encouraged her taste, and corrected her judgment; he made reading useful by talking to her of what she read, and heightened its attraction by judicious praise. In return for such services she loved him better than any body in the world except William; her heart was divided between the two.

line 2: which, properly] **1814** which properly   //   line 3: French, and] **1814** French and   //   line 4: History; but] **1814** History, but

Chapter 3

THE first event of any importance in the family was the death of Mr. Norris, which happened when Fanny was about fifteen, and necessarily introduced alterations and novelties. Mrs. Norris, on quitting the parsonage, removed first to the park, and afterwards to a small house of Sir Thomas's in the village, and consoled herself for the loss of her husband by considering that she could do very well without him, and for her reduction of income by the evident necessity of stricter economy.

The living was hereafter for Edmund, and had his uncle died a few years sooner, it would have been duly given to some friend to hold till he were old enough for orders. But Tom's extravagance had, previous to that event, been so great as to render a different disposal of the next presentation[1] necessary, and the younger brother must help to pay for the pleasures of the elder. There was another family-living actually held for Edmund; but though this circumstance had made the arrangement somewhat easier to Sir Thomas's conscience, he could not but feel it to be an act of injustice, and he earnestly tried to impress his eldest son with the same conviction, in the hope of its producing a better effect than any thing he had yet been able to say or do.

"I blush for you, Tom," said he, in his most dignified manner; "I blush for the expedient which I am driven on,

line 4: Mrs. Norris, on] 1814 Mrs. Norris on   //   line 9: economy.] 1814 economy,

26

and I trust I may pity your feelings as a brother on the occasion. You have robbed Edmund for ten, twenty, thirty years, perhaps for life, of more than half the income which ought to be his. It may hereafter be in my power, or in your's (I hope it will), to procure him better preferment;[2] but it must not be forgotten, that no benefit of that sort would have been beyond his natural claims on us, and that nothing can, in fact, be an equivalent for the certain advantage which he is now obliged to forego through the urgency of your debts."

Tom listened with some shame and some sorrow; but escaping as quickly as possible, could soon with cheerful self-ishness reflect, 1st, that he had not been half so much in debt as some of his friends; 2dly, that his father had made a most tiresome piece of work of it; and 3dly, that the future incumbent, whoever he might be, would, in all probability, die very soon.

On Mr. Norris's death, the presentation became the right of a Dr. Grant, who came consequently to reside at Mansfield, and on proving to be a hearty man of forty-five, seemed likely to disappoint Mr. Bertram's calculations. But "no, he was a short-neck'd, apoplectic sort of fellow, and, plied well with good things, would soon pop off."

He had a wife about fifteen years his junior, but no children, and they entered the neighbourhood with the usual fair report of being very respectable, agreeable people.

The time was now come when Sir Thomas expected his sister-in-law to claim her share in their niece, the change in Mrs. Norris's situation, and the improvement in Fanny's age, seeming not merely to do away any former objection to their living together, but even to give it the most decided eligibility; and as his own circumstances were rendered less fair than heretofore, by some recent losses on his West India Estate,[3] in addition to his eldest son's extravagance, it became not undesirable to himself to be relieved from the expense of her support, and the obligation of her future provision. In the fulness of his belief that such a thing must be, he mentioned its probability to his wife; and the first time of the subject's occurring to her again, happening to be when Fanny was present, she calmly observed to her, "So, Fanny, you are going to leave us, and live with my sister. How shall you like it?"

Fanny was too much surprised to do more than repeat her aunt's words, "Going to leave you?"

"Yes, my dear, why should you be astonished? You have been five years with us, and my sister always meant to take you when Mr. Norris died. But you must come up and tack on my patterns⁴ all the same."

The news was as disagreeable to Fanny as it had been unexpected. She had never received kindness from her aunt Norris, and could not love her.

"I shall be very sorry to go away," said she, with a faltering voice.

"Yes, I dare say you will; *that's* natural enough. I suppose you have had as little to vex you, since you came into this house, as any creature in the world."

"I hope I am not ungrateful, aunt," said Fanny, modestly.

"No, my dear; I hope not. I have always found you a very good girl."

"And am I never to live here again?"

"Never, my dear; but you are sure of a comfortable home. It can make very little difference to you, whether you are in one house or the other."

Fanny left the room with a very sorrowful heart; she could not feel the difference to be so small, she could not think of

line 4: wife; and] **1814** wife, and

living with her aunt with any thing like satisfaction. As soon as she met with Edmund, she told him her distress.

"Cousin," said she, "something is going to happen which I do not like at all; and though you have often persuaded me into being reconciled to things that I disliked at first, you will not be able to do it now. I am going to live entirely with my aunt Norris."

"Indeed!"

"Yes, my aunt Bertram has just told me so. It is quite settled. I am to leave Mansfield Park, and go to the White house, I suppose, as soon as she is removed there."

"Well, Fanny, and if the plan were not unpleasant to you, I should call it an excellent one."

"Oh! Cousin!"

"It has every thing else in its favour. My aunt is acting like a sensible woman in wishing for you. She is choosing a friend and companion exactly where she ought, and I am glad her love of money does not interfere. You will be what you ought to be to her. I hope it does not distress you very much, Fanny."

"Indeed it does. I cannot like it. I love this house and every thing in it. I shall love nothing there. You know how uncomfortable I feel with her."

"I can say nothing for her manner to you as a child; but it was the same with us all, or nearly so. She never knew how to be pleasant to children. But you are now of an age to be treated better; I think she *is* behaving better already; and when you are her only companion, you *must* be important to her."

"I can never be important to any one."

"What is to prevent you?"

"Every thing—my situation—my foolishness and awkwardness."

line 16: choosing] **1814** chusing // line 23: child; but] **1814** child, but // line 26: already; and] **1814** already, and

"As to your foolishness and awkwardness, my dear Fanny, believe me, you never have a shadow of either, but in using the words so improperly. There is no reason in the world why you should not be important where you are known. You have good sense, and a sweet temper, and I am sure you have a grateful heart, that could never receive kindness without wishing to return it. I do not know any better qualifications for a friend and companion."

"You are too kind," said Fanny, colouring at such praise; "how shall I ever thank you as I ought, for thinking so well of me. Oh! cousin, if I am to go away, I shall remember your goodness, to the last moment of my life."

"Why, indeed, Fanny, I should hope to be remembered at such a distance as the White house. You speak as if you were going two hundred miles off, instead of only across the park. But you will belong to us almost as much as ever. The two families will be meeting every day in the year. The only difference will be, that living with your aunt, you will necessarily be brought forward, as you ought to be. *Here*, there are too many, whom you can hide behind; but with *her* you will be forced to speak for yourself."

"Oh! do not say so."

"I must say it, and say it with pleasure. Mrs. Norris is much better fitted than my mother for having the charge of you now. She is of a temper to do a great deal for any body she really interests herself about, and she will force you to do justice to your natural powers."

Fanny sighed, and said, "I cannot see things as you do; but I ought to believe you to be right rather than myself, and I am very much obliged to you for trying to reconcile me to

line 11: cousin, if] **1814** cousin, If

what must be. If I could suppose my aunt really to care for me, it would be delightful to feel myself of consequence to any body!—*Here*, I know I am of none, and yet I love the place so well."

"The place, Fanny, is what you will not quit, though you quit the house. You will have as free a command of the park and gardens as ever. Even *your* constant little heart need not take fright at such a nominal change. You will have the same walks to frequent, the same library to choose from, the same people to look at, the same horse to ride."

"Very true. Yes, dear old grey poney. Ah! cousin, when I remember how much I used to dread riding, what terrors it gave me to hear it talked of as likely to do me good;—(Oh! how I have trembled at my uncle's opening his lips if horses were talked of) and then think of the kind pains you took to reason and persuade me out of my fears, and convince me that I should like it after a little while, and feel how right you proved to be, I am inclined to hope you may always prophesy as well."

"And I am quite convinced that your being with Mrs. Norris, will be as good for your mind, as riding has been for your health—and as much for your ultimate happiness, too."

So ended their discourse, which, for any very appropriate service it could render Fanny, might as well have been spared, for Mrs. Norris had not the smallest intention of taking her. It had never occurred to her, on the present occasion, but as a thing to be carefully avoided. To prevent its being expected, she had fixed on the smallest habitation which could rank as genteel among the buildings of Mansfield parish; the White house being only just large enough to receive herself and

line 9: choose] **1814** chuse   //   line 18: prophesy] **1814** prophecy her servants, and allow a spare room for a friend, of which she made a very particular point;—the spare-rooms at the parsonage had never been wanted, but the absolute necessity of a spare-room for a friend was now never forgotten. Not all her precautions, however, could save her from being suspected of something better; or, perhaps, her very display of the importance of a spare-room, might have misled Sir Thomas to suppose it really intended for Fanny. Lady Bertram soon brought the matter to a certainty, by carelessly observing to Mrs. Norris,—

"I think, sister, we need not keep Miss Lee any longer, when Fanny goes to live with you?"

Mrs. Norris almost started. "Live with me, dear Lady Bertram, what do you mean?"

"Is not she to live with you?—I thought you had settled it with Sir Thomas?"

"Me! never. I never spoke a syllable about it to Sir Thomas, nor he to me. Fanny live with me! the last thing in the world for me to think of, or for any body to wish that really knows us both. Good heaven! what could I do with Fanny?—Me! a poor helpless, forlorn widow, unfit for any thing, my spirits quite broke down, what could I do with a girl at her time of life, a girl of fifteen! the very age of all others to need most attention and care, and put the cheerfullest spirits to the test. Sure Sir Thomas could not seriously expect such a thing! Sir Thomas is too much my friend. Nobody that wishes me well, I am sure, would propose it. How came Sir Thomas to speak to you about it?"

"Indeed, I do not know. I suppose he thought it best."

"But what did he say?—He could not say he *wished* me to take Fanny. I am sure in his heart he could not wish me to do it."

"No, he only said he thought it very likely—and I thought so too. We both thought it would be a comfort to you. But if you do not like it, there is no more to be said. She is no incumbrance here."

"Dear sister! If you consider my unhappy state, how can she be any comfort to me? Here am I a poor desolate widow, deprived of the best of husbands, my health gone in attending and nursing him, my spirits still worse, all my peace in this world destroyed, with barely enough to support me in the rank of a gentlewoman, and enable me to live so as not to disgrace the memory of the dear departed—what possible comfort could I have in taking such a charge upon me as Fanny! If I could wish it for my own sake, I would not do so unjust a thing by the poor girl. She is in good hands, and sure of doing well. I must struggle through my sorrows and difficulties as I can."

"Then you will not mind living by yourself quite alone?"

"Dear Lady Bertram! what am I fit for but solitude? Now and then I shall hope to have a friend in my little cottage (I shall always have a bed for a friend); but the most part of my future days will be spent in utter seclusion. If I can but make both ends meet, that's all I ask for."

"I hope, sister, things are not so very bad with you neither—considering Sir Thomas says you will have six hundred a year."[5]

"Lady Bertram, I do not complain. I know I cannot live as I have done, but I must retrench where I can, and learn to be a better manager. I *have been* a liberal housekeeper enough, but

line 2: thought it] **1814** though it   //   line 14: hands, and] **1814** hands and //   line 17: alone?"/"Dear Lady Bertram!] **1814** alone?" "Dear Lady Bertram! //   line 22: all I ask for."/"I hope,] **1814** all I ask for." "I hope,   //   line 23: neither—considering Sir Thomas] **1814** neither—considering. Sir Thomas

I shall not be ashamed to practise economy now. My situation is as much altered as my income. A great many things were due from poor Mr. Norris as clergyman of the parish, that cannot be expected from me. It is unknown how much was consumed in our kitchen by odd comers and goers. At the White house, matters must be better looked after. I *must* live within my income, or I shall be miserable; and I own it would give me great satisfaction to be able to do rather more—to lay by a little at the end of the year."

"I dare say you will. You always do, don't you?"

"My object, Lady Bertram, is to be of use to those that come after me. It is for your children's good that I wish to be richer. I have nobody else to care for, but I should be very glad to think I could leave a little trifle among them, worth their having."

"You are very good, but do not trouble yourself about them. They are sure of being well provided for. Sir Thomas will take care of that."

"Why, you know Sir Thomas's means will be rather straitened, if the Antigua estate is to make such poor returns."[6]

"Oh! *that* will soon be settled. Sir Thomas has been writing about it, I know."

"Well, Lady Bertram," said Mrs. Norris, moving to go, "I can only say that my sole desire is to be of use to your family—and so if Sir Thomas should ever speak again about my taking Fanny, you will be able to say, that my health and spirits put it quite out of the question—besides that, I really should not have a bed to give her, for I must keep a spare room for a friend."

line 1: practise] **1814** practice   //   line 20: returns."/"Oh! *that*] **1814** returns." "Oh! *that*   //   line 22: about it, I] **1814** about it I   //   line 23: Norris, moving] **1814** Norris moving   //   line 29: friend.] **1814** friend."

Lady Bertram repeated enough of this conversation to her husband, to convince him how much he had mistaken his sister-in-law's views; and she was from that moment perfectly safe from all expectation, or the slightest allusion to it from him. He could not but wonder at her refusing to do any thing for a niece, whom she had been so forward to adopt; but as she took early care to make him, as well as Lady Bertram, understand that whatever she possessed was designed for their family, he soon grew reconciled to a distinction, which at the same time that it was advantageous and complimentary to them, would enable him better to provide for Fanny himself.

Fanny soon learnt how unnecessary had been her fears of a removal; and her spontaneous, untaught felicity on the discovery, conveyed some consolation to Edmund for his disappointment in what he had expected to be so essentially serviceable to her. Mrs. Norris took possession of the White house, the Grants arrived at the parsonage, and these events over, every thing at Mansfield went on for some time as usual.

The Grants showing a disposition to be friendly and sociable, gave great satisfaction in the main among their new acquaintance. They had their faults, and Mrs. Norris soon found them out. The Dr. was very fond of eating, and would have a good dinner every day; and Mrs. Grant, instead of contriving to gratify him at little expense, gave her cook as high wages as they did at Mansfield Park, and was scarcely ever seen in her offices. Mrs. Norris could not speak with any temper of such grievances, nor of the quantity of butter and eggs that were regularly consumed in the house. "Nobody loved plenty and hospitality more than herself—nobody more

line 20: showing] **1814** shewing // line 24: day; and] **1814** day, and // line 24: Grant, instead] **1814** Grant instead // line 26: Mansfield Park] **1814** Mansfield park

hated pitiful doings—the parsonage she believed had never been wanting in comforts of any sort, had never borne a bad character in *her time*, but this was a way of going on that she could not understand. A fine lady in a country parsonage was quite out of place. *Her* store-room she thought might have been good enough for Mrs. Grant to go into. Enquire where she would, she could not find out that Mrs. Grant had ever had more than five thousand pounds."

Lady Bertram listened without much interest to this sort of invective. She could not enter into the wrongs of an economist, but she felt all the injuries of beauty in Mrs. Grant's being so well settled in life without being handsome, and expressed her astonishment on that point almost as often, though not so diffusely, as Mrs. Norris discussed the other.

These opinions had been hardly canvassed a year, before another event arose of such importance in the family, as might fairly claim some place in the thoughts and conversation of the ladies. Sir Thomas found it expedient to go to Antigua himself, for the better arrangement of his affairs, and he took his eldest son with him in the hope of detaching him from some bad connections at home. They left England with the probability of being nearly a twelvemonth absent.

The necessity of the measure in a pecuniary light, and the hope of its utility to his son, reconciled Sir Thomas to the effort of quitting the rest of his family, and of leaving his daughters to the direction of others at their present most interesting time of life. He could not think Lady Bertram quite equal to supply his place with them, or rather to perform

line 14: diffusely, as] **1814** diffusely as   //   line 17: another] **1814** an other

what should have been her own; but in Mrs. Norris's watchful attention, and in Edmund's judgment, he had sufficient confidence to make him go without fears for their conduct.

Lady Bertram did not at all like to have her husband leave her; but she was not disturbed by any alarm for his safety, or solicitude for his comfort, being one of those persons who think nothing can be dangerous or difficult, or fatiguing to any body but themselves.

The Miss Bertrams were much to be pitied on the occasion; not for their sorrow, but for their want of it. Their father was no object of love to them, he had never seemed the friend of their pleasures, and his absence was unhappily most welcome. They were relieved by it from all restraint; and without aiming at one gratification that would probably have been forbidden by Sir Thomas, they felt themselves immediately at their own disposal, and to have every indulgence within their reach. Fanny's relief, and her consciousness of it, were quite equal to her cousins', but a more tender nature suggested that her feelings were ungrateful, and she really grieved because she could not grieve. "Sir Thomas, who had done so much for her and her brothers, and who was gone perhaps never to return! that she should see him go without a tear!—it was a shameful insensibility." He had said to her moreover, on the very last morning, that he hoped she might see William again in the course of the ensuing winter, and had charged her to write and invite him to Mansfield as soon as the squadron[7] to which he belonged should be known to be in England. "This was so thoughtful and kind!"—and would he only have smiled upon her and called her "my dear Fanny," while he said it, every former frown or cold address might have been forgotten. But

line 25: winter,] **1814** Winter,   //   line 29: it, every] **1814** it every he had ended his speech in a way to sink her in sad mortification, by adding, "If William does come to Mansfield, I hope you may be able to convince him that the many years which have passed since you parted, have not been spent on your side entirely without improvement—though I fear he must find his sister at sixteen in some respects too much like his sister at ten." She cried bitterly over this reflection when her uncle was gone; and her cousins, on seeing her with red eyes, set her down as a hypocrite.

line 8: cousins, on] **1814** cousins on

Chapter 4

TOM BERTRAM had of late spent so little of his time at home, that he could be only nominally missed; and Lady Bertram was soon astonished to find how very well they did even without his father, how well Edmund could supply his place in carving, talking to the steward, writing to the attorney, settling with the servants, and equally saving her from all possible fatigue or exertion in every particular, but that of directing her letters.

The earliest intelligence of the travellers' safe arrival in Antigua after a favourable voyage,[1] was received; though not before Mrs. Norris had been indulging in very dreadful fears, and trying to make Edmund participate them[2] whenever she could get him alone; and as she depended on being the first person made acquainted with any fatal catastrophe, she had already arranged the manner of breaking it to all the others, when Sir Thomas's assurances of their both being alive and well, made it necessary to lay by her agitation and affectionate preparatory speeches for a while.

The winter came and passed without their being called for; the accounts continued perfectly good;—and Mrs. Norris in promoting gaieties for her nieces, assisting their toilettes, displaying their accomplishments, and looking about for their future husbands, had so much to do as, in addition to all her own household cares, some interference in those of her sister, and Mrs. Grant's wasteful doings to overlook,[3] left her very little occasion to be occupied even in fears for the absent.

The Miss Bertrams were now fully established among the belles of the neighbourhood; and as they joined to beauty and brilliant acquirements, a manner naturally easy, and carefully formed to general civility and obligingness, they possessed its favour as well as its admiration. Their vanity was in such good order, that they seemed to be quite free from it, and gave themselves no airs; while the praises attending such behaviour, secured, and brought round by their aunt, served to strengthen them in believing they had no faults.

Lady Bertram did not go into public with her daughters. She was too indolent even to accept a mother's gratification in witnessing their success and enjoyment at the expense of any personal trouble, and the charge was made over to her sister, who desired nothing better than a post of such honourable representation,[4] and very thoroughly relished the means it afforded her of mixing in society without having horses to hire.

Fanny had no share in the festivities of the season; but she enjoyed being avowedly useful as her aunt's companion, when they called away the rest of the family; and as Miss Lee had left Mansfield, she naturally became every thing to Lady Bertram during the night of a ball or a party. She talked to her, listened to her, read to her; and the tranquillity of such evenings, her perfect security in such a *tête-à-tête* from any sound of unkindness, was unspeakably welcome to a mind which had seldom known a pause in its alarms or embarrassments.[5] As to her cousins' gaieties, she loved to hear an account of them, especially of the balls, and whom Edmund had danced with; but thought too lowly of her own situation to imagine she should ever be admitted to the same,

line 2: neighbourhood; and] **1814** neighbourhood, and   //   line 6: order, that] **1814** order that   //   line 24: *tête-à-tête*] **1814** *tête-à-tête*   //   line 29: danced with; but] **1814** danced wh ; but

and listened therefore without an idea of any nearer concern in them. Upon the whole, it was a comfortable winter to her; for though it brought no William to England, the never failing hope of his arrival was worth much.

The ensuing spring deprived her of her valued friend the old grey poney, and for some time she was in danger of feeling the loss in her health as well as in her affections, for in spite of the acknowledged importance of her riding on horseback, no measures were taken for mounting her again, "because," as it was observed by her aunts, "she might ride one of her cousin's horses at any time when they did not want them;" and as the Miss Bertrams regularly wanted their horses every fine day, and had no idea of carrying their obliging manners to the sacrifice of any real pleasure, that time of course never came. They took their cheerful rides in the fine mornings of April and May; and Fanny either sat at home the whole day with one aunt, or walked beyond her strength at the instigation of the other; Lady Bertram holding exercise to be as unnecessary for every body as it was unpleasant to herself; and Mrs. Norris, who was walking all day, thinking every body ought to walk as much. Edmund was absent at this time, or the evil would have been earlier remedied. When he returned to understand how Fanny was situated, and perceived its ill effects, there seemed with him but one thing to be done, and that "Fanny must have a horse," was the resolute declaration with which he opposed whatever could be urged by the supineness of his mother, or the economy of his aunt, to make it appear unimportant. Mrs. Norris could not help thinking that some steady old thing might be found among the numbers belonging to the Park, that would do vastly well, or that one might be borrowed

line 3: her; for] **1814** her, for // line 11: them;" and] **1814** them," and // line 19: herself; and] **1814** herself, and // line 23: and perceived] **1814** and perceive

of the steward, or that perhaps Dr. Grant might now and then lend them the poney he sent to the post. She could not but consider it as absolutely unnecessary, and even improper, that Fanny should have a regular lady's horse of her own in the style of her cousins. She was sure Sir Thomas had never intended it; and she must say, that to be making such a purchase in his absence, and adding to the great expenses of his stable at a time when a large part of his income was unsettled, seemed to her very unjustifiable. "Fanny must have a horse," was Edmund's only reply. Mrs. Norris could not see it in the same light. Lady Bertram did; she entirely agreed with her son as to the necessity of it, and as to its being considered necessary by his father;—she only pleaded against there being any hurry, she only wanted him to wait till Sir Thomas's return, and then Sir Thomas might settle it all himself. He would be at home in September, and where would be the harm of only waiting till September?

Though Edmund was much more displeased with his aunt than with his mother, as evincing least regard for her niece, he could not help paying more attention to what she said, and at length determined on a method of proceeding which would obviate the risk of his father's thinking he had done too much, and at the same time procure for Fanny the immediate means of exercise, which he could not bear she should be without. He had three horses of his own, but not one that would carry a woman. Two of them were hunters; the third, a useful road-horse: this third he resolved to exchange for one that his cousin might ride; he knew where such a one was to be met

line 6: it; and] **1814** it, and // line 12: by his father;—] **1814** by is
father;— // line 18: his aunt] **1814** his Aunt // line 19: mother, as]
1814 Mother, as // line 24: exercise, which] **1814** exercise which //
line 26: hunters; the] **1814** hunters, the // line 27: road-horse: this] **1814**
road-horse; this

with, and having once made up his mind, the whole business was soon completed. The new mare proved a treasure; with a very little trouble, she became exactly calculated for the purpose, and Fanny was then put in almost full possession of her. She had not supposed before, that any thing could ever suit her like the old grey poney; but her delight in Edmund's mare was far beyond any former pleasure of the sort; and the addition it was ever receiving in the consideration of that kindness from which her pleasure sprung, was beyond all her words to express. She regarded her cousin as an example of every thing good and great, as possessing worth, which no one but herself could ever appreciate, and as entitled to such gratitude from her, as no feelings could be strong enough to pay. Her sentiments towards him were compounded of all that was respectful, grateful, confiding, and tender.

As the horse continued in name as well as fact, the property of Edmund, Mrs. Norris could tolerate its being for Fanny's use; and had Lady Bertram ever thought about her own objection again, he might have been excused in her eyes, for not waiting till Sir Thomas's return in September, for when September came, Sir Thomas was still abroad, and without any near prospect of finishing his business. Unfavourable circumstances had suddenly arisen at a moment when he was beginning to turn all his thoughts towards England, and the very great uncertainty in which every thing was then involved, determined him on sending home his son, and waiting the final arrangement by himself. Tom arrived safely, bringing an excellent account of his father's health; but to very little purpose, as far as Mrs. Norris was concerned. Sir Thomas's sending away his son, seemed to her so like a parent's care, under the influence of a foreboding of evil to himself, that she could not help feeling dreadful presentiments; and as the long evenings of autumn came on, was so terribly haunted by these ideas, in the sad solitariness of her cottage, as to be obliged to take daily refuge in the dining room of the park. The return of winter engagements, however, was not without its effect; and in the course of their progress, her mind became so pleasantly occupied in superintending the fortunes of her eldest niece, as tolerably to quiet her nerves. "If poor Sir Thomas were fated never to return, it would be peculiarly consoling to see their dear Maria well married," she very often thought; always when they were in the company of men of fortune, and particularly on the introduction of a young man who had recently succeeded to one of the largest estates and finest places in the country.[6]

Mr. Rushworth was from the first struck with the beauty of Miss Bertram, and being inclined to marry, soon fancied himself in love. He was a heavy young man, with not more than common sense; but as there was nothing disagreeable in his figure or address, the young lady was well pleased with her conquest. Being now in her twenty-first year, Maria Bertram was beginning to think matrimony a duty; and as a marriage with Mr. Rushworth would give her the enjoyment of a larger income than her father's, as well as ensure her the house in town,[7] which was now a prime object, it became, by the same rule of moral obligation, her evident duty to marry Mr. Rushworth if she could. Mrs. Norris was most zealous in promoting the match, by every suggestion and contrivance, likely to enhance its desirableness to either party; and, among other means, by seeking an intimacy with the gentleman's mother, who at present lived with him, and to whom she even forced Lady Bertram to go through ten miles of indifferent road,[8] to pay a morning

line 11: estates and] **1814** estates, and   //   line 16: sense; but] **1814** sense, but   //   line 23: became, by] **1814** became by   //   line 27: and, among other means, by] **1814** and among other means by

visit. It was not long before a good understanding took place between this lady and herself. Mrs. Rushworth acknowledged herself very desirous that her son should marry, and declared that of all the young ladies she had ever seen, Miss Bertram seemed, by her amiable qualities and accomplishments, the best adapted to make him happy. Mrs. Norris accepted the compliment, and admired the nice discernment of character which could so well distinguish merit. Maria was indeed the pride and delight of them all—perfectly faultless—an angel; and of course, so surrounded by admirers, must be difficult[9] in her choice; but yet as far as Mrs. Norris could allow herself to decide on so short an acquaintance, Mr. Rushworth appeared precisely the young man to deserve and attach her.

After dancing with each other at a proper number of balls, the young people justified these opinions, and an engagement, with a due reference to the absent Sir Thomas, was entered into, much to the satisfaction of their respective families, and of the general lookers-on of the neighbourhood, who had, for many weeks past, felt the expediency of Mr. Rushworth's marrying Miss Bertram.

It was some months before Sir Thomas's consent could be received; but in the mean while, as no one felt a doubt of his most cordial pleasure in the connection, the intercourse of the two families was carried on without restraint, and no other attempt made at secrecy, than Mrs. Norris's talking of it every where as a matter not to be talked of at present.

Edmund was the only one of the family who could see a fault in the business; but no representation of his aunt's could induce him to find Mr. Rushworth a desirable companion. He could allow his sister to be the best judge of her own happiness, but he was not pleased that her happiness should centre in a large income; nor could he refrain from often saying to himself, in Mr. Rushworth's company, "If this man had not twelve thousand a year,[10] he would be a very stupid fellow."

Sir Thomas, however, was truly happy in the prospect of an alliance so unquestionably advantageous, and of which he heard nothing but the perfectly good and agreeable. It was a connection exactly of the right sort; in the same county, and the same interest;[11] and his most hearty concurrence was conveyed as soon as possible. He only conditioned that the marriage should not take place before his return, which he was again looking eagerly forward to. He wrote in April, and had strong hopes of settling every thing to his entire satisfaction, and leaving Antigua before the end of the summer.

Such was the state of affairs in the month of July, and Fanny had just reached her eighteenth year, when the society of the village received an addition in the brother and sister of Mrs. Grant, a Mr. and Miss Crawford, the children of her mother by a second marriage. They were young people of fortune. The son had a good estate in Norfolk, the daughter twenty thousand pounds.[12] As children, their sister had been always very fond of them; but, as her own marriage had been soon followed by the death of their common parent, which left them to the care of a brother of their father, of whom Mrs. Grant knew nothing, she had scarcely seen them since. In their uncle's house they had found a kind home. Admiral and Mrs. Crawford, though agreeing in nothing else, were united in affection for these children, or at least were no farther adverse in their feelings than that each had their favourite, to whom they showed the greatest fondness of the two. The Admiral delighted in the boy, Mrs. Crawford doated on the girl; and it was the lady's death which now

line 29: showed] **1814** shewed

obliged her *protegée*, after some months further trial at her uncle's house, to find another home. Admiral Crawford was a man of vicious conduct, who chose, instead of retaining his niece, to bring his mistress under his own roof; and to this Mrs. Grant was indebted for her sister's proposal of coming to her, a measure quite as welcome on one side, as it could be expedient on the other; for Mrs. Grant having by this time run through the usual resources of ladies residing in the country without a family of children; having more than filled her favourite sitting room with pretty furniture, and made a choice collection of plants and poultry, was very much in want of some variety at home. The arrival, therefore, of a sister whom she had always loved, and now hoped to retain with her as long as she remained single, was highly agreeable; and her chief anxiety was lest Mansfield should not satisfy the habits of a young woman who had been mostly used to London.

Miss Crawford was not entirely free from similar apprehensions, though they arose principally from doubts of her sister's style of living and tone of society; and it was not till after she had tried in vain to persuade her brother to settle with her at his own country-house, that she could resolve to hazard herself among her other relations. To any thing like a permanence of abode, or limitation of society, Henry Crawford had, unluckily, a great dislike; he could not accommodate his sister in an article of such importance, but he escorted her, with the utmost kindness, into Northamptonshire, and as readily engaged to fetch her away again at half an hour's notice, whenever she were weary of the place.

The meeting was very satisfactory on each side. Miss Crawford found a sister without preciseness or rusticity[13]—a

line 10: sitting room] **1814** sitting-room

sister's husband who looked the gentleman, and a house commodious and well fitted up; and Mrs. Grant received in those whom she hoped to love better than ever, a young man and woman of very prepossessing appearance. Mary Crawford was remarkably pretty; Henry, though not handsome, had air and countenance;[14] the manners of both were lively and pleasant, and Mrs. Grant immediately gave them credit for every thing else. She was delighted with each, but Mary was her dearest object; and having never been able to glory in beauty of her own, she thoroughly enjoyed the power of being proud of her sister's. She had not waited her arrival to look out for a suitable match for her; she had fixed on Tom Bertram; the eldest son of a Baronet was not too good for a girl of twenty thousand pounds, with all the elegance and accomplishments which Mrs. Grant foresaw in her; and being a warm-hearted, unreserved woman, Mary had not been three hours in the house before she told her what she had planned.

Miss Crawford was glad to find a family of such consequence so very near them, and not at all displeased either at her sister's early care, or the choice it had fallen on. Matrimony was her object, provided she could marry well, and having seen Mr. Bertram in town, she knew that objection could no more be made to his person than to his situation in life. While she treated it as a joke, therefore, she did not forget to think of it seriously. The scheme was soon repeated to Henry.

"And now," added Mrs. Grant, "I have thought of something to make it quite complete. I should dearly love to settle you both in this country, and therefore, Henry, you shall marry the youngest Miss Bertram, a nice, handsome,

line 28: Grant, "I] **1814** Grant; "I

good-humoured, accomplished girl, who will make you very happy."

Henry bowed and thanked her.

"My dear sister," said Mary, "if you can persuade him into any thing of the sort, it will be a fresh matter of delight to me, to find myself allied to any body so clever, and I shall only regret that you have not half-a-dozen daughters to dispose of. If you can persuade Henry to marry, you must have the address of a Frenchwoman.[15] All that English abilities can do, has been tried already. I have three very particular friends who have been all dying for him in their turn; and the pains which they, their mothers, (very clever women,) as well as my dear aunt and myself, have taken to reason, coax, or trick him into marrying, is inconceivable! He is the most horrible flirt that can be imagined. If your Miss Bertrams do not like to have their hearts broke, let them avoid Henry."

"My dear brother, I will not believe this of you."

"No, I am sure you are too good. You will be kinder than Mary. You will allow for the doubts of youth and inexperience. I am of a cautious temper, and unwilling to risk my happiness in a hurry. Nobody can think more highly of the matrimonial state than myself. I consider the blessing of a wife as most justly described in those discreet lines of the poet, "Heaven's *last* best gift."[16]

"There, Mrs. Grant, you see how he dwells on one word, and only look at his smile. I assure you he is very detestable— the admiral's lessons have quite spoiled him."

"I pay very little regard," said Mrs. Grant, "to what any young person says on the subject of marriage. If they profess a disinclination for it, I only set it down that they have not yet seen the right person."

line 12: women,) as] **1814** women) as

Dr. Grant laughingly congratulated Miss Crawford on feeling no disinclination to the state herself.

"Oh! yes, I am not at all ashamed of it. I would have every body marry if they can do it properly; I do not like to have people throw themselves away; but every body should marry as soon as they can do it to advantage."

Chapter 5

THE young people were pleased with each other from the first. On each side there was much to attract, and their acquaintance soon promised as early an intimacy as good manners would warrant. Miss Crawford's beauty did her no disservice with the Miss Bertrams. They were too handsome themselves to dislike any woman for being so too, and were almost as much charmed as their brothers, with her lively dark eye, clear brown complexion, and general prettiness. Had she been tall, full formed, and fair, it might have been more of a trial; but as it was, there could be no comparison, and she was most allowably a sweet pretty girl, while they were the finest young women in the country.

Her brother was not handsome; no, when they first saw him, he was absolutely plain, black and plain; but still he was the gentleman, with a pleasing address. The second meeting proved him not so very plain; he was plain, to be sure, but then he had so much countenance, and his teeth were so good, and he was so well made, that one soon forgot he was plain; and after a third interview, after dining in company with him at the parsonage, he was no longer allowed to be called so by any body. He was, in fact, the most agreeable young man the sisters had ever known, and they were equally delighted with him. Miss Bertram's engagement made him in equity the property of Julia, of which Julia was fully aware, and before he had been at Mansfield a week, she was quite ready to be fallen in love with.

Maria's notions on the subject were more confused and indistinct. She did not want to see or understand. "There could be no harm in her liking an agreeable man—every body knew her situation—Mr. Crawford must take care of himself." Mr. Crawford did not mean to be in any danger; the Miss Bertrams were worth pleasing, and were ready to be pleased; and he began with no object but of making them like him. He did not want them to die of love; but with sense and temper which ought to have made him judge and feel better, he allowed himself great latitude on such points.

"I like your Miss Bertrams exceedingly, sister," said he, as he returned from attending them to their carriage after the said dinner visit; "they are very elegant, agreeable girls."

"So they are, indeed, and I am delighted to hear you say it. But you like Julia best."

"Oh! yes, I like Julia best."

"But do you really? for Miss Bertram is in general thought the handsomest."

"So I should suppose. She has the advantage in every feature, and I prefer her countenance—but I like Julia best. Miss Bertram is certainly the handsomest, and I have found her the most agreeable, but I shall always like Julia best, because you order me."

"I shall not talk to you, Henry, but I know you *will* like her best at last."

"Do not I tell you, that I like her best *at first*?"

"And besides, Miss Bertram is engaged. Remember that, my dear brother. Her choice is made."

"Yes, and I like her the better for it. An engaged woman is always more agreeable than a disengaged. She is satisfied with herself. Her cares are over, and she feels that she may

line 14: are, indeed,] **1814** are indeed,

exert all her powers of pleasing without suspicion. All is safe with a lady engaged; no harm can be done."

"Why as to that—Mr. Rushworth is a very good sort of young man, and it is a great match for her."

"But Miss Bertram does not care three straws for him; *that* is your opinion of your intimate friend. *I* do not subscribe to it. I am sure Miss Bertram is very much attached to Mr. Rushworth. I could see it in her eyes, when he was mentioned. I think too well of Miss Bertram to suppose she would ever give her hand without her heart."

"Mary, how shall we manage him?"

"We must leave him to himself I believe. Talking does no good. He will be taken in at last."

"But I would not have him *taken in*, I would not have him duped; I would have it all fair and honourable."

"Oh! dear—Let him stand his chance and be taken in. It will do just as well. Every body is taken in at some period or other."

"Not always in marriage, dear Mary,"

"In marriage especially. With all due respect to such of the present company as chance to be married, my dear Mrs. Grant, there is not one in a hundred of either sex, who is not taken in when they marry. Look where I will, I see that it *is* so; and I feel that it *must* be so, when I consider that it is, of all transactions, the one in which people expect most from others, and are least honest themselves."

"Ah! You have been in a bad school for matrimony, in Hill Street."[1]

"My poor aunt had certainly little cause to love the state; but, however, speaking from my own observation, it is a manœuvring business.[2] I know so many who have married

line 26: themselves."] **1814** themselves,"

in the full expectation and confidence of some one particular advantage in the connection, or accomplishment or good quality in the person, who have found themselves entirely deceived, and been obliged to put up with exactly the reverse! What is this, but a take in?"

"My dear child, there must be a little imagination here. I beg your pardon, but I cannot quite believe you. Depend upon it, you see but half. You see the evil, but you do not see the consolation. There will be little rubs and disappointments every where, and we are all apt to expect too much; but then, if one scheme of happiness fails, human nature turns to another; if the first calculation is wrong, we make a second better; we find comfort somewhere—and those evil-minded observers, dearest Mary, who make much of a little, are more taken in and deceived than the parties themselves."

"Well done, sister! I honour your *esprit du corps*. When I am a wife, I mean to be just as staunch myself; and I wish my friends in general would be so too. It would save me many a heart-ache."

"You are as bad as your brother, Mary; but we will cure you both. Mansfield shall cure you both—and without any taking in. Stay with us and we will cure you."

The Crawfords, without wanting to be cured, were very willing to stay. Mary was satisfied with the parsonage as a present home, and Henry equally ready to lengthen his visit. He had come, intending to spend only a few days with them, but Mansfield promised well, and there was nothing to call him elsewhere. It delighted Mrs. Grant to keep them both with her, and Dr. Grant was exceedingly well contented to have it so; a talking pretty young woman like Miss Crawford,

line 19: heart-ache."] **1814** heart ache."

is always pleasant society to an indolent, stay-at-home man; and Mr. Crawford's being his guest was an excuse for drinking claret every day.

The Miss Bertrams' admiration[3] of Mr. Crawford was more rapturous than any thing which Miss Crawford's habits made her likely to feel. She acknowledged, however, that the Mr. Bertrams were very fine young men, that two such young men were not often seen together even in London, and that their manners, particularly those of the eldest, were very good. *He* had been much in London, and had more liveliness and gallantry than Edmund, and must, therefore, be preferred; and, indeed, his being the eldest was another strong claim. She had felt an early presentiment that she *should* like the eldest best. She knew it was her way.

Tom Bertram must have been thought pleasant, indeed, at any rate; he was the sort of young man to be generally liked, his agreeableness was of the kind to be oftener found agreeable than some endowments of a higher stamp, for he had easy manners, excellent spirits, a large acquaintance, and a great deal to say; and the reversion[4] of Mansfield Park, and a baronetcy, did no harm to all this. Miss Crawford soon felt, that he and his situation might do. She looked about her with due consideration, and found almost every thing in his favour, a park, a real park five miles round, a spacious modern-built house, so well placed and well screened as to deserve to be in any collection of engravings of gentlemen's seats[5] in the kingdom, and wanting only to be completely new furnished—pleasant sisters, a quiet mother, and an agreeable man himself—with the advantage of being tied up from much gaming at present, by a promise to his father, and of being Sir Thomas hereafter. It might do very well; she believed she should accept him; and she began accordingly to interest herself a little about the horse which he had to run at the B——[6] races.

These races were to call him away not long after their acquaintance began; and as it appeared that the family did not, from his usual goings on, expect him back again for many weeks, it would bring his passion to an early proof. Much was said on his side to induce her to attend the races, and schemes were made for a large party to them, with all the eagerness of inclination, but it would only do to be talked of.

And Fanny, what was *she* doing and thinking all this while? and what was *her* opinion of the new-comers? Few young ladies of eighteen could be less called on to speak their opinion than Fanny. In a quiet way, very little attended to, she paid her tribute of admiration to Miss Crawford's beauty; but as she still continued to think Mr. Crawford very plain, in spite of her two cousins having repeatedly proved the contrary, she never mentioned *him*. The notice which she excited herself, was to this effect. "I begin now to understand you all, except Miss Price," said Miss Crawford, as she was walking with the Mr. Bertrams. "Pray, is she out, or is she not?[7]—I am puzzled.—She dined at the parsonage, with the rest of you, which seemed like being *out*; and yet she says so little, that I can hardly suppose she *is*."

Edmund, to whom this was chiefly addressed, replied, "I believe I know what you mean—but I will not undertake to answer the question. My cousin is grown up. She has the age and sense of a woman, but the outs and not outs are beyond me."

"And yet in general, nothing can be more easily ascertained. The distinction is so broad. Manners as well as appearance are, generally speaking, so totally different. Till now, I could not have supposed it possible to be mistaken as to a girl's being out or not. A girl not out, has always the same sort of dress; a close bonnet[8] for instance, looks very demure, and never says a word. You may smile—but it is so I assure you—and except that it is sometimes carried a little too far, it is all very proper. Girls should be quiet and modest. The most objectionable part is, that the alteration of manners on being introduced into company is frequently too sudden. They sometimes pass in such very little time from reserve to quite the opposite— to confidence! *That* is the faulty part of the present system. One does not like to see a girl of eighteen or nineteen so immediately up to every thing—and perhaps when one has seen her hardly able to speak the year before. Mr. Bertram, I dare say *you* have sometimes met with such changes."

"I believe I have; but this is hardly fair; I see what you are at. You are quizzing[9] me and Miss Anderson."

"No indeed. Miss Anderson! I do not know who or what you mean. I am quite in the dark. But I *will* quiz you with a great deal of pleasure, if you will tell me what about."

"Ah! you carry it off very well, but I cannot be quite so far imposed on. You must have had Miss Anderson in your eye, in describing an altered young lady. You paint too accurately for mistake. It was exactly so. The Andersons of Baker Street.[10] We were speaking of them the other day, you know. Edmund, you have heard me mention Charles Anderson. The circumstance was precisely as this lady has represented it. When Anderson first introduced me to his family, about two years ago, his sister was not *out*, and I could not get her to speak to me. I sat there an hour one morning waiting for Anderson, with only her and a little girl or two in the room— the governess being sick or run away, and the mother in and

line 23: day, you] **1814** day you

out every moment with letters of business; and I could hardly get a word or a look from the young lady—nothing like a civil answer—she screwed up her mouth, and turned from me with such an air! I did not see her again for a twelvemonth. She was then *out*. I met her at Mrs. Holford's—and did not recollect her. She came up to me, claimed me as an acquaintance, stared me out of countenance,[11] and talked and laughed till I did not know which way to look. I felt that I must be the jest of the room at the time—and Miss Crawford, it is plain, has heard the story."

"And a very pretty story it is, and with more truth in it, I dare say, than does credit to Miss Anderson. It is too common a fault. Mothers certainly have not yet got quite the right way of managing their daughters. I do not know where the error lies. I do not pretend to set people right, but I do see that they are often wrong."

"Those who are showing the world what female manners *should be*," said Mr. Bertram, gallantly, "are doing a great deal to set them right."

"The error is plain enough," said the less courteous Edmund; "such girls are ill brought up. They are given wrong notions from the beginning. They are always acting upon motives of vanity—and there is no more real modesty in their behaviour *before* they appear in public than afterwards."

"I do not know," replied Miss Crawford hesitatingly. "Yes, I cannot agree with you there. It is certainly the modestest part of the business. It is much worse to have girls *not out*, give themselves the same airs and take the same liberties as if they were, which I *have* seen done. *That* is worse than any thing—quite disgusting!"

line 9: Crawford, it is plain, has] **1814** Crawford it is plain has // line 17: showing] **1814** shewing // line 21: Edmund; "such] **1814** Edmund, "such // line 25: Crawford hesitatingly] **1814** Crawford, hesitatingly

"Yes, *that* is very inconvenient indeed," said Mr. Bertram. "It leads one astray; one does not know what to do. The close bonnet and demure air you describe so well, (and nothing was ever juster,) tell one what is expected; but I got into a dreadful scrape last year from the want of them. I went down to Ramsgate for a week with a friend last September—just after my return from the West Indies—my friend Sneyd—you have heard me speak of Sneyd, Edmund; his father and mother and sisters were there, all new to me. When we reached Albion place[12] they were out; we went after them, and found them on the pier. Mrs. and the two Miss Sneyds, with others of their acquaintance. I made my bow in form, and as Mrs. Sneyd was surrounded by men, attached myself to one of her daughters, walked by her side all the way home, and made myself as agreeable as I could; the young lady perfectly easy in her manners, and as ready to talk as to listen. I had not a suspicion that I could be doing any thing wrong. They looked just the same; both well dressed, with veils and parasols like other girls; but I afterwards found that I had been giving all my attention to the youngest, who was not *out*, and had most excessively offended the eldest. Miss Augusta ought not to have been noticed for the next six months, and Miss Sneyd, I believe, has never forgiven me."

"That was bad indeed. Poor Miss Sneyd! Though I have no younger sister, I feel for her. To be neglected before one's time, must be very vexatious. But it was entirely the mother's fault. Miss Augusta should have been with her governess. Such half and half doings never prosper. But now I must be satisfied about Miss Price. Does she go to balls? Does she dine out every where, as well as at my sister's?"

line 3: so well, (and nothing was ever juster,)] **1814** so well (and nothing was ever juster) // line 23: forgiven me."] **1814** forgiven me.

"No," replied Edmund, "I do not think she has ever been to a ball. My mother seldom goes into company herself, and dines no where but with Mrs. Grant, and Fanny stays at home with *her*."

"Oh! then the point is clear. Miss Price is *not* out."

Chapter 6

MR. BERTRAM set off for ———, and Miss Crawford was
prepared to find a great chasm in their society, and to miss him
decidedly in the meetings which were now becoming almost
daily between the families; and on their all dining together at
the park soon after his going, she retook her chosen place near
the bottom of the table,[1] fully expecting to feel a most melancholy difference in the change of masters. It would be a very
flat business, she was sure. In comparison with his brother,
Edmund would have nothing to say. The soup would be sent
round in a most spiritless manner, wine drank without any
smiles, or agreeable trifling, and the venison cut up without
supplying one pleasant anecdote of any former haunch, or a
single entertaining story about "my friend such a one." She
must try to find amusement in what was passing at the upper
end of the table, and in observing Mr. Rushworth, who was
now making his appearance at Mansfield, for the first time
since the Crawfords' arrival. He had been visiting a friend in
a neighbouring county, and that friend having recently had
his grounds laid out by an improver,[2] Mr. Rushworth was
returned with his head full of the subject, and very eager to
be improving his own place in the same way; and though
not saying much to the purpose, could talk of nothing else.
The subject had been already handled in the drawing-room;
it was revived in the dining-parlour. Miss Bertram's attention and opinion was evidently his chief aim; and though her

deportment showed rather conscious superiority than any solicitude to oblige him, the mention of Sotherton Court, and the ideas attached to it, gave her a feeling of complacency, which prevented her from being very ungracious.

"I wish you could see Compton," said he, "it is the most complete thing! I never saw a place so altered in my life. I told Smith I did not know where I was. The approach[3] *now* is one of the finest things in the country. You see the house in the most surprising manner. I declare when I got back to Sotherton yesterday, it looked like a prison—quite a dismal old prison."

"Oh! for shame!" cried Mrs. Norris. "A prison, indeed! Sotherton Court is the noblest old place in the world."

"It wants improvement,[4] ma'am, beyond any thing. I never saw a place that wanted so much improvement in my life; and it is so forlorn, that I do not know what can be done with it."

"No wonder that Mr. Rushworth should think so at present," said Mrs. Grant to Mrs. Norris, with a smile; "but depend upon it, Sotherton will have *every* improvement in time which his heart can desire."

"I must try to do something with it," said Mr. Rushworth, "but I do not know what. I hope I shall have some good friend to help me."

"Your best friend upon such an occasion," said Miss Bertram, calmly, "would be Mr. Repton,[5] I imagine."

"That is what I was thinking of. As he has done so well by Smith, I think I had better have him at once. His terms are five guineas a day."[6]

---

line 1: showed] **1814** shewed   //   line 12: shame!" cried] **1814** shame, "cried // line 14: ma'am,] **1814** Ma'am,   //   line 16: forlorn, that] **1814** forlorn that

"Well, and if they were *ten*," cried Mrs. Norris, "I am sure *you* need not regard it. The expense need not be any impediment. If I were you, I should not think of the expense. I would have every thing done in the best style, and made as nice as possible. Such a place as Sotherton Court deserves every thing that taste and money can do. You have space to work upon there, and grounds that will well reward you. For my own part, if I had any thing within the fiftieth part of the size of Sotherton, I should be always planting and improving, for naturally I am excessively fond of it. It would be too ridiculous for me to attempt any thing where I am now, with my little half acre. It would be quite a burlesque. But if I had more room, I should take a prodigious delight in improving and planting. We did a vast deal in that way at the parsonage; we made it quite a different place from what it was when we first had it. You young ones do not remember much about it, perhaps. But if dear Sir Thomas were here, he could tell you what improvements we made; and a great deal more would have been done, but for poor Mr. Norris's sad state of health. He could hardly ever get out, poor man, to enjoy any thing, and *that* disheartened me from doing several things that Sir Thomas and I used to talk of. If it had not been for *that*, we should have carried on the garden wall, and made the plantation to shut out the churchyard, just as Dr. Grant has done. We were always doing something, as it was. It was only the spring twelvemonth before Mr. Norris's death, that we put in the apricot against the stable wall, which is now grown such a noble tree, and getting to such perfection, sir," addressing herself then to Dr. Grant.

line 25: churchyard] **1814** church-yard   //   line 29: sir,"] **1814** Sir,"

"The tree thrives well beyond a doubt, madam," replied Dr. Grant. "The soil is good; and I never pass it without regretting, that the fruit should be so little worth the trouble of gathering."

"Sir, it is a moor park,[7] we bought it as a moor park, and it cost us—that is, it was a present from Sir Thomas, but I saw the bill, and I know it cost seven shillings, and was charged as a moor park."

"You were imposed on, ma'am," replied Dr. Grant; "these potatoes have as much the flavour of a moor park apricot, as the fruit from that tree. It is an insipid fruit at the best; but a good apricot is eatable, which none from my garden are."

"The truth is, ma'am," said Mrs. Grant, pretending to whisper across the table to Mrs. Norris, "that Dr. Grant hardly knows what the natural taste of our apricot is; he is scarcely ever indulged with one, for it is so valuable a fruit, with a little assistance, and ours is such a remarkably large, fair sort, that what with early tarts and preserves, my cook contrives to get them all."

Mrs. Norris, who had begun to redden, was appeased, and, for a little while, other subjects took place of the improvements of Sotherton. Dr. Grant and Mrs. Norris were seldom good friends; their acquaintance had begun in dilapidations,[8] and their habits were totally dissimilar.

After a short interruption, Mr. Rushworth began again. "Smith's place is the admiration of all the country; and it was a mere nothing before Repton took it in hand. I think I shall have Repton."

line 7: seven shillings,] **1814** seven-shillings,   //   line 9: ma'am,"] **1814** Ma'am,"   //   line 9: Grant; "these] **1814** Grant, "these   //   line 13: ma'am,] **1814** Ma'am,   //   line 20: appeased, and, for] **1814** appeased, and for   //   line 27: mere nothing] **1814** mere othing

"Mr. Rushworth," said Lady Bertram, "if I were you, I would have a very pretty shrubbery. One likes to get out into a shrubbery[9] in fine weather."

Mr. Rushworth was eager to assure her ladyship of his acquiescence, and tried to make out something complimentary; but between his submission to *her* taste, and his having always intended the same himself, with the super-added objects of professing attention to the comfort of ladies in general, and of insinuating, that there was one only whom he was anxious to please, he grew puzzled; and Edmund was glad to put an end to his speech by a proposal of wine. Mr. Rushworth, however, though not usually a great talker, had still more to say on the subject next his heart. "Smith has not much above a hundred acres altogether in his grounds, which is little enough, and makes it more surprising that the place can have been so improved. Now, at Sotherton, we have a good seven hundred,[10] without reckoning the water meadows; so that I think, if so much could be done at Compton, we need not despair. There have been two or three fine old trees cut down that grew too near the house, and it opens the prospect amazingly, which makes me think that Repton, or any body of that sort, would certainly have the avenue at Sotherton down;[11] the avenue that leads from the west front to the top of the hill you know," turning to Miss Bertram particularly as he spoke. But Miss Bertram thought it most becoming to reply:

"The avenue! Oh! I do not recollect it. I really know very little of Sotherton."

Fanny, who was sitting on the other side of Edmund, exactly opposite Miss Crawford, and who had been attentively listening, now looked at him, and said in a low voice,

line 16: Now, at] **1814** Now at // line 26: to reply:] **1814** to reply.

"Cut down an avenue! What a pity! Does not it make you think of Cowper?"[12] 'Ye fallen avenues, once more I mourn your fate unmerited.'

He smiled as he answered, "I am afraid the avenue stands a bad chance, Fanny."

"I should like to see Sotherton before it is cut down, to see the place as it is now, in its old state; but I do not suppose I shall."

"Have you never been there? No, you never can; and unluckily it is out of distance for a ride. I wish we could contrive it."

"Oh! it does not signify. Whenever I do see it, you will tell me how it has been altered."

"I collect,"[13] said Miss Crawford, "that Sotherton is an old place, and a place of some grandeur. In any particular style of building?"

"The house was built in Elizabeth's time,[14] and is a large, regular, brick building—heavy, but respectable looking, and has many good rooms. It is ill placed. It stands in one of the lowest spots of the park; in that respect, unfavourable for improvement. But the woods are fine, and there is a stream, which, I dare say, might be made a good deal of.[15] Mr. Rushworth is quite right, I think, in meaning to give it a modern dress, and I have no doubt that it will be all done extremely well."

Miss Crawford listened with submission, and said to herself, "He is a well bred man; he makes the best of it."

"I do not wish to influence Mr. Rushworth," he continued, "but had I a place to new fashion, I should not put myself

---

line 2: of Cowper?"] **1814** of Cowper.   //   line 3: unmerited.'] **1814** unmerited.'"   //   line 15: grandeur. In] **1814** grandeur." "In   //   line 18: regular, brick] **1814** regular brick   //   line 18: respectable] **1814** respectably //   line 23: right, I think,] **1814** right I think,

into the hands of an improver. I would rather have an inferior degree of beauty, of my own choice, and acquired progressively. I would rather abide by my own blunders than by his."

"*You* would know what you were about of course—but that would not suit *me*. I have no eye or ingenuity for such matters, but as they are before me; and had I a place of my own in the country, I should be most thankful to any Mr. Repton who would undertake it, and give me as much beauty as he could for my money; and I should never look at it, till it was complete."

"It would be delightful to *me* to see the progress of it all," said Fanny.

"Ay—you have been brought up to it. It was no part of my education; and the only dose I ever had, being administered by not the first favourite in the world, has made me consider improvements *in hand* as the greatest of nuisances. Three years ago, the admiral, my honoured uncle, bought a cottage at Twickenham[16] for us all to spend our summers in; and my aunt and I went down to it quite in raptures; but it being excessively pretty, it was soon found necessary to be improved; and for three months we were all dirt and confusion, without a gravel walk to step on, or a bench fit for use. I would have every thing as complete as possible in the country, shrubberies and flower gardens, and rustic seats innumerable; but it must be all done without my care. Henry is different, he loves to be doing."

Edmund was sorry to hear Miss Crawford, whom he was much disposed to admire, speak so freely of her uncle. It did not suit his sense of propriety, and he was silenced, till induced by further smiles and liveliness, to put the matter by for the present.

line 13: Ay—] **1814** Aye—

"Mr. Bertram," said she, "I have tidings of my harp[17] at last. I am assured that it is safe at Northampton; and there it has probably been these ten days, in spite of the solemn assurances we have so often received to the contrary." Edmund expressed his pleasure and surprise. "The truth is, that our inquiries were too direct; we sent a servant, we went ourselves: this will not do seventy miles from London—but this morning we heard of it in the right way. It was seen by some farmer, and he told the miller, and the miller told the butcher, and the butcher's son-in-law left word at the shop."

"I am very glad that you have heard of it, by whatever means; and hope there will be no farther delay."

"I am to have it to-morrow; but how do you think it is to be conveyed? Not by a waggon or cart;—Oh! no, nothing of that kind could be hired in the village. I might as well have asked for porters and a hand-barrow."

"You would find it difficult, I dare say, just now, in the middle of a very late hay harvest, to hire a horse and cart?"

"I was astonished to find what a piece of work was made of it! To want a horse and cart in the country seemed impossible, so I told my maid to speak for one directly; and as I cannot look out of my dressing-closet without seeing one farm yard, nor walk in the shrubbery without passing another, I thought it would be only ask and have, and was rather grieved that I could not give the advantage to all. Guess my surprise, when I found that I had been asking the most unreasonable, most impossible thing in the world, had offended all the farmers, all the labourers, all the hay in the parish. As for Dr. Grant's bailiff,[18] I believe I had better keep out of *his* way; and my brother-in-law himself, who is all kindness in general, looked rather black upon me, when he found what I had been at."

line 5: inquiries] **1814** enquiries // line 6: ourselves: this] **1814** ourselves; this

"You could not be expected to have thought on the subject before, but when you *do* think of it, you must see the importance of getting in the grass. The hire of a cart at any time, might not be so easy as you suppose; our farmers are not in the habit of letting them out; but in harvest, it must be quite out of their power to spare a horse."

"I shall understand all your ways in time; but coming down with the true London maxim,[19] that every thing is to be got with money, I was a little embarrassed[20] at first by the sturdy independence of your country customs. However, I am to have my harp fetched to-morrow. Henry, who is good-nature itself, has offered to fetch it in his barouche.[21] Will it not be honourably conveyed?"

Edmund spoke of the harp as his favourite instrument, and hoped to be soon allowed to hear her. Fanny had never heard the harp at all, and wished for it very much.

"I shall be most happy to play to you both," said Miss Crawford; "at least, as long as you can like to listen; probably much longer, for I dearly love music myself, and where the natural taste is equal, the player must always be best off, for she is gratified in more ways than one. Now, Mr. Bertram, if you write to your brother, I entreat you to tell him that my harp *is* come, he heard so much of my misery about it. And you may say, if you please, that I shall prepare my most plaintive airs against his return, in compassion to his feelings, as I know his horse will lose."

"If I write, I will say whatever you wish me; but I do not at present foresee any occasion for writing."

"No, I dare say, nor if he were to be gone a twelvemonth, would you ever write to him, nor he to you, if it could be helped. The occasion would never be foreseen. What strange

line 18: probably much] **1814** probably, much   //   line 22: entreat] **1814** intreat

creatures brothers are! You would not write to each other but upon the most urgent necessity in the world; and when obliged to take up the pen to say that such a horse is ill, or such a relation dead, it is done in the fewest possible words. You have but one style among you. I know it perfectly. Henry, who is in every other respect exactly what a brother should be, who loves me, consults me, confides in me, and will talk to me by the hour together, has never yet turned the page in a letter; and very often it is nothing more than, 'Dear Mary, I am just arrived. Bath seems full, and every thing as usual. Your's sincerely.' That is the true manly style; that is a complete brother's letter."

"When they are at a distance from all their family," said Fanny, colouring for William's sake, "they can write long letters."

"Miss Price has a brother at sea," said Edmund, "whose excellence as a correspondent, makes her think you too severe upon us."

"At sea, has she?—In the King's service of course."[22]

Fanny would rather have had Edmund tell the story, but his determined silence obliged her to relate her brother's situation; her voice was animated in speaking of his profession,[23] and the foreign stations he had been on, but she could not mention the number of years that he had been absent without tears in her eyes. Miss Crawford civilly wished him an early promotion.

"Do you know any thing of my cousin's captain?" said Edmund; "Captain Marshall? You have a large acquaintance in the navy, I conclude?"

"Among Admirals,[24] large enough; but," with an air of grandeur, "we know very little of the inferior ranks. Post

line 28: "Captain Marshall?] **1814** "captain Marshall? //   line 30: but," with an air of grandeur, "we] **1814** but" with an air of grandeur; "we captains may be very good sort of men, but they do not belong to *us*. Of various admirals I could tell you a great deal; of them and their flags, and the gradation of their pay, and their bickerings and jealousies.[25] But in general, I can assure you that they are all passed over, and all very ill used. Certainly, my home at my uncle's brought me acquainted with a circle of admirals. Of *Rears*, and *Vices*,[26] I saw enough. Now, do not be suspecting me of a pun, I entreat."

Edmund again felt grave, and only replied, "It is a noble profession."

"Yes, the profession is well enough under two circumstances; if it make the fortune, and there be discretion in spending it. But, in short, it is not a favourite profession of mine. It has never worn an amiable form to *me*."

Edmund reverted to the harp, and was again very happy in the prospect of hearing her play.

The subject of improving grounds meanwhile was still under consideration among the others; and Mrs. Grant could not help addressing her brother, though it was calling his attention from Miss Julia Bertram. "My dear Henry, have *you* nothing to say? You have been an improver yourself, and from what I hear of Everingham, it may vie with any place in England. Its natural beauties, I am sure, are great. Everingham as it *used* to be was perfect in my estimation; such a happy fall of ground, and such timber![27] What would not I give to see it again!"

"Nothing could be so gratifying to me as to hear your opinion of it," was his answer. "But I fear there would be some disappointment. You would not find it equal to your present ideas. In extent it is a mere nothing—you would be surprised at its insignificance; and as for improvement, there

line 2: admirals I] **1814** admirals, I   //   line 28: it," was] **1814** it, was

was very little for me to do; too little—I should like to have been busy much longer."

"You are fond of the sort of thing?" said Julia.

"Excessively: but what with the natural advantages of the ground, which pointed out even to a very young eye what little remained to be done, and my own consequent resolutions, I had not been of age three months before Everingham was all that it is now. My plan was laid at Westminster[28]—a little altered perhaps at Cambridge, and at one and twenty executed. I am inclined to envy Mr. Rushworth for having so much happiness yet before him. I have been a devourer of my own."

"Those who see quickly, will resolve quickly and act quickly," said Julia. "*You* can never want employment. Instead of envying Mr. Rushworth, you should assist him with your opinion."

Mrs. Grant hearing the latter part of this speech, enforced it warmly, persuaded that no judgment could be equal to her brother's; and as Miss Bertram caught at the idea likewise, and gave it her full support, declaring that in her opinion it was infinitely better to consult with friends and disinterested advisers, than immediately to throw the business into the hands of a professional man, Mr. Rushworth was very ready to request the favour of Mr. Crawford's assistance; and Mr. Crawford after properly depreciating his own abilities, was quite at his service in any way that could be useful. Mr. Rushworth then began to propose Mr. Crawford's doing him the honour of coming over to Sotherton, and taking a bed there; when Mrs. Norris, as if reading in her two nieces' minds their little approbation of a plan which was to take Mr. Crawford away, interposed with an amendment. "There

line 4: "Excessively: but] **1814** "Excessively; but   //   line 5: ground, which]
1814 ground which

can be no doubt of Mr. Crawford's willingness; but why should not more of us go?—Why should not we make a little party? Here are many that would be interested in your improvements, my dear Mr. Rushworth, and that would like to hear Mr. Crawford's opinion on the spot, and that might be of some small use to you with *their* opinions; and for my own part I have been long wishing to wait upon your good mother again; nothing but having no horses of my own, could have made me so remiss; but now I could go and sit a few hours with Mrs. Rushworth while the rest of you walked about and settled things, and then we could all return to a late dinner here, or dine at Sotherton just as might be most agreeable to your mother, and have a pleasant drive home by moonlight. I dare say Mr. Crawford would take my two nieces and me in his barouche, and Edmund can go on horseback, you know, sister, and Fanny will stay at home with you."

Lady Bertram made no objection, and every one concerned in the going, was forward in expressing their ready concurrence, excepting Edmund, who heard it all and said nothing.

line 15: know, sister, and] **1814** know sister, and

Chapter 7

"WELL Fanny, and how do you like Miss Crawford *now?*" said Edmund the next day, after thinking some time on the subject himself. "How did you like her yesterday?"

"Very well—very much. I like to hear her talk. She entertains me; and she is so extremely pretty, that I have great pleasure in looking at her."

"It is her countenance that is so attractive. She has a wonderful play of feature! But was there nothing in her conversation that struck you Fanny, as not quite right?"

"Oh! yes, she ought not to have spoken of her uncle as she did. I was quite astonished. An uncle with whom she has been living so many years, and who, whatever his faults may be, is so very fond of her brother, treating him, they say, quite like a son. I could not have believed it!"

"I thought you would be struck. It was very wrong—very indecorous."

"And very ungrateful I think."

"Ungrateful is a strong word. I do not know that her uncle has any claim to her *gratitude*; his wife certainly had; and it is the warmth of her respect for her aunt's memory which misleads her here. She is awkwardly circumstanced. With such warm feelings and lively spirits it must be difficult to do justice to her affection for Mrs. Crawford, without throwing a shade on the admiral. I do not pretend to know which was

line 21: circumstanced. With] **1814** circumstanced With   //   line 24: the admiral.] **1814** the Admiral.

most to blame in their disagreements, though the admiral's present conduct might incline one to the side of his wife: but it is natural and amiable that Miss Crawford should acquit her aunt entirely. I do not censure her *opinions*; but there certainly *is* impropriety in making them public."

"Do not you think," said Fanny, after a little consideration, "that this impropriety is a reflection itself upon Mrs. Crawford, as her niece has been entirely brought up by her? She cannot have given her right notions of what was due to the admiral."

"That is a fair remark. Yes, we must suppose the faults of the niece to have been those of the aunt; and it makes one more sensible of the disadvantages she has been under. But I think her present home must do her good. Mrs. Grant's manners are just what they ought to be. She speaks of her brother with a very pleasing affection."

"Yes, except as to his writing her such short letters. She made me almost laugh; but I cannot rate so very highly the love or good nature of a brother, who will not give himself the trouble of writing any thing worth reading, to his sisters, when they are separated. I am sure William would never have used *me* so, under any circumstances. And what right had she to suppose, that *you* would not write long letters when you were absent?"

"The right of a lively mind, Fanny, seizing whatever may contribute to its own amusement or that of others; perfectly allowable, when untinctured by ill humour or roughness; and there is not a shadow of either in the countenance or manner of Miss Crawford, nothing sharp, or loud, or coarse. She is perfectly feminine, except in the instances we have been

line 1: admiral's] **1814** Admiral's   //   line 2: wife: but] **1814** wife; but   //
line 19: good nature] **1814** good-nature

speaking of. *There* she cannot be justified. I am glad you saw it all as I did."

Having formed her mind and gained her affections, he had a good chance of her thinking like him; though at this period, and on this subject, there began now to be some danger of dissimilarity, for he was in a line of admiration of Miss Crawford, which might lead him where Fanny could not follow. Miss Crawford's attractions did not lessen. The harp arrived,[1] and rather added to her beauty, wit, and good humour, for she played with the greatest obligingness, with an expression and taste which were peculiarly becoming, and there was something clever to be said at the close of every air. Edmund was at the parsonage every day to be indulged with his favourite instrument; one morning secured an invitation for the next, for the lady could not be unwilling to have a listener, and every thing was soon in a fair train.

A young woman, pretty, lively, with a harp as elegant as herself;[2] and both placed near a window, cut down to the ground, and opening on a little lawn, surrounded by shrubs in the rich foliage of summer, was enough to catch any man's heart. The season, the scene, the air, were all favourable to tenderness and sentiment. Mrs. Grant and her tambour frame[3] were not without their use; it was all in harmony; and as every thing will turn to account when love is once set going, even the sandwich tray, and Dr. Grant doing the honours of it, were worth looking at. Without studying the business, however, or knowing what he was about, Edmund was beginning, at the end of a week of such intercourse, to be a good deal in love; and to the credit of the lady it may be added, that without his being a man of the world or an elder

line 5: subject, there] **1814** subject there   //   line 9: arrived, and] **1814** arrived and   //   line 21: air, were] **1814** air were   //   line 28: beginning, at] **1814** beginning at

brother, without any of the arts of flattery or the gaieties of small talk, he began to be agreeable to her. She felt it to be so, though she had not foreseen and could hardly understand it; for he was not pleasant by any common rule, he talked no nonsense, he paid no compliments, his opinions were unbending, his attentions tranquil and simple. There was a charm, perhaps, in his sincerity, his steadiness, his integrity, which Miss Crawford might be equal to feel, though not equal to discuss with herself. She did not think very much about it, however; he pleased her for the present; she liked to have him near her; it was enough.

Fanny could not wonder that Edmund was at the parsonage every morning; she would gladly have been there too, might she have gone in uninvited and unnoticed to hear the harp; neither could she wonder, that when the evening stroll was over, and the two families parted again, he should think it right to attend Mrs. Grant and her sister to their home, while Mr. Crawford was devoted to the ladies of the park; but she thought it a very bad exchange, and if Edmund were not there to mix the wine and water for her, would rather go without it than not. She was a little surprised that he could spend so many hours with Miss Crawford, and not see more of the sort of fault which he had already observed, and of which *she* was almost always reminded by a something of the same nature whenever she was in her company; but so it was. Edmund was fond of speaking to her of Miss Crawford, but he seemed to think it enough that the admiral had since been spared; and she scrupled to point out her own remarks to him,[4] lest it should appear like ill-nature. The first actual pain which Miss Crawford occasioned her, was the consequence of an inclination to learn to ride, which the former caught soon after her being settled at Mansfield from the example of the young ladies at the park, and which, when Edmund's acquaintance with her increased, led to his encouraging the wish, and the offer of his own quiet mare for the purpose of her first attempts, as the best fitted for a beginner that either stable could furnish. No pain, no injury, however, was designed by him to his cousin in this offer: *she* was not to lose a day's exercise by it. The mare was only to be taken down to the parsonage half an hour before her ride were to begin; and Fanny, on its being first proposed, so far from feeling slighted, was almost overpowered with gratitude that he should be asking her leave for it.

Miss Crawford made her first essay[5] with great credit to herself, and no inconvenience to Fanny. Edmund, who had taken down the mare and presided at the whole, returned with it in excellent time, before either Fanny or the steady old coachman, who always attended her when she rode without her cousins, were ready to set forward. The second day's trial was not so guiltless. Miss Crawford's enjoyment of riding was such, that she did not know how to leave off. Active and fearless, and, though rather small, strongly made, she seemed formed for a horsewoman; and to the pure genuine pleasure of the exercise, something was probably added in Edmund's attendance and instructions, and something more in the conviction of very much surpassing her sex in general by her early progress, to make her unwilling to dismount. Fanny was ready and waiting, and Mrs. Norris was beginning to scold her for not being gone, and still no horse was announced, no Edmund appeared. To avoid her aunt, and look for him, she went out.

The houses, though scarcely half a mile apart, were not within sight of each other; but by walking fifty yards from the hall door, she could look down the park, and command

line 5: offer: *she*] **1814** offer; *she* // line 10: for it.] **1814** for it // line 20: horsewoman;] **1814** horse woman;

a view of the parsonage and all its demesnes, gently rising beyond the village road; and in Dr. Grant's meadow[6] she immediately saw the group—Edmund and Miss Crawford both on horseback, riding side by side, Dr. and Mrs. Grant, and Mr. Crawford, with two or three grooms, standing about and looking on. A happy party it appeared to her—all interested in one object—cheerful beyond a doubt, for the sound of merriment ascended even to her. It was a sound which did not make *her* cheerful; she wondered that Edmund should forget her, and felt a pang. She could not turn her eyes from the meadow, she could not help watching all that passed. At first Miss Crawford and her companion made the circuit of the field, which was not small, at a foot's pace; then, at *her* apparent suggestion, they rose into a canter; and to Fanny's timid nature it was most astonishing to see how well she sat. After a few minutes, they stopt entirely, Edmund was close to her, he was speaking to her, he was evidently directing her management of the bridle, he had hold of her hand; she saw it, or the imagination supplied what the eye could not reach.[7] She must not wonder at all this; what could be more natural than that Edmund should be making himself useful, and proving his good-nature by any one? She could not but think indeed that Mr. Crawford might as well have saved him the trouble; that it would have been particularly proper and becoming in a brother to have done it himself; but Mr. Crawford, with all his boasted good-nature, and all his coachmanship, probably knew nothing of the matter, and had no active kindness in comparison of Edmund. She began to think it rather hard upon the mare to have such double duty; if she were forgotten the poor mare should be remembered.

line 26: good-nature,] **1814** good nature,

Her feelings for one and the other were soon a little tran-quillized, by seeing the party in the meadow disperse, and Miss Crawford still on horseback, but attended by Edmund on foot, pass through a gate into the lane, and so into the park, and make towards the spot where she stood. She began then to be afraid of appearing rude and impatient; and walked to meet them with a great anxiety to avoid the suspicion.

"My dear Miss Price," said Miss Crawford, as soon as she was at all within hearing, "I am come to make my own apologies for keeping you waiting—but I have nothing in the world to say for myself—I knew it was very late, and that I was behaving extremely ill; and, therefore, if you please, you must forgive me. Selfishness must always be forgiven you know, because there is no hope of a cure."

Fanny's answer was extremely civil, and Edmund added his conviction that she could be in no hurry. "For there is more than time enough for my cousin to ride twice as far as she ever goes," said he, "and you have been promoting her comfort by preventing her from setting off half an hour sooner; clouds are now coming up, and she will not suffer from the heat as she would have done then. I wish *you* may not be fatigued by so much exercise. I wish you had saved yourself this walk home."

"No part of it fatigues me but getting off this horse, I assure you," said she, as she sprang down with his help; "I am very strong. Nothing ever fatigues me, but doing what I do not like. Miss Price, I give way to you with a very bad grace; but I sincerely hope you will have a pleasant ride, and that I may have nothing but good to hear of this dear, delightful, beautiful animal."

line 8: "My] **1814** 'My   //   line 25: help; "I am] **1814** help; I am   //
line 27: Miss Price, I] **1814** Miss Price I   //   line 27: grace; but] **1814** grace, but

The old coachman, who had been waiting about with his own horse, now joining them, Fanny was lifted on her's, and they set off across another part of the park; her feelings of discomfort not lightened by seeing, as she looked back, that the others were walking down the hill together to the village; nor did her attendant do her much good by his comments on Miss Crawford's great cleverness as a horsewoman, which he had been watching with an interest almost equal to her own.

"It is a pleasure to see a lady with such a good heart for riding!" said he. "I never see one sit a horse better. She did not seem to have a thought of fear. Very different from you, miss, when you first began, six years ago come next Easter. Lord bless me! how you did tremble when Sir Thomas first had you put on!"

In the drawing-room Miss Crawford was also celebrated. Her merit in being gifted by nature with strength and courage was fully appreciated by the Miss Bertrams; her delight in riding was like their own; her early excellence in it was like their own, and they had great pleasure in praising it.

"I was sure she would ride well," said Julia; "she has the make for it. Her figure is as neat as her brother's."

"Yes," added Maria, "and her spirits are as good, and she has the same energy of character. I cannot but think that good horsemanship has a great deal to do with the mind."

When they parted at night, Edmund asked Fanny whether she meant to ride the next day.

"No, I do not know, not if you want the mare," was her answer. "I do not want her at all for myself," said he; "but whenever you are next inclined to stay at home, I think Miss

line 1: coachman, who] **1814** coachman who   //   line 7: horsewoman,] **1814** horse woman,   //   line 11: you, miss,] **1814** you, Miss,   //   line 15: drawing-room] **1814** drawing room   //   line 20: said Julia; "she] **1814** said Julia, "she   //   line 28: he; "but] **1814** he, "but

Crawford would be glad to have her for a longer time—
for a whole morning in short. She has a great desire to get
as far as Mansfield common,[8] Mrs. Grant has been telling
her of its fine views, and I have no doubt of her being perfectly equal to it. But any morning will do for this. She
would be extremely sorry to interfere with you. It would be
very wrong if she did.—*She* rides only for pleasure, *you* for
health."

"I shall not ride to-morrow, certainly," said Fanny; "I have
been out very often lately, and would rather stay at home.
You know I am strong enough now to walk very well."

Edmund looked pleased, which must be Fanny's comfort, and the ride to Mansfield common took place the next
morning;—the party included all the young people but herself, and was much enjoyed at the time, and doubly enjoyed
again in the evening discussion. A successful scheme of this
sort generally brings on another; and the having been to
Mansfield-common, disposed them all for going somewhere
else the day after. There were many other views to be shewn,
and though the weather was hot, there were shady lanes wherever they wanted to go. A young party is always provided with
a shady lane. Four fine mornings successively were spent in
this manner, in shewing the Crawfords the country, and doing
the honours of its finest spots. Every thing answered; it was
all gaiety and good-humour, the heat only supplying inconvenience enough to be talked of with pleasure—till the fourth
day, when the happiness of one of the party was exceedingly
clouded. Miss Bertram was the one. Edmund and Julia were
invited to dine at the parsonage, and *she* was excluded. It was
meant and done by Mrs. Grant, with perfect good humour,

line 23: Crawfords] **1814** Crawford's   //   line 30: humour, on] **1814**
humour on

on Mr. Rushworth's account, who was partly expected at the park that day; but it was felt as a very grievous injury, and her good manners were severely taxed to conceal her vexation and anger, till she reached home. As Mr. Rushworth did *not* come, the injury was increased, and she had not even the relief of shewing her power over him; she could only be sullen to her mother, aunt, and cousin, and throw as great a gloom as possible over their dinner and dessert.

Between ten and eleven, Edmund and Julia walked into the drawing-room, fresh with the evening air, glowing and cheerful, the very reverse of what they found in the three ladies sitting there, for Maria would scarcely raise her eyes from her book, and Lady Bertram was half asleep; and even Mrs. Norris, discomposed by her niece's ill-humour, and having asked one or two questions about the dinner, which were not immediately attended to, seemed almost determined to say no more. For a few minutes, the brother and sister were too eager in their praise of the night and their remarks on the stars, to think beyond themselves; but when the first pause came, Edmund, looking around, said, "But where is Fanny?—Is she gone to bed?"

"No, not that I know of," replied Mrs. Norris; "she was here a moment ago."

Her own gentle voice speaking from the other end of the room, which was a very long one, told them that she was on the sofa. Mrs. Norris began scolding.

"That is a very foolish trick, Fanny, to be idling away all the evening upon a sofa. Why cannot you come and sit here, and employ yourself as *we* do?—If you have no work of your own, I can supply you from the poor-basket.[9] There is all the new calico that was bought last week, not touched yet. I am sure I almost broke my back by cutting it out. You should

83

learn to think of other people; and take my word for it, it is a shocking trick for a young person to be always lolling upon a sofa."

Before half this was said, Fanny was returned to her seat at the table, and had taken up her work again; and Julia, who was in high good-humour, from the pleasures of the day, did her the justice of exclaiming, "I must say, ma'am, that Fanny is as little upon the sofa as any body in the house."

"Fanny," said Edmund, after looking at her attentively; "I am sure you have the headach?"

She could not deny it, but said it was not very bad.

"I can hardly believe you," he replied; "I know your looks too well. How long have you had it?"

"Since a little before dinner. It is nothing but the heat."

"Did you go out in the heat?"

"Go out! to be sure she did," said Mrs. Norris; "would you have her stay within such a fine day as this? Were not we *all* out? Even your mother was out to-day for above an hour."

"Yes, indeed, Edmund," added her ladyship, who had been thoroughly awakened by Mrs. Norris's sharp reprimand to Fanny; "I was out above an hour. I sat three quarters of an hour in the flower garden, while Fanny cut the roses, and very pleasant it was I assure you, but very hot. It was shady enough in the alcove,[10] but I declare I quite dreaded the coming home again."

"Fanny has been cutting roses, has she?"

"Yes, and I am afraid they will be the last this year. Poor thing! *She* found it hot enough, but they were so full blown, that one could not wait."

"There was no help for it certainly," rejoined Mrs. Norris, in a rather softened voice; "but I question whether her

line 7: ma'am,] **1814** Ma'am,   //   line 10: headach?"] **1814** head-ache?"   //
line 16: Norris; "would] **1814** Norris; "Would

headach might not be caught *then*, sister. There is nothing so likely to give it as standing and stooping in a hot sun. But I dare say it will be well to-morrow. Suppose you let her have your aromatic vinegar;[11] I always forget to have mine filled."

"She has got it," said Lady Bertram; "she has had it ever since she came back from your house the second time."

"What!" cried Edmund; "has she been walking as well as cutting roses; walking across the hot park to your house, and doing it twice, ma'am?—No wonder her head aches."

Mrs. Norris was talking to Julia, and did not hear.

"I was afraid it would be too much for her," said Lady Bertram; "but when the roses were gathered, your aunt wished to have them,[12] and then you know they must be taken home."

"But were there roses enough to oblige her to go twice?"

"No; but they were to be put into the spare room to dry; and, unluckily, Fanny forgot to lock the door of the room and bring away the key, so she was obliged to go again."

Edmund got up and walked about the room, saying, "And could nobody be employed on such an errand but Fanny?— Upon my word, ma'am, it has been a very ill-managed business."

"I am sure I do not know how it was to have been done better," cried Mrs. Norris, unable to be longer deaf; "unless I had gone myself indeed; but I cannot be in two places at once; and I was talking to Mr. Green at that very time about your mother's dairymaid, by *her* desire, and had promised John Groom[13] to write to Mrs. Jefferies about his son, and the poor fellow was waiting for me half an hour. I think nobody can justly accuse me of sparing myself upon any occasion, but really I cannot do every thing at once. And as for Fanny's just

line 1: headach] **1814** head-ache // line 5: Lady Bertram;] **1814** lady Bertram; // line 9: ma'am?] **1814** Ma'am? // line 11: Lady Bertram;] **1814** lady Bertram; // line 20: ma'am,] **1814** Ma'am, stepping down to my house for me, it is not much above a quarter of a mile,[14] I cannot think I was unreasonable to ask it. How often do I pace it three times a-day, early and late, ay and in all weathers too, and say nothing about it."

"I wish Fanny had half your strength, ma'am."

"If Fanny would be more regular in her exercise, she would not be knocked up[15] so soon. She has not been out on horseback now this long while, and I am persuaded, that when she does not ride, she ought to walk. If she had been riding before, I should not have asked it of her. But I thought it would rather do her good after being stooping among the roses; for there is nothing so refreshing as a walk after a fatigue of that kind; and though the sun was strong, it was not so very hot. Between ourselves, Edmund," nodding significantly at his mother, "it was cutting the roses, and dawdling about in the flower-garden, that did the mischief."

"I am afraid it was, indeed," said the more candid Lady Bertram, who had overheard her, "I am very much afraid she caught the headach there, for the heat was enough to kill any body. It was as much as I could bear myself. Sitting and calling to Pug, and trying to keep him from the flower-beds, was almost too much for me."

Edmund said no more to either lady; but going quietly to another table, on which the supper tray yet remained, brought a glass of Madeira[16] to Fanny, and obliged her to drink the greater part. She wished to be able to decline it; but the tears which a variety of feelings created, made it easier to swallow than to speak.

Vexed as Edmund was with his mother and aunt, he was still more angry with himself. His own forgetfulness of her

line 3: a-day,] **1814** a day,   //   line 4: ay and] **1814** aye and   //   line 5: ma'am."] **1814** Ma'am."   //   line 6: exercise,] **1814** excercise,   //   line 19: headach] **1814** head-ache

was worse than any thing which they had done. Nothing of this would have happened had she been properly considered; but she had been left four days together without any choice of companions or exercise, and without any excuse for avoiding whatever her unreasonable aunts might require. He was ashamed to think that for four days together she had not had the power of riding, and very seriously resolved, however unwilling he must be to check a pleasure of Miss Crawford's, that it should never happen again.

Fanny went to bed with her heart as full as on the first evening of her arrival at the Park. The state of her spirits had probably had its share in her indisposition; for she had been feeling neglected, and been struggling against discontent and envy for some days past. As she leant on the sofa, to which she had retreated that she might not be seen, the pain of her mind had been much beyond that in her head; and the sudden change which Edmund's kindness had then occasioned, made her hardly know how to support herself.

Chapter 8

FANNY'S rides recommenced the very next day, and as it was a pleasant fresh-feeling morning, less hot than the weather had lately been, Edmund trusted that her losses both of health and pleasure would be soon made good. While she was gone, Mr. Rushworth arrived, escorting his mother, who came to be civil, and to shew her civility especially, in urging the execution of the plan for visiting Sotherton, which had been started a fortnight before, and which, in consequence of her subsequent absence from home, had since lain dormant. Mrs. Norris and her nieces were all well pleased with its revival, and an early day was named, and agreed to, provided Mr. Crawford should be disengaged; the young ladies did not forget that stipulation, and though Mrs. Norris would willingly have answered for his being so, they would neither authorize the liberty, nor run the risk; and at last on a hint from Miss Bertram, Mr. Rushworth discovered that the properest thing to be done, was for him to walk down to the parsonage directly, and call on Mr. Crawford, and inquire whether Wednesday would suit him or not.

Before his return Mrs. Grant and Miss Crawford came in. Having been out some time, and taken a different route to the house, they had not met him. Comfortable hopes, however, were given that he would find Mr. Crawford at home. The

line 4: While she was] **1814** While he was   //   line 6: especially, in] **1814** especially in   //   line 18: inquire] **1814** enquire   //   line 22: hopes, however, were] **1814** hopes however were

88

Sotherton scheme was mentioned of course. It was hardly possible indeed that any thing else should be talked of, for Mrs. Norris was in high spirits about it, and Mrs. Rushworth, a well-meaning, civil, prosing, pompous woman, who thought nothing of consequence, but as it related to her own and her son's concerns, had not yet given over pressing Lady Bertram to be of the party. Lady Bertram constantly declined it; but her placid manner of refusal made Mrs. Rushworth still think she wished to come, till Mrs. Norris's more numerous words and louder tone convinced her of the truth.

"The fatigue would be too much for my sister, a great deal too much I assure you, my dear Mrs. Rushworth. Ten miles there, and ten back, you know. You must excuse my sister on this occasion, and accept of our two dear girls and myself without her. Sotherton is the only place that could give her a *wish* to go so far, but it cannot be indeed. She will have a companion in Fanny Price you know, so it will all do very well; and as for Edmund, as he is not here to speak for himself, I will answer for his being most happy to join the party. He can go on horseback, you know."

Mrs. Rushworth being obliged to yield to Lady Bertram's staying at home, could only be sorry. "The loss of her Ladyship's company would be a great drawback, and she should have been extremely happy to have seen the young lady too, Miss Price, who had never been at Sotherton yet, and it was a pity she should not see the place."

"You are very kind, you are all kindness, my dear madam," cried Mrs. Norris; "but as to Fanny, she will have opportunities in plenty of seeing Sotherton. She has time enough before her; and her going now is quite out of the question. Lady Bertram could not possibly spare her."

line 8: it; but] **1814** it, but

"Oh! no—I cannot do without Fanny."

Mrs. Rushworth proceeded next, under the conviction that every body must be wanting to see Sotherton, to include Miss Crawford in the invitation; and though Mrs. Grant, who had not been at the trouble of visiting Mrs. Rushworth on her coming into the neighbourhood, civilly declined it on her own account, she was glad to secure any pleasure for her sister; and Mary, properly pressed and persuaded, was not long in accepting her share of the civility. Mr. Rushworth came back from the parsonage successful; and Edmund made his appearance just in time to learn what had been settled for Wednesday, to attend Mrs. Rushworth to her carriage, and walk half way down the park with the two other ladies.

On his return to the breakfast-room, he found Mrs. Norris trying to make up her mind as to whether Miss Crawford's being of the party were desirable or not, or whether her brother's barouche would not be full without her. The Miss Bertrams laughed at the idea, assuring her that the barouche would hold four perfectly well, independent of the box, on which *one* might go with him.

"But why is it necessary," said Edmund, "that Crawford's carriage, or his *only* should be employed? Why is no use to be made of my mother's chaise? I could not, when the scheme was first mentioned the other day, understand why a visit from the family were not to be made in the carriage of the family."

"What!" cried Julia: "go box'd up three in a post-chaise in this weather when we may have seats in a barouche![1] No, my dear Edmund, that will not quite do."

"Besides," said Maria, "I know that Mr. Crawford depends upon taking us. After what passed at first, he would claim it as a promise."

line 21: necessary," said Edmund, "that] **1814** necessary, said Edmund, that // line 26: "What!" cried Julia: "go] **1814** "What! cried Julia. Go

"And my dear Edmund," added Mrs. Norris, "taking out *two* carriages when *one* will do, would be trouble for nothing; and between ourselves, coachman is not very fond of the roads between this and Sotherton; he always complains bitterly of the narrow lanes scratching his carriage, and you know one should not like to have dear Sir Thomas when he comes home find all the varnish scratched off."

"That would not be a very handsome reason for using Mr. Crawford's," said Maria; "but the truth is, that Wilcox is a stupid old fellow, and does not know how to drive. I will answer for it that we shall find no inconvenience from narrow roads on Wednesday."

"There is no hardship, I suppose, nothing unpleasant," said Edmund, "in going on the barouche box."

"Unpleasant!" cried Maria: "Oh! dear, I believe it would be generally thought the favourite seat. There can be no comparison as to one's view of the country. Probably, Miss Crawford will choose the barouche box herself."

"There can be no objection then to Fanny's going with you; there can be no doubt of your having room for her."

"Fanny!" repeated Mrs. Norris; "my dear Edmund, there is no idea of her going with us. She stays with her aunt. I told Mrs. Rushworth so. She is not expected."

"You can have no reason I imagine madam," said he, addressing his mother, "for wishing Fanny *not* to be of the party, but as it relates to yourself, to your own comfort. If you could do without her, you would not wish to keep her at home?"

line 13: hardship, I] **1814** hardship I   //   line 15: Maria: "Oh!] **1814** Maria; "Oh!   //   line 15: it would be] **1814** it could be   //   line 18: choose] **1814** chuse   //   line 18: box herself."] **1814** box-herself"   //   line 21: Mrs. Norris; "my] **1814** Mrs. Norris, "my   //   line 24: he, addressing his mother, "for] **1814** he addressing his mother, for   //   line 26: party, but] **1814** party, "but

"To be sure not, but I *cannot* do without her."

"You can, if I stay at home with you, as I mean to do."

There was a general cry out at this. "Yes," he continued, "there is no necessity for my going, and I mean to stay at home. Fanny has a great desire to see Sotherton. I know she wishes it very much. She has not often a gratification of the kind, and I am sure ma'am you would be glad to give her the pleasure now?"

"Oh! yes, very glad, if your aunt sees no objection."

Mrs. Norris was very ready with the only objection which could remain, their having positively assured Mrs. Rushworth, that Fanny could not go, and the very strange appearance there would consequently be in taking her, which seemed to her a difficulty quite impossible to be got over. It must have the strangest appearance! It would be something so very unceremonious, so bordering on disrespect for Mrs. Rushworth, whose own manners were such a pattern of good-breeding and attention, that she really did not feel equal to it. Mrs. Norris had no affection for Fanny, and no wish of procuring her pleasure at any time, but her opposition to Edmund *now* arose more from partiality for her own scheme because it *was* her own, than from any thing else. She felt that she had arranged every thing extremely well, and that any alteration must be for the worse. When Edmund, therefore, told her in reply, as he did when she would give him the hearing, that she need not distress herself on Mrs. Rushworth's account, because he had taken the opportunity as he walked with her through the hall, of mentioning Miss Price as one who would probably be of the party, and had directly received a very sufficient invitation for his cousin,[2] Mrs. Norris was too much vexed to submit with a very good grace, and would

line 3: this. "Yes] **1814** this, "Yes // line 7: ma'am] **1814** Ma'am //
line 31: grace, and] **1814** grace and

only say, "Very well, very well, just as you choose, settle it your own way, I am sure I do not care about it."

"It seems very odd," said Maria, "that you should be staying at home instead of Fanny."

"I am sure she ought to be very much obliged to you," added Julia, hastily leaving the room as she spoke, from a consciousness that she ought to offer to stay at home herself.

"Fanny will feel quite as grateful as the occasion requires," was Edmund's only reply, and the subject dropt.

Fanny's gratitude when she heard the plan, was in fact much greater than her pleasure. She felt Edmund's kindness with all, and more than all, the sensibility which he, unsuspicious of her fond attachment, could be aware of; but that he should forego any enjoyment on her account gave her pain, and her own satisfaction in seeing Sotherton would be nothing without him.

The next meeting of the two Mansfield families produced another alteration in the plan, and one that was admitted with general approbation. Mrs. Grant offered herself as companion for the day to Lady Bertram in lieu of her son, and Dr. Grant was to join them at dinner. Lady Bertram was very well pleased to have it so, and the young ladies were in spirits again. Even Edmund was very thankful for an arrangement which restored him to his share of the party; and Mrs. Norris thought it an excellent plan, and had it at her tongue's end, and was on the point of proposing it when Mrs. Grant spoke.

Wednesday was fine, and soon after breakfast the barouche arrived, Mr. Crawford driving his sisters; and as every body was ready, there was nothing to be done but for Mrs. Grant to alight and the others to take their places. The place of

line 1: choose,] 1814 chuse,   //   line 29: sisters; and] 1814 sisters, and all places, the envied seat, the post of honour, was unappropriated. To whose happy lot was it to fall? While each of the Miss Bertrams were meditating how best, and with most appearance of obliging the others, to secure it, the matter was settled by Mrs. Grant's saying, as she stepped from the carriage, "As there are five of you, it will be better that one should sit with Henry, and as you were saying lately, that you wished you could drive, Julia, I think this will be a good opportunity for you to take a lesson."

Happy Julia! Unhappy Maria! The former was on the barouche-box in a moment, the latter took her seat within, in gloom and mortification; and the carriage drove off amid the good wishes of the two remaining ladies, and the barking of pug in his mistress's arms.

Their road was through a pleasant country;[3] and Fanny, whose rides had never been extensive, was soon beyond her knowledge, and was very happy in observing all that was new, and admiring all that was pretty. She was not often invited to join in the conversation of the others, nor did she desire it. Her own thoughts and reflections were habitually her best companions; and in observing the appearance of the country, the bearings of the roads, the difference of soil, the state of the harvest, the cottages, the cattle, the children, she found entertainment that could only have been heightened by having Edmund to speak to of what she felt. That was the only point of resemblance between her and the lady who sat by her; in every thing but a value for Edmund, Miss Crawford was very unlike her. She had none of Fanny's delicacy of taste, of mind, of feeling; she saw nature, inanimate nature, with little observation; her attention was all for men and women, her talents for the light and lively. In looking back after Edmund,

line 10: Happy Julia!] **1814** "Happy Julia! // line 11: barouche-box] **1814** barouche box // line 30: men and women,] **1814** man and women,

however, when there was any stretch of road behind them, or when he gained on them in ascending a considerable hill, they were united, and a "there he is" broke at the same moment from them both, more than once.

For the first seven miles Miss Bertram had very little real comfort; her prospect always ended in Mr. Crawford and her sister sitting side by side full of conversation and merriment; and to see only his expressive profile as he turned with a smile to Julia, or to catch the laugh of the other was a perpetual source of irritation, which her own sense of propriety could but just smooth over. When Julia looked back, it was with a countenance of delight, and whenever she spoke to them, it was in the highest spirits; "her view of the country was charming, she wished they could all see it, &c." but her only offer of exchange was addressed to Miss Crawford, as they gained the summit of a long hill, and was not more inviting than this, "Here is a fine burst of country. I wish you had my seat, but I dare say you will not take it, let me press you ever so much," and Miss Crawford could hardly answer, before they were moving again at a good pace.

When they came within the influence of Sotherton associations, it was better for Miss Bertram, who might be said to have two strings to her bow. She had Rushworth-feelings, and Crawford-feelings, and in the vicinity of Sotherton, the former had considerable effect. Mr. Rushworth's consequence was hers. She could not tell Miss Crawford that "those woods belonged to Sotherton," she could not carelessly observe that "she believed it was now all Mr. Rushworth's property on each side of the road," without elation of heart; and it was a pleasure to increase with their approach to

line 19: answer, before] **1814** answer before   //   line 23: Rushworth-feelings, and] **1814** Rushworth-feelings and

the capital freehold mansion, and ancient manorial residence of the family,[4] with all its rights of Court-Leet and Court-Baron.[5]

"Now we shall have no more rough road, Miss Crawford, our difficulties are over. The rest of the way is such as it ought to be. Mr. Rushworth has made it[6] since he succeeded to the estate. Here begins the village. Those cottages are really a disgrace. The church spire is reckoned remarkably handsome. I am glad the church is not so close to the Great House as often happens in old places. The annoyance of the bells must be terrible. There is the parsonage; a tidy looking house, and I understand the clergyman and his wife are very decent people. Those are alms-houses,[7] built by some of the family. To the right is the steward's house; he is a very respectable man. Now we are coming to the lodge gates;[8] but we have nearly a mile through the park still. It is not ugly, you see, at this end; there is some fine timber, but the situation of the house is dreadful. We go down hill to it for half-a-mile, and it is a pity, for it would not be an ill-looking place if it had a better approach."

Miss Crawford was not slow to admire; she pretty well guessed Miss Bertram's feelings, and made it a point of honour to promote her enjoyment to the utmost. Mrs. Norris was all delight and volubility; and even Fanny had something to say in admiration, and might be heard with complacency. Her eye was eagerly taking in every thing within her reach; and after being at some pains to get a view of the house, and observing that "it was a sort of building which she could not look at but with respect," she added, "Now, where is the avenue? The house fronts the east, I perceive. The avenue,

line 26: reach; and] **1814** reach, and

therefore, must be at the back of it. Mr. Rushworth talked of the west front."

"Yes, it is exactly behind the house; begins at a little distance, and ascends for half-a-mile to the extremity of the grounds. You may see something of it here—something of the more distant trees. It is oak entirely."

Miss Bertram could now speak with decided information of what she had known nothing about, when Mr. Rushworth had asked her opinion, and her spirits were in as happy a flutter as vanity and pride could furnish, when they drove up to the spacious stone steps before the principal entrance.

Chapter 9

MR. RUSHWORTH was at the door to receive his fair lady, and the whole party were welcomed by him with due attention. In the drawing-room they were met with equal cordiality by the mother, and Miss Bertram had all the distinction with each that she could wish. After the business of arriving was over, it was first necessary to eat, and the doors were thrown open to admit them through one or two intermediate rooms into the appointed dining-parlour, where a collation[1] was prepared with abundance and elegance. Much was said, and much was ate, and all went well. The particular object of the day was then considered. How would Mr. Crawford like, in what manner would he choose, to take a survey of the grounds?—Mr. Rushworth mentioned his curricle.[2] Mr. Crawford suggested the greater desirableness of some carriage which might convey more than two. "To be depriving themselves of the advantage of other eyes and other judgments, might be an evil even beyond the loss of present pleasure."

Mrs. Rushworth proposed that the chaise[3] should be taken also; but this was scarcely received as an amendment; the young ladies neither smiled nor spoke. Her next proposition, of shewing the house[4] to such of them as had not been there before, was more acceptable, for Miss Bertram was pleased

line 12: choose,] **1814** chuse,

to have its size displayed, and all were glad to be doing something.

The whole party rose accordingly, and under Mrs. Rushworth's guidance were shewn through a number of rooms, all lofty, and many large, and amply furnished in the taste of fifty years back, with shining floors, solid mahogany, rich damask, marble, gilding and carving,[5] each handsome in its way. Of pictures there were abundance, and some few good, but the larger part were family portraits, no longer any thing to any body but Mrs. Rushworth, who had been at great pains to learn all that the housekeeper could teach, and was now almost equally well qualified to shew the house. On the present occasion, she addressed herself chiefly to Miss Crawford and Fanny, but there was no comparison in the willingness of their attention, for Miss Crawford, who had seen scores of great houses, and cared for none of them, had only the appearance of civilly listening, while Fanny, to whom every thing was almost as interesting as it was new, attended with unaffected earnestness to all that Mrs. Rushworth could relate of the family in former times, its rise and grandeur, regal visits and loyal efforts,[6] delighted to connect any thing with history already known, or warm her imagination with scenes of the past.

The situation of the house excluded the possibility of much prospect from any of the rooms, and while Fanny and some of the others were attending Mrs. Rushworth, Henry Crawford was looking grave and shaking his head at the windows. Every room on the west front looked across a lawn to the beginning of the avenue immediately beyond tall iron palisades[7] and gates.

line 28: west front] **1814** West front

Having visited many more rooms than could be supposed to be of any other use than to contribute to the window tax,[8] and find employment for housemaids, "Now," said Mrs. Rushworth, "we are coming to the chapel, which properly we ought to enter from above, and look down upon; but as we are quite among friends, I will take you in this way, if you will excuse me."

They entered. Fanny's imagination had prepared her for something grander than a mere, spacious, oblong room,[9] fitted up for the purpose of devotion—with nothing more striking or more solemn than the profusion of mahogany, and the crimson velvet cushions appearing over the ledge of the family gallery above. "I am disappointed," said she, in a low voice, to Edmund. "This is not my idea of a chapel. There is nothing awful here, nothing melancholy, nothing grand. Here are no aisles, no arches, no inscriptions, no banners. No banners, cousin, to be 'blown by the night wind of Heaven.' No signs that a 'Scottish monarch sleeps below.'"[10]

"You forget, Fanny, how lately all this has been built, and for how confined a purpose, compared with the old chapels of castles and monasteries. It was only for the private use of the family. They have been buried, I suppose, in the parish church. *There* you must look for the banners and the atchievements."

"It was foolish of me not to think of all that, but I am disappointed."

Mrs. Rushworth began her relation. "This chapel was fitted up as you see it, in James the Second's time.[11] Before that period, as I understand, the pews were only wainscot;[12] and there is some reason to think that the linings and cushions

---

line 13: disappointed," said] **1814** disappointed, cousin," said // line 14: voice, to] **1814** voice to // line 29: wainscot;] **1814** wainscoat;

of the pulpit and family-seat were only purple cloth;[13] but this is not quite certain. It is a handsome chapel, and was formerly in constant use both morning and evening. Prayers were always read in it by the domestic chaplain,[14] within the memory of many. But the late Mr. Rushworth left it off."

"Every generation has its improvements," said Miss Crawford, with a smile, to Edmund.

Mrs. Rushworth was gone to repeat her lesson to Mr. Crawford; and Edmund, Fanny, and Miss Crawford, remained in a cluster together.

"It is a pity," cried Fanny, "that the custom should have been discontinued. It was a valuable part of former times. There is something in a chapel and chaplain so much in character with a great house, with one's ideas of what such a household should be![15] A whole family assembling regularly for the purpose of prayer, is fine!"

"Very fine indeed!" said Miss Crawford, laughing. "It must do the heads of the family a great deal of good to force all the poor housemaids and footmen to leave business and pleasure, and say their prayers here twice a day, while they are inventing excuses themselves for staying away."

"*That* is hardly Fanny's idea of a family assembling," said Edmund. "If the master and mistress do *not* attend themselves, there must be more harm than good in the custom."

"At any rate, it is safer to leave people to their own devices on such subjects. Every body likes to go their own way—to choose their own time and manner of devotion. The obligation of attendance, the formality, the restraint, the length of time—altogether it is a formidable thing, and what nobody

line 1: family-seat] **1814** family seat // line 10: Miss Crawford, remained] **1814** Miss Crawford remained // line 28: choose] **1814** chuse // line 30: thing, and] **1814** thing and

likes: and if the good people who used to kneel and gape in that gallery could have foreseen that the time would ever come when men and women might lie another ten minutes in bed, when they woke with a headach, without danger of reprobation, because chapel was missed, they would have jumped with joy and envy. Cannot you imagine with what unwilling feelings the former belles of the house of Rushworth did many a time repair to this chapel? The young Mrs. Eleanors and Mrs. Bridgets[16]—starched up into seeming piety, but with heads full of something very different—especially if the poor chaplain were not worth looking at—and, in those days, I fancy parsons[17] were very inferior even to what they are now."

For a few moments she was unanswered. Fanny coloured and looked at Edmund, but felt too angry for speech; and *he* needed a little recollection before he could say, "Your lively mind can hardly be serious even on serious subjects.[18] You have given us an amusing sketch, and human nature cannot say it was not so. We must all feel *at times* the difficulty of fixing our thoughts as we could wish; but if you are supposing it a frequent thing, that is to say, a weakness grown into a habit from neglect, what could be expected from the *private* devotions of such persons? Do you think the minds which are suffered, which are indulged in wanderings in a chapel, would be more collected in a closet?"[19]

"Yes, very likely. They would have two chances at least in their favour. There would be less to distract the attention from without, and it would not be tried so long."

"The mind which does not struggle against itself under *one* circumstance, would find objects to distract it in the *other*, I believe; and the influence of the place and of example may

line 1: likes: and] **1814** likes; and   //   line 4: headach,] **1814** head-ache,

often rouse better feelings than are begun with. The greater length of the service, however, I admit to be sometimes too hard a stretch upon the mind. One wishes it were not so—but I have not yet left Oxford long enough to forget what chapel prayers are."[20]

While this was passing, the rest of the party being scattered about the chapel, Julia called Mr. Crawford's attention to her sister, by saying, "Do look at Mr. Rushworth and Maria, standing side by side, exactly as if the ceremony were going to be performed. Have not they completely the air of it?"

Mr. Crawford smiled his acquiescence, and stepping forward to Maria, said, in a voice which she only could hear, "I do not like to see Miss Bertram so near the altar."

Starting, the lady instinctively moved a step or two, but recovering herself in a moment, affected to laugh, and asked him, in a tone not much louder, "if he would give her away?"

"I am afraid I should do it very awkwardly," was his reply, with a look of meaning.

Julia joining them at the moment, carried on the joke.

"Upon my word, it is really a pity that it should not take place directly, if we had but a proper license,[21] for here we are altogether, and nothing in the world could be more snug and pleasant." And she talked and laughed about it with so little caution, as to catch the comprehension of Mr. Rushworth and his mother, and expose her sister to the whispered gallantries of her lover, while Mrs. Rushworth spoke with proper smiles and dignity of its being a most happy event to her whenever it took place.

"If Edmund were but in orders!" cried Julia, and running to where he stood with Miss Crawford and Fanny; "My dear Edmund, if you were but in orders now, you might perform the ceremony directly. How unlucky that you are not ordained,[22] Mr. Rushworth and Maria are quite ready."

Miss Crawford's countenance, as Julia spoke, might have amused a disinterested observer. She looked almost aghast under the new idea she was receiving. Fanny pitied her. "How distressed she will be at what she said just now," passed across her mind.

"Ordained!" said Miss Crawford; "what, are you to be a clergyman?"

"Yes, I shall take orders soon after my father's return—probably at Christmas."[23]

Miss Crawford rallying her spirits, and recovering her complexion, replied only, "If I had known this before, I would have spoken of the cloth[24] with more respect," and turned the subject.

The chapel was soon afterwards left to the silence and stillness which reigned in it with few interruptions throughout the year. Miss Bertram, displeased with her sister, led the way, and all seemed to feel that they had been there long enough.

The lower part of the house had been now entirely shown, and Mrs. Rushworth, never weary in the cause, would have proceeded towards the principal stair-case, and taken them through all the rooms above, if her son had not interposed with a doubt of there being time enough. "For if," said he, with the sort of self-evident proposition which many a clearer head does not always avoid—"we are *too* long going over the house, we shall not have time for what is to be done out of doors. It is past two, and we are to dine at five."[25]

Mrs. Rushworth submitted, and the question of surveying the grounds, with the who and the how, was likely to be more fully agitated, and Mrs. Norris was beginning to arrange by what junction of carriages and horses most could be done, when the young people, meeting with an outward

line 1: countenance, as] **1814** countenance as   //   line 18: shown,] **1814** shewn,

door, temptingly open on a flight of steps which led immediately to turf and shrubs, and all the sweets of pleasure-grounds,[26] as by one impulse, one wish for air and liberty, all walked out.

"Suppose we turn down here for the present," said Mrs. Rushworth, civilly taking the hint and following them. "Here are the greatest number of our plants, and here are the curious pheasants."

"Query," said Mr. Crawford, looking round him, "whether we may not find something to employ us here, before we go farther? I see walls of great promise.[27] Mr. Rushworth, shall we summon a council on this lawn?"

"James," said Mrs. Rushworth to her son, "I believe the wilderness[28] will be new to all the party. The Miss Bertrams have never seen the wilderness yet."

No objection was made, but for some time there seemed no inclination to move in any plan, or to any distance. All were attracted at first by the plants or the pheasants, and all dispersed about in happy independence. Mr. Crawford was the first to move forward, to examine the capabilities of that end of the house. The lawn, bounded on each side by a high wall, contained beyond the first planted ærea, a bowling-green, and beyond the bowling-green a long terrace walk, backed by iron palissades, and commanding a view over them into the tops of the trees of the wilderness immediately adjoining. It was a good spot for fault-finding. Mr. Crawford was soon followed by Miss Bertram and Mr. Rushworth, and when after a little time the others began to form into parties, these three were found in busy consultation on the terrace by Edmund, Miss Crawford and Fanny, who seemed as naturally to unite, and who after a short participation of their regrets

line 9: Crawford, looking] **1814** Crawford looking // line 11: Rushworth, shall] **1814** Rushworth shall // line 13: Rushworth to] **1814** Rushworth, to

and difficulties, left them and walked on. The remaining three, Mrs. Rushworth, Mrs. Norris, and Julia, were still far behind; for Julia, whose happy star no longer prevailed, was obliged to keep by the side of Mrs. Rushworth, and restrain her impatient feet to that lady's slow pace, while her aunt, having fallen in with the housekeeper, who was come out to feed the pheasants, was lingering behind in gossip with her. Poor Julia, the only one out of the nine not tolerably satisfied with their lot, was now in a state of complete penance, and as different from the Julia of the barouche-box as could well be imagined. The politeness which she had been brought up to practise as a duty, made it impossible for her to escape; while the want of that higher species of self-command, that just consideration of others, that knowledge of her own heart, that principle of right[29] which had not formed any essential part of her education, made her miserable under it.

"This is insufferably hot," said Miss Crawford when they had taken one turn on the terrace, and were drawing a second time to the door in the middle which opened to the wilderness. "Shall any of us object to being comfortable? Here is a nice little wood, if one can but get into it. What happiness if the door should not be locked—but of course it is, for in these great places, the gardeners are the only people who can go where they like."

The door, however, proved not to be locked, and they were all agreed in turning joyfully through it, and leaving the unmitigated glare of day behind. A considerable flight of steps landed them in the wilderness, which was a planted wood of about two acres, and though chiefly of larch and laurel, and beech cut down,[30] and though laid out with too

line 10: barouche-box] **1814** barouche box   //   line 12: duty, made] **1814** duty made   //   line 12: escape; while] **1814** escape, while   //   line 25: locked,] **1814** lock'd,

much regularity, was darkness and shade, and natural beauty, compared with the bowling-green and the terrace. They all felt the refreshment of it, and for some time could only walk and admire. At length, after a short pause, Miss Crawford began with, "So you are to be a clergyman, Mr. Bertram. This is rather a surprise to me."

"Why should it surprise you? You must suppose me designed for some profession, and might perceive that I am neither a lawyer, nor a soldier, nor a sailor."

"Very true; but, in short, it had not occurred to me. And you know there is generally an uncle or a grandfather to leave a fortune to the second son."

"A very praiseworthy practice," said Edmund, "but not quite universal. I am one of the exceptions, and *being* one, must do something for myself."

"But why are you to be a clergyman? I thought *that* was always the lot of the youngest, where there were many to choose before him."

"Do you think the church itself never chosen then?"

"*Never* is a black word. But yes, in the *never* of conversation which means *not very often*, I do think it. For what is to be done in the church? Men love to distinguish themselves, and in either of the other lines, distinction may be gained, but not in the church. A clergyman is nothing."

"The *nothing* of conversation has its gradations, I hope, as well as the *never*. A clergyman cannot be high in state or fashion. He must not head mobs, or set the ton[31] in dress. But I cannot call that situation nothing, which has the charge of all that is of the first importance to mankind, individually or collectively considered, temporally and eternally—which has the guardianship of religion and morals, and consequently of

line 13: praiseworthy] **1814** praise-worthy   //   line 18: choose] **1814** chuse   //   line 30: eternally—which] **1814** eternally,—which

the manners which result from their influence. No one here can call the *office*[32] nothing. If the man who holds it is so, it is by the neglect of his duty, by foregoing its just importance, and stepping out of his place to appear what he ought not to appear."

"*You* assign greater consequence to the clergyman than one has been used to hear given, or than I can quite comprehend. One does not see much of this influence and importance in society, and how can it be acquired where they are so seldom seen themselves? How can two sermons a week, even supposing them worth hearing, supposing the preacher to have the sense to prefer Blair's to his own,[33] do all that you speak of? govern the conduct and fashion the manners of a large congregation for the rest of the week? One scarcely sees a clergyman out of his pulpit."

"*You* are speaking of London, *I* am speaking of the nation at large."

"The metropolis, I imagine, is a pretty fair sample of the rest."

"Not, I should hope, of the proportion of virtue to vice throughout the kingdom. We do not look in great cities for our best morality. It is not there, that respectable people of any denomination can do most good; and it certainly is not there, that the influence of the clergy can be most felt. A fine preacher is followed and admired; but it is not in fine preaching only that a good clergyman will be useful in his parish and his neighbourhood, where the parish and neighbourhood are of a size capable of knowing his private character, and observing his general conduct, which in London can rarely be the case. The clergy are lost there in the crowds of their parishioners. They are known to the largest part only as preachers.

line 16: London, *I*] **1814** London. *I*

And with regard to their influencing public manners, Miss Crawford must not misunderstand me, or suppose I mean to call them the arbiters of good breeding, the regulators of refinement and courtesy, the masters of the ceremonies of life. The *manners* I speak of, might rather be called *conduct*, perhaps, the result of good principles; the effect, in short, of those doctrines which it is their duty to teach and recommend; and it will, I believe, be every where found, that as the clergy are, or are not what they ought to be, so are the rest of the nation."

"Certainly," said Fanny with gentle earnestness.

"There," cried Miss Crawford, "you have quite convinced Miss Price already."

"I wish I could convince Miss Crawford too."

"I do not think you ever will," said she with an arch smile; "I am just as much surprised now as I was at first that you should intend to take orders. You really are fit for something better. Come, do change your mind. It is not too late. Go into the law."

"Go into the law! with as much ease as I was told to go into this wilderness."

"Now you are going to say something about law being the worst wilderness of the two, but I forestall you; remember I have forestalled you."

"You need not hurry when the object is only to prevent my saying a bon-mot, for there is not the least wit in my nature. I am a very matter of fact, plain spoken being, and may blunder on the borders of a repartee for half an hour together without striking it out."

A general silence succeeded. Each was thoughtful. Fanny made the first interruption by saying, "I wonder that I should be tired with only walking in this sweet wood; but the next

line 8: found, that] **1814** found that   //   line 25: bon-mot,] **1814** bon mot,   //   line 31: wood; but] **1814** wood, but

time we come to a seat, if it is not disagreeable to you, I should be glad to sit down for a little while."

"My dear Fanny," cried Edmund, immediately drawing her arm within his, "how thoughtless I have been! I hope you are not very tired. Perhaps," turning to Miss Crawford, "my other companion may do me the honour of taking an arm."

"Thank you, but I am not at all tired." She took it, however, as she spoke, and the gratification of having her do so, of feeling such a connection for the first time, made him a little forgetful of Fanny. "You scarcely touch me," said he. "You do not make me of any use. What a difference in the weight of a woman's arm from that of a man! At Oxford I have been a good deal used to have a man lean on me for the length of a street,[34] and you are only a fly in the comparison."

"I am really not tired, which I almost wonder at; for we must have walked at least a mile in this wood. Do not you think we have?"

"Not half a mile," was his sturdy answer; for he was not yet so much in love as to measure distance, or reckon time, with feminine lawlessness.

"Oh! you do not consider how much we have wound about. We have taken such a very serpentine course; and the wood itself must be half a mile long in a straight line, for we have never seen the end of it yet, since we left the first great path."

"But if you remember, before we left that first great path, we saw directly to the end of it. We looked down the whole vista, and saw it closed by iron gates, and it could not have been more than a furlong in length."[35]

"Oh! I know nothing of your furlongs, but I am sure it is a very long wood; and that we have been winding in and out ever since we came into it; and therefore when I

line 5: tired. Perhaps,"] **1814** tired." "Perhaps,"

say that we have walked a mile in it, I must speak within compass."[36]

"We have been exactly a quarter of an hour here," said Edmund, taking out his watch. "Do you think we are walking four miles an hour?"

"Oh! do not attack me with your watch. A watch is always too fast or too slow. I cannot be dictated to by a watch."

A few steps farther brought them out at the bottom of the very walk they had been talking of; and standing back, well shaded and sheltered, and looking over a ha-ha into the park,[37] was a comfortable-sized bench, on which they all sat down.

"I am afraid you are very tired, Fanny," said Edmund, observing her; "why would not you speak sooner? This will be a bad day's amusement for you, if you are to be knocked up. Every sort of exercise fatigues her so soon, Miss Crawford, except riding."

"How abominable in you, then, to let me engross her horse as I did all last week! I am ashamed of you and of myself, but it shall never happen again."

"*Your* attentiveness and consideration make me more sensible of my own neglect. Fanny's interest seems in safer hands with you than with me."

"That she should be tired now, however, gives me no surprise; for there is nothing in the course of one's duties so fatiguing as what we have been doing this morning[38]— seeing a great house, dawdling from one room to another— straining one's eyes and one's attention—hearing what one does not understand—admiring what one does not care for.— It is generally allowed to be the greatest bore in the world,

line 4: watch. "Do] **1814** watch. Do // line 14: her; "why] **1814** her. "why // line 20: again."] **1814** again"

and Miss Price has found it so, though she did not know it."

"I shall soon be rested," said Fanny; "to sit in the shade on a fine day, and look upon verdure, is the most perfect refreshment."

After sitting a little while, Miss Crawford was up again. "I must move," said she, "resting fatigues me.—I have looked across the ha-ha till I am weary. I must go and look through that iron gate at the same view, without being able to see it so well."

Edmund left the seat likewise. "Now, Miss Crawford, if you will look up the walk, you will convince yourself that it cannot be half a mile long, or half half a mile."

"It is an immense distance," said she; "I see *that* with a glance."

He still reasoned with her, but in vain. She would not calculate, she would not compare. She would only smile and assert. The greatest degree of rational consistency could not have been more engaging, and they talked with mutual satisfaction. At last it was agreed, that they should endeavour to determine the dimensions of the wood by walking a little more about it. They would go to one end of it, in the line they were then in (for there was a straight green walk along the bottom by the side of the ha-ha,) and perhaps turn a little way in some other direction, if it seemed likely to assist them, and be back in a few minutes. Fanny said she was rested, and would have moved too, but this was not suffered. Edmund urged her remaining where she was with an earnestness which she could not resist, and she was left on the bench to think with pleasure of her cousin's care, but with great regret that she was not stronger. She watched them till they had turned the corner, and listened till all sound of them had ceased.

Chapter 10

A QUARTER of an hour, twenty minutes, passed away, and Fanny was still thinking of Edmund, Miss Crawford, and herself, without interruption from any one. She began to be surprised at being left so long, and to listen with an anxious desire of hearing their steps and their voices again. She listened, and at length she heard; she heard voices and feet approaching; but she had just satisfied herself that it was not those she wanted, when Miss Bertram, Mr. Rushworth, and Mr. Crawford, issued from the same path which she had trod herself, and were before her.

"Miss Price all alone!" and "My dear Fanny, how comes this?" were the first salutations. She told her story. "Poor dear Fanny," cried her cousin, "how ill you have been used by them! You had better have staid with us."

Then seating herself with a gentleman on each side, she resumed the conversation which had engaged them before, and discussed the possibility of improvements with much animation. Nothing was fixed on—but Henry Crawford was full of ideas and projects, and, generally speaking, whatever he proposed was immediately approved, first by her, and then by Mr. Rushworth, whose principal business seemed to be to hear the others, and who scarcely risked an original thought

line 3: herself, without] **1814** herself without   //   line 13: them! You] **1814** them. You

of his own beyond a wish that they had seen his friend Smith's place.

After some minutes spent in this way, Miss Bertram observing the iron gate, expressed a wish of passing through it into the park, that their views and their plans might be more comprehensive. It was the very thing of all others to be wished, it was the best, it was the only way of proceeding with any advantage, in Henry Crawford's opinion; and he directly saw a knoll[1] not half a mile off, which would give them exactly the requisite command of the house. Go therefore they must to that knoll, and through that gate; but the gate was locked. Mr. Rushworth wished he had brought the key; he had been very near thinking whether he should not bring the key; he was determined he would never come without the key again; but still this did not remove the present evil. They could not get through; and as Miss Bertram's inclination for so doing did by no means lessen, it ended in Mr. Rushworth's declaring outright that he would go and fetch the key. He set off accordingly.

"It is undoubtedly the best thing we can do now, as we are so far from the house already," said Mr. Crawford, when he was gone.

"Yes, there is nothing else to be done. But now, sincerely, do not you find the place altogether worse than you expected?"

"No, indeed, far otherwise. I find it better, grander, more complete in its style, though that style may not be the best. And to tell you the truth," speaking rather lower, "I do not think that *I* shall ever see Sotherton again with so much pleasure as I do now. Another summer will hardly improve it to me."

line 16: through; and] **1814** through, and

After a moment's embarrassment the lady replied, "You are too much a man of the world[2] not to see with the eyes of the world. If other people think Sotherton improved, I have no doubt that you will."

"I am afraid I am not quite so much the man of the world as might be good for me in some points. My feelings are not quite so evanescent, nor my memory of the past under such easy dominion as one finds to be the case with men of the world."

This was followed by a short silence. Miss Bertram began again. "You seemed to enjoy your drive here very much this morning. I was glad to see you so well entertained. You and Julia were laughing the whole way."

"Were we? Yes, I believe we were; but I have not the least recollection at what. Oh! I believe I was relating to her some ridiculous stories of an old Irish groom of my uncle's. Your sister loves to laugh."

"You think her more light-hearted than I am."

"More easily amused," he replied, "consequently you know," smiling, "better company. I could not have hoped to entertain *you* with Irish anecdotes during a ten miles' drive."

"Naturally, I believe, I am as lively as Julia, but I have more to think of now."

"You have undoubtedly—and there are situations in which very high spirits would denote insensibility. Your prospects, however, are too fair to justify want of spirits. You have a very smiling scene before you."

"Do you mean literally or figuratively? Literally, I conclude. Yes, certainly, the sun shines and the park looks very cheerful. But unluckily that iron gate, that ha-ha, give me a feeling of

line 21: miles' drive.] **1814** miles drive.   //   line 28: Literally, I] **1814** Literally I   //   line 30: ha-ha,] **1814** Ha, Ha,

restraint and hardship. I cannot get out, as the starling said."[3]
As she spoke, and it was with expression, she walked to the
gate; he followed her. "Mr. Rushworth is so long fetching
this key!"

"And for the world you would not get out without the key
and without Mr. Rushworth's authority and protection, or I
think you might with little difficulty pass round the edge of
the gate, here, with my assistance;[4] I think it might be done, if
you really wished to be more at large, and could allow yourself
to think it not prohibited."

"Prohibited! nonsense! I certainly can get out that way,
and I will. Mr. Rushworth will be here in a moment you
know—we shall not be out of sight."

"Or if we are, Miss Price will be so good as to tell him, that
he will find us near that knoll, the grove of oak on the knoll."

Fanny, feeling all this to be wrong, could not help
making an effort to prevent it. "You will hurt yourself, Miss
Bertram," she cried, "you will certainly hurt yourself against
those spikes—you will tear your gown—you will be in danger
of slipping into the ha-ha. You had better not go."

Her cousin was safe on the other side, while these words
were spoken, and smiling with all the good-humour of
success, she said, "Thank you, my dear Fanny, but I and
my gown are alive and well, and so good bye."

Fanny was again left to her solitude, and with no increase of
pleasant feelings, for she was sorry for almost all that she had
seen and heard, astonished at Miss Bertram, and angry with
Mr. Crawford. By taking a circuitous, and as it appeared to
her, very unreasonable direction to the knoll, they were soon
beyond her eye; and for some minutes longer she remained

line 11: way, and] **1814** way and   //   line 20: ha-ha.] **1814** Ha-Ha.   //
line 23: success, she] **1814** success she

without sight or sound of any companion. She seemed to have the little wood all to herself. She could almost have thought, that Edmund and Miss Crawford had left it, but that it was impossible for Edmund to forget her so entirely.

She was again roused from disagreeable musings by sudden footsteps, somebody was coming at a quick pace down the principal walk. She expected Mr. Rushworth, but it was Julia, who hot and out of breath, and with a look of disappointment, cried out on seeing her, "Heyday! Where are the others? I thought Maria and Mr. Crawford were with you."

Fanny explained.

"A pretty trick, upon my word! I cannot see them any where," looking eagerly into the park. "But they cannot be very far off, and I think I am equal to as much as Maria, even without help."

"But, Julia, Mr. Rushworth will be here in a moment with the key. Do wait for Mr. Rushworth."

"Not I, indeed. I have had enough of the family for one morning. Why, child, I have but this moment escaped from his horrible mother. Such a penance as I have been enduring, while you were sitting here so composed and so happy! It might have been as well, perhaps, if you had been in my place, but you always contrive to keep out of these scrapes."

This was a most unjust reflection, but Fanny could allow for it, and let it pass; Julia was vexed, and her temper was hasty, but she felt that it would not last, and therefore taking no notice, only asked her if she had not seen Mr. Rushworth.

"Yes, yes, we saw him. He was posting away,[5] as if upon life and death, and could but just spare time to tell us his errand, and where you all were."

line 12: trick, upon] **1814** trick upon   //   line 19: Why, child,] **1814** Why child,   //   line 29: away, as] **1814** away as

"It is a pity that he should have so much trouble for nothing."

"*That* is Miss Maria's concern. I am not obliged to punish myself for *her* sins. The mother I could not avoid, as long as my tiresome aunt was dancing about with the housekeeper, but the son I *can* get away from."

And she immediately scrambled across the fence,[6] and walked away, not attending to Fanny's last question of whether she had seen any thing of Miss Crawford and Edmund. The sort of dread in which Fanny now sat of seeing Mr. Rushworth prevented her thinking so much of their continued absence, however, as she might have done. She felt that he had been very ill-used, and was quite unhappy in having to communicate what had passed. He joined her within five minutes after Julia's exit; and though she made the best of the story, he was evidently mortified and displeased in no common degree. At first he scarcely said any thing; his looks only expressed his extreme surprise and vexation, and he walked to the gate and stood there, without seeming to know what to do.

"They desired me to stay—my cousin Maria charged me to say that you would find them at that knoll, or thereabouts."

"I do not believe I shall go any further," said he sullenly; "I see nothing of them. By the time I get to the knoll, they may be gone some where else. I have had walking enough."

And he sat down with a most gloomy countenance by Fanny.

line 7: fence, and] **1814** fence and   //   line 11: Rushworth prevented] **1814** Rushworth, prevented   //   line 22: knoll, or] **1814** Knoll or   //   line 23: he sullenly;] **1814** he, sullenly;   //   line 24: knoll,] **1814** Knoll,

"I am very sorry," said she; "it is very unlucky." And she longed to be able to say something more to the purpose.

After an interval of silence, "I think they might as well have staid for me," said he.

"Miss Bertram thought you would follow her."

"I should not have had to follow her if she had staid."

This could not be denied, and Fanny was silenced. After another pause, he went on: "Pray, Miss Price, are you such a great admirer of this Mr. Crawford as some people are? For my part, I can see nothing in him."

"I do not think him at all handsome."

"Handsome! Nobody can call such an under-sized man handsome. He is not five foot nine.[7] I should not wonder if he was not more than five foot eight. I think he is an ill-looking fellow. In my opinion, these Crawfords are no addition at all. We did very well without them."

A small sigh escaped Fanny here, and she did not know how to contradict him.

"If I had made any difficulty about fetching the key, there might have been some excuse, but I went the very moment she said she wanted it."

"Nothing could be more obliging than your manner, I am sure, and I dare say you walked as fast as you could; but still it is some distance, you know, from this spot to the house, quite into the house; and when people are waiting, they are bad judges of time, and every half minute seems like five."

He got up and walked to the gate again, and "wished he had had the key about him at the time." Fanny thought she discerned in his standing there, an indication of relenting, which

line 8: pause, he] **1814** pause he   //   line 8: on: "Pray,] **1814** on. "Pray   //
line 23: could; but] **1814** could, but

encouraged her to another attempt, and she said, therefore, "It is a pity you should not join them. They expected to have a better view of the house from that part of the park, and will be thinking how it may be improved; and nothing of that sort, you know, can be settled without you."

She found herself more successful in sending away, than in retaining a companion. Mr. Rushworth was worked on. "Well," said he, "if you really think I had better go; it would be foolish to bring the key for nothing." And letting himself out, he walked off without further ceremony.

Fanny's thoughts were now all engrossed by the two who had left her so long ago, and getting quite impatient, she resolved to go in search of them. She followed their steps along the bottom walk, and had just turned up into another, when the voice and the laugh of Miss Crawford once more caught her ear; the sound approached, and a few more windings brought them before her. They were just returned into the wilderness from the park, to which a side gate, not fastened, had tempted them very soon after their leaving her, and they had been across a portion of the park into the very avenue which Fanny had been hoping the whole morning to reach at last; and had been sitting down under one of the trees. This was their history. It was evident that they had been spending their time pleasantly, and were not aware of the length of their absence. Fanny's best consolation was in being assured that Edmund had wished for her very much, and that he should certainly have come back for her, had she not been tired already; but this was not quite sufficient to do away the pain of having been left a whole hour, when he had talked of only a few minutes, nor to banish the sort of curiosity she felt, to know what they had been conversing about all that time; and the result of the whole was to her disappointment and depression, as they prepared, by general agreement, to return to the house.

On reaching the bottom of the steps to the terrace, Mrs. Rushworth and Mrs. Norris presented themselves at the top, just ready for the wilderness, at the end of an hour and half from their leaving the house. Mrs. Norris had been too well employed to move faster. Whatever cross accidents had occurred to intercept the pleasures of her nieces, she had found a morning of complete enjoyment—for the house-keeper, after a great many courtesies on the subject of pheas-ants, had taken her to the dairy, told her all about their cows, and given her the receipt for a famous cream cheese; and since Julia's leaving them, they had been met by the gardener, with whom she had made a most satisfactory acquaintance, for she had set him right as to his grandson's illness, convinced him it was an ague, and promised him a charm[8] for it; and he, in return, had shewn her all his choicest nursery of plants, and actually presented her with a very curious specimen of heath.[9]

On this rencontre they all returned to the house together, there to lounge away the time as they could with sofas, and chit-chat, and Quarterly Reviews,[10] till the return of the others, and the arrival of dinner. It was late before the Miss Bertrams and the two gentlemen came in, and their ramble did not appear to have been more than partially agreeable, or at all productive of any thing useful with regard to the object of the day. By their own accounts they had been all walking after each other, and the junction which had taken place at last seemed, to Fanny's observation, to have been as much too late for re-establishing harmony, as it confessedly had been

line 2: to return to] **1814** to re-return to // line 4: themselves at] **1814** themselvess at // line 16: it; and] **1814** it, and

for determining on any alteration. She felt, as she looked at Julia and Mr. Rushworth, that her's was not the only dissatisfied bosom amongst them; there was gloom on the face of each. Mr. Crawford and Miss Bertram were much more gay, and she thought that he was taking particular pains, during dinner, to do away any little resentment of the other two, and restore general good humour.

Dinner was soon followed by tea and coffee, a ten miles' drive home allowed no waste of hours, and from the time of their sitting down to table, it was a quick succession of busy nothings till the carriage came to the door, and Mrs. Norris, having fidgetted about, and obtained a few pheasant's eggs and a cream cheese from the housekeeper, and made abundance of civil speeches to Mrs. Rushworth, was ready to lead the way. At the same moment Mr. Crawford approaching Julia, said, "I hope I am not to lose my companion, unless she is afraid of the evening air in so exposed a seat." The request had not been foreseen, but was very graciously received, and Julia's day was likely to end almost as well as it began. Miss Bertram had made up her mind to something different, and was a little disappointed—but her conviction of being really the one preferred, comforted her under it, and enabled her to receive Mr. Rushworth's parting attentions as she ought. He was certainly better pleased to hand her into the barouche than to assist her in ascending the box—and his complacency seemed confirmed by the arrangement.

"Well, Fanny, this has been a fine day for you, upon my word!" said Mrs. Norris, as they drove through the park. "Nothing but pleasure from beginning to end! I am sure you ought to be very much obliged to your aunt Bertram and me,

line 31: aunt Bertram] **1814** Aunt Bertram

for contriving to let you go. A pretty good day's amusement you have had!"

Maria was just discontented enough to say directly, "I think *you* have done pretty well yourself, ma'am. Your lap seems full of good things, and here is a basket of something between us, which has been knocking my elbow unmercifully."

"My dear, it is only a beautiful little heath, which that nice old gardener would make me take; but if it is in your way, I will have it in my lap directly. There Fanny, you shall carry that parcel for me—take great care of it—do not let it fall; it is a cream cheese, just like the excellent one we had at dinner. Nothing would satisfy that good old Mrs. Whitaker, but my taking one of the cheeses. I stood out as long as I could, till the tears almost came into her eyes, and I knew it was just the sort that my sister would be delighted with. That Mrs. Whitaker is a treasure! She was quite shocked when I asked her whether wine was allowed at the second table,[11] and she has turned away two housemaids for wearing white gowns.[12] Take care of the cheese, Fanny. Now I can manage the other parcel and the basket very well."

"What else have you been spunging?"[13] said Maria, half pleased that Sotherton should be so complimented.

"Spunging, my dear! It is nothing but four of those beautiful pheasant's eggs, which Mrs. Whitaker would quite force upon me; she would not take a denial. She said it must be such an amusement to me, as she understood I lived quite alone, to have a few living creatures of that sort; and so to be sure it will. I shall get the dairy maid to set them under the first spare hen, and if they come to good I can have them moved to my own house and borrow a coop; and it will be a great delight to me in my lonely hours to attend

line 4: ma'am.] **1814** Ma'am.

to them. And if I have good luck, your mother shall have some."

It was a beautiful evening, mild and still, and the drive was as pleasant as the serenity of nature could make it; but when Mrs. Norris ceased speaking it was altogether a silent drive to those within. Their spirits were in general exhausted—and to determine whether the day had afforded most pleasure or pain, might occupy the meditations of almost all.

Chapter 11

THE day at Sotherton, with all its imperfections, afforded the Miss Bertrams much more agreeable feelings than were derived from the letters from Antigua, which soon afterwards reached Mansfield. It was much pleasanter to think of Henry Crawford than of their father; and to think of their father in England again within a certain period, which these letters obliged them to do, was a most unwelcome exercise.

November was the black month fixed for his return. Sir Thomas wrote of it with as much decision as experience and anxiety could authorize. His business was so nearly concluded as to justify him in proposing to take his passage in the September packet,[1] and he consequently looked forward with the hope of being with his beloved family again early in November.

Maria was more to be pitied than Julia, for to her the father brought a husband, and the return of the friend[2] most solicitous for her happiness, would unite her to the lover, on whom she had chosen that happiness should depend. It was a gloomy prospect, and all that she could do was to throw a mist over it, and hope when the mist cleared away, she should see something else. It would hardly be *early* in November, there were generally delays, a bad passage or *something*; that favouring *something* which every body who shuts their eyes while they look, or their understandings while they reason, feels the

line 10: authorize.] **1814** authorise.

comfort of. It would probably be the middle of November at least; the middle of November was three months off. Three months comprised thirteen weeks. Much might happen in thirteen weeks.

Sir Thomas would have been deeply mortified by a suspicion of half that his daughters felt on the subject of his return, and would hardly have found consolation in a knowledge of the interest it excited in the breast of another young lady. Miss Crawford, on walking up with her brother to spend the evening at Mansfield Park, heard the good news; and though seeming to have no concern in the affair beyond politeness, and to have vented all her feelings in a quiet congratulation, heard it with an attention not so easily satisfied. Mrs. Norris gave the particulars of the letters, and the subject was dropt; but after tea, as Miss Crawford was standing at an open window with Edmund and Fanny looking out on a twilight scene, while the Miss Bertrams, Mr. Rushworth, and Henry Crawford, were all busy with candles at the piano-forte, she suddenly revived it by turning round towards the group, and saying, "How happy Mr. Rushworth looks! He is thinking of November."

Edmund looked round at Mr. Rushworth too, but had nothing to say. "Your father's return will be a very interesting event."

"It will, indeed, after such an absence; an absence not only long, but including so many dangers."

"It will be the fore-runner also of other interesting events; your sister's marriage, and your taking orders."

"Yes."

"Don't be affronted," said she laughing; "but it does put me in mind of some of the old heathen heroes, who after performing great exploits in a foreign land, offered sacrifices to the gods on their safe return."

"There is no sacrifice in the case," replied Edmund with a serious smile, and glancing at the piano-forte again, "it is entirely her own doing."

"Oh! yes, I know it is. I was merely joking. She has done no more than what every young woman would do; and I have no doubt of her being extremely happy. My other sacrifice of course you do not understand."

"My taking orders I assure you is quite as voluntary as Maria's marrying."

"It is fortunate that your inclination and your father's convenience should accord so well. There is a very good living kept for you, I understand, hereabouts."

"Which you suppose has biassed me."

"But *that* I am sure it has not," cried Fanny.

"Thank you for your good word, Fanny, but it is more than I would affirm myself. On the contrary, the knowing that there was such a provision for me, probably did bias me. Nor can I think it wrong that it should. There was no natural disinclination to be overcome, and I see no reason why a man should make a worse clergyman for knowing that he will have a competence[3] early in life. I was in safe hands. I hope I should not have been influenced myself in a wrong way, and I am sure my father was too conscientious to have allowed it. I have no doubt that I was biassed, but I think it was blamelessly."

"It is the same sort of thing," said Fanny, after a short pause, "as for the son of an admiral to go into the navy, or the son of a general to be in the army, and nobody sees any thing wrong in that. Nobody wonders that they should prefer the line where their friends can serve them best, or suspects them to be less in earnest in it than they appear."

line 2: again, "it] **1814** again, "It

"No, my dear Miss Price, and for reasons good. The profession, either navy or army, is its own justification. It has every thing in its favour; heroism, danger, bustle, fashion. Soldiers and sailors are always acceptable in society. Nobody can wonder that men are soldiers and sailors."

"But the motives of a man who takes orders with the certainty of preferment,[4] may be fairly suspected, you think?" said Edmund. "To be justified in your eyes, he must do it in the most complete uncertainty of any provision."

"What! take orders without a living! No, that is madness indeed, absolute madness!"

"Shall I ask you how the church is to be filled, if a man is neither to take orders with a living, nor without? No, for you certainly would not know what to say. But I must beg some advantage to the clergyman from your own argument. As he cannot be influenced by those feelings which you rank highly as temptation and reward to the soldier and sailor in their choice of a profession, as heroism, and noise, and fashion are all against him, he ought to be less liable to the suspicion of wanting sincerity or good intentions in the choice of his."

"Oh! no doubt he is very sincere in preferring an income ready made, to the trouble of working for one; and has the best intentions of doing nothing all the rest of his days but eat, drink, and grow fat. It is indolence Mr. Bertram, indeed. Indolence and love of ease—a want of all laudable ambition, of taste for good company, or of inclination to take the trouble of being agreeable, which make men clergymen. A clergyman has nothing to do but to be slovenly and selfish—read the newspaper, watch the weather, and quarrel with his wife. His curate[5] does all the work, and the business of his own life is to dine."

line 27: clergymen. A clergyman] **1814** Clergymen. A Clergyman   //
line 30: curate] **1814** Curate

"There are such clergymen, no doubt, but I think they are not so common as to justify Miss Crawford in esteeming it their general character. I suspect that in this comprehensive and (may I say) common-place censure, you are not judging from yourself, but from prejudiced persons, whose opinions you have been in the habit of hearing. It is impossible that your own observation can have given you much knowledge of the clergy. You can have been personally acquainted with very few of a set of men you condemn so conclusively. You are speaking what you have been told at your uncle's table."

"I speak what appears to me the general opinion; and where an opinion is general, it is usually correct. Though *I* have not seen much of the domestic lives of clergymen, it is seen by too many to leave any deficiency of information."

"Where any one body of educated men, of whatever denomination, are condemned indiscriminately, there must be a deficiency of information, or (smiling) of something else. Your uncle, and his brother admirals, perhaps, knew little of clergymen beyond the chaplains whom, good or bad, they were always wishing away."

"Poor William! He has met with great kindness from the chaplain of the Antwerp,"[6] was a tender apostrophe of Fanny's, very much to the purpose of her own feelings, if not of the conversation.

"I have been so little addicted to take my opinions from my uncle," said Miss Crawford, "that I can hardly suppose;— and since you push me so hard, I must observe, that I am not entirely without the means of seeing what clergymen are, being at this present time the guest of my own brother,

line 1: clergymen, no] **1814** Clergymen, no   //   line 8: clergy.] **1814** Clergy. //   line 10: uncle's] **1814** Uncle's   //   line 18: admirals,] **1814** Admirals, //   line 22: chaplain] **1814** Chaplain   //   line 26: suppose;—and] **1814** suppose, and

Dr. Grant. And though Dr. Grant is most kind and obliging to me, and though he is really a gentleman, and I dare say a good scholar and clever, and often preaches good sermons, and is very respectable, *I* see him to be an indolent selfish bon vivant, who must have his palate consulted in every thing, who will not stir a finger for the convenience of any one, and who, moreover, if the cook makes a blunder, is out of humour with his excellent wife. To own the truth, Henry and I were partly driven out this very evening, by a disappointment about a green goose,[7] which he could not get the better of. My poor sister was forced to stay and bear it."

"I do not wonder at your disapprobation, upon my word. It is a great defect of temper, made worse by a very faulty habit of self-indulgence; and to see your sister suffering from it, must be exceedingly painful to such feelings as your's. Fanny, it goes against us. We cannot attempt to defend Dr. Grant."

"No," replied Fanny, "but we need not give up his profession for all that; because, whatever profession Dr. Grant had chosen, he would have taken a—not a good temper into it; and as he must either in the navy or army have had a great many more people under his command than he has now, I think more would have been made unhappy by him as a sailor or soldier than as a clergyman. Besides, I cannot but suppose that whatever there may be to wish otherwise in Dr. Grant, would have been in a greater danger of becoming worse in a more active and worldly profession, where he would have had less time and obligation—where he might have escaped that knowledge of himself, the *frequency*, at least, of that knowledge which it is impossible he should escape as he is now. A

line 4: bon vivant,] **1814** Bon vivant, // line 20: the navy or army] **1814** the Navy or Army // line 22: sailor or soldier] **1814** Sailor or Soldier // line 23: clergyman] **1814** Clergyman

man—a sensible man like Dr. Grant, cannot be in the habit of teaching others their duty every week, cannot go to church twice every Sunday and preach such very good sermons in so good a manner as he does, without being the better for it himself. It must make him think, and I have no doubt that he oftener endeavours to restrain himself than he would if he had been any thing but a clergyman."

"We cannot prove the contrary, to be sure—but I wish you a better fate Miss Price, than to be the wife of a man whose amiableness depends upon his own sermons;[8] for though he may preach himself into a good humour every Sunday, it will be bad enough to have him quarrelling about green geese from Monday morning till Saturday night."

"I think the man who could often quarrel with Fanny," said Edmund, affectionately, "must be beyond the reach of any sermons."

Fanny turned farther into the window; and Miss Crawford had only time to say in a pleasant manner, "I fancy Miss Price has been more used to deserve praise than to hear it;" when being earnestly invited by the Miss Bertrams to join in a glee,[9] she tripped off to the instrument, leaving Edmund looking after her in an ecstasy of admiration of all her many virtues, from her obliging manners down to her light and graceful tread.[10]

"There goes good humour I am sure," said he presently. "There goes a temper which would never give pain! How well she walks! and how readily she falls in with the inclination of others! joining them the moment she is asked. What a pity," he added, after an instant's reflection, "that she should have been in such hands!"

line 7: clergyman."] **1814** Clergyman." // line 19: hear it;" when] **1814** hear it," when

Fanny agreed to it, and had the pleasure of seeing him continue at the window with her, in spite of the expected glee; and of having his eyes soon turned like her's towards the scene without, where all that was solemn and soothing, and lovely, appeared in the brilliancy of an unclouded night, and the contrast of the deep shade of the woods. Fanny spoke her feelings. "Here's harmony!" said she, "Here's repose! Here's what may leave all painting and all music behind, and what poetry only can attempt to describe. Here's what may tranquillize every care, and lift the heart to rapture! When I look out on such a night as this, I feel as if there could be neither wickedness nor sorrow in the world; and there certainly would be less of both if the sublimity of Nature[11] were more attended to, and people were carried more out of themselves by contemplating such a scene."

"I like to hear your enthusiasm,[12] Fanny. It is a lovely night, and they are much to be pitied who have not been taught to feel in some degree as you do—who have not at least been given a taste for nature in early life. They lose a great deal."

"*You* taught me to think and feel on the subject, cousin."

"I had a very apt scholar. There's Arcturus looking very bright."

"Yes, and the bear. I wish I could see Cassiopeia."[13]

"We must go out on the lawn for that. Should you be afraid?"

"Not in the least. It is a great while since we have had any star-gazing."

"Yes, I do not know how it has happened." The glee began. "We will stay till this is finished, Fanny," said he, turning his back on the window; and as it advanced, she had the

line 8: all painting and all music behind, and what poetry] **1814** all Painting, and all Music behind, and what Poetry mortification of seeing him advance too, moving forward by gentle degrees towards the instrument, and when it ceased, he was close by the singers, among the most urgent in requesting to hear the glee again.

Fanny sighed alone at the window till scolded away by Mrs. Norris's threats of catching cold.

Chapter 12

SIR THOMAS was to return in November, and his eldest son had duties to call him earlier home. The approach of September brought tidings of Mr. Bertram first in a letter to the gamekeeper,[1] and then in a letter to Edmund; and by the end of August, he arrived himself, to be gay, agreeable, and gallant again as occasion served, or Miss Crawford demanded, to tell of races and Weymouth,[2] and parties and friends, to which she might have listened six weeks before with some interest, and altogether to give her the fullest conviction, by the power of actual comparison, of her preferring his younger brother.

It was very vexatious, and she was heartily sorry for it; but so it was; and so far from now meaning to marry the elder, she did not even want to attract him beyond what the simplest claims of conscious beauty required; his lengthened absence from Mansfield, without any thing but pleasure in view, and his own will to consult, made it perfectly clear that he did not care about her; and his indifference was so much more than equalled by her own, that were he now to step forth the owner of Mansfield Park, the Sir Thomas complete, which he was to be in time, she did not believe she could accept him.

The season and duties which brought Mr. Bertram back to Mansfield, took Mr. Crawford into Norfolk. Everingham

line 4: gamekeeper,] **1814** game-keeper, // line 16: any thing] **1814** anything // line 20: Mansfield Park,] **1814** Mansfield park,

134

could not do without him in the beginning of September.[3] He went for a fortnight; a fortnight of such dulness to the Miss Bertrams, as ought to have put them both on their guard, and made even Julia admit in her jealousy of her sister, the absolute necessity of distrusting his attentions, and wishing him not to return; and a fortnight of sufficient leisure in the intervals of shooting and sleeping, to have convinced the gentleman that he ought to keep longer away, had he been more in the habit of examining his own motives, and of reflecting to what the indulgence of his idle vanity was tending; but, thoughtless and selfish from prosperity and bad example, he would not look beyond the present moment. The sisters, handsome, clever, and encouraging, were an amusement to his sated mind; and finding nothing in Norfolk to equal the social pleasures of Mansfield, he gladly returned to it at the time appointed, and was welcomed thither quite as gladly by those whom he came to trifle with farther.

Maria, with only Mr. Rushworth to attend to her, and doomed to the repeated details of his day's sport, good or bad, his boast of his dogs, his jealousy of his neighbours, his doubts of their qualification, and his zeal after poachers,[4]— subjects which will not find their way to female feelings without some talent on one side, or some attachment on the other, had missed Mr. Crawford grievously; and Julia, unengaged and unemployed, felt all the right of missing him much more. Each sister believed herself the favourite. Julia might be justified in so doing by the hints of Mrs. Grant, inclined to credit what she wished, and Maria by the hints of Mr. Crawford himself. Every thing returned into the same channel as before his absence; his manners being to each so animated and agreeable, as to lose no ground with either,

line 2: dulness] **1814** dullness // line 24: grievously; and] **1814** grievously, and // line 26: favourite. Julia] **1814** favourite; Julia

and just stopping short of the consistence, the steadiness, the solicitude, and the warmth which might excite general notice.

Fanny was the only one of the party who found any thing to dislike; but since the day at Sotherton, she could never see Mr. Crawford with either sister without observation, and seldom without wonder or censure; and had her confidence in her own judgment been equal to her exercise of it in every other respect, had she been sure that she was seeing clearly, and judging candidly,⁵ she would probably have made some important communications to her usual confidant. As it was, however, she only hazarded a hint, and the hint was lost. "I am rather surprised," said she, "that Mr. Crawford should come back again so soon, after being here so long before, full seven weeks; for I had understood he was so very fond of change and moving about, that I thought something would certainly occur when he was once gone, to take him elsewhere. He is used to much gayer places than Mansfield."

"It is to his credit," was Edmund's answer, "and I dare say it gives his sister pleasure. She does not like his unsettled habits."

"What a favourite he is with my cousins!"

"Yes, his manners to women are such as must please. Mrs. Grant, I believe, suspects him of a preference for Julia; I have never seen much symptom of it, but I wish it may be so. He has no faults but what a serious attachment would remove."

"If Miss Bertram were not engaged," said Fanny, cautiously, "I could sometimes almost think that he admired her more than Julia."

"Which is, perhaps, more in favour of his liking Julia best, than you, Fanny, may be aware; for I believe it often happens,

line 3: any thing] **1814** anything

136

that a man, before he has quite made up his own mind, will distinguish the sister or intimate friend of the woman he is really thinking of, more than the woman herself. Crawford has too much sense to stay here if he found himself in any danger from Maria; and I am not at all afraid for her, after such a proof as she has given, that her feelings are not strong."

Fanny supposed she must have been mistaken, and meant to think differently in future; but with all that submission to Edmund could do, and all the help of the coinciding looks and hints which she occasionally noticed in some of the others, and which seemed to say that Julia was Mr. Crawford's choice, she knew not always what to think. She was privy, one evening, to the hopes of her aunt Norris on this subject, as well as to her feelings, and the feelings of Mrs. Rushworth, on a point of some similarity, and could not help wondering as she listened; and glad would she have been not to be obliged to listen, for it was while all the other young people were dancing, and she sitting, most unwillingly, among the chaperons at the fire, longing for the re-entrance of her elder cousin, on whom all her own hopes of a partner then depended. It was Fanny's first ball, though without the preparation or splendour of many a young lady's first ball, being the thought only of the afternoon, built on the late acquisition of a violin player in the servants' hall, and the possibility of raising five couple with the help of Mrs. Grant and a new intimate friend of Mr. Bertram's just arrived on a visit. It had, however, been a very happy one to Fanny through four dances, and she was quite grieved to be losing even a quarter of an hour.—While waiting and wishing, looking now at the dancers and now at the door, this dialogue between the two above-mentioned ladies was forced on her.

line 31: ladies] **1814** Ladies

"I think, ma'am," said Mrs. Norris—her eyes directed towards Mr. Rushworth and Maria, who were partners for the second time—"we shall see some happy faces again now."

"Yes, ma'am, indeed"—replied the other, with a stately simper—"there will be some satisfaction in looking on *now*, and I think it was rather a pity they should have been obliged to part. Young folks in their situation should be excused complying with the common forms.[6]—I wonder my son did not propose it."

"I dare say he did, ma'am.—Mr. Rushworth is never remiss. But dear Maria has such a strict sense of propriety, so much of that true delicacy which one seldom meets with now-a-days, Mrs. Rushworth, that wish of avoiding particularity!—Dear ma'am, only look at her face at this moment;—how different from what it was the two last dances!"

Miss Bertram did indeed look happy, her eyes were sparkling with pleasure, and she was speaking with great animation, for Julia and her partner, Mr. Crawford, were close to her; they were all in a cluster together. How she had looked before, Fanny could not recollect, for she had been dancing with Edmund herself, and had not thought about her.

Mrs. Norris continued, "It is quite delightful, ma'am, to see young people so properly happy, so well suited, and so much the thing! I cannot but think of dear Sir Thomas's delight. And what do you say, ma'am, to the chance of another match? Mr. Rushworth has set a good example, and such things are very catching."

line 1: "I think, ma'am,"] **1814** "I think Ma'am," //   line 4: "Yes, ma'am,] **1814** "Yes, Ma'am, //   line 10: did, ma'am.] **1814** did, Ma'am. //   line 14: Dear ma'am,] **1814** dear Ma'am, //   line 24: delightful, ma'am,] **1814** delightful, Ma'am, //   line 27: say, ma'am,] **1814** say, Ma'am,

Mrs. Rushworth, who saw nothing but her son, was quite at a loss. "The couple above,[7] ma'am. Do you see no symptoms there?"

"Oh! dear—Miss Julia and Mr. Crawford. Yes, indeed, a very pretty match. What is his property?"

"Four thousand a year."

"Very well.—Those who have not more, must be satisfied with what they have.—Four thousand a year is a pretty estate, and he seems a very genteel, steady young man, so I hope Miss Julia will be very happy."

"It is not a settled thing, ma'am, yet.—We only speak of it among friends. But I have very little doubt it *will be*.—He is growing extremely particular in his attentions."

Fanny could listen no farther. Listening and wondering were all suspended for a time, for Mr. Bertram was in the room again, and though feeling it would be a great honour to be asked by him, she thought it must happen. He came towards their little circle; but instead of asking her to dance, drew a chair near her, and gave her an account of the present state of a sick horse, and the opinion of the groom, from whom he had just parted. Fanny found that it was not to be, and in the modesty of her nature immediately felt that she had been unreasonable in expecting it. When he had told of his horse, he took a newspaper from the table, and looking over it said in a languid way, "If you want to dance, Fanny, I will stand up with you."—With more than equal civility the offer was declined;—she did not wish to dance.—"I am glad of it," said he in a much brisker tone, and throwing down the newspaper again—"for I am tired to death. I only wonder how the good people can keep it up so long.—They had need be *all* in love, to find any amusement in such folly—and so

line 2: above, ma'am.] **1814** above, Ma'am.   //   line 11: thing, ma'am,] **1814** thing, Ma'am,

they are, I fancy.—If you look at them, you may see they are so many couple of lovers—all but Yates and Mrs. Grant—and, between ourselves, she, poor woman! must want a lover as much as any one of them. A desperate dull life her's must be with the doctor," making a sly face as he spoke towards the chair of the latter, who proving, however, to be close at his elbow, made so instantaneous a change of expression and subject necessary, as Fanny, in spite of every thing, could hardly help laughing at.—"A strange business this in America,[8] Dr. Grant!—What is your opinion?—I always come to you to know what I am to think of public matters."

"My dear Tom," cried his aunt soon afterwards, "as you are not dancing, I dare say you will have no objection to join us in a rubber;[9] shall you?"—then, leaving her seat, and coming to him to enforce the proposal, added in a whisper—"We want to make a table for Mrs. Rushworth, you know.—Your mother is quite anxious about it, but cannot very well spare time to sit down herself, because of her fringe. Now, you and I and Dr. Grant will just do; and though *we* play but half-crowns,[10] you know you may bet half-guineas with *him*."

"I should be most happy," replied he aloud, and jumping up with alacrity, "it would give me the greatest pleasure—but that I am this moment going to dance. Come, Fanny,"—taking her hand—"do not be dawdling any longer, or the dance will be over."

Fanny was led off very willingly, though it was impossible for her to feel much gratitude towards her cousin, or distinguish, as he certainly did, between the selfishness of another person and his own.

line 3: and, between ourselves, she,] **1814** and between ourselves she, // line 12: aunt] **1814** Aunt // line 17: mother] **1814** Mother // line 20: half-guineas] **1814** half guineas // · line 22: "it would] **1814** it would // line 27: cousin,] **1814** Cousin,

"A pretty modest request upon my word!" he indignantly exclaimed as they walked away. "To want to nail me to a card table for the next two hours with herself and Dr. Grant, who are always quarrelling, and that poking old woman, who knows no more of whist than of algebra. I wish my good aunt would be a little less busy! And to ask me in such a way too! without ceremony, before them all, so as to leave me no possibility of refusing! *That* is what I dislike most particularly. It raises my spleen more than any thing, to have the pretence of being asked, of being given a choice, and at the same time addressed in such a way as to oblige one to do the very thing—whatever it be! If I had not luckily thought of standing up with you, I could not have got out of it. It is a great deal too bad. But when my aunt has got a fancy in her head, nothing can stop her."

line 5: algebra.] **1814** Algebra.

Chapter 13

THE HONOURABLE[1] JOHN YATES, this new friend, had
not much to recommend him beyond habits of fashion and
expense, and being the younger son of a lord with a tolerable independence;[2] and Sir Thomas would probably have
thought his introduction at Mansfield by no means desirable. Mr. Bertram's acquaintance with him had begun at
Weymouth, where they had spent ten days together in the
same society, and the friendship, if friendship it might be
called, had been proved and perfected by Mr. Yates's being
invited to take Mansfield in his way, whenever he could, and
by his promising to come; and he did come rather earlier than
had been expected, in consequence of the sudden breaking-up
of a large party assembled for gaiety at the house of another
friend, which he had left Weymouth to join. He came on the
wings of disappointment, and with his head full of acting, for
it had been a theatrical party; and the play, in which he had
borne a part, was within two days of representation, when the
sudden death of one of the nearest connections of the family
had destroyed the scheme and dispersed the performers. To
be so near happiness, so near fame, so near the long paragraph in praise of the private theatricals at Ecclesford,[3] the
seat of the Right Hon. Lord Ravenshaw, in Cornwall, which
would of course have immortalized the whole party for at

line 3: lord] **1814** Lord   //   line 4: independence;] **1814** independance;

142

least a twelvemonth! and being so near, to lose it all, was an injury to be keenly felt, and Mr. Yates could talk of nothing else. Ecclesford and its theatre, with its arrangements and dresses, rehearsals and jokes, was his never-failing subject, and to boast of the past his only consolation.

Happily for him, a love of the theatre is so general, an itch for acting so strong among young people, that he could hardly out-talk the interest of his hearers. From the first casting of the parts, to the epilogue, it was all bewitching, and there were few who did not wish to have been a party concerned, or would have hesitated to try their skill. The play had been Lovers' Vows,[4] and Mr. Yates was to have been Count Cassel. "A trifling part," said he, "and not at all to my taste, and such a one as I certainly would not accept again; but I was determined to make no difficulties. Lord Ravenshaw and the duke had appropriated the only two characters worth playing before I reached Ecclesford; and though Lord Ravenshaw offered to resign his to me, it was impossible to take it, you know. I was sorry for *him* that he should have so mistaken his powers, for he was no more equal to the Baron! A little man, with a weak voice, always hoarse after the first ten minutes! It must have injured the piece materially; but *I* was resolved to make no difficulties. Sir Henry thought the duke not equal to Frederick, but that was because Sir Henry wanted the part himself; whereas it was certainly in the best hands of the two. I was surprised to see Sir Henry such a stick. Luckily the strength of the piece did not depend upon him. Our Agatha was inimitable, and the duke was thought very great by many. And upon the whole it would certainly have gone off wonderfully."

line 12: Lovers' Vows,] **1814** Lover's Vows,   //   line 16: duke] **1814** Duke //   line 23: duke] **1814** Duke

"It was a hard case, upon my word;" and, "I do think you were very much to be pitied;" were the kind responses of listening sympathy.

"It is not worth complaining about, but to be sure the poor old dowager[5] could not have died at a worse time; and it is impossible to help wishing, that the news could have been suppressed for just the three days we wanted. It was but three days; and being only a grandmother, and all happening two hundred miles off, I think there would have been no great harm, and it *was* suggested, I know; but Lord Ravenshaw, who I suppose is one of the most correct men in England, would not hear of it."

"An after-piece[6] instead of a comedy," said Mr. Bertram. "Lovers' Vows were at an end, and Lord and Lady Ravenshaw left to act my Grandmother[7] by themselves. Well, the jointure[8] may comfort *him*; and perhaps, between friends, he began to tremble for his credit and his lungs in the Baron, and was not sorry to withdraw; and to make *you* amends, Yates, I think we must raise a little theatre at Mansfield, and ask you to be our manager."[9]

This, though the thought of the moment, did not end with the moment; for the inclination to act was awakened, and in no one more strongly than in him who was now master of the house; and who having so much leisure as to make almost any novelty a certain good, had likewise such a degree of lively talents and comic taste, as were exactly adapted to the novelty of acting. The thought returned again and again. "Oh! for the Ecclesford theatre and scenery to try something with." Each sister could echo the wish; and Henry Crawford, to whom, in all the riot of his gratifications[10] it was yet an

line 8: grandmother,] **1814** grand-mother,   //   line 14: "Lovers' Vows] **1814** "Lover's Vows untasted pleasure, was quite alive at the idea. "I really believe," said he, "I could be fool enough at this moment to undertake any character that ever was written, from Shylock or Richard III.[11] down to the singing hero of a farce in his scarlet coat and cocked hat. I feel as if I could be any thing or every thing, as if I could rant and storm, or sigh, or cut capers[12] in any tragedy or comedy in the English language. Let us be doing something. Be it only half a play—an act—a scene; what should prevent us? Not these countenances I am sure," looking towards the Miss Bertrams, "and for a theatre, what signifies a theatre? We shall be only amusing ourselves. Any room in this house might suffice."

"We must have a curtain," said Tom Bertram, "a few yards of green baize for a curtain,[13] and perhaps that may be enough."

"Oh! quite enough," cried Mr. Yates, "with only just a side wing or two run up, doors in flat, and three or four scenes to be let down;[14] nothing more would be necessary on such a plan as this. For mere amusement among ourselves, we should want nothing more."

"I believe we must be satisfied with *less*," said Maria. "There would not be time, and other difficulties would arise. We must rather adopt Mr. Crawford's views, and make the *performance*, not the *theatre*, our object. Many parts of our best plays are independent of scenery."

"Nay," said Edmund, who began to listen with alarm. "Let us do nothing by halves. If we are to act, let it be in a theatre completely fitted up with pit, box, and gallery, and let us have a play entire from beginning to end; so as it be a German play,[15] no matter what, with a good tricking, shifting after-piece, and a figure-dance, and a horn-pipe, and a song between the acts.[16] If we do not out do Ecclesford, we do nothing."

"Now, Edmund, do not be disagreeable," said Julia. "Nobody loves a play better than you do, or can have gone much farther to see one."

"True, to see real acting, good hardened real acting; but I would hardly walk from this room to the next to look at the raw efforts of those who have not been bred to the trade,[17]—a set of gentlemen and ladies, who have all the disadvantages of education and decorum to struggle through."

After a short pause, however, the subject still continued, and was discussed with unabated eagerness, every one's inclination increasing by the discussion, and a knowledge of the inclination of the rest; and though nothing was settled but that Tom Bertram would prefer a comedy, and his sisters and Henry Crawford a tragedy, and that nothing in the world could be easier than to find a piece which would please them all, the resolution to act something or other, seemed so decided, as to make Edmund quite uncomfortable. He was determined to prevent it, if possible, though his mother, who equally heard the conversation which passed at table, did not evince the least disapprobation.

The same evening afforded him an opportunity of trying his strength. Maria, Julia, Henry Crawford, and Mr. Yates, were in the billiard-room.[18] Tom returning from them into the drawing-room, where Edmund was standing thoughtfully by the fire, while Lady Bertram was on the sofa at a little distance, and Fanny close beside her arranging her work, thus began as he entered. "Such a horribly vile billiard-table as ours, is not to be met with, I believe, above ground! I can stand it no longer, and I think, I may say, that nothing shall ever tempt me to it again. But one good thing I have just ascertained. It is the very room for a theatre, precisely the

line 4: hardened] **1814** harden'd // line 23: billiard-room.] **1814** billiard room. // line 25: Lady Bertram] **1814** lady Bertram

shape and length for it, and the doors at the farther end, communicating with each other[19] as they may be made to do in five minutes, by merely moving the book-case in my father's room, is the very thing we could have desired, if we had set down to wish for it. And my father's room will be an excellent green-room.[20] It seems to join the billiard-room on purpose."

"You are not serious, Tom, in meaning to act?" said Edmund in a low voice, as his brother approached the fire.

"Not serious! never more so, I assure you. What is there to surprise you in it?"

"I think it would be very wrong. In a *general* light, private theatricals are open to some objections,[21] but as *we* are circumstanced, I must think it would be highly injudicious, and more than injudicious, to attempt any thing of the kind. It would show great want of feeling on my father's account, absent as he is, and in some degree of constant danger;[22] and it would be imprudent, I think, with regard to Maria, whose situation is a very delicate one, considering every thing, extremely delicate."

"You take up a thing so seriously! as if we were going to act three times a week till my father's return, and invite all the country. But it is not to be a display of that sort. We mean nothing but a little amusement among ourselves, just to vary the scene, and exercise our powers in something new. We want no audience, no publicity. We may be trusted, I think, in choosing some play most perfectly unexceptionable, and I can conceive no greater harm or danger to any of us in conversing in the elegant written language of some respectable author than in chattering in words of our own. I have no fears, and

line 6: billiard-room] **1814** billiard room   //   line 9: the fire.] **1814** the fire."   //   line 27: choosing] **1814** chusing

no scruples. And as to my father's being absent, it is so far from an objection, that I consider it rather as a motive; for the expectation of his return must be a very anxious period to my mother, and if we can be the means of amusing that anxiety, and keeping up her spirits for the next few weeks, I shall think our time very well spent, and so I am sure will he.—It is a *very* anxious period for her."

As he said this, each looked towards their mother. Lady Bertram, sunk back in one corner of the sofa, the picture of health, wealth, ease, and tranquillity, was just falling into a gentle doze, while Fanny was getting through the few difficulties of her work for her.

Edmund smiled and shook his head.

"By Jove! this won't do—cried Tom, throwing himself into a chair with a hearty laugh. To be sure, my dear mother, your anxiety—I was unlucky there."

"What is the matter?" asked her ladyship in the heavy tone of one half roused,—"I was not asleep."

"Oh! dear, no ma'am—nobody suspected you—Well, Edmund," he continued, returning to the former subject, posture, and voice, as soon as Lady Bertram began to nod again—"But *this* I *will* maintain—that we shall be doing no harm."

"I cannot agree with you—I am convinced that my father would totally disapprove it."

"And I am convinced to the contrary.—Nobody is fonder of the exercise of talent in young people, or promotes it more,

line 2: objection, that] **1814** objection that // line 14: won't do] **1814** wont do // line 15: mother, your] **1814** Mother, your // line 17: ladyship] **1814** Ladyship // line 19: ma'am—nobody] **1814** Ma'am—Nobody // line 19: Well, Edmund,"] **1814** Well Edmund," // line 24: father] **1814** Father // line 27: people, or] **1814** people or // line 27: more, than] **1814** more than

than my father; and for any thing of the acting, spouting, reciting kind, I think he has always a decided taste. I am sure he encouraged it in us as boys. How many a time have we mourned over the dead body of Julius Cæsar, and *to be'd* and not *to be'd*,[23] in this very room, for his amusement! And I am sure, *my name was Norval*,[24] every evening of my life through one Christmas holidays."

"It was a very different thing.—You must see the difference yourself. My father wished us, as school-boys, to speak well, but he would never wish his grown up daughters to be acting plays. His sense of decorum is strict."

"I know all that," said Tom, displeased. "I know my father as well as you do, and I'll take care that his daughters do nothing to distress him. Manage your own concerns, Edmund, and I'll take care of the rest of the family."

"If you are resolved on acting," replied the persevering Edmund, "I must hope it will be in a very small and quiet way; and I think a theatre ought not to be attempted.—It would be taking liberties with my father's house in his absence which could not be justified."

"For every thing of that nature, I will be answerable,"—said Tom, in a decided tone.—"His house shall not be hurt. I have quite as great an interest[25] in being careful of his house as you can have; and as to such alterations as I was suggesting just now, such as moving a bookcase, or unlocking a door, or even as using the billiard-room for the space of a week without

line 1: my father; and] **1814** my father, and // line 1: acting, spouting, reciting] **1814** Acting, Spouting, Reciting // line 5: amusement!] **1814** amusement. // line 6: through] **1814** though // line 9: father] **1814** Father // line 12: Tom, displeased.] **1814** Tom displeased. // line 12: father as] **1814** Father as // line 19: my father's house] **1814** my Father's house // line 21: answerable,"—said Tom,] **1814** answerable"—said Tom, // line 25: bookcase,] **1814** Book case, // line 26: billiard-room] **1814** Billiard room,

playing at billiards in it, you might just as well suppose he would object to our sitting more in this room, and less in the breakfast-room, than we did before he went away, or to my sister's piano forte[26] being moved from one side of the room to the other.—Absolute nonsense!"

"The innovation, if not wrong as an innovation, will be wrong as an expense."

"Yes, the expense of such an undertaking would be prodigious! Perhaps it might cost a whole twenty pounds.[27]—Something of a Theatre we must have undoubtedly, but it will be on the simplest plan;—a green curtain and a little carpenter's work—and that's all; and as the carpenter's work may be all done at home by Christopher Jackson himself, it will be too absurd to talk of expense;—and as long as Jackson is employed, every thing will be right with Sir Thomas.—Don't imagine that nobody in this house can see or judge but yourself.—Don't act yourself, if you do not like it, but don't expect to govern every body else."

"No, as to acting myself," said Edmund, "*that* I absolutely protest against."

Tom walked out of the room as he said it, and Edmund was left to sit down and stir the fire in thoughtful vexation.

Fanny, who had heard it all, and borne Edmund company in every feeling throughout the whole, now ventured to say, in her anxiety to suggest some comfort, "Perhaps they may not be able to find any play to suit them. Your brother's taste, and your sisters', seem very different."

---

line 1: billiards] **1814** Billiards   //   line 3: breakfast-room,] **1814** breakfast room,   //   line 6: innovation,] **1814** Innovation,   //   line 6: as an innovation,] **1814** as an Innovation,   //   line 9: twenty pounds.] **1814** Twenty pounds   //   line 26: brother's taste,] **1814** Brother's taste,   //   line 27: sisters',] **1814** Sisters,

"I have no hope there, Fanny. If they persist in the scheme they will find something—I shall speak to my sisters, and try to dissuade *them*, and that is all I can do."

"I should think my aunt Norris would be on your side."

"I dare say she would; but she has no influence with either Tom or my sisters that could be of any use; and if I cannot convince them myself, I shall let things take their 'course, without attempting it through her. Family squabbling is the greatest evil of all, and we had better do any thing than be altogether by the ears."[28]

His sisters, to whom he had an opportunity of speaking the next morning, were quite as impatient of his advice, quite as unyielding to his representation,[29] quite as determined in the cause of pleasure, as Tom.—Their mother had no objection to the plan, and they were not in the least afraid of their father's disapprobation.—There could be no harm in what had been done in so many respectable families, and by so many women of the first consideration; and it must be scrupulousness run mad, that could see any thing to censure in a plan like their's, comprehending only brothers and sisters, and intimate friends, and which would never be heard of beyond themselves. Julia *did* seem inclined to admit that Maria's situation might require particular caution and delicacy—but that could not extend to *her*—*she* was at liberty; and Maria evidently considered her engagement as only raising her so much more above restraint, and leaving her less occasion than Julia, to consult either father or mother. Edmund had little

line 2: sisters, and] **1814** sisters and // line 4: aunt Norris] **1814** Aunt Norris // line 6: sisters] **1814** Sisters. // line 14: pleasure, as Tom.] **1814** pleasure as om. // line 14: mother] **1814** Mother // line 16: father's] **1814** Father's // line 20: like their's,] **1814** like theirs, // line 27: father or mother.] **1814** Father or Mother.

to hope, but he was still urging the subject, when Henry Crawford entered the room, fresh from the Parsonage, calling out, "No want of hands in our Theatre, Miss Bertram. No want of under strappers[30]—My sister desires her love, and hopes to be admitted into the company, and will be happy to take the part of any old Duenna or tame Confidante,[31] that you may not like to do yourselves."

Maria gave Edmund a glance, which meant, "What say you now? Can we be wrong if Mary Crawford feels the same?" And Edmund silenced, was obliged to acknowledge that the charm of acting might well carry fascination to the mind of genius;[32] and with the ingenuity of love, to dwell more on the obliging, accommodating purport of the message than on any thing else.

The scheme advanced. Opposition was vain; and as to Mrs. Norris, he was mistaken in supposing she would wish to make any. She started no difficulties that were not talked down in five minutes by her eldest nephew and niece, who were all-powerful with her; and, as the whole arrangement was to bring very little expense to any body, and none at all to herself, as she foresaw in it all the comforts of hurry, bustle and importance, and derived the immediate advantage of fancying herself obliged to leave her own house, where she had been living a month at her own cost, and take up her abode in their's, that every hour might be spent in their service; she was, in fact, exceedingly delighted with the project.

line 5: company,] **1814** Company, // line 8: glance, which] **1814** glance which // line 12: genius;] **1814** Genius; // line 12: of love,] **1814** of Love, // line 18: all-powerful] **1814** all powerful // line 25: their's,] **1814** theirs,

Chapter 14

Fanny seemed nearer being right than Edmund had supposed. The business of finding a play that would suit every body, proved to be no trifle; and the carpenter had received his orders and taken his measurements, had suggested and removed at least two sets of difficulties, and having made the necessity of an enlargement of plan and expense fully evident, was already at work, while a play was still to seek. Other preparations were also in hand. An enormous roll of green baize had arrived from Northampton, and been cut out by Mrs. Norris (with a saving, by her good management, of full three quarters of a yard), and was actually forming into a curtain by the housemaids, and still the play was wanting; and as two or three days passed away in this manner, Edmund began almost to hope that none might ever be found.

There were, in fact, so many things to be attended to, so many people to be pleased, so many best characters required, and above all, such a need that the play should be at once both tragedy and comedy, that there did seem as little chance of a decision, as any thing pursued by youth and zeal could hold out.

On the tragic side were the Miss Bertrams, Henry Crawford, and Mr. Yates; on the comic, Tom Bertram, not *quite* alone, because it was evident that Mary Crawford's wishes, though politely kept back, inclined the same way;

line 11: a yard), and] **1814** a yard) and   //   line 22: comic, Tom] **1814** comic Tom but his determinateness and his power, seemed to make allies unnecessary; and independent of this great irreconcileable difference, they wanted a piece containing very few characters in the whole, but every character first-rate, and three principal women. All the best plays were run over in vain. Neither Hamlet, nor Macbeth, nor Othello, nor Douglas, nor the Gamester, presented any thing that could satisfy even the tragedians; and the Rivals, the School for Scandal, Wheel of Fortune, Heir at Law,[1] and a long etcetera, were successively dismissed with yet warmer objections. No piece could be proposed that did not supply somebody with a difficulty, and on one side or the other it was a continual repetition of, "Oh! no, *that* will never do. Let us have no ranting tragedies. Too many characters—Not a tolerable woman's part in the play—Any thing but *that*, my dear Tom. It would be impossible to fill it up—One could not expect any body to take such a part—Nothing but buffoonery from beginning to end. *That* might do, perhaps, but for the low parts—If I *must* give my opinion, I have always thought it the most insipid play in the English language—*I* do not wish to make objections, I shall be happy to be of any use, but I think we could not choose worse."

Fanny looked on and listened, not unamused to observe the selfishness which, more or less disguised, seemed to govern them all, and wondering how it would end. For her own gratification she could have wished that something might be acted, for she had never seen even half a play, but every thing of higher consequence was against it.

"This will never do," said Tom Bertram at last. "We are wasting time most abominably. Something must be fixed on. No matter what, so that something is chosen. We must not

line 21: choose] **1814** chuse

be so nice.[2] A few characters, too many must not frighten us. We must *double* them. We must descend a little. If a part is insignificant, the greater our credit in making any thing of it. From this moment *I* make no difficulties. I take any part you choose to give me, so as it be comic. Let it but be comic, I condition for nothing more."

For about the fifth time he then proposed the Heir at Law, doubting only whether to prefer Lord Duberley or Dr. Pangloss[3] for himself, and very earnestly, but very unsuccessfully, trying to persuade the others that there were some fine tragic parts in the rest of the Dramatis Personæ.

The pause which followed this fruitless effort was ended by the same speaker, who taking up one of the many volumes of plays that lay on the table, and turning it over, suddenly exclaimed, "Lovers' Vows! And why should not Lovers' Vows do for *us* as well as for the Ravenshaws? How came it never to be thought of before? It strikes me as if it would do exactly. What say you all?—Here are two capital tragic parts for Yates and Crawford, and here is the rhyming butler for me—if nobody else wants it—a trifling part, but the sort of thing I should not dislike, and as I said before, I am determined to take any-thing and do my best. And as for the rest, they may be filled up by any-body. It is only Count Cassel and Anhalt."

The suggestion was generally welcome. Every body was growing weary of indecision, and the first idea with every body was, that nothing had been proposed before so likely to suit them all. Mr. Yates was particularly pleased; he had been sighing and longing to do the Baron at Ecclesford, had grudged every rant[4] of Lord Ravenshaw's, and been

line 5: choose] **1814** chuse   //   line 15: Lovers' Vows!] **1814** Lovers Vows!   //   line 15: Lovers' Vows] **1814** Lovers Vows   //   line 19: rhyming butler] **1814** rhyming Butler   //   line 22: any-thing] **1814** anything   //   line 23: any-body.] **1814** anybody.

forced to re-rant it all in his own room. To storm through
Baron Wildenhaim was the height of his theatrical ambition, and with the advantage of knowing half the scenes by
heart already, he did now with the greatest alacrity offer his
services for the part. To do him justice, however, he did not
resolve to appropriate it—for remembering that there was
some very good ranting ground in Frederick, he professed
an equal willingness for that. Henry Crawford was ready to
take either. Whichever Mr. Yates did not choose, would perfectly satisfy him, and a short parley of compliment[5] ensued.
Miss Bertram feeling all the interest of an Agatha[6] in the
question, took on her to decide it, by observing to Mr. Yates,
that this was a point in which height and figure ought to be
considered, and that *his* being the tallest, seemed to fit him
peculiarly for the Baron. She was acknowledged to be quite
right, and the two parts being accepted accordingly, she was
certain of the proper Frederick. Three of the characters were
now cast, besides Mr. Rushworth, who was always answered
for by Maria as willing to do any thing; when Julia, meaning
like her sister to be Agatha, began to be scrupulous on Miss
Crawford's account.

"This is not behaving well by the absent," said she. "Here
are not women enough. Amelia and Agatha may do for Maria
and me, but here is nothing for your sister, Mr. Crawford."

Mr. Crawford desired *that* might not be thought of; he was
very sure his sister had no wish of acting, but as she might be
useful, and that she would not allow herself to be considered
in the present case. But this was immediately opposed by
Tom Bertram, who asserted the part of Amelia to be in every
respect the property of Miss Crawford if she would accept it.
"It falls as naturally, as necessarily to her," said he, "as Agatha

line 1: The storm] **1814** To storm // line 9: choose,] **1814** chuse, //
line 19: any thing;] **1814** anything;

does to one or other of my sisters. It can be no sacrifice on their side, for it is highly comic."

A short silence followed. Each sister looked anxious; for each felt the best claim to Agatha, and was hoping to have it pressed on her by the rest. Henry Crawford, who meanwhile had taken up the play, and with seeming carelessness was turning over the first act, soon settled the business. "I must entreat Miss *Julia* Bertram," said he, "not to engage in the part of Agatha, or it will be the ruin of all my solemnity. You must not, indeed you must not—(turning to her.) I could not stand your countenance dressed up in woe and paleness. The many laughs we have had together would infallibly come across me, and Frederick and his knapsack would be obliged to run away."

Pleasantly, courteously it was spoken; but the manner was lost in the matter to Julia's feelings. She saw a glance at Maria, which confirmed the injury to herself; it was a scheme— a trick; she was slighted, Maria was preferred; the smile of triumph which Maria was trying to suppress shewed how well it was understood, and before Julia could command herself enough to speak, her brother gave his weight against her too, by saying, "Oh! yes, Maria must be Agatha. Maria will be the best Agatha. Though Julia fancies she prefers tragedy, I would not trust her in it. There is nothing of tragedy about her. She has not the look of it. Her features are not tragic features, and she walks too quick, and speaks too quick, and would not keep her countenance. She had better do the old countrywoman; the Cottager's wife; you had, indeed, Julia. Cottager's wife is a very pretty part I assure you. The old lady relieves the high-flown benevolence of her husband with a good deal of spirit. You shall be Cottager's wife."

line 10: not, indeed you] **1814** not, indeed, you // line 16: Maria, which] **1814** Maria which

"Cottager's wife!" cried Mr. Yates. "What are you talking of? The most trivial, paltry, insignificant part; the merest common-place—not a tolerable speech in the whole. Your sister do that! It is an insult to propose it. At Ecclesford the governess was to have done it. We all agreed that it could not be offered to any body else. A little more justice, Mr. Manager, if you please. You do not deserve the office, if you cannot appreciate the talents of your company a little better."

"Why as to *that*, my good friend, till I and my company have really acted there must be some guess-work; but I mean no disparagement to Julia. We cannot have two Agathas, and we must have one Cottager's wife; and I am sure I set her the example of moderation myself in being satisfied with the old Butler. If the part is trifling she will have more credit in making something of it; and if she is so desperately bent against every thing humorous, let her take Cottager's speeches instead of Cottager's wife's, and so change the parts all through; *he* is solemn and pathetic enough I am sure. It could make no difference in the play; and as for Cottager himself, when he has got his wife's speeches, *I* would undertake him with all my heart."

"With all your partiality for Cottager's wife," said Henry Crawford, "it will be impossible to make any thing of it fit for your sister, and we must not suffer her good nature to be imposed on. We must not *allow* her to accept the part. She must not be left to her own complaisance. Her talents will be wanted in Amelia. Amelia is a character more difficult to be well represented than even Agatha. I consider Amelia as the most difficult character in the whole piece. It requires great powers, great nicety, to give her playfulness and

line 22: heart.] **1814** heart." // line 24: any thing] **1814** anything simplicity without extravagance. I have seen good actresses fail in the part. Simplicity, indeed, is beyond the reach of almost every actress by profession. It requires a delicacy of feeling which they have not. It requires a gentlewoman—a Julia Bertram. You *will* undertake it I hope?" turning to her with a look of anxious entreaty, which softened her a little; but while she hesitated what to say, her brother again interposed with Miss Crawford's better claim.

"No, no, Julia must not be Amelia. It is not at all the part for her. She would not like it. She would not do well. She is too tall and robust. Amelia should be a small, light, girlish, skipping figure. It is fit for Miss Crawford and Miss Crawford only. She looks the part, and I am persuaded will do it admirably."

Without attending to this, Henry Crawford continued his supplication. "You must oblige us," said he, "indeed you must. When you have studied the character, I am sure you will feel it suit you. Tragedy may be your choice, but it will certainly appear that comedy chooses *you*. You will be to visit me in prison with a basket of provisions; you will not refuse to visit me in prison? I think I see you coming in with your basket."

The influence of his voice was felt. Julia wavered: but was he only trying to soothe and pacify her, and make her over-look the previous affront? She distrusted him. The slight had been most determined. He was, perhaps, but at treach-erous play with her. She looked suspiciously at her sister; Maria's countenance was to decide it; if she were vexed and alarmed—but Maria looked all serenity and satisfaction, and Julia well knew that on this ground Maria could not be happy but at her expense. With hasty indignation therefore, and a

line 5: hope?" turning] **1814** hope?" Turning // line 6: entreaty, which] **1814** entreaty which // line 19: chooses] **1814** chuses // line 22: wavered: but] **1814** wavered; but // line 23: to soothe] **1814** too soothe

tremulous voice, she said to him, "You do not seem afraid of not keeping your countenance when I come in with a basket of provisions—though one might have supposed—but it is only as Agatha that I was to be so overpowering!"—She stopped—Henry Crawford looked rather foolish, and as if he did not know what to say. Tom Bertram began again,

"Miss Crawford must be Amelia.—She will be an excellent Amelia."

"Do not be afraid of *my* wanting the character," cried Julia with angry quickness;—"I am *not* to be Agatha, and I am sure I will do nothing else; and as to Amelia, it is of all parts in the world the most disgusting to me. I quite detest her. An odious, little, pert, unnatural, impudent girl. I have always protested against comedy, and this is comedy in its worst form." And so saying, she walked hastily out of the room, leaving awkward feelings to more than one, but exciting small compassion in any except Fanny, who had been a quiet auditor of the whole, and who could not think of her as under the agitations of *jealousy*, without great pity.

A short silence succeeded her leaving them; but her brother soon returned to business and Lovers' Vows, and was eagerly looking over the play, with Mr. Yates's help, to ascertain what scenery would be necessary—while Maria and Henry Crawford conversed together in an under voice, and the declaration with which she began of, "I am sure I would give up the part to Julia most willingly, but that though I shall probably do it very ill, I feel persuaded *she* would do it worse," was doubtless receiving all the compliments it called for.

line 1: voice, she] **1814** voice she   //   line 13: world the] **1814** world, the   //   line 20: *jealousy*,] **1814** *Jealousy*,   //   line 22: Lovers' Vows,] **1814** Lovers Vows,

When this had lasted some time, the division of the party was completed by Tom Bertram and Mr. Yates walking off together to consult farther in the room now beginning to be called *the Theatre*, and Miss Bertram's resolving to go down to the Parsonage herself with the offer of Amelia to Miss Crawford; and Fanny remained alone.

The first use she made of her solitude was to take up the volume which had been left on the table, and begin to acquaint herself with the play of which she had heard so much. Her curiosity was all awake, and she ran through it with an eagerness which was suspended only by intervals of astonishment, that it could be chosen in the present instance—that it could be proposed and accepted in a private Theatre! Agatha and Amelia appeared to her in their different ways so totally improper for home representation—the situation of one, and the language of the other, so unfit to be expressed by any woman of modesty, that she could hardly suppose her cousins could be aware of what they were engaging in; and longed to have them roused as soon as possible by the remonstrance which Edmund would certainly make.

line 2: Tom Bertram and] **1814** Tom Bertram, and

Chapter 15

MISS CRAWFORD accepted the part very readily, and soon after Miss Bertram's return from the Parsonage, Mr. Rushworth arrived, and another character was consequently cast. He had the offer of Count Cassel and Anhalt, and at first did not know which to choose, and wanted Miss Bertram to direct him, but upon being made to understand the different style of the characters, and which was which, and recollecting that he had once seen the play in London, and had thought Anhalt a very stupid fellow, he soon decided for the Count. Miss Bertram approved the decision, for the less he had to learn the better; and though she could not sympathize in his wish that the Count and Agatha might be to act together, nor wait very patiently while he was slowly turning over the leaves with the hope of still discovering such a scene, she very kindly took his part in hand, and curtailed every speech that admitted being shortened;—besides pointing out the necessity of his being very much dressed, and choosing his colours. Mr. Rushworth liked the idea of his finery very well, though affecting to despise it, and was too much engaged with what his own appearance would be, to think of the others, or draw any of those conclusions, or feel any of that displeasure, which Maria had been half prepared for.

line 5: choose,] **1814** chuse,   //   line 17: dressed, and choosing] **1814** dress'd and chusing   //   line 19: finery very] **1814** finery, very

Thus much was settled before Edmund, who had been out all the morning, knew any thing of the matter; but when he entered the drawing-room before dinner, the buz of discussion was high between Tom, Maria, and Mr. Yates; and Mr. Rushworth stepped forward with great alacrity to tell him the agreeable news.

"We have got a play," said he.—"It is to be Lovers' Vows; and I am to be Count Cassel, and am to come in first with a blue dress, and a pink satin cloak, and afterwards am to have another fine fancy suit by way of a shooting dress.—I do not know how I shall like it."

Fanny's eyes followed Edmund, and her heart beat for him as she heard this speech, and saw his look, and felt what his sensations must be.

"Lovers' Vows!"—in a tone of the greatest amazement, was his only reply to Mr. Rushworth; and he turned towards his brother and sisters as if hardly doubting a contradiction.[1]

"Yes," cried Mr. Yates.—"After all our debatings and difficulties, we find there is nothing that will suit us altogether so well, nothing so unexceptionable, as Lovers' Vows. The wonder is that it should not have been thought of before. My stupidity was abominable, for here we have all the advantage of what I saw at Ecclesford; and it is so useful to have any thing of a model!—We have cast almost every part."

"But what do you do for women?" said Edmund gravely, and looking at Maria.

Maria blushed in spite of herself as she answered, "I take the part which Lady Ravenshaw was to have done, and (with a bolder eye) Miss Crawford is to be Amelia."

line 3: drawing-room] **1814** drawing room   //   line 7: to be Lovers' Vows;] **1814** to be called Lovers Vows;   //   line 15: "Lovers' Vows!"] **1814** "Lovers Vows!"   //   line 20: unexceptionable, as Lovers' Vows.] **1814** unexceptionable as Lovers Vows.

"I should not have thought it the sort of play to be so easily filled up, with *us*," replied Edmund, turning away to the fire where sat his mother, aunt, and Fanny, and seating himself with a look of great vexation.

Mr. Rushworth followed him to say, "I come in three times, and have two and forty speeches. That's something, is not it?—But I do not much like the idea of being so fine.—I shall hardly know myself in a blue dress, and a pink satin cloak."

Edmund could not answer him.—In a few minutes Mr. Bertram was called out of the room to satisfy some doubts of the carpenter, and being accompanied by Mr. Yates, and followed soon afterwards by Mr. Rushworth, Edmund almost immediately took the opportunity of saying, "I cannot before Mr. Yates speak what I feel as to this play, without reflecting on his friends at Ecclesford—but I must now, my dear Maria, tell *you*, that I think it exceedingly unfit for private representation, and that I hope you will give it up.—I cannot but suppose you *will* when you have read it carefully over.— Read only the first Act aloud, to either your mother or aunt, and see how you can approve it.—It will not be necessary to send you to your *father's* judgment, I am convinced."

"We see things very differently," cried Maria—"I am perfectly acquainted with the play, I assure you—and with a very few omissions, and so forth, which will be made, of course, I can see nothing objectionable in it; and *I* am not the *only* young woman you find, who thinks it very fit for private representation."

line 3: mother, aunt, and] **1814** Mother, Aunt, and // line 5: to say, "I] **1814** to say "I // line 20: mother or aunt,] **1814** Mother or Aunt, // line 22: *father's* judgment, I am convinced."] **1814** *Father's* judgment, I am convinced.

"I am sorry for it," was his answer—"But in this matter it is *you* who are to lead. *You* must set the example.—If others have blundered, it is your place to put them right, and shew them what true delicacy is.—In all points of decorum, *your* conduct must be law to the rest of the party."

This picture of her consequence had some effect, for no one loved better to lead than Maria;—and with far more good humour she answered, "I am much obliged to you, Edmund;—you mean very well, I am sure—but I still think you see things too strongly; and I really cannot undertake to harangue all the rest upon a subject of this kind.—*There* would be the greatest indecorum I think."

"Do you imagine that I could have such an idea in my head? No—let your conduct be the only harangue.—Say that, on examining the part, you feel yourself unequal to it, that you find it requiring more exertion and confidence than you can be supposed to have.—Say this with firmness, and it will be quite enough.—All who can distinguish, will understand your motive.—The play will be given up, and your delicacy honoured as it ought."

"Do not act any thing improper, my dear," said Lady Bertram. "Sir Thomas would not like it.—Fanny, ring the bell; I must have my dinner.—To be sure Julia is dressed by this time."

"I am convinced, madam," said Edmund, preventing Fanny, "that Sir Thomas would not like it."

"There, my dear, do you hear what Edmund says?"

"If I were to decline the part," said Maria with renewed zeal, "Julia would certainly take it."

"What!"—cried Edmund, "if she knew your reasons!"

line 2: example.—If] **1814** example,—If // line 3: blundered,] **1814** blunder'd, // line 14: Say that, on] **1814** Say that on // line 23: dressed] **1814** dress'd // line 25: madam,] **1814** Madam,

"Oh! she might think the difference between us—the difference in our situations—that *she* need not be so scrupulous as *I* might feel necessary. I am sure she would argue so. No, you must excuse me, I cannot retract my consent. It is too far settled; every body would be so disappointed. Tom would be quite angry: and if we are so very nice, we shall never act any thing."

"I was just going to say the very same thing," said Mrs. Norris. "If every play is to be objected to, you will act nothing—and the preparations will be all so much money thrown away—and I am sure *that* would be a discredit to us all. I do not know the play; but, as Maria says, if there is any thing a little too warm (and it is so with most of them) it can be easily left out.—We must not be over precise Edmund. As Mr. Rushworth is to act too, there can be no harm.—I only wish Tom had known his own mind when the carpenters began, for there was the loss of half a day's work about those side-doors.—The curtain will be a good job, however. The maids do their work very well, and I think we shall be able to send back some dozens of the rings.—There is no occasion to put them so very close together. I *am* of some use I hope in preventing waste and making the most of things. There should always be one steady head to superintend so many young ones. I forgot to tell Tom of something that happened to me this very day.—I had been looking about me in the poultry yard, and was just coming out, when who should I see but Dick Jackson making up to the servants' hall door with two bits of deal board[2] in his hand, bringing them to father, you may be sure; mother had chanced to send him of

line 6: angry: and] **1814** angry; and   //   line 12: play; but,] **1814** play, but,   //   line 18: side-doors.] **1814** side doors.   //   line 27: servants' hall door] **1814** Servants' Hall door   //   line 29: mother] **1814** Mother

a message to father, and then father had bid him bring up them two bits of board, for he could not no how do without them. I knew what all this meant, for the servants' dinner bell was ringing at the very moment over our heads, and as I hate such encroaching people, (the Jacksons are very encroaching, I have always said so,—just the sort of people to get all they can.) I said to the boy directly—(a great lubberly[3] fellow of ten years old you know, who ought to be ashamed of himself,) *I'll* take the boards to your father, Dick; so get you home again as fast as you can.—The boy looked very silly and turned away without offering a word, for I believe I might speak pretty sharp; and I dare say it will cure him of coming marauding about the house for one while,—I hate such greediness—so good as your father is to the family, employing the man all the year round!"

Nobody was at the trouble of an answer; the others soon returned, and Edmund found that to have endeavoured to set them right must be his only satisfaction.

Dinner passed heavily. Mrs. Norris related again her triumph over Dick Jackson, but neither play nor preparation were otherwise much talked of, for Edmund's disapprobation was felt even by his brother, though he would not have owned it. Maria, wanting Henry Crawford's animating support, thought the subject better avoided. Mr. Yates, who was trying to make himself agreeable to Julia, found her gloom less impenetrable on any topic than that of his regret at her secession from their company, and Mr. Rushworth having

line 1: father,] **1814** Father,   //   line 1: father] **1814** Father   //   line 2: board, for] **1814** board for   //   line 3: servants' dinner] **1814** Servants' dinner   //   line 8: himself,)] **1814** himself),   //   line 9: father,] **1814** Father,   //   line 13: one while,] **1814** on ewhile,   //   line 14: father] **1814** Father

only his own part, and his own dress in his head, had soon talked away all that could be said of either.

But the concerns of the theatre were suspended only for an hour or two; there was still a great deal to be settled; and the spirits of evening giving fresh courage, Tom, Maria, and Mr. Yates, soon after their being re-assembled in the drawing-room, seated themselves in committee at a separate table, with the play open before them, and were just getting deep in the subject when a most welcome interruption was given by the entrance of Mr. and Miss Crawford, who, late and dark and dirty as it was, could not help coming, and were received with the most grateful joy.

"Well, how do you go on?" and "What have you settled?" and "Oh! we can do nothing without you," followed the first salutations; and Henry Crawford was soon seated with the other three at the table, while his sister made her way to Lady Bertram, and with pleasant attention was complimenting *her*. "I must really congratulate your ladyship," said she, "on the play being chosen; for though you have borne it with exemplary patience, I am sure you must be sick of all our noise and difficulties. The actors may be glad, but the by-standers must be infinitely more thankful for a decision; and I do sincerely give you joy, madam, as well as Mrs. Norris, and every body else who is in the same predicament," glancing half fearfully, half slily, beyond Fanny to Edmund.

She was very civilly answered by Lady Bertram, but Edmund said nothing. His being only a by-stander was not disclaimed. After continuing in chat with the party round the fire a few minutes, Miss Crawford returned to the party round the table; and standing by them, seemed to interest herself in

line 7: drawing-room,] **1814** drawing room,   //   line 19: chosen; for] **1814** chosen, for   //   line 23: joy, madam,] **1814** joy, Madam,   //   line 27: by-stander] **1814** bye-stander

their arrangements till, as if struck by a sudden recollection, she exclaimed, "My good friends, you are most composedly at work upon these cottages and ale-houses, inside and out—but pray let me know my fate in the meanwhile. Who is to be Anhalt? What gentleman among you am I to have the pleasure of making love to?"[4]

For a moment no one spoke; and then many spoke together to tell the same melancholy truth—that they had not yet got any Anhalt. "Mr. Rushworth was to be Count Cassel, but no one had yet undertaken Anhalt."

"I had my choice of the parts," said Mr. Rushworth; "but I thought I should like the Count best—though I do not much relish the finery I am to have."

"You chose very wisely, I am sure," replied Miss Crawford, with a brightened look. "Anhalt is a heavy part."

"*The Count* has two and forty speeches," returned Mr. Rushworth, "which is no trifle."

"I am not at all surprised," said Miss Crawford, after a short pause, "at this want of an Anhalt. Amelia deserves no better. Such a forward young lady may well frighten the men."

"I should be but too happy in taking the part if it were possible," cried Tom, "but unluckily the Butler and Anhalt are in together. I will not entirely give it up, however—I will try what can be done—I will look it over again."

"Your *brother* should take the part," said Mr. Yates, in a low voice. "Do not you think he would?"

"*I* shall not ask him," replied Tom, in a cold, determined manner.

Miss Crawford talked of something else, and soon afterwards rejoined the party at the fire. "They do not want me at all," said she, seating herself. "I only puzzle them,[5] and oblige

line 5: you am] 1814 you, am   //   line 31: herself. "I] 1814 herself. I them to make civil speeches. Mr. Edmund Bertram, as you do not act yourself, you will be a disinterested adviser; and, therefore, I apply to *you*. What shall we do for an Anhalt? Is it practicable for any of the others to double it? What is your advice?"

"My advice," said he, calmly, "is that you change the play."

"*I* should have no objection," she replied; "for though I should not particularly dislike the part of Amelia if well supported—that is, if every thing went well—I shall be sorry to be an inconvenience—but as they do not choose to hear your advice at *that table*—(looking round)—it certainly will not be taken."

Edmund said no more.

"If *any* part could tempt *you* to act, I suppose it would be Anhalt," observed the lady, archly, after a short pause—"for he is a clergyman you know."

"*That* circumstance would by no means tempt me," he replied, "for I should be sorry to make the character ridiculous by bad acting. It must be very difficult to keep Anhalt from appearing a formal, solemn lecturer; and the man who chooses the profession itself, is, perhaps, one of the last who would wish to represent it on the stage."

Miss Crawford was silenced; and with some feelings of resentment and mortification, moved her chair considerably nearer the tea-table, and gave all her attention to Mrs. Norris, who was presiding there.

"Fanny," cried Tom Bertram, from the other table, where the conference was eagerly carrying on, and the conversation incessant, "we want your services."

line 1: Bertram, as] **1814** Bertram as   //   line 11: choose] **1814** chuse   //
line 21: lecturer; and] **1814** lecturer, and   //   line 22: chooses] **1814** chuses

Fanny was up in a moment, expecting some errand, for the habit of employing her in that way was not yet overcome, in spite of all that Edmund could do.

"Oh! we do not want to disturb you from your seat. We do not want your *present* services. We shall only want you in our play. You must be Cottager's wife."

"Me!" cried Fanny, sitting down again with a most frightened look. "Indeed you must excuse me. I could not act any thing if you were to give me the world. No, indeed, I cannot act."

"Indeed but you must, for we cannot excuse you. It need not frighten you; it is a nothing of a part, a mere nothing, not above half a dozen speeches altogether, and it will not much signify if nobody hears a word you say, so you may be as creepmouse⁶ as you like, but we must have you to look at."

"If you are afraid of half a dozen speeches," cried Mr. Rushworth, "what would you do with such a part as mine? I have forty-two to learn."

"It is not that I am afraid of learning by heart," said Fanny, shocked to find herself at that moment the only speaker in the room, and to feel that almost every eye was upon her; "but I really cannot act."

"Yes, yes, you can act well enough for *us*. Learn your part, and we will teach you all the rest. You have only two scenes, and as I shall be Cottager, I'll put you in and push you about; and you will do it very well I'll answer for it."

"No, indeed, Mr. Bertram, you must excuse me. You cannot have an idea. It would be absolutely impossible for me. If I were to undertake it, I should only disappoint you."

"Phoo! Phoo! Do not be so shamefaced. You'll do it very well. Every allowance will be made for you. We do not expect

line 15: creepmouse] **1814** cr epmouse

perfection. You must get a brown gown, and a white apron, and a mob cap, and we must make you a few wrinkles, and a little of the crows-foot at the corner of your eyes, and you will be a very proper, little old woman."

"You must excuse me, indeed you must excuse me," cried Fanny, growing more and more red from excessive agitation, and looking distressfully at Edmund, who was kindly observing her, but unwilling to exasperate his brother by interference, gave her only an encouraging smile. Her entreaty had no effect on Tom; he only said again what he had said before; and it was not merely Tom, for the requisition[7] was now backed by Maria and Mr. Crawford, and Mr. Yates, with an urgency which differed from his, but in being more gentle or more ceremonious, and which altogether was quite overpowering to Fanny; and before she could breathe after it, Mrs. Norris completed the whole, by thus addressing her in a whisper at once angry and audible: "What a piece of work here is about nothing.—I am quite ashamed of you, Fanny, to make such a difficulty of obliging your cousins in a trifle of this sort,—So kind as they are to you!—Take the part with a good grace, and let us hear no more of the matter, I entreat."

"Do not urge her, madam," said Edmund. "It is not fair to urge her in this manner.—You see she does not like to act.— Let her choose for herself as well as the rest of us.—Her judgment may be quite as safely trusted.—Do not urge her any more."

"I am not going to urge her,"—replied Mrs. Norris sharply, "but I shall think her a very obstinate, ungrateful girl, if she does not do what her aunt and cousins wish her—very ungrateful indeed, considering who and what she is."

line 17: audible: "What] **1814** audible, "What // line 19: cousins] **1814** Cousins // line 22: madam,"] **1814** Madam," // line 24: choose] **1814** chuse // line 29: her aunt and cousins] **1814** her Aunt, and Cousins

Edmund was too angry to speak; but Miss Crawford looking for a moment with astonished eyes at Mrs. Norris, and
then at Fanny, whose tears were beginning to show themselves, immediately said with some keenness, "I do not like
my situation; this *place* is too hot for me"—and moved away
her chair to the opposite side of the table close to Fanny, saying to her in a kind low whisper as she placed herself, "Never
mind, my dear Miss Price—this is a cross evening,—every
body is cross and teasing—but do not let us mind them;" and
with pointed attention continued to talk to her and endeavour
to raise her spirits, in spite of being out of spirits herself.—By
a look at her brother, she prevented any farther entreaty from
the theatrical board, and the really good feelings by which
she was almost purely governed, were rapidly restoring her
to all the little she had lost in Edmund's favour.

Fanny did not love Miss Crawford; but she felt very much
obliged to her for her present kindness; and when from taking notice of her work and wishing *she* could work as well,
and begging for the pattern, and supposing Fanny was now
preparing for her *appearance* as of course she would come out
when her cousin was married, Miss Crawford proceeded to
inquire if she had heard lately from her brother at sea, and
said that she had quite a curiosity to see him, and imagined him a very fine young man, and advised Fanny to get
his picture drawn before he went to sea again[8]—She could
not help admitting it to be very agreeable flattery, or help
listening, and answering with more animation than she had
intended.

The consultation upon the play still went on, and Miss
Crawford's attention was first called from Fanny by Tom
Bertram's telling her, with infinite regret, that he found it

line 8: every body] **1814** everybody // line 9: teasing] **1814** teizing //
line 13: theatrical] **1814** Theatrical // line 22: inquire] **1814** enquire

absolutely impossible for him to undertake the part of Anhalt
in addition to the Butler;—he had been most anxiously trying
to make it out to be feasible,—but it would not do,—he must
give it up.—"But there will not be the smallest difficulty in
filling it," he added.—"We have but to speak the word; we
may pick and choose.—I could name at this moment at least
six young men within six miles of us, who are wild to be
admitted into our company, and there are one or two that
would not disgrace us.—I should not be afraid to trust either
of the Olivers or Charles Maddox.—Tom Oliver is a very
clever fellow, and Charles Maddox is as gentlemanlike a man
as you will see any where, so I will take my horse early to-
morrow morning, and ride over to Stoke,[9] and settle with one
of them."

While he spoke, Maria was looking apprehensively round
at Edmund in full expectation that he must oppose such an
enlargement of the plan as this—so contrary to all their first
protestations; but Edmund said nothing.—After a moment's
thought, Miss Crawford calmly replied, "As far as I am concerned, I can have no objection to anything that you all think
eligible. Have I ever seen either of the gentlemen?—Yes,
Mr. Charles Maddox dined at my sister's one day, did not
he Henry?—A quiet-looking young man. I remember him.
Let *him* be applied to, if you please, for it will be less unpleasant to me than to have a perfect stranger."

Charles Maddox was to be the man.—Tom repeated his
resolution of going to him early on the morrow; and though
Julia, who had scarcely opened her lips before, observed in a
sarcastic manner, and with a glance, first at Maria, and then
at Edmund, that "the Mansfield Theatricals would enliven

line 5: it," he added.—"We] **1814** it, he added.—We   //   line 6: choose.]
1814 chuse.   //   line 22: sister's] **1814** Sister's

the whole neighbourhood exceedingly"—Edmund still held his peace, and shewed his feelings only by a determined gravity.

"I am not very sanguine as to our play"—said Miss Crawford in an under voice, to Fanny, after some consideration; "and I can tell Mr. Maddox, that I shall shorten some of *his* speeches, and a great many of *my own*, before we rehearse together.—It will be very disagreeable, and by no means what I expected."

line 1: neighbourhood exceedingly"] **1814** neighbourhood, exceedingly"

Chapter 16

It was not in Miss Crawford's power to talk Fanny into any real forgetfulness of what had passed.—When the evening was over, she went to bed full of it, her nerves still agitated by the shock of such an attack from her cousin Tom, so public and so persevered in, and her spirits sinking under her aunt's unkind reflection and reproach. To be called into notice in such a manner, to hear that it was but the prelude to something so infinitely worse, to be told that she must do what was so impossible as to act; and then to have the charge of obstinacy and ingratitude follow it, enforced with such a hint at the dependence of her situation, had been too distressing at the time, to make the remembrance when she was alone much less so,—especially with the superadded dread of what the morrow might produce in continuation of the subject. Miss Crawford had protected her only for the time; and if she were applied to again among themselves with all the authoritative urgency that Tom and Maria were capable of; and Edmund perhaps away—what should she do? She fell asleep before she could answer the question, and found it quite as puzzling when she awoke the next morning. The little white attic, which had continued her sleeping room ever since her first entering the family, proving incompetent to suggest any reply, she had recourse, as soon as she was dressed, to another

line 6: aunt's] **1814** Aunt's // line 8: something] **1814** some thing // line 10: ingratitude follow it,] **1814** ingratitude, follow it, // line 11: dependence] **1814** dependance

apartment, more spacious and more meet[1] for walking about in, and thinking, and of which she had now for some time been almost equally mistress. It had been their school-room; so called till the Miss Bertrams would not allow it to be called so any longer, and inhabited as such to a later period. There Miss Lee had lived, and there they had read and written, and talked and laughed, till within the last three years, when she had quitted them.—The room had then become useless, and for some time was quite deserted, except by Fanny, when she visited her plants, or wanted one of the books, which she was still glad to keep there, from the deficiency of space and accommodation in her little chamber above;—but gradually, as her value for the comforts of it increased, she had added to her possessions, and spent more of her time there; and having nothing to oppose her, had so naturally and so artlessly worked herself into it, that it was now generally admitted to be her's. The East room as it had been called, ever since Maria Bertram was sixteen, was now considered Fanny's, almost as decidedly as the white attic;—the smallness of the one making the use of the other so evidently reasonable, that the Miss Bertrams, with every superiority in their own apartments, which their own sense of superiority could demand, were entirely approving it;—and Mrs. Norris having stipulated for there never being a fire in it on Fanny's account, was tolerably resigned to her having the use of what nobody else wanted, though the terms in which she sometimes spoke of the indulgence, seemed to imply that it was the best room in the house.

The aspect was so favourable, that even without a fire it was habitable in many an early spring, and late autumn morning, to such a willing mind as Fanny's, and while there was a gleam

line 19: attic;] **1814** Attic;

of sunshine, she hoped not to be driven from it entirely, even when winter came. The comfort of it in her hours of leisure was extreme. She could go there after any thing unpleasant below, and find immediate consolation in some pursuit, or some train of thought at hand.—Her plants, her books—of which she had been a collector, from the first hour of her commanding a shilling[2]—her writing desk, and her works of charity and ingenuity, were all within her reach;—or if indisposed for employment, if nothing but musing would do, she could scarcely see an object in that room which had not an interesting remembrance connected with it.—Every thing was a friend, or bore her thoughts to a friend; and though there had been sometimes much of suffering to her—though her motives had been often misunderstood, her feelings disregarded, and her comprehension undervalued; though she had known the pains of tyranny, of ridicule, and neglect, yet almost every recurrence of either had led to something consolatory; her aunt Bertram had spoken for her, or Miss Lee had been encouraging, or what was yet more frequent or more dear—Edmund had been her champion and her friend;—he had supported her cause, or explained her meaning, he had told her not to cry, or had given her some proof of affection which made her tears delightful—and the whole was now so blended together, so harmonized by distance,[3] that every former affliction had its charm. The room was most dear to her, and she would not have changed its furniture for the handsomest in the house, though what had been originally plain, had suffered all the ill-usage of children—and its greatest elegancies and ornaments were a faded footstool of Julia's work,[4] too ill done for the drawing-room, three transparencies, made in a rage for transparencies, for the

line 15: undervalued;] **1814** under valued;   //   line 18: aunt Bertram] **1814** Aunt Bertram   //   line 29: footstool] **1814** foot-stool

three lower panes of one window, where Tintern Abbey held its station between a cave in Italy, and a moonlight lake in Cumberland;[5] a collection of family profiles thought unworthy of being anywhere else, over the mantlepiece, and by their side and pinned against the wall, a small sketch of a ship sent four years ago from the Mediterranean by William, with H. M. S. Antwerp at the bottom, in letters as tall as the mainmast.

To this nest of comforts Fanny now walked down to try its influence on an agitated, doubting spirit—to see if by looking at Edmund's profile she could catch any of his counsel, or by giving air to her geraniums she might inhale a breeze of mental strength herself. But she had more than fears of her own perseverance to remove; she had begun to feel undecided as to what she *ought to do*; and as she walked round the room her doubts were increasing. Was she *right* in refusing what was so warmly asked, so strongly wished for? What might be so essential to a scheme on which some of those to whom she owed the greatest complaisance,[6] had set their hearts? Was it not ill-nature—selfishness—and a fear of exposing herself? And would Edmund's judgment, would his persuasion of Sir Thomas's disapprobation of the whole, be enough to justify her in a determined denial in spite of all the rest? It would be so horrible to her to act, that she was inclined to suspect the truth and purity of her own scruples, and as she looked around her, the claims of her cousins to being obliged, were strengthened by the sight of present upon present that she had received from them. The table between the windows was covered with work-boxes and netting-boxes,[7] which had been given her at different times, principally by Tom; and she grew bewildered as to the amount of the debt which all these kind

line 4: mantlepiece,] **1814** mantle piece, // line 8: mainmast.] **1814** main-mast.

remembrances produced. A tap at the door roused her in the midst of this attempt to find her way to her duty, and her gentle "come in," was answered by the appearance of one, before whom all her doubts were wont to be laid. Her eyes brightened at the sight of Edmund.

"Can I speak with you, Fanny, for a few minutes?" said he.

"Yes, certainly."

"I want to consult. I want your opinion."

"My opinion!" she cried, shrinking from such a compliment, highly as it gratified her.

"Yes, your advice and opinion. I do not know what to do. This acting scheme gets worse and worse you see. They have chosen almost as bad a play as they could; and now, to complete the business, are going to ask the help of a young man very slightly known to any of us. This is the end of all the privacy and propriety which was talked about at first. I know no harm of Charles Maddox; but the excessive intimacy which must spring from his being admitted among us in this manner, is highly objectionable, the *more* than intimacy—the familiarity. I cannot think of it with any patience—and it does appear to me an evil of such magnitude as must, *if possible*, be prevented. Do not you see it in the same light?"

"Yes, but what can be done? Your brother is so determined?"

"There is but *one* thing to be done, Fanny. I must take Anhalt myself. I am well aware that nothing else will quiet Tom."

Fanny could not answer him.

"It is not at all what I like," he continued. "No man can like being driven into the *appearance* of such inconsistency. After

line 17: Maddox; but] **1814** Maddox, but

being known to oppose the scheme from the beginning, there is absurdity in the face of my joining them *now*, when they are exceeding their first plan in every respect; but I can think of no other alternative. Can you, Fanny?"

"No," said Fanny, slowly, "not immediately—but——"

"But what? I see your judgment is not with me. Think it a little over. Perhaps you are not so much aware as I am, of the mischief that *may*, of the unpleasantness that *must*, arise from a young man's being received in this manner—domesticated among us—authorized to come at all hours—and placed suddenly on a footing which must do away all restraints. To think only of the license which every rehearsal must tend to create. It is all very bad! Put yourself in Miss Crawford's place, Fanny. Consider what it would be to act Amelia with a stranger. She has a right to be felt for, because she evidently feels for herself. I heard enough of what she said to you last night, to understand her unwillingness to be acting with a stranger; and as she probably engaged in the part with different expectations—perhaps, without considering the subject enough to know what was likely to be, it would be ungenerous, it would be really wrong to expose her to it. Her feelings ought to be respected. Does not it strike you so, Fanny? You hesitate."

"I am sorry for Miss Crawford; but I am more sorry to see you drawn in to do what you had resolved against, and what you are known to think will be disagreeable to my uncle. It will be such a triumph to the others!"

"They will not have much cause of triumph, when they see how infamously I act. But, however, triumph there certainly will be, and I must brave it. But if I can be the means of

line 8: unpleasantness] **1814** unpleasantnesses   //   line 12: license] **1814** licence   //   line 27: others!"] **1814** others?"

restraining the publicity of the business, of limiting the exhibition, of concentrating our folly,[8] I shall be well repaid. As I
am now, I have no influence, I can do nothing; I have offended
them, and they will not hear me; but when I have put them
in good humour by this concession, I am not without hopes
of persuading them to confine the representation within a
much smaller circle than they are now in the high road
for. This will be a material gain. My object is to confine
it to Mrs. Rushworth and the Grants. Will not this be worth
gaining?"

"Yes, it will be a great point."

"But still it has not your approbation. Can you mention
any other measure by which I have a chance of doing equal
good?"

"No, I cannot think of any thing else."

"Give me your approbation, then, Fanny. I am not comfortable without it."

"Oh! cousin."

"If you are against me, I ought to distrust myself—and
yet—— But it is absolutely impossible to let Tom go on in
this way, riding about the country in quest of any body who
can be persuaded to act—no matter whom; the look of a
gentleman is to be enough. I thought *you* would have entered
more into Miss Crawford's feelings."

"No doubt she will be very glad. It must be a great relief
to her," said Fanny, trying for greater warmth of manner.

"She never appeared more amiable than in her behaviour
to you last night. It gave her a very strong claim on my good
will."

line 15: any thing] **1814** anything   //   line 19: —and yet—— But]
1814 —and yet. But   //   line 21: any body] **1814** anybody

"She *was* very kind indeed, and I am glad to have her spared.". . . .

She could not finish the generous effusion. Her conscience stopt her in the middle, but Edmund was satisfied.

"I shall walk down immediately after breakfast," said he, "and am sure of giving pleasure there. And now, dear Fanny, I will not interrupt you any longer. You want to be reading. But I could not be easy till I had spoken to you, and come to a decision. Sleeping or waking, my head has been full of this matter all night. It is an evil—but I am certainly making it less than it might be. If Tom is up, I shall go to him directly and get it over; and when we meet at breakfast we shall be all in high good humour at the prospect of acting the fool together with such unanimity. *You* in the meanwhile will be taking a trip into China, I suppose. How does Lord Macartney go on?[9]—(opening a volume on the table and then taking up some others.) And here are Crabbe's Tales, and the Idler, at hand to relieve you, if you tire of your great book. I admire your little establishment exceedingly; and as soon as I am gone, you will empty your head of all this nonsense of acting, and sit comfortably down to your table. But do not stay here to be cold."

He went; but there was no reading, no China, no composure for Fanny. He had told her the most extraordinary, the most inconceivable, the most unwelcome news; and she could think of nothing else. To be acting! After all his objections—objections so just and so public! After all that she had heard him say, and seen him look, and known him to be feeling. Could it be possible? Edmund so inconsistent. Was he

line 1: kind indeed, and] **1814** kind, indeed, and   //   line 2: spared." . . . .] **1814** spared."   //   line 19: your little] **1814** you little   //   line 21: your table.] **1814** you table.

not deceiving himself? Was he not wrong? Alas! it was all Miss Crawford's doing. She had seen her influence in every speech, and was miserable. The doubts and alarms as to her own conduct, which had previously distressed her, and which had all slept while she listened to him, were become of little consequence now. This deeper anxiety swallowed them up. Things should take their course; she cared not how it ended. Her cousins might attack, but could hardly tease her. She was beyond their reach; and if at last obliged to yield—no matter—it was all misery *now*.

line 8: tease] **1814** teize

Chapter 17

I T was, indeed, a triumphant day to Mr. Bertram and Maria. Such a victory over Edmund's discretion had been beyond their hopes, and was most delightful. There was no longer any thing to disturb them in their darling project, and they congratulated each other in private on the jealous weakness to which they attributed the change, with all the glee of feelings gratified in every way. Edmund might still look grave, and say he did not like the scheme in general, and must disapprove the play in particular; their point was gained; he was to act, and he was driven to it by the force of selfish inclinations only. Edmund had descended from that moral elevation which he had maintained before, and they were both as much the better as the happier for the descent.

They behaved very well, however, *to him* on the occasion, betraying no exultation beyond the lines about the corners of the mouth, and seemed to think it as great an escape to be quit of the intrusion of Charles Maddox, as if they had been forced into admitting him against their inclination. "To have it quite in their own family circle was what they had particularly wished. A stranger among them would have been the destruction of all their comfort," and when Edmund, pursuing that idea, gave a hint of his hope as to the limitation of the audience, they were ready, in the complaisance of the moment, to promise any thing. It was all good

line 4: any thing.] **1814** anything.   //   line 24: any thing.] **1814** anything.

humour and encouragement. Mrs. Norris offered to contrive his dress, Mr. Yates assured him, that Anhalt's last scene with the Baron admitted a good deal of action and emphasis,[1] and Mr. Rushworth undertook to count his speeches.

"Perhaps," said Tom, "*Fanny* may be more disposed to oblige us now. Perhaps you may persuade *her*."

"No, she is quite determined. She certainly will not act."

"Oh! very well." And not another word was said: but Fanny felt herself again in danger, and her indifference to the danger was beginning to fail her already.

There were not fewer smiles at the parsonage than at the park on this change in Edmund; Miss Crawford looked very lovely in her's, and entered with such an instantaneous renewal of cheerfulness into the whole affair, as could have but one effect on him. "He was certainly right in respecting such feelings; he was glad he had determined on it." And the morning wore away in satisfactions very sweet, if not very sound. One advantage resulted from it to Fanny; at the earnest request of Miss Crawford, Mrs. Grant had with her usual good humour agreed to undertake the part for which Fanny had been wanted—and this was all that occurred to gladden *her* heart during the day; and even this, when imparted by Edmund, brought a pang with it, for it was Miss Crawford to whom she was obliged, it was Miss Crawford whose kind exertions were to excite her gratitude, and whose merit in making them was spoken of with a glow of admiration. She was safe; but peace and safety were unconnected here. Her mind had been never farther from peace. She could not feel that she had done wrong herself, but she was disquieted in every other way. Her heart and her judgment were

line 3: Baron admitted] **1814** Baron, admitted // line 8: very well." And] **1814** very well. And // line 8: said: but] **1814** said; but // line 27: unconnected] **1814** connected

equally against Edmund's decision; she could not acquit his unsteadiness; and his happiness under it made her wretched. She was full of jealousy and agitation. Miss Crawford came with looks of gaiety which seemed an insult, with friendly expressions towards herself which she could hardly answer calmly. Every body around her was gay and busy, prosperous and important, each had their object of interest, their part, their dress, their favourite scene, their friends and confederates, all were finding employment in consultations and comparisons, or diversion in the playful conceits they suggested. She alone was sad and insignificant; she had no share in any thing; she might go or stay, she might be in the midst of their noise, or retreat from it to the solitude of the East room, without being seen or missed. She could almost think any thing would have been preferable to this. Mrs. Grant was of consequence; *her* good nature had honourable mention— her taste and her time were considered—her presence was wanted—she was sought for and attended, and praised; and Fanny was at first in some danger of envying her the character she had accepted. But reflection brought better feelings, and shewed her that Mrs. Grant was entitled to respect, which could never have belonged to *her*, and that had she received even the greatest, she could never have been easy in joining a scheme which, considering only her uncle, she must condemn altogether.

Fanny's heart was not absolutely the only saddened one amongst them, as she soon began to acknowledge herself.— Julia was a sufferer too, though not quite so blamelessly.

Henry Crawford had trifled with her feelings; but she had very long allowed and even sought his attentions, with a jealousy of her sister so reasonable as ought to have been their

line 13: East room,] **1814** east room,   //   line 26: saddened] **1814** sadden'd

cure; and now that the conviction of his preference for Maria had been forced on her, she submitted to it without any alarm for Maria's situation, or any endeavour at rational tranquillity for herself.—She either sat in gloomy silence, wrapt in such gravity as nothing could subdue, no curiosity touch, no wit amuse; or allowing the attentions of Mr. Yates, was talking with forced gaiety to him alone, and ridiculing the acting of the others.

For a day or two after the affront was given, Henry Crawford had endeavoured to do it away by the usual attack of gallantry and compliment, but he had not cared enough about it to persevere against a few repulses; and becoming soon too busy with his play to have time for more than one flirtation, he grew indifferent to the quarrel, or rather thought it a lucky occurrence, as quietly putting an end to what might ere long have raised expectations in more than Mrs. Grant.— She was not pleased to see Julia excluded from the play, and sitting by disregarded; but as it was not a matter which really involved her happiness, as Henry must be the best judge of his own, and as he did assure her, with a most persuasive smile, that neither he nor Julia had ever had a serious thought of each other, she could only renew her former caution as to the elder sister, entreat him not to risk his tranquillity by too much admiration[2] there, and then gladly take her share in any thing that brought cheerfulness to the young people in general, and that did so particularly promote the pleasure of the two so dear to her.

"I rather wonder Julia is not in love with Henry," was her observation to Mary.

"I dare say she is," replied Mary, coldly. "I imagine both sisters are."

line 23: sister, entreat] **1814** Sister, intreat

"Both! no, no, that must not be. Do not give him a hint of it. Think of Mr. Rushworth."

"You had better tell Miss Bertram to think of Mr. Rushworth. It may do *her* some good. I often think of Mr. Rushworth's property and independence, and wish them in other hands—but I never think of *him*. A man might represent the county with such an estate; a man might escape a profession and represent the county."

"I dare say he *will* be in parliament soon. When Sir Thomas comes, I dare say he will be in for some borough, but there has been nobody to put him in the way of doing any thing yet."[3]

"Sir Thomas is to achieve mighty things when he comes home," said Mary, after a pause. "Do you remember Hawkins Browne's 'Address to Tobacco,' in imitation of Pope?[4]—

> "Blest leaf! whose aromatic gales dispense
> "To Templars modesty, to Parsons sense."

I will parody them:

> Blest Knight! whose dictatorial looks dispense
> To Children affluence, to Rushworth sense.

Will not that do, Mrs. Grant? Every thing seems to depend upon Sir Thomas's return."

"You will find his consequence very just and reasonable when you see him in his family, I assure you. I do not think we do so well without him. He has a fine dignified manner, which suits the head of such a house, and keeps every body in

line 14: Browne's 'Address to Tobacco,' in] **1814** Browne's address to Tobacco, in // lines 14–20: imitation of Pope?—] **1814** *This is presented as*: imitation of Pope?—'Blest leaf, whose aromatic gales dispense, to Templars modesty, to Parsons sense.' I will parody them. Blest Knight! whose dictatorial looks dispense, to Children affluence, to Rushworth sense Will not that do, Mrs. Grant?

their place. Lady Bertram seems more of a cipher now than when he is at home; and nobody else can keep Mrs. Norris in order. But, Mary, do not fancy that Maria Bertram cares for Henry. I am sure *Julia* does not, or she would not have flirted as she did last night with Mr. Yates; and though he and Maria are very good friends, I think she likes Sotherton too well to be inconstant."

"I would not give much for Mr. Rushworth's chance, if Henry stept in before the articles were signed."[5]

"If you have such a suspicion, something must be done, and as soon as the play is all over, we will talk to him seriously, and make him know his own mind; and if he means nothing, we will send him off, though he is Henry, for a time."

Julia *did* suffer, however, though Mrs. Grant discerned it not, and though it escaped the notice of many of her own family likewise. She had loved, she did love still, and she had all the suffering which a warm temper and a high spirit were likely to endure under the disappointment of a dear, though irrational hope, with a strong sense of ill-usage. Her heart was sore and angry, and she was capable only of angry consolations. The sister with whom she was used to be on easy terms, was now become her greatest enemy; they were alienated from each other, and Julia was not superior to the hope of some distressing end to the attentions which were still carrying on there, some punishment to Maria for conduct so shameful towards herself, as well as towards Mr. Rushworth. With no material fault of temper, or difference of opinion, to prevent their being very good friends while their interests were the same, the sisters, under such a trial as this, had not affection or principle enough to make them merciful or just, to give them honour or compassion. Maria felt her triumph, and pursued

line 1: cipher] **1814** cypher   //   line 12: mind; and] **1814** mind, and

her purpose careless of Julia; and Julia could never see Maria distinguished by Henry Crawford, without trusting that it would create jealousy, and bring a public disturbance at last.

Fanny saw and pitied much of this in Julia; but there was no outward fellowship between them. Julia made no communication, and Fanny took no liberties. They were two solitary sufferers, or connected only by Fanny's consciousness.

The inattention of the two brothers and the aunt to Julia's discomposure, and their blindness to its true cause, must be imputed to the fulness of their own minds. They were totally preoccupied. Tom was engrossed by the concerns of his theatre, and saw nothing that did not immediately relate to it. Edmund, between his theatrical and his real part, between Miss Crawford's claims and his own conduct, between love and consistency, was equally unobservant; and Mrs. Norris was too busy in contriving and directing the general little matters of the company, superintending their various dresses with economical expedient, for which nobody thanked her, and saving, with delighted integrity, half-a-crown[6] here and there to the absent Sir Thomas, to have leisure for watching the behaviour, or guarding the happiness of his daughters.

line 8: aunt to] **1814** aunt, to   //   line 18: expedient, for] **1814** expedient for   //   line 19: saving, with] **1814** saving with

Chapter 18

EVERY thing was now in a regular train; theatre, actors, actresses, and dresses, were all getting forward: but though no other great impediments arose, Fanny found, before many days were past, that it was not all uninterrupted enjoyment to the party themselves, and that she had not to witness the continuance of such unanimity and delight, as had been almost too much for her at first. Every body began to have their vexation. Edmund had many. Entirely against *his* judgment, a scene painter arrived from town,[1] and was at work, much to the increase of the expenses, and what was worse, of the eclat[2] of their proceedings; and his brother, instead of being really guided by him as to the privacy of the representation, was giving an invitation to every family who came in his way. Tom himself began to fret over the scene painter's slow progress, and to feel the miseries of waiting. He had learned his part—all his parts—for he took every trifling one that could be united with the Butler, and began to be impatient to be acting; and every day thus unemployed, was tending to increase his sense of the insignificance of all his parts together, and make him more ready to regret that some other play had not been chosen.

Fanny, being always a very courteous listener, and often the only listener at hand, came in for the complaints and distresses of most of them. *She* knew that Mr. Yates was in

line 2: forward: but] **1814** forward; but // line 17: Butler, and] **1814** butler and

general thought to rant dreadfully, that Mr. Yates was disappointed in Henry Crawford, that Tom Bertram spoke so quick he would be unintelligible, that Mrs. Grant spoilt every thing by laughing, that Edmund was behind-hand with his part, and that it was misery to have any thing to do with Mr. Rushworth, who was wanting a prompter through every speech. She knew, also, that poor Mr. Rushworth could seldom get any body to rehearse with him; *his* complaint came before her as well as the rest; and so decided to her eye was her cousin Maria's avoidance of him, and so needlessly often the rehearsal of the first scene between her and Mr. Crawford,[3] that she had soon all the terror of other complaints from *him.*—So far from being all satisfied and all enjoying, she found every body requiring something they had not, and giving occasion of discontent to the others.—Every body had a part either too long or too short;—nobody would attend as they ought, nobody would remember on which side they were to come in—nobody but the complainer would observe any directions.

Fanny believed herself to derive as much innocent enjoyment from the play as any of them;—Henry Crawford acted well, and it was a pleasure to *her* to creep into the theatre, and attend the rehearsal of the first act—in spite of the feelings it excited in some speeches for Maria.[4]—Maria she also thought acted well—too well;—and after the first rehearsal or two, Fanny began to be their only audience—and sometimes as prompter, sometimes as spectator—was often very useful.—As far as she could judge, Mr. Crawford was considerably the best actor of all; he had more confidence than Edmund, more judgment than Tom, more talent and taste than Mr. Yates.—She did not like him as a man, but she must

line 21: play] **1814** Play   //   line 22: theatre,] **1814** Theatre,   //   line 24: Maria she] **1814** Maria, she admit him to be the best actor, and on this point there were not many who differed from her. Mr. Yates, indeed, exclaimed against his tameness and insipidity—and the day came at last, when Mr. Rushworth turned to her with a black look, and said—"Do you think there is any thing so very fine in all this? For the life and soul of me, I cannot admire him;—and between ourselves, to see such an undersized, little, mean-looking man, set up for a fine actor, is very ridiculous in my opinion."

From this moment there was a return of his former jealousy, which Maria, from increasing hopes of Crawford, was at little pains to remove; and the chances of Mr. Rushworth's ever attaining to the knowledge of his two and forty speeches became much less. As to his ever making any thing *tolerable* of them, nobody had the smallest idea of that except his mother—*She*, indeed, regretted that his part was not more considerable, and deferred coming over to Mansfield till they were forward enough in their rehearsal to comprehend all his scenes, but the others aspired at nothing beyond his remembering the catchword,⁵ and the first line of his speech, and being able to follow the prompter through the rest. Fanny, in her pity and kind-heartedness, was at great pains to teach him how to learn, giving him all the helps and directions in her power, trying to make an artificial memory for him, and learning every word of his part herself, but without his being much the forwarder.

Many uncomfortable, anxious, apprehensive feelings she certainly had; but with all these, and other claims on her time and attention, she was as far from finding herself without employment or utility amongst them, as without a companion

line 10: moment there] **1814** moment, there // line 11: Maria, from] **1814** Maria from // line 16: mother] **1814** Mother // line 22: kind-heartedness,] **1814** kindheartedness,

in uneasiness; quite as far from having no demand on her leisure as on her compassion. The gloom of her first anticipations was proved to have been unfounded. She was occasionally useful to all; she was perhaps as much at peace as any.

There was a great deal of needle-work to be done moreover, in which her help was wanted; and that Mrs. Norris thought her quite as well off as the rest, was evident by the manner in which she claimed it: "Come Fanny," she cried, "these are fine times for you, but you must not be always walking from one room to the other and doing the lookings on, at your ease, in this way,—I want you here.—I have been slaving myself till I can hardly stand, to contrive Mr. Rushworth's cloak without sending for any more satin; and now I think you may give me your help in putting it together.—There are but three seams, you may do them in a trice.—It would be lucky for me if I had nothing but the executive part[6] to do.—*You* are best off, I can tell you; but if nobody did more than *you*, we should not get on very fast."

Fanny took the work very quietly, without attempting any defence; but her kinder aunt Bertram observed on her behalf,

"One cannot wonder, sister, that Fanny *should* be delighted; it is all new to her, you know,—you and I used to be very fond of a play ourselves—and so am I still;—and as soon as I am a little more at leisure, *I* mean to look in at their rehearsals too. What is the play about, Fanny, you have never told me?"

"Oh! sister, pray do not ask her now; for Fanny is not one of those who can talk and work at the same time.—It is about Lovers' Vows."

line 5: needle-work] **1814** needlework // line 6: wanted; and] **1814** wanted, and // line 8: it: "Come] **1814** it, "Come // line 17: you; but] **1814** you, but // line 19: quietly, without] **1814** quietly without // line 21: sister,] **1814** Sister, // line 24: rehearsals] **1814** Rehearsals // line 28: Lovers' Vows."] **1814** Lovers Vows."

"I believe," said Fanny to her aunt Bertram, "there will be three acts rehearsed to-morrow evening, and that will give you an opportunity of seeing all the actors at once."

"You had better stay till the curtain is hung," interposed Mrs. Norris—"the curtain will be hung in a day or two,—there is very little sense in a play without a curtain—and I am much mistaken if you do not find it draw up into very handsome festoons."[7]

Lady Bertram seemed quite resigned to waiting.—Fanny did not share her aunt's composure; she thought of the morrow a great deal,—for if the three acts were rehearsed, Edmund and Miss Crawford would then be acting together for the first time;—the third act would bring a scene between them[8] which interested her most particularly, and which she was longing and dreading to see how they would perform. The whole subject of it was love—a marriage of love was to be described by the gentleman, and very little short of a declaration of love be made by the lady.

She had read, and read the scene again with many painful, many wondering emotions, and looked forward to their representation of it as a circumstance almost too interesting. She did not *believe* they had yet rehearsed it, even in private.

The morrow came, the plan for the evening continued, and Fanny's consideration of it did not become less agitated. She worked very diligently under her aunt's directions, but her diligence and her silence concealed a very absent, anxious mind; and about noon she made her escape with her work to the East room, that she might have no concern in another, and, as she deemed it, most unnecessary rehearsal of the first

line 1: believe," said] **1814** believe" said // line 2: acts] **1814** Acts // line 5: a day or two,] **1814** a day of two, // line 22: rehearsed it, even] **1814** rehearsed it even // line 29: East room,] **1814** east room,

act, which Henry Crawford was just proposing, desirous at once of having her time to herself, and of avoiding the sight of Mr. Rushworth. A glimpse, as she passed through the hall, of the two ladies walking up from the parsonage, made no change in her wish of retreat, and she worked and meditated in the East room, undisturbed, for a quarter of an hour, when a gentle tap at the door was followed by the entrance of Miss Crawford.

"Am I right?—Yes; this is the East room. My dear Miss Price, I beg your pardon, but I have made my way to you on purpose to entreat your help."

Fanny, quite surprised, endeavoured to show herself mistress of the room by her civilities, and looked at the bright bars of her empty grate with concern.

"Thank you—I am quite warm, very warm. Allow me to stay here a little while, and do have the goodness to hear me my third act. I have brought my book, and if you would but rehearse it with me, I should be *so* obliged! I came here to-day intending to rehearse it with Edmund—by ourselves—against the evening, but he is not in the way;[9] and if he *were*, I do not think I could go through it with *him*, till I have hardened myself a little, for really there *is* a speech or two—You will be so good, won't you?"

Fanny was most civil in her assurances, though she could not give them in a very steady voice.

"Have you ever happened to look at the part I mean?" continued Miss Crawford, opening her book. "Here it is. I did not think much of it at first—but, upon my word—. There, look at *that* speech, and *that*, and *that*. How am I ever to look him in the face and say such things? Could you do it? But then he is your cousin, which makes all the difference.

line 6: East room,] **1814** east room,   //   line 9: the East] **1814** the east   //   line 11: entreat] **1814** intreat   //   line 12: show] **1814** shew

You must rehearse it with me, that I may fancy *you* him, and get on by degrees. You *have* a look of *his* sometimes."

"Have I?—I will do my best with the greatest readiness— but I must *read* the part, for I can *say* very little of it."

"*None* of it, I suppose. You are to have the book of course. Now for it. We must have two chairs at hand for you to bring forward to the front of the stage.[10] There—very good school-room chairs, not made for a theatre, I dare say; much more fitted for little girls to sit and kick their feet against when they are learning a lesson. What would your governess and your uncle say to see them used for such a purpose? Could Sir Thomas look in upon us just now, he would bless himself, for we are rehearsing all over the house. Yates is storming away in the dining room. I heard him as I came up stairs, and the theatre is engaged of course by those indefatigable rehearsers, Agatha and Frederick. If *they* are not perfect, I *shall* be surprised. By the bye, I looked in upon them five minutes ago, and it happened to be exactly at one of the times when they were trying *not* to embrace,[11] and Mr. Rushworth was with me. I thought he began to look a little queer, so I turned it off as well as I could, by whispering to him, 'We shall have an excellent Agatha, there is something so *maternal* in her manner, so completely *maternal* in her voice and countenance.' Was not that well done of me? He brightened up directly. Now for my soliloquy."

She began, and Fanny joined in with all the modest feeling which the idea of representing Edmund was so strongly calculated to inspire; but with looks and voice so truly feminine, as to be no very good picture of a man. With such an Anhalt, however, Miss Crawford had courage enough, and they had got through half the scene, when a tap at the door brought a

line 16: Frederick.] **1814** Frederic.

pause, and the entrance of Edmund the next moment, suspended it all.

Surprise, consciousness, and pleasure, appeared in each of the three on this unexpected meeting; and as Edmund was come on the very same business that had brought Miss Crawford, consciousness and pleasure were likely to be more than momentary in *them*. He too had his book, and was seeking Fanny, to ask her to rehearse with him, and help him to prepare for the evening, without knowing Miss Crawford to be in the house; and great was the joy and animation of being thus thrown together—of comparing schemes—and sympathizing in praise of Fanny's kind offices.

She could not equal them in their warmth. *Her* spirits sank under the glow of theirs, and she felt herself becoming too nearly nothing to both, to have any comfort in having been sought by either. They must now rehearse together. Edmund proposed, urged, entreated it—till the lady, not very unwilling at first, could refuse no longer—and Fanny was wanted only to prompt and observe them. She was invested, indeed, with the office of judge and critic, and earnestly desired to exercise it and tell them all their faults; but from doing so every feeling within her shrank, she could not, would not, dared not attempt it; had she been otherwise qualified for criticism, her conscience must have restrained her from venturing at disapprobation. She believed herself to feel too much of it in the aggregate for honesty or safety in particulars. To prompt them must be enough for her; and it was sometimes *more* than enough; for she could not always pay attention to the book. In watching them she forgot herself; and agitated by the increasing spirit of Edmund's manner, had once closed

line 8: help him to prepare] **1814** help him prepare   //   line 12: sympathizing] **1814** sympathising   //   line 29: she forgot herself;] **1814** she forget herself;

the page and turned away exactly as he wanted help. It was imputed to very reasonable weariness, and she was thanked and pitied; but she deserved their pity, more than she hoped they would ever surmise. At last the scene was over, and Fanny forced herself to add her praise to the compliments each was giving the other; and when again alone and able to recall the whole, she was inclined to believe their performance would, indeed, have such nature and feeling in it, as must ensure their credit, and make it a very suffering exhibition to herself. Whatever might be its effect, however, she must stand the brunt of it again that very day.

The first regular rehearsal of the three first acts was certainly to take place in the evening; Mrs. Grant and the Crawfords were engaged to return for that purpose as soon as they could after dinner; and every one concerned was looking forward with eagerness. There seemed a general diffusion of cheerfulness on the occasion; Tom was enjoying such an advance towards the end, Edmund was in spirits from the morning's rehearsal, and little vexations seemed every where smoothed away. All were alert and impatient; the ladies moved soon, the gentlemen soon followed them,[12] and with the exception of Lady Bertram, Mrs. Norris, and Julia, every body was in the theatre at an early hour, and having lighted it up as well as its unfinished state admitted, were waiting only the arrival of Mrs. Grant and the Crawfords to begin.

They did not wait long for the Crawfords, but there was no Mrs. Grant. She could not come. Dr. Grant, professing an indisposition, for which he had little credit with his fair sister-in-law, could not spare his wife.

"Dr. Grant is ill," said she, with mock solemnity. "He has been ill ever since he did not eat any of the pheasant to day. He

line 8: it, as] **1814** it as

fancied it tough—sent away his plate—and has been suffering ever since."

Here was disappointment! Mrs. Grant's non-attendance was sad indeed. Her pleasant manners and cheerful conformity made her always valuable amongst them—but *now* she was absolutely necessary.[13] They could not act, they could not rehearse with any satisfaction without her. The comfort of the whole evening was destroyed. What was to be done? Tom, as Cottager, was in despair. After a pause of perplexity, some eyes began to be turned towards Fanny, and a voice or two, to say, "If Miss Price would be so good as to *read* the part." She was immediately surrounded by supplications, every body asked it, even Edmund said, "Do Fanny, if it is not *very* disagreeable to you."

But Fanny still hung back. She could not endure the idea of it. Why was not Miss Crawford to be applied to as well? Or why had not she rather gone to her own room, as she had felt to be safest, instead of attending the rehearsal at all? She had known it would irritate and distress her—she had known it her duty to keep away. She was properly punished.

"You have only to *read* the part," said Henry Crawford, with renewed entreaty.

"And I do believe she can say every word of it," added Maria, "for she could put Mrs. Grant right the other day in twenty places. Fanny, I am sure you know the part."

Fanny could not say she did *not*—and as they all persevered—as Edmund repeated his wish, and with a look of even fond dependence on her good nature, she must yield. She would do her best. Every body was satisfied—and she was left to the tremors of a most palpitating heart, while the others prepared to begin.

line 22: entreaty.] **1814** intreaty.

They *did* begin—and being too much engaged in their own noise, to be struck by unusual noise[14] in the other part of the house, had proceeded some way, when the door of the room was thrown open, and Julia appearing at it, with a face all aghast, exclaimed, "My father is come! He is in the hall at this moment."

END OF VOLUME I

MANSFIELD PARK

Volume II

Chapter 1

How is the consternation of the party to be described? To the greater number it was a moment of absolute horror. Sir Thomas in the house! All felt the instantaneous conviction. Not a hope of imposition or mistake was harboured any where. Julia's looks were an evidence of the fact that made it indisputable; and after the first starts and exclamations, not a word was spoken for half a minute; each with an altered countenance was looking at some other, and almost each was feeling it a stroke the most unwelcome, most ill-timed, most appalling! Mr. Yates might consider it only as a vexatious interruption for the evening, and Mr. Rushworth might imagine it a blessing, but every other heart was sinking under some degree of self-condemnation or undefined alarm, every other heart was suggesting "What will become of us? what is to be done now?" It was a terrible pause; and terrible to every ear were the corroborating sounds of opening doors and passing footsteps.

Julia was the first to move and speak again. Jealousy and bitterness had been suspended: selfishness was lost in the common cause; but at the moment of her appearance, Frederick was listening with looks of devotion to Agatha's narrative, and pressing her hand to his heart,[1] and as soon as she could notice this, and see that, in spite of the shock of her words, he still kept his station and retained her sister's hand, her

line 21: narrative, and] **1814** narrative and   //   line 23: this, and] **1814** this and   //   line 23: that, in] **1814** that in

wounded heart swelled again with injury, and looking as red as she had been white before, she turned out of the room, saying "*I* need not be afraid of appearing before him."

Her going roused the rest; and at the same moment, the two brothers stepped forward, feeling the necessity of doing something. A very few words between them were sufficient. The case admitted no difference of opinion; they must go to the drawing-room directly. Maria joined them with the same intent, just then the stoutest of the three; for the very circumstance which had driven Julia away, was to her the sweetest support. Henry Crawford's retaining her hand at such a moment, a moment of such peculiar proof and importance, was worth ages of doubt and anxiety. She hailed it as an earnest of the most serious determination, and was equal even to encounter her father. They walked off, utterly heedless of Mr. Rushworth's repeated question of, "Shall I go too?—Had not I better go too?—Will not it be right for me to go too?" but they were no sooner through the door than Henry Crawford undertook to answer the anxious inquiry, and encouraging him by all means to pay his respects to Sir Thomas without delay, sent him after the others with delighted haste.

Fanny was left with only the Crawfords and Mr. Yates. She had been quite overlooked by her cousins; and as her own opinion of her claims on Sir Thomas's affection was much too humble to give her any idea of classing herself with his children, she was glad to remain behind and gain a little breathing time. Her agitation and alarm exceeded all that was endured by the rest, by the right of a disposition which not even innocence could keep from suffering. She was nearly fainting: all her former habitual dread of her uncle was returning, and with it compassion for him and for almost every one

line 23: cousins; and] **1814** cousins, and

of the party on the development[2] before him—with solicitude on Edmund's account indescribable. She had found a seat, where in excessive trembling she was enduring all these fearful thoughts, while the other three, no longer under any restraint, were giving vent to their feelings of vexation, lamenting over such an unlooked-for premature arrival as a most untoward event, and without mercy wishing poor Sir Thomas had been twice as long on his passage, or were still in Antigua.

The Crawfords were more warm on the subject than Mr. Yates, from better understanding the family and judging more clearly of the mischief that must ensue. The ruin of the play was to them a certainty, they felt the total destruction of the scheme to be inevitably at hand; while Mr. Yates considered it only as a temporary interruption, a disaster for the evening, and could even suggest the possibility of the rehearsal being renewed after tea, when the bustle of receiving Sir Thomas were over and he might be at leisure to be amused by it. The Crawfords laughed at the idea; and having soon agreed on the propriety of their walking quietly home and leaving the family to themselves, proposed Mr. Yates's accompanying them and spending the evening at the Parsonage. But Mr. Yates, having never been with those who thought much of parental claims, or family confidence,[3] could not perceive that any thing of the kind was necessary, and therefore, thanking them, said, "he preferred remaining where he was that he might pay his respects to the old gentleman handsomely since he *was* come; and besides, he did not think it would be fair by the others to have every body run away."

Fanny was just beginning to collect herself, and to feel that if she staid longer behind it might seem disrespectful,

line 1: before him] **1814** before them   //   line 22: Yates, having] **1814** Yates having   //   line 30: herself, and] **1814** herself and

when this point was settled, and being commissioned with the brother and sister's apology, saw them preparing to go as she quitted the room herself to perform the dreadful duty of appearing before her uncle.

Too soon did she find herself at the drawing-room door, and after pausing a moment for what she knew would not come, for a courage which the outside of no door had ever supplied to her, she turned the lock in desperation, and the lights of the drawing-room and all the collected family were before her. As she entered, her own name caught her ear. Sir Thomas was at that moment looking round him, and saying "But where is Fanny?—Why do not I see my little Fanny?" And on perceiving her, came forward with a kindness which astonished and penetrated her, calling her his dear Fanny, kissing her affectionately, and observing with decided pleasure how much she was grown! Fanny knew not how to feel, nor where to look. She was quite oppressed. He had never been so kind, so *very* kind to her in his life. His manner seemed changed; his voice was quick[4] from the agitation of joy, and all that had been awful in his dignity seemed lost in tenderness. He led her nearer the light and looked at her again—inquired particularly after her health, and then correcting himself, observed, that he need *not* inquire, for her appearance spoke sufficiently on that point. A fine blush having succeeded the previous paleness of her face, he was justified in his belief of her equal improvement in health and beauty. He inquired next after her family, especially William; and his kindness altogether was such as made her reproach herself for loving him so little, and thinking his return a misfortune; and when, on having courage to lift her eyes to his face, she saw that he was grown thinner and had the burnt,

line 2: sister's] **1814** sisters

fagged, worn look of fatigue and a hot climate, every tender feeling was increased, and she was miserable in considering how much unsuspected vexation was probably ready to burst on him.

Sir Thomas was indeed the life of the party, who at his suggestion now seated themselves round the fire. He had the best right to be the talker; and the delight of his sensations in being again in his own house, in the centre of his family, after such a separation, made him communicative and chatty in a very unusual degree; and he was ready to give every information as to his voyage, and answer every question of his two sons almost before it was put. His business in Antigua had latterly been prosperously rapid, and he came directly from Liverpool,[5] having had an opportunity of making his passage thither in a private vessel, instead of waiting for the packet; and all the little particulars of his proceedings and events, his arrivals and departures, were most promptly delivered, as he sat by Lady Bertram and looked with heartfelt satisfaction on the faces around him—interrupting himself more than once, however, to remark on his good fortune in finding them all at home—coming unexpectedly as he did—all collected together exactly as he could have wished, but dared not depend on. Mr. Rushworth was not forgotten; a most friendly reception and warmth of hand-shaking had already met him, and with pointed attention he was now included in the objects most intimately connected with Mansfield. There was nothing disagreeable in Mr. Rushworth's appearance, and Sir Thomas was liking him already.

By not one of the circle was he listened to with such unbroken unalloyed enjoyment as by his wife, who was really extremely happy to see him, and whose feelings were so

line 8: family, after] **1814** family after

warmed by his sudden arrival, as to place her nearer agitation than she had been for the last twenty years. She had been *almost* fluttered for a few minutes, and still remained so sensibly animated as to put away her work, move Pug from her side, and give all her attention and all the rest of her sofa to her husband. She had no anxieties for any body to cloud *her* pleasure; her own time had been irreproachably spent during his absence; she had done a great deal of carpet work[6] and made many yards of fringe; and she would have answered as freely for the good conduct and useful pursuits of all the young people as for her own. It was so agreeable to her to see him again, and hear him talk, to have her ear amused and her whole comprehension filled by his narratives, that she began particularly to feel how dreadfully she must have missed him, and how impossible it would have been for her to bear a lengthened absence.[7]

Mrs. Norris was by no means to be compared in happiness to her sister. Not that *she* was incommoded by many fears of Sir Thomas's disapprobation when the present state of his house should be known, for her judgment had been so blinded, that except by the instinctive caution with which she had whisked away Mr. Rushworth's pink satin cloak as her brother-in-law entered, she could hardly be said to shew any sign of alarm; but she was vexed by the *manner* of his return. It had left her nothing to do. Instead of being sent for out of the room, and seeing him first, and having to spread the happy news through the house, Sir Thomas, with a very reasonable dependance perhaps on the nerves of his wife and children, had sought no confidant but the butler, and had been following him almost instantaneously into the drawing-room. Mrs. Norris felt herself defrauded of an office on which she

line 21: blinded, that] **1814** blinded that // line 22: whisked] **1814** whisk'd // line 27: Sir Thomas, with] **1814** Sir Thomas with

had always depended, whether his arrival or his death were to be the thing unfolded; and was now trying to be in a bustle without having any thing to bustle about, and labouring to be important where nothing was wanted but tranquillity and silence. Would Sir Thomas have consented to eat, she might have gone to the house-keeper with troublesome directions, and insulted the footmen with injunctions of dispatch; but Sir Thomas resolutely declined all dinner; he would take nothing, nothing till tea came—he would rather wait for tea. Still Mrs. Norris was at intervals urging something different, and in the most interesting moment of his passage to England, when the alarm of a French privateer[8] was at the height, she burst through his recital with the proposal of soup. "Sure, my dear Sir Thomas, a basin of soup would be a much better thing for you than tea. Do have a basin of soup."

Sir Thomas could not be provoked. "Still the same anxiety for every body's comfort, my dear Mrs. Norris," was his answer. "But indeed I would rather have nothing but tea."

"Well then, Lady Bertram, suppose you speak for tea directly, suppose you hurry Baddeley a little, he seems behind hand to-night." She carried this point, and Sir Thomas's narrative proceeded.

At length there was a pause. His immediate communications were exhausted, and it seemed enough to be looking joyfully around him, now at one, now at another of the beloved circle; but the pause was not long: in the elation of her spirits Lady Bertram became talkative, and what were the sensations of her children upon hearing her say, "How do you think the young people have been amusing themselves lately, Sir Thomas? They have been acting. We have been all alive with acting."

line 14: basin] **1814** bason   //   line 15: basin] **1814** bason   //   line 30: lately, Sir Thomas?] **1814** lately Sir Thomas?

"Indeed! and what have you been acting?"

"Oh! They'll tell you all about it."

"The *all* will be soon told," cried Tom hastily, and with affected unconcern; "but it is not worth while to bore my father with it now. You will hear enough of it to-morrow, sir. We have just been trying, by way of doing something, and amusing my mother, just within the last week, to get up a few scenes, a mere trifle. We have had such incessant rains almost since October began,[9] that we have been nearly confined to the house for days together. I have hardly taken out a gun since the 3d. Tolerable sport the first three days, but there has been no attempting any thing since. The first day I went over Mansfield Wood, and Edmund took the copses beyond Easton, and we brought home six brace[10] between us, and might each have killed six times as many; but we respect your pheasants, sir, I assure you, as much as you could desire. I do not think you will find your woods by any means worse stocked than they were. *I* never saw Mansfield Wood so full of pheasants in my life as this year. I hope you will take a day's sport there yourself, sir, soon."

For the present the danger was over, and Fanny's sick feelings subsided; but when tea was soon afterwards brought in, and Sir Thomas, getting up, said that he found he could not be any longer in the house without just looking into his own dear room, every agitation was returning. He was gone before any thing had been said to prepare him for the change he must find there; and a pause of alarm followed his disappearance. Edmund was the first to speak:

"Something must be done," said he.

"It is time to think of our visitors," said Maria, still feeling her hand pressed to Henry Crawford's heart, and caring little

line 5: to-morrow, sir.] **1814** to-morrow, Sir.   //   line 16: pheasants, sir,] **1814** pheasants, Sir,   //   line 20: yourself, sir,] **1814** yourself, Sir,

for any thing else.—"Where did you leave Miss Crawford, Fanny?"

Fanny told of their departure, and delivered their message. "Then poor Yates is all alone," cried Tom. "I will go and fetch him. He will be no bad assistant when it all comes out."

To the Theatre he went, and reached it just in time to witness the first meeting of his father and his friend. Sir Thomas had been a good deal surprized to find candles burning in his room; and on casting his eye round it, to see other symptoms of recent habitation, and a general air of confusion in the furniture. The removal of the book-case from before the billiard room door struck him especially, but he had scarcely more than time to feel astonished at all this, before there were sounds from the billiard room to astonish him still further. Some one was talking there in a very loud accent—he did not know the voice—*more* than talking—almost hallooing. He stept to the door, rejoicing at that moment in having the means of immediate communication, and opening it, found himself on the stage of a theatre, and opposed to a ranting young man, who appeared likely to knock him down backwards. At the very moment of Yates perceiving Sir Thomas, and giving perhaps the very best start[11] he had ever given in the whole course of his rehearsals, Tom Bertram entered at the other end of the room; and never had he found greater difficulty in keeping his countenance. His father's looks of solemnity and amazement on this his first appearance on any stage, and the gradual metamorphosis of the impassioned Baron Wildenhaim into the well-bred and easy Mr. Yates, making his bow and apology to Sir Thomas Bertram, was such an exhibition, such a piece of true acting as he would not

line 8: surprized] **1814** surprised   //   line 14: further.] **1814** farther.   //   line 18: it, found] **1814** it found   //   line 28: Wildenheim [**1814** Wildenhaim

have lost upon any account. It would be the last—in all probability the last scene on that stage; but he was sure there could not be a finer. The house[12] would close with the greatest eclat.

There was little time, however, for the indulgence of any images of merriment. It was necessary for him to step forward too and assist the introduction, and with many awkward sensations he did his best. Sir Thomas received Mr. Yates with all the appearance of cordiality which was due to his own character,[13] but was really as far from pleased with the necessity of the acquaintance as with the manner of its commencement. Mr. Yates's family and connections were sufficiently known to him, to render his introduction as the "particular friend," another of the hundred particular friends of his son, exceedingly unwelcome; and it needed all the felicity of being again at home, and all the forbearance it could supply, to save Sir Thomas from anger on finding himself thus bewildered[14] in his own house, making part of a ridiculous exhibition in the midst of theatrical nonsense, and forced in so untoward a moment to admit the acquaintance of a young man whom he felt sure of disapproving, and whose easy indifference and volubility in the course of the first five minutes seemed to mark him the most at home of the two.

Tom understood his father's thoughts, and heartily wishing he might be always as well disposed to give them but partial expression, began to see more clearly than he had ever done before that there might be some ground of offence—that there might be some reason for the glance his father gave towards the ceiling and stucco of the room;[15] and that when he inquired with mild gravity after the fate of the billiard table, he was not proceeding beyond a very allowable curiosity. A few minutes were enough for such unsatisfactory sensations

line 15: supply, to] **1814** supply to

on each side; and Sir Thomas, having exerted himself so far as to speak a few words of calm approbation in reply to an eager appeal of Mr. Yates, as to the happiness of the arrangement, the three gentlemen returned to the drawing-room together, Sir Thomas with an increase of gravity which was not lost on all.

"I come from your theatre," said he composedly, as he sat down; "I found myself in it rather unexpectedly. Its vicinity to my own room—but in every respect indeed it took me by surprize, as I had not the smallest suspicion of your acting having assumed so serious a character. It appears a neat job, however, as far as I could judge by candle-light, and does my friend Christopher Jackson credit." And then he would have changed the subject, and sipped his coffee in peace over domestic matters of a calmer hue; but Mr. Yates, without discernment to catch Sir Thomas's meaning, or diffidence, or delicacy, or discretion enough to allow him to lead the discourse while he mingled among the others with the least obtrusiveness himself, would keep him on the topic of the theatre, would torment him with questions and remarks relative to it, and finally would make him hear the whole history of his disappointment at Ecclesford. Sir Thomas listened most politely, but found much to offend his ideas of decorum and confirm his ill opinion of Mr. Yates's habits of thinking from the beginning to the end of the story; and when it was over, could give him no other assurance of sympathy than what a slight bow conveyed.

"This was in fact the origin of *our* acting," said Tom after a moment's thought. "My friend Yates brought the infection[16]

line 1: side; and] **1814** side, and   //   line 1: Sir Thomas, having] **1814** Sir Thomas having   //   line 7: composedly, as] **1814** composedly as   //   line 10: surprize,] **1814** surprize,   //   line 16: diffidence, or delicacy, or] **1814** diffidence or delicacy or

from Ecclesford, and it spread as those things always spread you know, sir—the faster probably from *your* having so often encouraged the sort of thing in us formerly. It was like treading old ground again."

Mr. Yates took the subject from his friend as soon as possible, and immediately gave Sir Thomas an account of what they had done and were doing, told him of the gradual increase of their views, the happy conclusion of their first difficulties, and present promising state of affairs; relating every thing with so blind an interest as made him not only totally unconscious of the uneasy movements of many of his friends as they sat, the change of countenance, the fidget, the hem! of unquietness, but prevented him even from seeing the expression of the face on which his own eyes were fixed—from seeing Sir Thomas's dark brow contract as he looked with inquiring earnestness at his daughters and Edmund, dwelling particularly on the latter, and speaking a language, a remonstrance, a reproof, which *he* felt at his heart. Not less acutely was it felt by Fanny, who had edged back her chair behind her aunt's end of the sofa, and, screened from notice herself, saw all that was passing before her. Such a look of reproach at Edmund from his father she could never have expected to witness; and to feel that it was in any degree deserved, was an aggravation indeed. Sir Thomas's look implied, "On your judgment, Edmund, I depended; what have you been about?"—She knelt in spirit to her uncle,[17] and her bosom swelled to utter, "Oh! not to *him*. Look so to all the others, but not to *him*!"

Mr. Yates was still talking. "To own the truth, Sir Thomas, we were in the middle of a rehearsal when you arrived this evening. We were going through the three first acts, and

line 2: know, sir] **1814** know, Sir   //   line 20: sofa, and, screened] **1814** sofa, and screened

not unsuccessfully upon the whole. Our company is now so dispersed from the Crawfords being gone home, that nothing more can be done to-night; but if you will give us the honour of your company to-morrow evening, I should not be afraid of the result. We bespeak your indulgence,[18] you understand, as young performers; we bespeak your indulgence."

"My indulgence shall be given, sir," replied Sir Thomas gravely, "but without any other rehearsal."—And with a relenting smile he added, "I come home to be happy and indulgent." Then turning away towards any or all of the rest, he tranquilly said, "Mr. and Miss Crawford were mentioned in my last letters from Mansfield. Do you find them agreeable acquaintance?"

Tom was the only one at all ready with an answer, but he being entirely without particular regard for either, without jealousy either in love or acting, could speak very handsomely of both. "Mr. Crawford was a most pleasant gentleman-like man;—his sister a sweet, pretty, elegant, lively girl."

Mr. Rushworth could be silent no longer. "I do not say he is not gentleman-like, considering; but you should tell your father he is not above five feet eight, or he will be expecting a well-looking man."

Sir Thomas did not quite understand this, and looked with some surprize at the speaker.

"If I must say what I think," continued Mr. Rushworth, "in my opinion it is very disagreeable to be always rehearsing. It is having too much of a good thing. I am not so fond of acting

line 2: dispersed from] **1814** dispersed, from // line 4: evening, I] **1814** evening I // line 5: indulgence, you understand, as] **1814** indulgence you understand as // line 7: given, sir,"] **1814** given, Sir," // line 18: sweet, pretty,] **1814** sweet pretty, // line 20: gentleman-like, considering;] **1814** gentleman-like considering; // line 24: surprize] **1814** surprise // line 25: I think," continued Mr. Rushworth, "in] **1814** I think, continued Mr. Rushworth, in

as I was at first. I think we are a great deal better employed, sitting comfortably here among ourselves, and doing nothing."

Sir Thomas looked again, and then replied with an approving smile, "I am happy to find our sentiments on this subject so much the same. It gives me sincere satisfaction. That I should be cautious and quick-sighted, and feel many scruples which my children do *not* feel, is perfectly natural; and equally so that *my* value for domestic tranquillity, for a home which shuts out noisy pleasures, should much exceed theirs. But at your time of life to feel all this, is a most favourable circumstance for yourself and for every body connected with you; and I am sensible of the importance of having an ally of such weight."

Sir Thomas meant to be giving Mr. Rushworth's opinion in better words than he could find himself. He was aware that he must not expect a genius in Mr. Rushworth; but as a well-judging steady young man, with better notions than his elocution would do justice to, he intended to value him very highly. It was impossible for many of the others not to smile. Mr. Rushworth hardly knew what to do with so much meaning; but by looking, as he really felt, most exceedingly pleased with Sir Thomas's good opinion, and saying scarcely any thing, he did his best towards preserving that good opinion a little longer.

line 7: quick-sighted,] **1814** quick sighted,   //   line 22: looking, as] **1814** looking as

Chapter 2

EDMUND's first object the next morning was to see his father alone, and give him a fair statement of the whole acting scheme, defending his own share in it as far only as he could then, in a soberer moment, feel his motives to deserve, and acknowledging with perfect ingenuousness that his concession had been attended with such partial good as to make his judgment in it very doubtful. He was anxious, while vindicating himself, to say nothing unkind of the others; but there was only one amongst them whose conduct he could mention without some necessity of defence or palliation. "We have all been more or less to blame," said he, "every one of us, excepting Fanny. Fanny is the only one who has judged rightly throughout, who has been consistent. *Her* feelings have been steadily against it from first to last. She never ceased to think of what was due to you. You will find Fanny every thing you could wish."

Sir Thomas saw all the impropriety of such a scheme among such a party, and at such a time, as strongly as his son had ever supposed he must; he felt it too much indeed for many words;[1] and having shaken hands with Edmund,[2] meant to try to lose the disagreeable impression, and forget how much he had been forgotten himself as soon as he could,

line 4: then, in a soberer moment, feel] **1814** then in a soberer moment feel
line 7: anxious, while vindicating himself, to] **1814** anxious while vindicating himself to // line 11: blame," said he, "every one of us, excepting Fanny.] **1814** blame, said he, every one of us excepting Fanny.

after the house had been cleared of every object enforcing the remembrance, and restored to its proper state. He did not enter into any remonstrance with his other children: he was more willing to believe they felt their error, than to run the risk of investigation. The reproof of an immediate conclusion of every thing, the sweep of every preparation would be sufficient.

There was one person, however, in the house whom he could not leave to learn his sentiments merely through his conduct. He could not help giving Mrs. Norris a hint of his having hoped, that her advice might have been interposed to prevent what her judgment must certainly have disapproved. The young people had been very inconsiderate in forming the plan; they ought to have been capable of a better decision themselves; but they were young, and, excepting Edmund, he believed of unsteady characters; and with greater surprize therefore he must regard her acquiescence in their wrong measures, her countenance of their unsafe amusements, than that such measures and such amusements should have been suggested. Mrs. Norris was a little confounded, and as nearly being silenced as ever she had been in her life; for she was ashamed to confess having never seen any of the impropriety which was so glaring to Sir Thomas, and would not have admitted that her influence was insufficient, that she might have talked in vain. Her only resource was to get out of the subject as fast as possible, and turn the current of Sir Thomas's ideas into a happier channel. She had a great deal to insinuate in her own praise as to *general* attention to the interest and comfort of his family, much exertion and many sacrifices to glance at in the form of hurried walks and sudden removals from her own fire-side, and many excellent hints

line 15: young, and, excepting] **1814** young, and excepting // line 16: surprize] **1814** surprise

of distrust and economy to Lady Bertram and Edmund to detail, whereby a most considerable saving had always arisen, and more than one bad servant been detected. But her chief strength lay in Sotherton. Her greatest support and glory was in having formed the connection with the Rushworths. *There* she was impregnable. She took to herself all the credit of bringing Mr. Rushworth's admiration of Maria to any effect. "If I had not been active," said she, "and made a point of being introduced to his mother, and then prevailed on my sister to pay the first visit, I am as certain as I sit here, that nothing would have come of it—for Mr. Rushworth is the sort of amiable modest young man who wants a great deal of encouragement, and there were girls enough on the catch for him if we had been idle. But I left no stone unturned. I was ready to move heaven and earth to persuade my sister, and at last I did persuade her. You know the distance to Sotherton; it was in the middle of winter, and the roads almost impassable, but I did persuade her."

"I know how great, how justly great your influence is with Lady Bertram and her children, and am the more concerned that it should not have been"——

"My dear Sir Thomas, if you had seen the state of the roads *that* day! I thought we should never have got through them, though we had the four horses of course; and poor old coachman would attend us, out of his great love and kindness, though he was hardly able to sit the box on account of the rheumatism which I had been doctoring him for, ever since Michaelmas. I cured him at last;[3] but he was very bad all the winter—and this was such a day, I could not help going to him up in his room before we set off to advise him not to venture: he was putting on his wig—so I said, 'Coachman,

line 25: us, out] **1814** us out // line 31: said, 'Coachman,] **1814** said, "Coachman,

you had much better not go, your Lady and I shall be very safe; you know how steady Stephen is, and Charles has been upon the leaders[4] so often now, that I am sure there is no fear.' But, however, I soon found it would not do; he was bent upon going, and as I hate to be worrying and officious, I said no more; but my heart quite ached for him at every jolt, and when we got into the rough lanes about Stoke, where what with frost and snow upon beds of stones, it was worse than any thing you can imagine, I was quite in an agony about him. And then the poor horses too!—To see them straining away! You know how I always feel for the horses. And when we got to the bottom of Sandcroft Hill, what do you think I did? You will laugh at me—but I got out and walked up. I did indeed. It might not be saving them much, but it was something, and I could not bear to sit at my ease, and be dragged up at the expense of those noble animals. I caught a dreadful cold, but *that* I did not regard. My object was accomplished in the visit."

"I hope we shall always think the acquaintance worth any trouble that might be taken to establish it. There is nothing very striking in Mr. Rushworth's manners, but I was pleased last night with what appeared to be his opinion on *one* subject—his decided preference of a quiet family-party to the bustle and confusion of acting. He seemed to feel exactly as one could wish."

"Yes, indeed,—and the more you know of him, the better you will like him. He is not a shining character, but he has a thousand good qualities! and is so disposed to look up to you, that I am quite laughed at about it, for every body considers it as my doing. 'Upon my word, Mrs. Norris,' said Mrs. Grant,

line 3: fear.'] **1814** fear."   //   line 16: expense] **1814** expence   //   line 22: family-party] **1814** family party   //   line 25: indeed,—and] **1814** indeed, and   //   line 29: 'Upon my word, Mrs. Norris,'] **1814** "Upon my word, Mrs. Norris,"

the other day, 'if Mr. Rushworth were a son of your own he could not hold Sir Thomas in greater respect.'"

Sir Thomas gave up the point, foiled by her evasions, disarmed by her flattery; and was obliged to rest satisfied with the conviction that where the present pleasure of those she loved was at stake, her kindness did sometimes overpower her judgment.

It was a busy morning with him. Conversation with any of them occupied but a small part of it. He had to reinstate himself in all the wonted concerns of his Mansfield life, to see his steward and his bailiff—to examine and compute—and, in the intervals of business, to walk into his stables and his gardens, and nearest plantations;[5] but active and methodical, he had not only done all this before he resumed his seat as master of the house at dinner, he had also set the carpenter to work in pulling down what had been so lately put up in the billiard room, and given the scene painter his dismissal, long enough to justify the pleasing belief of his being then at least as far off as Northampton. The scene painter was gone, having spoilt only the floor of one room, ruined all the coachman's sponges, and made five of the under-servants idle and dissatisfied; and Sir Thomas was in hopes that another day or two would suffice to wipe away every outward memento of what had been, even to the destruction of every unbound[6] copy of "Lovers' Vows" in the house, for he was burning all that met his eye.

Mr. Yates was beginning now to understand Sir Thomas's intentions, though as far as ever from understanding their source. He and his friend had been out with their guns the

line 1: day, 'if] **1814** day, "if // line 2: respect.'"] **1814** respect." // line 3: point, foiled] **1814** point; foiled // line 11: and, in the intervals of business, to] **1814** and in the intervals of business to // line 23: suffice] **1814** suffice // line 25: "Lovers' Vows"] **1814** "Lover's Vows"

chief of the morning, and Tom had taken the opportunity of explaining, with proper apologies for his father's particularity, what was to be expected. Mr. Yates felt it as acutely as might be supposed. To be a second time disappointed in the same way was an instance of very severe ill-luck; and his indignation was such, that had it not been for delicacy towards his friend and his friend's youngest sister, he believed he should certainly attack the Baronet on the absurdity of his proceedings, and argue him into a little more rationality. He believed this very stoutly while he was in Mansfield Wood, and all the way home; but there was a something in Sir Thomas, when they sat round the same table, which made Mr. Yates think it wiser to let him pursue his own way, and feel the folly of it without opposition. He had known many disagreeable fathers before, and often been struck with the inconveniences they occasioned, but never in the whole course of his life, had he seen one of that class, so unintelligibly moral, so infamously tyrannical as Sir Thomas. He was not a man to be endured but for his children's sake, and he might be thankful to his fair daughter Julia that Mr. Yates did yet mean to stay a few days longer under his roof.

The evening passed with external smoothness, though almost every mind was ruffled; and the music which Sir Thomas called for from his daughters helped to conceal the want of real harmony. Maria was in a good deal of agitation. It was of the utmost consequence to her that Crawford should now lose no time in declaring himself, and she was disturbed that even a day should be gone by without seeming to advance that point. She had been expecting to see him the whole morning—and all the evening too was still expecting him. Mr. Rushworth had set off early with the great news for Sotherton; and she had fondly hoped for such an immediate eclaircissement[7] as might save him the trouble of ever coming back again. But they had seen no one from the Parsonage—not a creature, and had heard no tidings beyond a friendly note of congratulation and inquiry from Mrs. Grant to Lady Bertram. It was the first day for many, many weeks, in which the families had been wholly divided. Four-and-twenty hours had never passed before, since August began, without bringing them together in some way or other. It was a sad anxious day; and the morrow, though differing in the sort of evil, did by no means bring less. A few moments of feverish enjoyment were followed by hours of acute suffering. Henry Crawford was again in the house; he walked up with Dr. Grant, who was anxious to pay his respects to Sir Thomas, and at rather an early hour they were ushered into the breakfast-room, where were most of the family. Sir Thomas soon appeared, and Maria saw with delight and agitation the introduction of the man she loved to her father. Her sensations were indefinable, and so were they a few minutes afterwards upon hearing Henry Crawford, who had a chair between herself and Tom, ask the latter in an under voice, whether there were any plan for resuming the play after the present happy interruption, (with a courteous glance at Sir Thomas,) because in that case, he should make a point of returning to Mansfield, at any time required by the party; he was going away immediately, being to meet his uncle at Bath[8] without delay, but if there were any prospect of a renewal of "Lovers' Vows," he should hold himself positively engaged, he should break through every other claim, he should absolutely condition with his uncle for attending them whenever he might be wanted. The play should not be lost by *his* absence.

line 2: Parsonage] **1814** parsonage   //   line 5: Four-and-twenty] **1814** Four and twenty   //   line 21: interruption, (with] **1814** interruption (with   // line 22: Sir Thomas,)] **1814** Sir Thomas)   //   line 26: "Lovers' Vows," he] **1814** "Lovers Vows" he

"From Bath, Norfolk, London, York—wherever I may be," said he, "I will attend you from any place in England, at an hour's notice."

It was well at that moment that Tom had to speak and not his sister. He could immediately say with easy fluency, "I am sorry you are going—but as to our play, *that* is all over—entirely at an end (looking significantly at his father). The painter was sent off yesterday, and very little will remain of the theatre to-morrow.—I knew how *that* would be from the first.—It is early for Bath.—You will find nobody there."

"It is about my uncle's usual time."

"When do you think of going?"

"I may perhaps get as far as Banbury[9] to-day."

"Whose stables do you use at Bath?" was the next question; and while this branch of the subject was under discussion, Maria, who wanted neither pride nor resolution, was preparing to encounter her share of it with tolerable calmness.

To her he soon turned, repeating much of what he had already said, with only a softened air and stronger expressions of regret. But what availed his expressions or his air?—He was going—and if not voluntarily going, voluntarily intending to stay away; for, excepting what might be due to his uncle, his engagements were all self-imposed.—He might talk of necessity, but she knew his independence.—The hand which had so pressed her's to his heart!—The hand and the heart were alike motionless and passive now![10] Her spirit supported her, but the agony of her mind was severe.—She had not long to endure what arose from listening to language, which his actions contradicted, or to bury the tumult of her feelings under the restraint of society; for general civilities soon called

line 1: be," said] **1814** be" said   //   line 13: to-day."] **1814** to day."   //
line 22: away; for, excepting] **1814** away, for excepting   //   line 25: her's to
his heart!—The] **1814** hers to his heart! The

his notice from her, and the farewell visit, as it then became openly acknowledged, was a very short one.—He was gone— he had touched her hand for the last time, he had made his parting bow, and she might seek directly all that solitude could do for her. Henry Crawford was gone—gone from the house, and within two hours afterwards from the parish; and so ended all the hopes his selfish vanity had raised in Maria and Julia Bertram.

Julia could rejoice that he was gone.—His presence was beginning to be odious to her; and if Maria gained him not, she was now cool enough to dispense with any other revenge.—She did not want exposure to be added to desertion.—Henry Crawford gone, she could even pity her sister.

With a purer spirit did Fanny rejoice in the intelligence.— She heard it at dinner and felt it a blessing. By all the others it was mentioned with regret, and his merits honoured with due gradation of feeling, from the sincerity of Edmund's too par- tial regard, to the unconcern of his mother speaking entirely by rote. Mrs. Norris began to look about her and wonder that his falling in love with Julia had come to nothing; and could almost fear that she had been remiss herself in forwarding it; but with so many to care for, how was it possible for even *her* activity to keep pace with her wishes?

Another day or two, and Mr. Yates was gone likewise. In *his* departure Sir Thomas felt the chief interest; wanting to be alone with his family, the presence of a stranger superior to Mr. Yates must have been irksome; but of him, trifling and confident, idle and expensive, it was every way vexatious. In himself he was wearisome, but as the friend of Tom and the admirer[11] of Julia he became offensive. Sir Thomas had

line 19: regard, to] **1814** regard to

been quite indifferent to Mr. Crawford's going or staying—but his good wishes for Mr. Yates's having a pleasant journey, as he walked with him to the hall door, were given with genuine satisfaction. Mr. Yates had staid to see the destruction of every theatrical preparation at Mansfield, the removal of every thing appertaining to the play; he left the house in all the soberness of its general character; and Sir Thomas hoped, in seeing him out of it, to be rid of the worst object connected with the scheme, and the last that must be inevitably reminding him of its existence.

Mrs. Norris contrived to remove one article from his sight that might have distressed him. The curtain over which she had presided with such talent and such success, went off with her to her cottage, where she happened to be particularly in want of green baize.

line 7: hoped, in] **1814** hoped in

Chapter 3

SIR THOMAS'S return made a striking change in the
ways of the family, independent of Lovers' Vows. Under his
government, Mansfield was an altered place. Some members of their society sent away and the spirits of many others
saddened, it was all sameness and gloom, compared with
the past; a sombre family-party rarely enlivened. There was
little intercourse with the Parsonage. Sir Thomas drawing
back from intimacies in general, was particularly disinclined,
at this time, for any engagements but in one quarter. The
Rushworths were the only addition to his own domestic
circle which he could solicit.

Edmund did not wonder that such should be his father's
feelings, nor could he regret any thing but the exclusion of
the Grants. "But they," he observed to Fanny, "have a claim.
They seem to belong to us—they seem to be part of ourselves.
I could wish my father were more sensible of their very great
attention to my mother and sisters while he was away. I am
afraid they may feel themselves neglected. But the truth is
that my father hardly knows them. They had not been here a
twelvemonth when he left England. If he knew them better,
he would value their society as it deserves, for they are in fact
exactly the sort of people he would like. We are sometimes a
little in want of animation among ourselves; my sisters seem

line 2: Lovers' Vows.] **1814** Lover's vows.   //   line 5: gloom, compared]
1814 gloom compared   //   line 6: family-party] **1814** family party   //
line 7: Parsonage.] **1814** parsonage.   //   line 13: any thing] **1814** anything

out of spirits, and Tom is certainly not at his ease. Dr. and Mrs. Grant would enliven us, and make our evenings pass away with more enjoyment even to my father."

"Do you think so?" said Fanny. "In my opinion, my uncle would not like *any* addition. I think he values the very quietness you speak of, and that the repose of his own family-circle is all he wants. And it does not appear to me that we are more serious than we used to be; I mean before my uncle went abroad. As well as I can recollect, it was always much the same. There was never much laughing in his presence; or, if there is any difference, it is not more I think than such an absence has a tendency to produce at first. There must be a sort of shyness. But I cannot recollect that our evenings formerly were ever merry, except when my uncle was in town. No young people's are, I suppose, when those they look up to are at home."

"I believe you are right, Fanny," was his reply, after a short consideration. "I believe our evenings are rather returned to what they were, than assuming a new character. The novelty was in their being lively.—Yet, how strong the impression that only a few weeks will give! I have been feeling as if we had never lived so before."

"I suppose I am graver than other people," said Fanny. "The evenings do not appear long to me. I love to hear my uncle talk of the West Indies. I could listen to him for an hour together. It entertains *me* more than many other things have done—but then I am unlike other people I dare say."

"Why should you dare say *that*? (smiling)—Do you want to be told that you are only unlike other people in being more wise and discreet? But when did you or any body ever get a compliment from me, Fanny? Go to my father if you want to

line 6: family-circle] **1814** family circle // line 9: recollect, it] **1814** recollect it // line 17: Fanny," was] **1814** Fanny" was

be complimented. He will satisfy you. Ask your uncle what he thinks, and you will hear compliments enough; and though they may be chiefly on your person, you must put up with it, and trust to his seeing as much beauty of mind in time."

Such language was so new to Fanny that it quite embarrassed her.

"Your uncle thinks you very pretty, dear Fanny—and that is the long and the short of the matter. Any body but myself would have made something more of it, and any body but you would resent that you had not been thought very pretty before; but the truth is, that your uncle never did admire you till now—and now he does. Your complexion is so improved!—and you have gained so much countenance![1]— and your figure—Nay, Fanny, do not turn away about it—it is but an uncle. If you cannot bear an uncle's admiration[2] what is to become of you? You must really begin to harden yourself to the idea of being worth looking at.—You must try not to mind growing up into a pretty woman."

"Oh! don't talk so, don't talk so," cried Fanny, distressed by more feelings than he was aware of; but seeing that she was distressed, he had done with the subject, and only added more seriously, "Your uncle is disposed to be pleased with you in every respect; and I only wish you would talk to him more.— You are one of those who are too silent in the evening circle."

"But I do talk to him more than I used. I am sure I do. Did not you hear me ask him about the slave-trade[3] last night?"

"I did—and was in hopes the question would be followed up by others. It would have pleased your uncle to be inquired of farther."

"And I longed to do it—but there was such a dead silence! And while my cousins were sitting by without speaking a

line 8: Any body] **1814** Anybody // line 14: it—it] **1814** it—It // line 21: subject, and] **1814** subject and // line 26: slave-trade] **1814** slave trade

word, or seeming at all interested in the subject, I did not like—I thought it would appear as if I wanted to set myself off at their expense, by shewing a curiosity and pleasure in his information which he must wish his own daughters to feel."

"Miss Crawford was very right in what she said of you the other day—that you seemed almost as fearful of notice and praise as other women were of neglect. We were talking of you at the Parsonage, and those were her words. She has great discernment. I know nobody who distinguishes characters better.—For so young a woman it is remarkable! She certainly understands *you* better than you are understood by the greater part of those who have known you so long; and with regard to some others, I can perceive, from occasional lively hints, the unguarded expressions of the moment, that she could define *many* as accurately, did not delicacy forbid it. I wonder what she thinks of my father! She must admire him as a fine looking man, with most gentleman-like, dignified, consistent manners; but perhaps having seen him so seldom, his reserve may be a little repulsive.[4] Could they be much together I feel sure of their liking each other. He would enjoy her liveliness—and she has talents to value his powers.[5] I wish they met more frequently!—I hope she does not suppose there is any dislike on his side."

"She must know herself too secure of the regard of all the rest of you," said Fanny with half a sigh, "to have any such apprehension. And Sir Thomas's wishing just at first to be only with his family is so very natural, that she can argue nothing from that. After a little while I dare say we shall be meeting again in the same sort of way, allowing for the difference of the time of year."

line 13: perceive, from] **1814** perceive from // line 15: accurately, did] **1814** accurately did

"This is the first October that she has passed in the country since her infancy. I do not call Tunbridge or Cheltenham[6] the country; and November is a still more serious month, and I can see that Mrs. Grant is very anxious for her not finding Mansfield dull as winter comes on."

Fanny could have said a great deal, but it was safer to say nothing, and leave untouched all Miss Crawford's resources, her accomplishments, her spirits, her importance, her friends, lest it should betray her into any observations seemingly unhandsome. Miss Crawford's kind opinion of herself deserved at least a grateful forbearance, and she began to talk of something else.

"To-morrow, I think, my uncle dines at Sotherton, and you and Mr. Bertram too. We shall be quite a small party at home. I hope my uncle may continue to like Mr. Rushworth."

"That is impossible, Fanny. He must like him less after to-morrow's visit, for we shall be five hours in his company. I should dread the stupidity of the day, if there were not a much greater evil to follow—the impression it must leave on Sir Thomas. He cannot much longer deceive himself. I am sorry for them all, and would give something that Rushworth and Maria had never met."

In this quarter, indeed, disappointment was impending over Sir Thomas. Not all his good-will for Mr. Rushworth, not all Mr. Rushworth's deference for him, could prevent him from soon discerning some part of the truth—that Mr. Rushworth was an inferior young man, as ignorant in business as in books, with opinions in general unfixed, and without seeming much aware of it himself.

He had expected a very different son-in-law; and beginning to feel grave on Maria's account, tried to understand *her* feelings. Little observation there was necessary to tell him that indifference was the most favourable state they could be in. Her behaviour to Mr. Rushworth was careless and cold. She could not, did not like him. Sir Thomas resolved to speak seriously to her. Advantageous as would be the alliance, and long standing and public as was the engagement, her happiness must not be sacrificed to it. Mr. Rushworth had perhaps been accepted on too short an acquaintance, and on knowing him better she was repenting.

With solemn kindness Sir Thomas addressed her; told her his fears, inquired into her wishes, entreated her to be open and sincere, and assured her that every inconvenience should be braved, and the connection entirely given up, if she felt herself unhappy in the prospect of it. He would act for her and release her. Maria had a moment's struggle as she listened, and only a moment's: when her father ceased, she was able to give her answer immediately, decidedly, and with no apparent agitation. She thanked him for his great attention, his paternal kindness, but he was quite mistaken in supposing she had the smallest desire of breaking through her engagement, or was sensible of any change of opinion or inclination since her forming it. She had the highest esteem for Mr. Rushworth's character and disposition, and could not have a doubt of her happiness with him.

Sir Thomas was satisfied; too glad to be satisfied perhaps to urge the matter quite so far as his judgment might have dictated to others. It was an alliance which he could not have relinquished without pain; and thus he reasoned. Mr. Rushworth was young enough to improve;—Mr. Rushworth must and would improve in good society; and if Maria could now speak so securely of her happiness with him, speaking certainly without the prejudice, the blindness of love, she ought to be believed. Her feelings probably were not acute; he had never supposed them to be so; but her comforts might not be less on that account, and if she could dispense with seeing her husband a leading, shining character, there would certainly be every thing else in her favour. A well-disposed young woman, who did not marry for love, was in general but the more attached to her own family, and the nearness of Sotherton to Mansfield must naturally hold out the greatest temptation, and would, in all probability, be a continual supply of the most amiable and innocent enjoyments. Such and such-like were the reasonings of Sir Thomas—happy to escape the embarrassing evils of a rupture,[7] the wonder, the reflections, the reproach that must attend it, happy to secure a marriage which would bring him such an addition of respectability and influence, and very happy to think any thing of his daughter's disposition that was most favourable for the purpose.

To her the conference closed as satisfactorily as to him. She was in a state of mind to be glad that she had secured her fate beyond recall—that she had pledged herself anew to Sotherton—that she was safe from the possibility of giving Crawford the triumph of governing her actions, and destroying her prospects; and retired in proud resolve, determined only to behave more cautiously to Mr. Rushworth in future, that her father might not be again suspecting her.

Had Sir Thomas applied to his daughter within the first three or four days after Henry Crawford's leaving Mansfield, before her feelings were at all tranquillized, before she had given up every hope of him, or absolutely resolved on enduring his rival, her answer might have been different; but after another three or four days, when there was no return, no letter, no message—no symptom of a softened heart—no hope of advantage from separation—her mind became cool

line 6: would, in all probability, be] **1814** would in all probability be   //
line 8: such-like] **1814** such like   //   line 19: actions, and] **1814** actions and

enough to seek all the comfort that pride and self-revenge[8] could give.

Henry Crawford had destroyed her happiness, but he should not know that he had done it; he should not destroy her credit, her appearance, her prosperity too. He should not have to think of her as pining in the retirement of Mansfield for *him*, rejecting Sotherton and London, independence and splendour for *his* sake. Independence was more needful than ever; the want of it at Mansfield more sensibly felt. She was less and less able to endure the restraint which her father imposed. The liberty which his absence had given was now become absolutely necessary. She must escape from him and Mansfield as soon as possible, and find consolation in fortune and consequence, bustle and the world,[9] for a wounded spirit. Her mind was quite determined and varied not.

To such feelings, delay, even the delay of much preparation, would have been an evil, and Mr. Rushworth could hardly be more impatient for the marriage than herself. In all the important preparations of the mind she was complete; being prepared for matrimony by an hatred of home, restraint, and tranquillity; by the misery of disappointed affection, and contempt of the man she was to marry. The rest might wait. The preparations of new carriages and furniture might wait for London and spring, when her own taste could have fairer play.

The principals[10] being all agreed in this respect, it soon appeared that a very few weeks would be sufficient for such arrangements as must precede the wedding.

Mrs. Rushworth was quite ready to retire, and make way for the fortunate young woman whom her dear son had selected;—and very early in November removed herself, her

line 21: affection, and] **1814** affection and

maid, her footman, and her chariot, with true dowager pro-priety, to Bath—there to parade over the wonders of Sother-ton in her evening-parties—enjoying them as thoroughly perhaps in the animation of a card-table as she had ever done on the spot—and before the middle of the same month the ceremony had taken place, which gave Sotherton another mistress.

It was a very proper wedding. The bride was elegantly dressed—the two bridemaids were duly inferior—her father gave her away—her mother stood with salts in her hand,[11] expecting to be agitated—her aunt tried to cry—and the ser-vice was impressively read by Dr. Grant. Nothing could be objected to when it came under the discussion of the neigh-bourhood, except that the carriage which conveyed the bride and bridegroom and Julia from the church door to Sotherton, was the same chaise which Mr. Rushworth had used for a twelvemonth before. In every thing else the etiquette of the day might stand the strictest investigation.

It was done, and they were gone. Sir Thomas felt as an anxious father must feel, and was indeed experiencing much of the agitation which his wife had been apprehensive of for herself, but had fortunately escaped. Mrs. Norris, most happy to assist in the duties of the day, by spending it at the Park to support her sister's spirits, and drinking the health of Mr. and Mrs. Rushworth in a supernumerary glass or two, was all joyous delight—for she had made the match—she had done every thing—and no one would have supposed, from her confident triumph, that she had ever heard of conjugal

line 1: chariot, with true dowager propriety, to] **1814** chariot with true dowager propriety to   //   line 3: evening-parties] **1814** evening parties   //   line 4: card-table] **1814** card table   //   line 10: hand, expecting] **1814** hand expecting   //   line 15: Julia from] **1814** Julia, from //   line 19: done, and] **1814** done and   //   line 27: supposed, from] **1814** supposed from

infelicity in her life, or could have the smallest insight into the disposition of the niece who had been brought up under her eye.

The plan of the young couple was to proceed after a few days to Brighton,[12] and take a house there for some weeks. Every public place was new to Maria, and Brighton is almost as gay in winter as in summer. When the novelty of amusement there were over, it would be time for the wider range of London.

Julia was to go with them to Brighton. Since rivalry between the sisters had ceased, they had been gradually recovering much of their former good understanding; and were at least sufficiently friends to make each of them exceedingly glad to be with the other at such a time. Some other companion than Mr. Rushworth was of the first consequence to his lady, and Julia was quite as eager for novelty and pleasure as Maria, though she might not have struggled through so much to obtain them, and could better bear a subordinate situation.

Their departure made another material change at Mansfield, a chasm which required some time to fill up. The family circle became greatly contracted, and though the Miss Bertrams had latterly added little to its gaiety, they could not but be missed. Even their mother missed them—and how much more their tender-hearted cousin, who wandered about the house, and thought of them, and felt for them, with a degree of affectionate regret which they had never done much to deserve!

line 16: lady,] **1814** Lady,   //   line 28: deserve!] **1814** deserve.

Chapter 4

FANNY'S consequence increased on the departure of her cousins. Becoming, as she then did, the only young woman in the drawing-room, the only occupier of that interesting division of a family in which she had hitherto held so humble a third, it was impossible for her not to be more looked at, more thought of and attended to, than she had ever been before; and "where is Fanny?" became no uncommon question, even without her being wanted for any one's convenience.

Not only at home did her value increase, but at the Parsonage too. In that house which she had hardly entered twice a year since Mr. Norris's death, she became a welcome, an invited guest; and in the gloom and dirt of a November day, most acceptable to Mary Crawford. Her visits there, beginning by chance, were continued by solicitation. Mrs. Grant, really eager to get any change for her sister, could by the easiest self-deceit persuade herself that she was doing the kindest thing by Fanny, and giving her the most important opportunities of improvement[1] in pressing her frequent calls.

Fanny, having been sent into the village on some errand by her aunt Norris, was overtaken by a heavy shower close to the Parsonage, and being descried from one of the windows endeavouring to find shelter under the branches and lingering leaves of an oak just beyond their premises, was forced,

line 2: Becoming, as] **1814** Becoming as   //   line 19: Fanny, having] **1814** Fanny having   //   line 21: windows endeavouring] **1814** windows, endeavouring

though not without some modest reluctance on her part, to come in. A civil servant she had withstood; but when Dr. Grant himself went out with an umbrella, there was nothing to be done but to be very much ashamed and to get into the house as fast as possible; and to poor Miss Crawford, who had just been contemplating the dismal rain in a very desponding state of mind, sighing over the ruin of all her plan of exercise for that morning, and of every chance of seeing a single creature beyond themselves for the next twenty-four hours; the sound of a little bustle at the front door, and the sight of Miss Price dripping with wet in the vestibule, was delightful. The value of an event on a wet day in the country, was most forcibly brought before her. She was all alive again directly, and among the most active in being useful to Fanny, in detecting her to be wetter than she would at first allow, and providing her with dry clothes; and Fanny, after being obliged to submit to all this attention, and to being assisted and waited on by mistresses and maids, being also obliged on returning down stairs, to be fixed in their drawing-room for an hour while the rain continued, the blessing of something fresh to see and think of was thus extended to Miss Crawford, and might carry on her spirits to the period of dressing and dinner.

The two sisters were so kind to her and so pleasant, that Fanny might have enjoyed her visit could she have believed herself not in the way, and could she have foreseen that the weather would certainly clear at the end of the hour, and save her from the shame of having Dr. Grant's carriage and horses out to take her home, with which she was threatened. As to anxiety for any alarm that her absence in such weather might occasion at home, she had nothing to suffer on that score; for as her being out was known only to her two aunts, she was

line 16: Fanny, after] **1814** Fanny after

perfectly aware that none would be felt, and that in whatever cottage aunt Norris might chuse to establish her during the rain, her being in such cottage would be indubitable to aunt Bertram.

It was beginning to look brighter, when Fanny, observing a harp in the room, asked some questions about it, which soon led to an acknowledgment of her wishing very much to hear it, and a confession, which could hardly be believed, of her having never yet heard it since its being in Mansfield. To Fanny herself it appeared a very simple and natural circumstance. She had scarcely ever been at the Parsonage since the instrument's arrival, there had been no reason that she should; but Miss Crawford, calling to mind an early-expressed wish on the subject, was concerned at her own neglect;—and "shall I play to you now?"—and "what will you have?" were questions immediately following with the readiest good humour.

She played accordingly; happy to have a new listener, and a listener who seemed so much obliged, so full of wonder at the performance, and who shewed herself not wanting in taste. She played till Fanny's eyes, straying to the window on the weather's being evidently fair, spoke what she felt must be done.

"Another quarter of an hour," said Miss Crawford, "and we shall see how it will be. Do not run away the first moment of its holding up. Those clouds look alarming."

"But they are passed over," said Fanny.—"I have been watching them.—This weather is all from the south."

"South or north, I know a black cloud when I see it; and you must not set forward while it is so threatening. And besides, I want to play something more to you—a very pretty

line 5: Fanny, observing] **1814** Fanny observing   //   line 8: confession, which] **1814** confession which   //   line 13: Miss Crawford, calling] **1814** Miss Crawford calling

piece—and your cousin Edmund's prime favourite. You must stay and hear your cousin's favourite."

Fanny felt that she must; and though she had not waited for that sentence to be thinking of Edmund, such a memento made her particularly awake to his idea,[2] and she fancied him sitting in that room again and again, perhaps in the very spot where she sat now, listening with constant delight to the favourite air, played, as it appeared to her, with superior tone and expression; and though pleased with it herself, and glad to like whatever was liked by him, she was more sincerely impatient to go away at the conclusion of it than she had been before; and on this being evident, she was so kindly asked to call again, to take them in her walk whenever she could, to come and hear more of the harp, that she felt it necessary to be done, if no objection arose at home.

Such was the origin of the sort of intimacy which took place between them within the first fortnight after the Miss Bertrams' going away, an intimacy resulting principally from Miss Crawford's desire of something new, and which had little reality in Fanny's feelings. Fanny went to her every two or three days; it seemed a kind of fascination; she could not be easy without going, and yet it was without loving her, without ever thinking like her, without any sense of obligation for being sought after now when nobody else was to be had; and deriving no higher pleasure from her conversation than occasional amusement, and *that* often at the expense of her judgment, when it was raised by pleasantry on people or subjects which she wished to be respected. She went however, and they sauntered about together many an half hour in Mrs. Grant's shrubbery, the weather being unusually mild for the time of year; and venturing sometimes even to sit down on one of the benches now comparatively unsheltered, remaining there perhaps till in the midst of some tender ejaculation of Fanny's, on the sweets of so protracted an autumn, they were forced by the sudden swell of a cold gust shaking down the last few yellow leaves about them, to jump up and walk for warmth.

"This is pretty—very pretty," said Fanny, looking around her as they were thus sitting together one day: "Every time I come into this shrubbery I am more struck with its growth and beauty. Three years ago, this was nothing but a rough hedgerow[3] along the upper side of the field, never thought of as any thing, or capable of becoming any thing; and now it is converted into a walk, and it would be difficult to say whether most valuable as a convenience or an ornament; and perhaps in another three years we may be forgetting—almost forgetting what it was before. How wonderful, how very wonderful the operations of time, and the changes of the human mind!" And following the latter train of thought, she soon afterwards added: "If any one faculty of our nature may be called *more* wonderful than the rest, I do think it is memory.[4] There seems something more speakingly[5] incomprehensible in the powers, the failures, the inequalities of memory, than in any other of our intelligences. The memory is sometimes so retentive, so serviceable, so obedient—at others, so bewildered and so weak—and at others again, so tyrannic, so beyond controul!—We are to be sure a miracle every way—but our powers of recollecting and of forgetting, do seem peculiarly past finding out."

Miss Crawford, untouched and inattentive, had nothing to say; and Fanny, perceiving it, brought back her own mind to what she thought must interest.

line 11: any thing,] **1814** anything,   //   line 11: any thing;] **1814** anything;   //   line 28: Miss Crawford, untouched] **1814** Miss Crawford untouched   //   line 29: Fanny, perceiving it,] **1814** Fanny perceiving it,

"It may seem impertinent in *me* to praise, but I must admire the taste Mrs. Grant has shewn in all this. There is such a quiet simplicity in the plan of the walk!—not too much attempted!"

"Yes," replied Miss Crawford carelessly, "it does very well for a place of this sort. One does not think of extent *here*—and between ourselves, till I came to Mansfield, I had not imagined a country parson[6] ever aspired to a shrubbery or any thing of the kind."

"I am so glad to see the evergreens[7] thrive!" said Fanny in reply. "My uncle's gardener always says the soil here is better than his own, and so it appears from the growth of the laurels and evergreens in general.—The evergreen!—How beautiful, how welcome, how wonderful the evergreen!—When one thinks of it, how astonishing a variety of nature!—In some countries we know the tree that sheds its leaf is the variety,[8] but that does not make it less amazing, that the same soil and the same sun should nurture plants differing in the first rule and law of their existence. You will think me rhapsodizing;[9] but when I am out of doors, especially when I am sitting out of doors, I am very apt to get into this sort of wondering strain. One cannot fix one's eyes on the commonest natural production without finding food for a rambling fancy."

"To say the truth," replied Miss Crawford, "I am something like the famous Doge at the court of Lewis XIV,[10] and may declare that I see no wonder in this shrubbery equal to seeing myself in it. If any body had told me a year ago that this place would be my home, that I should be spending month after month here, as I have done, I certainly should not have believed them!—I have now been here nearly five months! and moreover the quietest five months I ever passed."

line 7: Mansfield, I] **1814** Mansfield I

"*Too* quiet for you I believe."

"I should have thought so *theoretically* myself, but"—and her eyes brightened as she spoke—"take it all and all, I never spent so happy a summer.—But then"—with a more thoughtful air and lowered voice—"there is no saying what it may lead to."

Fanny's heart beat quick, and she felt quite unequal to surmizing or soliciting any thing more. Miss Crawford however, with renewed animation, soon went on:

"I am conscious of being far better reconciled to a country residence than I had ever expected to be. I can even suppose it pleasant to spend *half* the year in the country, under certain circumstances—very pleasant. An elegant, moderate-sized house in the centre of family connections—continual engagements among them—commanding the first society in the neighbourhood—looked-up to perhaps as leading it even more than those of larger fortune, and turning from the cheerful round of such amusements to nothing worse than a tête-à-tête with the person one feels most agreeable in the world. There is nothing frightful in such a picture, is there, Miss Price? One need not envy the new Mrs. Rushworth with such a home as *that*." "Envy Mrs. Rushworth!" was all that Fanny attempted to say. "Come, come, it would be very unhandsome in us to be severe on Mrs. Rushworth, for I look forward to our owing her a great many gay, brilliant, happy hours. I expect we shall be all very much at Sotherton another year. Such a match as Miss Bertram has made is a public blessing, for the first pleasures of Mr. Rushworth's wife must be to fill her house, and give the best balls in the country."

line 8: surmizing] **1814** surmising // line 8: any thing] **1814** anything //
line 9: however, with renewed animation, soon] **1814** however with renewed
animation soon // line 20: is there, Miss Price?] **1814** is there Miss Price?

Fanny was silent—and Miss Crawford relapsed into thoughtfulness, till suddenly looking up at the end of a few minutes, she exclaimed, "Ah! here he is." It was not Mr. Rushworth, however, but Edmund, who then appeared walking towards them with Mrs. Grant. "My sister and Mr. Bertram—I am so glad your eldest cousin is gone that he *may* be Mr. Bertram again. There is something in the sound of Mr. *Edmund* Bertram so formal, so pitiful, so younger-brother-like, that I detest it."

"How differently we feel!" cried Fanny. "To me, the sound of *Mr.* Bertram is so cold and nothing-meaning—so entirely without warmth or character!—It just stands for a gentleman, and that's all. But there is nobleness in the name of Edmund.[11] It is a name of heroism and renown—of kings, princes, and knights; and seems to breathe the spirit of chivalry and warm affections."

"I grant you the name is good in itself, and *Lord* Edmund or *Sir* Edmund sound delightfully; but sink it under the chill, the annihilation of a Mr.—and Mr. Edmund is no more than Mr. John or Mr. Thomas. Well, shall we join and disappoint them of half their lecture upon sitting down out of doors at this time of year, by being up before they can begin?"

Edmund met them with particular pleasure. It was the first time of his seeing them together since the beginning of that better acquaintance which he had been hearing of with great satisfaction. A friendship between two so very dear to him was exactly what he could have wished; and to the credit of the lover's understanding be it stated, that he did not by any means consider Fanny as the only, or even as the greater gainer by such a friendship.

line 12: gentleman, and] **1814** gentleman and

"Well," said Miss Crawford, "and do not you scold us for our imprudence? What do you think we have been sitting down for but to be talked to about it, and entreated and supplicated never to do so again?"

"Perhaps I might have scolded," said Edmund, "if either of you had been sitting down alone; but while you do wrong together I can overlook a great deal."

"They cannot have been sitting long," cried Mrs. Grant, "for when I went up for my shawl I saw them from the stair-case window, and then they were walking."

"And really," added Edmund, "the day is so mild, that your sitting down for a few minutes can be hardly thought imprudent. Our weather must not always be judged by the Calendar. We may sometimes take greater liberties in November than in May."

"Upon my word," cried Miss Crawford, "you are two of the most disappointing and unfeeling kind friends I ever met with! There is no giving you a moment's uneasiness. You do not know how much we have been suffering, nor what chills we have felt! But I have long thought Mr. Bertram one of the worst subjects to work on, in any little manœuvre against common sense that a woman could be plagued with. I had very little hope of *him* from the first; but you, Mrs. Grant, my sister, my own sister, I think I had a right to alarm you a little."

"Do not flatter yourself, my dearest Mary. You have not the smallest chance of moving me. I have my alarms, but they are quite in a different quarter: and if I could have altered the weather, you would have had a good sharp east wind blowing on you the whole time—for here are some of my plants which Robert *will* leave out because the nights are so

line 8: Grant, "for] **1814** Grant, for // line 11: mild, that] **1814** mild that // line 14: Calendar.] **1814** calendar. // line 23: you, Mrs. Grant,] **1814** you Mrs. Grant,

mild, and I know the end of it will be that we shall have a sudden change of weather, a hard frost setting in all at once, taking every body (at least Robert) by surprize, and I shall lose every one; and what is worse, cook has just been telling me that the turkey, which I particularly wished not to be dressed till Sunday, because I know how much more Dr. Grant would enjoy it on Sunday after the fatigues of the day, will not keep beyond to-morrow. These are something like grievances, and make me think the weather most unseasonably close."

"The sweets of housekeeping in a country village!" said Miss Crawford archly. "Commend me to the nurseryman and the poulterer."[12]

"My dear child, commend Dr. Grant to the deanery of Westminster or St. Paul's,[13] and I should be as glad of your nurseryman and poulterer as you could be. But we have no such people in Mansfield. What would you have me do?"

"Oh! you can do nothing but what you do already; be plagued very often and never lose your temper."

"Thank you—but there is no escaping these little vexations, Mary, live where we may; and when you are settled in town and I come to see you, I dare say I shall find you with yours, in spite of the nurseryman and the poulterer—or perhaps on their very account. Their remoteness and unpunctuality, or their exorbitant charges and frauds will be drawing forth bitter lamentations."

"I mean to be too rich to lament or to feel any thing of the sort. A large income is the best recipé for happiness I ever heard of. It certainly may secure all the myrtle and turkey part of it."[14]

line 3: surprize,] **1814** surprise,   //   line 5: turkey, which] **1814** turkey which   //   line 8: to-morrow.] **1814** tomorrow.

"You intend to be very rich," said Edmund, with a look which, to Fanny's eye, had a great deal of serious meaning.

"To be sure. Do not you?—Do not we all?"

"I cannot intend any thing which it must be so completely beyond my power to command. Miss Crawford may chuse her degree of wealth. She has only to fix on her number of thousands a year, and there can be no doubt of their coming. My intentions are only not to be poor."

"By moderation and economy, and bringing down your wants to your income, and all that. I understand you—and a very proper plan it is for a person at your time of life, with such limited means and indifferent connections.—What can *you* want but a decent maintenance? You have not much time before you; and your relations are in no situation to do any thing for you, or to mortify you by the contrast of their own wealth and consequence. Be honest and poor, by all means— but I shall not envy you; I do not much think I shall even respect you. I have a much greater respect for those that are honest and rich."

"Your degree of respect for honesty, rich or poor, is precisely what I have no manner of concern with. I do not mean to be poor. Poverty is exactly what I have determined against. Honesty, in the something between, in the middle state of worldly circumstances, is all that I am anxious for your not looking down on."

"But I do look down upon it, if it might have been higher. I must look down upon any thing contented with obscurity when it might rise to distinction."

line 2: which, to Fanny's eye, had] **1814** which to Fanny's eye had   //
line 4: any thing] **1814** anything   //   line 10: income, and] **1814** income
and //   line 14: any thing] **1814** anything   //   line 16: poor, by] **1814** poor
by   //   line 17: shall even respect] **1814** shall ever respect   //   line 27: any
thing] **1814** anything

"But how may it rise?—How may my honesty at least rise to any distinction?"

This was not so very easy a question to answer, and occasioned an "Oh!" of some length from the fair lady before she could add "You ought to be in parliament, or you should have gone into the army ten years ago."

"*That* is not much to the purpose now; and as to my being in parliament, I believe I must wait till there is an especial assembly for the representation of younger sons who have little to live on. No, Miss Crawford," he added, in a more serious tone, "there *are* distinctions which I should be miserable if I thought myself without any chance—absolutely without chance or possibility of obtaining—but they are of a different character."

A look of consciousness as he spoke, and what seemed a consciousness of manner on Miss Crawford's side as she made some laughing answer, was sorrowful food for Fanny's observation; and finding herself quite unable to attend as she ought to Mrs. Grant, by whose side she was now following the others, she had nearly resolved on going home immediately, and only waited for courage to say so, when the sound of the great clock at Mansfield Park, striking three, made her feel that she had really been much longer absent than usual, and brought the previous self-inquiry of whether she should take leave or not just then, and how, to a very speedy issue. With undoubting decision she directly began her adieus; and Edmund began at the same time to recollect, that his mother had been inquiring for her, and that he had walked down to the Parsonage on purpose to bring her back.

line 22: Mansfield Park,] **1814** Mansfield park, // line 25: then, and]
1814 then and

Fanny's hurry increased; and without in the least expecting Edmund's attendance, she would have hastened away alone; but the general pace was quickened, and they all accompanied her into the house through which it was necessary to pass. Dr. Grant was in the vestibule, and as they stopt to speak to him, she found from Edmund's manner that he *did* mean to go with her.—He too was taking leave.—She could not but be thankful.—In the moment of parting, Edmund was invited by Dr. Grant to eat his mutton[15] with him the next day; and Fanny had barely time for an unpleasant feeling on the occasion, when Mrs. Grant, with sudden recollection, turned to her and asked for the pleasure of her company too. This was so new an attention, so perfectly new a circumstance in the events of Fanny's life, that she was all surprize and embarrassment; and while stammering out her great obligation, and her—"but she did not suppose it would be in her power," was looking at Edmund for his opinion and help.— But Edmund, delighted with her having such an happiness offered, and ascertaining with half a look, and half a sentence, that she had no objection but on her aunt's account, could not imagine that his mother would make any difficulty of sparing her, and therefore gave his decided open advice that the invitation should be accepted; and though Fanny would not venture, even on his encouragement, to such a flight of audacious independence, it was soon settled that if nothing were heard to the contrary, Mrs. Grant might expect her.

"And you know what your dinner will be," said Mrs. Grant, smiling—"the turkey—and I assure you a very fine one; for,

---

line 1: increased; and] **1814** increased, and   //   line 2: attendance, she] **1814** attendance she   //   line 8: parting, Edmund] **1814** parting Edmund   //   line 11: Grant, with sudden recollection, turned] **1814** Grant with sudden recollection turned   //   line 14: surprize] **1814** surprise   //   line 26: Grant might] **1814** Grant migh   //   line 28: for, my] **1814** for my

my dear"—turning to her husband—"cook insists upon the turkey's being dressed to-morrow."

"Very well, very well," cried Dr. Grant, "all the better. I am glad to hear you have any thing so good in the house. But Miss Price and Mr. Edmund Bertram, I dare say, would take their chance. We none of us want to hear the bill of fare. A friendly meeting, and not a fine dinner, is all we have in view. A turkey or a goose, or a leg of mutton, or whatever you and your cook chuse to give us."

The two cousins walked home together; and except in the immediate discussion of this engagement, which Edmund spoke of with the warmest satisfaction, as so particularly desirable for her in the intimacy which he saw with so much pleasure established, it was a silent walk—for having finished that subject, he grew thoughtful and indisposed for any other.

line 2: to-morrow."] **1814** tomorrow."

Chapter 5

"B U T why should Mrs. Grant ask Fanny?" said Lady Bertram. "How came she to think of asking Fanny?—Fanny never dines there, you know, in this sort of way. I cannot spare her, and I am sure she does not want to go.—Fanny, you do not want to go, do you?"

"If you put such a question to her," cried Edmund, preventing his cousin's speaking, "Fanny will immediately say, no; but I am sure, my dear mother, she would like to go; and I can see no reason why she should not."

"I cannot imagine why Mrs. Grant should think of asking her.—She never did before.—She used to ask your sisters now and then, but she never asked Fanny."

"If you cannot do without me, ma'am," said Fanny, in a self-denying tone—

"But my mother will have my father with her all the evening."

"To be sure, so I shall."

"Suppose you take my father's opinion, ma'am."

"That's well thought of. So I will, Edmund. I will ask Sir Thomas, as soon as he comes in, whether I can do without her."

"As you please, ma'am, on that head; but I meant my father's opinion as to the *propriety* of the invitation's being accepted or not; and I think he will consider it a right thing by

line 3: there, you know, in] **1814** there you know in

253

Mrs. Grant, as well as by Fanny, that being the *first* invitation[1] it should be accepted."

"I do not know. We will ask him. But he will be very much surprized that Mrs. Grant should ask Fanny at all."

There was nothing more to be said, or that could be said to any purpose, till Sir Thomas were present; but the subject involving, as it did, her own evening's comfort for the morrow, was so much uppermost in Lady Bertram's mind, that half an hour afterwards, on his looking in for a minute in his way from his plantation to his dressing-room, she called him back again, when he had almost closed the door, with "Sir Thomas, stop a moment—I have something to say to you."

Her tone of calm languor, for she never took the trouble of raising her voice, was always heard and attended to; and Sir Thomas came back. Her story began; and Fanny immediately slipped out of the room; for to hear herself the subject of any discussion with her uncle, was more than her nerves could bear. She was anxious, she knew—more anxious perhaps than she ought to be—for what was it after all whether she went or staid?—but if her uncle were to be a great while considering and deciding, and with very grave looks, and those grave looks directed to her, and at last decide against her, she might not be able to appear properly submissive and indifferent. Her cause meanwhile went on well. It began, on Lady Bertram's part, with, "I have something to tell you that will surprize you. Mrs. Grant has asked Fanny to dinner!"

"Well," said Sir Thomas, as if waiting more to accomplish the surprize.

"Edmund wants her to go. But how can I spare her?"

---

line 4: surprized] **1814** surprised   //   line 18: anxious, she] **1814** anxious she   //   line 24: began, on Lady Bertram's part, with,] **1814** began on Lady Bertram's part with,   //   line 26: surprize] **1814** surprise   //   line 28: surprize.] **1814** surprise.

"She will be late," said Sir Thomas, taking out his watch, "but what is your difficulty?"

Edmund found himself obliged to speak and fill up the blanks in his mother's story. He told the whole, and she had only to add, "So strange! for Mrs. Grant never used to ask her."

"But is not it very natural," observed Edmund, "that Mrs. Grant should wish to procure so agreeable a visitor for her sister?"

"Nothing can be more natural," said Sir Thomas, after a short deliberation; "nor, were there no sister in the case, could any thing in my opinion be more natural. Mrs. Grant's shewing civility to Miss Price, to Lady Bertram's niece, could never want explanation. The only surprize I can feel is that this should be the *first* time of its being paid. Fanny was perfectly right in giving only a conditional answer. She appears to feel as she ought. But as I conclude that she must wish to go, since all young people like to be together, I can see no reason why she should be denied the indulgence."

"But can I do without her, Sir Thomas?"

"Indeed I think you may."

"She always makes tea, you know, when my sister is not here."

"Your sister perhaps may be prevailed on to spend the day with us, and I shall certainly be at home."

"Very well, then, Fanny may go, Edmund."

The good news soon followed her. Edmund knocked at her door in his way to his own.

"Well, Fanny, it is all happily settled, and without the smallest hesitation on your uncle's side. He had but one opinion. You are to go."

line 12: any thing] **1814** anything   //   line 14: surprize] **1814** surprise   //
line 22: tea, you] **1814** tea you

"Thank you, I am *so* glad," was Fanny's instinctive reply; though when she had turned from him and shut the door, she could not help feeling, "And yet, why should I be glad? for am I not certain of seeing or hearing something there to pain me?"

In spite of this conviction, however, she was glad. Simple as such an engagement might appear in other eyes, it had novelty and importance in her's, for excepting the day at Sotherton, she had scarcely ever dined out before; and though now going only half a mile and only to three people, still it was dining out, and all the little interests of preparation were enjoyments in themselves. She had neither sympathy nor assistance from those who ought to have entered into her feelings and directed her taste; for Lady Bertram never thought of being useful to any body, and Mrs. Norris, when she came on the morrow, in consequence of an early call and invitation from Sir Thomas, was in a very ill humour, and seemed intent only on lessening her niece's pleasure, both present and future, as much as possible.

"Upon my word, Fanny, you are in high luck to meet with such attention and indulgence! You ought to be very much obliged to Mrs. Grant for thinking of you, and to your aunt for letting you go, and you ought to look upon it as something extraordinary: for I hope you are aware that there is no real occasion for your going into company in this sort of way, or ever dining out at all; and it is what you must not depend upon ever being repeated. Nor must you be fancying, that the invitation is meant as any particular compliment to *you*; the compliment is intended to your uncle and aunt, and me. Mrs. Grant thinks it a civility due to *us* to take a little notice of you, or else it would never have come into her head, and

line 3: feeling, "And] **1814** feeling, "and

you may be very certain, that if your cousin Julia had been at home, you would not have been asked at all."

Mrs. Norris had now so ingeniously done away all Mrs. Grant's part of the favour, that Fanny, who found herself expected to speak, could only say that she was very much obliged to her aunt Bertram for sparing her, and that she was endeavouring to put her aunt's evening work in such a state as to prevent her being missed.

"Oh! depend upon it, your aunt can do very well without you, or you would not be allowed to go. *I* shall be here, so you may be quite easy about your aunt. And I hope you will have a very *agreeable* day[2] and find it all mighty *delightful*. But I must observe, that five is the very awkwardest of all possible numbers to sit down to table; and I cannot but be surprized that such an *elegant* lady as Mrs. Grant should not contrive better! And round their enormous great wide table too, which fills up the room so dreadfully! Had the Doctor been contented to take my dining table when I came away, as any body in their senses would have done, instead of having that absurd new one of his own, which is wider, literally wider than the dinner table here—how infinitely better it would have been! and how much more he would have been respected! for people are never respected when they step out of their proper sphere. Remember *that*, Fanny. Five, only five to be sitting round that table! However, you will have dinner enough on it for ten I dare say."

Mrs. Norris fetched breath and went on again.

"The nonsense and folly of people's stepping out of their rank and trying to appear above themselves, makes me think it right to give *you* a hint, Fanny, now that you are going into company without any of us; and I do beseech and intreat you

line 15: surprized] **1814** surprised   //   line 17: Doctor] **1814** doctor   //
line 19: any body] **1814** anybody   //   line 20: own, which] **1814** own which

not to be putting yourself forward, and talking and giving your opinion as if you were one of your cousins—as if you were dear Mrs. Rushworth or Julia. *That* will never do, believe me. Remember, wherever you are, you must be the lowest and last;³ and though Miss Crawford is in a manner at home, at the Parsonage, you are not to be taking place of her.⁴ And as to coming away at night, you are to stay just as long as Edmund chuses. Leave him to settle *that*."

"Yes, ma'am, I should not think of any thing else."

"And if it should rain, which I think exceedingly likely, for I never saw it more threatening for a wet evening in my life— you must manage as well as you can, and not be expecting the carriage to be sent for you. I certainly do not go home to night, and, therefore, the carriage will not be out on my account; so you must make up your mind to what may happen, and take your things accordingly."

Her niece thought it perfectly reasonable. She rated her own claims to comfort as low even as Mrs. Norris could; and when Sir Thomas, soon afterwards, just opening the door, said, "Fanny, at what time would you have the carriage come round?" she felt a degree of astonishment which made it impossible for her to speak.

"My dear Sir Thomas!" cried Mrs. Norris, red with anger, "Fanny can walk."

"Walk!" repeated Sir Thomas, in a tone of most unanswerable dignity, and coming farther into the room.—"My niece walk to a dinner engagement at this time of the year! Will twenty minutes after four⁵ suit you?"

"Yes, sir," was Fanny's humble answer, given with the feelings almost of a criminal towards Mrs. Norris; and not bearing to remain with her in what might seem a state of triumph,

line 9: any thing] **1814** anything   //   line 14: and, therefore,] **1814** and therefore,   //   line 20: door, said,] **1814** door said,

she followed her uncle out of the room, having staid behind him only long enough to hear these words spoken in angry agitation:

"Quite unnecessary!—a great deal too kind! But Edmund goes;—true—it is upon Edmund's account. I observed he was hoarse on Thursday night."

But this could not impose on Fanny. She felt that the carriage was for herself and herself alone; and her uncle's consideration of her, coming immediately after such representations from her aunt, cost her some tears of gratitude when she was alone.

The coachman drove round to a minute; another minute brought down the gentleman, and as the lady had, with a most scrupulous fear of being late, been many minutes seated in the drawing room, Sir Thomas saw them off in as good time as his own correctly punctual habits required.

"Now I must look at you, Fanny," said Edmund, with the kind smile of an affectionate brother, "and tell you how I like you; and as well as I can judge by this light, you look very nicely indeed. What have you got on?"

"The new dress that my uncle was so good as to give me on my cousin's marriage. I hope it is not too fine; but I thought I ought to wear it as soon as I could, and that I might not have such another opportunity all the winter. I hope you do not think me too fine."

"A woman can never be too fine while she is all in white. No, I see no finery about you; nothing but what is perfectly proper. Your gown seems very pretty. I like these glossy spots. Has not Miss Crawford a gown something the same?"

In approaching the Parsonage they passed close by the stable-yard and coach-house.—

line 9: her, coming] **1814** her coming // line 22: fine; but] **1814** fine, but

"Hey day!" said Edmund, "here's company, here's a carriage! who have they got to meet us?" And letting down the side-glass to distinguish, "'Tis Crawford's, Crawford's barouche, I protest! There are his own two men pushing it back into its old quarters. He is here of course. This is quite a surprize, Fanny. I shall be very glad to see him."

There was no occasion, there was no time for Fanny to say how very differently she felt; but the idea of having such another to observe her, was a great increase of the trepidation with which she performed the very aweful ceremony of walking into the drawing-room.

In the drawing-room Mr. Crawford certainly was; having been just long enough arrived to be ready for dinner; and the smiles and pleased looks of the three others standing round him, shewed how welcome was his sudden resolution of coming to them for a few days on leaving Bath. A very cordial meeting passed between him and Edmund; and with the exception of Fanny, the pleasure was general; and even to *her*, there might be some advantage in his presence, since every addition to the party must rather forward her favourite indulgence of being suffered to sit silent and unattended to. She was soon aware of this herself; for though she must submit, as her own propriety of mind directed, in spite of her aunt Norris's opinion, to being the principal lady in company, and to all the little distinctions consequent thereon, she found, while they were at table, such a happy flow of conversation prevailing in which she was not required to take any part—there was so much to be said between the brother and sister about Bath, so much between the two young men about hunting, so much of politics between Mr. Crawford

line 4: barouche, I] **1814** barouche I // line 6: surprize,] **1814** surprize, // line 10: aweful] **1814** awful // line 23: directed, in] **1814** directed in // line 26: found, while] **1814** found while

and Dr. Grant, and of every thing, and all together between Mr. Crawford and Mrs. Grant, as to leave her the fairest prospect of having only to listen in quiet, and of passing a very agreeable day. She could not compliment the newly-arrived gentleman however with any appearance of interest in a scheme for extending his stay at Mansfield, and sending for his hunters from Norfolk, which, suggested by Dr. Grant, advised by Edmund, and warmly urged by the two sisters, was soon in possession of his mind, and which he seemed to want to be encouraged even by her to resolve on. Her opinion was sought as to the probable continuance of the open weather, but her answers were as short and indifferent as civility allowed. She could not wish him to stay, and would much rather not have him speak to her.

Her two absent cousins, especially Maria, were much in her thoughts on seeing him; but no embarrassing remembrance affected *his* spirits. Here he was again on the same ground where all had passed before, and apparently as willing to stay and be happy without the Miss Bertrams, as if he had never known Mansfield in any other state. She heard them spoken of by him only in a general way, till they were all re-assembled in the drawing-room, when Edmund, being engaged apart in some matter of business with Dr. Grant, which seemed entirely to engross them, and Mrs. Grant occupied at the tea-table, he began talking of them with more particularity to his other sister. With a significant smile, which made Fanny quite hate him, he said, "So! Rushworth and his fair bride are at Brighton, I understand—Happy man!"

"Yes, they have been there—about a fortnight, Miss Price, have they not?—And Julia is with them."

line 21: way, till] **1814** way till   //   line 22: Edmund, being] **1814** Edmund being   //   line 28: Brighton, I] **1814** Brighton I   //   line 29: fortnight, Miss] **1814** fortnight Miss

"And Mr. Yates, I presume, is not far off."

"Mr. Yates!—Oh! we hear nothing of Mr. Yates. I do not imagine he figures much in the letters to Mansfield Park; do you, Miss Price?—I think my friend Julia knows better than to entertain her father with Mr. Yates."

"Poor Rushworth and his two-and-forty speeches!" continued Crawford. "Nobody can ever forget them. Poor fellow!—I see him now;—his toil and his despair. Well, I am much mistaken if his lovely Maria will ever want him to make two-and-forty speeches to her"—adding, with a momentary seriousness, "She is too good for him—much too good." And then changing his tone again to one of gentle gallantry,[6] and addressing Fanny, he said, "You were Mr. Rushworth's best friend. Your kindness and patience can never be forgotten, your indefatigable patience in trying to make it possible for him to learn his part—in trying to give him a brain which nature had denied—to mix up an understanding for him out of the superfluity of your own! *He* might not have sense enough himself to estimate your kindness, but I may venture to say that it had honour from all the rest of the party."

Fanny coloured, and said nothing.

"It is as a dream, a pleasant dream!" he exclaimed, breaking forth again after few minutes musing. "I shall always look back on our theatricals with exquisite pleasure. There was such an interest, such an animation, such a spirit diffused! Every body felt it. We were all alive. There was employment, hope, solicitude, bustle, for every hour of the day. Always some little objection, some little doubt, some little anxiety to be got over. I never was happier."

line 6: two-and-forty] **1814** two and forty // line 10: two-and-forty] **1814** two and forty // line 10: adding, with] **1814** adding with

With silent indignation, Fanny repeated to herself, "Never happier!—never happier than when doing what you must know was not justifiable!—never happier than when behaving so dishonourably and unfeelingly!—Oh! what a corrupted mind!"

"We were unlucky, Miss Price," he continued in a lower tone, to avoid the possibility of being heard by Edmund, and not at all aware of her feelings, "we certainly were very unlucky. Another week, only one other week, would have been enough for us. I think if we had had the disposal of events—if Mansfield Park had had the government of the winds just for a week or two about the equinox,[7] there would have been a difference. Not that we would have endangered his safety by any tremendous weather—but only by a steady contrary wind, or a calm. I think, Miss Price, we would have indulged ourselves with a week's calm in the Atlantic at that season."

He seemed determined to be answered; and Fanny, averting her face, said with a firmer tone than usual, "As far as *I* am concerned, sir, I would not have delayed his return for a day. My uncle disapproved it all so entirely when he did arrive, that in my opinion, every thing had gone quite far enough."

She had never spoken so much at once to him in her life before, and never so angrily to any one; and when her speech was over, she trembled and blushed at her own daring. He was surprized; but after a few moments silent consideration of her, replied in a calmer, graver tone, and as if the candid result of conviction, "I believe you are right. It was more pleasant than prudent. We were getting too noisy." And then turning the conversation, he would have engaged her on some other

line 7: tone, to] **1814** tone to   //   line 27: surprized;] **1814** surprised;   //
line 28: calmer, graver] **1814** calmer graver

subject, but her answers were so shy and reluctant that he could not advance in any.

Miss Crawford, who had been repeatedly eyeing Dr. Grant and Edmund, now observed, "Those gentlemen must have some very interesting point to discuss."

"The most interesting in the world," replied her brother—"how to make money—how to turn a good income into a better. Dr. Grant is giving Bertram instructions about the living[8] he is to step into so soon. I find he takes orders in a few weeks. They were at it in the dining-parlour. I am glad to hear Bertram will be so well off. He will have a very pretty income to make ducks and drakes with,[9] and earned without much trouble. I apprehend he will not have less than seven hundred a year. Seven hundred a year is a fine thing for a younger brother; and as of course he will still live at home,[10] it will be all for his *menus plaisirs*;[11] and a sermon at Christmas and Easter, I suppose, will be the sum total of sacrifice."

His sister tried to laugh off her feelings by saying, "Nothing amuses me more than the easy manner with which every body settles the abundance of those who have a great deal less than themselves. You would look rather blank, Henry, if your menus plaisirs were to be limited to seven hundred a year."

"Perhaps I might; but all *that* you know is entirely comparative. Birthright and habit must settle the business. Bertram is certainly well off for a cadet of even a Baronet's family. By the time he is four or five-and-twenty he will have seven hundred a year, and nothing to do for it."

line 10: dining-parlour.] **1814** dining parlour. // line 17: Easter, I suppose, will] **1814** Easter I suppose will // line 28: five-and-twenty] **1814** five and twenty

Miss Crawford *could* have said that there would be a some-thing to do and to suffer for it, which she could not think lightly of; but she checked herself and let it pass; and tried to look calm and unconcerned when the two gentlemen shortly afterwards joined them.

"Bertram," said Henry Crawford, "I shall make a point of coming to Mansfield to hear you preach your first sermon. I shall come on purpose to encourage a young beginner. When is it to be? Miss Price, will not you join me in encouraging your cousin? Will not you engage to attend with your eyes steadily fixed on him the whole time—as I shall do—not to lose a word; or only looking off just to note down any sentence pre-eminently beautiful? We will provide ourselves with tablets and a pencil.[12] When will it be? You must preach at Mansfield, you know, that Sir Thomas and Lady Bertram may hear you."

"I shall keep clear of you, Crawford, as long as I can," said Edmund, "for you would be more likely to disconcert me, and I should be more sorry to see you trying at it, than almost any other man."

"Will he not feel this?" thought Fanny. "No, he can feel nothing as he ought."

The party being now all united, and the chief talkers attracting each other, she remained in tranquillity; and as a whist table was formed after tea—formed really for the amusement of Dr. Grant, by his attentive wife, though it was not to be supposed so—and Miss Crawford took her harp, she had nothing to do but to listen, and her tran-quillity remained undisturbed the rest of the evening, except when Mr. Crawford now and then addressed to her a ques-tion or observation, which she could not avoid answering.

line 15: Mansfield, you know, that] **1814** Mansfield you know that

Miss Crawford was too much vexed by what had passed to be in a humour for any thing but music. With that, she soothed herself and amused her friend.

The assurance of Edmund's being so soon to take orders, coming upon her like a blow that had been suspended, and still hoped uncertain and at a distance, was felt with resentment and mortification. She was very angry with him. She had thought her influence more. She *had* begun to think of him—she felt that she had—with great regard, with almost decided intentions; but she would now meet him with his own cool feelings. It was plain that he could have no serious views, no true attachment, by fixing himself in a situation which he must know she would never stoop to. She would learn to match him in his indifference. She would henceforth admit his attentions without any idea beyond immediate amusement. If *he* could so command his affections, *her's* should do her no harm.

line 2: any thing] **1814** anything

Chapter 6

HENRY CRAWFORD had quite made up his mind by the next morning to give another fortnight to Mansfield, and having sent for his hunters[1] and written a few lines of explanation to the Admiral, he looked round at his sister as he sealed and threw the letter from him, and seeing the coast clear of the rest of the family, said, with a smile, "And how do you think I mean to amuse myself, Mary, on the days that I do not hunt? I am grown too old to go out more than three times a week; but I have a plan for the intermediate days, and what do you think it is?"

"To walk and ride with me, to be sure."

"Not exactly, though I shall be happy to do both, but *that* would be exercise only to my body, and I must take care of my mind. Besides *that* would be all recreation and indulgence, without the wholesome alloy of labour, and I do not like to eat the bread of idleness.[2] No, my plan is to make Fanny Price in love with me."

"Fanny Price! Nonsense! No, no. You ought to be satisfied with her two cousins."

"But I cannot be satisfied without Fanny Price, without making a small hole in Fanny Price's heart. You do not seem properly aware of her claims to notice. When we talked of her last night, you none of you seemed sensible of the wonderful improvement that has taken place in her looks within the last six weeks. You see her every day, and therefore do not notice it, but I assure you, she is quite a different creature from what she was in the autumn. She was then merely a quiet, modest, not plain looking girl, but she is now absolutely pretty. I used to think she had neither complexion nor countenance; but in that soft skin of her's, so frequently tinged with a blush as it was yesterday, there is decided beauty; and from what I observed of her eyes and mouth, I do not despair of their being capable of expression enough when she has any thing to express. And then—her air, her manner, her tout ensemble[3] is so indescribably improved! She must be grown two inches, at least, since October."

"Phoo! phoo! This is only because there were no tall women to compare her with, and because she has got a new gown, and you never saw her so well dressed before. She is just what she was in October, believe me. The truth is, that she was the only girl in company for you to notice, and you must have a somebody. I have always thought her pretty—not strikingly pretty—but 'pretty enough' as people say; a sort of beauty that grows on one. Her eyes should be darker, but she has a sweet smile; but as for this wonderful degree of improvement, I am sure it may all be resolved into a better style of dress and your having nobody else to look at; and therefore, if you do set about a flirtation with her, you never will persuade me that it is in compliment to her beauty, or that it proceeds from any thing but your own idleness and folly."

Her brother gave only a smile to this accusation, and soon afterwards said, "I do not quite know what to make of Miss Fanny. I do not understand her. I could not tell what she would be at yesterday. What is her character?—Is she solemn?—Is she queer?—Is she prudish?[4] Why did she draw back and look so grave at me? I could hardly get her to speak. I never was so long in company with a girl in my life—trying

line 4: her's,] **1814** hers,   //   line 7: any thing] **1814** anything   //   line 9: most be [**1814** must be   //   line 23: any thing] **1814** anything

to entertain her—and succeed so ill! Never met with a girl who looked so grave on me! I must try to get the better of this. Her looks say, 'I will not like you, I am determined not to like you,' and I say, she shall."

"Foolish fellow! And so this is her attraction after all! This it is—her not caring about you—which gives her such a soft skin and makes her so much taller, and produces all these charms and graces! I do desire that you will not be making her really unhappy; a *little* love perhaps may animate and do her good, but I will not have you plunge her deep,[5] for she is as good a little creature as ever lived, and has a great deal of feeling."

"It can be but for a fortnight," said Henry, "and if a fortnight can kill her, she must have a constitution which nothing could save. No, I will not do her any harm, dear little soul! I only want her to look kindly on me, to give me smiles as well as blushes, to keep a chair for me by herself wherever we are, and be all animation when I take it and talk to her; to think as I think, be interested in all my possessions and pleasures, try to keep me longer at Mansfield, and feel when I go away that she shall be never happy again. I want nothing more."

"Moderation itself!" said Mary. "I can have no scruples now. Well, you will have opportunities enough of endeavouring to recommend yourself, for we are a great deal together."

And without attempting any further remonstrance, she left Fanny to her fate—a fate which, had not Fanny's heart been guarded in a way unsuspected by Miss Crawford, might have been a little harder than she deserved; for although there doubtless are such unconquerable young ladies of eighteen (or one should not read about them)[6] as are never to be persuaded into love against their judgment by all that talent,

line 4: shall. [**1814** shall." // line 11: lived, and] **1814** lived and // line 25: further] **1814** farther

269

manner, attention, and flattery can do, I have no inclination to believe Fanny one of them, or to think that with
so much tenderness of disposition, and so much taste as
belonged to her, she could have escaped heart-whole from
the courtship (though the courtship only of a fortnight) of
such a man as Crawford, in spite of there being some previous ill-opinion of him to be overcome, had not her affection
been engaged elsewhere. With all the security which love
of another and disesteem of him could give to the peace of
mind he was attacking, his continued attentions—continued,
but not obtrusive, and adapting themselves more and more
to the gentleness and delicacy of her character,—obliged her
very soon to dislike him less than formerly. She had by no
means forgotten the past, and she thought as ill of him as
ever; but she felt his powers; he was entertaining, and his
manners were so improved, so polite, so seriously and blamelessly polite, that it was impossible not to be civil to him in
return.

A very few days were enough to effect this; and at the
end of those few days, circumstances arose which had a tendency rather to forward his views of pleasing her, inasmuch
as they gave her a degree of happiness which must dispose
her to be pleased with every body. William, her brother, the
so long absent and dearly loved brother, was in England
again. She had a letter from him herself, a few hurried happy
lines, written as the ship came up Channel, and sent into
Portsmouth, with the first boat that left the Antwerp, at
anchor, in Spithead;[7] and when Crawford walked up with
the newspaper in his hand, which he had hoped would bring
the first tidings, he found her trembling with joy over this

line 12: character,—obliged] **1814** character, obliged   //   line 15: powers;
he] **1814** powers, he

270

letter, and listening with a glowing, grateful countenance to the kind invitation which her uncle was most collectedly dictating in reply.

It was but the day before, that Crawford had made himself thoroughly master of the subject, or had in fact become at all aware of her having such a brother, or his being in such a ship, but the interest then excited had been very properly lively, determining him on his return to town to apply for information as to the probable period of the Antwerp's return from the Mediterranean,[8] &c.; and the good luck which attended his early examination of ship news, the next morning, seemed the reward of his ingenuity in finding out such a method of pleasing her, as well as of his dutiful attention to the Admiral, in having for many years taken in the paper esteemed to have the earliest naval intelligence.[9] He proved, however, to be too late. All those fine first feelings, of which he had hoped to be the excitor, were already given. But his intention, the kindness of his intention, was thankfully acknowledged—quite thankfully and warmly, for she was elevated beyond the common timidity of her mind by the flow of her love for William.

This dear William would soon be amongst them. There could be no doubt of his obtaining leave of absence immediately, for he was still only a midshipman;[10] and as his parents, from living on the spot, must already have seen him and be seeing him perhaps daily, his direct holidays might with justice be instantly given to the sister, who had been his best correspondent through a period of seven years, and the uncle who had done most for his support and advancement; and accordingly the reply to her reply, fixing a very early day for his arrival, came as soon as possible; and scarcely ten days had passed since Fanny had been in the agitation of her first

line 1: glowing, grateful] **1814** glowing grateful // line 30: possible; and] **1814** possible and dinner visit, when she found herself in an agitation of a higher nature—watching in the hall, in the lobby, on the stairs, for the first sound of the carriage which was to bring her a brother.

It came happily while she was thus waiting; and there being neither ceremony nor fearfulness to delay the moment of meeting, she was with him as he entered the house, and the first minutes of exquisite feeling had no interruption and no witnesses, unless the servants chiefly intent upon opening the proper doors could be called such. This was exactly what Sir Thomas and Edmund had been separately conniving at, as each proved to the other by the sympathetic alacrity with which they both advised Mrs. Norris's continuing where she was, instead of rushing out into the hall as soon as the noises of the arrival reached them.

William and Fanny soon shewed themselves; and Sir Thomas had the pleasure of receiving, in his protégé, certainly a very different person from the one he had equipped seven years ago, but a young man of an open, pleasant countenance, and frank, unstudied, but feeling and respectful manners, and such as confirmed him his friend.

It was long before Fanny could recover from the agitating happiness of such an hour as was formed by the last thirty minutes of expectation and the first of fruition; it was some time even before her happiness could be said to make her happy, before the disappointment inseparable from the alteration of person had vanished, and she could see in him the same William as before, and talk to him, as her heart had been yearning to do, through many a past year. That time, however, did gradually come, forwarded by an affection on his side as warm as her own, and much less incumbered by refinement or self-distrust. She was the first object of his love,

line 2: stairs, for] **1814** stairs for   //   line 4: waiting; and] **1814** waiting, and   //   line 16: receiving, in] **1814** receiving in

but it was a love which his stronger spirits, and bolder temper, made it as natural for him to express as to feel. On the morrow they were walking about together with true enjoyment, and every succeeding morrow renewed a tête-à-tête, which Sir Thomas could not but observe with complacency,[11] even before Edmund had pointed it out to him.

Excepting the moments of peculiar delight, which any marked or unlooked-for instance of Edmund's consideration of her in the last few months had excited, Fanny had never known so much felicity in her life, as in this unchecked, equal, fearless intercourse with the brother and friend, who was opening all his heart to her, telling her all his hopes and fears, plans, and solicitudes respecting that long thought of, dearly earned, and justly valued blessing of promotion—who could give her direct and minute information of the father and mother, brothers and sisters, of whom she very seldom heard—who was interested in all the comforts and all the little hardships of her home, at Mansfield—ready to think of every member of that home as she directed, or differing only by a less scrupulous opinion, and more noisy abuse of their aunt Norris—and with whom (perhaps the dearest indulgence of the whole) all the evil and good of their earliest years could be gone over again, and every former united pain and pleasure retraced with the fondest recollection. An advantage this, a strengthener of love, in which even the conjugal tie is beneath the fraternal. Children of the same family, the same blood, with the same first associations and habits, have some means of enjoyment in their power, which no subsequent connections can supply; and it must be by a long and unnatural estrangement, by a divorce which no subsequent connection can justify, if such precious remains of the earliest

line 11: equal, fearless] **1814** equal fearless

attachments are ever entirely outlived. Too often, alas! it is so.—Fraternal love, sometimes almost every thing, is at others worse than nothing. But with William and Fanny Price, it was still a sentiment in all its prime and freshness, wounded by no opposition of interest, cooled by no separate attachment, and feeling the influence of time and absence only in its increase.

An affection so amiable was advancing each in the opinion of all who had hearts to value any thing good. Henry Crawford was as much struck with it as any. He honoured the warm hearted, blunt fondness of the young sailor, which led him to say, with his hand stretched towards Fanny's head, "Do you know, I begin to like that queer fashion[12] already, though when I first heard of such things being done in England I could not believe it, and when Mrs. Brown, and the other women, at the Commissioner's, at Gibraltar,[13] appeared in the same trim, I thought they were mad; but Fanny can reconcile me to any thing"—and saw, with lively admiration, the glow of Fanny's cheek, the brightness of her eye, the deep interest, the absorbed attention, while her brother was describing any of the imminent hazards, or terrific[14] scenes, which such a period, at sea, must supply.

It was a picture which Henry Crawford had moral taste[15] enough to value. Fanny's attractions increased—increased two-fold—for the sensibility which beautified her complexion and illumined her countenance, was an attraction in itself. He was no longer in doubt of the capabilities of her heart. She had feeling, genuine feeling. It would be something to be loved by such a girl, to excite the first ardours of her young, unsophisticated mind! She interested him more than he had foreseen. A fortnight was not enough. His stay became indefinite.

line 8: any thing] **1814** anything   //   line 17: any thing"] **1814** anything"

William was often called on by his uncle to be the talker. His recitals were amusing in themselves to Sir Thomas, but the chief object in seeking them, was to understand the recitor, to know the young man by his histories; and he listened to his clear, simple, spirited details with full satisfaction—seeing in them, the proof of good principles, professional knowledge, energy, courage, and cheerfulness— every thing that could deserve or promise well. Young as he was, William had already seen a great deal. He had been in the Mediterranean—in the West Indies—in the Mediterranean[16] again—had been often taken on shore by the favour of his Captain,[17] and in the course of seven years had known every variety of danger, which sea and war together could offer. With such means in his power he had a right to be listened to; and though Mrs. Norris could fidget about the room, and disturb every body in quest of two needlefulls of thread or a second hand shirt button in the midst of her nephew's account of a shipwreck or an engagement, every body else was attentive;[18] and even Lady Bertram could not hear of such horrors unmoved, or without sometimes lifting her eyes from her work to say, "Dear me! how disagreeable.—I wonder any body can ever go to sea."

To Henry Crawford they gave a different feeling. He longed to have been at sea, and seen and done and suffered as much. His heart was warmed, his fancy fired, and he felt the highest respect for a lad who, before he was twenty, had gone through such bodily hardships, and given such proofs of mind.[19] The glory of heroism, of usefulness, of exertion, of endurance, made his own habits of selfish indulgence appear in shameful contrast; and he wished he had been a William Price, distinguishing himself and working his way to fortune

line 16: every body in] **1814** every body, in // line 19: attentive; and] **1814** attentive, and

and consequence with so much self-respect and happy ardour, instead of what he was!

The wish was rather eager than lasting. He was roused from the reverie of retrospection and regret produced by it, by some inquiry from Edmund as to his plans for the next day's hunting; and he found it was as well to be a man of fortune at once with horses and grooms at his command. In one respect it was better, as it gave him the means of conferring a kindness where he wished to oblige. With spirits, courage, and curiosity up to any thing, William expressed an inclination to hunt; and Crawford could mount him without the slightest inconvenience to himself, and with only some scruples to obviate in Sir Thomas, who knew better than his nephew the value of such a loan, and some alarms to reason away in Fanny. She feared for William; by no means convinced by all that he could relate of his own horsemanship in various countries, of the scrambling parties in which he had been engaged, the rough horses and mules he had ridden, or his many narrow escapes from dreadful falls, that he was at all equal to the management of a high-fed hunter in an English fox-chase; nor till he returned safe and well, without accident or discredit, could she be reconciled to the risk, or feel any of that obligation to Mr. Crawford for lending the horse which he had fully intended it should produce. When it was proved however to have done William no harm, she could allow it to be a kindness, and even reward the owner with a smile when the animal was one minute tendered to his use again; and the next, with the greatest cordiality, and in a manner not to be resisted, made over to his use entirely so long as he remained in Northamptonshire.

line 18: ridden, or] **1814** ridden or

Chapter 7

THE intercourse of the two families was at this period more nearly restored to what it had been in the autumn, than any member of the old intimacy had thought ever likely to be again. The return of Henry Crawford, and the arrival of William Price, had much to do with it, but much was still owing to Sir Thomas's more than toleration of the neighbourly attempts at the Parsonage. His mind, now disengaged from the cares which had pressed on him at first, was at leisure to find the Grants and their young inmates really worth visiting; and though infinitely above scheming or contriving for any the most advantageous matrimonial establishment that could be among the apparent possibilities of any one most dear to him, and disdaining even as a littleness the being quick-sighted on such points, he could not avoid perceiving in a grand and careless way that Mr. Crawford was somewhat distinguishing his niece—nor perhaps refrain (though unconsciously) from giving a more willing assent to invitations on that account.

His readiness, however, in agreeing to dine at the Parsonage, when the general invitation was at last hazarded, after many debates and many doubts as to whether it were worth while, "because Sir Thomas seemed so ill inclined! and Lady Bertram was so indolent!"—proceeded from good breeding and good-will alone, and had nothing to do with

Mr. Crawford, but as being one in an agreeable group; for it was in the course of that very visit, that he first began to think, that any one in the habit of such idle observations *would have thought* that Mr. Crawford was the admirer of Fanny Price.

The meeting was generally felt to be a pleasant one, being composed in a good proportion of those who would talk and those who would listen; and the dinner itself was elegant and plentiful, according to the usual style of the Grants, and too much according to the usual habits of all to raise any emotion except in Mrs. Norris, who could never behold either the wide table or the number of dishes on it with patience, and who did always contrive to experience some evil from the passing of the servants behind her chair, and to bring away some fresh conviction of its being impossible among so many dishes but that some must be cold.

In the evening it was found, according to the predetermination of Mrs. Grant and her sister, that after making up the Whist table there would remain sufficient for a round game,[1] and every body being as perfectly complying and without a choice as on such occasions they always are, Speculation[2] was decided on almost as soon as Whist;[3] and Lady Bertram soon found herself in the critical situation of being applied to for her own choice between the games, and being required either to draw a card for Whist or not. She hesitated. Luckily Sir Thomas was at hand.

"What shall I do, Sir Thomas?—Whist and Speculation; which will amuse me most?"[4]

Sir Thomas, after a moment's thought, recommended Speculation. He was a Whist player himself, and perhaps might feel that it would not much amuse him to have her for a partner.

line 1: Mr. Crawford, but] **1814** Mr. Crawford but   //   line 19: complying and] **1814** complying, and

"Very well," was her ladyship's contented answer—"then Speculation if you please, Mrs. Grant. I know nothing about it, but Fanny must teach me."

Here Fanny interposed however with anxious protestations of her own equal ignorance; she had never played the game nor seen it played in her life; and Lady Bertram felt a moment's indecision again—but upon every body's assuring her that nothing could be so easy, that it was the easiest game on the cards, and Henry Crawford's stepping forward with a most earnest request to be allowed to sit between her ladyship and Miss Price, and teach them both, it was so settled; and Sir Thomas, Mrs. Norris, and Dr. and Mrs. Grant, being seated at the table of prime intellectual state and dignity, the remaining six, under Miss Crawford's direction, were arranged round the other. It was a fine arrangement for Henry Crawford, who was close to Fanny, and with his hands full of business, having two persons cards to manage as well as his own—for though it was impossible for Fanny not to feel herself mistress of the rules of the game in three minutes, he had yet to inspirit her play, sharpen her avarice, and harden her heart, which, especially in any competition with William, was a work of some difficulty; and as for Lady Bertram, he must continue in charge of all her fame and fortune through the whole evening; and if quick enough to keep her from looking at her cards when the deal began, must direct her in whatever was to be done with them to the end of it.

He was in high spirits, doing every thing with happy ease, and pre-eminent in all the lively turns, quick resources, and playful impudence that could do honour to the game; and the round table was altogether a very comfortable contrast to the steady sobriety and orderly silence of the other.

line 14: six, under Miss Crawford's direction, were] **1814** six under Miss Crawford's direction were

Twice had Sir Thomas inquired into the enjoyment and success of his lady, but in vain; no pause was long enough for the time his measured manner needed; and very little of her state could be known till Mrs. Grant was able, at the end of the first rubber, to go to her and pay her compliments.

"I hope your ladyship is pleased with the game."

"Oh! dear, yes.—Very entertaining indeed. A very odd game. I do not know what it is all about. I am never to see my cards; and Mr. Crawford does all the rest."

"Bertram," said Crawford some time afterwards, taking the opportunity of a little languor in the game, "I have never told you what happened to me yesterday in my ride home." They had been hunting together, and were in the midst of a good run, and at some distance from Mansfield, when his horse being found to have flung a shoe, Henry Crawford had been obliged to give up, and make the best of his way back. "I told you I lost my way after passing that old farm house, with the yew trees, because I can never bear to ask; but I have not told you that, with my usual luck—for I never do wrong without gaining by it—I found myself in due time in the very place which I had a curiosity to see. I was suddenly, upon turning the corner of a steepish downy field,⁵ in the midst of a retired little village between gently rising hills; a small stream before me to be forded, a church standing on a sort of knoll to my right—which church was strikingly large and handsome for the place, and not a gentleman or half a gentleman's house to be seen excepting one—to be presumed the Parsonage, within a stone's throw of the said knoll and church. I found myself in short in Thornton Lacey."

"It sounds like it," said Edmund; "but which way did you turn after passing Sewell's farm?"

line 4: able, at the end of the first rubber, to] **1814** able at the end of the first rubber to // line 19: that, with] **1814** that with

"I answer no such irrelevant and insidious questions; though were I to answer all that you could put in the course of an hour, you would never be able to prove that it was *not* Thornton Lacey—for such it certainly was."

"You inquired then?"

"No, I never inquire. But I *told* a man mending a hedge that it was Thornton Lacey, and he agreed to it."

"You have a good memory. I had forgotten having ever told you half so much of the place."

Thornton Lacey was the name of his impending living, as Miss Crawford well knew; and her interest in a negociation for William Price's knave increased.

"Well," continued Edmund, "and how did you like what you saw?"

"Very much indeed. You are a lucky fellow. There will be work for five summers at least before the place is live-able."

"No, no, not so bad as that. The farm-yard must be moved,[6] I grant you; but I am not aware of any thing else. The house is by no means bad, and when the yard is removed, there may be a very tolerable approach to it."

"The farm-yard must be cleared away entirely, and planted up to shut out the blacksmith's shop. The house must be turned[7] to front the east instead of the north—the entrance and principal rooms, I mean, must be on that side, where the view is really very pretty; I am sure it may be done. And *there* must be your approach—through what is at present the garden. You must make a new garden at what is now the back of the house; which will be giving it the best aspect in the world—sloping to the south-east. The ground seems precisely formed for it. I rode fifty yards up the lane between

line 11: interest in a] **1814** interest for a   //   line 24: rooms, I mean, must] **1814** rooms I mean must   //   line 24: side, where] **1814** side where   //   line 27: make a new] **1814** make you a new

the church and the house in order to look about me; and saw how it might all be. Nothing can be easier. The meadows beyond what *will be* the garden, as well as what now *is*, sweeping round from the lane I stood in to the north-east, that is, to the principal road through the village, must be all laid together of course; very pretty meadows they are, finely sprinkled with timber. They belong to the living, I suppose. If not, you must purchase them. Then the stream—something must be done with the stream; but I could not quite determine what. I had two or three ideas."

"And I have two or three ideas also," said Edmund, "and one of them is that very little of your plan for Thornton Lacey will ever be put in practice. I must be satisfied with rather less ornament and beauty. I think the house and premises may be made comfortable, and given the air of a gentleman's residence[8] without any very heavy expense, and that must suffice me; and I hope may suffice all who care about me."

Miss Crawford, a little suspicious and resentful of a certain tone of voice and a certain half-look attending the last expression of his hope, made a hasty finish of her dealings with William Price, and securing his knave at an exorbitant rate, exclaimed, "There, I will stake my last like a woman of spirit. No cold prudence for me. I am not born to sit still and do nothing. If I lose the game, it shall not be from not striving for it."

The game was her's, and only did not pay her for what she had given to secure it. Another deal proceeded, and Crawford began again about Thornton Lacey.

"My plan may not be the best possible; I had not many minutes to form it in: but you must do a good deal. The place deserves it, and you will find yourself not satisfied with much

line 4: north-east,] **1814** north east,   //   line 26: her's,] **1814** hers,

less than it is capable of.—(Excuse me, your ladyship must not see your cards. There, let them lie just before you.) The place deserves it, Bertram. You talk of giving it the air of a gentleman's residence. *That* will be done, by the removal of the farm-yard, for, independent of that terrible nuisance, I never saw a house of the kind which had in itself so much the air of a gentleman's residence, so much the look of a something above a mere Parsonage House, above the expenditure of a few hundreds a year. It is not a scrambling collection of low single rooms, with as many roofs as windows—it is not cramped into the vulgar compactness of a square farm-house—it is a solid,[9] roomy, mansion-like looking house, such as one might suppose a respectable old country family had lived in from generation to generation, through two centuries at least, and were now spending from two to three thousand a year in." Miss Crawford listened, and Edmund agreed to this. "The air of a gentleman's residence, therefore, you cannot but give it, if you do any thing. But it is capable of much more. (Let me see, Mary; Lady Bertram bids a dozen[10] for that queen; no, no, a dozen is more than it is worth. Lady Bertram does *not* bid a dozen. She will have nothing to say to it. Go on, go on.) By some such improvements as I have suggested, (I do not really require you to proceed upon my plan, though by the bye I doubt any body's striking out a better)—you may give it a higher character. You may raise it into a *place*.[11] From being the mere gentleman's residence, it becomes, by judicious improvement, the residence of a man of education, taste, modern manners, good connections. All this may be stamped on it; and that house receive such an

line 5: for, independent] **1814** for independent   //   line 12: solid, roomy,] **1814** solid walled, roomy,   //   line 23: suggested, (I] **1814** suggested, I   //   line 25: better)—you] **1814** better. You   //   line 27: improvement, the] **1814** improvement the

air as to make its owner be set down as the great land-holder of the parish, by every creature travelling the road; especially as there is no real squire's house to dispute the point; a circumstance between ourselves to enhance the value of such a situation in point of privilege and independence beyond all calculation. *You* think with me, I hope—(turning with a softened voice to Fanny).—Have you ever seen the place?"

Fanny gave a quick negative, and tried to hide her interest in the subject by an eager attention to her brother, who was driving as hard a bargain and imposing on her as much as he could; but Crawford pursued with "No, no, you must not part with the queen. You have bought her too dearly, and your brother does not offer half her value. No, no, sir, hands off—hands off. Your sister does not part with the queen. She is quite determined. The game will be yours, turning to her again—it will certainly be yours."

"And Fanny had much rather it were William's," said Edmund, smiling at her. "Poor Fanny! not allowed to cheat herself as she wishes!"

"Mr. Bertram," said Miss Crawford, a few minutes afterwards, "you know Henry to be such a capital improver, that you cannot possibly engage in any thing of the sort at Thornton Lacey, without accepting his help. Only think how useful he was at Sotherton! Only think what grand things were produced there by our all going with him one hot day in August to drive about the grounds, and see his genius take fire. There we went, and there we came home again; and what was done there is not to be told!"

Fanny's eyes were turned on Crawford for a moment with an expression more than grave, even reproachful; but on catching his were instantly withdrawn. With something of

line 6: me, I] **1814** me I // line 7: Fanny).—Have] **1814** Fanny)—Have // line 13: no, sir,] **1814** no, Sir,

consciousness he shook his head at his sister, and laughingly replied, "I cannot say there was much done at Sotherton; but it was a hot day, and we were all walking after each other and bewildered." As soon as a general buz gave him shelter, he added, in a low voice directed solely at Fanny, "I should be sorry to have my powers of *planning* judged of by the day at Sotherton. I see things very differently now. Do not think of me as I appeared then."

Sotherton was a word to catch Mrs. Norris, and being just then in the happy leisure which followed securing the odd trick[12] by Sir Thomas's capital play and her own, against Dr. and Mrs. Grant's great hands, she called out in high good-humour, "Sotherton! Yes, that is a place indeed, and we had a charming day there. William, you are quite out of luck; but the next time you come I hope dear Mr. and Mrs. Rushworth will be at home, and I am sure I can answer for your being kindly received by both. Your cousins are not of a sort to forget their relations, and Mr. Rushworth is a most amiable man. They are at Brighton now, you know—in one of the best houses there, as Mr. Rushworth's fine fortune gives them a right to be. I do not exactly know the distance, but when you get back to Portsmouth, if it is not very far off, you ought to go over and pay your respects to them; and I could send a little parcel by you that I want to get conveyed to your cousins."

"I should be very happy, aunt—but Brighton is almost by Beachey Head;[13] and if I could get so far, I could not expect to be welcome in such a smart place as that—poor scrubby[14] midshipman as I am."

Mrs. Norris was beginning an eager assurance of the affability he might depend on, when she was stopped by

line 5: added, in] **1814** added in   //   line 19: now, you know] **1814** now you know

Sir Thomas's saying with authority, "I do not advise your going to Brighton, William, as I trust you may soon have more convenient opportunities of meeting, but my daughters would be happy to see their cousins any where; and you will find Mr. Rushworth most sincerely disposed to regard all the connections of our family as his own."

"I would rather find him private secretary to the first Lord[15] than any thing else," was William's only answer, in an under voice, not meant to reach far, and the subject dropped.

As yet Sir Thomas had seen nothing to remark in Mr. Crawford's behaviour; but when the Whist table broke up at the end of the second rubber, and leaving Dr. Grant and Mrs. Norris to dispute over their last play, he became a looker-on at the other, he found his niece the object of attentions, or rather of professions of a somewhat pointed character.

Henry Crawford was in the first glow of another scheme about Thornton Lacey, and not being able to catch Edmund's ear, was detailing it to his fair neighbour with a look of considerable earnestness. His scheme was to rent the house himself the following winter, that he might have a home of his own in that neighbourhood; and it was not merely for the use of it in the hunting season, (as he was then telling her,) though *that* consideration had certainly some weight, feeling as he did, that in spite of all Dr. Grant's very great kindness, it was impossible for him and his horses to be accommodated where they now were without material inconvenience; but his attachment to that neighbourhood did not depend upon one amusement or one season of the year: he had set his heart upon having a something there that he could come to at any time, a little homestall[16] at his command where all the holidays of his year might be spent, and he might find himself continuing, improving, and *perfecting* that friendship and intimacy with the Mansfield Park family which was increasing in value to him every day. Sir Thomas heard and was not offended. There was no want of respect in the young man's address; and Fanny's reception of it was so proper and modest, so calm and uninviting, that he had nothing to censure in her. She said little, assented only here and there, and betrayed no inclination either of appropriating any part of the compliment to herself or of strengthening his views in favour of Northamptonshire. Finding by whom he was observed, Henry Crawford addressed himself on the same subject to Sir Thomas, in a more every day tone, but still with feeling.

"I want to be your neighbour, Sir Thomas, as you have perhaps heard me telling Miss Price. May I hope for your acquiescence and for your not influencing your son against such a tenant?"

Sir Thomas, politely bowing, replied—"It is the only way, sir, in which I could *not* wish you established as a permanent neighbour; but I hope, and believe, that Edmund will occupy his own house at Thornton Lacey. Edmund, am I saying too much?"

Edmund, on this appeal, had first to hear what was going on, but on understanding the question, was at no loss for an answer.

"Certainly, sir, I have no idea but of residence.[17] But, Crawford, though I refuse you as a tenant, come to me as a friend. Consider the house as half your own every winter, and we will add to the stables on your own improved plan, and with all the improvements of your improved plan that may occur to you this spring."

line 5: uninviting, that] **1814** uninviting that // line 17: Thomas, politely] **1814** Thomas politely // line 25: But, Crawford,] **1814** But Crawford,

"We shall be the losers," continued Sir Thomas. "His going, though only eight miles, will be an unwelcome contraction of our family circle; but I should have been deeply mortified, if any son of mine could reconcile himself to doing less. It is perfectly natural that you should not have thought much on the subject, Mr. Crawford. But a parish has wants and claims which can be known only by a clergyman constantly resident, and which no proxy can be capable of satisfying to the same extent. Edmund might, in the common phrase, do the duty of Thornton, that is, he might read prayers and preach, without giving up Mansfield Park; he might ride over, every Sunday, to a house nominally inhabited, and go through divine service; he might be the clergyman of Thornton Lacey every seventh day, for three or four hours, if that would content him. But it will not. He knows that human nature needs more lessons than a weekly sermon can convey, and that if he does not live among his parishioners and prove himself by constant attention their well-wisher and friend, he does very little either for their good or his own."

Mr. Crawford bowed his acquiescence.

"I repeat again," added Sir Thomas, "that Thornton Lacey is the only house in the neighbourhood in which I should *not* be happy to wait on Mr. Crawford as occupier."

Mr. Crawford bowed his thanks.

"Sir Thomas," said Edmund, "undoubtedly understands the duty of a parish priest.—We must hope his son may prove that *he* knows it too."

Whatever effect Sir Thomas's little harangue might really produce on Mr. Crawford, it raised some awkward sensations in two of the others, two of his most attentive listeners, Miss Crawford and Fanny.—One of whom, having never before understood that Thornton was so soon and so completely to be his home, was pondering with downcast eyes on what it would be, *not* to see Edmund every day; and the other, startled from the agreeable fancies she had been previously indulging on the strength of her brother's description, no longer able, in the picture she had been forming of a future Thornton, to shut out the church, sink the clergyman, and see only the respectable, elegant, modernized, and occasional residence of a man of independent fortune—was considering Sir Thomas, with decided ill-will, as the destroyer of all this, and suffering the more from that involuntary forbearance which his character and manner commanded, and from not daring to relieve herself by a single attempt at throwing ridicule on his cause.

All the agreeable of *her* speculation was over for that hour. It was time to have done with cards if sermons prevailed, and she was glad to find it necessary to come to a conclusion and be able to refresh her spirits by a change of place and neighbour.

The chief of the party were now collected irregularly round the fire, and waiting the final break up. William and Fanny were the most detached. They remained together at the otherwise deserted card-table, talking very comfortably and not thinking of the rest, till some of the rest began to think of them. Henry Crawford's chair was the first to be given a direction towards them, and he sat silently observing them for a few minutes; himself in the meanwhile observed by Sir Thomas, who was standing in chat with Dr. Grant.

"This is the Assembly night,"[18] said William. "If I were at Portsmouth, I should be at it perhaps."

"But you do not wish yourself at Portsmouth, William?"

"No, Fanny, that I do not. I shall have enough of Portsmouth, and of dancing too, when I cannot have you.

line 4: able, in] **1814** able in // line 16: place and neighbour.] **1814** place and neighbours.

And I do not know that there would be any good in going to the Assembly, for I might not get a partner. The Portsmouth girls turn up their noses at any body who has not a commission.[19] One might as well be nothing as a midshipman. One *is* nothing indeed. You remember the Gregorys; they are grown up amazing fine girls, but they will hardly speak to *me*, because Lucy is courted by a lieutenant."

"Oh! shame, shame!—But never mind it, William. (Her own cheeks in a glow of indignation as she spoke.) It is not worth minding. It is no reflection on *you*; it is no more than what the greatest admirals have all experienced, more or less, in their time. You must think of that; you must try to make up your mind to it as one of the hardships which fall to every sailor's share—like bad weather and hard living—only with this advantage, that there will be an end to it, that there will come a time when you will have nothing of that sort to endure. When you are a lieutenant!—only think, William, when you are a lieutenant, how little you will care for any nonsense of this kind."

"I begin to think I shall never be a lieutenant, Fanny. Every body gets made but me."

"Oh! my dear William, do not talk so, do not be so desponding. My uncle says nothing, but I am sure he will do every thing in his power to get you made. He knows, as well as you do, of what consequence it is."

She was checked by the sight of her uncle much nearer to them than she had any suspicion of, and each found it necessary to talk of something else.

"Are you fond of dancing, Fanny?"

"Yes, very;—only I am soon tired."

line 3: any body] **1814** anybody // line 18: lieutenant, how] **1814** lieutenant how // line 24: knows, as] **1814** knows as

"I should like to go to a ball with you and see you dance. Have you never any balls at Northampton?—I should like to see you dance, and I'd dance with you if you *would*, for nobody would know who I was here, and I should like to be your partner once more. We used to jump about together many a time, did not we? when the hand-organ was in the street?[20] I am a pretty good dancer in my way, but I dare say you are a better."—And turning to his uncle, who was now close to them—"Is not Fanny a very good dancer, sir?"

Fanny, in dismay at such an unprecedented question, did not know which way to look, or how to be prepared for the answer. Some very grave reproof, or at least the coldest expression of indifference must be coming to distress her brother, and sink her to the ground. But, on the contrary, it was no worse than, "I am sorry to say that I am unable to answer your question. I have never seen Fanny dance since she was a little girl; but I trust we shall both think she acquits herself like a gentlewoman when we do see her, which perhaps we may have an opportunity of doing ere long."

"I have had the pleasure of seeing your sister dance, Mr. Price," said Henry Crawford, leaning forward, "and will engage to answer every inquiry which you can make on the subject, to your entire satisfaction. But I believe (seeing Fanny look distressed) it must be at some other time. There is *one* person in company who does not like to have Miss Price spoken of."

True enough, he had once seen Fanny dance; and it was equally true that he would now have answered for her gliding about with quiet, light elegance, and in admirable time, but in fact he could not for the life of him recall what her dancing

line 4: here, and] **1814** here and // line 14: But, on the contrary, it] **1814** But on the contrary it

had been, and rather took it for granted that she had been present than remembered any thing about her.

He passed, however, for an admirer of her dancing; and Sir Thomas, by no means displeased, prolonged the conversation on dancing in general, and was so well engaged in describing the balls of Antigua, and listening to what his nephew could relate of the different modes of dancing which had fallen within his observation, that he had not heard his carriage announced, and was first called to the knowledge of it by the bustle of Mrs. Norris.

"Come, Fanny, Fanny, what are you about? We are going. Do not you see your aunt is going? Quick, quick. I cannot bear to keep good old Wilcox waiting. You should always remember the coachman and horses. My dear Sir Thomas, we have settled it that the carriage should come back for you, and Edmund, and William."

Sir Thomas could not dissent, as it had been his own arrangement, previously communicated to his wife and sister; but *that* seemed forgotten by Mrs. Norris, who must fancy that she settled it all herself.

Fanny's last feeling in the visit was disappointment—for the shawl which Edmund was quietly taking from the servant to bring and put round her shoulders, was seized by Mr. Crawford's quicker hand, and she was obliged to be indebted to his more prominent attention.

line 2: any thing] **1814** anything

Chapter 8

WILLIAM's desire of seeing Fanny dance, made more than a momentary impression on his uncle. The hope of an opportunity, which Sir Thomas had then given, was not given to be thought of no more. He remained steadily inclined to gratify so amiable a feeling—to gratify any body else who might wish to see Fanny dance, and to give pleasure to the young people in general; and having thought the matter over and taken his resolution in quiet independence, the result of it appeared the next morning at breakfast, when, after recalling and commending what his nephew had said, he added, "I do not like, William, that you should leave Northamptonshire without this indulgence. It would give me pleasure to see you both dance. You spoke of the balls at Northampton. Your cousins have occasionally attended them; but they would not altogether suit us now. The fatigue would be too much for your aunt. I believe, we must not think of a Northampton ball. A dance at home would be more eligible, and if"—

"Ah! my dear Sir Thomas," interrupted Mrs. Norris, "I knew what was coming. I knew what you were going to say. If dear Julia were at home, or dearest Mrs. Rushworth at Sotherton, to afford a reason, an occasion for such a thing, you would be tempted to give the young people a dance at Mansfield. I know you would. If *they* were at home to grace

line 5: any body else] **1814** anybody else   //   line 9: when, after] **1814** when after   //   line 20: Rushworth at] **1814** Rushworth, at   //   line 21: a thing, you] **1814** a thing, yu   //   line 23: If *they* were] **1814** If they were the ball, a ball you would have this very Christmas. Thank your uncle, William, thank your uncle."

"My daughters," replied Sir Thomas, gravely interposing, "have their pleasures at Brighton, and I hope are very happy; but the dance which I think of giving at Mansfield, will be for their cousins. Could we be all assembled, our satisfaction would undoubtedly be more complete, but the absence of some is not to debar the others of amusement."

Mrs. Norris had not another word to say. She saw decision in his looks, and her surprize and vexation required some minutes silence to be settled into composure. A ball at such a time! His daughters absent and herself not consulted! There was comfort, however, soon at hand. *She* must be the doer of every thing; Lady Bertram would of course be spared all thought and exertion, and it would all fall upon *her*. She should have to do the honours of the evening, and this reflection quickly restored so much of her good humour as enabled her to join in with the others, before their happiness and thanks were all expressed.

Edmund, William, and Fanny, did, in their different ways, look and speak as much grateful pleasure in the promised ball, as Sir Thomas could desire. Edmund's feelings were for the other two. His father had never conferred a favour or shewn a kindness more to his satisfaction.

Lady Bertram was perfectly quiescent and contented, and had no objections to make. Sir Thomas engaged for its giving her very little trouble, and she assured him, "that she was not at all afraid of the trouble, indeed she could not imagine there would be any."

Mrs. Norris was ready with her suggestions as to the rooms he would think fittest to be used, but found it all prearranged;

line 10: surprize] **1814** surprise   //   line 14: of couse [**1814** of course

and when she would have conjectured and hinted about the day, it appeared that the day was settled too. Sir Thomas had been amusing himself with shaping a very complete outline of the business; and as soon as she would listen quietly, could read his list of the families to be invited, from whom he calculated, with all necessary allowance for the shortness of the notice, to collect young people enough to form twelve or fourteen couple; and could detail the considerations which had induced him to fix on the 22d, as the most eligible day. William was required to be at Portsmouth on the 24th; the 22d would therefore be the last day of his visit; but where the days were so few it would be unwise to fix on any earlier. Mrs. Norris was obliged to be satisfied with thinking just the same, and with having been on the point of proposing the 22d herself, as by far the best day for the purpose.

The ball was now a settled thing, and before the evening a proclaimed thing to all whom it concerned. Invitations were sent with dispatch, and many a young lady went to bed that night with her head full of happy cares as well as Fanny.—To her, the cares were sometimes almost beyond the happiness; for young and inexperienced, with small means of choice and no confidence in her own taste—the "how she should be dressed" was a point of painful solicitude; and the almost solitary ornament in her possession, a very pretty amber cross which William had brought her from Sicily,[1] was the greatest distress of all, for she had nothing but a bit of ribbon to fasten it to; and though she had worn it in that manner once, would it be allowable at such a time, in the midst of all the rich ornaments which she supposed all the other young ladies would appear in? And yet not to wear it! William had wanted to buy her a gold chain too, but the purchase had been beyond his

line 16: evening a] **1814** evening, a   //   line 18: dispatch, and] **1814** dispatch and   //   line 19: cares as] **1814** cares, as   //   line 28: time, in] **1814** time in

means, and therefore not to wear the cross might be mortifying him. These were anxious considerations; enough to sober her spirits even under the prospect of a ball given principally for her gratification.

The preparations meanwhile went on, and Lady Bertram continued to sit on her sofa without any inconvenience from them. She had some extra visits from the housekeeper, and her maid was rather hurried in making up a new dress for her; Sir Thomas gave orders and Mrs. Norris ran about, but all this gave *her* no trouble, and as she had foreseen, "there was in fact no trouble in the business."

Edmund was at this time particularly full of cares; his mind being deeply occupied in the consideration of two important events now at hand, which were to fix his fate in life— ordination and matrimony—events of such a serious character as to make the ball, which would be very quickly followed by one of them, appear of less moment in his eyes than in those of any other person in the house. On the 23d he was going to a friend near Peterborough[2] in the same situation as himself, and they were to receive ordination in the course of the Christmas week. Half his destiny would then be determined—but the other half might not be so very smoothly wooed. His duties would be established, but the wife who was to share, and animate, and reward those duties[3] might yet be unattainable. He knew his own mind, but he was not always perfectly assured of knowing Miss Crawford's. There were points on which they did not quite agree, there were moments in which she did not seem propitious, and though trusting altogether to her affection, so far as to be resolved (almost resolved) on bringing it to a decision within a very short time, as soon as the variety of business before him

line 16: ball, which] **1814** ball which   //   line 19: Peterborough in] **1814** Peterborough, in

were arranged, and he knew what he had to offer her—he had many anxious feelings, many doubting hours as to the result. His conviction of her regard for him was sometimes very strong; he could look back on a long course of encouragement, and she was as perfect in disinterested attachment as in every thing else. But at other times doubt and alarm intermingled with his hopes, and when he thought of her acknowledged disinclination for privacy and retirement, her decided preference of a London life—what could he expect but a determined rejection? unless it were an acceptance even more to be deprecated, demanding such sacrifices of situation and employment on his side as conscience must forbid.

The issue of all depended on one question. Did she love him well enough to forego what had used to be essential points—did she love him well enough to make them no longer essential? And this question, which he was continually repeating to himself, though oftenest answered with a "Yes," had sometimes its "No."

Miss Crawford was soon to leave Mansfield, and on this circumstance the "no" and the "yes" had been very recently in alternation. He had seen her eyes sparkle as she spoke of the dear friend's letter, which claimed a long visit from her in London, and of the kindness of Henry, in engaging to remain where he was till January, that he might convey her thither; he had heard her speak of the pleasure of such a journey with an animation which had "no" in every tone. But this had occurred on the first day of its being settled, within the first hour of the burst of such enjoyment, when nothing but the friends she was to visit, was before her. He had since heard her express herself differently—with other feelings—more chequered feelings; he had heard her tell Mrs. Grant that

line 1: were arranged,] **1814** was arranged,

she should leave her with regret; that she began to believe neither the friends nor the pleasures she was going to were worth those she left behind; and that though she felt she must go, and knew she should enjoy herself when once away, she was already looking forward to being at Mansfield again. Was there not a "yes" in all this?

With such matters to ponder over, and arrange, and re-arrange, Edmund could not, on his own account, think very much of the evening, which the rest of the family were looking forward to with a more equal degree of strong interest. Independent of his two cousins enjoyment in it, the evening was to him of no higher value than any other appointed meeting of the two families might be. In every meeting there was a hope of receiving further confirmation of Miss Crawford's attachment; but the whirl of a ball-room perhaps was not particularly favourable to the excitement or expression of serious feelings. To engage her early for the two first dances, was all the command of individual happiness which he felt in his power, and the only preparation for the ball which he could enter into, in spite of all that was passing around him on the subject, from morning till night.

Thursday was the day of the ball: and on Wednesday morning, Fanny, still unable to satisfy herself, as to what she ought to wear, determined to seek the counsel of the more enlightened, and apply to Mrs. Grant and her sister, whose acknowledged taste would certainly bear her blameless; and as Edmund and William were gone to Northampton, and she had reason to think Mr. Crawford likewise out, she walked

line 1: should leave] 1814 would leave   //   line 1: regret; that] 1814 regret, that   //   line 3: behind; and] 1814 behind, and   //   line 8: not, on his own account, think] 1814 not on his own account think   //   line 14: further confirmation] 1814 farther confirmation   //   line 15: attachment; but] 1814 attachment, but   //   line 22: ball: and] 1814 ball; and

down to the Parsonage without much fear of wanting an opportunity for private discussson; and the privacy of such a discussion was a most important part of it to Fanny, being more than half ashamed of her own solicitude.

She met Miss Crawford within a few yards of the Parsonage, just setting out to call on her, and as it seemed to her, that her friend, though obliged to insist on turning back, was unwilling to lose her walk, she explained her business at once and observed that if she would be so kind as to give her opinion, it might be all talked over as well without doors as within. Miss Crawford appeared gratified by the application, and after a moment's thought, urged Fanny's returning with her in a much more cordial manner than before, and proposed their going up into her room, where they might have a comfortable coze,⁴ without disturbing Dr. and Mrs. Grant, who were together in the drawing-room. It was just the plan to suit Fanny; and with a great deal of gratitude on her side for such ready and kind attention, they proceeded in doors and upstairs, and were soon deep in the interesting subject. Miss Crawford, pleased with the appeal, gave her all her best judgment and taste, made every thing easy by her suggestions, and tried to make every thing agreeable by her encouragement. The dress being settled in all its grander parts,—"But what shall you have by way of necklace?" said Miss Crawford. "Shall not you wear your brother's cross?" And as she spoke she was undoing a small parcel, which Fanny had observed in her hand when they met. Fanny acknowledged her wishes and doubts on this point; she did not know how either to wear the cross, or to refrain from wearing it. She was answered by having a small trinket-box placed before her, and being requested to chuse from among several gold chains and necklaces. Such had been the parcel with which Miss Crawford was provided, and such the object of her intended visit; and in the kindest manner she now urged Fanny's taking one for the cross and to keep for her sake, saying every thing she could think of to obviate the scruples which were making Fanny start back at first with a look of horror at the proposal.

"You see what a collection I have," said she, "more by half than I ever use or think of. I do not offer them as new. I offer nothing but an old necklace. You must forgive the liberty and oblige me."

Fanny still resisted, and from her heart. The gift was too valuable. But, Miss Crawford persevered, and argued the case with so much affectionate earnestness through all the heads[5] of William and the cross, and the ball, and herself, as to be finally successful. Fanny found herself obliged to yield, that she might not be accused of pride or indifference, or some other littleness; and having with modest reluctance given her consent, proceeded to make the selection. She looked and looked, longing to know which might be least valuable; and was determined in her choice at last, by fancying there was one necklace more frequently placed before her eyes than the rest. It was of gold prettily worked; and though Fanny would have preferred a longer and a plainer chain as more adapted for her purpose, she hoped in fixing on this, to be chusing what Miss Crawford least wished to keep. Miss Crawford smiled her perfect approbation; and hastened to complete the gift by putting the necklace round her and making her see how well it looked.

Fanny had not a word to say against its becomingness, and excepting what remained of her scruples, was exceedingly pleased with an acquisition so very apropos. She would rather perhaps have been obliged to some other person. But this

line 9: resisted, and] **1814** resisted and // line 12: herself, as] **1814** herself as // line 13: yield, that] **1814** yield that // line 20: worked; and] **1814** worked, and

was an unworthy feeling. Miss Crawford had anticipated her wants with a kindness which proved her a real friend. "When I wear this necklace I shall always think of you," said she, "and feel how very kind you were."

"You must think of somebody else too when you wear that necklace," replied Miss Crawford. "You must think of Henry, for it was his choice in the first place. He gave it to me, and with the necklace I make over to you all the duty of remembering the original giver. It is to be a family remembrancer.[6] The sister is not to be in your mind without bringing the brother too."

Fanny, in great astonishment and confusion, would have returned the present instantly. To take what had been the gift of another person—of a brother too—impossible!—it must not be!—and with an eagerness and embarrassment quite diverting to her companion, she laid down the necklace again on its cotton, and seemed resolved either to take another or none at all. Miss Crawford thought she had never seen a prettier consciousness.[7] "My dear child," said she laughing, "what are you afraid of? Do you think Henry will claim the necklace as mine, and fancy you did not come honestly by it?—or are you imagining he would be too much flattered by seeing round your lovely throat an ornament which his money purchased three years ago, before he knew there was such a throat in the world?—or perhaps—looking archly— you suspect a confederacy between us, and that what I am now doing is with his knowledge and at his desire?"

With the deepest blushes Fanny protested against such a thought.

"Well then," replied Miss Crawford more seriously but without at all believing her, "to convince me that you suspect

line 18: Crawfurd [**1814** Crawford

no trick, and are as unsuspicious of compliment as I have always found you, take the necklace, and say no more about it. Its being a gift of my brother's need not make the smallest difference in your accepting it, as I assure you it makes none in my willingness to part with it. He is always giving me something or other. I have such innumerable presents from him that it is quite impossible for me to value, or for him to remember half. And as for this necklace, I do not suppose I have worn it six times; it is very pretty—but I never think of it; and though you would be most heartily welcome to any other in my trinket-box, you have happened to fix on the very one which, if I have a choice, I would rather part with and see in your possession than any other. Say no more against it, I entreat you. Such a trifle is not worth half so many words."

Fanny dared not make any further opposition; and with renewed but less happy thanks accepted the necklace again, for there was an expression in Miss Crawford's eyes which she could not be satisfied with.

It was impossible for her to be insensible of Mr. Crawford's change of manners. She had long seen it. He evidently tried to please her—he was gallant—he was attentive—he was something like what he had been to her cousins: he wanted, she supposed, to cheat her of her tranquillity as he had cheated them; and whether he might not have some concern in this necklace!—She could not be convinced that he had not, for Miss Crawford, complaisant[8] as a sister, was careless as a woman and a friend.

Reflecting and doubting, and feeling that the possession of what she had so much wished for, did not bring much satisfaction, she now walked home again—with a change rather than a diminution of cares since her treading that path before.

line 3: brother's need] **1814** brother's, need   //   line 13: it, I] **1814** it I   //
line 15: further] **1814** farther

Chapter 9

ON reaching home, Fanny went immediately up stairs to deposit this unexpected acquisition, this doubtful good of a necklace, in some favourite box in the east room which held all her smaller treasures; but on opening the door, what was her surprize to find her cousin Edmund there writing at the table! Such a sight having never occurred before, was almost as wonderful as it was welcome.

"Fanny," said he directly, leaving his seat and his pen, and meeting her with something in his hand, "I beg your pardon for being here. I came to look for you, and after waiting a little while in hope of your coming in, was making use of your inkstand to explain my errand. You will find the beginning of a note to yourself; but I can now speak my business, which is merely to beg your acceptance of this little trifle—a chain for William's cross. You ought to have had it a week ago, but there has been a delay from my brother's not being in town by several days so soon as I expected; and I have only just now received it at Northampton. I hope you will like the chain itself, Fanny. I endeavoured to consult the simplicity of your taste, but at any rate I know you will be kind to my intentions, and consider it, as it really is, a token of the love of one of your oldest friends."

And so saying, he was hurrying away, before Fanny, overpowered by a thousand feelings of pain and pleasure, could

line 5: surprize] **1814** surprise   //   line 8: pen, and] **1814** pen and   //
line 21: it, as] **1814** it as

attempt to speak; but quickened by one sovereign wish she then called out, "Oh! cousin, stop a moment, pray stop."

He turned back.

"I cannot attempt to thank you," she continued in a very agitated manner, "thanks are out of the question. I feel much more than I can possibly express. Your goodness in thinking of me in such a way is beyond"—

"If this is all you have to say, Fanny," smiling and turning away again—

"No, no, it is not. I want to consult you."

Almost unconsciously she had now undone the parcel he had just put into her hand, and seeing before her, in all the niceness[1] of jewellers' packing, a plain gold chain perfectly simple and neat, she could not help bursting forth again. "Oh! this is beautiful indeed! this is the very thing, precisely what I wished for! this is the only ornament I have ever had a desire to possess. It will exactly suit my cross. They must and shall be worn together. It comes too in such an acceptable moment. Oh! cousin, you do not know how acceptable it is."

"My dear Fanny, you feel these things a great deal too much. I am most happy that you like the chain, and that it should be here in time for to-morrow: but your thanks are far beyond the occasion. Believe me, I have no pleasure in the world superior to that of contributing to yours. No, I can safely say, I have no pleasure so complete, so unalloyed. It is without a drawback."

Upon such expressions of affection, Fanny could have lived an hour without saying another word; but Edmund, after waiting a moment, obliged her to bring down her mind from its heavenly flight by saying, "But what is it that you want to consult me about?"

line 12: her, in] **1814** her in   //   line 13: jewellers'] **1814** jeweller's

It was about the necklace, which she was now most earnestly longing to return, and hoped to obtain his approbation of her doing. She gave the history of her recent visit, and now her raptures might well be over, for Edmund was so struck with the circumstance, so delighted with what Miss Crawford had done, so gratified by such a coincidence of conduct between them, that Fanny could not but admit the superior power of *one* pleasure over his own mind, though it might have its drawback. It was some time before she could get his attention to her plan, or any answer to her demand of his opinion; he was in a reverie of fond reflection, uttering only now and then a few half sentences of praise; but when he did awake and understand, he was very decided in opposing what she wished.

"Return the necklace! No, my dear Fanny, upon no account. It would be mortifying her severely. There can hardly be a more unpleasant sensation than the having any thing returned on our hands, which we have given with a reasonable hope of its contributing to the comfort of a friend. Why should she lose a pleasure which she has shewn herself so deserving of?"

"If it had been given to me in the first instance," said Fanny, "I should not have thought of returning it; but being her brother's present, is not it fair to suppose that she would rather not part with it, when it is not wanted?"

"She must not suppose it not wanted,[2] not acceptable at least; and its having been originally her brother's gift makes no difference, for as she was not prevented from offering, nor you from taking it on that account, it ought not to affect your keeping it. No doubt it is handsomer than mine, and fitter for a ball-room."

"No, it is not handsomer, not at all handsomer in its way, and for my purpose not half so fit. The chain will agree with William's cross beyond all comparison better than the necklace."

"For one night, Fanny, for only one night, if it *be* a sacrifice—I am sure you will, upon consideration, make that sacrifice rather than give pain to one who has been so studious of your comfort. Miss Crawford's attentions to you have been—not more than you were justly entitled to—I am the last person to think that *could be*—but they have been invariable; and to be returning them with what must have something the *air* of ingratitude, though I know it could never have the *meaning*, is not in your nature I am sure. Wear the necklace, as you are engaged to do to-morrow evening, and let the chain, which was not ordered with any reference to the ball, be kept for commoner occasions. This is my advice. I would not have the shadow of a coolness between the two whose intimacy I have been observing with the greatest pleasure, and in whose characters there is so much general resemblance in true generosity and natural delicacy as to make the few slight differences, resulting principally from situation, no reasonable hindrance to a perfect friendship. I would not have the shadow of a coolness arise," he repeated, his voice sinking a little, "between the two dearest objects I have on earth."

He was gone as he spoke; and Fanny remained to tranquillise herself as she could. She was one of his two dearest—that must support her. But the other!—the first! She had never heard him speak so openly before, and though it told her no more than what she had long perceived, it was a stab;—for it told of his own convictions and views. They were decided. He would marry Miss Crawford. It was a stab, in spite of every long-standing expectation; and she was obliged

line 4: will, upon consideration, make] **1814** will upon consideration make

to repeat again and again that she was one of his two dearest, before the words gave her any sensation. Could she believe Miss Crawford to deserve him, it would be—Oh! how different would it be—how far more tolerable! But he was deceived in her; he gave her merits which she had not; her faults were what they had ever been, but he saw them no longer. Till she had shed many tears over this deception, Fanny could not subdue her agitation; and the dejection which followed could only be relieved by the influence of fervent prayers for his happiness.

It was her intention, as she felt it to be her duty, to try to overcome all that was excessive, all that bordered on selfishness in her affection for Edmund. To call or to fancy it a loss, a disappointment, would be a presumption; for which she had not words strong enough to satisfy her own humility. To think of him as Miss Crawford might be justified in thinking, would in her be insanity. To her, he could be nothing under any circumstances—nothing dearer than a friend. Why did such an idea occur to her even enough to be reprobated and forbidden? It ought not to have touched on the confines of her imagination. She would endeavour to be rational, and to deserve the right of judging of Miss Crawford's character and the privilege of true solicitude for him by a sound intellect and an honest heart.

She had all the heroism of principle,[3] and was determined to do her duty; but having also many of the feelings of youth and nature, let her not be much wondered at if, after making all these good resolutions on the side of self-government, she seized the scrap of paper on which Edmund had begun writing to her, as a treasure beyond all her hopes, and reading with the tenderest emotion these words, "My very dear Fanny, you must do me the favour to accept"—locked it up with the chain, as the dearest part of the gift. It was the only thing approaching to a letter which she had ever received from him; she might never receive another; it was impossible that she ever should receive another so perfectly gratifying in the occasion and the style. Two lines more prized had never fallen from the pen of the most distinguished author— never more completely blessed the researches of the fondest biographer.[4] The enthusiasm of a woman's love is even beyond the biographer's. To her, the hand-writing itself, independent of any thing it may convey, is a blessedness. Never were such characters cut by any other human being, as Edmund's commonest hand-writing gave! This specimen, written in haste as it was, had not a fault; and there was a felicity in the flow of the first four words, in the arrangement of "My very dear Fanny," which she could have looked at for ever.

Having regulated her thoughts and comforted her feelings by this happy mixture of reason and weakness, she was able, in due time, to go down and resume her usual employments near her aunt Bertram, and pay her the usual observances without any apparent want of spirits.

Thursday, predestined to hope and enjoyment, came; and opened with more kindness to Fanny than such self-willed, unmanageable days often volunteer, for soon after breakfast a very friendly note was brought from Mr. Crawford to William stating, that as he found himself obliged to go to London on the morrow for a few days, he could not help trying to procure a companion; and therefore hoped that if William could make up his mind to leave Mansfield half a day earlier than had been proposed, he would accept a place in his carriage. Mr. Crawford meant to be in town by his uncle's accustomary late dinner-hour,[5] and William was invited to

line 17: able, in due time, to] **1814** able in due time to   //   line 21: self-willed, unmanageable] **1814** self willed, unmanageable

dine with him at the Admiral's. The proposal was a very pleasant one to William himself, who enjoyed the idea of travelling post[6] with four horses and such a good humoured agreeable friend; and in likening it to going up with dispatches,[7] was saying at once every thing in favour of its happiness and dignity which his imagination could suggest; and Fanny, from a different motive, was exceedingly pleased: for the original plan was that William should go up by the mail[8] from Northampton the following night which would not have allowed him an hour's rest before he must have got into a Portsmouth coach; and though this offer of Mr. Crawford's would rob her of many hours of his company, she was too happy in having William spared from the fatigue of such a journey, to think of any thing else. Sir Thomas approved of it for another reason. His nephew's introduction to Admiral Crawford might be of service. The Admiral he believed had interest. Upon the whole, it was a very joyous note. Fanny's spirits lived on it half the morning, deriving some accession of pleasure from its writer being himself to go away.

As for the ball so near at hand, she had too many agitations and fears to have half the enjoyment in anticipation which she ought to have had, or must have been supposed to have, by the many young ladies looking forward to the same event in situations more at ease, but under circumstances of less novelty, less interest, less peculiar gratification than would be attributed to her. Miss Price, known only by name to half the people invited, was now to make her first appearance, and must be regarded as the Queen of the evening. Who could be happier than Miss Price? But Miss Price had not been brought up to the trade of *coming out*;[9] and had she

line 6: Fanny, from a different motive, was] **1814** Fanny from a different motive was // line 17: whole, it] **1814** whole it

known in what light this ball was, in general, considered respecting her, it would very much have lessened her comfort by increasing the fears she already had, of doing wrong and being looked at. To dance without much observation or any extraordinary fatigue, to have strength and partners for about half the evening, to dance a little with Edmund, and not a great deal with Mr. Crawford, to see William enjoy himself, and be able to keep away from her aunt Norris, was the height of her ambition, and seemed to comprehend her greatest possibility of happiness. As these were the best of her hopes, they could not always prevail; and in the course of a long morning, spent principally with her two aunts, she was often under the influence of much less sanguine views. William, determined to make this last day a day of thorough enjoyment, was out snipe shooting;[10] Edmund, she had too much reason to suppose, was at the Parsonage; and left alone to bear the worrying of Mrs. Norris, who was cross because the house-keeper would have her own way with the supper, and whom *she* could not avoid though the house-keeper might, Fanny was worn down at last to think every thing an evil belonging to the ball, and when sent off with a parting worry to dress, moved as languidly towards her own room, and felt as incapable of happiness as if she had been allowed no share in it.

As she walked slowly up stairs she thought of yesterday; it had been about the same hour that she had returned from the Parsonage, and found Edmund in the east room.—"Suppose I were to find him there again to-day!" said she to herself in a fond indulgence of fancy.

line 1: was, in general, considered] **1814** was in general considered   //
line 8: Norris, was] **1814** Norris was   //   line 12: morning, spent] **1814**
morning spent   //   line 16: suppose, was] **1814** suppose was

"Fanny," said a voice at that moment near her. Starting and looking up, she saw across the lobby she had just reached Edmund himself, standing at the head of a different staircase. He came towards her. "You look tired and fagged, Fanny. You have been walking too far."

"No, I have not been out at all."

"Then you have had fatigues within doors, which are worse. You had better have gone out."

Fanny, not liking to complain, found it easiest to make no answer; and though he looked at her with his usual kindness, she believed he had soon ceased to think of her countenance. He did not appear in spirits; something unconnected with her was probably amiss. They proceeded up stairs together, their rooms being on the same floor above.

"I come from Dr. Grant's," said Edmund presently. "You may guess my errand there, Fanny." And he looked so conscious, that Fanny could think but of one errand, which turned her too sick for speech.—"I wished to engage Miss Crawford for the two first dances," was the explanation that followed, and brought Fanny to life again, enabling her, as she found she was expected to speak, to utter something like an inquiry as to the result.

"Yes," he answered, "she is engaged to me; but (with a smile that did not sit easy) she says it is to be the last time that she ever will dance with me. She is not serious. I think, I hope, I am sure she is not serious—but I would rather not hear it. She never has danced with a clergyman she says, and she never *will*. For my own sake, I could wish there had been no ball

line 2: up, she] **1814** up she // line 4: came towards] **1814** come towards // line 17: conscious, that] **1814** conscious that // line 20: her, as] **1814** her as // line 26: not hear it.] **1814** not hear.

just at—I mean not this very week, this very day—to-morrow I leave home."

Fanny struggled for speech, and said, "I am very sorry that any thing has occurred to distress you. This ought to be a day of pleasure. My uncle meant it so."

"Oh! yes, yes, and it will be a day of pleasure. It will all end right. I am only vexed for a moment. In fact, it is not that I consider the ball as ill-timed;—what does it signify? But, Fanny,"—stopping her by taking her hand, and speaking low and seriously, "you know what all this means. You see how it is; and could tell me, perhaps better than I could tell you, how and why I am vexed. Let me talk to you a little. You are a kind, kind listener. I have been pained by her manner this morning, and cannot get the better of it. I know her disposition to be as sweet and faultless as your own, but the influence of her former companions makes her seem, gives to her conversation, to her professed opinions, sometimes a tinge of wrong. She does not *think* evil, but she speaks[11] it—speaks it in playfulness—and though I know it to be playfulness, it grieves me to the soul."

"The effect of education," said Fanny gently.

Edmund could not but agree to it. "Yes, that uncle and aunt! They have injured the finest mind!—for sometimes, Fanny, I own to you, it does appear more than manner; it appears as if the mind itself was tainted."

Fanny imagined this to be an appeal to her judgment, and therefore, after a moment's consideration, said, "If you only want me as a listener, cousin, I will be as useful as I can; but I am not qualified for an adviser. Do not ask advice of *me*. I am not competent."

line 3: speech, and] **1814** speech and // line 9: But, Fanny,"] **1814** But Fanny," // line 27: therefore, after] **1814** therefore after

"You are right, Fanny, to protest against such an office, but you need not be afraid. It is a subject on which I should never ask advice. It is the sort of subject on which it had better never be asked; and few I imagine do ask it, but when they want to be influenced against their conscience. I only want to talk to you."

"One thing more. Excuse the liberty—but take care *how* you talk to me. Do not tell me any thing now, which hereafter you may be sorry for. The time may come—"

The colour rushed into her cheeks as she spoke.

"Dearest Fanny!" cried Edmund, pressing her hand to his lips, with almost as much warmth as if it had been Miss Crawford's, "you are all considerate thought!—But it is unnecessary here. The time will never come. No such time as you allude to will ever come. I begin to think it most improbable; the chances grow less and less. And even if it should—there will be nothing to be remembered by either you or me, that we need be afraid of, for I can never be ashamed of my own scruples; and if they are removed, it must be by changes that will only raise her character the more by the recollection of the faults she once had. You are the only being upon earth to whom I should say what I have said; but you have always known my opinion of her; you can bear me witness, Fanny, that I have never been blinded. How many a time have we talked over her little errors! You need not fear me. I have almost given up every serious idea of her; but I must be a blockhead indeed if, whatever befell me, I could think of your kindness and sympathy without the sincerest gratitude."

He had said enough to shake the experience of eighteen. He had said enough to give Fanny some happier feelings than

line 8: any thing] **1814** anything // line 22: earth to] **1814** earth, to

she had lately known, and with a brighter look, she answered, "Yes, cousin, I am convinced that *you* would be incapable of any thing else, though perhaps some might not. I cannot be afraid of hearing any thing you wish to say. Do not check yourself. Tell me whatever you like."

They were now on the second floor, and the appearance of a housemaid prevented any further conversation. For Fanny's present comfort it was concluded perhaps at the happiest moment; had he been able to talk another five minutes, there is no saying that he might not have talked away all Miss Crawford's faults and his own despondence. But as it was, they parted with looks on his side of grateful affection, and with some very precious sensations on her's. She had felt nothing like it for hours. Since the first joy from Mr. Crawford's note to William had worn away, she had been in a state absolutely their reverse; there had been no comfort around, no hope within her. Now, every thing was smiling. William's good fortune returned again upon her mind, and seemed of greater value than at first. The ball too—such an evening of pleasure before her! It was now a real animation! and she began to dress for it with much of the happy flutter which belongs to a ball. All went well—she did not dislike her own looks; and when she came to the necklaces again, her good fortune seemed complete, for upon trial the one given her by Miss Crawford would by no means go through the ring of the cross. She had, to oblige Edmund, resolved to wear it—but it was too large for the purpose. His therefore must be worn; and having, with delightful feelings, joined the chain and the cross, those memorials of the two most beloved of her heart, those dearest tokens so formed for each other by every thing real and imaginary—and put them round

line 13: on her's.] **1814** on hers.   //   line 28: having, with delightful feelings, joined] **1814** having with delightful feelings joined

her neck, and seen and felt how full of William and Edmund they were, she was able, without an effort, to resolve on wearing Miss Crawford's necklace too. She acknowledged it to be right. Miss Crawford had a claim; and when it was no longer to encroach on, to interfere with the stronger claims, the truer kindness of another, she could do her justice even with pleasure to herself. The necklace really looked very well; and Fanny left her room at last, comfortably satisfied with herself and all about her.

Her aunt Bertram had recollected her on this occasion, with an unusual degree of wakefulness. It had really occurred to her, unprompted, that Fanny, preparing for a ball, might be glad of better help than the upper housemaid's, and when dressed herself, she actually sent her own maid to assist her; too late of course to be of any use. Mrs. Chapman had just reached the attic floor, when Miss Price came out of her room completely dressed, and only civilities were necessary— but Fanny felt her aunt's attention almost as much as Lady Bertram or Mrs. Chapman could do themselves.

line 2: able, without an effort, to] **1814** able without an effort to   //
line 14: maid] **1814** woman

Chapter 10

HER uncle and both her aunts were in the drawing-room when Fanny went down. To the former she was an interesting object, and he saw with pleasure the general elegance of her appearance and her being in remarkably good looks. The neatness and propriety of her dress was all that he would allow himself to commend in her presence, but upon her leaving the room again soon afterwards, he spoke of her beauty with very decided praise.

"Yes," said Lady Bertram, "she looks very well. I sent Chapman to her."

"Look well! Oh yes," cried Mrs. Norris, "she has good reason to look well with all her advantages: brought up in this family as she has been, with all the benefit of her cousins' manners before her. Only think, my dear Sir Thomas, what extraordinary advantages you and I have been the means of giving her. The very gown you have been taking notice of, is your own generous present to her when dear Mrs. Rushworth married. What would she have been if we had not taken her by the hand?"

Sir Thomas said no more; but when they sat down to table the eyes of the two young men assured him, that the subject might be gently touched again when the ladies withdrew, with more success. Fanny saw that she was approved; and the consciousness of looking well, made her look still better.

line 7: afterwards, he] **1814** afterwards he   //   line 13: been, with] **1814** been with   //   line 18: been if] **1814** been, if

316

From a variety of causes she was happy, and she was soon made still happier; for in following her aunts out of the room, Edmund, who was holding open the door, said as she passed him, "You must dance with me, Fanny; you must keep two dances for me; any two that you like, except the first." She had nothing more to wish for. She had hardly ever been in a state so nearly approaching high spirits in her life. Her cousins' former gaiety on the day of a ball was no longer surprizing to her; she felt it to be indeed very charming, and was actually practising her steps about the drawing-room as long as she could be safe from the notice of her aunt Norris, who was entirely taken up at first in fresh arranging and injuring the noble fire which the butler had prepared.

Half an hour followed, that would have been at least languid under any other circumstances, but Fanny's happiness still prevailed. It was but to think[1] of her conversation with Edmund; and what was the restlessness of Mrs. Norris? What were the yawns of Lady Bertram?

The gentlemen joined them; and soon after began the sweet expectation of a carriage, when a general spirit of ease and enjoyment seemed diffused, and they all stood about and talked and laughed, and every moment had its pleasure and its hope. Fanny felt that there must be a struggle in Edmund's cheerfulness, but it was delightful to see the effort so successfully made.

When the carriages were really heard, when the guests began really to assemble, her own gaiety of heart was much subdued; the sight of so many strangers threw her back into herself; and besides the gravity and formality of the first great circle, which the manners of neither Sir Thomas nor Lady

---

line 8: surprizing] **1814** surprising // line 19: them; and] **1814** them, and // line 29: herself; and] **1814** herself, and

Bertram were of a kind to do away, she found herself occasionally called on to endure something worse. She was introduced here and there by her uncle, and forced to be spoken to, and to curtsey, and speak again. This was a hard duty, and she was never summoned to it, without looking at William, as he walked about at his ease in the back ground of the scene, and longing to be with him.

The entrance of the Grants and Crawfords was a favourable epoch. The stiffness of the meeting soon gave way before their popular manners and more diffused intimacies:—little groups were formed and every body grew comfortable. Fanny felt the advantage; and, drawing back from the toils of civility, would have been again most happy, could she have kept her eyes from wandering between Edmund and Mary Crawford. *She* looked all loveliness—and what might not be the end of it? Her own musings were brought to an end on perceiving Mr. Crawford before her, and her thoughts were put into another channel by his engaging her almost instantly for the two first dances. Her happiness on this occasion was very much à-la-mortal, finely chequered.[2] To be secure of a partner at first, was a most essential good—for the moment of beginning was now growing seriously near, and she so little understood her own claims as to think, that if Mr. Crawford had not asked her, she must have been the last to be sought after, and should have received a partner only through a series of inquiry, and bustle, and interference which would have been terrible; but at the same time there was a pointedness in his manner of asking her, which she did not like, and she saw his eye glancing for a moment at her necklace—with a smile—she thought there was a smile—which made her blush

line 12: advantage; and, drawing] **1814** advantage, and drawing   //   line 12: civility, would] **1814** civility would   //   line 20: à-la-mortal,] **1814** a-la-mortal,

and feel wretched. And though there was no second glance to disturb her, though his object seemed then to be only quietly agreeable, she could not get the better of her embarrassment, heightened as it was by the idea of his perceiving it, and had no composure till he turned away to some one else. Then she could gradually rise up to the genuine satisfaction of having a partner, a voluntary partner secured against the dancing began.[3]

When the company were moving into the ball-room she found herself for the first time near Miss Crawford, whose eyes and smiles were immediately and more unequivocally directed as her brother's had been, and who was beginning to speak on the subject, when Fanny, anxious to get the story over, hastened to give the explanation of the second necklace—the real chain. Miss Crawford listened; and all her intended compliments and insinuations to Fanny were forgotten; she felt only one thing; and her eyes, bright as they had been before, shewing they could yet be brighter, she exclaimed with eager pleasure, "Did he? Did Edmund? That was like himself. No other man would have thought of it. I honour him beyond expression." And she looked around as if longing to tell him so. He was not near, he was attending a party of ladies out of the room; and Mrs. Grant coming up to the two girls and taking an arm of each, they followed with the rest.

Fanny's heart sunk, but there was no leisure for thinking long even of Miss Crawford's feelings. They were in the ball-room, the violins were playing, and her mind was in a flutter that forbad its fixing on any thing serious. She must watch the general arrangements and see how every thing was done.

In a few minutes Sir Thomas came to her, and asked if she were engaged; and the "Yes, sir, to Mr. Crawford," was exactly what he had intended to hear. Mr. Crawford was not far off;

Sir Thomas brought him to her, saying something which discovered to Fanny, that *she* was to lead the way and open the ball; an idea that had never occurred to her before. Whenever she had thought on the minutiæ of the evening, it had been as a matter of course that Edmund would begin with Miss Crawford, and the impression was so strong, that though *her uncle* spoke the contrary, she could not help an exclamation of surprize, a hint of her unfitness, an entreaty even to be excused. To be urging her opinion against Sir Thomas's, was a proof of the extremity of the case, but such was her horror at the first suggestion, that she could actually look him in the face and say she hoped it might be settled otherwise; in vain however;—Sir Thomas smiled, tried to encourage her, and then looked too serious and said too decidedly—"It must be so, my dear," for her to hazard another word; and she found herself the next moment conducted by Mr. Crawford to the top of the room,[4] and standing there to be joined by the rest of the dancers, couple after couple as they were formed.

She could hardly believe it. To be placed above so many elegant young women! The distinction was too great. It was treating her like her cousins! And her thoughts flew to those absent cousins with most unfeigned and truly tender regret, that they were not at home to take their own place in the room, and have their share of a pleasure which would have been so very delightful to them. So often as she had heard them wish for a ball at home as the greatest of all felicities! And to have them away when it was given—and for *her* to be opening the ball—and with Mr. Crawford too! She hoped they would not envy her that distinction *now*; but when she looked back to the state of things in the autumn, to what they had all been to each other when once dancing in that house

line 8: surprize,] **1814** surprize,   //   line 29: *now*; but] **1814** *now*, but

before, the present arrangement was almost more than she could understand herself.

The ball began. It was rather honour than happiness to Fanny, for the first dance at least; her partner was in excellent spirits and tried to impart them to her, but she was a great deal too much frightened to have any enjoyment, till she could suppose herself no longer looked at. Young, pretty, and gentle, however, she had no awkwardnesses that were not as good as graces, and there were few persons present that were not disposed to praise her. She was attractive, she was modest, she was Sir Thomas's niece, and she was soon said to be admired by Mr. Crawford. It was enough to give her general favour. Sir Thomas himself was watching her progress down the dance with much complacency; he was proud of his niece, and without attributing all her personal beauty, as Mrs. Norris seemed to do, to her transplantation to Mansfield, he was pleased with himself for having supplied every thing else;—education and manners she owed to him.

Miss Crawford saw much of Sir Thomas's thoughts as he stood, and having, in spite of all his wrongs towards her, a general prevailing desire of recommending herself to him, took an opportunity of stepping aside to say something agreeable of Fanny. Her praise was warm, and he received it as she could wish, joining in it as far as discretion, and politeness, and slowness of speech would allow, and certainly appearing to greater advantage on the subject, than his lady did, soon afterwards, when Mary, perceiving her on a sofa very near, turned round before she began to dance, to compliment her on Miss Price's looks.

line 3: honour than] **1814** honour then // line 14: complacency;] **1814** complaceney; // line 20: having, in] **1814** having in // line 21: general prevailing] **1814** generally prevailing // line 27: Mary, perceiving] **1814** Mary perceiving // line 28: began to dance,] **1814** began the dance,

"Yes, she does look very well," was Lady Bertram's placid reply. "Chapman helped her dress. I sent Chapman to her." Not but that she was really pleased to have Fanny admired; but she was so much more struck with her own kindness in sending Chapman to her, that she could not get it out of her head.

Miss Crawford knew Mrs. Norris too well to think of gratifying *her* by commendation of Fanny; to her, it was as the occasion offered.—"Ah! ma'am, how much we want dear Mrs. Rushworth and Julia to night!" and Mrs. Norris paid her with as many smiles and courteous words as she had time for, amid so much occupation as she found for herself, in making up card-tables, giving hints to Sir Thomas, and trying to move all the chaperons to a better part of the room.

Miss Crawford blundered most towards Fanny herself, in her intentions to please. She meant to be giving her little heart a happy flutter, and filling her with sensations of delightful self-consequence; and misinterpreting Fanny's blushes, still thought she must be doing so—when she went to her after the two first dances and said, with a significant look, "perhaps *you* can tell me why my brother goes to town to-morrow. He says, he has business there, but will not tell me what. The first time he ever denied me his confidence! But this is what we all come to. All are supplanted sooner or later. Now, I must apply to you for information. Pray what is Henry going for?"

Fanny protested her ignorance as steadily as her embarrassment allowed.

"Well, then," replied Miss Crawford laughing, "I must suppose it to be purely for the pleasure of conveying your brother and talking of you by the way."

line 18: self-consequence; and] **1814** self-consequence, and

Fanny was confused, but it was the confusion of discontent; while Miss Crawford wondered she did not smile, and thought her over-anxious, or thought her odd, or thought her any thing rather than insensible of pleasure in Henry's attentions. Fanny had a good deal of enjoyment in the course of the evening—but Henry's attentions had very little to do with it. She would much rather *not* have been asked by him again so very soon, and she wished she had not been obliged to suspect that his previous inquiries of Mrs. Norris, about the supper-hour, were all for the sake of securing her at that part of the evening. But it was not to be avoided; he made her feel that she was the object of all; though she could not say that it was unpleasantly done, that there was indelicacy or ostentation in his manner—and sometimes, when he talked of William, he was really not un-agreeable, and shewed even a warmth of heart which did him credit. But still his attentions made no part of her satisfaction. She was happy whenever she looked at William, and saw how perfectly he was enjoying himself, in every five minutes that she could walk about with him and hear his account of his partners; she was happy in knowing herself admired, and she was happy in having the two dances with Edmund still to look forward to, during the greatest part of the evening, her hand being so eagerly sought after, that her indefinite engagement with *him* was in continual perspective. She was happy even when they did take place; but not from any flow of spirits on his side, or any such expressions of tender gallantry as had blessed the morning. His mind was fagged, and her happiness sprung from being the friend with whom it could find repose. "I am worn out with civility," said he. "I have been talking incessantly all night, and with nothing to say. But with *you*, Fanny,

line 4: any thing] **1814** anything

there may be peace. You will not want to be talked to. Let us have the luxury of silence." Fanny would hardly even speak her agreement. A weariness arising probably, in great measure, from the same feelings which he had acknowledged in the morning, was peculiarly to be respected, and they went down their two dances together with such sober tranquillity as might satisfy any looker-on, that Sir Thomas had been bringing up no wife for his younger son.

The evening had afforded Edmund little pleasure. Miss Crawford had been in gay spirits when they first danced together, but it was not her gaiety that could do him good; it rather sank than raised his comfort; and afterwards—for he found himself still impelled to seek her again, she had absolutely pained him by her manner of speaking of the profession to which he was now on the point of belonging. They had talked—and they had been silent—he had reasoned— she had ridiculed—and they had parted at last with mutual vexation. Fanny, not able to refrain entirely from observing them, had seen enough to be tolerably satisfied. It was barbarous to be happy when Edmund was suffering. Yet some happiness must and would arise, from the very conviction, that he did suffer.

When her two dances with him were over, her inclination and strength for more were pretty well at an end; and Sir Thomas having seen her rather walk than dance down the shortening set, breathless and with her hand at her side, gave his orders for her sitting down entirely. From that time, Mr. Crawford sat down likewise.

"Poor Fanny!" cried William, coming for a moment to visit her and working away his partner's fan as if for life:—"how soon she is knocked up! Why, the sport is but just begun. I

line 30: for life:—"how] **1814** for life. "How

hope we shall keep it up these two hours. How can you be tired so soon?"

"So soon! my good friend," said Sir Thomas, producing his watch with all necessary caution—"it is three o'clock, and your sister is not used to these sort of hours."

"Well then, Fanny, you shall not get up to-morrow before I go. Sleep as long as you can and never mind me."

"Oh! William."

"What! Did she think of being up before you set off?"

"Oh! yes, sir," cried Fanny, rising eagerly from her seat to be nearer her uncle, "I must get up and breakfast with him. It will be the last time you know, the last morning."

"You had better not.—He is to have breakfasted and be gone by half past nine.—Mr. Crawford, I think you call for him at half past nine?"

Fanny was too urgent, however, and had too many tears in her eyes for denial; and it ended in a gracious, "Well, well," which was permission.

"Yes, half past nine," said Crawford to William, as the latter was leaving them, "and I shall be punctual, for there will be no kind sister to get up for *me*." And in a lower tone to Fanny, "I shall have only a desolate house to hurry from. Your brother will find my ideas of time and his own very different to-morrow."

After a short consideration, Sir Thomas asked Crawford to join the early breakfast party in that house instead of eating alone; he should himself be of it; and the readiness with which his invitation was accepted, convinced him that the suspicions whence, he must confess to himself, this very ball had in great measure sprung, were well founded. Mr. Crawford was in love with Fanny. He had a pleasing anticipation of what

line 23: own very] 1814 own, very // line 27: it; and] 1814 it, and

would be. His niece, meanwhile, did not thank him for what he had just done. She had hoped to have William all to herself, the last morning. It would have been an unspeakable indulgence. But though her wishes were overthrown there was no spirit of murmuring within her.[5] On the contrary, she was so totally unused to have her pleasure consulted, or to have any thing take place at all in the way she could desire, that she was more disposed to wonder and rejoice in having carried her point so far, than to repine at the counteraction which followed.

Shortly afterwards, Sir Thomas was again interfering a little with her inclination, by advising her to go immediately to bed. "Advise" was his word, but it was the advice of absolute power, and she had only to rise and, with Mr. Crawford's very cordial adieus, pass quietly away; stopping at the entrance door, like the Lady of Branxholm Hall, "one moment and no more,"[6] to view the happy scene, and take a last look at the five or six determined couple, who were still hard at work—and then, creeping slowly up the principal staircase, pursued by the ceaseless country-dance, feverish with hopes and fears, soup and negus,[7] sore footed and fatigued, restless and agitated, yet feeling, in spite of every thing, that a ball was indeed delightful.

In thus sending her away, Sir Thomas perhaps might not be thinking merely of her health. It might occur to him, that Mr. Crawford had been sitting by her long enough, or he might mean to recommend her as a wife by shewing her persuadableness.

line 7: any thing] **1814** anything   //   line 22: feeling, in spite of every thing, that] **1814** feeling in spite of every thing that

Chapter 11

THE ball was over—and the breakfast was soon over too; the last kiss was given, and William was gone. Mr. Crawford had, as he foretold, been very punctual, and short and pleasant had been the meal.

After seeing William to the last moment, Fanny walked back into the breakfast-room with a very saddened heart to grieve over the melancholy change; and there her uncle kindly left her to cry in peace, conceiving perhaps that the deserted chair of each young man might exercise her tender enthusiasm, and that the remaining cold pork bones and mustard in William's plate, might but divide her feelings with the broken egg-shells in Mr. Crawford's. She sat and cried *con amore*[1] as her uncle intended, but it was con amore fraternal and no other. William was gone, and she now felt as if she had wasted half his visit in idle cares and selfish solicitudes unconnected with him.

Fanny's disposition was such that she could never even think of her aunt Norris in the meagreness and cheerlessness of her own small house, without reproaching herself for some little want of attention to her when they had been last together; much less could her feelings acquit her of having done and said and thought every thing by William, that was due to him for a whole fortnight.

It was a heavy, melancholy day.—Soon after the second breakfast,[2] Edmund bad them good bye for a week, and mounted his horse for Peterborough, and then all were gone. Nothing remained of last night but remembrances, which she had nobody to share in. She talked to her aunt Bertram—she must talk to somebody of the ball, but her aunt had seen so little of what passed, and had so little curiosity, that it was heavy work. Lady Bertram was not certain of any body's dress, or any body's place at supper, but her own. "She could not recollect what it was that she had heard about one of the Miss Maddoxes, or what it was that Lady Prescott had noticed in Fanny; she was not sure whether Colonel Harrison had been talking of Mr. Crawford or of William, when he said he was the finest young man in the room; somebody had whispered something to her, she had forgot to ask Sir Thomas what it could be." And these were her longest speeches and clearest communications; the rest was only a languid "Yes—yes—very well—did you? did he?—I did not see *that*—I should not know one from the other." This was very bad. It was only better than Mrs. Norris's sharp answers would have been; but she being gone home with all the supernumerary jellies to nurse a sick maid, there was peace and good humour in their little party, though it could not boast much beside.

The evening was heavy like the day—"I cannot think what is the matter with me!" said Lady Bertram, when the tea-things were removed. "I feel quite stupid. It must be sitting up so late last night. Fanny, you must do something to keep me awake. I cannot work. Fetch the cards,—I feel so very stupid."

line 2: week, and] **1814** week and // line 7: curiosity, that] **1814** curiosity that // line 9: any body's] **1814** anybody's // line 11: Miss Maddoxes,] **1814** Miss Maddox', // line 13: William, when] **1814** William when // line 20: been; but] **1814** been, but

The cards were brought, and Fanny played at cribbage[3] with her aunt till bed-time; and as Sir Thomas was reading to himself, no sounds were heard in the room for the next two hours beyond the reckonings of the game—"And *that* makes thirty-one;—four in hand and eight in crib.—You are to deal, ma'am; shall I deal for you?" Fanny thought and thought again of the difference which twenty-four hours had made in that room, and all that part of the house. Last night it had been hope and smiles, bustle and motion, noise and brilliancy in the drawing-room, and out of the drawing-room, and every where. Now it was languor, and all but solitude.

A good night's rest improved her spirits. She could think of William the next day more cheerfully, and as the morning afforded her an opportunity of talking over Thursday night with Mrs. Grant and Miss Crawford, in a very handsome style, with all the heightenings of imagination and all the laughs of playfulness which are so essential to the shade of a departed ball, she could afterwards bring her mind without much effort into its everyday state, and easily conform to the tranquillity of the present quiet week.[4]

They were indeed a smaller party than she had ever known there for a whole day together, and *he* was gone on whom the comfort and cheerfulness of every family-meeting and every meal chiefly depended. But this must be learned to be endured. He would soon be always gone; and she was thankful that she could now sit in the same room with her uncle, hear his voice, receive his questions, and even answer

---

line 1: brought, and] **1814** brought and // line 4: "And *that*] **1814** And *that* // line 5: crib.—You] **1814** crib. "You // line 10: drawing-room, and] **1814** drawing-room and // line 10: drawing-room, and] **1814** drawing room and // line 11: languor, and] **1814** languor and // line 24: family-meeting] **1814** family meeting

them without such wretched feelings as she had formerly known.

"We miss our two young men," was Sir Thomas's observation on both the first and second day, as they formed their very reduced circle after dinner; and in consideration of Fanny's swimming eyes, nothing more was said on the first day than to drink their good health; but on the second it led to something farther. William was kindly commended and his promotion hoped for. "And there is no reason to suppose," added Sir Thomas, "but that his visits to us may now be tolerably frequent. As to Edmund, we must learn to do without him. This will be the last winter of his belonging to us,[5] as he has done." "Yes," said Lady Bertram, "but I wish he was not going away. They are all going away I think. I wish they would stay at home."

This wish was levelled principally at Julia, who had just applied for permission to go to town with Maria; and as Sir Thomas thought it best for each daughter that the permission should be granted, Lady Bertram, though in her own good nature she would not have prevented it, was lamenting the change it made in the prospect of Julia's return, which would otherwise have taken place about this time. A great deal of good sense followed on Sir Thomas's side, tending to reconcile his wife to the arrangement. Every thing that a considerate parent *ought* to feel was advanced for her use; and every thing that an affectionate mother *must* feel in promoting her children's enjoyment, was attributed to her nature. Lady Bertram agreed to it all with a calm "Yes"—and at the end of a quarter of an hour's silent consideration, spontaneously observed, "Sir Thomas, I have been thinking—and

line 11: Edmund, we] **1814** Edmund we   //   line 17: Maria; and] **1814** Maria, and

I am very glad we took Fanny as we did, for now the others are away, we feel the good of it."

Sir Thomas immediately improved this compliment by adding, "Very true. We shew Fanny what a good girl we think her by praising her to her face—she is now a very valuable companion. If we have been kind to *her*, she is now quite as necessary to *us*."

"Yes," said Lady Bertram presently—"and it is a comfort to think that we shall always have *her*."

Sir Thomas paused, half smiled, glanced at his niece, and then gravely replied, "She will never leave us, I hope, till invited to some other home that may reasonably promise her greater happiness than she knows here."

"And *that* is not very likely to be, Sir Thomas. Who should invite her? Maria might be very glad to see her at Sotherton now and then, but she would not think of asking her to live there—and I am sure she is better off here—and besides I cannot do without her."

The week which passed so quietly and peaceably at the great house in Mansfield, had a very different character at the Parsonage. To the young lady at least in each family, it brought very different feelings. What was tranquillity and comfort to Fanny was tediousness and vexation to Mary. Something arose from difference of disposition and habit— one so easily satisfied, the other so unused to endure; but still more might be imputed to difference of circumstances. In some points of interest they were exactly opposed to each other. To Fanny's mind, Edmund's absence was really in its cause and its tendency a relief. To Mary it was every way painful. She felt the want of his society every day, almost every hour; and was too much in want of it to derive any

line 2: away, we] **1814** away we   //   line 11: us, I hope,] **1814** us I hope, thing but irritation from considering the object for which he went. He could not have devised any thing more likely to raise his consequence than this week's absence, occurring as it did at the very time of her brother's going away, of William Price's going too, and completing the sort of general break-up of a party which had been so animated. She felt it keenly. They were now a miserable trio, confined within doors by a series of rain and snow, with nothing to do and no variety to hope for. Angry as she was with Edmund for adhering to his own notions and acting on them in defiance of her, (and she had been so angry that they had hardly parted friends at the ball,) she could not help thinking of him continually when absent, dwelling on his merit and affection, and long-ing again for the almost daily meetings they lately had. His absence was unnecessarily long. He should not have planned such an absence—he should not have left home for a week, when her own departure from Mansfield was so near. Then she began to blame herself. She wished she had not spoken so warmly in their last conversation. She was afraid she had used some strong—some contemptuous expressions in speaking of the clergy, and *that* should not have been. It was ill-bred—it was wrong. She wished such words unsaid with all her heart.

Her vexation did not end with the week. All this was bad, but she had still more to feel when Friday came round again and brought no Edmund—when Saturday came and still no Edmund—and when, through the slight communication with the other family which Sunday produced, she learnt that he had actually written home to defer his return, having promised to remain some days longer with his friend!

If she had felt impatience and regret before—if she had been sorry for what she said, and feared its too strong effect

line 25: no Edmund—when] **1814** no Edmund.—When

on him, she now felt and feared it all tenfold more. She had, moreover, to contend with one disagreeable emotion entirely new to her—jealousy. His friend Mr. Owen had sisters— He might find them attractive. But at any rate his staying away at a time, when, according to all preceding plans, she was to remove to London, meant something that she could not bear. Had Henry returned, as he talked of doing, at the end of three or four days, she should now have been leaving Mansfield. It became absolutely necessary for her to get to Fanny and try to learn something more. She could not live any longer in such solitary wretchedness; and she made her way to the Park, through difficulties of walking which she had deemed unconquerable a week before, for the chance of hearing a little in addition, for the sake of at least hearing his name.

The first half hour was lost, for Fanny and Lady Bertram were together, and unless she had Fanny to herself she could hope for nothing. But at last Lady Bertram left the room— and then almost immediately Miss Crawford thus began, with a voice as well regulated as she could—"And how do *you* like your cousin Edmund's staying away so long?—Being the only young person at home, I consider *you* as the greatest sufferer.—You must miss him. Does his staying longer surprize you?"

"I do not know," said Fanny hesitatingly.—"Yes—I had not particularly expected it."

"Perhaps he will always stay longer than he talks of. It is the general way all young men do."

"He did not, the only time he went to see Mr. Owen before."

line 5: when, according to all preceding plans,] **1814** when according to all preceding plans   //   line 22: home, I] **1814** home I   //   line 24: surprize] **1814** surprise

"He finds the house more agreeable *now.*—He is a very—a very pleasing young man himself, and I cannot help being rather concerned at not seeing him again before I go to London, as will now undoubtedly be the case.—I am looking for Henry every day, and as soon as he comes there will be nothing to detain me at Mansfield. I should like to have seen him once more, I confess. But you must give my compliments to him. Yes—I think it must be compliments. Is not there a something wanted, Miss Price, in our language—a some-thing between compliments and—and love—to suit the sort of friendly acquaintance we have had together?—So many months acquaintance!—But compliments may be sufficient here.—Was his letter a long one?—Does he give you much account of what he is doing?—Is it Christmas gaieties that he is staying for?"

"I only heard a part of the letter; it was to my uncle—but I believe it was very short; indeed I am sure it was but a few lines. All that I heard was that his friend had pressed him to stay longer, and that he had agreed to do so. A *few* days longer, or *some* days longer, I am not quite sure which."

"Oh! if he wrote to his father—But I thought it might have been to Lady Bertram or you. But if he wrote to his father, no wonder he was concise. Who could write chat to Sir Thomas? If he had written to you, there would have been more particulars. You would have heard of balls and parties.— He would have sent you a description of every thing and every body. How many Miss Owens are there?"

"Three grown up."

"Are they musical?"

"I do not at all know. I never heard."

line 20: longer, or] **1814** longer or

"That is the first question, you know," said Miss Crawford, trying to appear gay and unconcerned, "which every woman who plays herself is sure to ask about another. But it is very foolish to ask questions about any young ladies—about any three sisters just grown up; for one knows, without being told, exactly what they are—all very accomplished and pleasing, and *one* very pretty. There is a beauty in every family.—It is a regular thing. Two play on the piano-forte, and one on the harp—and all sing—or would sing if they were taught—or sing all the better for not being taught—or something like it."

"I know nothing of the Miss Owens," said Fanny calmly.

"You know nothing and you care less, as people say. Never did tone express indifference plainer. Indeed how can one care for those one has never seen?—Well, when your cousin comes back, he will find Mansfield very quiet;—all the noisy ones gone, your brother and mine and myself. I do not like the idea of leaving Mrs. Grant now the time draws near. She does not like my going."

Fanny felt obliged to speak. "You cannot doubt your being missed by many," said she. "You will be very much missed."

Miss Crawford turned her eye on her, as if wanting to hear or see more, and then laughingly said, "Oh! yes, missed as every noisy evil is missed when it is taken away; that is, there is a great difference felt. But I am not fishing; don't compliment me. If I *am* missed, it will appear. I may be discovered by those who want to see me. I shall not be in any doubtful, or distant, or unapproachable region."

Now Fanny could not bring herself to speak, and Miss Crawford was disappointed; for she had hoped to hear some pleasant assurance of her power, from one who she thought must know; and her spirits were clouded again.

"The Miss Owens," said she soon afterwards—"Suppose you were to have one of the Miss Owens settled at Thornton Lacey; how should you like it? Stranger things have happened. I dare say they are trying for it. And they are quite in the right, for it would be a very pretty establishment for them. I do not at all wonder or blame them.—It is every body's duty to do as well for themselves as they can. Sir Thomas Bertram's son is somebody; and now, he is in their own line. Their father is a clergyman and their brother is a clergyman, and they are all clergymen together. He is their lawful property, he fairly belongs to them. You don't speak, Fanny—Miss Price—you don't speak.—But honestly now, do not you rather expect it than otherwise?"

"No," said Fanny stoutly, "I do not expect it at all."

"Not at all!"—cried Miss Crawford with alacrity. "I wonder at that. But I dare say you know exactly—I always imagine you are—perhaps you do not think him likely to marry at all—or not at present."

"No, I do not," said Fanny softly—hoping she did not err either in the belief or the acknowledgment of it.

Her companion looked at her keenly; and gathering greater spirit from the blush soon produced from such a look, only said, "He is best off as he is," and turned the subject.

line 14: expect it at all."] **1814** expect it all."   //   line 15: all!"—cried] **1814** all,"—cried

Chapter 12

MISS CRAWFORD'S uneasiness was much lightened by this conversation, and she walked home again in spirits which might have defied almost another week of the same small party in the same bad weather, had they been put to the proof; but as that very evening brought her brother down from London again in quite, or more than quite, his usual cheerfulness, she had nothing further to try her own. His still refusing to tell her what he had gone for, was but the promotion of gaiety; a day before it might have irritated, but now it was a pleasant joke—suspected only of concealing something planned as a pleasant surprize to herself. And the next day *did* bring a surprize to her. Henry had said he should just go and ask the Bertrams how they did, and be back in ten minutes—but he was gone above an hour; and when his sister, who had been waiting for him to walk with her in the garden, met him at last most impatiently in the sweep,[1] and cried out, "My dear Henry, where can you possibly have been all this time?" he had only to say that he had been sitting with Lady Bertram and Fanny.

"Sitting with them an hour and half!" exclaimed Mary.

But this was only the beginning of her surprize.

"Yes, Mary," said he, drawing her arm within his, and walking along the sweep as if not knowing where he was "—I could not get away sooner—Fanny looked so lovely!—I am

line 7: further] **1814** farther // line 11: surprize] **1814** surprise // line 12: surprize] **1814** surprise // line 21: surprize.] **1814** surprise.

quite determined, Mary. My mind is entirely made up. Will it astonish you? No—You must be aware that I am quite determined to marry Fanny Price."

The surprize was now complete; for in spite of whatever his consciousness might suggest, a suspicion of his having any such views[2] had never entered his sister's imagination; and she looked so truly the astonishment she felt, that he was obliged to repeat what he had said, and more fully and more solemnly. The conviction of his determination once admitted, it was not unwelcome. There was even pleasure with the surprize. Mary was in a state of mind to rejoice in a connection with the Bertram family, and to be not displeased with her brother's marrying a little beneath him.

"Yes, Mary," was Henry's concluding assurance. "I am fairly caught. You know with what idle designs I began—but this is the end of them. I have (I flatter myself) made no inconsiderable progress in her affections; but my own are entirely fixed."

"Lucky, lucky girl!" cried Mary as soon as she could speak— "what a match for her! My dearest Henry, this must be my *first* feeling; but my *second*, which you shall have as sincerely, is that I approve your choice from my soul, and foresee your happiness as heartily as I wish and desire it. You will have a sweet little wife; all gratitude and devotion. Exactly what you deserve. What an amazing match for her! Mrs. Norris often talks of her luck; what will she say now? The delight of all the family indeed! And she has some *true* friends in it. How *they* will rejoice! But tell me all about it. Talk to me for ever. When did you begin to think seriously about her?"

Nothing could be more impossible than to answer such a question, though nothing be more agreeable than to have it

line 4: surprize] **1814** surprise   //   line 4: complete; for in] **1814** complete, for, in   //   line 11: surprize.] **1814** surprise.

asked. "How the pleasing plague had stolen on him"[3] he could not say, and before he had expressed the same sentiment with a little variation of words three times over, his sister eagerly interrupted him with, "Ah! my dear Henry, and this is what took you to London! This was your business! You chose to consult the Admiral, before you made up your mind."

But this he stoutly denied. He knew his uncle too well to consult him on any matrimonial scheme. The Admiral hated marriage, and thought it never pardonable in a young man of independent fortune.

"When Fanny is known to him," continued Henry, "he will doat on her. She is exactly the woman to do away every prejudice of such a man as the Admiral, for she is exactly such a woman as he thinks does not exist in the world. She is the very impossibility he would describe—if indeed he has now delicacy of language enough to embody his own ideas. But till it is absolutely settled—settled beyond all interference, he shall know nothing of the matter. No, Mary, you are quite mistaken. You have not discovered my business yet!"

"Well, well, I am satisfied. I know now to whom it must relate, and am in no hurry for the rest. Fanny Price— Wonderful—quite wonderful!—That Mansfield should have done so much for—that *you* should have found your fate in Mansfield! But you are quite right, you could not have chosen better. There is not a better girl in the world, and you do not want for fortune; and as to her connections, they are more than good. The Bertrams are undoubtedly some of the first people in this country. She is niece to Sir Thomas Bertram; that will be enough for the world. But go on, go on. Tell me more. What are your plans? Does she know her own happiness?"

"No."

"What are you waiting for?"

"For—for very little more than opportunity. Mary, she is not like her cousins; but I think I shall not ask in vain."

"Oh! no, you cannot. Were you even less pleasing—supposing her not to love you already, (of which however I can have little doubt,) you would be safe. The gentleness and gratitude of her disposition would secure her all your own immediately. From my soul I do not think she would marry you *without* love; that is, if there is a girl in the world capable of being uninfluenced by ambition, I can suppose it her; but ask her to love you, and she will never have the heart to refuse."

As soon as her eagerness could rest in silence, he was as happy to tell as she could be to listen, and a conversation followed almost as deeply interesting to her as to himself, though he had in fact nothing to relate but his own sensations, nothing to dwell on but Fanny's charms.—Fanny's beauty of face and figure, Fanny's graces of manner and goodness of heart were the exhaustless theme. The gentleness, modesty, and sweetness of her character were warmly expatiated on, that sweetness which makes so essential a part of every woman's worth in the judgment of man, that though he sometimes loves where it is not, he can never believe it absent. Her temper he had good reason to depend on and to praise. He had often seen it tried. Was there one of the family, excepting Edmund, who had not in some way or other continually exercised her patience and forbearance? Her affections were evidently strong. To see her with her brother! What could more delightfully prove that the warmth of her heart was equal to its gentleness?—What could be more encouraging to a man who had her love in view? Then, her understanding was beyond every suspicion, quick and clear;

line 4: already, (of] **1814** already (of   //   line 5: doubt,) you] **1814** doubt) you

and her manners were the mirror of her own modest and elegant mind. Nor was this all. Henry Crawford had too much sense not to feel the worth of good principles in a wife, though he was too little accustomed to serious reflection to know them by their proper name; but when he talked of her having such a steadiness and regularity of conduct, such a high notion of honour, and such an observance of decorum as might warrant any man in the fullest dependence on her faith and integrity, he expressed what was inspired by the knowledge of her being well principled and religious.[4]

"I could so wholly and absolutely confide in her," said he; "and *that* is what I want."

Well might his sister, believing as she really did that his opinion of Fanny Price was scarcely beyond her merits, rejoice in her prospects.

"The more I think of it," she cried, "the more am I convinced that you are doing quite right, and though I should never have selected Fanny Price as the girl most likely to attach you, I am now persuaded she is the very one to make you happy. Your wicked project upon her peace turns out a clever thought indeed. You will both find your good in it."

"It was bad, very bad in me against such a creature![5] but I did not know her then. And she shall have no reason to lament the hour that first put it into my head. I will make her very happy, Mary, happier than she has ever yet been herself, or ever seen any body else. I will not take her from Northamptonshire. I shall let Everingham, and rent a place in this neighbourhood—perhaps Stanwix Lodge.[6] I shall let a seven years' lease of Everingham. I am sure of an excellent

line 31: years' lease] **1814** year's lease

tenant at half a word. I could name three people now, who would give me my own terms and thank me."

"Ha!" cried Mary, "settle in Northamptonshire! That is pleasant! Then we shall be all together."

When she had spoken it, she recollected herself, and wished it unsaid; but there was no need of confusion,[7] for her brother saw her only as the supposed inmate[8] of Mansfield Parsonage, and replied but to invite her in the kindest manner to his own house, and to claim the best right in her.

"You must give us more than half your time," said he; "I cannot admit Mrs. Grant to have an equal claim with Fanny and myself, for we shall both have a right in you. Fanny will be so truly your sister!"

Mary had only to be grateful and give general assurances; but she was now very fully purposed to be the guest of neither brother nor sister many months longer.

"You will divide your year between London and Northamptonshire?"

"Yes."

"That's right; and in London, of course, a house of your own; no longer with the Admiral. My dearest Henry, the advantage to you of getting away from the Admiral before your manners are hurt by the contagion of his, before you have contracted any of his foolish opinions, or learnt to sit over your dinner, as if it were the best blessing of life!—*You* are not sensible of the gain, for your regard for him has blinded you; but, in my estimation, your marrying early may be the saving of you. To have seen you grow like the Admiral in word or deed, look or gesture, would have broken my heart."

line 28: but, in my estimation, your] **1814** but in my estimation your   //
line 30: broken my] **1814** broke my

"Well, well, we do not think quite alike here. The Admiral has his faults, but he is a very good man, and has been more than a father to me. Few fathers would have let me have my own way half so much. You must not prejudice Fanny against him. I must have them love one another."

Mary refrained from saying what she felt, that there could not be two persons in existence, whose characters and manners were less accordant; time would discover it to him; but she could not help *this* reflection on the Admiral. "Henry, I think so highly of Fanny Price, that if I could suppose the next Mrs. Crawford would have half the reason which my poor ill used aunt had to abhor the very name, I would prevent the marriage, if possible; but I know you, I know that a wife you *loved* would be the happiest of women and that even when you ceased to love, she would yet find in you the liberality and good-breeding of a gentleman."

The impossibility of not doing every thing in the world to make Fanny Price happy, or of ceasing to love Fanny Price, was of course the ground-work of his eloquent answer.

"Had you seen her this morning, Mary," he continued, "attending with such ineffable sweetness and patience, to all the demands of her aunt's stupidity, working with her, and for her, her colour beautifully heightened as she leant over the work, then returning to her seat to finish a note which she was previously engaged in writing for that stupid woman's service, and all this with such unpretending gentleness, so much as if it were a matter of course that she was not to have a moment at her own command, her hair arranged as neatly as it always is, and one little curl falling forward as she wrote, which she now and then shook back, and in the midst of all this, still speaking at intervals to *me*, or listening, and as if she liked to listen to what I said. Had you seen her so, Mary, you would not have implied the possibility of her power over my heart ever ceasing."

"My dearest Henry," cried Mary, stopping short, and smiling in his face, "how glad I am to see you so much in love! It quite delights me. But what will Mrs. Rushworth and Julia say?"

"I care neither what they say, nor what they feel. They will now see what sort of woman it is that can attach me, that can attach a man of sense. I wish the discovery may do them any good. And they will now see their cousin treated as she ought to be, and I wish they may be heartily ashamed of their own abominable neglect and unkindness. They will be angry," he added, after a moment's silence, and in a cooler tone, "Mrs. Rushworth will be very angry. It will be a bitter pill to her; that is, like other bitter pills, it will have two moments ill-flavour, and then be swallowed and forgotten; for I am not such a coxcomb as to suppose her feelings more lasting than other women's, though *I* was the object of them. Yes, Mary, my Fanny will feel a difference indeed, a daily, hourly difference, in the behaviour of every being who approaches her; and it will be the completion of my happiness to know that I am the doer of it, that I am the person to give the consequence so justly her due. Now she is dependent, helpless, friendless, neglected, forgotten."

"Nay, Henry, not by all, not forgotten by all, not friendless or forgotten. Her cousin Edmund never forgets her."

"Edmund—True, I believe he is (generally speaking) kind to her; and so is Sir Thomas in his way, but it is the way of a rich, superior, longworded, arbitrary uncle. What can Sir Thomas and Edmund together do, what *do* they do for her happiness, comfort, honour, and dignity in the world to what I *shall* do?"

Chapter 13

HENRY CRAWFORD was at Mansfield Park again the next morning, and at an earlier hour than common visiting warrants. The two ladies were together in the breakfast-room, and fortunately for him, Lady Bertram was on the very point of quitting it as he entered. She was almost at the door, and not chusing by any means to take so much trouble in vain, she still went on, after a civil reception, a short sentence about being waited for, and a "Let Sir Thomas know," to the servant.

Henry, overjoyed to have her go, bowed and watched her off, and without losing another moment, turned instantly to Fanny, and taking out some letters said, with a most animated look, "I must acknowledge myself infinitely obliged to any creature who gives me such an opportunity of seeing you alone: I have been wishing it more than you can have any idea. Knowing as I do what your feelings as a sister are, I could hardly have borne that any one in the house should share with you in the first knowledge of the news I now bring. He is made. Your brother is a Lieutenant. I have the infinite satisfaction of congratulating you on your brother's promotion. Here are the letters which announce it, this moment come to hand. You will, perhaps, like to see them."

Fanny could not speak, but he did not want her to speak. To see the expression of her eyes, the change of her complexion, the progress of her feelings, their doubt, confusion, and felicity, was enough. She took the letters as he gave them. The first was from the Admiral to inform his nephew, in a few words, of his having succeeded in the object he had undertaken, the promotion of young Price, and inclosing two more, one from the Secretary of the First Lord to a friend, whom the Admiral had set to work in the business, the other from that friend to himself, by which it appeared that his Lordship had the very great happiness of attending to the recommendation of Sir Charles, that Sir Charles was much delighted in having such an opportunity of proving his regard for Admiral Crawford, and that the circumstance of Mr. William Price's commission as second Lieutenant of H. M. sloop Thrush,[1] being made out, was spreading general joy through a wide circle of great people.

While her hand was trembling under these letters, her eye running from one to the other, and her heart swelling with emotion, Crawford thus continued, with unfeigned eagerness, to express his interest in the event.

"I will not talk of my own happiness," said he, "great as it is, for I think only of yours. Compared with you, who has a right to be happy? I have almost grudged myself my own prior knowledge of what you ought to have known before all the world. I have not lost a moment, however. The post was late this morning, but there has not been since, a moment's delay. How impatient, how anxious, how wild I have been on the subject, I will not attempt to describe; how severely mortified, how cruelly disappointed, in not having it finished while I was in London! I was kept there from day to day in the hope of it, for nothing less dear to me than such an object would have detained me half the time from Mansfield. But though my uncle entered into my wishes with all the warmth I could desire, and exerted himself immediately, there were

line 10: Crawford,] **1814** Crauford, // line 16: continued, with] **1814** continued with

difficulties from the absence of one friend, and the engagements of another, which at last I could no longer bear to stay
the end of, and knowing in what good hands I left the cause,
I came away on Monday, trusting that many posts would not
pass before I should be followed by such very letters as these.
My uncle, who is the very best man in the world, has exerted
himself, as I knew he would after seeing your brother. He
was delighted with him. I would not allow myself yesterday
to say *how* delighted, or to repeat half that the Admiral said
in his praise. I deferred it all, till his praise should be proved
the praise of a friend, as this day *does* prove it. *Now* I may
say that even *I* could not require William Price to excite a
greater interest, or be followed by warmer wishes and higher
commendation, than were most voluntarily bestowed by my
uncle, after the evening they passed together."

"Has this been all *your* doing then?" cried Fanny. "Good
Heaven! how very, very kind! Have you really—was it by *your*
desire—I beg your pardon, but I am bewildered. Did Admiral
Crawford apply?—how was it?—I am stupified."

Henry was most happy to make it more intelligible, by
beginning at an earlier stage, and explaining very particularly
what he had done. His last journey to London had been
undertaken with no other view than that of introducing her
brother in Hill-street, and prevailing on the Admiral to exert
whatever interest he might have for getting him on. This had
been his business. He had communicated it to no creature; he
had not breathed a syllable of it even to Mary; while uncertain
of the issue, he could not have borne any participation of his
feelings, but this had been his business; and he spoke with
such a glow of what his solicitude had been, and used such
strong expressions, was so abounding in the *deepest interest*,
in *twofold motives*, in *views and wishes more than could be told*,
that Fanny could not have remained insensible of his drift,

had she been able to attend; but her heart was so full and her senses still so astonished, that she could listen but imperfectly even to what he told her of William, and saying only when he paused, "How kind! how very kind! Oh! Mr. Crawford, we are infinitely obliged to you. Dearest, dearest William!" She jumped up and moved in haste towards the door, crying out, "I will go to my uncle. My uncle ought to know it as soon as possible." But this could not be suffered. The opportunity was too fair, and his feelings too impatient. He was after her immediately. "She must not go, she must allow him five minutes longer," and he took her hand and led her back to her seat, and was in the middle of his further explanation, before she had suspected for what she was detained. When she did understand it, however, and found herself expected to believe that *she* had created sensations which his heart had never known before, and that every thing he had done for William, was to be placed to the account of his excessive and unequalled attachment to her, she was exceedingly distressed, and for some moments unable to speak. She considered it all as nonsense, as mere trifling and gallantry, which meant only to deceive for the hour; she could not but feel that it was treating her improperly and unworthily, and in such a way as she had not deserved; but it was like himself, and entirely of a piece with what she had seen before; and she would not allow herself to shew half the displeasure she felt, because he had been conferring an obligation, which no want of delicacy on his part could make a trifle to her. While her heart was still bounding with joy and gratitude on William's behalf, she could not be severely resentful of any thing that injured only herself; and after having twice drawn back her hand, and twice attempted in vain to turn away from him, she got up

line 12: further] **1814** farther

348

and said only, with much agitation, "Don't, Mr. Crawford, pray don't. I beg you would not. This is a sort of talking which is very unpleasant to me. I must go away. I cannot bear it." But he was still talking on, describing his affection, soliciting a return, and, finally, in words so plain as to bear but one meaning even to *her*, offering himself, hand, fortune, every thing to her acceptance. It was so; he had said it. Her astonishment and confusion increased; and though still not knowing how to suppose him serious, she could hardly stand. He pressed for an answer.

"No, no, no," she cried, hiding her face. "This is all nonsense. Do not distress me. I can hear no more of this. Your kindness to William makes me more obliged to you than words can express; but I do not want, I cannot bear, I must not listen to such—No, no, don't think of me. But you are *not* thinking of me. I know it is all nothing."

She had burst away from him, and at that moment Sir Thomas was heard speaking to a servant in his way towards the room they were in. It was no time for further assurances or entreaty, though to part with her at a moment when her modesty alone seemed to his sanguine and pre-assured mind to stand in the way of the happiness he sought, was a cruel necessity.—She rushed out at an opposite door from the one her uncle was approaching, and was walking up and down the east room in the utmost confusion of contrary feeling, before Sir Thomas's politeness or apologies were over, or he had reached the beginning of the joyful intelligence, which his visitor came to communicate.

She was feeling, thinking, trembling, about every thing; agitated, happy, miserable, infinitely obliged, absolutely

line 25: contrary feeling,] **1814** contrary feelings,   //   line 26: politeness or apologies] **1814** politeness and apologies   //   line 29: trembling, about] **1814** trembling about

angry. It was all beyond belief! He was inexcusable, incomprehensible!—But such were his habits, that he could do nothing without a mixture of evil. He had previously made her the happiest of human beings, and now he had insulted— she knew not what to say—how to class or how to regard it. She would not have him be serious, and yet what could excuse the use of such words and offers, if they meant but to trifle?

But William was a Lieutenant.—*That* was a fact beyond a doubt and without an alloy. She would think of it for ever and forget all the rest. Mr. Crawford would certainly never address her so again: he must have seen how unwelcome it was to her; and in that case, how gratefully she could esteem him for his friendship to William!

She would not stir farther from the east-room than the head of the great staircase, till she had satisfied herself of Mr. Crawford's having left the house; but when convinced of his being gone, she was eager to go down and be with her uncle, and have all the happiness of his joy as well as her own, and all the benefit of his information or his conjectures as to what would now be William's destination. Sir Thomas was as joyful as she could desire, and very kind and communicative; and she had so comfortable a talk with him about William as to make her feel as if nothing had occurred to vex her, till she found towards the close that Mr. Crawford was engaged to return and dine there that very day. This was a most unwelcome hearing, for though *he* might think nothing of what had passed, it would be quite distressing to her to see him again so soon.

She tried to get the better of it, tried very hard as the dinner hour approached, to feel and appear as usual; but it was quite impossible for her not to look most shy and uncomfortable

line 14: farther] **1814** further // line 17: gone, she] **1814** gone she

when their visitor entered the room. She could not have supposed it in the power of any concurrence of circumstances to give her so many painful sensations on the first day of hearing of William's promotion.

Mr. Crawford was not only in the room; he was soon close to her. He had a note to deliver from his sister. Fanny could not look at him, but there was no consciousness of past folly in his voice. She opened her note immediately, glad to have any thing to do, and happy as she read it, to feel that the fidgettings of her aunt Norris, who was also to dine there, screened her a little from view.

"My DEAR FANNY, for so I may now always call you, to the infinite relief of a tongue that has been stumbling at *Miss Price* for at least the last six weeks—I cannot let my brother go without sending you a few lines of general congratulation, and giving my most joyful consent and approval.—Go on, my dear Fanny, and without fear; there can be no difficulties worth naming. I chuse to suppose that the assurance of *my* consent will be something; so, you may smile upon him with your sweetest smiles this afternoon, and send him back to me even happier than he goes.

Yours affectionately,

M. C."

These were not expressions to do Fanny any good; for though she read in too much haste and confusion to form the clearest judgment of Miss Crawford's meaning, it was evident that she meant to compliment her on her brother's attachment and even to *appear* to believe it serious. She did not know what to do, or what to think. There was wretchedness in the

line 9: happy as] **1814** happy, as // line 22: Yours] **1814** Your's //
line 24: good; for] **1814** good, for

idea of its being serious; there was perplexity and agitation every way. She was distressed whenever Mr. Crawford spoke to her, and he spoke to her much too often; and she was afraid there was a something in his voice and manner in addressing her, very different from what they were when he talked to the others. Her comfort in that day's dinner was quite destroyed; she could hardly eat any thing; and when Sir Thomas good humouredly observed, that joy had taken away her appetite, she was ready to sink with shame, from the dread of Mr. Crawford's interpretation; for though nothing could have tempted her to turn her eyes to the right hand where he sat, she felt that *his* were immediately directed towards her.

She was more silent than ever. She would hardly join even when William was the subject, for his commission came all from the right hand too, and there was pain in the connection.

She thought Lady Bertram sat longer than ever, and began to be in despair of ever getting away; but at last they were in the drawing-room and she was able to think as she would, while her aunts finished the subject of William's appointment in their own style.

Mrs. Norris seemed as much delighted with the saving it would be to Sir Thomas, as with any part of it. "*Now* William would be able to keep himself, which would make a vast difference to his uncle, for it was unknown how much he had cost his uncle; and indeed it would make some difference in *her* presents too. She was very glad that she had given William what she did at parting, very glad indeed that it had been in her power, without material inconvenience just at that time, to give him something rather considerable; that is, for *her*, with *her* limited means, for now it would all be useful in helping to fit up his cabin. She knew he must be at some expense, that he would have many things to buy, though to be sure his father and mother would be able to put him in the way of getting every thing very cheap—but she was very glad that she had contributed her mite towards it."

"I am glad you gave him something considerable," said Lady Bertram, with most unsuspicious calmness—"for *I* gave him only 10*l*."

"Indeed!" cried Mrs. Norris, reddening. "Upon my word, he must have gone off with his pockets well lined! and at no expense for his journey to London either!"

"Sir Thomas told me 10*l*. would be enough."

Mrs. Norris, being not at all inclined to question its sufficiency, began to take the matter in another point.

"It is amazing," said she, "how much young people cost their friends, what with bringing them up and putting them out in the world! They little think how much it comes to, or what their parents, or their uncles and aunts pay for them in the course of the year. Now, here are my sister Price's children;—take them all together, I dare say nobody would believe what a sum they cost Sir Thomas every year, to say nothing of what *I* do for them."

"Very true, sister, as you say. But, poor things! they cannot help it; and you know it makes very little difference to Sir Thomas. Fanny, William must not forget my shawl, if he goes to the East Indies; and I shall give him a commission for any thing else that is worth having, I wish he may go to the East Indies, that I may have my shawl. I think I will have two shawls,[2] Fanny."

Fanny, meanwhile, speaking only when she could not help it, was very earnestly trying to understand what Mr. and Miss Crawford were at. There was every thing in the world

line 5: must [**1814** most // line 11: Mrs. Norris, being] **1814** Mrs. Norris being // line 18: children;—take] **1814** children; take // line 25: any thing] **1814** anything // line 25: having, I] **1814** having. I

against their being serious, but his words and manner. Every thing natural, probable, reasonable was against it; all their habits and ways of thinking, and all her own demerits.— How could *she* have excited serious attachment in a man, who had seen so many, and been admired by so many, and flirted with so many, infinitely her superiors—who seemed so little open to serious impressions, even where pains had been taken to please him—who thought so slightly, so carelessly, so unfeelingly on all such points—who was every thing to every body, and seemed to find no one essential to him?—And further, how could it be supposed that his sister, with all her high and worldly notions of matrimony, would be forwarding any thing of a serious nature in such a quarter? Nothing could be more unnatural in either. Fanny was ashamed of her own doubts. Every thing might be possible rather than serious attachment or serious approbation of it toward her. She had quite convinced herself of this before Sir Thomas and Mr. Crawford joined them. The difficulty was in maintaining the conviction quite so absolutely after Mr. Crawford was in the room; for once or twice a look seemed forced on her which she did not know how to class among the common meaning; in any other man at least, she would have said that it meant something very earnest, very pointed. But she still tried to believe it no more than what he might often have expressed towards her cousins and fifty other women.

She thought he was wishing to speak to her unheard by the rest. She fancied he was trying for it the whole evening at intervals, whenever Sir Thomas was out of the room, or at all engaged with Mrs. Norris, and she carefully refused him every opportunity.

line 13: any thing] **1814** anything // line 16: toward her.] **1814** towards her.

At last—it seemed an at last to Fanny's nervousness, though not remarkably late,—he began to talk of going away; but the comfort of the sound was impaired by his turning to her the next moment, and saying, "Have you nothing to send to Mary? No answer to her note? She will be disappointed if she receives nothing from you. Pray write to her, if it be only a line."

"Oh! yes, certainly," cried Fanny, rising in haste, the haste of embarrassment and of wanting to get away—"I will write directly."

She went accordingly to the table, where she was in the habit of writing for her aunt, and prepared her materials without knowing what in the world to say! She had read Miss Crawford's note only once; and how to reply to any thing so imperfectly understood was most distressing. Quite unpractised in such sort of note-writing, had there been time for scruples and fears as to style, she would have felt them in abundance; but something must be instantly written, and with only one decided feeling, that of wishing not to appear to think any thing really intended, she wrote thus, in great trembling both of spirits and hand:

"I AM very much obliged to you, my dear Miss Crawford, for your kind congratulations, as far as they relate to my dearest William. The rest of your note I know means nothing; but I am so unequal to any thing of the sort, that I hope you will excuse my begging you to take no further notice. I have seen too much of Mr. Crawford not to understand his manners; if he understood me as well, he would, I dare say,

line 2: late,—he] **1814** late, he   //   line 14: any thing] **1814** anything   //
line 20: any thing] **1814** anything   //   line 24: nothing; but] **1814** nothing,
but   //   line 25: any thing] **1814** anything   //   line 28: would, I dare say,
behave] **1814** would I dare say behave

behave differently. I do not know what I write, but it would be a great favour of you never to mention the subject again. With thanks for the honour of your note,

> I remain, dear Miss Crawford,
>
> &c. &c."

The conclusion was scarcely intelligible from increasing fright, for she found that Mr. Crawford, under pretence of receiving the note, was coming towards her.

"You cannot think I mean to hurry you," said he, in an under voice, perceiving the amazing trepidation with which she made up the note; "you cannot think I have any such object. Do not hurry yourself, I entreat."

"Oh! I thank you, I have quite done, just done—it will be ready in a moment—I am very much obliged to you—if you will be so good as to give *that* to Miss Crawford."

The note was held out and must be taken; and as she instantly and with averted eyes walked towards the fireplace, where sat the others, he had nothing to do but to go in good earnest.

Fanny thought she had never known a day of greater agitation, both of pain and pleasure; but happily the pleasure was not of a sort to die with the day—for every day would restore the knowledge of William's advancement, whereas the pain she hoped would return no more. She had no doubt that her note must appear excessively ill-written, that the language would disgrace a child, for her distress had allowed no arrangement; but at least it would assure them both of her being neither imposed on, nor gratified by Mr. Crawford's attentions.

END OF VOLUME II

line 9: he, in] **1814** he in   //   line 12: entreat."] **1814** intreat."

MANSFIELD PARK
Volume III

Chapter 1

FANNY had by no means forgotten Mr. Crawford, when she awoke the next morning; but she remembered the purport of her note, and was not less sanguine, as to its effect, than she had been the night before. If Mr. Crawford would but go away!—That was what she most earnestly desired;—go and take his sister with him, as he was to do, and as he returned to Mansfield on purpose to do. And why it was not done already, she could not devise, for Miss Crawford certainly wanted no delay.—Fanny had hoped, in the course of his yesterday's visit, to hear the day named; but he had only spoken of their journey as what would take place ere long.

Having so satisfactorily settled the conviction her note would convey, she could not but be astonished to see Mr. Crawford, as she accidentally did, coming up to the house again, and at an hour as early as the day before.—His coming might have nothing to do with her, but she must avoid seeing him if possible; and being then in her way up stairs, she resolved there to remain, during the whole of his visit, unless actually sent for; and as Mrs. Norris was still in the house, there seemed little danger of her being wanted.

She sat some time in a good deal of agitation, listening, trembling, and fearing to be sent for every moment; but as no footsteps approached the east room, she grew gradually composed, could sit down, and be able to employ herself,

line 23: east room,] **1814** East room,

359

and able to hope that Mr. Crawford had come, and would go without her being obliged to know any thing of the matter.

Nearly half an hour had passed, and she was growing very comfortable, when suddenly the sound of a step in regular approach was heard—a heavy step, an unusual step in that part of the house; it was her uncle's; she knew it as well as his voice; she had trembled at it as often, and began to tremble again, at the idea of his coming up to speak to her, whatever might be the subject.—It was indeed Sir Thomas, who opened the door, and asked if she were there, and if he might come in. The terror of his former occasional visits to that room seemed all renewed, and she felt as if he were going to examine her again in French and English.

She was all attention, however, in placing a chair for him, and trying to appear honoured; and in her agitation, had quite overlooked the deficiences of her apartment, till he, stopping short as he entered, said, with much surprise, "Why have you no fire to-day?"

There was snow on the ground, and she was sitting in a shawl. She hesitated.

"I am not cold, Sir—I never sit here long at this time of year."

"But,—you have a fire in general?"

"No, Sir."

"How comes this about; here must be some mistake. I understood that you had the use of this room by way of making you perfectly comfortable.—In your bed-chamber I know you *cannot* have a fire. Here is some great misapprehension which must be rectified. It is highly unfit for you to

line 7: uncle's;] **1814** unc l's;

sit—be it only half an hour a day, without a fire. You are not strong. You are chilly. Your aunt cannot be aware of this."

Fanny would rather have been silent, but being obliged to speak, she could not forbear, in justice to the aunt she loved best, from saying something in which the words "my aunt Norris" were distinguishable.

"I understand," cried her uncle recollecting himself, and not wanting to hear more—"I understand. Your aunt Norris has always been an advocate, and very judiciously, for young people's being brought up without unnecessary indulgences; but there should be moderation in every thing.—She is also very hardy herself, which of course will influence her in her opinion of the wants of others. And on another account too, I can perfectly comprehend.—I know what her sentiments have always been. The principle was good in itself, but it may have been, and I believe *has been* carried too far in your case.—I am aware that there has been sometimes, in some points, a misplaced distinction; but I think too well of you, Fanny, to suppose you will ever harbour resentment on that account.—You have an understanding, which will prevent you from receiving things only in part, and judging partially by the event.—You will take in the whole of the past, you will consider times, persons, and probabilities, and you will feel that *they* were not least your friends who were educating and preparing you for that mediocrity of condition which *seemed* to be your lot.—Though their caution may prove eventually unnecessary, it was kindly meant; and of this you may be assured, that every advantage of affluence will be doubled by the little privations and restrictions that may have been imposed. I am sure you will not disappoint my opinion of

line 5: words "my] **1814** words, "my

you, by failing at any time to treat your aunt Norris with the respect and attention that are due to her.—But enough of this. Sit down, my dear. I must speak to you for a few minutes, but I will not detain you long."

Fanny obeyed, with eyes cast down and colour rising.— After a moment's pause, Sir Thomas, trying to suppress a smile, went on.

"You are not aware, perhaps, that I have had a visitor this morning.—I had not been long in my own room, after breakfast, when Mr. Crawford was shewn in.—His errand you may probably conjecture."

Fanny's colour grew deeper and deeper; and her uncle perceiving that she was embarrassed to a degree that made either speaking or looking up quite impossible, turned away his own eyes, and without any farther pause, proceeded in his account of Mr. Crawford's visit.

Mr. Crawford's business had been to declare himself the lover of Fanny, make decided proposals for her, and intreat the sanction of the uncle, who seemed to stand in the place of her parents; and he had done it all so well, so openly, so liberally, so properly, that Sir Thomas, feeling, moreover, his own replies, and his own remarks to have been very much to the purpose—was exceedingly happy to give the particulars of their conversation—and, little aware of what was passing in his niece's mind, conceived that by such details he must be gratifying her far more than himself. He talked therefore for several minutes without Fanny's daring to interrupt him.—She had hardly even attained the wish to do it. Her mind was in too much confusion. She had changed her position, and with her eyes fixed intently on one of the windows, was listening to her uncle, in the utmost perturbation and dismay.—For a moment he ceased, but she had barely become conscious of it, when, rising from his chair, he said, "And now, Fanny, having performed one part of my commission, and shewn you every thing placed on a basis the most assured and satisfactory, I may execute the remainder by prevailing on you to accompany me down stairs, where—though I cannot but presume on having been no unacceptable companion myself, I must submit to your finding one still better worth listening to.—Mr. Crawford, as you have perhaps foreseen, is yet in the house. He is in my room, and hoping to see you there."

There was a look, a start, an exclamation, on hearing this, which astonished Sir Thomas; but what was his increase of astonishment on hearing her exclaim—"Oh! no, Sir, I cannot, indeed I cannot go down to him. Mr. Crawford ought to know—he must know that—I told him enough yesterday to convince him—he spoke to me on this subject yesterday—and I told him without disguise that it was very disagreeable to me, and quite out of my power to return his good opinion."

"I do not catch your meaning," said Sir Thomas, sitting down again,—"Out of your power to return his good opinion! what is all this? I know he spoke to you yesterday, and (as far as I understand), received as much encouragement to proceed as a well-judging young woman could permit herself to give. I was very much pleased with what I collected to have been your behaviour on the occasion; it shewed a discretion highly to be commended. But now, when he has made his overtures so properly, and honourably—what are your scruples *now*?"

"You are mistaken, Sir,"—cried Fanny, forced by the anxiety of the moment even to tell her uncle that he was wrong—"You are quite mistaken. How could Mr. Crawford say such a thing? I gave him no encouragement yesterday—On the

line 12: "Oh! no, Sir,] **1814** "Oh! no Sir, // line 18: Sir Thomas, sitting] **1814** Sir Thomas sitting // line 28: uncle] **1814** Uncle // line 30: thing? I] **1814** thing; I // line 30: encouragement] **1814** encouragemen

contrary, I told him—I cannot recollect my exact words—but I am sure I told him that I would not listen to him, that it was very unpleasant to me in every respect, and that I begged him never to talk to me in that manner again.—I am sure I said as much as that and more; and I should have said still more,—if I had been quite certain of his meaning any thing seriously, but I did not like to be—I could not bear to be—imputing more than might be intended. I thought it might all pass for nothing with *him*."

She could say no more; her breath was almost gone.

"Am I to understand," said Sir Thomas, after a few moments silence, "that you mean to *refuse* Mr. Crawford?"

"Yes, Sir."

"Refuse him?"

"Yes, Sir."

"Refuse Mr. Crawford! Upon what plea? For what reason?"

"I—I cannot like him, Sir, well enough to marry him."

"This is very strange!" said Sir Thomas, in a voice of calm displeasure. "There is something in this which my comprehension does not reach. Here is a young man wishing to pay his addresses to you, with every thing to recommend him; not merely situation in life, fortune, and character, but with more than common agreeableness, with address and conversation pleasing to every body. And he is not an acquaintance of to-day, you have now known him some time. His sister, moreover, is your intimate friend, and he has been doing *that* for your brother, which I should suppose would have been almost sufficient recommendation to you, had there been no other. It is very uncertain when my interest might have got William on. He has done it already."

line 19: "There is] **1814** There is   //   line 27: your brother,] you brother,

"Yes," said Fanny, in a faint voice, and looking down with fresh shame; and she did feel almost ashamed of herself, after such a picture as her uncle had drawn, for not liking Mr. Crawford.

"You must have been aware," continued Sir Thomas, presently,[1] "you must have been some time aware of a particularity in Mr. Crawford's manners to you. This cannot have taken you by surprise. You must have observed his attentions; and though you always received them very properly, (I have no accusation to make on that head,) I never perceived them to be unpleasant to you. I am half inclined to think, Fanny, that you do not quite know your own feelings."

"Oh! yes, Sir, indeed I do. His attentions were always—what I did not like."

Sir Thomas looked at her with deeper surprise. "This is beyond me," said he. "This requires explanation. Young as you are, and having seen scarcely any one, it is hardly possible that your affections——"

He paused and eyed her fixedly. He saw her lips formed into a *no*, though the sound was inarticulate, but her face was like scarlet. That, however, in so modest a girl might be very compatible with innocence; and chusing at least to appear satisfied, he quickly added, "No, no, I know *that* is quite out of the question—quite impossible. Well, there is nothing more to be said."

And for a few minutes he did say nothing. He was deep in thought. His niece was deep in thought likewise, trying to harden and prepare herself against farther questioning. She would rather die than own the truth, and she hoped by a little reflection to fortify herself beyond betraying it.

"Independently of the interest which Mr. Crawford's *choice* seemed to justify," said Sir Thomas, beginning again, and

very composedly, "his wishing to marry at all so early is rec-
ommendatory to me. I am an advocate for early marriages,
where there are means in proportion, and would have every
young man, with a sufficient income, settle as soon after four
and twenty as he can. This is so much my opinion, that I am
sorry to think how little likely my own eldest son, your cousin,
Mr. Bertram, is to marry early; but at present, as far as I can
judge, matrimony makes no part of his plans or thoughts. I
wish he were more likely to fix." Here was a glance at Fanny.
"Edmund I consider from his disposition and habits as much
more likely to marry early than his brother. *He*, indeed, I have
lately thought has seen the woman he could love, which, I
am convinced, my eldest son has not. Am I right? Do you
agree with me, my dear?"

"Yes, Sir."

It was gently, but it was calmly said, and Sir Thomas was
easy on the score of the cousins. But the removal of his alarm
did his niece no service; as her unaccountableness was confirmed, his displeasure increased; and getting up and walking
about the room, with a frown, which Fanny could picture
to herself, though she dared not lift up her eyes, he shortly
afterwards, and in a voice of authority, said, "Have you any
reason, child, to think ill of Mr. Crawford's temper?"

"No, Sir."

She longed to add, "but of his principles I have;" but her
heart sunk under the appalling prospect of discussion, explanation, and probably non-conviction. Her ill opinion of him
was founded chiefly on observations, which, for her cousin's
sake,[2] she could scarcely dare mention to their father. Maria
and Julia—and especially Maria, were so closely implicated
in Mr. Crawford's misconduct, that she could not give his
character, such as she believed it, without betraying them.
She had hoped that to a man like her uncle, so discerning, so

honourable, so good, the simple acknowledgment of settled *dislike* on her side, would have been sufficient. To her infinite grief she found it was not.

Sir Thomas came towards the table where she sat in trembling wretchedness, and with a good deal of cold sternness, said, "It is of no use, I perceive, to talk to you. We had better put an end to this most mortifying conference. Mr. Crawford must not be kept longer waiting. I will, therefore, only add, as thinking it my duty to mark my opinion of your conduct— that you have disappointed every expectation I had formed, and proved yourself of a character the very reverse of what I had supposed. For I *had*, Fanny, as I think my behaviour must have shewn, formed a very favourable opinion of you from the period of my return to England. I had thought you peculiarly free from wilfulness of temper, self-conceit, and every tendency to that independence of spirit,[3] which prevails so much in modern days, even in young women, and which in young women is offensive and disgusting beyond all common offence. But you have now shewn me that you can be wilful and perverse, that you can and will decide for yourself, without any consideration or deference for those who have surely some right to guide you—without even asking their advice. You have shewn yourself very, very different from any thing that I had imagined. The advantage or disadvantage of your family—of your parents—your brothers and sisters—never seems to have had a moment's share in your thoughts on this occasion. How *they* might be benefited, how *they* must rejoice in such an establishment for you—is nothing to *you*. You think only of yourself; and because you do not feel for Mr. Crawford exactly what a young, heated fancy imagines to be necessary for happiness, you resolve to refuse

line 24: any thing] **1814** anything

367

him at once, without wishing even for a little time to consider of it—a little more time for cool consideration, and for really examining your own inclinations—and are, in a wild fit of folly, throwing away from you such an opportunity of being settled in life, eligibly, honourably, nobly settled, as will, probably, never occur to you again. Here is a young man of sense, of character, of temper, of manners, and of fortune, exceedingly attached to you, and seeking your hand in the most handsome and disinterested way; and let me tell you, Fanny, that you may live eighteen years longer in the world, without being addressed by a man of half Mr. Crawford's estate, or a tenth part of his merits. Gladly would I have bestowed either of my own daughters on him. Maria is nobly married—but had Mr. Crawford sought Julia's hand, I should have given it to him with superior and more heartfelt satisfaction than I gave Maria's to Mr. Rushworth." After half a moment's pause—"And I should have been very much surprised had either of my daughters, on receiving a proposal of marriage at any time, which might carry with it only *half* the eligibility of *this*, immediately and peremptorily, and without paying my opinion or my regard the compliment of any consultation, put a decided negative on it. I should have been much surprised, and much hurt, by such a proceeding. I should have thought it a gross violation of duty and respect. *You* are not to be judged by the same rule. You do not owe me the duty of a child. But, Fanny, if your heart can acquit you of *ingratitude*—"

He ceased. Fanny was by this time crying so bitterly, that angry as he was, he would not press that article farther. Her heart was almost broke by such a picture of what she appeared

line 21: regard the] **1814** regard, the // line 26: But, Fanny, if] **1814** But, Fanny, if

to him; by such accusations, so heavy, so multiplied, so rising in dreadful gradation! Self-willed, obstinate, selfish, and ungrateful. He thought her all this. She had deceived his expectations; she had lost his good opinion. What was to become of her?

"I am very sorry," said she inarticulately through her tears, "I am very sorry indeed."

"Sorry! yes, I hope you are sorry; and you will probably have reason to be long sorry for this day's transactions."

"If it were possible for me to do otherwise," said she with another strong effort, "but I am so perfectly convinced that I could never make him happy, and that I should be miserable myself."

Another burst of tears; but in spite of that burst, and in spite of that great black word *miserable*, which served to introduce it, Sir Thomas began to think a little relenting, a little change of inclination, might have something to do with it; and to augur favourably from the personal intreaty of the young man himself. He knew her to be very timid, and exceedingly nervous; and thought it not improbable that her mind might be in such a state, as a little time, a little pressing, a little patience, and a little impatience, a judicious mixture of all on the lover's side, might work their usual effect on. If the gentleman would but persevere, if he had but love enough to persevere—Sir Thomas began to have hopes; and these reflections having passed across his mind and cheered it, "Well," said he, in a tone of becoming gravity, but of less anger, "well, child, dry up your tears. There is no use in these tears; they can do no good. You must now come down stairs with me. Mr. Crawford has been kept waiting too long already. You must give him your own answer; we cannot

line 10: otherwise," said] **1814** otherwise, "said

expect him to be satisfied with less; and you only can explain to him the grounds of that misconception of your sentiments, which, unfortunately for himself, he certainly has imbibed. I am totally unequal to it."

But Fanny shewed such reluctance, such misery, at the idea of going down to him, that Sir Thomas, after a little consideration, judged it better to indulge her. His hopes from both gentleman and lady suffered a small depression in consequence; but when he looked at his niece, and saw the state of feature and complexion which her crying had brought her into, he thought there might be as much lost as gained by an immediate interview. With a few words, therefore, of no particular meaning, he walked off by himself, leaving his poor niece to sit and cry over what had passed, with very wretched feelings.

Her mind was all disorder. The past, present, future, every thing was terrible. But her uncle's anger gave her the severest pain of all. Selfish and ungrateful! to have appeared so to him! She was miserable for ever. She had no one to take her part, to counsel, or speak for her. Her only friend was absent. He might have softened his father; but all, perhaps all, would think her selfish and ungrateful. She might have to endure the reproach again and again; she might hear it, or see it, or know it to exist for ever in every connection about her. She could not but feel some resentment against Mr. Crawford; yet, if he really loved her, and were unhappy too!—it was all wretchedness together.

In about a quarter of an hour her uncle returned; she was almost ready to faint at the sight of him. He spoke calmly, however, without austerity, without reproach, and she revived a little. There was comfort too in his words, as well as his

line 26: were unhappy] **1814** was unhappy

manner, for he began with, "Mr. Crawford is gone; he has just left me. I need not repeat what has passed. I do not want to add to any thing you may now be feeling, by an account of what he has felt. Suffice it, that he has behaved in the most gentleman-like and generous manner; and has confirmed me in a most favourable opinion of his understanding, heart, and temper. Upon my representation of what you were suffering, he immediately, and with the greatest delicacy, ceased to urge to see you for the present."

Here Fanny, who had looked up, looked down again. "Of course," continued her uncle, "it cannot be supposed but that he should request to speak with you alone, be it only for five minutes; a request too natural, a claim too just to be denied. But there is no time fixed, perhaps to-morrow, or whenever your spirits are composed enough. For the present you have only to tranquillize yourself. Check these tears; they do but exhaust you. If, as I am willing to suppose, you wish to shew me any observance, you will not give way to these emotions, but endeavour to reason yourself into a stronger frame of mind. I advise you to go out, the air will do you good; go out for an hour on the gravel,[4] you will have the shrubbery to yourself and will be the better for air and exercise. And, Fanny, (turning back again for a moment) I shall make no mention below of what has passed; I shall not even tell your aunt Bertram. There is no occasion for spreading the disappointment; say nothing about it yourself."

This was an order to be most joyfully obeyed; this was an act of kindness which Fanny felt at her heart. To be spared from her aunt Norris's interminable reproaches!—he left her in a glow of gratitude. Any thing might be bearable rather

line 22: yourself and] **1814** yourself, and

than such reproaches. Even to see Mr. Crawford would be less overpowering.

She walked out directly as her uncle recommended, and followed his advice throughout, as far as she could; did check her tears, did earnestly try to compose her spirits, and strengthen her mind. She wished to prove to him that she did desire his comfort, and sought to regain his favour; and he had given her another strong motive for exertion, in keeping the whole affair from the knowledge of her aunts. Not to excite suspicion by her look or manner was now an object worth attaining; and she felt equal to almost any thing that might save her from her aunt Norris.

She was struck, quite struck, when on returning from her walk, and going into the east room again, the first thing which caught her eye was a fire lighted and burning. A fire! it seemed too much; just at that time to be giving her such an indulgence, was exciting even painful gratitude. She wondered that Sir Thomas could have leisure to think of such a trifle again; but she soon found, from the voluntary information of the housemaid, who came in to attend it, that so it was to be every day. Sir Thomas had given orders for it.

"I must be a brute indeed, if I can be really ungrateful!" said she in soliloquy; "Heaven defend me from being ungrateful!"

She saw nothing more of her uncle, nor of her aunt Norris, till they met at dinner. Her uncle's behaviour to her was then as nearly as possible what it had been before; she was sure he did not mean there should be any change, and that it was only her own conscience that could fancy any; but her aunt was soon quarrelling with her: and when she found how much and how unpleasantly her having only walked out without her aunt's knowledge could be dwelt on, she felt all the reason she had to bless the kindness which saved her from the same spirit of reproach, exerted on a more momentous subject.

"If I had known you were going out, I should have got you just to go as far as my house with some orders for Nanny," said she, "which I have since, to my very great inconvenience, been obliged to go and carry myself. I could very ill spare the time, and you might have saved me the trouble, if you would only have been so good as to let us know you were going out. It would have made no difference to you, I suppose, whether you had walked in the shrubbery, or gone to my house."

"I recommended the shrubbery to Fanny as the dryest place," said Sir Thomas.

"Oh," said Mrs. Norris with a moment's check, "that was very kind of you, Sir Thomas; but you do not know how dry the path is to my house. Fanny would have had quite as good a walk there, I assure you; with the advantage of being of some use, and obliging her aunt: it is all her fault. If she would but have let us know she was going out—but there is a something about Fanny, I have often observed it before,—she likes to go her own way to work; she does not like to be dictated to; she takes her own independent walk whenever she can; she certainly has a little spirit of secrecy, and independence, and nonsense, about her, which I would advise her to get the better of."

As a general reflection on Fanny, Sir Thomas thought nothing could be more unjust, though he had been so lately expressing the same sentiments himself, and he tried to turn the conversation; tried repeatedly before he could succeed; for Mrs. Norris had not discernment enough to perceive, either now, or at any other time, to what degree he thought well of his niece, or how very far he was from wishing to have his own children's merits set off by the depreciation of hers.

line 11: "Oh," said] **1814** "Oh!" said   //   line 14: there, I] **1814** there I   //
line 30: hers.] **1814** her's.

She was talking *at* Fanny, and resenting this private walk half through the dinner.

It was over, however, at last; and the evening set in with more composure to Fanny, and more cheerfulness of spirits than she could have hoped for after so stormy a morning; but she trusted, in the first place, that she had done right, that her judgment had not misled her; for the purity of her intentions she could answer; and she was willing to hope, secondly, that her uncle's displeasure was abating, and would abate farther as he considered the matter with more impartiality, and felt, as a good man must feel, how wretched, and how unpardonable, how hopeless and how wicked it was, to marry without affection.

When the meeting with which she was threatened for the morrow was past, she could not but flatter herself that the subject would be finally concluded, and Mr. Crawford once gone from Mansfield, that every thing would soon be as if no such subject had existed. She would not, could not believe, that Mr. Crawford's affection for her could distress him long; his mind was not of that sort. London would soon bring its cure. In London he would soon learn to wonder at his infatuation, and be thankful for the right reason[5] in her, which had saved him from its evil consequences.

While Fanny's mind was engaged in these sort of hopes, her uncle was soon after tea called out of the room; an occurrence too common to strike her, and she thought nothing of it till the butler re-appeared ten minutes afterwards, and advancing decidedly towards herself, said, "Sir Thomas wishes to speak with you, Ma'am, in his own room." Then it occurred to her what might be going on; a suspicion rushed over her mind which drove the colour from her cheeks; but instantly rising, she was preparing to obey, when Mrs. Norris called out, "Stay,

stay, Fanny! what are you about?—where are you going?—
don't be in such a hurry. Depend upon it, it is not you that are
wanted; depend upon it it is me; (looking at the butler) but
you are so very eager to put yourself forward. What should
Sir Thomas want you for? It is me, Baddeley, you mean; I
am coming this moment. You mean me, Baddeley, I am sure;
Sir Thomas wants me, not Miss Price."

But Baddeley was stout. "No, Ma'am, it is Miss Price,
I am certain of its being Miss Price." And there was a half
smile with the words which meant, "I do not think *you* would
answer the purpose at all."

Mrs. Norris, much discontented, was obliged to compose
herself to work again; and Fanny, walking off in agitating
consciousness, found herself, as she anticipated, in another
minute alone with Mr. Crawford.

line 3: depend upon it is me;[**1814** depend upon it it is me;   //   line 8: "No,
Ma'am,] **1814** "No Ma'am,   //   line 12: Mrs. Norris, much discontented,
was] **1814** Mrs. Norris much discontented was

Chapter 2

THE conference was neither so short, nor so conclusive, as the lady had designed. The gentleman was not so easily satisfied. He had all the disposition to persevere that Sir Thomas could wish him. He had vanity, which strongly inclined him, in the first place, to think she did love him, though she might not know it herself; and which, secondly, when constrained at last to admit that she did know her own present feelings, convinced him that he should be able in time to make those feelings what he wished.

He was in love, very much in love; and it was a love which, operating on an active, sanguine spirit, of more warmth than delicacy, made her affection appear of greater consequence, because it was withheld, and determined him to have the glory, as well as the felicity, of forcing her to love him.

He would not despair: he would not desist. He had every well grounded reason for solid attachment; he knew her to have all the worth that could justify the warmest hopes of lasting happiness with her; her conduct at this very time, by speaking the disinterestedness and delicacy of her character (qualities which he believed most rare indeed), was of a sort to heighten all his wishes, and confirm all his resolutions. He knew not that he had a pre-engaged heart to attack. Of *that*, he had no suspicion. He considered her rather as one who had never thought on the subject enough to be in danger; who had been guarded by youth, a youth of mind as lovely as of person; whose modesty had prevented her from understanding his attentions, and who was still overpowered by the suddenness of addresses so wholly unexpected, and the novelty of a situation which her fancy had never taken into account.

Must it not follow of course, that when he was understood, he should succeed?—he believed it fully. Love such as his, in a man like himself, must with perseverance secure a return, and at no great distance; and he had so much delight in the idea of obliging her to love him in a very short time, that her not loving him now was scarcely regretted. A little difficulty to be overcome, was no evil to Henry Crawford. He rather derived spirits from it. He had been apt to gain hearts too easily. His situation was new and animating.

To Fanny, however, who had known too much opposition all her life, to find any charm in it, all this was unintelligible. She found that he did mean to persevere; but how he could, after such language from her as she felt herself obliged to use, was not to be understood. She told him, that she did not love him, could not love him, was sure she never should love him: that such a change was quite impossible, that the subject was most painful to her, that she must intreat him never to mention it again, to allow her to leave him at once, and let it be considered as concluded for ever. And when farther pressed, had added, that in her opinion their dispositions were so totally dissimilar, as to make mutual affection incompatible; and that they were unfitted for each other by nature, education, and habit. All this she had said, and with the earnestness of sincerity; yet this was not enough, for he immediately denied there being anything uncongenial in their characters, or anything unfriendly in their situations; and positively declared, that he would still love, and still hope!

Fanny knew her own meaning, but was no judge of her own manner. Her manner was incurably gentle, and she was not aware how much it concealed the sternness of her purpose. Her diffidence, gratitude, and softness, made every expression of indifference seem almost an effort of self-denial; seem at least, to be giving nearly as much pain to herself as to him. Mr. Crawford was no longer the Mr. Crawford who, as the clandestine, insidious, treacherous admirer of Maria Bertram, had been her abhorrence, whom she had hated to see or to speak to, in whom she could believe no good quality to exist, and whose power, even of being agreeable, she had barely acknowledged. He was now the Mr. Crawford who was addressing herself with ardent, disinterested, love; whose feelings were apparently become all that was honourable and upright, whose views of happiness were all fixed on a marriage of attachment; who was pouring out his sense of her merits, describing and describing again his affection, proving, as far as words could prove it, and in the language, tone, and spirit of a man of talent too, that he sought her for her gentleness, and her goodness; and to complete the whole, he was now the Mr. Crawford who had procured William's promotion!

Here was a change! and here were claims which could not but operate. She might have disdained him in all the dignity of angry virtue, in the grounds of Sotherton, or the theatre at Mansfield Park; but he approached her now with rights that demanded different treatment. She must be courteous, and she must be compassionate. She must have a sensation of being honoured, and whether thinking of herself or her brother, she must have a strong feeling of gratitude. The effect of the whole was a manner so pitying and agitated, and words intermingled with her refusal so expressive of obligation and concern, that to a temper of vanity and hope like Crawford's the truth, or at least the strength of her indifference, might well be questionable; and he was not so irrational as Fanny considered him, in the professions of persevering, assiduous, and not desponding attachment which closed the interview.

It was with reluctance that he suffered her to go, but there was no look of despair in parting to bely his words, or give her hopes of his being less unreasonable than he professed himself.

Now she was angry. Some resentment did arise at a perseverance so selfish and ungenerous. Here was again a want of delicacy and regard for others which had formerly so struck and disgusted her. Here was again a something of the same Mr. Crawford whom she had so reprobated before. How evidently was there a gross want of feeling and humanity where his own pleasure was concerned—And, alas! how always known no principle[1] to supply as a duty what the heart was deficient in. Had her own affections been as free—as perhaps they ought to have been—he never could have engaged them.

So thought Fanny in good truth and sober sadness,[2] as she sat musing over that too great indulgence and luxury of a fire upstairs—wondering at the past and present, wondering at what was yet to come, and in a nervous agitation which made nothing clear to her but the persuasion of her being never under any circumstances able to love Mr. Crawford, and the felicity of having a fire to sit over and think of it.

Sir Thomas was obliged or obliged himself to wait till the morrow for a knowledge of what had passed between the young people. He then saw Mr. Crawford, and received his account.—The first feeling was disappointment: he had hoped better things; he had thought that an hour's intreaty from a young man like Crawford could not have worked so

line 27: Mr. Crawford, and] **1814** Mr. Crawford and   //   line 28: disappointment: he] **1814** disappointment; he

little change on a gentle tempered girl like Fanny; but there was speedy comfort in the determined views and sanguine perseverance of the lover; and when seeing such confidence of success in the principal, Sir Thomas was soon able to depend on it himself.

Nothing was omitted, on his side, of civility, compliment, or kindness, that might assist the plan. Mr. Crawford's steadiness was honoured, and Fanny was praised, and the connection was still the most desirable in the world. At Mansfield Park Mr. Crawford would always be welcome; he had only to consult his own judgment and feelings as to the frequency of his visits, at present or in future. In all his niece's family and friends there could be but one opinion, one wish on the subject; the influence of all who loved her must incline one way.

Every thing was said that could encourage, every encouragement received with grateful joy, and the gentlemen parted the best of friends.

Satisfied that the cause was now on a footing the most proper and hopeful, Sir Thomas resolved to abstain from all farther importunity with his niece, and to shew no open interference. Upon her disposition he believed kindness might be the best way of working. Intreaty should be from one quarter only. The forbearance of her family on a point, respecting which she could be in no doubt of their wishes, might be their surest means of forwarding it. Accordingly, on this principle Sir Thomas took the first opportunity of saying to her, with a mild gravity, intended to be overcoming, "Well, Fanny, I have seen Mr. Crawford again, and learn from him exactly how matters stand between you. He is a most extraordinary young man, and whatever be the event, you must feel that

line 1: tempered] **1814** temper'd   //   line 9: Mansfield Park] **1814** Mansfield park

you have created an attachment of no common character; though, young as you are, and little acquainted with the transient, varying, unsteady nature of love, as it generally exists, you cannot be struck as I am with all that is wonderful in a perseverance of this sort, against discouragement. With him, it is entirely a matter of feeling; he claims no merit in it, perhaps is entitled to none. Yet, having chosen so well, his constancy has a respectable stamp. Had his choice been less unexceptionable, I should have condemned his persevering."

"Indeed, Sir," said Fanny, "I am very sorry that Mr. Crawford should continue to——I know that it is paying me a very great compliment, and I feel most undeservedly honoured, but I am so perfectly convinced, and I have told him so, that it never will be in my power——"

"My dear," interrupted Sir Thomas, "there is no occasion for this. Your feelings are as well known to me, as my wishes and regrets must be to you. There is nothing more to be said or done. From this hour, the subject is never to be revived between us. You will have nothing to fear, or to be agitated about. You cannot suppose me capable of trying to persuade you to marry against your inclinations. Your happiness and advantage are all that I have in view, and nothing is required of you but to bear with Mr. Crawford's endeavours to convince you, that they may not be incompatible with his. He proceeds at his own risk. You are on safe ground. I have engaged for your seeing him whenever he calls, as you might have done, had nothing of this sort occurred. You will see him with the rest of us, in the same manner, and as much as you can, dismissing the recollection of every thing unpleasant. He leaves Northamptonshire so soon, that even this slight sacrifice cannot be often demanded. The future must be very uncertain.

line 9: persevering."] **1814** persevering.

And now, my dear Fanny, this subject is closed between us."

The promised departure was all that Fanny could think of with much satisfaction. Her uncle's kind expressions, however, and forbearing manner, were sensibly felt; and when she considered how much of the truth was unknown to him, she believed she had no right to wonder at the line of conduct he pursued. He who had married a daughter to Mr. Rushworth. Romantic delicacy³ was certainly not to be expected from him. She must do her duty, and trust that time might make her duty easier than it now was.

She could not, though only eighteen, suppose Mr. Crawford's attachment would hold out for ever; she could not but imagine that steady, unceasing discouragement from herself would put an end to it in time. How much time she might, in her own fancy, allot for its dominion, is another concern. It would not be fair to enquire into a young lady's exact estimate of her own perfections.

In spite of his intended silence, Sir Thomas found himself once more obliged to mention the subject to his niece, to prepare her briefly for its being imparted to her aunts; a measure which he would still have avoided, if possible, but which became necessary from the totally opposite feelings of Mr. Crawford, as to any secrecy of proceeding. He had no idea of concealment. It was all known at the parsonage, where he loved to talk over the future with both his sisters; and it would be rather gratifying to him to have enlightened witnesses of the progress of his success. When Sir Thomas understood this, he felt the necessity of making his own wife and sister-in-law acquainted with the business without delay; though on Fanny's account, he almost dreaded the effect of the communication to Mrs. Norris as much as Fanny herself. He deprecated her mistaken, but well-meaning zeal. Sir Thomas, indeed, was, by this time, not very far from classing Mrs. Norris as one of those well-meaning people, who are always doing mistaken and very disagreeable things.

Mrs. Norris, however, relieved him. He pressed for the strictest forbearance and silence towards their niece; she not only promised, but did observe it. She only looked her increased ill-will. Angry she was, bitterly angry; but she was more angry with Fanny for having received such an offer, than for refusing it. It was an injury and affront to Julia, who ought to have been Mr. Crawford's choice; and, independently of that, she disliked Fanny, because she had neglected her; and she would have grudged such an elevation to one whom she had been always trying to depress.

Sir Thomas gave her more credit for discretion on the occasion than she deserved; and Fanny could have blessed her for allowing her only to see her displeasure, and not to hear it.

Lady Bertram took it differently. She had been a beauty, and a prosperous beauty, all her life; and beauty and wealth were all that excited her respect. To know Fanny to be sought in marriage by a man of fortune, raised her, therefore, very much in her opinion. By convincing her that Fanny *was* very pretty, which she had been doubting about before, and that she would be advantageously married, it made her feel a sort of credit in calling her niece.

"Well, Fanny," said she, as soon as they were alone together afterwards,—and she really had known something like impatience, to be alone with her, and her countenance, as she

line 3: well-meaning] **1814** well meaning

spoke, had extraordinary animation—"Well, Fanny, I have had a very agreeable surprise this morning. I must just speak of it *once*, I told Sir Thomas I must *once*, and then I shall have done. I give you joy, my dear niece."—And looking at her complacently, she added, "Humph—We certainly are a handsome family."

Fanny coloured, and doubted at first what to say; when hoping to assail her on her vulnerable side, she presently answered—

"My dear aunt, *you* cannot wish me to do differently from what I have done, I am sure. *You* cannot wish me to marry; for you would miss me, should not you?—Yes, I am sure you would miss me too much for that."

"No, my dear, I should not think of missing you, when such an offer as this comes in your way. I could do very well without you, if you were married to a man of such good estate as Mr. Crawford. And you must be aware, Fanny, that it is every young woman's duty to accept such a very unexceptionable offer as this."

This was almost the only rule of conduct, the only piece of advice, which Fanny had ever received from her aunt in the course of eight years and a half.—It silenced her. She felt how unprofitable contention would be. If her aunt's feelings were against her, nothing could be hoped from attacking her understanding. Lady Bertram was quite talkative.

"I will tell you what, Fanny," said she.—"I am sure he fell in love with you at the ball, I am sure the mischief was done that evening. You did look remarkably well. Every body said so. Sir Thomas said so. And you know you had Chapman to help you dress. I am very glad I sent Chapman to you. I shall tell

line 4: niece."—And] **1814** niece."—and // line 5: added, "Humph] **1814** added "Humph // line 9: answered—] **1814** answered,

Sir Thomas that I am sure it was done that evening."—And still pursuing the same cheerful thoughts, she soon afterwards added,—"And I will tell you what, Fanny—which is more than I did for Maria—the next time pug has a litter[4] you shall have a puppy."

line 3: added,—"And] **1814** added.—"And

Chapter 3

EDMUND had great things to hear on his return. Many surprises were awaiting him. The first that occurred was not least in interest,—the appearance of Henry Crawford and his sister walking together through the village, as he rode into it.—He had concluded,—he had meant them to be far distant. His absence had been extended beyond a fortnight purposely to avoid Miss Crawford. He was returning to Mansfield with spirits ready to feed on melancholy remembrances, and tender associations, when her own fair self was before him, leaning on her brother's arm; and he found himself receiving a welcome, unquestionably friendly from the woman whom, two moments before, he had been thinking of as seventy miles off, and as farther, much farther from him in inclination than any distance could express.

Her reception of him was of a sort which he could not have hoped for, had he expected to see her. Coming as he did from such a purport[1] fulfilled as had taken him away, he would have expected any thing rather than a look of satisfaction, and words of simple, pleasant meaning. It was enough to set his heart in a glow, and to bring him home in the properest state for feeling the full value of the other joyful surprises at hand.

William's promotion, with all its particulars, he was soon master of; and with such a secret provision of comfort within

line 18: any thing] **1814** anything   //   line 18: satisfaction, and] **1814** satisfaction and his own breast to help the joy, he found in it a source of most gratifying sensation, and unvarying cheerfulness all dinner-time.

After dinner, when he and his father were alone, he had Fanny's history; and then all the great events of the last fort-night, and the present situation of matters at Mansfield were known to him.

Fanny suspected what was going on. They sat so much longer than usual in the dining parlour, that she was sure they must be talking of her; and when tea at last brought them away, and she was to be seen by Edmund again, she felt dreadfully guilty. He came to her, sat down by her, took her hand, and pressed it kindly; and at that moment she thought that, but for the occupation and the scene which the tea-things afforded, she must have betrayed her emotion in some unpardonable excess.

He was not intending, however, by such action, to be con-veying to her that unqualified approbation and encourage-ment which her hopes drew from it. It was designed only to express his participation in all that interested her, and to tell her that he had been hearing what quickened every feeling of affection. He was, in fact, entirely on his father's side of the question. His surprise was not so great as his father's, at her refusing Crawford, because, so far from supposing her to consider him with anything like a preference, he had always believed it to be rather the reverse, and could imagine her to be taken perfectly unprepared, but Sir Thomas could not regard the connection as more desirable than he did. It had every recommendation to him, and while honouring her for what she had done under the influence of her present indiffer-ence, honouring her in rather stronger terms than Sir Thomas

line 2: dinner-time.] **1814** dinner time.   //   line 14: tea-things] **1814** tea things

could quite echo, he was most earnest in hoping, and sanguine in believing, that it would be a match at last, and that, united by mutual affection, it would appear that their dispositions were as exactly fitted to make them blessed in each other, as he was now beginning seriously to consider them. Crawford had been too precipitate. He had not given her time to attach herself. He had begun at the wrong end. With such powers as his, however, and such a disposition as hers, Edmund trusted that every thing would work out a happy conclusion. Meanwhile, he saw enough of Fanny's embarrassment to make him scrupulously guard against exciting it a second time, by any word, or look, or movement.

Crawford called the next day, and on the score of Edmund's return, Sir Thomas felt himself more than licensed to ask him to stay dinner; it was really a necessary compliment. He staid of course, and Edmund had then ample opportunity for observing how he sped[2] with Fanny, and what degree of immediate encouragement for him might be extracted from her manners; and it was so little, so very very little, (every chance, every possibility of it, resting upon her embarrassment only, if there was not hope in her confusion, there was hope in nothing else,) that he was almost ready to wonder at his friend's perseverance.—Fanny was worth it all; he held her to be worth every effort of patience, every exertion of mind—but he did not think he could have gone on himself with any woman breathing, without something more to warm his courage than his eyes could discern in hers. He was very willing to hope that Crawford saw clearer; and this was the most comfortable conclusion for his friend that he could come to from all that he observed to pass before, and at, and after dinner.

line 8: hers,] **1814** her's,   //   line 22: else,) that] **1814** else) that   //
line 27: hers.] **1814** her's.   //   line 29: friend that] **1814** friend, that

In the evening a few circumstances occurred which he thought more promising. When he and Crawford walked into the drawing-room, his mother and Fanny were sitting as intently and silently at work as if there were nothing else to care for. Edmund could not help noticing their apparently deep tranquillity.

"We have not been so silent all the time," replied his mother. "Fanny has been reading to me, and only put the book down upon hearing you coming."—And sure enough there was a book on the table which had the air of being very recently closed, a volume of Shakespeare.—"She often reads to me out of those books;³ and she was in the middle of a very fine speech of that man's—What's his name, Fanny?—when we heard your footsteps."

Crawford took the volume. "Let me have the pleasure of finishing that speech to your ladyship," said he. "I shall find it immediately." And by carefully giving way to the inclination of the leaves, he did find it, or within a page or two, quite near enough to satisfy Lady Bertram, who assured him, as soon as he mentioned the name of Cardinal Wolsey,⁴ that he had got the very speech.—Not a look, or an offer of help had Fanny given; not a syllable for or against. All her attention was for her work. She seemed determined to be interested by nothing else. But taste was too strong in her. She could not abstract her mind five minutes; she was forced to listen; his reading was capital, and her pleasure in good reading extreme. To *good* reading, however, she had been long used; her uncle read well—her cousins all—Edmund very well; but in Mr. Crawford's reading there was a variety of excellence beyond what she had ever met with. The King, the Queen, Buckingham, Wolsey, Cromwell, all were given in turn; for

line 3: drawing-room,] **1814** drawing room,   //   line 29: reading there]
1814 reading, there

with the happiest knack, the happiest power of jumping and guessing, he could always light, at will, on the best scene, or the best speeches of each; and whether it were dignity or pride, or tenderness or remorse, or whatever were to be expressed, he could do it with equal beauty.—It was truly dramatic.—His acting had first taught Fanny what pleasure a play might give, and his reading brought all his acting before her again; nay, perhaps with greater enjoyment, for it came unexpectedly, and with no such drawback as she had been used to suffer in seeing him on the stage with Miss Bertram.

Edmund watched the progress of her attention, and was amused and gratified by seeing how she gradually slackened in the needle-work, which, at the beginning, seemed to occupy her totally; how it fell from her hand while she sat motionless over it—and at last, how the eyes which had appeared so studiously to avoid him throughout the day, were turned and fixed on Crawford, fixed on him for minutes, fixed on him in short till the attraction drew Crawford's upon her, and the book was closed, and the charm was broken. Then, she was shrinking again into herself, and blushing and working as hard as ever; but it had been enough to give Edmund encouragement for his friend, and as he cordially thanked him, he hoped to be expressing Fanny's secret feelings too.

"That play must be a favourite with you," said he; "You read as if you knew it well."

"It will be a favourite I believe from this hour," replied Crawford;—"but I do not think I have had a volume of Shakespeare in my hand before, since I was fifteen.—I once saw Henry the 8th acted.—Or I have heard of it from some-body who did—I am not certain which. But Shakespeare one gets acquainted with without knowing how. It is a part of an

line 13: beginning, seemed] **1814** beginning seemed // line 24: he; "You] **1814** he, "You // line 27: Crawford;—"but] **1814** Crawford;—but

Englishman's constitution. His thoughts and beauties are so spread abroad that one touches them every where, one is intimate with him by instinct.—No man of any brain can open at a good part of one of his plays, without falling into the flow of his meaning immediately."

"No doubt, one is familiar with Shakespeare in a degree," said Edmund, "from one's earliest years. His celebrated passages are quoted by every body; they are in half the books we open,[5] and we all talk Shakespeare, use his similies, and describe with his descriptions; but this is totally distinct from giving his sense as you gave it. To know him in bits and scraps, is common enough; to know him pretty thoroughly, is, perhaps, not uncommon; but to read him well aloud, is no everyday talent."[6]

"Sir, you do me honour;" was Crawford's answer, with a bow of mock gravity.

Both gentlemen had a glance at Fanny, to see if a word of accordant praise could be extorted from her; yet both feeling that it could not be. Her praise had been given in her attention; *that* must content them.

Lady Bertram's admiration was expressed, and strongly too. "It was really like being at a play," said she.—"I wish Sir Thomas had been here."

Crawford was excessively pleased.—If Lady Bertram, with all her incompetency and languor, could feel this, the inference of what her niece, alive and enlightened as she was, must feel, was elevating.

"You have a great turn for acting, I am sure, Mr. Crawford," said her Ladyship soon afterwards—"and I will tell you what, I think you will have a theatre, some time or other, at your house in Norfolk. I mean when you are settled there. I do, indeed. I think you will fit up a theatre at your house in Norfolk."

"Do you, Ma'am?" cried he with quickness. "No, no, that will never be. Your Ladyship is quite mistaken. No theatre at Everingham! Oh! no."—And he looked at Fanny with an expressive smile, which evidently meant, "that lady will never allow a theatre at Everingham."

Edmund saw it all, and saw Fanny so determined *not* to see it, as to make it clear that the voice was enough to convey the full meaning of the protestation; and such a quick consciousness of compliment, such a ready comprehension of a hint, he thought, was rather favourable than not.

The subject of reading aloud was farther discussed. The two young men were the only talkers, but they, standing by the fire, talked over the too common neglect of the qualification, the total inattention to it, in the ordinary school-system for boys, the consequently natural—yet in some instances almost unnatural degree of ignorance and uncouthness of men, of sensible and well-informed men, when suddenly called to the necessity of reading aloud, which had fallen within their notice, giving instances of blunders, and failures with their secondary causes, the want of management of the voice, of proper modulation and emphasis, of foresight and judgment, all proceeding from the first cause, want of early attention and habit; and Fanny was listening again with great entertainment.[7]

"Even in my profession"—said Edmund with a smile—"how little the art of reading has been studied! how little a clear manner, and good delivery, have been attended to! I speak rather of the past, however, than the present—There is now a spirit of improvement abroad;[8] but among those who were ordained twenty, thirty, forty years ago, the larger number, to judge by their performance, must have thought reading was reading, and preaching was preaching. It is different now. The subject is more justly considered. It is felt

that distinctness and energy may have weight in recommending the most solid truths; and, besides, there is more general
observation and taste, a more critical knowledge diffused,
than formerly; in every congregation, there is a larger proportion who know a little of the matter, and who can judge and
criticize."

Edmund had already gone through the service[9] once since
his ordination; and upon this being understood, he had
a variety of questions from Crawford as to his feelings
and success; questions which being made—though with the
vivacity of friendly interest and quick taste—without any
touch of that spirit of banter or air of levity which Edmund
knew to be most offensive to Fanny, he had true pleasure in
satisfying; and when Crawford proceeded to ask his opinion
and give his own as to the properest manner in which particular passages in the service should be delivered, shewing it
to be a subject on which he had thought before, and thought
with judgment, Edmund was still more and more pleased.
This would be the way to Fanny's heart. She was not to be
won by all that gallantry and wit, and good nature together,
could do; or at least, she would not be won by them nearly
so soon, without the assistance of sentiment and feeling, and
seriousness on serious subjects.[10]

"Our liturgy,"[11] observed Crawford, "has beauties, which
not even a careless, slovenly style of reading can destroy; but
it has also redundancies and repetitions, which require good
reading not to be felt. For myself, at least, I must confess
being not always so attentive as I ought to be—(here was
a glance at Fanny) that nineteen times out of twenty I am
thinking how such a prayer ought to be read, and longing to

line 1: energy may] **1814** energy, may   //   line 8: ordination;] **1814**
Ordination;   //   line 14: satisfying; and] **1814** satisfying, and   //   line 26:
redundancies] **1814** renundancies

have it to read myself—Did you speak?" stepping eagerly to Fanny, and addressing her in a softened voice; and upon her saying, "No," he added, "Are you sure you did not speak? I saw your lips move. I fancied you might be going to tell me I *ought* to be more attentive, and not *allow* my thoughts to wander. Are not you going to tell me so?"

"No, indeed, you know your duty too well for me to—even supposing—"

She stopt, felt herself getting into a puzzle, and could not be prevailed on to add another word, not by dint of several minutes of supplication and waiting. He then returned to his former station, and went on as if there had been no such tender interruption.

"A sermon, well delivered, is more uncommon even than prayers well read. A sermon, good in itself, is no rare thing. It is more difficult to speak well than to compose well; that is, the rules and trick of composition are oftener an object of study. A thoroughly good sermon, thoroughly well delivered, is a capital gratification. I can never hear such a one without the greatest admiration and respect, and more than half a mind to take orders and preach myself. There is something in the eloquence of the pulpit,[12] when it is really eloquence, which is entitled to the highest praise and honour. The preacher who can touch and affect such an heterogeneous mass of hearers, on subjects limited, and long worn thread-bare in all common hands; who can say any thing new or striking, any thing that rouses the attention, without offending the taste, or wearing out the feelings of his hearers, is a man whom one could not (in his public capacity) honour enough. I should like to be such a man."

line 3: "Are] **1814** "are // line 20: respect, and more] **1814** respect, and, more // line 24: touch and affect] **1814** touch and effect // line 30: man."] **1814** man.

Edmund laughed.

"I should indeed. I never listened to a distinguished preacher in my life, without a sort of envy. But then, I must have a London audience. I could not preach, but to the educated; to those who were capable of estimating my composition. And I do not know that I should be fond of preaching often; now and then, perhaps, once or twice in the spring, after being anxiously expected for half a dozen Sundays together; but not for a constancy; it would not do for a constancy."[13]

Here Fanny, who could not but listen, involuntarily shook her head, and Crawford was instantly by her side again, intreating to know her meaning; and as Edmund perceived, by his drawing in a chair, and sitting down close by her, that it was to be a very thorough attack, that looks and undertones were to be well tried, he sank as quietly as possible into a corner, turned his back, and took up a newspaper, very sincerely wishing that dear little Fanny might be persuaded into explaining away that shake of the head to the satisfaction of her ardent lover; and as earnestly trying to bury every sound of the business from himself in murmurs of his own, over the various advertisements[14] of "a most desirable estate in South Wales"—"To Parents and Guardians"—and a "Capital season'd Hunter."

Fanny, meanwhile, vexed with herself for not having been as motionless as she was speechless, and grieved to the heart to see Edmund's arrangements, was trying, by every thing in the power of her modest gentle nature, to repulse Mr. Crawford, and avoid both his looks and enquiries; and he unrepulsable was persisting in both.

line 6: And I] **1814** And, I   //   line 28: Mr. Crawford, and] **1814** Mr. Crawford and

"What did that shake of the head mean?" said he. "What was it meant to express? Disapprobation, I fear. But of what?—What had I been saying to displease you?—Did you think me speaking improperly?—lightly, irreverently on the subject?—Only tell me if I was. Only tell me if I was wrong. I want to be set right. Nay, nay, I entreat you; for one moment put down your work. What did that shake of the head mean?"

In vain was her "Pray, Sir, don't—pray, Mr. Crawford," repeated twice over; and in vain did she try to move away—In the same low eager voice, and the same close neighbourhood, he went on, re-urging the same questions as before. She grew more agitated and displeased.

"How can you, Sir? You quite astonish me—I wonder how you can"—

"Do I astonish you?"—said he. "Do you wonder? Is there any thing in my present intreaty that you do not understand? I will explain to you instantly all that makes me urge you in this manner, all that gives me an interest in what you look and do, and excites my present curiosity. I will not leave you to wonder long."

In spite of herself, she could not help half a smile, but she said nothing.

"You shook your head at my acknowledging that I should not like to engage in the duties of a clergyman always for a constancy. Yes, that was the word. Constancy, I am not afraid of the word. I would spell it, read it, write it with any body. I see nothing alarming in the word. Did you think I ought?"

line 2: Disapprobation, I] **1814** Disapprobation I   //   line 5: wrong. I want] **1814** wrong. want   //   line 9: pray, Mr. Crawford,"] **1814** pray Mr. Crawford,"   //   line 25: clergyman] **1814** Clergyman   //   line 26: Constancy, I] **1814** Constancy. I

"Perhaps, Sir," said Fanny, wearied at last into speaking—
"perhaps, Sir, I thought it was a pity you did not always know
yourself as well as you seemed to do at that moment."

Crawford, delighted to get her to speak at any rate, was
determined to keep it up; and poor Fanny, who had hoped
to silence him by such an extremity of reproof, found herself
sadly mistaken, and that it was only a change from one object
of curiosity and one set of words to another. He had always
something to intreat the explanation of. The opportunity was
too fair. None such had occurred since his seeing her in her
uncle's room, none such might occur again before his leaving
Mansfield. Lady Bertram's being just on the other side of the
table was a trifle, for she might always be considered as only
half awake, and Edmund's advertisements were still of the
first utility.

"Well," said Crawford, after a course of rapid questions
and reluctant answers—"I am happier than I was, because I
now understand more clearly your opinion of me. You think
me unsteady—easily swayed by the whim of the moment—
easily tempted—easily put aside. With such an opinion, no
wonder that——But we shall see.—It is not by protestations
that I shall endeavour to convince you I am wronged, it is
not by telling you that my affections are steady. My conduct
shall speak for me—absence, distance, time shall speak for
me.—*They* shall prove, that as far as you can be deserved by
any body, I do deserve you.—You are infinitely my superior
in merit; all *that* I know.—You have qualities which I had
not before supposed to exist in such a degree in any human
creature. You have some touches of the angel in you, beyond
what—not merely beyond what one sees, because one never
sees any thing like it—but beyond what one fancies might be.

line 3: seemed] **1814** semed // line 11: uncle's] **1814** Uncle's // line 17:
answers—"I] **1814** answers—I // line 18: me. You] **1814** me, You

397

But still I am not frightened. It is not by equality of merit that you can be won. That is out of the question. It is he who sees and worships your merit the strongest, who loves you most devotedly, that has the best right to a return. There I build my confidence. By that right I do and will deserve you; and when once convinced that my attachment is what I declare it, I know you too well not to entertain the warmest hopes— Yes, dearest, sweetest Fanny—Nay—(seeing her draw back displeased) forgive me. Perhaps I have as yet no right—but by what other name can I call you? Do you suppose you are ever present to my imagination under any other? No, it is 'Fanny' that I think of all day, and dream of all night.—You have given the name such reality of sweetness,[15] that nothing else can now be descriptive of you."

Fanny could hardly have kept her seat any longer, or have refrained from at least trying to get away in spite of all the too public opposition she foresaw to it, had it not been for the sound of approaching relief, the very sound which she had been long watching for, and long thinking strangely delayed.

The solemn procession, headed by Baddely, of tea-board, urn, and cake-bearers,[16] made its appearance, and delivered her from a grievous imprisonment of body and mind. Mr. Crawford was obliged to move. She was at liberty, she was busy, she was protected.

Edmund was not sorry to be admitted again among the number of those who might speak and hear. But though the conference had seemed full long to him, and though on looking at Fanny he saw rather a flush of vexation, he inclined to hope that so much could not have been said and listened to, without some profit to the speaker.

line 30: profit] **1814** prfiot

Chapter 4

EDMUND had determined that it belonged entirely to Fanny to chuse whether her situation with regard to Crawford should be mentioned between them or not; and that if she did not lead the way, it should never be touched on by him; but after a day or two of mutual reserve, he was induced by his father to change his mind, and try what his influence might do for his friend.

A day, and a very early day, was actually fixed for the Crawfords' departure; and Sir Thomas thought it might be as well to make one more effort for the young man before he left Mansfield, that all his professions and vows of unshaken attachment might have as much hope to sustain them as possible.

Sir Thomas was most cordially anxious for the perfection of Mr. Crawford's character in that point. He wished him to be a model of constancy; and fancied the best means of effecting it would be by not trying him too long.

Edmund was not unwilling to be persuaded to engage in the business; he wanted to know Fanny's feelings. She had been used to consult him in every difficulty, and he loved her too well to bear to be denied her confidence now; he hoped to be of service to her, he thought he must be of service to her, whom else had she to open her heart to? If she did not need counsel, she must need the comfort of communication. Fanny estranged from him, silent and reserved, was an unnatural state of things; a state which he must break through, and which he could easily learn to think she was wanting him to break through.

"I will speak to her, Sir; I will take the first opportunity of speaking to her alone," was the result of such thoughts as these; and upon Sir Thomas's information of her being at that very time walking alone in the shrubbery, he instantly joined her.

"I am come to walk with you, Fanny," said he. "Shall I?"— (drawing her arm within his,) "it is a long while since we have had a comfortable walk together."

She assented to it all rather by look than word. Her spirits were low.

"But, Fanny," he presently added, "in order to have a comfortable walk, something more is necessary than merely pacing this gravel together. You must talk to me. I know you have something on your mind. I know what you are thinking of. You cannot suppose me uninformed. Am I to hear of it from every body but Fanny herself?"

Fanny, at once agitated and dejected, replied, "If you hear of it from every body, cousin, there can be nothing for me to tell."

"Not of facts, perhaps; but of feelings, Fanny. No one but you can tell me them. I do not mean to press you, however. If it is not what you wish yourself, I have done. I had thought it might be a relief."

"I am afraid we think too differently, for me to find any relief in talking of what I feel."

"Do you suppose that we think differently? I have no idea of it. I dare say, that on a comparison of our opinions, they would be found as much alike as they have been used to be: to the

line 20: Fanny, at] **1814** Fanny at

point—I consider Crawford's proposals as most advantageous and desirable, if you could return his affection. I consider it as most natural that all your family should wish you could return it; but that as you cannot, you have done exactly as you ought in refusing him. Can there be any disagreement between us here?"

"Oh no! But I thought you blamed me. I thought you were against me. This is such a comfort!"

"This comfort you might have had sooner, Fanny, had you sought it. But how could you possibly suppose me against you? How could you imagine me an advocate for marriage without love? Were I even careless in general on such matters, how could you imagine me so where *your* happiness was at stake?"

"My uncle thought me wrong, and I knew he had been talking to you."

"As far as you have gone, Fanny, I think you perfectly right. I may be sorry, I may be surprised—though hardly *that*, for you had not had time to attach yourself; but I think you perfectly right. Can it admit of a question? It is disgraceful to us if it does. You did not love him—nothing could have justified your accepting him."

Fanny had not felt so comfortable for days and days.

"So far your conduct has been faultless, and they were quite mistaken who wished you to do otherwise. But the matter does not end here. Crawford's is no common attachment; he perseveres, with the hope of creating that regard which had not been created before. This, we know, must be a work of time. But (with an affectionate smile), let him succeed at last, Fanny, let him succeed at last. You have proved yourself upright and disinterested, prove yourself grateful and

line 7: you were] **1814** you was // line 8: comfort!"] **1814** comfort."

tender-hearted; and then you will be the perfect model of a woman, which I have always believed you born for."

"Oh! never, never, never; he never will succeed with me." And she spoke with a warmth which quite astonished Edmund, and which she blushed at the recollection of herself, when she saw his look, and heard him reply, "Never, Fanny, so very determined and positive! This is not like yourself, your rational self."

"I mean," she cried, sorrowfully, correcting herself, "that I *think*, I never shall, as far as the future can be answered for—I think I never shall return his regard."

"I must hope better things. I am aware, more aware than Crawford can be, that the man who means to make you love him (you having due notice of his intentions), must have very up-hill work, for there are all your early attachments, and habits, in battle array; and before he can get your heart for his own use, he has to unfasten it from all the holds upon things animate and inanimate, which so many years growth have confirmed, and which are considerably tightened for the moment by the very idea of separation. I know that the apprehension of being forced to quit Mansfield will for a time be arming you against him. I wish he had not been obliged to tell you what he was trying for. I wish he had known you as well as I do, Fanny. Between us, I think we should have won you. My theoretical and his practical knowledge together, could not have failed. He should have worked upon my plans. I must hope, however, that time proving him (as I firmly believe it will), to deserve you by his steady affection, will give him his reward. I cannot suppose that you have not the *wish* to love him—the natural wish of gratitude. You must have some feeling of that sort. You must be sorry for your own indifference."

line 6: Fanny, so] **1814** Fanny!—so

"We are so totally unlike," said Fanny, avoiding a direct answer, "we are so very, very different in all our inclinations and ways, that I consider it as quite impossible we should ever be tolerably happy together, even if I *could* like him. There never were two people more dissimilar. We have not one taste in common. We should be miserable."

"You are mistaken, Fanny. The dissimilarity is not so strong. You are quite enough alike. You *have* tastes in common. You have moral and literary tastes in common. You have both warm hearts and benevolent feelings; and Fanny, who that heard him read, and saw you listen to Shakespeare the other night, will think you unfitted as companions? You forget yourself: there is a decided difference in your tempers, I allow. He is lively, you are serious; but so much the better; his spirits will support yours. It is your disposition to be easily dejected, and to fancy difficulties greater than they are. His cheerfulness will counteract this. He sees difficulties no where; and his pleasantness and gaiety will be a constant support to you. Your being so far unlike, Fanny, does not in the smallest degree make against the probability of your happiness together: do not imagine it. I am myself convinced that it is rather a favourable circumstance. I am perfectly persuaded that the tempers had better be unlike; I mean unlike in the flow of the spirits, in the manners, in the inclination for much or little company, in the propensity to talk or to be silent, to be grave or to be gay. Some opposition here is, I am thoroughly convinced, friendly to matrimonial happiness. I exclude extremes of course; and a very close resemblance in all those points would be the likeliest way to produce an extreme. A counteraction, gentle and continual, is the best safeguard of manners and conduct."

line 4: him. There] **1814** him There   //   line 13: tempers, I] **1814** tempers I // line 15: yours.] **1814** your's.   //   line 26: here is, I] **1814** here, is, I

Full well could Fanny guess where his thoughts were now. Miss Crawford's power was all returning. He had been speaking of her cheerfully from the hour of his coming home. His avoiding her was quite at an end. He had dined at the parsonage only the preceding day.

After leaving him to his happier thoughts for some minutes, Fanny feeling it due to herself, returned to Mr. Crawford, and said, "It is not merely in *temper* that I consider him as totally unsuited to myself; though in *that* respect, I think the difference between us too great, infinitely too great; his spirits often oppress me—but there is something in him which I object to still more. I must say, cousin, that I cannot approve his character. I have not thought well of him from the time of the play. I then saw him behaving, as it appeared to me, so very improperly and unfeelingly, I may speak of it now because it is all over—so improperly by poor Mr. Rushworth, not seeming to care how he exposed or hurt him, and paying attentions to my cousin Maria, which—in short, at the time of the play, I received an impression which will never be got over."

"My dear Fanny," replied Edmund, scarcely hearing her to the end, "let us not, any of us, be judged by what we appeared at that period of general folly. The time of the play, is a time which I hate to recollect. Maria was wrong, Crawford was wrong, we were all wrong together; but none so wrong as myself. Compared with me, all the rest were blameless. I was playing the fool with my eyes open."

"As a by-stander," said Fanny, "perhaps I saw more than you did; and I do think that Mr. Rushworth was sometimes very jealous."

"Very possibly. No wonder. Nothing could be more improper than the whole business. I am shocked whenever

I think that Maria could be capable of it; but if she could undertake the part, we must not be surprised at the rest."

"Before the play, I am much mistaken, if *Julia* did not think he was paying her attentions."

"Julia!—I have heard before from some one of his being in love with Julia, but I could never see any thing of it. And Fanny, though I hope I do justice to my sisters' good qualities, I think it very possible that they might, one or both, be more desirous of being admired by Crawford, and might shew that desire rather more unguardedly than was perfectly prudent. I can remember that they were evidently fond of his society; and with such encouragement, a man like Crawford, lively, and it may be a little unthinking, might be led on to—There could be nothing very striking, because it is clear that he had no pretensions; his heart was reserved for you. And I must say, that its being for you, has raised him inconceivably in my opinion. It does him the highest honour; it shews his proper estimation of the blessing of domestic happiness, and pure attachment. It proves him unspoilt by his uncle. It proves him, in short, every thing that I had been used to wish to believe him, and feared he was not."

"I am persuaded that he does not think as he ought, on serious subjects."[1]

"Say rather, that he has not thought at all upon serious subjects, which I believe to be a good deal the case. How could it be otherwise, with such an education and adviser? Under the disadvantages, indeed, which both have had, is it not wonderful that they should be what they are? Crawford's *feelings*, I am ready to acknowledge, have hitherto been too much his guides. Happily, those feelings have generally been

line 6: any thing] **1814** anything // line 7: sisters' good] **1814** sisters good

good. You will supply the rest; and a most fortunate man he is to attach himself to such a creature—to a woman, who firm as a rock in her own principles, has a gentleness of character so well adapted to recommend them. He has chosen his partner, indeed, with rare felicity. He will make you happy, Fanny, I know he will make you happy; but you will make him every thing."

"I would not engage in such a charge," cried Fanny in a shrinking accent—"in such an office of high responsibility!"

"As usual, believing yourself unequal to anything!—fancying every thing too much for you! Well, though I may not be able to persuade you into different feelings, you will be persuaded into them I trust. I confess myself sincerely anxious that you may. I have no common interest in Crawford's well doing. Next to your happiness, Fanny, his has the first claim on me. You are aware of my having no common interest in Crawford."

Fanny was too well aware of it, to have anything to say; and they walked on together some fifty yards in mutual silence and abstraction. Edmund first began again:—

"I was very much pleased by her manner of speaking of it yesterday, particularly pleased, because I had not depended upon her seeing every thing in so just a light. I knew she was very fond of you, but yet I was afraid of her not estimating your worth to her brother, quite as it deserved, and of her regretting that he had not rather fixed on some woman of distinction, or fortune. I was afraid of the bias of those worldly maxims, which she has been too much used to hear. But it was very different. She spoke of you, Fanny, just as she ought. She desires the connection as warmly as your uncle or myself. We had a long talk about it. I should not have mentioned the subject, though very anxious to know her sentiments—but

I had not been in the room five minutes, before she began, introducing it with all that openness of heart, and sweet peculiarity of manner, that spirit and ingenuousness, which are so much a part of herself. Mrs. Grant laughed at her for her rapidity."

"Was Mrs. Grant in the room, then?"

"Yes, when I reached the house I found the two sisters together by themselves; and when once we had begun, we had not done with you, Fanny, till Crawford and Dr. Grant came in."

"It is above a week since I saw Miss Crawford."

"Yes, she laments it; yet owns it may have been best. You will see her, however, before she goes. She is very angry with you, Fanny; you must be prepared for that. She calls herself very angry, but you can imagine her anger. It is the regret and disappointment of a sister, who thinks her brother has a right to every thing he may wish for, at the first moment. She is hurt, as you would be for William; but she loves and esteems you with all her heart."

"I knew she would be very angry with me."

"My dearest Fanny," cried Edmund, pressing her arm closer to him, "do not let the idea of her anger distress you. It is anger to be talked of, rather than felt. Her heart is made for love and kindness, not for resentment. I wish you could have overheard her tribute of praise; I wish you could have seen her countenance, when she said that you *should* be Henry's wife. And I observed, that she always spoke of you as 'Fanny,' which she was never used to do; and it had a sound of most sisterly cordiality."

"And Mrs. Grant, did she say—did she speak—was she there all the time?"

"Yes, she was agreeing exactly with her sister. The surprise of your refusal, Fanny, seems to have been unbounded. That you could refuse such a man as Henry Crawford, seems more than they can understand. I said what I could for you; but in good truth, as they stated the case—you must prove yourself to be in your senses as soon as you can, by a different conduct; nothing else will satisfy them. But this is teazing you. I have done. Do not turn away from me."

"I *should* have thought," said Fanny, after a pause of recollection and exertion, "that every woman must have felt the possibility of a man's not being approved, not being loved by some one of her sex, at least, let him be ever so generally agreeable. Let him have all the perfections in the world, I think it ought not to be set down as certain, that a man must be acceptable to every woman he may happen to like himself. But even supposing it is so, allowing Mr. Crawford to have all the claims which his sisters think he has, how was I to be prepared to meet him with any feeling answerable to his own? He took me wholly by surprise. I had not an idea that his behaviour to me before had any meaning; and surely I was not to be teaching myself to like him only because he was taking, what seemed, very idle notice of me. In my situation, it would have been the extreme of vanity to be forming expectations on Mr. Crawford. I am sure his sisters, rating him as they do, must have thought it so, supposing he had meant nothing. How then was I to be—to be in love with him the moment he said he was with me? How was I to have an attachment at his service, as soon as it was asked for? His sisters should consider me as well as him. The higher his deserts, the more improper for me ever to have thought of him. And, and—we think very differently of the nature of women, if they can imagine a woman so very soon capable of returning an affection as this seems to imply."

line 19: him only] **1814** him, only

"My dear, dear Fanny, now I have the truth. I know this to be the truth; and most worthy of you are such feelings. I had attributed them to you before. I thought I could understand you. You have now given exactly the explanation which I ventured to make for you to your friend and Mrs. Grant, and they were both better satisfied, though your warm-hearted friend was still run away with a little, by the enthusiasm of her fondness for Henry. I told them, that you were of all human creatures the one, over whom habit had most power, and novelty least: and that the very circumstance of the novelty of Crawford's addresses was against him. Their being so new and so recent was all in their disfavour; that you could tolerate nothing that you were not used to; and a great deal more to the same purpose, to give them a knowledge of your character. Miss Crawford made us laugh by her plans of encouragement for her brother. She meant to urge him to persevere in the hope of being loved in time, and of having his addresses most kindly received at the end of about ten years' happy marriage."

Fanny could with difficulty give the smile that was here asked for. Her feelings were all in revolt. She feared she had been doing wrong, saying too much, overacting the caution which she had been fancying necessary, in guarding against one evil, laying herself open to another, and to have Miss Crawford's liveliness repeated to her at such a moment, and on such a subject, was a bitter aggravation.

Edmund saw weariness and distress in her face, and immediately resolved to forbear all farther discussion; and not even to mention the name of Crawford again, except as it might be connected with what *must* be agreeable to her. On this principle, he soon afterwards observed, "They go on Monday. You are sure therefore of seeing your friend either to-morrow

line 10: least: and] **1814** least; and

or Sunday. They really go on Monday! and I was within a trifle of being persuaded to stay at Lessingby till that very day! I had almost promised it. What a difference it might have made! Those five or six days more at Lessingby might have been felt all my life!"

"You were near staying there?"

"Very. I was most kindly pressed, and had nearly consented. Had I received any letter from Mansfield, to tell me how you were all going on, I believe I should certainly have stayed; but I knew nothing that had happened here for a fortnight, and felt that I had been away long enough."

"You spent your time pleasantly there."

"Yes; that is, it was the fault of my own mind if I did not. They were all very pleasant. I doubt their finding me so. I took uneasiness with me, and there was no getting rid of it till I was in Mansfield again."

"The Miss Owens—you liked them, did not you?"

"Yes, very well. Pleasant, good-humoured, unaffected girls. But I am spoilt, Fanny, for common female society. Good-humoured, unaffected girls, will not do for a man who has been used to sensible women. They are two distinct orders of being. You and Miss Crawford have made me too nice."

Still, however, Fanny was oppressed and wearied; he saw it in her looks; it could not be talked away, and attempting it no more, he led her directly with the kind authority of a privileged guardian into the house.

line 4: made!] **1814** made.   //   line 5: life!"] **1814** life."   //   line 24: looks; it] **1814** looks, it

Chapter 5

EDMUND now believed himself perfectly acquainted with all that Fanny could tell, or could leave to be conjectured of her sentiments, and he was satisfied.—It had been, as he before presumed, too hasty a measure on Crawford's side, and time must be given to make the idea first familiar, and then agreeable to her. She must be used to the consideration of his being in love with her, and then a return of affection might not be very distant.

He gave this opinion as the result of the conversation, to his father; and recommended there being nothing more said to her, no farther attempts to influence or persuade; but that every thing should be left to Crawford's assiduities, and the natural workings of her own mind.

Sir Thomas promised that it should be so. Edmund's account of Fanny's disposition he could believe to be just, he supposed she had all those feelings, but he must consider it as very unfortunate that she *had*; for, less willing than his son to trust to the future, he could not help fearing that if such very long allowances of time and habit were necessary for her, she might not have persuaded herself into receiving his addresses properly, before the young man's inclination for paying them were over. There was nothing to be done, however, but to submit quietly, and hope the best.

line 10: father;] **1814** Father;

The promised visit from her "friend," as Edmund called Miss Crawford, was a formidable threat to Fanny, and she lived in continual terror of it. As a sister, so partial and so angry, and so little scrupulous of what she said; and in another light, so triumphant and secure, she was in every way an object of painful alarm. Her displeasure, her penetration, and her happiness were all fearful to encounter; and the dependence of having others present when they met, was Fanny's only support in looking forward to it. She absented herself as little as possible from Lady Bertram, kept away from the east room, and took no solitary walk in the shrubbery, in her caution to avoid any sudden attack.

She succeeded. She was safe in the breakfast-room, with her aunt, when Miss Crawford did come; and the first misery over, and Miss Crawford looking and speaking with much less particularity of expression than she had anticipated, Fanny began to hope there would be nothing worse to be endured than an half-hour of moderate agitation. But here she hoped too much, Miss Crawford was not the slave of opportunity. She was determined to see Fanny alone, and therefore said to her tolerably soon, in a low voice, "I must speak to you for a few minutes somewhere;" words that Fanny felt all over her, in all her pulses, and all her nerves. Denial was impossible. Her habits of ready submission, on the contrary, made her almost instantly rise and lead the way out of the room. She did it with wretched feelings, but it was inevitable.

They were no sooner in the hall than all restraint of countenance was over on Miss Crawford's side. She immediately shook her head at Fanny with arch, yet affectionate reproach, and taking her hand, seemed hardly able to help beginning directly. She said nothing, however, but, "Sad, sad girl! I do

line 10: east room,] **1814** East-room,   //   line 13: breakfast-room, with her aunt,] **1814** Breakfast-room with her Aunt,

not know when I shall have done scolding you," and had discretion enough to reserve the rest till they might be secure of having four walls to themselves. Fanny naturally turned up stairs, and took her guest to the apartment which was now always fit for comfortable use; opening the door, however, with a most aching heart, and feeling that she had a more distressing scene before her than ever that spot had yet witnessed. But the evil ready to burst on her, was at least delayed by the sudden change in Miss Crawford's ideas; by the strong effect on her mind which the finding herself in the east room again produced.

"Ha!" she cried, with instant animation, "am I here again? The east room. Once only was I in this room before!"—and after stopping to look about her, and seemingly to retrace all that had then passed, she added, "Once only before. Do you remember it? I came to rehearse. Your cousin came too; and we had a rehearsal. You were our audience and prompter. A delightful rehearsal. I shall never forget it. Here we were, just in this part of the room; here was your cousin, here was I, here were the chairs.—Oh! why will such things ever pass away?"

Happily for her companion, she wanted no answer. Her mind was entirely self-engrossed. She was in a reverie of sweet remembrances.

"The scene we were rehearsing was so very remarkable! The subject of it so very—very—what shall I say? He was to be describing and recommending matrimony to me. I think I see him now, trying to be as demure and composed as Anhalt ought, through the two long speeches.[1] 'When two sympathetic hearts meet in the marriage state, matrimony may be called a happy life.' I suppose no time can ever wear out the

line 13: east room.] **1814** East room.

impression I have of his looks and voice, as he said those words. It was curious, very curious, that we should have such a scene to play! If I had the power of recalling any one week of my existence, it should be that week, that acting week. Say what you would, Fanny, it should be *that*; for I never knew such exquisite happiness in any other. His sturdy spirit to bend as it did! Oh! it was sweet beyond expression. But alas! that very evening destroyed it all. That very evening brought your most unwelcome uncle. Poor Sir Thomas, who was glad to see you? Yet, Fanny, do not imagine I would now speak disrespectfully of Sir Thomas, though I certainly did hate him for many a week. No, I do him justice now. He is just what the head of such a family should be. Nay, in sober sadness,[2] I believe I now love you all." And having said so, with a degree of tenderness and consciousness which Fanny had never seen in her before, and now thought only too becoming, she turned away for a moment to recover herself. "I have had a little fit since I came into this room, as you may perceive," said she presently, with a playful smile, "but it is over now; so let us sit down and be comfortable; for as to scolding you, Fanny, which I came fully intending to do, I have not the heart for it when it comes to the point." And embracing her very affectionately,—"Good, gentle Fanny! when I think of this being the last time of seeing you; for I do not know how long—I feel it quite impossible to do any thing but love you."

Fanny was affected. She had not foreseen anything of this, and her feelings could seldom withstand the melancholy influence of the word "last."[3] She cried as if she had loved Miss Crawford more than she possibly could; and Miss Crawford, yet farther softened by the sight of such

line 4: existence, it] **1814** existence, It   //   line 22: point." And] **1814** point. And   //   line 26: you."] **1814** you"

emotion, hung about her with fondness, and said, "I hate to leave you. I shall see no one half so amiable where I am going. Who says we shall not be sisters? I know we shall. I feel that we are born to be connected; and those tears convince me that you feel it too, dear Fanny."

Fanny roused herself, and replying only in part, said, "But you are only going from one set of friends to another. You are going to a very particular friend."

"Yes, very true. Mrs. Fraser has been my intimate friend for years. But I have not the least inclination to go near her. I can think only of the friends I am leaving; my excellent sister, yourself, and the Bertrams in general. You have all so much more *heart* among you, than one finds in the world at large. You all give me a feeling of being able to trust and confide in you; which, in common intercourse, one knows nothing of. I wish I had settled with Mrs. Fraser not to go to her till after Easter, a much better time for the visit—but now I cannot put her off. And when I have done with her, I must go to her sister, Lady Stornaway, because *she* was rather my most particular friend of the two; but I have not cared much for *her* these three years."

After this speech, the two girls sat many minutes silent, each thoughtful; Fanny meditating on the different sorts of friendship in the world, Mary on something of less philosophic tendency. *She* first spoke again.

"How perfectly I remember my resolving to look for you up stairs; and setting off to find my way to the east room, without having an idea whereabouts it was! How well I remember what I was thinking of as I came along; and my looking in and seeing you here, sitting at this table at work; and then your cousin's astonishment when he opened the door at seeing

line 15: intercourse, one] **1814** intercourse one

me here! To be sure, your uncle's returning that very evening! There never was anything quite like it."

Another short fit of abstraction followed—when, shaking it off, she thus attacked her companion.

"Why, Fanny, you are absolutely in a reverie! Thinking, I hope, of one who is always thinking of you. Oh! that I could transport you for a short time into our circle in town, that you might understand how your power over Henry is thought of there! Oh! the envyings and heart-burnings of dozens and dozens! the wonder, the incredulity that will be felt at hearing what you have done! For as to secrecy, Henry is quite the hero of an old romance,[4] and glories in his chains. You should come to London, to know how to estimate your conquest. It you were to see how is courted, and how I am courted for his sake! Now I am well aware, that I shall not be half so welcome to Mrs. Fraser in consequence of his situation with you. When she comes to know the truth, she will very likely wish me in Northamptonshire again; for there is a daughter of Mr. Fraser by a first wife, whom she is wild to get married, and wants Henry to take. Oh! she has been trying for him to such a degree! Innocent and quiet as you sit here, you cannot have an idea of the *sensation* that you will be occasioning, of the curiosity there will be to see you, of the endless questions I shall have to answer! Poor Margaret Fraser will be at me for ever about your eyes and your teeth, and how you do your hair, and who makes your shoes. I wish Margaret were married, for my poor friend's sake, for I look upon the Frasers to be about as unhappy as most other married people. And yet it was a most desirable match for Janet at the time. We were all delighted. She could not do otherwise than accept him, for he was rich, and she had nothing; but

line 27: were married,] **1814** was married,

he turns out ill-tempered, and *exigeant*;[5] and wants a young woman, a beautiful young woman of five-and-twenty, to be as steady as himself. And my friend does not manage him well; she does not seem to know how to make the best of it. There is a spirit of irritation, which, to say nothing worse, is certainly very ill-bred. In their house I shall call to mind the conjugal manners of Mansfield Parsonage with respect. Even Dr. Grant does shew a thorough confidence in my sister, and a certain consideration for her judgment, which makes one feel there *is* attachment; but of that, I shall see nothing with the Frasers. I shall be at Mansfield for ever, Fanny. My own sister as a wife, Sir Thomas Bertram as a husband, are my standards of perfection. Poor Janet has been sadly taken in; and yet there was nothing improper on her side; she did not run into the match inconsiderately, there was no want of foresight. She took three days to consider of his proposals; and during those three days asked the advice of every body connected with her, whose opinion was worth having; and especially applied to my late dear aunt, whose knowledge of the world made her judgment very generally and deservedly looked up to by all the young people of her acquaintance; and she was decidedly in favour of Mr. Fraser. This seems as if nothing were a security for matrimonial comfort! I have not so much to say for my friend Flora, who jilted a very nice young man in the Blues,[6] for the sake of that horrid Lord Stornaway, who has about as much sense, Fanny, as Mr. Rushworth, but much worse looking, and with a blackguard character. I *had* my doubts at the time about her being right, for he has not even the air of a gentleman, and now, I am sure, she was wrong. By the by, Flora Ross was dying for Henry the first winter she came out. But were I to attempt to tell you of all

line 30: By the by,] **1814** By the bye,

the women whom I have known to be in love with him, I should never have done. It is you only, you, insensible Fanny, who can think of him with any thing like indifference. But are you so insensible as you profess yourself? No, no, I see you are not."

There was indeed so deep a blush over Fanny's face at that moment, as might warrant strong suspicion in a pre-disposed mind.

"Excellent creature! I will not teaze you. Every thing shall take its course. But dear Fanny, you must allow that you were not so absolutely unprepared to have the question asked as your cousin fancies. It is not possible, but that you must have had some thoughts on the subject, some surmises as to what might be. You must have seen that he was trying to please you, by every attention in his power. Was not he devoted to you at the ball? And then before the ball, the necklace! Oh! you received it just as it was meant. You were as conscious as heart could desire. I remember it perfectly."

"Do you mean then that your brother knew of the necklace beforehand? Oh! Miss Crawford, *that* was not fair."

"Knew of it! it was his own doing entirely, his own thought. I am ashamed to say, that it had never entered my head; but I was delighted to act on his proposal, for both your sakes."

"I will not say," replied Fanny, "that I was not half afraid at the time of its being so; for there was something in your look that frightened me—but not at first—I was as unsuspicious of it at first!—indeed, indeed I was. It is as true as that I sit here. And had I had an idea of it, nothing should have induced me to accept the necklace. As to your brother's behaviour, certainly I was sensible of a particularity, I had been sensible of it some little time, perhaps two or three weeks; but then

line 3: any thing] **1814** anything   //   line 11: asked as] **1814** asked, as   //
line 25: time of] **1814** time, of   //   line 31: two or] **1814** too or

I considered it as meaning nothing, I put it down as simply being his way, and was as far from supposing as from wishing him to have any serious thoughts of me. I had not, Miss Crawford, been an inattentive observer of what was passing between him and some part of this family in the summer and autumn. I was quiet, but I was not blind. I could not but see that Mr. Crawford allowed himself in gallantries[7] which did mean nothing."

"Ah! I cannot deny it. He has now and then been a sad flirt, and cared very little for the havock he might be making in young ladies' affections. I have often scolded him for it, but it is his only fault; and there is this to be said, that very few young ladies have any affections worth caring for. And then, Fanny, the glory of fixing one who has been shot at by so many; of having it in one's power to pay off the debts of one's sex! Oh, I am sure it is not in woman's nature to refuse such a triumph."

Fanny shook her head. "I cannot think well of a man who sports with any woman's feelings; and there may often be a great deal more suffered than a stander-by can judge of."

"I do not defend him. I leave him entirely to your mercy; and when he has got you at Everingham, I do not care how much you lecture him. But this I will say, that his fault, the liking to make girls a little in love with him, is not half so dangerous to a wife's happiness, as a tendency to fall in love himself, which he has never been addicted to. And I do seriously and truly believe that he is attached to you in a way that he never was to any woman before; that he loves you with all his heart, and will love you as nearly for ever as possible. If any man ever loved a woman for ever, I think Henry will do as much for you."

Fanny could not avoid a faint smile, but had nothing to say.

"I cannot imagine Henry ever to have been happier," continued Mary, presently, "than when he had succeeded in getting your brother's commission."

She had made a sure push at Fanny's feelings here.

"Oh! yes. How very, very kind of him!"

"I know he must have exerted himself very much, for I know the parties he had to move. The Admiral hates trouble, and scorns asking favours; and there are so many young men's claims to be attended to in the same way, that a friendship and energy, not very determined, is easily put by. What a happy creature William must be! I wish we could see him."

Poor Fanny's mind was thrown into the most distressing of all its varieties. The recollection of what had been done for William was always the most powerful disturber of every decision against Mr. Crawford; and she sat thinking deeply of it till Mary, who had been first watching her complacently, and then musing on something else, suddenly called her attention, by saying, "I should like to sit talking with you here all day, but we must not forget the ladies below, and so good bye, my dear, my amiable, my excellent Fanny, for though we shall nominally part in the breakfast parlour, I must take leave of you here. And I do take leave, longing for a happy re-union, and trusting, that when we meet again, it will be under circumstances which may open our hearts to each other without any remnant or shadow of reserve."

A very, very kind embrace, and some agitation of manner, accompanied these words.

"I shall see your cousin in town soon; he talks of being there tolerably soon; and Sir Thomas, I dare say, in the course of the spring; and your eldest cousin and the Rushworths and Julia I am sure of meeting again and again, and all but you. I

line 20: excellent Fanny,] **1814** excellent, Fanny,

have two favours to ask, Fanny; one is your correspondence. You must write to me. And the other, that you will often call on Mrs. Grant and make her amends for my being gone."

The first, at least, of these favours Fanny would rather not have been asked; but it was impossible for her to refuse the correspondence; it was impossible for her even not to accede to it more readily than her own judgment authorised. There was no resisting so much apparent affection. Her disposition was peculiarly calculated to value a fond treatment, and from having hitherto known so little of it, she was the more overcome by Miss Crawford's. Besides, there was gratitude towards her, for having made their tête à tête so much less painful than her fears had predicted.

It was over, and she had escaped without reproaches and without detection. Her secret was still her own; and while that was the case, she thought she could resign herself to almost every thing.

In the evening there was another parting. Henry Crawford came and sat some time with them; and her spirits not being previously in the strongest state, her heart was softened for a while towards him—because he really seemed to feel.— Quite unlike his usual self, he scarcely said any thing. He was evidently oppressed, and Fanny must grieve for him, though hoping she might never see him again till he were the husband of some other woman.

When it came to the moment of parting, he would take her hand, he would not be denied it; he said nothing, however, or nothing that she heard, and when he had left the room, she was better pleased that such a token of friendship had passed.[8]

On the morrow the Crawfords were gone.

line 3: gone."] **1814** gone.   //   line 12: tête à tête] **1814** tète a tète   //   line 29: pleased that] **1814** pleased, that   //   line 30: Crawfords] **1814** Crawford's

Chapter 6

MR. CRAWFORD gone, Sir Thomas's next object was, that he should be missed, and he entertained great hope that his niece would find a blank in the loss of those attentions which at the time she had felt, or fancied an evil. She had tasted of consequence in its most flattering form; and he did hope that the loss of it, the sinking again into nothing, would awaken very wholesome regrets in her mind.—He watched her with this idea—but he could hardly tell with what success. He hardly knew whether there were any difference in her spirits or not. She was always so gentle and retiring, that her emotions were beyond his discrimination. He did not understand her; he felt that he did not; and therefore applied to Edmund to tell him how she stood affected on the present occasion, and whether she were more or less happy than she had been.

Edmund did not discern any symptom of regret, and thought his father a little unreasonable in supposing the first three or four days could produce any.

What chiefly surprised Edmund was, that Crawford's sister, the friend and companion, who had been so much to her, should not be more visibly regretted. He wondered that Fanny spoke so seldom of *her*, and had so little voluntarily to say of her concern at this separation.

line 19: Edmund was,] **1814** Edmund, was,

Alas! it was this sister, this friend and companion, who was now the chief bane of Fanny's comfort.—If she could have believed Mary's future fate as unconnected with Mansfield, as she was determined the brother's should be, if she could have hoped her return thither, to be as distant as she was much inclined to think his, she would have been light of heart indeed; but the more she recollected and observed, the more deeply was she convinced that every thing was now in a fairer train for Miss Crawford's marrying Edmund than it had ever been before.—On his side, the inclination was stronger, on hers less equivocal. His objections, the scruples of his integrity, seemed all done away—nobody could tell how; and the doubts and hesitations of her ambition were equally got over—and equally without apparent reason. It could only be imputed to increasing attachment. His good and her bad feelings yielded to love, and such love must unite them. He was to go to town, as soon as some business relative to Thornton Lacey were completed—perhaps, within a fortnight, he talked of going, he loved to talk of it; and when once with her again, Fanny could not doubt the rest.—Her acceptance must be as certain as his offer; and yet, there were bad feelings still remaining which made the prospect of it most sorrowful to her, independently—she believed independently of self.

In their very last conversation, Miss Crawford, in spite of some amiable sensations, and much personal kindness, had still been Miss Crawford, still shewn a mind led astray and bewildered, and without any suspicion of being so; darkened, yet fancying itself light.[1] She might love, but she did not deserve Edmund by any other sentiment. Fanny believed there was scarcely a second feeling in common between them;

line 11: hers] **1814** her's   //   line 12: away—nobody could tell how; and] **1814** away; nobody could tell how—and   //   line 15: good and] **1814** good, and

and she may be forgiven by older sages, for looking on the chance of Miss Crawford's future improvement as nearly desperate, for thinking that if Edmund's influence in this season of love, had already done so little in clearing her judgment, and regulating her notions, his worth would be finally wasted on her even in years of matrimony.

Experience might have hoped more for any young people, so circumstanced, and impartiality would not have denied to Miss Crawford's nature, that participation of the general nature of women, which would lead her to adopt the opinions of the man she loved and respected, as her own.—But as such were Fanny's persuasions, she suffered very much from them, and could never speak of Miss Crawford without pain.

Sir Thomas, meanwhile, went on with his own hopes, and his own observations, still feeling a right, by all his knowledge of human nature, to expect to see the effect of the loss of power and consequence, on his niece's spirits, and the past attentions of the lover producing a craving for their return; and he was soon afterwards able to account for his not yet completely and indubitably seeing all this, by the prospect of another visitor, whose approach he could allow to be quite enough to support the spirits he was watching.—William had obtained a ten days' leave of absence to be given to Northamptonshire, and was coming, the happiest of lieutenants, because the latest made, to shew his happiness and describe his uniform.[2]

He came; and he would have been delighted to shew his uniform there too, had not cruel custom prohibited its appearance except on duty. So the uniform remained at Portsmouth, and Edmund conjectured that before Fanny had any chance of seeing it, all its own freshness, and all the freshness of its wearer's feelings, must be worn away. It would be sunk into a badge of disgrace; for what can be more unbecoming, or more worthless, than the uniform of a lieutenant, who has been a lieutenant a year or two, and sees others made commanders before him? So reasoned Edmund, till his father made him the confident of a scheme which placed Fanny's chance of seeing the 2d lieutenant of H. M. S. Thrush, in all his glory in another light.

This scheme was that she should accompany her brother back to Portsmouth, and spend a little time with her own family. It had occurred to Sir Thomas, in one of his dignified musings, as a right and desirable measure; but before he absolutely made up his mind, he consulted his son. Edmund considered it every way, and saw nothing but what was right. The thing was good in itself, and could not be done at a better time; and he had no doubt of it being highly agreeable to Fanny. This was enough to determine Sir Thomas; and a decisive "then so it shall be," closed that stage of the business; Sir Thomas retiring from it with some feelings of satisfaction, and views of good over and above what he had communicated to his son, for his prime motive in sending her away, had very little to do with the propriety of her seeing her parents again, and nothing at all with any idea of making her happy. He certainly wished her to go willingly, but he as certainly wished her to be heartily sick of home before her visit ended; and that a little abstinence from the elegancies and luxuries of Mansfield Park, would bring her mind into a sober state, and incline her to a juster estimate of the value of that home of greater permanence, and equal comfort, of which she had the offer.

It was a medicinal project upon his niece's understanding, which he must consider as at present diseased. A residence of eight or nine years in the abode of wealth and plenty had

line 10: measure; but] **1814** measure, but

a little disordered her powers of comparing and judging. Her Father's house would, in all probability, teach her the value of a good income; and he trusted that she would be the wiser and happier woman, all her life, for the experiment he had devised.

Had Fanny been at all addicted to raptures, she must have had a strong attack of them, when she first understood what was intended, when her uncle first made her the offer of visiting the parents and brothers, and sisters, from whom she had been divided, almost half her life, of returning for a couple of months to the scenes of her infancy, with William for the protector and companion of her journey; and the certainty of continuing to see William to the last hour of his remaining on land. Had she ever given way to bursts of delight, it must have been then, for she was delighted, but her happiness was of a quiet, deep, heart-swelling sort; and though never a great talker, she was always more inclined to silence when feeling most strongly. At the moment she could only thank and accept. Afterwards, when familiarized with the visions of enjoyment so suddenly opened, she could speak more largely to William and Edmund of what she felt; but still there were emotions of tenderness that could not be clothed in words— The remembrance of all her earliest pleasures, and of what she had suffered in being torn from them, came over her with renewed strength, and it seemed as if to be at home again, would heal every pain that had since grown out of the separation. To be in the centre of such a circle, loved by so many, and more loved by all than she had ever been before, to feel affection without fear or restraint, to feel herself the equal of those who surrounded her, to be at peace from all mention of the Crawfords, safe from every look which

line 22: words—The] **1814** words,—The

could be fancied a reproach on their account!—This was a prospect to be dwelt on with a fondness that could be but half acknowledged.

Edmund too—to be two months from *him*, (and perhaps, she might be allowed to make her absence three) must do her good. At a distance unassailed by his looks or his kindness, and safe from the perpetual irritation of knowing his heart, and striving to avoid his confidence, she should be able to reason herself into a properer state; she should be able to think of him as in London, and arranging every thing there, without wretchedness.——What might have been hard to bear at Mansfield, was to become a slight evil at Portsmouth.

The only drawback was the doubt of her Aunt Bertram's being comfortable without her. She was of use to no one else; but *there* she might be missed to a degree that she did not like to think of; and that part of the arrangement was, indeed, the hardest for Sir Thomas to accomplish, and what only *he* could have accomplished at all.

But he was master at Mansfield Park. When he had really resolved on any measure, he could always carry it through; and now by dint of long talking on the subject, explaining and dwelling on the duty of Fanny's sometimes seeing her family, he did induce his wife to let her go; obtaining it rather from submission, however, than conviction, for Lady Bertram was convinced of very little more than that Sir Thomas thought Fanny ought to go, and therefore that she must. In the calmness of her own dressing-room, in the impartial flow of her own meditations, unbiassed by his bewildering statements, she could not acknowledge any necessity for Fanny's ever

line 9: state; she] **1814** state: she   //   line 11: wretchedness.——What]
1814 wretchedness.—What   //   line 23: obtaining it] **1814** obtaining t   //
line 25: than that] **1814** than, that   //   line 27: dressing-room,] **1814**
dressing room,

going near a Father and Mother who had done without her so long, while she was so useful to herself.—And as to the not missing her, which under Mrs. Norris's discussion was the point attempted to be proved, she set herself very steadily against admitting any such thing.

Sir Thomas had appealed to her reason, conscience, and dignity. He called it a sacrifice, and demanded it of her goodness and self-command as such. But Mrs. Norris wanted to persuade her that Fanny could be very well spared—(*She* being ready to give up all her own time to her as requested) and in short could not really be wanted or missed.

"That may be, sister,"—was all Lady Bertram's reply—"I dare say you are very right, but I am sure I shall miss her very much."

The next step was to communicate with Portsmouth. Fanny wrote to offer herself; and her mother's answer, though short, was so kind, a few simple lines expressed so natural and motherly a joy in the prospect of seeing her child again, as to confirm all the daughter's views of happiness in being with her—convincing her that she should now find a warm and affectionate friend in the "Mamma" who had certainly shewn no remarkable fondness for her formerly; but this she could easily suppose to have been her own fault, or her own fancy. She had probably alienated Love by the helplessness and fretfulness of a fearful temper, or been unreasonable in wanting a larger share than any one among so many could deserve. Now, when she knew better how to be useful and how to forbear, and when her mother could be no longer occupied by the incessant demands of a house full of little children, there would be leisure and inclination for every comfort,[3] and they should soon be what mother and daughter ought to be to each other.

William was almost as happy in the plan as his sister. It would be the greatest pleasure to him to have her there to the last moment before he sailed, and perhaps find her there still when he came in, from his first cruise![4] And besides, he wanted her so very much to see the Thrush before she went out of harbour (the Thrush was certainly the finest sloop in the service). And there were several improvements in the dock-yard,[5] too, which he quite longed to shew her.

He did not scruple to add, that her being at home for a while would be a great advantage to every body.

"I do not know how it is," said he, "but we seem to want some of your nice[6] ways and orderliness at my father's. The house is always in confusion. You will set things going in a better way, I am sure. You will tell my mother how it all ought to be, and you will be so useful to Susan, and you will teach Betsey, and make the boys love and mind you. How right and comfortable it will all be!"

By the time Mrs. Price's answer arrived, there remained but a very few days more to be spent at Mansfield; and for part of one of those days the young travellers were in a good deal of alarm on the subject of their journey, for when the mode of it came to be talked of, and Mrs. Norris found that all her anxiety to save her Brother-in-law's money was vain, and that in spite of her wishes and hints for a less expensive conveyance of Fanny, they were to travel post, when she saw Sir Thomas actually give William notes for the purpose,[7] she was struck with the idea of there being room for a third in the carriage, and suddenly seized with a strong inclination to go with them—to go and see her poor dear sister Price. She proclaimed her thoughts. She must say that she had more

line 4: cruise!] **1814** cruize!

than half a mind to go with the young people; it would be such an indulgence to her; she had not seen her poor dear sister Price for more than twenty years; and it would be a help to the young people in their journey to have her older head to manage for them; and she could not help thinking her poor dear sister Price would feel it very unkind of her not to come by such an opportunity.

William and Fanny were horror-struck at the idea.

All the comfort of their comfortable journey would be destroyed at once. With woeful countenances they looked at each other. Their suspense lasted an hour or two. No one interfered to encourage or dissuade. Mrs. Norris was left to settle the matter by herself; and it ended to the infinite joy of her nephew and niece, in the recollection that she could not possibly be spared from Mansfield Park at present; that she was a great deal too necessary to Sir Thomas and Lady Bertram for her to be able to answer it to herself to leave them even for a week, and therefore must certainly sacrifice every other pleasure to that of being useful to them.

It had, in fact, occurred to her, that, though taken to Portsmouth for nothing, it would be hardly possible for her to avoid paying her own expenses back again. So, her poor dear sister Price was left to all the disappointment of her missing such an opportunity; and another twenty years' absence, perhaps, begun.

Edmund's plans were affected by this Portsmouth journey, this absence of Fanny's. He too had a sacrifice to make to Mansfield Park, as well as his aunt. He had intended, about this time, to be going to London, but he could not leave his father and mother just when every body else of most importance to their comfort, was leaving them; and with an effort, felt but not boasted of, he delayed for a week or two longer a journey which he was looking forward to, with the hope of its fixing his happiness for ever.

He told Fanny of it. She knew so much already, that she must know every thing. It made the substance of one other confidential discourse about Miss Crawford; and Fanny was the more affected from feeling it to be the last time in which Miss Crawford's name would ever be mentioned between them with any remains of liberty. Once afterwards, she was alluded to by him. Lady Bertram had been telling her niece in the evening to write to her soon and often, and promising to be a good correspondent herself; and Edmund, at a convenient moment, then added, in a whisper, "And *I* shall write to you, Fanny, when I have any thing worth writing about; any thing to say, that I think you will like to hear, and that you will not hear so soon from any other quarter." Had she doubted his meaning while she listened, the glow in his face, when she looked up at him, would have been decisive.

For this letter she must try to arm herself. That a letter from Edmund should be a subject of terror! She began to feel that she had not yet gone through all the changes of opinion and sentiment, which the progress of time and variation of circumstances occasion in this world of changes. The vicissitudes of the human mind[8] had not yet been exhausted by her.

Poor Fanny! though going, as she did, willingly and eagerly, the last evening at Mansfield Park must still be wretchedness. Her heart was completely sad at parting. She had tears for every room in the house, much more for every beloved inhabitant. She clung to her aunt, because she would miss her; she kissed the hand of her uncle with struggling sobs, because she had displeased him; and as for Edmund, she could neither

line 19: terror!] **1814** terror.   //   line 29: her; she] **1814** her, she   //
line 31: him; and] **1814** him, and

speak, nor look, nor think, when the last moment came with *him*, and it was not till it was over that she knew he was giving her the affectionate farewell of a brother.

All this passed over night, for the journey was to begin very early in the morning; and when the small, diminished party met at breakfast, William and Fanny were talked of as already advanced one stage.

Chapter 7

THE novelty of travelling, and the happiness of being with William, soon produced their natural effect on Fanny's spirits, when Mansfield Park was fairly left behind, and by the time their first stage was ended, and they were to quit Sir Thomas's carriage, she was able to take leave of the old coachman, and send back proper messages, with cheerful looks.

Of pleasant talk between the brother and sister, there was no end. Every thing supplied an amusement to the high glee of William's mind, and he was full of frolic and joke, in the intervals of their higher-toned subjects, all of which ended, if they did not begin, in praise of the Thrush, conjectures how she would be employed, schemes for an action with some superior force, which (supposing the first lieutenant out of the way—and William was not very merciful to the first lieutenant) was to give himself the next step as soon as possible, or speculations upon prize money,[1] which was to be generously distributed at home, with only the reservation of enough to make the little cottage comfortable, in which he and Fanny were to pass all their middle and latter life together.

Fanny's immediate concerns, as far as they involved Mr. Crawford, made no part of their conversation. William knew what had passed, and from his heart lamented that his

line 5: carriage,] **1814** Carriage, // line 7: sister, there] **1814** sister there // line 14: not very merciful] **1814** not always merciful // line 23: heart lamented] **1814** heart, lamented

sister's feelings should be so cold towards a man whom he must consider as the first of human characters; but he was of an age to be all for love,[2] and therefore unable to blame; and knowing her wish on the subject, he would not distress her by the slightest allusion.

She had reason to suppose herself not yet forgotten by Mr. Crawford.—She had heard repeatedly from his sister within the three weeks which had passed since their leaving Mansfield, and in each letter there had been a few lines from himself, warm and determined like his speeches. It was a correspondence which Fanny found quite as unpleasant as she had feared. Miss Crawford's style of writing, lively and affectionate, was itself an evil, independent of what she was thus forced into reading from the brother's pen, for Edmund would never rest till she had read the chief of the letter to him, and then she had to listen to his admiration of her language, and the warmth of her attachments.—There had, in fact, been so much of message, of allusion, of recollection, so much of Mansfield in every letter, that Fanny could not but suppose it meant for him to hear; and to find herself forced into a purpose of that kind, compelled into a correspondence which was bringing her the addresses of the man she did not love, and obliging her to administer to the adverse passion of the man she did, was cruelly mortifying. Here, too, her present removal promised advantage. When no longer under the same roof with Edmund, she trusted that Miss Crawford would have no motive for writing, strong enough to overcome the trouble, and that at Portsmouth their correspondence would dwindle into nothing.

With such thoughts as these among ten hundred others, Fanny proceeded in her journey, safely and cheerfully, and as

line 24: Here, too,] **1814** Here too,

expeditiously as could rationally be hoped in the dirty month of February. They entered Oxford, but she could take only a hasty glimpse of Edmund's College as they passed along, and made no stop any where, till they reached Newbury,[3] where a comfortable meal, uniting dinner and supper, wound up the enjoyments and fatigues of the day.

The next morning saw them off again at an early hour; and with no events and no delays they regularly advanced, and were in the environs of Portsmouth while there was yet daylight for Fanny to look around her, and wonder at the new buildings.—They passed the Drawbridge,[4] and entered the town; and the light was only beginning to fail, as, guided by William's powerful voice, they were rattled into a narrow street, leading from the high street, and drawn up before the door of a small house now inhabited by Mr. Price.

Fanny was all agitation and flutter—all hope and apprehension. The moment they stopt, a trollopy-looking[5] maid-servant, seemingly in waiting for them at the door, stept forward, and more intent on telling the news, than giving them any help, immediately began with "the Thrush is gone out of harbour,[6] please Sir, and one of the officers has been here to"——She was interrupted by a fine tall boy of eleven years old, who rushing out of the house, pushed the maid aside, and while William was opening the chaise door himself, called out, "you are just in time. We have been looking for you this half hour. The Thrush went out of harbour this morning. I saw her. It was a beautiful sight. And they think she will have her orders in a day or two. And Mr. Campbell was here at four o'clock, to ask for you; he has got one of the Thrush's boats, and is going off to her at six, and hoped you would be here in time to go with him."

line 20: with "the] **1814** with, "the // line 29: you; he] **1814** you, he

A stare or two at Fanny, as William helped her out of the carriage, was all the voluntary notice which this brother bestowed;—but he made no objection to her kissing him, though still entirely engaged in detailing farther particulars of the Thrush's going out of harbour, in which he had a strong right of interest, being to commence his career of seamanship in her at this very time.

Another moment, and Fanny was in the narrow entrance-passage of the house, and in her mother's arms, who met her there with looks of true kindness, and with features which Fanny loved the more, because they brought her aunt Bertram's before her; and there were her two sisters, Susan, a well-grown fine girl of fourteen, and Betsey, the youngest of the family, about five—both glad to see her in their way, though with no advantage of manner in receiving her. But manner Fanny did not want. Would they but love her, she should be satisfied.

She was then taken into a parlour, so small that her first conviction was of its being only a passage-room to something better, and she stood for a moment expecting to be invited on; but when she saw there was no other door, and that there were signs of habitation before her, she called back her thoughts, reproved herself, and grieved lest they should have been suspected. Her mother, however, could not stay long enough to suspect any thing. She was gone again to the street door, to welcome William. "Oh! my dear William, how glad I am to see you. But have you heard about the Thrush? She is gone out of harbour already, three days before we had any thought of it; and I do not know what I am to do about Sam's things, they will never be ready in time; for she may have her orders to-morrow, perhaps. It takes me quite unawares. And

line 25: any thing.] **1814** anything.

now you must be off for Spithead too. Campbell has been here, quite in a worry about you; and now, what shall we do? I thought to have had such a comfortable evening with you, and here every thing comes upon me at once."

Her son answered cheerfully, telling her that every thing was always for the best; and making light of his own inconvenience, in being obliged to hurry away so soon.

"To be sure, I had much rather she had stayed in harbour, that I might have sat a few hours with you in comfort; but as there is a boat ashore, I had better go off at once, and there is no help for it. Whereabouts does the Thrush lay at Spithead? Near the Canopus? But no matter—here's Fanny in the parlour, and why should we stay in the passage?—Come, mother, you have hardly looked at your own dear Fanny yet."

In they both came, and Mrs. Price having kindly kissed her daughter again, and commented a little on her growth, began with very natural solicitude to feel for their fatigues and wants as travellers.

"Poor dears! how tired you must both be!—and now what will you have? I began to think you would never come. Betsey and I have been watching for you this half hour. And when did you get anything to eat? And what would you like to have now? I could not tell whether you would be for some meat, or only a dish of tea[7] after your journey, or else I would have got something ready. And now I am afraid Campbell will be here, before there is time to dress a steak,[8] and we have no butcher at hand. It is very inconvenient to have no butcher in the street. We were better off in our last house. Perhaps you would like some tea, as soon as it can be got."

They both declared they should prefer it to anything. "Then, Betsey, my dear, run into the kitchen, and see if

line 12: Spithead?] **1814** Spithead!

Rebecca has put the water on; and tell her to bring in the tea-things as soon as she can. I wish we could get the bell mended—but Betsey is a very handy little messenger."

Betsey went with alacrity; proud to shew her abilities before her fine new sister.

"Dear me!" continued the anxious mother, "what a sad fire we have got, and I dare say you are both starved with cold.⁹ Draw your chair nearer, my dear. I cannot think what Rebecca has been about. I am sure I told her to bring some coals half an hour ago. Susan, *you* should have taken care of the fire."

"I was up stairs, mamma, moving my things;" said Susan, in a fearless, self-defending tone, which startled Fanny. "You know you had but just settled that my sister Fanny and I should have the other room; and I could not get Rebecca to give me any help."

Farther discussion was prevented by various bustles; first, the driver came to be paid—then there was a squabble between Sam and Rebecca, about the manner of carrying up his sister's trunk, which he would manage all his own way; and lastly in walked Mr. Price himself, his own loud voice preceding him, as with something of the oath kind he kicked away his son's portmanteau, and his daughter's band-box¹⁰ in the passage, and called out for a candle; no candle was brought, however, and he walked into the room.

Fanny, with doubting feelings, had risen to meet him, but sank down again on finding herself undistinguished in the dusk, and unthought of. With a friendly shake of his son's hand, and an eager voice, he instantly began—"Ha! welcome back, my boy. Glad to see you. Have you heard the news? The

line 12: fearless, self-defending] **1814** fearless self-defending // line 12: Fanny. "You] **1814** Fanny. "you // line 20: lastly in] **1814** lastly, in

Thrush went out of harbour this morning. Sharp is the word, you see. By G—, you are just in time. The doctor[11] has been here enquiring for you; he has got one of the boats, and is to be off for Spithead by six, so you had better go with him. I have been to Turner's about your mess;[12] it is all in a way to be done. I should not wonder if you had your orders to-morrow; but you cannot sail with this wind, if you are to cruize to the westward; and Captain Walsh thinks you will certainly have a cruize to the westward, with the Elephant.[13] By G—, I wish you may.[14] But old Scholey was saying just now, that he thought you would be sent first to the Texel.[15] Well, well, we are ready, whatever happens. But by G—, you lost a fine sight by not being here in the morning to see the Thrush go out of harbour. I would not have been out of the way for a thousand pounds. Old Scholey ran in at breakfast time, to say she had slipped her moorings[16] and was coming out. I jumped up, and made but two steps to the platform.[17] If ever there was a perfect beauty afloat, she is one; and there she lays at Spithead, and anybody in England would take her for an eight-and-twenty.[18] I was upon the platform two hours this afternoon, looking at her. She lays close to the Endymion, between her and the Cleopatra, just to the eastward of the sheer hulk."[19]

"Ha!" cried William, "*that's* just where I should have put her myself. It's the best birth at Spithead. But here is my sister, Sir, here is Fanny;" turning and leading her forward;—"it is so dark you do not see her."

line 1: Sharp is the word,] **1814** Alert is the word,   //   line 5: your mess; it] **1814** your things, it   //   line 16: she had slipped her moorings and was coming out.] **1814** she was under weigh.   //   line 17: the platform.] **1814** the point.   //   line 21: lays close to the Endymion, between her and the Cleopatra, just to the eastward of the sheer hulk."] **1814** lays just astern of the Endymion, with the Cleopatra to larboard."   //   line 25: myself. It's the best birth at Spithead. But] **1814** myself. But

With an acknowledgment that he had quite forgot her, Mr. Price now received his daughter; and, having given her a cordial hug, and observed that she was grown into a woman, and he supposed would be wanting a husband soon, seemed very much inclined to forget her again.

Fanny shrunk back to her seat, with feelings sadly pained by his language and his smell of spirits; and he talked on only to his son, and only of the Thrush, though William, warmly interested, as he was, in that subject, more than once tried to make his father think of Fanny, and her long absence and long journey.

After sitting some time longer, a candle was obtained; but, as there was still no appearance of tea, nor, from Betsey's reports from the kitchen, much hope of any under a considerable period, William determined to go and change his dress, and make the necessary preparations for his removal on board directly, that he might have his tea in comfort afterwards.

As he left the room, two rosy-faced boys, ragged and dirty, about eight and nine years old, rushed into it just released from school, and coming eagerly to see their sister, and tell that the Thrush was gone out of harbour; Tom and Charles: Charles had been born since Fanny's going away, but Tom she had often helped to nurse, and now felt a particular pleasure in seeing again. Both were kissed very tenderly, but Tom she wanted to keep by her, to try to trace the features of the baby she had loved, and talked to,[20] of his infant preference of herself. Tom, however, had no mind for such treatment: he came home, not to stand and be talked to, but to run about and make a noise; and both boys had soon burst away from her, and slammed the parlour door till her temples ached.

line 1: acknowledgment] **1814** acknowledgement   //   line 21: Charles: Charles] **1814** Charles; Charles   //   line 27: treatment: he] **1814** treatment; he   //   line 30: her, and] **1814** her and

She had now seen all that were at home; there remained only two brothers between herself and Susan, one of whom was a clerk in a public office in London, and the other midshipman on board an Indiaman.[21] But though she had *seen* all the members of the family, she had not yet *heard* all the noise they could make. Another quarter of an hour brought her a great deal more. William was soon calling out from the landing-place of the second story, for his mother and for Rebecca. He was in distress for something that he had left there, and did not find again. A key was mislaid, Betsey accused of having got at his new hat, and some slight, but essential alteration of his uniform waistcoat, which he had been promised to have done for him, entirely neglected.

Mrs. Price, Rebecca, and Betsey, all went up to defend themselves, all talking together, but Rebecca loudest, and the job was to be done, as well as it could, in a great hurry; William trying in vain to send Betsey down again, or keep her from being troublesome where she was; the whole of which, as almost every door in the house was open, could be plainly distinguished in the parlour, except when drowned at intervals by the superior noise of Sam, Tom, and Charles chasing each other up and down stairs, and tumbling about and hallooing.

Fanny was almost stunned. The smallness of the house, and thinness of the walls, brought every thing so close to her, that, added to the fatigue of her journey, and all her recent agitation, she hardly knew how to bear it. *Within* the room all was tranquil enough, for Susan having disappeared with the others, there were soon only her father and herself remaining; and he taking out a newspaper— the accustomary loan of a neighbour, applied himself to

line 3: was a clerk] **1814** was clerk

studying it, without seeming to recollect her existence. The solitary candle was held between himself and the paper, without any reference to her possible convenience; but she had nothing to do, and was glad to have the light screened from her aching head, as she sat in bewildered, broken, sorrowful contemplation.

She was at home. But alas! it was not such a home, she had not such a welcome, as——she checked herself; she was unreasonable. What right had she to be of importance to her family? She could have none, so long lost sight of! William's concerns must be dearest—they always had been—and he had every right. Yet to have so little said or asked about herself—to have scarcely an enquiry made after Mansfield! It did pain her to have Mansfield forgotten; the friends who had done so much—the dear, dear friends! But here, one subject swallowed up all the rest. Perhaps it must be so. The destination of the Thrush must be now pre-eminently interesting. A day or two might shew the difference. *She* only was to blame. Yet she thought it would not have been so at Mansfield. No, in her uncle's house there would have been a consideration of times and seasons, a regulation of subject, a propriety, an attention towards every body which there was not here.

The only interruption which thoughts like these received for nearly half an hour, was from a sudden burst of her father's, not at all calculated to compose them. At a more than ordinary pitch of thumping and hallooing in the passage, he exclaimed, "Devil take those young dogs! How they are singing out! Ay, Sam's voice louder than all the rest! That boy is fit for a boatswain.[22] Holla—you there—Sam—stop your confounded pipe, or I shall be after you."

This threat was so palpably disregarded, that though within five minutes afterwards the three boys all burst into

line 28: Ay, Sam's] **1814** Aye, Sam's

the room together and sat down, Fanny could not consider it as a proof of any thing more than their being for the time thoroughly fagged, which their hot faces and panting breaths seemed to prove—especially as they were still kicking each other's shins, and hallooing out at sudden starts immediately under their father's eye.

The next opening of the door brought something more welcome; it was for the tea-things, which she had begun almost to despair of seeing that evening. Susan and an attendant girl, whose inferior appearance informed Fanny, to her great surprise, that she had previously seen the upper servant brought in every thing necessary for the meal; Susan looking as she put the kettle on the fire and glanced at her sister, as if divided between the agreeable triumph of shewing her activity and usefulness, and the dread of being thought to demean herself by such an office. "She had been into the kitchen," she said, "to hurry Sally and help make the toast, and spread the bread and butter—or she did not know when they should have got tea—and she was sure her sister must want something after her journey."

Fanny was very thankful. She could not but own that she should be very glad of a little tea, and Susan immediately set about making it, as if pleased to have the employment all to herself; and with only a little unnecessary bustle, and some few injudicious attempts at keeping her brothers in better order than she could, acquitted herself very well. Fanny's spirit was as much refreshed as her body; her head and heart were soon the better for such well-timed kindness. Susan had an open, sensible countenance; she was like William—and Fanny hoped to find her like him in disposition and good will towards herself.

line 8: tea-things,] **1814** tea things,   //   line 11: servant brought] **1814** servant, brought

In this more placid state of things William re-entered, followed not far behind by his mother and Betsey. He, complete in his Lieutenant's uniform, looking and moving all the taller, firmer, and more graceful for it, and with the happiest smile over his face, walked up directly to Fanny—who, rising from her seat, looked at him for a moment in speechless admiration, and then threw her arms round his neck to sob out her various emotions of pain and pleasure.

Anxious not to appear unhappy, she soon recovered herself: and wiping away her tears, was able to notice and admire all the striking parts of his dress—listening with reviving spirits to his cheerful hopes of being on shore some part of every day before they sailed, and even of getting her to Spithead to see the sloop.

The next bustle brought in Mr. Campbell, the Surgeon of the Thrush, a very well behaved young man, who came to call for his friend, and for whom there was with some contrivance found a chair, and with some hasty washing of the young tea-maker's, a cup and saucer; and after another quarter of an hour of earnest talk between the gentlemen, noise rising upon noise, and bustle upon bustle, men and boys at last all in motion together, the moment came for setting off; every thing was ready, William took leave, and all of them were gone—for the three boys, in spite of their mother's intreaty, determined to see their brother and Mr. Campbell to the sally-port;[23] and Mr. Price walked off at the same time to carry back his neighbour's newspaper.

Something like tranquillity might now be hoped for, and accordingly, when Rebecca had been prevailed on to carry away the tea-things, and Mrs. Price had walked about the room some time looking for a shirt sleeve, which Betsey at

line 26: sally-port;] **1814** salley-port;

last hunted out from a drawer in the kitchen, the small party of females were pretty well composed, and the mother having lamented again over the impossibility of getting Sam ready in time, was at leisure to think of her eldest daughter and the friends she had come from.

A few enquiries began; but one of the earliest—"How did her sister Bertram manage about her servants? Was she as much plagued as herself to get tolerable servants?"—soon led her mind away from Northamptonshire, and fixed it on her own domestic grievances; and the shocking character of all the Portsmouth servants, of whom she believed her own two were the very worst, engrossed her completely. The Bertrams were all forgotten in detailing the faults of Rebecca, against whom Susan had also much to depose, and little Betsey a great deal more, and who did seem so thoroughly without a single recommendation, that Fanny could not help modestly presuming that her mother meant to part with her when her year was up.[24]

"Her year!" cried Mrs. Price; "I am sure I hope I shall be rid of her before she has staid a year, for that will not be up till November. Servants are come to such a pass, my dear, in Portsmouth, that it is quite a miracle if one keeps them more than half-a-year. I have no hope of ever being settled; and if I was to part with Rebecca, I should only get something worse. And yet I do not think I am a very difficult mistress to please—and I am sure the place is easy enough, for there is always a girl under her, and I often do half the work myself."

Fanny was silent; but not from being convinced that there might not be a remedy found for some of these evils. As she now sat looking at Betsey, she could not but think particularly of another sister, a very pretty little girl, whom

line 9: Northamptonshire, and] **1814** Northamptonshire and // line 17: her when] **1814** her, when // line 25: yet I] **1814** yet, I

445

she had left there not much younger when she went into Northamptonshire, who had died a few years afterwards. There had been something remarkably amiable about her. Fanny, in those early days, had preferred her to Susan; and when the news of her death had at last reached Mansfield, had for a short time been quite afflicted.—The sight of Betsey brought the image of little Mary back again, but she would not have pained her mother by alluding to her, for the world.—While considering her with these ideas, Betsey, at a small distance, was holding out something to catch her eyes, meaning to screen it at the same time from Susan's.

"What have you got there, my love?" said Fanny, "come and shew it to me."

It was a silver knife. Up jumped Susan, claiming it as her own, and trying to get it away; but the child ran to her mother's protection, and Susan could only reproach, which she did very warmly, and evidently hoping to interest Fanny on her side. "It was very hard that she was not to have her *own* knife; it was her own knife; little sister Mary had left it to her upon her death-bed, and she ought to have had it to keep herself long ago. But mamma kept it from her, and was always letting Betsey get hold of it; and the end of it would be that Betsey would spoil it, and get it for her own, though mamma had *promised* her that Betsey should not have it in her own hands."

Fanny was quite shocked. Every feeling of duty, honour, and tenderness was wounded by her sister's speech and her mother's reply.

"Now, Susan," cried Mrs. Price in a complaining voice, "now, how can you be so cross? You are always quarrelling

line 14: Susan, claiming] **1814** Susan claiming // line 20: death-bed,]
1814 death bed, // line 23: be that] **1814** be, that // line 26: honour,
and] **1814** honour and

about that knife. I wish you would not be so quarrelsome. Poor little Betsey; how cross Susan is to you! But you should not have taken it out, my dear, when I sent you to the drawer. You know I told you not to touch it, because Susan is so cross about it. I must hide it another time, Betsey. Poor Mary little thought it would be such a bone of contention when she gave it me to keep, only two hours before she died. Poor little soul! she could but just speak to be heard, and she said so prettily, 'Let sister Susan have my knife, mamma, when I am dead and buried.'—Poor little dear! she was so fond of it, Fanny, that she would have it lay by her in bed, all through her illness. It was the gift of her good godmother, old Mrs. Admiral Maxwell, only six weeks before she was taken for death. Poor little sweet creature! Well, she was taken away from evil to come. My own Betsey, (fondling her), *you* have not the luck of such a good godmother. Aunt Norris lives too far off, to think of such little people as you."

Fanny had indeed nothing to convey from aunt Norris, but a message to say she hoped her god-daughter was a good girl, and learnt her book. There had been at one moment a slight murmur in the drawing-room at Mansfield Park, about sending her a Prayer-book; but no second sound had been heard of such a purpose. Mrs. Norris, however, had gone home and taken down two old Prayer-books of her husband, with that idea, but upon examination, the ardour of generosity went off. One was found to have too small a print for a child's eyes, and the other to be too cumbersome for her to carry about.

Fanny fatigued and fatigued again, was thankful to accept the first invitation of going to bed; and before Betsey had finished her cry at being allowed to sit up only one hour

line 22: Prayer-book;] **1814** Prayer book;   //   line 24: old Prayer-books]
1814 old Prayer books

extraordinary in honour of sister, she was off, leaving all below in confusion and noise again, the boys begging for toasted cheese, her father calling out for his rum and water, and Rebecca never where she ought to be.

There was nothing to raise her spirits in the confined and scantily-furnished chamber that she was to share with Susan. The smallness of the rooms above and below indeed, and the narrowness of the passage and staircase, struck her beyond her imagination. She soon learnt to think with respect of her own little attic at Mansfield Park, in *that* house reckoned too small for anybody's comfort.

Chapter 8

COULD Sir Thomas have seen all his niece's feelings, when she wrote her first letter to her aunt, he would not have despaired; for though a good night's rest, a pleasant morning, the hope of soon seeing William again, and the comparatively quiet state of the house, from Tom and Charles being gone to school, Sam on some project of his own, and her father on his usual lounges, enabled her to express herself cheerfully on the subject of home, there were still to her own perfect consciousness, many drawbacks suppressed. Could he have seen only half that she felt before the end of a week, he would have thought Mr. Crawford sure of her, and been delighted with his own sagacity.

Before the week ended, it was all disappointment. In the first place, William was gone. The Thrush had had her orders, the wind had changed, and he was sailed within four days from their reaching Portsmouth; and during those days, she had seen him only twice, in a short and hurried way, when he had come ashore on duty. There had been no free conversation, no walk on the ramparts,[1] no visit to the dock-yard, no acquaintance with the Thrush—nothing of all that they had planned and depended on. Every thing in that quarter failed her, except William's affection. His last thought on leaving home was for her. He stepped back again to the door to say, "Take care of Fanny, mother. She is tender, and not

line 10: before] **1814** besore

used to rough it like the rest of us. I charge you, take care of Fanny."

William was gone;—and the home he had left her in was—Fanny could not conceal it from herself—in almost every respect, the very reverse of what she could have wished. It was the abode of noise, disorder, and impropriety. Nobody was in their right place, nothing was done as it ought to be. She could not respect her parents, as she had hoped. On her father, her confidence had not been sanguine, but he was more negligent of his family, his habits were worse, and his manners coarser, than she had been prepared for. He did not want abilities; but he had no curiosity, and no information beyond his profession; he read only the newspaper and the navy-list;[2] he talked only of the dockyard, the harbour, Spithead, and the Motherbank;[3] he swore and he drank, he was dirty and gross. She had never been able to recal anything approaching to tenderness in his former treatment of herself. There had remained only a general impression of roughness and loudness; and now he scarcely ever noticed her, but to make her the object of a coarse joke.

Her disappointment in her mother was greater; *there* she had hoped much, and found almost nothing. Every flattering scheme of being of consequence to her soon fell to the ground. Mrs. Price was not unkind—but, instead of gaining on her affection and confidence[4] and becoming more and more dear, her daughter never met with greater kindness from her, than on the first day of her arrival. The instinct of nature[5] was soon satisfied, and Mrs. Price's attachment had no other source. Her heart and her time were already quite full; she had neither leisure nor affection to bestow on Fanny. Her daughters never had been much to her. She

line 3: in was—] **1814** in, was—   //   line 23: her soon] **1814** her, soon

was fond of her sons, especially of William, but Betsey was the first of her girls whom she had ever much regarded. To her she was most injudiciously indulgent. William was her pride; Betsey, her darling; and John, Richard, Sam, Tom, and Charles, occupied all the rest of her maternal solicitude, alternately her worries and her comforts. These shared her heart; her time was given chiefly to her house and her servants. Her days were spent in a kind of slow bustle; all was busy without getting on, always behindhand and lamenting it, without altering her ways; wishing to be an economist, without contrivance or regularity; dissatisfied with her servants, without skill to make them better, and whether helping, or reprimanding, or indulging them, without any power of engaging their respect.

Of her two sisters, Mrs. Price very much more resembled Lady Bertram than Mrs. Norris. She was a manager by necessity, without any of Mrs. Norris's inclination for it, or any of her activity. Her disposition was naturally easy and indolent, like Lady Bertram's; and a situation of similar affluence and do-nothing-ness would have been much more suited to her capacity, than the exertions and self-denials of the one, which her imprudent marriage had placed her in. She might have made just as good a woman of consequence as Lady Bertram, but Mrs. Norris would have been a more respectable mother of nine children, on a small income.

Much of all this, Fanny could not but be sensible of. She might scruple to make use of the words, but she must and did feel that her mother was a partial, ill-judging parent, a dawdle, a slattern, who neither taught nor restrained her children, whose house was the scene of mismanagement and

line 3: her she] **1814** her, she   //   line 8: all was busy] **1814** always busy   //
line 9: behindhand] **1814** behind hand   //   line 12: helping, or] **1814**
helping or

discomfort from beginning to end, and who had no talent, no conversation, no affection towards herself; no curiosity to know her better, no desire of her friendship, and no inclination for her company that could lessen her sense of such feelings.

Fanny was very anxious to be useful, and not to appear above her home, or in any way disqualified or disinclined, by her foreign education, from contributing her help to its comforts, and therefore set about working for Sam immediately, and by working early and late, with perseverance and great dispatch, did so much, that the boy was shipped off at last, with more than half his linen ready. She had great pleasure in feeling her usefulness, but could not conceive how they would have managed without her.

Sam, loud and overbearing as he was, she rather regretted when he went, for he was clever and intelligent, and glad to be employed in any errand in the town; and though spurning the remonstrances of Susan, given as they were—though very reasonable in themselves, with ill-timed and powerless warmth, was beginning to be influenced by Fanny's services, and gentle persuasions; and she found that the best of the three younger ones was gone in him; Tom and Charles being at least as many years as they were his juniors distant from that age of feeling and reason, which might suggest the expediency of making friends, and of endeavouring to be less disagreeable. Their sister soon despaired of making the smallest impression on *them*; they were quite untameable by any means of address which she had spirits or time to attempt. Every afternoon brought a return of their riotous games all over the house; and she very early learnt to sigh at the approach of Saturday's constant half holiday.

line 9: therefore set] **1814** therefore, set   //   line 23: at least] **1814** as least

Betsey too, a spoilt child, trained up to think the alphabet her greatest enemy, left to be with the servants at her pleasure, and then encouraged to report any evil of them, she was almost as ready to despair of being able to love or assist; and of Susan's temper, she had many doubts. Her continual disagreements with her mother, her rash squabbles with Tom and Charles, and petulance with Betsey, were at least so distressing to Fanny, that though admitting they were by no means without provocation, she feared the disposition that could push them to such length must be far from amiable, and from affording any repose to herself.

Such was the home which was to put Mansfield out of her head, and teach her to think of her cousin Edmund with moderated feelings. On the contrary, she could think of nothing but Mansfield, its beloved inmates, its happy ways. Every thing where she now was was in full contrast to it. The elegance, propriety, regularity, harmony—and perhaps, above all, the peace and tranquillity of Mansfield, were brought to her remembrance every hour of the day, by the prevalence of every thing opposite to them *here*.

The living in incessant noise was to a frame and temper, delicate and nervous like Fanny's, an evil which no superadded elegance or harmony could have entirely atoned for. It was the greatest misery of all. At Mansfield, no sounds of contention, no raised voice, no abrupt bursts, no tread of violence was ever heard; all proceeded in a regular course of cheerful orderliness; every body had their due importance; every body's feelings were consulted. If tenderness could be ever supposed wanting, good sense and good breeding supplied its place; and as to the little irritations, sometimes

line 10: length must] **1814** length, must // line 16: was was] **1814** was, was // line 23: harmony could] **1814** harmony, could // line 29: sense and] **1814** sense, and

453

introduced by aunt Norris, they were short, they were trifling, they were as a drop of water to the ocean, compared with the ceaseless tumult of her present abode. Here, every body was noisy, every voice was loud, (excepting, perhaps, her mother's, which resembled the soft monotony of Lady Bertram's, only worn into fretfulness.)—Whatever was wanted, was halloo'd for, and the servants halloo'd out their excuses from the kitchen. The doors were in constant banging, the stairs were never at rest, nothing was done without a clatter, nobody sat still, and nobody could command attention when they spoke.

In a review of the two houses, as they appeared to her before the end of a week, Fanny was tempted to apply to them Dr. Johnson's celebrated judgment[6] as to matrimony and celibacy, and say, that though Mansfield Park might have some pains, Portsmouth could have no pleasures.

line 14: Mansfield Park might] **1814** Mansfield Park, might

Chapter 9

FANNY was right enough in not expecting to hear from Miss Crawford now, at the rapid rate in which their correspondence had begun; Mary's next letter was after a decidedly longer interval than the last, but she was not right in supposing that such an interval would be felt a great relief to herself.—Here was another strange revolution of mind!—She was really glad to receive the letter when it did come. In her present exile from good society, and distance from every thing that had been wont to interest her, a letter from one belonging to the set where her heart lived, written with affection, and some degree of elegance, was thoroughly acceptable.—The usual plea of increasing engagements was made in excuse for not having written to her earlier, "and now that I have begun," she continued, "my letter will not be worth your reading, for there will be no little offering of love at the end, no three or four lines passionées[1] from the most devoted H. C. in the world, for Henry is in Norfolk; business called him to Everingham ten days ago, or perhaps he only pretended the call, for the sake of being travelling at the same time that you were. But there he is, and, by the by, his absence may sufficiently account for any remissness of his sister's in writing, for there has been no 'well, Mary, when do you write to Fanny?—is not it time for you to write to Fanny?' to spur

line 13: her earlier,] **1814** her her earlier, // line 14: continued, my [**1814** continued, "my // line 20: by the by,] **1814** by the bye, // line 22: well, Mary,] **1814** well Mary,

455

me on. At last, after various attempts at meeting, I have seen your cousins, 'dear Julia and dearest Mrs. Rushworth;' they found me at home yesterday, and we were glad to see each other again. We *seemed very* glad to see each other, and I do really think we were a little.—We had a vast deal to say.— Shall I tell you how Mrs. Rushworth looked when your name was mentioned? I did not use to think her wanting in self-possession, but she had not quite enough for the demands of yesterday. Upon the whole Julia was in the best looks of the two, at least after you were spoken of. There was no recovering the complexion from the moment that I spoke of 'Fanny,' and spoke of her as a sister should.—But Mrs. Rushworth's day of good looks will come; we have cards for her first party on the 28th.—Then she will be in beauty, for she will open one of the best houses in Wimpole Street.[2] I was in it two years ago, when it was Lady Lascelles's, and prefer it to almost any I know in London, and certainly she will then feel—to use a vulgar phrase—that she has got her pennyworth for her penny. Henry could not have afforded her such a house. I hope she will recollect it, and be satisfied, as well she may, with moving the queen of a palace, though the king may appear best in the back ground; and as I have no desire to tease her, I shall never *force* your name upon her again. She will grow sober by degrees.—From all that I hear and guess, Baron Wildenhaim's attentions to Julia continue, but I do not know that he has any serious encouragement. She ought to do better. A poor honourable is no catch, and I cannot imagine any liking in the case, for, take away his rants, and the poor Baron has nothing. What a difference a vowel makes!— if his rents were but equal to his rants!—Your cousin Edmund moves slowly; detained, perchance, by parish duties. There

line 7: self-possession,] **1814** self possession,   //   line 22: ground; and] **1814** ground, and   //   line 23: tease] **1814** teize

may be some old woman at Thornton Lacey to be converted.[3] I am unwilling to fancy myself neglected for a *young* one. Adieu, my dear sweet Fanny, this is a long letter from London; write me a pretty one in reply to gladden Henry's eyes, when he comes back—and send me an account of all the dashing young captains whom you disdain for his sake."

There was great food for meditation in this letter, and chiefly for unpleasant meditation; and yet, with all the uneasiness it supplied, it connected her with the absent, it told her of people and things about whom she had never felt so much curiosity as now, and she would have been glad to have been sure of such a letter every week. Her correspondence with her aunt Bertram was her only concern of higher interest.

As for any society in Portsmouth, that could at all make amends for deficiencies at home, there were none within the circle of her father's and mother's acquaintance to afford her the smallest satisfaction; she saw nobody in whose favour she could wish to overcome her own shyness and reserve. The men appeared to her all coarse, the women all pert, every body under-bred; and she gave as little contentment as she received from introductions either to old or new acquaintance. The young ladies who approached her at first with some respect, in consideration of her coming from a Baronet's family, were soon offended by what they termed "airs"— for as she neither played on the pianoforte nor wore fine pelisses,[4] they could, on farther observation, admit no right of superiority.

The first solid consolation which Fanny received for the evils of home, the first which her judgment could entirely approve, and which gave any promise of durability, was in a better knowledge of Susan, and a hope of being of service to

line 23: respect, in] **1814** repect in

her. Susan had always behaved pleasantly to herself, but the determined character of her general manners had astonished and alarmed her, and it was at least a fortnight before she began to understand a disposition so totally different from her own. Susan saw that much was wrong at home, and wanted to set it right. That a girl of fourteen, acting only on her own unassisted reason, should err in the method of reform was not wonderful; and Fanny soon became more disposed to admire the natural light of the mind which could so early distinguish justly, than to censure severely the faults of conduct to which it led. Susan was only acting on the same truths, and pursuing the same system, which her own judgment acknowledged, but which her more supine and yielding temper would have shrunk from asserting. Susan tried to be useful, where *she* could only have gone away and cried; and that Susan was useful she could perceive; that things, bad as they were, would have been worse but for such interposition, and that both her mother and Betsey were restrained from some excesses of very offensive indulgence and vulgarity.

In every argument with her mother, Susan had in point of reason the advantage, and never was there any maternal tenderness to buy her off. The blind fondness which was for ever producing evil around her, *she* had never known. There was no gratitude for affection past or present, to make her better bear with its excesses to the others.

All this became gradually evident, and gradually placed Susan before her sister as an object of mingled compassion and respect. That her manner was wrong, however, at times very wrong—her measures often ill-chosen and ill-timed, and her looks and language very often indefensible, Fanny could not cease to feel; but she began to hope they might

line 10: severely the] **1814** severely, the   //   line 29: ill-timed,] **1814** ill timed,

be rectified. Susan, she found, looked up to her and wished for her good opinion; and new as any thing like an office of authority was to Fanny, new as it was to imagine herself capable of guiding or informing any one, she did resolve to give occasional hints to Susan, and endeavour to exercise for her advantage the juster notions of what was due to every body, and what would be wisest for herself, which her own more favoured education had fixed in her.

Her influence, or at least the consciousness and use of it, originated in an act of kindness by Susan, which after many hesitations of delicacy, she at last worked herself up to. It had very early occurred to her, that a small sum of money might, perhaps, restore peace for ever on the sore subject of the silver knife, canvassed as it now was continually, and the riches which she was in possession of herself, her uncle having given her 10*l.* at parting, made her as able as she was willing to be generous. But she was so wholly unused to confer favours, except on the very poor, so unpractised in removing evils, or bestowing kindnesses among her equals, and so fearful of appearing to elevate herself as a great lady at home, that it took some time to determine that it would not be unbecoming in her to make such a present. It was made, however, at last; a silver knife was bought for Betsey, and accepted with great delight, its newness giving it every advantage over the other that could be desired; Susan was established in the full possession of her own, Betsey handsomely declaring that now she had got one so much prettier herself, she should never want *that* again—and no reproach seemed conveyed to the equally satisfied mother, which Fanny had almost feared to be impossible. The deed thoroughly answered; a source of domestic altercation was entirely done away, and it was the

line 23: last; a] **1814** last, a

means of opening Susan's heart to her, and giving her something more to love and be interested in. Susan shewed that she had delicacy; pleased as she was to be mistress of property which she had been struggling for at least two years, she yet feared that her sister's judgment had been against her, and that a reproof was designed her for having so struggled as to make the purchase necessary for the tranquillity of the house.

Her temper was open. She acknowledged her fears, blamed herself for having contended so warmly, and from that hour Fanny understanding the worth of her disposition, and perceiving how fully she was inclined to seek her good opinion and refer to her judgment, began to feel again the blessing of affection, and to entertain the hope of being useful to a mind so much in need of help, and so much deserving it. She gave advice; advice too sound to be resisted by a good understanding, and given so mildly and considerately as not to irritate an imperfect temper; and she had the happiness of observing its good effects not unfrequently; more was not expected by one, who, while seeing all the obligation and expediency of submission and forbearance, saw also with sympathetic acuteness of feeling, all that must be hourly grating to a girl like Susan. Her greatest wonder on the subject soon became—not that Susan should have been provoked into disrespect and impatience against her better knowledge—but that so much better knowledge, so many good notions, should have been hers at all; and that, brought up in the midst of negligence and error, she should have formed such proper opinions of what ought to be—she, who had had no cousin Edmund to direct her thoughts or fix her principles.

line 26: hers] **1814** her's   //   line 29: who had had no] **1814** who had no

The intimacy thus begun between them was a material advantage to each. By sitting together up stairs, they avoided a great deal of the disturbance of the house; Fanny had peace, and Susan learnt to think it no misfortune to be quietly employed. They sat without a fire; but *that* was a privation familiar even to Fanny, and she suffered the less because reminded by it of the east-room. It was the only point of resemblance. In space, light, furniture, and prospect, there was nothing alike in the two apartments; and she often heaved a sigh at the remembrance of all her books and boxes, and various comforts there. By degrees the girls came to spend the chief of the morning up stairs, at first only in working and talking; but after a few days, the remembrance of the said books grew so potent and stimulative, that Fanny found it impossible not to try for books again. There were none in her father's house; but wealth is luxurious and daring—and some of hers found its way to a circulating library.[5] She became a subscriber—amazed at being any thing in *propria persona*, amazed at her own doings in every way; to be a renter, a chuser of books! And to be having any one's improvement in view in her choice! But so it was. Susan had read nothing, and Fanny longed to give her a share in her own first pleasures, and inspire a taste for the biography and poetry which she delighted in herself.

In this occupation she hoped, moreover, to bury some of the recollections of Mansfield which were too apt to seize her mind if her fingers only were busy; and especially at this time, hoped it might be useful in diverting her thoughts from pursuing Edmund to London, whither, on the authority of

line 1: them was] **1814** them, was   //   line 17: hers] **1814** her's   //
line 18: any thing] **1814** anything

her aunt's last letter, she knew he was gone. She had no doubt of what would ensue. The promised notification was hanging over her head. The postman's knock[6] within the neighbourhood was beginning to bring its daily terrors—and if reading could banish the idea for even half an hour, it was something gained.

Chapter 10

A WEEK was gone since Edmund might be supposed in town, and Fanny had heard nothing of him. There were three different conclusions to be drawn from his silence, between which her mind was in fluctuation; each of them at times being held the most probable. Either his going had been again delayed, or he had yet procured no opportunity of seeing Miss Crawford alone—or, he was too happy for letter writing!

One morning about this time, Fanny having now been nearly four weeks from Mansfield—a point which she never failed to think over and calculate every day—as she and Susan were preparing to remove as usual up stairs, they were stopt by the knock of a visitor, whom they felt they could not avoid, from Rebecca's alertness in going to the door, a duty which always interested her beyond any other.

It was a gentleman's voice; it was a voice that Fanny was just turning pale about, when Mr. Crawford walked into the room.

Good sense, like hers, will always act when really called upon; and she found that she had been able to name him to her mother, and recal her remembrance of the name, as that of "William's friend," though she could not previously have believed herself capable of uttering a syllable at such a moment. The consciousness of his being known there only as William's friend, was some support. Having introduced him,

line 12: avoid, from] **1814** avoid from   //   line 18: hers,] **1814** her's,

however, and being all re-seated, the terrors that occurred of what this visit might lead to were overpowering, and she fancied herself on the point of fainting away.

While trying to keep herself alive, their visitor, who had at first approached her with as animated a countenance as ever, was wisely and kindly keeping his eyes away, and giving her time to recover, while he devoted himself entirely to her mother, addressing her, and attending to her with the utmost politeness and propriety, at the same time with a degree of friendliness—of interest at least—which was making his manner perfect.

Mrs. Price's manners were also at their best. Warmed by the sight of such a friend to her son, and regulated by the wish of appearing to advantage before him, she was overflowing with gratitude, artless, maternal gratitude, which could not be unpleasing. Mr. Price was out, which she regretted very much. Fanny was just recovered enough to feel that *she* could not regret it; for to her many other sources of uneasiness was added the severe one of shame for the home in which he found her. She might scold herself for the weakness, but there was no scolding it away. She was ashamed, and she would have been yet more ashamed of her father, than of all the rest.

They talked of William, a subject on which Mrs. Price could never tire; and Mr. Crawford was as warm in his commendation, as even her heart could wish. She felt that she had never seen so agreeable a man in her life; and was only astonished to find, that so great and so agreeable as he was, he should be come down to Portsmouth neither on a visit to the port-admiral, nor the commissioner, nor yet with the intention of going over to the island, nor of seeing the Dock-yard.[1]

line 2: to were] **1814** to, were // line 19: added the] **1814** added, the

Nothing of all that she had been used to think of as the proof of importance, or the employment of wealth, had brought him to Portsmouth. He had reached it late the night before, was come for a day or two, was staying at the Crown,[2] had accidentally met with a navy officer or two of his acquaintance, since his arrival, but had no object of that kind in coming.

By the time he had given all this information, it was not unreasonable to suppose, that Fanny might be looked at and spoken to; and she was tolerably able to bear his eye, and hear that he had spent half an hour with his sister, the evening before his leaving London; that she had sent her best and kindest love, but had had no time for writing; that he thought himself lucky in seeing Mary for even half an hour, having spent scarcely twenty-four hours in London after his return from Norfolk, before he set off again; that her cousin Edmund was in town, had been in town, he understood, a few days; that he had not seen him, himself, but that he was well, had left them all well at Mansfield, and was to dine, as yesterday, with the Frasers.

Fanny listened collectedly even to the last-mentioned circumstance; nay, it seemed a relief to her worn mind to be at any certainty; and the words, "then by this time it is all settled," passed internally, without more evidence of emotion than a faint blush.

After talking a little more about Mansfield, a subject in which her interest was most apparent, Crawford began to hint at the expediency of an early walk;—"It was a lovely morning, and at that season of the year[3] a fine morning so often turned off, that it was wisest for everybody not to delay their exercise;" and such hints producing nothing, he

line 2: wealth, had] **1814** wealth had // line 17: town, he understood, a few days; that] **1814** town he understood, a few days, that

soon proceeded to a positive recommendation to Mrs. Price and her daughters, to take their walk without loss of time. Now they came to an understanding. Mrs. Price, it appeared, scarcely ever stirred out of doors, except of a Sunday; she owned she could seldom, with her large family, find time for a walk.—"Would she not then persuade her daughters to take advantage of such weather, and allow him the pleasure of attending them?"—Mrs. Price was greatly obliged, and very complying. "Her daughters were very much confined— Portsmouth was a sad place⁴—they did not often get out— and she knew they had some errands in the town, which they would be very glad to do."—And the consequence was, that Fanny, strange as it was—strange, awkward, and distressing—found herself and Susan, within ten minutes, walking towards the High Street, with Mr. Crawford.

It was soon pain upon pain, confusion upon confusion; for they were hardly in the High Street, before they met her father, whose appearance was not the better from its being Saturday.⁵ He stopt; and, ungentlemanlike as he looked, Fanny was obliged to introduce him to Mr. Crawford. She could not have a doubt of the manner in which Mr. Crawford must be struck. He must be ashamed and disgusted altogether. He must soon give her up, and cease to have the smallest inclination for the match; and yet, though she had been so much wanting his affection to be cured, this was a sort of cure that would be almost as bad as the complaint; and I believe, there is scarcely a young lady in the united kingdoms, who would not rather put up with the misfortune of being sought by a clever, agreeable man, than have him driven away by the vulgarity of her nearest relations.

line 9: complying. "Her] **1814** complying.—"Her

Mr. Crawford probably could not regard his future father-in-law with any idea of taking him for a model in dress; but (as Fanny instantly, and to her great relief discerned), her father was a very different man, a very different Mr. Price in his behaviour to this most highly-respected stranger, from what he was in his own family at home. His manners now, though not polished, were more than passable; they were grateful, animated, manly; his expressions were those of an attached father, and a sensible man;—his loud tones did very well in the open air, and there was not a single oath to be heard. Such was his instinctive compliment to the good manners of Mr. Crawford; and be the consequence what it might, Fanny's immediate feelings were infinitely soothed.

The conclusion of the two gentlemen's civilities was an offer of Mr. Price's to take Mr. Crawford into the dock-yard, which Mr. Crawford, desirous of accepting as a favour, what was intended as such, though he had seen the dock-yard again and again; and hoping to be so much the longer with Fanny, was very gratefully disposed to avail himself of, if the Miss Prices were not afraid of the fatigue; and as it was somehow or other ascertained, or inferred, or at least acted upon, that they were not at all afraid, to the dock-yard they were all to go; and, but for Mr. Crawford, Mr. Price would have turned thither directly, without the smallest consideration for his daughter's errands in the High Street. He took care, however, that they should be allowed to go to the shops they came out expressly to visit; and it did not delay them long, for Fanny could so little bear to excite impatience, or be waited for, that before the gentlemen, as they stood at the door, could do more than begin upon the last naval regulations, or settle the number

line 20: and as] **1814** and, as

of three deckers[6] now in commission, their companions were ready to proceed.

They were then to set forward for the dock-yard at once, and the walk would have been conducted (according to Mr. Crawford's opinion) in a singular manner, had Mr. Price been allowed the entire regulation of it, as the two girls, he found, would have been left to follow, and keep up with them, or not, as they could, while they walked on together at their own hasty pace. He was able to introduce some improvement occasionally, though by no means to the extent he wished; he absolutely would not walk away from them; and, at any crossing, or any crowd, when Mr. Price was only calling out, "Come, girls—come, Fan—come, Sue—take care of yourselves—keep a sharp look out," he would give them his particular attendance.

Once fairly in the dock-yard, he began to reckon upon some happy intercourse with Fanny, as they were very soon joined by a brother lounger of Mr. Price's, who was come to take his daily survey of how things went on, and who must prove a far more worthy companion than himself; and after a time the two officers seemed very well satisfied in going about together and discussing matters of equal and never-failing interest, while the young people sat down upon some timbers in the yard, or found a seat on board a vessel in the stocks[7] which they all went to look at. Fanny was most conveniently in want of rest. Crawford could not have wished her more fatigued or more ready to sit down; but he could have wished her sister away. A quick looking girl of Susan's age was the very worst third in the world—totally different from Lady Bertram—all eyes and ears; and there was no introducing the main point before her. He must content himself with being

line 13: "Come, girls] **1814** "Come girls   //   line 25: stocks which] **1814** stocks, which

only generally agreeable, and letting Susan have her share of entertainment, with the indulgence, now and then, of a look or hint for the better informed and conscious Fanny. Norfolk was what he had mostly to talk of; there he had been some time, and every thing there was rising in importance from his present schemes. Such a man could come from no place, no society, without importing something to amuse; his journeys and his acquaintance were all of use, and Susan was entertained in a way quite new to her. For Fanny, somewhat more was related than the accidental agreeableness of the parties he had been in. For her approbation, the particular reason of his going into Norfolk at all, at this unusual time of year,[8] was given. It had been real business, relative to the renewal of a lease in which the welfare of a large and (he believed) industrious family was at stake. He had suspected his agent[9] of some underhand dealing—of meaning to bias him against the deserving—and he had determined to go himself, and thoroughly investigate the merits of the case. He had gone, had done even more good than he had foreseen, had been useful to more than his first plan had comprehended, and was now able to congratulate himself upon it, and to feel, that in performing a duty, he had secured agreeable recollections for his own mind. He had introduced himself to some tenants, whom he had never seen before; he had begun making acquaintance with cottages whose very existence, though on his own estate, had been hitherto unknown to him. This was aimed, and well aimed, at Fanny. It was pleasing to hear him speak so properly; here, he had been acting as he ought to do. To be the friend of the poor and oppressed! Nothing could be more grateful to her, and she was on the point of giving him an approving look when it was all frightened off,

line 7: society, without] **1814** society without // line 17: deserving—and] **1814** deserving, and // line 24: before; he] **1814** before, he

by his adding a something too pointed of his hoping soon to have an assistant, a friend, a guide in every plan of utility or charity for Everingham, a somebody that would make Everingham and all about it, a dearer object than it had ever been yet.

She turned away, and wished he would not say such things. She was willing to allow he might have more good qualities than she had been wont to suppose. She began to feel the possibility of his turning out well at last; but he was and must ever be completely unsuited to her, and ought not to think of her.

He perceived that enough had been said of Everingham, and that it would be as well to talk of something else, and turned to Mansfield. He could not have chosen better; that was a topic to bring back her attention and her looks almost instantly. It was a real indulgence to her to hear or to speak of Mansfield. Now so long divided from every body who knew the place, she felt it quite the voice of a friend when he mentioned it, and led the way to her fond exclamations in praise of its beauties and comforts, and by his honourable tribute to its inhabitants allowed her to gratify her own heart in the warmest eulogium, in speaking of her uncle as all that was clever and good, and her aunt as having the sweetest of all sweet tempers.

He had a great attachment to Mansfield himself; he said so; he looked forward with the hope of spending much, very much of his time there—always there, or in the neighbourhood. He particularly built upon a very happy summer and autumn there this year; he felt that it would be so; he depended upon it; a summer and autumn infinitely superior

line 16: her to] **1814** her, to

to the last. As animated, as diversified, as social—but with circumstances of superiority undescribable.

"Mansfield, Sotherton, Thornton Lacey," he continued, "what a society will be comprised in those houses! And at Michaelmas, perhaps, a fourth may be added, some small hunting-box[10] in the vicinity of every thing so dear—for as to any partnership in Thornton Lacey, as Edmund Bertram once good-humouredly proposed, I hope I foresee two objections, two fair, excellent, irresistible objections to that plan."

Fanny was doubly silenced here; though when the moment was passed, could regret that she had not forced herself into the acknowledged comprehension of one half of his meaning, and encouraged him to say something more of his sister and Edmund. It was a subject which she must learn to speak of, and the weakness that shrunk from it would soon be quite unpardonable.

When Mr. Price and his friend had seen all that they wished, or had time for, the others were ready to return; and in the course of their walk back, Mr. Crawford contrived a minute's privacy for telling Fanny that his only business in Portsmouth was to see her, that he was come down for a couple of days on her account and hers only, and because he could not endure a longer total separation. She was sorry, really sorry; and yet, in spite of this and the two or three other things which she wished he had not said, she thought him altogether improved since she had seen him; he was much more gentle, obliging, and attentive to other people's feelings than he had ever been at Mansfield; she had never seen him so agreeable—so *near* being agreeable; his behaviour to

line 6: hunting-box] **1814** hunting box // line 9: irresistible] **1814** irresistable // line 22: hers] **1814** her's // line 27: gentle, obliging,] **1814** gentle obliging,

her father could not offend, and there was something particularly kind and proper in the notice he took of Susan. He was decidedly improved. She wished the next day over, she wished he had come only for one day—but it was not so very bad as she would have expected; the pleasure of talking of Mansfield was so very great!

Before they parted, she had to thank him for another pleasure, and one of no trivial kind. Her father asked him to do them the honour of taking his mutton with them, and Fanny had time for only one thrill of horror, before he declared himself prevented by a prior engagement. He was engaged to dinner already both for that day and the next; he had met with some acquaintance at the Crown who would not be denied; he should have the honour, however, of waiting on them again on the morrow, &c. and so they parted— Fanny in a state of actual felicity from escaping so horrible an evil!

To have had him join their family dinner-party and see all their deficiencies would have been dreadful! Rebecca's cookery and Rebecca's waiting, and Betsey's eating at table without restraint, and pulling every thing about as she chose, were what Fanny herself was not yet enough inured to, for her often to make a tolerable meal. *She* was nice only from natural delicacy, but *he* had been brought up in a school of luxury and epicurism.[11]

line 12: next; he] **1814** next, he

Chapter 11

THE Prices were just setting off for church the next day when Mr. Crawford appeared again. He came—not to stop—but to join them; he was asked to go with them to the Garrison chapel,[1] which was exactly what he had intended, and they all walked thither together.

The family were now seen to advantage. Nature had given them no inconsiderable share of beauty, and every Sunday dressed them in their cleanest skins and best attire. Sunday always brought this comfort to Fanny, and on this Sunday she felt it more than ever. Her poor mother now did not look so very unworthy of being Lady Bertram's sister as she was but too apt to look. It often grieved her to the heart—to think of the contrast between them—to think that where nature had made so little difference, circumstances should have made so much, and that her mother, as handsome as Lady Bertram, and some years her junior, should have an appearance so much more worn and faded, so comfortless, so slatternly, so shabby. But Sunday made her a very creditable and tolerably cheerful looking Mrs. Price, coming abroad with a fine family of children, feeling a little respite of her weekly cares, and only discomposed if she saw her boys run into danger, or Rebecca pass by with a flower in her hat.

In chapel they were obliged to divide, but Mr. Crawford took care not to be divided from the female branch; and after

line 10: now did] **1814** now, did

chapel he still continued with them, and made one in the family party on the ramparts.

Mrs. Price took her weekly walk on the ramparts every fine Sunday throughout the year, always going directly after morning service and staying till dinner-time. It was her public place; there she met her acquaintance, heard a little news, talked over the badness of the Portsmouth servants, and wound up her spirits for the six days ensuing.

Thither they now went; Mr. Crawford most happy to consider the Miss Prices as his peculiar charge; and before they had been there long—somehow or other—there was no saying how—Fanny could not have believed it—but he was walking between them with an arm of each under his, and she did not know how to prevent or put an end to it. It made her uncomfortable for a time—but yet there were enjoyments in the day and in the view which would be felt.

The day was uncommonly lovely. It was really March; but it was April in its mild air, brisk soft wind, and bright sun, occasionally clouded for a minute; and every thing looked so beautiful under the influence of such a sky, the effects of the shadows pursuing each other, on the ships at Spithead and the island beyond, with the ever-varying hues of the sea now at high water, dancing in its glee and dashing against the ramparts with so fine a sound, produced altogether such a combination of charms for Fanny, as made her gradually almost careless of the circumstances under which she felt them. Nay, had she been without his arm, she would soon have known that she needed it, for she wanted strength for a two hours' saunter of this kind, coming as it generally did upon a week's previous inactivity. Fanny was

line 1: them, and] **1814** them and   //   line 5: dinner-time.] **1814** dinner time.

beginning to feel the effect of being debarred from her usual, regular exercise; she had lost ground as to health since her being in Portsmouth, and but for Mr. Crawford and the beauty of the weather, would soon have been knocked up now.

The loveliness of the day, and of the view, he felt like herself. They often stopt with the same sentiment and taste, leaning against the wall, some minutes, to look and admire; and considering he was not Edmund, Fanny could not but allow that he was sufficiently open to the charms of nature, and very well able to express his admiration. She had a few tender reveries now and then, which he could sometimes take advantage of, to look in her face without detection; and the result of these looks was, that though as bewitching as ever, her face was less blooming than it ought to be.—She *said* she was very well, and did not like to be supposed otherwise; but take it all in all, he was convinced that her present residence could not be comfortable, and, therefore, could not be salutary[2] for her, and he was growing anxious for her being again at Mansfield, where her own happiness, and his in seeing her, must be so much greater.

"You have been here a month, I think?" said he.

"No. Not quite a month.—It is only four weeks to-morrow since I left Mansfield."

"You are a most accurate and honest reckoner. I should call that a month."

"I did not arrive here till Tuesday evening."

"And it is to be a two months' visit, is not it?"

"Yes.—My uncle talked of two months. I suppose it will not be less."

"And how are you to be conveyed back again? Who comes for you?"

475

"I do not know. I have heard nothing about it yet from my aunt. Perhaps I may be to stay longer. It may not be convenient for me to be fetched exactly at the two months' end."

After a moment's reflection, Mr. Crawford replied, "I know Mansfield, I know its way, I know its faults towards *you*. I know the danger of your being so far forgotten, as to have your comforts give way to the imaginary convenience of any single being in the family. I am aware that you may be left here week after week, if Sir Thomas cannot settle every thing for coming himself, or sending your aunt's maid for you, without involving the slightest alteration of the arrangements which he may have laid down for the next quarter of a year. This will not do. Two months is an ample allowance, I should think six weeks quite enough.—I am considering your sister's health," said he, addressing himself to Susan, "which I think the confinement of Portsmouth unfavourable to. She requires constant air and exercise. When you know her as well as I do, I am sure you will agree that she does, and that she ought never to be long banished from the free air, and liberty of the country.—If, therefore, (turning again to Fanny) you find yourself growing unwell, and any difficulties arise about your returning to Mansfield— without waiting for the two months to be ended—*that* must not be regarded as of any consequence, if you feel yourself at all less strong, or comfortable than usual, and will only let my sister know it, give her only the slightest hint, she and I will immediately come down, and take you back to Mansfield. You know the ease, and the pleasure with which this would be done. You know all that would be felt on the occasion."

line 15: allowance, I] **1814** allowance. I

Fanny thanked him, but tried to laugh it off.

"I am perfectly serious,"—he replied,—"as you perfectly know.—And I hope you will not be cruelly concealing any tendency to indisposition.—Indeed, you shall *not*, it shall not be in your power, for so long only as you positively say, in every letter to Mary, 'I am well.'—and I know you cannot speak or write a falsehood,—so long only shall you be considered as well."

Fanny thanked him again, but was affected and distressed to a degree that made it impossible for her to say much, or even to be certain of what she ought to say.—This was towards the close of their walk. He attended them to the last, and left them only at the door of their own house, when he knew them to be going to dinner, and therefore pretended to be waited for elsewhere.

"I wish you were not so tired,"—said he, still detaining Fanny after all the others were in the house; "I wish I left you in stronger health.—Is there any thing I can do for you in town? I have half an idea of going into Norfolk again soon. I am not satisfied about Maddison.—I am sure he still means to impose on me if possible, and get a cousin of his own into a certain mill, which I design for somebody else.—I must come to an understanding with him. I must make him know that I will not be tricked on the south side of Everingham, any more than on the north, that I will be master of my own property. I was not explicit enough with him before.—The mischief such a man does on an estate, both as to the credit of his employer, and the welfare of the poor, is inconceivable. I have a great mind to go back into Norfolk directly, and put every thing at once on such a footing as cannot be afterwards swerved from.—Maddison is a clever fellow; I do not wish to

line 6: Mary, 'I] **1814** Mary 'I   //   line 16: tired,"—said] **1814** tired," said

displace him—provided he does not try to displace *me*;[3]—but it would be simple to be duped by a man who has no right of creditor to dupe me—and worse than simple to let him give me a hard-hearted, griping fellow for a tenant, instead of an honest man, to whom I have given half a promise already.— Would not it be worse than simple? Shall I go?—Do you advise it?"

"I advise!—you know very well what is right."

"Yes. When you give me your opinion, I always know what is right. Your judgment is my rule of right."

"Oh, no!—do not say so. We have all a better guide in ourselves,[4] if we would attend to it, than any other person can be. Good bye; I wish you a pleasant journey to-morrow."

"Is there nothing I can do for you in town?"

"Nothing, I am much obliged to you."

"Have you no message for anybody?"

"My love to your sister, if you please; and when you see my cousin—my cousin Edmund, I wish you would be so good as to say that—I suppose I shall soon hear from him."

"Certainly; and if he is lazy or negligent, I will write his excuses myself—"

He could say no more, for Fanny would be no longer detained. He pressed her hand, looked at her, and was gone. *He* went to while away the next three hours as he could, with his other acquaintance, till the best dinner that a capital inn afforded, was ready for their enjoyment, and *she* turned in to her more simple one immediately.

Their general fare bore a very different character; and could he have suspected how many privations, besides that of exercise, she endured in her father's house, he would have wondered that her looks were not much more affected than he

line 4: instead] **1814** in stead

found them. She was so little equal to Rebecca's puddings, and Rebecca's hashes,[5] brought to table as they all were, with such accompaniments of half-cleaned plates, and not half-cleaned knives and forks, that she was very often constrained to defer her heartiest meal, till she could send her brothers in the evening for biscuits and buns.[6] After being nursed up at Mansfield, it was too late in the day to be hardened at Portsmouth; and though Sir Thomas, had be known all, might have thought his niece in the most promising way of being starved, both mind and body, into a much juster value for Mr. Crawford's good company and good fortune, he would probably have feared to push his experiment farther, lest she might die under the cure.

Fanny was out of spirits all the rest of the day. Though tolerably secure of not seeing Mr. Crawford again, she could not help being low. It was parting with somebody of the nature of a friend; and though in one light glad to have him gone, it seemed as if she was now deserted by everybody; it was a sort of renewed separation from Mansfield; and she could not think of his returning to town, and being frequently with Mary and Edmund, without feelings so near akin to envy, as made her hate herself for having them.

Her dejection had no abatement from anything passing around her; a friend or two of her father's, as always happened if he was not with them, spent the long, long evening there; and from six o'clock to half past nine, there was little intermission of noise or grog. She was very low. The wonderful improvement which she still fancied in Mr. Crawford, was the nearest to administering comfort of anything within the current of her thoughts. Not considering in how different a circle she had been just seeing him, nor how much might be owing to contrast, she was quite persuaded of his being astonishingly more gentle, and regardful of others, than formerly.

And if in little things, must it not be so in great? So anxious for her health and comfort, so very feeling as he now expressed himself, and really seemed, might not it be fairly supposed, that he would not much longer persevere in a suit so distressing to her?

line 4: a suit so] **1814** a pursuit so

Chapter 12

IT was presumed that Mr. Crawford was travelling back to London, on the morrow, for nothing more was seen of him at Mr. Price's; and two days afterwards, it was a fact ascertained to Fanny by the following letter from his sister, opened and read by her, on another account, with the most anxious curiosity:—

"I have to inform you, my dearest Fanny, that Henry has been down to Portsmouth to see you; that he had a delightful walk with you to the Dock-yard last Saturday, and one still more to be dwelt on the next day, on the ramparts; when the balmy air, the sparkling sea, and your sweet looks and conversation were altogether in the most delicious harmony, and afforded sensations which are to raise ecstacy even in retrospect. This, as well as I understand, is to be the substance of my information. He makes me write, but I do not know what else is to be communicated, except this said visit to Portsmouth, and these two said walks, and his introduction to your family, especially to a fair sister of your's, a fine girl of fifteen,[1] who was of the party on the ramparts, taking her first lesson, I presume, in love. I have not time for writing much, but it would be out of place if I had, for this is to be a mere letter of business, penned for the purpose of conveying necessary information, which could not be delayed without risk of evil. My dear, dear Fanny, if I had you here, how I would talk to you!—You should listen to me till you were tired, and advise me till you were still tired more; but it is impossible to put an hundredth part of my great mind[2] on paper, so I will abstain altogether, and leave you to guess what you like. I have no news for you. You have politics of course; and it would be too bad to plague you with the names of people and parties, that fill up my time. I ought to have sent you an account of your cousin's first party, but I was lazy, and now it is too long ago; suffice it, that every thing was just as it ought to be, in a style that any of her connections must have been gratified to witness, and that her own dress and manners did her the greatest credit. My friend Mrs. Fraser is mad for such a house, and it would not make *me* miserable. I go to Lady Stornaway after Easter. She seems in high spirits, and very happy. I fancy Lord S. is very good-humoured and pleasant in his own family, and I do not think him so very ill-looking as I did, at least one sees many worse. He will not do by the side of your cousin Edmund. Of the last-mentioned hero, what shall I say? If I avoided his name entirely, it would look suspicious. I will say, then, that we have seen him two or three times, and that my friends here are very much struck with his gentleman-like appearance. Mrs. Fraser (no bad judge), declares she knows but three men in town who have so good a person, height, and air; and I must confess, when he dined here the other day, there were none to compare with him, and we were a party of sixteen. Luckily there is no distinction of dress now-a-days[3] to tell tales, but—but—but.

Your's, affectionately."

"I had almost forgot (it was Edmund's fault, he gets into my head more than does me good), one very material thing I had to say from Henry and myself, I mean about our taking

line 1: still tired more;] **1814** tired still more;   //   line 26: now-a-days] **1814** now a days

you back into Northamptonshire. My dear little creature, do not stay at Portsmouth to lose your pretty looks. Those vile sea-breezes are the ruin of beauty and health. My poor aunt always felt affected, if within ten miles of the sea, which the Admiral of course never believed, but I know it was so. I am at your service and Henry's, at an hour's notice. I should like the scheme, and we would make a little circuit, and shew you Everingham in our way, and perhaps you would not mind passing through London, and seeing the inside of St. George's, Hanover-Square.[4] Only keep your cousin Edmund from me at such a time, I should not like to be tempted. What a long letter!—one word more. Henry I find has some idea of going into Norfolk again upon some business that *you* approve, but this cannot possibly be permitted before the middle of next week, that is, he cannot any how be spared till after the 14th, for *we* have a party that evening. The value of a man like Henry on such an occasion, is what you can have no conception of; so you must take it upon my word, to be inestimable. He will see the Rushworths, which I own I am not sorry for—having a little curiosity—and so I think has he, though he will not acknowledge it."

This was a letter to be run through eagerly, to be read deliberately, to supply matter for much reflection, and to leave every thing in greater suspense than ever. The only certainty to be drawn from it was, that nothing decisive had yet taken place. Edmund had not yet spoken. How Miss Crawford really felt—how she meant to act, or might act without or against her meaning—whether his importance to her were quite what it had been before the last separation—whether if lessened it were likely to lessen more, or to recover itself, were subjects for endless conjecture, and to be thought of

line 28: were quite] **1814** was quite

on that day and many days to come, without producing any conclusion. The idea that returned the oftenest, was that Miss Crawford, after proving herself cooled and staggered[5] by a return to London habits, would yet prove herself in the end too much attached to him, to give him up. She would try to be more ambitious than her heart would allow. She would hesitate, she would teaze, she would condition, she would require a great deal, but she would finally accept. This was Fanny's most frequent expectation. A house in town!— *that* she thought must be impossible. Yet there was no saying what Miss Crawford might not ask. The prospect for her cousin grew worse and worse. The woman who could speak of him, and speak only of his appearance!—What an unworthy attachment!—To be deriving support from the commendations of Mrs. Fraser! *She* who had known him intimately half a year! Fanny was ashamed of her. Those parts of the letter which related only to Mr. Crawford and herself, touched her in comparison, slightly. Whether Mr. Crawford went into Norfolk before or after the 14th, was certainly no concern of her's, though, every thing considered, she thought he *would* go without delay. That Miss Crawford should endeavour to secure a meeting between him and Mrs. Rushworth, was all in her worst line of conduct, and grossly unkind and ill-judged; but she hoped *he* would not be actuated by any such degrading curiosity. He acknowledged no such inducement, and his sister ought to have given him credit for better feelings than her own.

She was yet more impatient for another letter from town after receiving this, than she had been before; and for a few days, was so unsettled by it altogether, by what had come, and what might come, that her usual readings and conversation

line 9: expectations. [**1814** expectation. // line 14: attachment!—To] **1814** attachment! To

with Susan were much suspended. She could not command her attention as she wished. If Mr. Crawford remembered her message to her cousin, she thought it very likely, *most* likely, that he would write to her at all events; it would be most consistent with his usual kindness, and till she got rid of this idea, till it gradually wore off, by no letters appearing in the course of three or four days more, she was in a most restless, anxious state.

At length, a something like composure succeeded. Suspense must be submitted to, and must not be allowed to wear her out, and make her useless. Time did something, her own exertions something more, and she resumed her attentions to Susan, and again awakened the same interest in them.

Susan was growing very fond of her, and though without any of the early delight in books, which had been so strong in Fanny, with a disposition much less inclined to sedentary pursuits, or to information for information's sake, she had so strong a desire of not *appearing* ignorant, as with a good clear understanding, made her a most attentive, profitable, thankful pupil. Fanny was her oracle. Fanny's explanations and remarks were a most important addition to every essay, or every chapter of history.[6] What Fanny told her of former times, dwelt more on her mind than the pages of Goldsmith; and she paid her sister the compliment of preferring her style to that of any printed author. The early habit of reading was wanting.

Their conversations, however, were not always on subjects so high as history or morals. Others had their hour; and of lesser matters, none returned so often, or remained so long between them, as Mansfield Park, a description of the people, the manners, the amusements, the ways of Mansfield Park. Susan, who had an innate taste for the genteel and well-appointed, was eager to hear, and Fanny could not but indulge herself in dwelling on so beloved a theme. She hoped it was not wrong; though after a time, Susan's very great admiration of every thing said or done in her uncle's house, and earnest longing to go into Northamptonshire, seemed almost to blame her for exciting feelings which could not be gratified.

Poor Susan was very little better fitted for home than her elder sister; and as Fanny grew thoroughly to understand this, she began to feel that when her own release from Portsmouth came, her happiness would have a material drawback in leaving Susan behind. That a girl so capable of being made every thing good, should be left in such hands, distressed her more and more. Were *she* likely to have a home to invite her to, what a blessing it would be!—And had it been possible for her to return Mr. Crawford's regard, the probability of his being very far from objecting to such a measure, would have been the greatest increase of all her own comforts. She thought he was really good-tempered, and could fancy his entering into a plan of that sort, most pleasantly.

line 19: sort, most] **1814** sort most

Chapter 13

SEVEN weeks of the two months were very nearly gone, when the one letter, the letter from Edmund so long expected, was put into Fanny's hands. As she opened and saw its length she prepared herself for a minute detail of happiness and a profusion of love and praise towards the fortunate creature, who was now mistress of his fate. These were the contents.

"*Mansfield Park.*

"My dear Fanny,

"Excuse me that I have not written before, Crawford told me that you were wishing to hear from me, but I found it impossible to write from London, and persuaded myself that you would understand my silence.—Could I have sent a few happy lines, they should not have been wanting, but nothing of that nature was ever in my power.—I am returned to Mansfield in a less assured state than when I left it. My hopes are much weaker.—You are probably aware of this already.—So very fond of you as Miss Crawford is, it is most natural that she should tell you enough of her own feelings, to furnish a tolerable guess at mine.—I will not be prevented, however, from making my own communication. Our confidences in you need not clash.—I ask no questions.—There is something soothing in the idea, that we have the same friend, and that whatever unhappy differences of opinion may exist

line 9: before, Crawford] **1814** before. Crawford

between us, we are united in our love of you.—It will be a comfort to me to tell you how things now are, and what are my present plans, if plans I can be said to have.—I have been returned since Saturday. I was three weeks in London, and saw her (for London) very often. I had every attention from the Frasers that could be reasonably expected. I dare say I was *not* reasonable in carrying with me hopes of an intercourse at all like that of Mansfield. It was her manner, however, rather than any unfrequency of meeting. Had she been different when I did see her, I should have made no complaint, but from the very first she was altered; my first reception was so unlike what I had hoped, that I had almost resolved on leaving London again directly.—I need not particularize. You know the weak side of her character, and may imagine the sentiments and expressions which were torturing me. She was in high spirits, and surrounded by those who were giving all the support of their own bad sense to her too lively mind. I do not like Mrs. Fraser. She is a cold-hearted, vain woman, who has married entirely from convenience, and though evidently unhappy in her marriage, places her disappointment, not to faults of judgement or temper, or disproportion of age, but to her being after all, less affluent than many of her acquaintance, especially than her sister, Lady Stornaway, and is the determined supporter of every thing mercenary and ambitious, provided it be only mercenary and ambitious enough. I look upon her intimacy with those two sisters, as the greatest misfortune of her life and mine. They have been leading her astray for years. Could she be detached from them!—and sometimes I do not despair of it, for the affection appears to me principally on their side. They are very fond of her; but I am sure she does not love them as she loves you. When I

line 13: particularize.] **1814** particularise.   //   line 28: them!—and] **1814** them, and

think of her great attachment to you, indeed, and the whole of her judicious, upright conduct as a sister, she appears a very different creature, capable of every thing noble, and I am ready to blame myself for a too harsh construction of a playful manner. I cannot give her up, Fanny. She is the only woman in the world whom I could ever think of as a wife. If I did not believe that she had some regard for me, of course I should not say this, but I do believe it. I am convinced, that she is not without a decided preference. I have no jealousy of any individual. It is the influence of the fashionable world altogether that I am jealous of. It is the habits of wealth that I fear. Her ideas are not higher than her own fortune may warrant, but they are beyond what our incomes united could authorise. There is comfort, however, even here. I could better bear to lose her, because not rich enough, than because of my profession. That would only prove her affection not equal to sacrifices, which, in fact, I am scarcely justified in asking; and if I am refused, *that*, I think, will be the honest motive. Her prejudices, I trust, are not so strong as they were. You have my thoughts exactly as they arise, my dear Fanny; perhaps they are some times contradictory, but it will not be a less faithful picture of my mind. Having once begun, it is a pleasure to me to tell you all I feel. I cannot give her up. Connected, as we already are, and, I hope, are to be, to give up Mary Crawford, would be to give up the society of some of those most dear to me, to banish myself from the very houses and friends whom, under any other distress, I should turn to for consolation. The loss of Mary I must consider as comprehending the loss of Crawford and of Fanny. Were it a decided thing, an actual refusal, I hope I should know how to bear it, and how to endeavour to weaken her hold on my heart—and in the course of a few years—but I am writing nonsense—were I refused, I must bear it; and till I am, I can never cease to try for her. This is the truth. The only question is *how*? What may be the likeliest means? I have sometimes thought of going to London again after Easter, and sometimes resolved on doing nothing till she returns to Mansfield. Even now, she speaks with pleasure of being in Mansfield in June; but June is at a great distance, and I believe I shall write to her. I have nearly determined on explaining myself by letter. To be at an early certainty is a material object. My present state is miserably irksome. Considering every thing, I think a letter will be decidedly the best method of explanation. I shall be able to write much that I could not say, and shall be giving her time for reflection before she resolves on her answer, and I am less afraid of the result of reflection than of an immediate hasty impulse; I think I am. My greatest danger would lie in her consulting Mrs. Fraser, and I at a distance, unable to help my own cause. A letter exposes to all the evil of consultation, and where the mind is any thing short of perfect decision, an adviser may, in an unlucky moment, lead it to do what it may afterwards regret. I must think this matter over a little. This long letter, full of my own concerns alone, will be enough to tire even the friendship of a Fanny. The last time I saw Crawford was at Mrs. Fraser's party. I am more and more satisfied with all that I see and hear of him. There is not a shadow of wavering. He thoroughly knows his own mind, and acts up to his resolutions—an inestimable quality. I could not see him, and my eldest sister in the same room, without recollecting what you once told me, and I acknowledge that they did not meet as friends. There was marked coolness on her side. They scarcely spoke. I saw him draw back surprised, and I was sorry that Mrs. Rushworth should resent any former supposed slight to Miss Bertram. You will

line 28: marked coolness] **1814** marked coldness

wish to hear my opinion of Maria's degree of comfort as a wife. There is no appearance of unhappiness. I hope they get on pretty well together. I dined twice in Wimpole Street, and might have been there oftener, but it is mortifying to be with Rushworth as a brother. Julia seems to enjoy London exceedingly. I had little enjoyment there—but have less here. We are not a lively party. You are very much wanted. I miss you more than I can express. My mother desires her best love, and hopes to hear from you soon. She talks of you almost every hour, and I am sorry to find how many weeks more she is likely to be without you. My Father means to fetch you himself, but it will not be till after Easter, when he has business in town. You are happy at Portsmouth, I hope, but this must not be a yearly visit. I want you at home, that I may have your opinion about Thornton Lacey. I have little heart for extensive improvements till I know that it will ever have a mistress. I think I shall certainly write. It is quite settled that the Grants go to Bath; they leave Mansfield on Monday. I am glad of it. I am not comfortable enough to be fit for any body; but your aunt seems to feel out of luck that such an article of Mansfield news should fall to my pen instead of her's. Your's ever, my dearest Fanny."

"I never will—no, I certainly never will wish for a letter again," was Fanny's secret declaration, as she finished this. "What do they bring but disappointment and sorrow?—Not till after Easter!—How shall I bear it?—And my poor aunt talking of me every hour!"

Fanny checked the tendency of these thoughts as well as she could, but she was within half a minute of starting the idea, that Sir Thomas was quite unkind, both to her aunt and to herself.—As for the main subject of the letter—there was nothing in that to soothe irritation. She was almost vexed into displeasure, and anger, against Edmund. "There is no good in this delay," said she. "Why is not it settled?—He is blinded, and nothing will open his eyes, nothing can, after having had truths before him so long in vain.—He will marry her, and be poor and miserable. God grant that her influence do not make him cease to be respectable!"—She looked over the letter again. "'So very fond of me!' 'tis nonsense all. She loves nobody but herself and her brother. Her friends leading her astray for years![1] She is quite as likely to have led *them* astray. They have all, perhaps, been corrupting one another; but if they are so much fonder of her than she is of them, she is the less likely to have been hurt, except by their flattery. 'The only woman in the world, whom he could ever think of as a wife.' I firmly believe it. It is an attachment to govern his whole life. Accepted or refused, his heart is wedded to her for ever. 'The loss of Mary, I must consider as comprehending the loss of Crawford and Fanny.' Edmund, you do not know *me*. The families would never be connected, if you did not connect them! Oh! write, write. Finish it at once. Let there be an end of this suspense. Fix, commit, condemn yourself."

Such sensations, however, were too near a kin to resentment to be long guiding Fanny's soliloquies. She was soon more softened and sorrowful.—His warm regard, his kind expressions, his confidential treatment touched her strongly. He was only too good to every body.—It was a letter, in short, which she would not but have had for the world, and which could never be valued enough. This was the end of it.

Every body at all addicted to letter writing, without having much to say, which will include a large proportion of the

line 2: settled?" [**1814** settled?   //   line 12: flattery. 'The] **1814** flattery.—'The   //   line 16: ever. 'The] **1814** ever.—The   //   line 17: and Fanny.'] **1814** and Fanny.—   //   line 19: connect them!] **1814** connect them.   //   line 23: sorrowful.] **1814** sorrowfu.

female world at least, must feel with Lady Bertram, that she was out of luck in having such a capital piece of Mansfield news, as the certainty of the Grants going to Bath, occur at a time when she could make no advantage of it, and will admit that it must have been very mortifying to her to see it fall to the share of her thankless son, and treated as concisely as possible at the end of a long letter, instead of having it to spread over the largest part of a page of her own.—For though Lady Bertram rather shone in the epistolary line, having early in her marriage, from the want of other employment, and the circumstance of Sir Thomas's being in Parliament, got into the way of making and keeping correspondents,[2] and formed for herself a very creditable, common-place, amplifying style, so that a very little matter was enough for her; she could not do entirely without any; she must have something to write about, even to her niece, and being so soon to lose all the benefit of Dr. Grant's gouty symptoms and Mrs. Grant's morning calls, it was very hard upon her to be deprived of one of the last epistolary uses she could put them to.

There was a rich amends, however, preparing for her. Lady Bertram's hour of good luck came. Within a few days from the receipt of Edmund's letter, Fanny had one from her aunt, beginning thus:—

"My dear Fanny,
"I take up my pen to communicate some very alarming intelligence, which I make no doubt will give you much concern."

This was a great deal better than to have to take up the pen to acquaint her with all the particulars of the Grants' intended journey, for the present intelligence was of a nature to

line 29: Grants' intended] **1814** Grant's intended

promise occupation for the pen for many days to come, being no less than the dangerous illness of her eldest son, of which they had received notice by express,[3] a few hours before.

Tom had gone from London with a party of young men to Newmarket,[4] where a neglected fall, and a good deal of drinking, had brought on a fever; and when the party broke up, being unable to move, had been left by himself at the house of one of these young men, to the comforts of sickness and solitude, and the attendance only of servants. Instead of being soon well enough to follow his friends, as he had then hoped, his disorder increased considerably, and it was not long before he thought so ill of himself, as to be as ready as his physician[5] to have a letter dispatched to Mansfield.

"This distressing intelligence, as you may suppose," observed her Ladyship, after giving the substance of it, "has agitated us exceedingly, and we cannot prevent ourselves from being greatly alarmed, and apprehensive for the poor invalid, whose state Sir Thomas fears may be very critical; and Edmund kindly proposes attending his brother immediately, but I am happy to add, that Sir Thomas will not leave me on this distressing occasion, as it would be too trying for me. We shall greatly miss Edmund in our small circle, but I trust and hope he will find the poor invalid in a less alarming state than might be apprehended, and that he will be able to bring him to Mansfield shortly, which Sir Thomas proposes should be done, and thinks best on every account, and I flatter myself, the poor sufferer will soon be able to bear the removal without material inconvenience or injury. As I have little doubt of your feeling for us, my dear Fanny, under these distressing circumstances, I will write again very soon."

line 21: as it would be] **1814** as is would be

Fanny's feelings on the occasion were indeed considerably more warm and genuine than her aunt's style of writing. She felt truly for them all. Tom dangerously ill, Edmund gone to attend him, and the sadly small party remaining at Mansfield, were cares to shut out every other care, or almost every other. She could just find selfishness enough to wonder whether Edmund *had* written to Miss Crawford before this summons came, but no sentiment dwelt long with her, that was not purely affectionate and disinterestedly anxious. Her aunt did not neglect her; she wrote again and again; they were receiving frequent accounts from Edmund, and these accounts were as regularly transmitted to Fanny, in the same diffuse style, and the same medley of trusts, hopes, and fears, all following and producing each other at hap-hazard. It was a sort of playing at being frightened. The sufferings which Lady Bertram did not see, had little power over her fancy; and she wrote very comfortably about agitation and anxiety, and poor invalids, till Tom was actually conveyed to Mansfield, and her own eyes had beheld his altered appearance. Then, a letter which she had been previously preparing for Fanny, was finished in a different style, in the language of real feeling and alarm; then, she wrote as she might have spoken. "He is just come, my dear Fanny, and is taken up stairs; and I am so shocked to see him, that I do not know what to do. I am sure he has been very ill. Poor Tom, I am quite grieved for him, and very much frightened, and so is Sir Thomas; and how glad I should be, if you were here to comfort me. But Sir Thomas hopes he will be better to-morrow, and says we must consider his journey."

The real solicitude now awakened in the maternal bosom was not soon over. Tom's extreme impatience to be removed to

line 10: neglec [**1814** neglect

Mansfield, and experience those comforts of home and family which had been little thought of in uninterrupted health, had probably induced his being conveyed thither too early, as a return of fever came on, and for a week he was in a more alarming state than ever. They were all very seriously frightened. Lady Bertram wrote her daily terrors to her niece, who might now be said to live upon letters, and pass all her time between suffering from that of to-day, and looking forward to to-morrow's. Without any particular affection for her eldest cousin, her tenderness of heart made her feel that she could not spare him; and the purity of her principles added yet a keener solicitude,[6] when she considered how little useful, how little self-denying his life had (apparently) been.

Susan was her only companion and listener on this, as on more common occasions. Susan was always ready to hear and to sympathize. Nobody else could be interested in so remote an evil as illness, in a family above an hundred miles off—not even Mrs. Price, beyond a brief question or two if she saw her daughter with a letter in her hand, and now and then the quiet observation of "My poor sister Bertram must be in a great deal of trouble."

So long divided, and so differently situated, the ties of blood were little more than nothing. An attachment, originally as tranquil as their tempers, was now become a mere name. Mrs. Price did quite as much for Lady Bertram, as Lady Bertram would have done for Mrs. Price. Three or four Prices might have been swept away, any or all, except Fanny and William, and Lady Bertram would have thought little about it; or perhaps might have caught from Mrs. Norris's lips the cant[7] of its being a very happy thing, and a great blessing to their poor dear sister Price to have them so well provided for.

Chapter 14

AT about the week's end from his return to Mansfield, Tom's immediate danger was over, and he was so far pronounced safe, as to make his mother perfectly easy; for being now used to the sight of him in his suffering, helpless state, and hearing only the best, and never thinking beyond what she heard, with no disposition for alarm, and no aptitude at a hint, Lady Bertram was the happiest subject in the world for a little medical imposition. The fever was subdued; the fever had been his complaint, of course he would soon be well again; Lady Bertram could think nothing less, and Fanny shared her aunt's security, till she received a few lines from Edmund, written purposely to give her a clearer idea of his brother's situation, and acquaint her with the apprehensions which he and his father had imbibed from the physician, with respect to some strong hectic[1] symptoms, which seemed to seize the frame on the departure of the fever. They judged it best that Lady Bertram should not be harassed by alarms which, it was to be hoped, would prove unfounded; but there was no reason why Fanny should not know the truth. They were apprehensive for his lungs.[2]

A very few lines from Edmund shewed her the patient and the sick room in a juster and stronger light than all Lady Bertram's sheets of paper could do. There was hardly any one in the house who might not have described, from personal observation, better than herself; not one who was not more useful at times to her son. She could do nothing but glide in quietly and look at him; but, when able to talk or be talked to, or read to, Edmund was the companion he preferred. His aunt worried him by her cares, and Sir Thomas knew not how to bring down his conversation or his voice to the level of irritation and feebleness. Edmund was all in all. Fanny would certainly believe him so at least, and must find that her estimation of him was higher than ever when he appeared as the attendant, supporter, cheerer of a suffering brother. There was not only the debility of recent illness to assist; there was also, as she now learnt, nerves much affected, spirits much depressed to calm and raise; and her own imagination added that there must be a mind to be properly guided.

The family were not consumptive, and she was more inclined to hope than fear for her cousin—except when she thought of Miss Crawford—but Miss Crawford gave her the idea of being the child of good luck, and to her selfishness and vanity it would be good luck to have Edmund the only son.

Even in the sick chamber, the fortunate Mary was not forgotten. Edmund's letter had this postscript. "On the subject of my last, I had actually begun a letter when called away by Tom's illness, but I have now changed my mind, and fear to trust the influence of friends. When Tom is better, I shall go."

Such was the state of Mansfield, and so it continued, with scarcely any change till Easter. A line occasionally added by Edmund to his mother's letter was enough for Fanny's information. Tom's amendment was alarmingly slow.

Easter came—particularly late this year,[3] as Fanny had most sorrowfully considered, on first learning that she had no chance of leaving Portsmouth till after it. It came, and she had yet heard nothing of her return—nothing even of the going to London, which was to precede her return. Her aunt often expressed a wish for her, but there was no notice, no message from the uncle on whom all depended. She supposed he could not yet leave his son, but it was a cruel, a terrible delay to her. The end of April was coming on; it would soon be almost three months instead of two that she had been absent from them all, and that her days had been passing in a state of penance,[4] which she loved them too well to hope they would thoroughly understand;—and who could yet say when there might be leisure to think of, or fetch her?

Her eagerness, her impatience, her longings to be with them, were such as to bring a line or two of Cowper's Tirocinium for ever before her.—"With what intense desire she wants her home,"[5] was continually on her tongue, as the truest description of a yearning which she could not suppose any school-boy's bosom to feel more keenly.

When she had been coming to Portsmouth, she had loved to call it her home, had been fond of saying that she was going home; the word had been very dear to her; and so it still was, but it must be applied to Mansfield. *That* was now the home. Portsmouth was Portsmouth; Mansfield was home. They had been long so arranged in the indulgence of her secret meditations; and nothing was more consolatory to her than to find her aunt using the same language.—"I cannot but say, I much regret your being from home at this distressing time, so very trying to my spirits.—I trust and hope, and sincerely wish you may never be absent from home so long again"—were most delightful sentences to her. Still, however, it was her private regale.[6]—Delicacy to her parents made her careful not to betray such a preference of her uncle's house: it was always, "when I go back into Northamptonshire, or when I return to Mansfield, I shall do so and so."—For a

line 12: her.—"With] **1814** her. "With   //   line 30: "it was always,[**1814** it was always,

great while it was so; but at last the longing grew stronger, it overthrew caution, and she found herself talking of what she should do when she went home, before she was aware.—She reproached herself, coloured and looked fearfully towards her Father and Mother. She need not have been uneasy. There was no sign of displeasure, or even of hearing her. They were perfectly free from any jealousy of Mansfield. She was as welcome to wish herself there, as to be there.

It was sad to Fanny to lose all the pleasures of spring. She had not known before what pleasures she *had* to lose in passing March and April in a town. She had not known before, how much the beginnings and progress of vegetation had delighted her.—What animation both of body and mind, she had derived from watching the advance of that season which cannot, in spite of its capriciousness, be unlovely, and seeing its increasing beauties, from the earliest flowers, in the warmest divisions of her aunt's garden,[7] to the opening of leaves of her uncle's plantations, and the glory of his woods.[8]—To be losing such pleasures was no trifle; to be losing them, because she was in the midst of closeness and noise, to have confinement, bad air, bad smells,[9] substituted for liberty, freshness, fragrance, and verdure, was infinitely worse;—but even these incitements to regret, were feeble, compared with what arose from the conviction of being missed, by her best friends, and the longing to be useful to those who were wanting her!

Could she have been at home, she might have been of service to every creature in the house. She felt that she must have been of use to all. To all, she must have saved some trouble of head or hand; and were it only in supporting the spirits of her aunt Bertram, keeping her from the evil of solitude, or the still greater evil of a restless, officious companion, too apt to be heightening danger in order to enhance her own importance, her being there would have been a general good. She loved to fancy how she could have read to her aunt, how she could have talked to her, and tried at once to make her feel the blessing of what was, and prepare her mind for what might be; and how many walks up and down stairs she might have saved her, and how many messages she might have carried.

It astonished her that Tom's sisters could be satisfied with remaining in London at such a time—through an illness, which had now, under different degrees of danger, lasted several weeks. *They* might return to Mansfield when they chose; travelling could be no difficulty to *them*, and she could not comprehend how both could still keep away. If Mrs. Rushworth could imagine any interfering obligations, Julia was certainly able to quit London whenever she chose.— It appeared from one of her aunt's letters, that Julia had offered to return if wanted—but this was all.—It was evident that she would rather remain where she was.

Fanny was disposed to think the influence of London very much at war with all respectable attachments. She saw the proof of it in Miss Crawford, as well as in her cousins; *her* attachment to Edmund had been respectable, the most respectable part of her character, her friendship for herself, had at least been blameless. Where was either sentiment now? It was so long since Fanny had had any letter from her, that she had some reason to think lightly of the friendship which had been so dwelt on.—It was weeks since she had heard any thing of Miss Crawford or of her other connections in town, except through Mansfield, and she was beginning to suppose that she might never know whether Mr. Crawford had gone into Norfolk again or not, till they met, and might never hear

line 9: illness, which] **1814** illness which   //   line 23: friendship for herself,] **1814** friendship for her herself,

from his sister any more this spring, when the following letter was received to revive old, and create some new sensations.

"Forgive me, my dear Fanny, as soon as you can, for my long silence, and behave as if you could forgive me directly. This is my modest request and expectation, for you are so good, that I depend upon being treated better than I deserve—and I write now to beg an immediate answer. I want to know the state of things at Mansfield Park, and you, no doubt, are perfectly able to give it. One should be a brute not to feel for the distress they are in—and from what I hear, poor Mr. Bertram has a bad chance of ultimate recovery. I thought little of his illness at first. I looked upon him as the sort of person to be made a fuss with, and to make a fuss himself in any trifling disorder, and was chiefly concerned for those who had to nurse him; but now it is confidently asserted that he is really in a decline, that the symptoms are most alarming, and that part of the family, at least, are aware of it. If it be so, I am sure you must be included in that part, that discerning part, and therefore intreat you to let me know how far I have been rightly informed. I need not say how rejoiced I shall be to hear there has been any mistake, but the report is so prevalent, that I confess I cannot help trembling. To have such a fine young man cut off in the flower of his days,[10] is most melancholy. Poor Sir Thomas will feel it dreadfully. I really am quite agitated on the subject. Fanny, Fanny, I see you smile, and look cunning, but upon my honour, I never bribed a physician in my life. Poor young man!—If he is to die, there will be *two* poor young men less in the world; and with a fearless face and bold voice would I say to any one, that wealth and consequence could fall into no hands more deserving of them. It was a foolish precipitation last Christmas, but the evil of a few days may be blotted out in part. Varnish and gilding hide many stains. It will be but the loss of the Esquire after his name. With real affection, Fanny, like mine, more might be overlooked. Write to me by return of post, judge of my anxiety, and do not trifle with it. Tell me the real truth, as you have it from the fountain head. And now, do not trouble yourself to be ashamed of either my feelings or your own. Believe me, they are not only natural, they are philanthropic and virtuous. I put it to your conscience, whether 'Sir Edmund' would not do more good with all the Bertram property, than any other possible 'Sir.' Had the Grants been at home, I would not have troubled you, but you are now the only one I can apply to for the truth, his sisters not being within my reach. Mrs. R. has been spending the Easter with the Aylmers at Twickenham (as to be sure you know), and is not yet returned; and Julia is with the cousins, who live near Bedford Square;[11] but I forgot their name and street. Could I immediately apply to either, however, I should still prefer you, because it strikes me, that they have all along been so unwilling to have their own amusements cut up, as to shut their eyes to the truth. I suppose, Mrs. R.'s Easter holidays will not last much longer; no doubt they are thorough holidays to her. The Aylmers are pleasant people; and her husband away, she can have nothing but enjoyment. I give her credit for promoting his going dutifully down to Bath, to fetch his mother; but how will she and the dowager agree in one house? Henry is not at hand, so I have nothing to say from him. Do not you think Edmund would have been in town again long ago, but for this illness?—Yours ever, Mary."

"I had actually began folding my letter, when Henry walked in; but he brings no intelligence to prevent my sending it. Mrs. R. knows a decline is apprehended; he saw her this

line 16: Bedford Square;] Bedford-Square; // line 28: Yours ever,] **1814** Your's ever,

morning, she returns to Wimpole Street to-day, the old lady is come. Now do not make yourself uneasy with any queer fancies, because he has been spending a few days at Richmond.[12] He does it every spring. Be assured, he cares for nobody but you. At this very moment, he is wild to see you, and occupied only in contriving the means for doing so, and for making his pleasure conduce to yours. In proof, he repeats, and more eagerly, what he said at Portsmouth, about our conveying you home, and I join him in it with all my soul. Dear Fanny, write directly, and tell us to come. It will do us all good. He and I can go to the Parsonage, you know, and be no trouble to our friends at Mansfield Park. It would really be gratifying to see them all again, and a little addition of society might be of infinite use to them; and, as to yourself, you must feel yourself to be so wanted there, that you cannot in conscience (conscientious as you are,) keep away, when you have the means of returning. I have not time or patience to give half Henry's messages; be satisfied, that the spirit of each and every one is unalterable affection."

Fanny's disgust at the greater part of this letter, with her extreme reluctance to bring the writer of it and her cousin Edmund together, would have made her (as she felt), incapable of judging impartially whether the concluding offer might be accepted or not. To herself, individually, it was most tempting. To be finding herself, perhaps, within three days, transported to Mansfield, was an image of the greatest felicity—but it would have been a material drawback, to be owing such felicity to persons in whose feelings and conduct, at the present moment, she saw so much to condemn; the sister's feelings—the brother's conduct—*her* cold-hearted

line 1: Wimpole Street] **1814** Wimpole-Street // line 7: yours.] **1814** your's. // line 14: and, as] **1814** and as // line 16: are,)] **1814** are),

ambition—*his* thoughtless vanity. To have him still the acquaintance, the flirt, perhaps, of Mrs. Rushworth!—She was mortified. She had thought better of him. Happily, however, she was not left to weigh and decide between opposite inclinations and doubtful notions of right; there was no occasion to determine, whether she ought to keep Edmund and Mary asunder or not. She had a rule to apply to, which settled every thing. Her awe of her uncle, and her dread of taking a liberty with him, made it instantly plain to her, what she had to do. She must absolutely decline the proposal. If he wanted, he would send for her; and even to offer an early return, was a presumption which hardly any thing would have seemed to justify. She thanked Miss Crawford, but gave a decided negative.—"Her uncle, she understood, meant to fetch her; and as her cousin's illness had continued so many weeks without her being thought at all necessary, she must suppose her return would be unwelcome at present, and that she should be felt an incumbrance."

Her representation of her cousin's state at this time, was exactly according to her own belief of it, and such as she supposed would convey to the sanguine mind of her correspondent, the hope of every thing she was wishing for. Edmund would be forgiven for being a clergyman, it seemed, under certain conditions of wealth; and this she suspected, was all the conquest of prejudice, which he was so ready to congratulate himself upon. She had only learnt to think nothing of consequence but money.

line 12: any thing] **1814** anything //   line 19: time,] **1814** tine, //   line 24: this she] **1814** this, she

Chapter 15

As Fanny could not doubt that her answer was conveying a real disappointment, she was rather in expectation, from her knowledge of Miss Crawford's temper, of being urged again; and though no second letter arrived for the space of a week, she had still the same feeling when it did come.

On receiving it, she could instantly decide on its containing little writing, and was persuaded of its having the air of a letter of haste and business. Its object was unquestionable; and two moments were enough to start the probability of its being merely to give her notice that they should be in Portsmouth that very day, and to throw her into all the agitation of doubting what she ought to do in such a case. If two moments, however, can surround with difficulties, a third can disperse them; and before she had opened the letter, the possibility of Mr. and Miss Crawford's having applied to her uncle and obtained his permission, was giving her ease. This was the letter.

"A most scandalous, ill-natured rumour has just reached me, and I write, dear Fanny, to warn you against giving the least credit to it, should it spread into the country. Depend upon it there is some mistake, and that a day or two will clear it up—at any rate, that Henry is blameless, and in spite of a moment's *etourderie*[1] thinks of nobody but you. Say not a word of it—hear nothing, surmise nothing, whisper nothing, till I write again. I am sure it will be all hushed up, and nothing proved but Rushworth's folly. If they are gone, I would lay my life they are only gone to Mansfield Park, and Julia with them. But why would not you let us come for you? I wish you may not repent it.

"Yours, &c."

Fanny stood aghast. As no scandalous, ill-natured rumour had reached her, it was impossible for her to understand much of this strange letter. She could only perceive that it must relate to Wimpole Street and Mr. Crawford, and only conjecture that something very imprudent had just occurred in that quarter to draw the notice of the world, and to excite her jealousy, in Miss Crawford's apprehension, if she heard it. Miss Crawford need not be alarmed for her. She was only sorry for the parties concerned and for Mansfield, if the report should spread so far; but she hoped it might not. If the Rushworths were gone themselves to Mansfield, as was to be inferred from what Miss Crawford said, it was not likely that any thing unpleasant should have preceded them, or at least should make any impression.

As to Mr. Crawford, she hoped it might give him a knowledge of his own disposition, convince him that he was not capable of being steadily attached to any one woman in the world, and shame him from persisting any longer in addressing herself.

It was very strange! She had begun to think he really loved her, and to fancy his affection for her something more than common—and his sister still said that he cared for nobody else. Yet there must have been some marked display of attentions to her cousin, there must have been some strong indiscretion, since her correspondent was not of a sort to regard a slight one.

line 5: "Yours,] **1814** "Your's,   //   line 18: any thing] **1814** anything

Very uncomfortable she was and must continue till she heard from Miss Crawford again. It was impossible to banish the letter from her thoughts, and she could not relieve herself by speaking of it to any human being. Miss Crawford need not have urged secrecy with so much warmth, she might have trusted to her sense of what was due to her cousin.

The next day came and brought no second letter. Fanny was disappointed. She could still think of little else all the morning; but when her father came back in the afternoon with the daily newspaper as usual, she was so far from expecting any elucidation through such a channel, that the subject was for a moment out of her head.

She was deep in other musing. The remembrance of her first evening in that room, of her father and his newspaper came across her. No candle was *now* wanted.[2] The sun was yet an hour and half above the horizon. She felt that she had, indeed, been three months there; and the sun's rays falling strongly into the parlour, instead of cheering, made her still more melancholy; for sun shine appeared to her a totally different thing in a town and in the country. Here, its power was only a glare, a stifling, sickly glare, serving but to bring forward stains and dirt that might otherwise have slept. There was neither health nor gaiety in sun-shine in a town. She sat in a blaze of oppressive heat, in a cloud of moving dust; and her eyes could only wander from the walls marked by her father's head, to the table cut and knotched by her brothers, where stood the tea-board never thoroughly cleaned, the cups and saucers wiped in streaks, the milk a mixture of motes floating in thin blue, and the bread and butter growing every minute more greasy than even Rebecca's hands had first produced it. Her father read his newspaper, and her mother lamented over the ragged carpet as usual, while the tea was in preparation—and wished Rebecca would mend it; and Fanny was first roused by his calling out to her, after humphing and considering over a particular paragraph—"What's the name of your great cousins in town, Fan?"

A moment's recollection enabled her to say, "Rushworth, Sir."

"And don't they live in Wimpole Street?"

"Yes, Sir."

"Then, there's the devil to pay among them, that's all. There, (holding out the paper to her)—much good may such fine relations do you. I don't know what Sir Thomas may think of such matters; he may be too much of the courtier and fine gentleman to like his daughter the less. But by G— if she belonged to *me*, I'd give her the rope's end[3] as long as I could stand over her. A little flogging for man and woman too, would be the best way of preventing such things."

Fanny read to herself that "it was with infinite concern the newspaper[4] had to announce to the world, a matrimonial *fracas*[5] in the family of Mr. R. of Wimpole Street; the beautiful Mrs. R. whose name had not long been enrolled in the lists of hymen,[6] and who had promised to become so brilliant a leader in the fashionable world, having quitted her husband's roof in company with the well known and captivating Mr. C. the intimate friend and associate of Mr. R. and it was not known, even to the editor of the newspaper, whither they were gone."

"It is a mistake, Sir," said Fanny instantly; "it must be a mistake—it cannot be true—it must mean some other people."

She spoke from the instinctive wish of delaying shame, she spoke with a resolution which sprung from despair, for she spoke what she did not, could not believe herself. It had been the shock of conviction as she read. The truth rushed on her;

and how she could have spoken at all, how she could even have breathed—was afterwards matter of wonder to herself.

Mr. Price cared too little about the report, to make her much answer. "It might be all a lie, he acknowledged; but so many fine ladies were going to the devil now-a-days that way, that there was no answering for anybody."

"Indeed, I hope it is not true," said Mrs. Price plaintively, "it would be so very shocking!—If I have spoken once to Rebecca about that carpet, I am sure I have spoke at least a dozen times; have not I, Betsey?—And it would not be ten minutes work."

The horror of a mind like Fanny's, as it received the conviction of such guilt, and began to take in some part of the misery that must ensue, can hardly be described. At first, it was a sort of stupefaction; but every moment was quickening her perception of the horrible evil. She could not doubt; she dared not indulge a hope of the paragraph being false. Miss Crawford's letter, which she had read so often as to make every line her own, was in frightful conformity with it. Her eager defence of her brother, her hope of its being *hushed up*, her evident agitation, were all of a piece with something very bad; and if there was a woman of character in existence, who could treat as a trifle this sin of the first magnitude, who could try to gloss it over, and desire to have it unpunished, she could believe Miss Crawford to be the woman! Now she could see her own mistake as to *who* were gone—or *said* to be gone. It was not Mr. and Mrs. Rushworth, it was Mrs. Rushworth and Mr. Crawford.

Fanny seemed to herself never to have been shocked before. There was no possibility of rest. The evening passed, without a pause of misery, the night was totally sleepless. She passed

line 6: anybody."] **1814** anybody. // line 8: spoken once] **1814** spoke once

only from feelings of sickness to shudderings of horror; and from hot fits of fever to cold. The event was so shocking, that there were moments even when her heart revolted from it as impossible—when she thought it could not be. A woman married only six months ago, a man professing himself devoted, even *engaged*, to another—that other her near relation—the whole family, both families connected as they were by tie upon tie, all friends, all intimate together!—it was too horrible a confusion of guilt, too gross a complication of evil, for human nature, not in a state of utter barbarism, to be capable of!—yet her judgment told her it was so. *His* unsettled affections, wavering with his vanity, *Maria's* decided attachment, and no sufficient principle on either side, gave it possibility—Miss Crawford's letter stampt it a fact.

What would be the consequence? Whom would it not injure? Whose views might it not effect?[7] Whose peace would it not cut up for ever? Miss Crawford herself—Edmund; but it was dangerous, perhaps, to tread such ground. She confined herself, or tried to confine herself to the simple, indubitable family-misery which must envelope all, if it were indeed a matter of certified guilt and public exposure. The mother's sufferings, the father's—there, she paused. Julia's, Tom's, Edmund's—there, a yet longer pause. They were the two on whom it would fall most horribly. Sir Thomas's parental solicitude, and high sense of honour and decorum, Edmund's upright principles, unsuspicious temper, and genuine strength of feeling, made her think it scarcely possible for them to support life and reason under such disgrace; and it appeared to her, that as far as this world alone was concerned, the greatest blessing to every one of kindred with Mrs. Rushworth would be instant annihilation.

line 11: yet her] **1814** yet, her // line 13: attachment, and] **1814** attachment—and // line 16: effect?] **1814** affect?

Nothing happened the next day, or the next, to weaken her terrors. Two posts came in, and brought no refutation, public or private. There was no second letter to explain away the first, from Miss Crawford; there was no intelligence from Mansfield, though it was now full time for her to hear again from her aunt. This was an evil omen. She had, indeed, scarcely the shadow of a hope to soothe her mind, and was reduced to so low and wan and trembling a condition as no mother—not unkind, except Mrs. Price, could have over-looked, when the third day did bring the sickening knock, and a letter was again put into her hands. It bore the London postmark, and came from Edmund.

"Dear Fanny,
    You know our present wretchedness. May God support you under *your* share. We have been here two days, but there is nothing to be done. They cannot be traced. You may not have heard of the last blow—Julia's elopement; she is gone to Scotland with Yates. She left London a few hours before we entered it. At any other time, this would have been felt dreadfully. Now it seems nothing, yet it is an heavy aggrava-tion. My father is not overpowered. More cannot be hoped. He is still able to think and act; and I write, by his desire, to propose your returning home. He is anxious to get you there for my mother's sake. I shall be at Portsmouth the morning after you receive this, and hope to find you ready to set off for Mansfield. My Father wishes you to invite Susan to go with you, for a few months. Settle it as you like; say what is proper; I am sure you will feel such an instance of his kind-ness at such a moment! Do justice to his meaning,[8] however I may confuse it. You may imagine something of my present

line 12: postmark,] **1814** post-mark,   //   line 14: You know] **1814** "You know

state. There is no end of the evil let loose upon us. You will see me early, by the mail.[9] Your's, &c."

Never had Fanny more wanted a cordial.[10] Never had she felt such a one as this letter contained. To-morrow! to leave Portsmouth to-morrow! She was, she felt she was, in the greatest danger of being exquisitely happy, while so many were miserable. The evil which brought such good to her! She dreaded lest she should learn to be insensible of it. To be going so soon, sent for so kindly, sent for as a comfort, and with leave to take Susan, was altogether such a combination of blessings as set her heart in a glow, and for a time, seemed to distance every pain, and make her incapable of suitably sharing the distress even of those whose distress she thought of most. Julia's elopement could affect her comparatively but little; she was amazed and shocked; but it could not occupy her, could not dwell on her mind. She was obliged to call herself to think of it, and acknowledge it to be terrible and grievous, or it was escaping her, in the midst of all the agitating, pressing, joyful cares attending this summons to herself.

There is nothing like employment, active, indispensable employment, for relieving sorrow.[11] Employment, even melancholy, may dispel melancholy, and her occupations were hopeful. She had so much to do, that not even the horrible story of Mrs. Rushworth (now fixed to the last point of certainty), could affect her as it had done before. She had not time to be miserable. Within twenty-four hours she was hoping to be gone; her father and mother must be spoken to, Susan prepared, every thing got ready. Business followed business; the day was hardly long enough. The happiness she

line 2: Your's, &c. [**1814** Your's, &c." // line 19: pressing, joyful] **1814** pressing joyful // line 26: her as] **1814** her, as

was imparting too, happiness very little alloyed by the black communication which must briefly precede it—the joyful consent of her father and mother to Susan's going with her— the general satisfaction with which the going of both seemed regarded—and the ecstacy of Susan herself, was all serving to support her spirits.

The affliction of the Bertrams was little felt in the family. Mrs. Price talked of her poor sister for a few minutes—but how to find any thing to hold Susan's clothes, because Rebecca took away all the boxes and spoilt them, was much more in her thoughts, and as for Susan, now unexpectedly gratified in the first wish of her heart, and knowing nothing personally of those who had sinned, or of those who were sorrowing—if she could help rejoicing from beginning to end, it was as much as ought to be expected from human virtue at fourteen.

As nothing was really left for the decision of Mrs. Price, or the good offices of Rebecca, every thing was rationally and duly accomplished, and the girls were ready for the morrow. The advantage of much sleep to prepare them for their journey, was impossible. The cousin who was travelling towards them, could hardly have less than visited their agitated spirits,[12] one all happiness, the other all varying and indescribable perturbation.

By eight in the morning, Edmund was in the house. The girls heard his entrance from above, and Fanny went down. The idea of immediately seeing him, with the knowledge of what he must be suffering, brought back all her own first feelings. He so near her, and in misery. She was ready to sink, as she entered the parlour. He was alone, and met her instantly; and she found herself pressed to his heart with only

line 9: any thing] **1814** anything   //   line 31: instantly;] **1814** intantly;

these words, just articulate, "My Fanny—my only sister—my only comfort now." She could say nothing; nor for some minutes could he say more.

He turned away to recover himself, and when he spoke again, though his voice still faltered, his manner showed the wish of self-command, and the resolution of avoiding any farther allusion. "Have you breakfasted?—When shall you be ready?—Does Susan go?"—were questions following each other rapidly. His great object was to be off as soon as possible. When Mansfield was considered, time was precious; and the state of his own mind made him find relief only in motion. It was settled that he should order the carriage to the door in half an hour; Fanny answered for their having breakfasted, and being quite ready in half an hour. He had already ate, and declined staying for their meal. He would walk round the ramparts, and join them with the carriage. He was gone again, glad to get away even from Fanny.

He looked very ill; evidently suffering under violent emotions, which he was determined to suppress. She knew it must be so, but it was terrible to her.

The carriage came; and he entered the house again at the same moment, just in time to spend a few minutes with the family, and be a witness—but that he saw nothing—of the tranquil manner in which the daughters were parted with, and just in time to prevent their sitting down to the breakfast table, which by dint of much unusual activity, was quite and completely ready as the carriage drove from the door. Fanny's last meal in her father's house was in character with her first; she was dismissed from it as hospitably as she had been welcomed.

line 5: showed] **1814** shewed

How her heart swelled with joy and gratitude, as she passed the barriers of Portsmouth,[13] and how Susan's face wore its broadest smiles, may be easily conceived. Sitting forwards, however, and screened by her bonnet, those smiles were unseen.

The journey was likely to be a silent one. Edmund's deep sighs often reached Fanny. Had he been alone with her, his heart must have opened in spite of every resolution; but Susan's presence drove him quite into himself, and his attempts to talk on indifferent subjects could never be long supported.

Fanny watched him with never-failing solicitude, and sometimes catching his eye, revived an affectionate smile,[14] which comforted her; but the first day's journey passed without her hearing a word from him on the subjects that were weighing him down. The next morning produced a little more. Just before their setting out from Oxford, while Susan was stationed at a window, in eager observation of the departure of a large family from the inn, the other two were standing by the fire; and Edmund, particularly struck by the alteration in Fanny's looks, and from his ignorance of the daily evils of her father's house, attributing an undue share of the change, attributing *all* to the recent event, took her hand, and said in a low, but very expressive tone, "No wonder—you must feel it—you must suffer. How a man who had once loved, could desert you! But *your's*—your regard was new compared with——Fanny, think of *me!*"

The first division of their journey occupied a long day, and brought them almost knocked up, to Oxford;[15] but the second was over at a much earlier hour. They were in the environs of Mansfield long before the usual dinner-time, and as they

line 8: opened in] **1814** opened, in // line 13: eye, revived an] **1814** eye, received an

approached the beloved place, the hearts of both sisters sank a little. Fanny began to dread the meeting with her aunts and Tom, under so dreadful a humiliation; and Susan to feel with some anxiety, that all her best manners, all her lately acquired knowledge of what was practised here, was on the point of being called into action. Visions of good and ill breeding, of old vulgarisms and new gentilities were before her; and she was meditating much upon silver forks, napkins, and finger glasses.[16] Fanny had been every where awake to the difference of the country since February; but, when they entered the Park, her perceptions and her pleasures were of the keenest sort. It was three months, full three months, since her quitting it; and the change was from winter to summer. Her eye fell every where on lawns and plantations of the freshest green; and the trees, though not fully clothed, were in that delightful state, when farther beauty is known to be at hand, and when, while much is actually given to the sight, more yet remains for the imagination. Her enjoyment, however, was for herself alone. Edmund could not share it. She looked at him, but he was leaning back, sunk in a deeper gloom than ever, and with eyes closed as if the view of cheerfulness oppressed him, and the lovely scenes of home must be shut out.

It made her melancholy again; and the knowledge of what must be enduring there, invested even the house, modern, airy, and well situated as it was, with a melancholy aspect.

By one of the suffering party within, they were expected with such impatience as she had never known before. Fanny had scarcely passed the solemn-looking servants, when Lady Bertram came from the drawing room to meet her; came with no indolent step; and, falling on her neck,[17] said, "Dear Fanny! now I shall be comfortable."

line 4: lately acquired] **1814** lately-acquired

Chapter 16

IT had been a miserable party, each of the three believing themselves most miserable. Mrs. Norris, however, as most attached to Maria, was really the greatest sufferer. Maria was her first favourite, the dearest of all; the match had been her own contriving, as she had been wont with such pride of heart to feel and say, and this conclusion of it almost overpowered her.

She was an altered creature, quieted, stupified, indifferent to every thing that passed. The being left with her sister and nephew, and all the house under her care, had been an advantage entirely thrown away; she had been unable to direct or dictate, or even fancy herself useful. When really touched by affliction, her active powers had been all benumbed; and neither Lady Bertram nor Tom had received from her the smallest support or attempt at support. She had done no more for them, than they had done for each other. They had been all solitary, helpless, and forlorn alike; and now the arrival of the others only established her superiority in wretchedness. Her companions were relieved, but there was no good for *her*. Edmund was almost as welcome to his brother, as Fanny to her aunt; but Mrs. Norris, instead of having comfort from either, was but the more irritated by the sight of the person whom, in the blindness of her anger, she could have charged as the dæmon of the piece.[1] Had Fanny accepted Mr. Crawford, this could not have happened.

Susan, too, was a grievance. She had not spirits to notice her in more than a few repulsive[2] looks, but she felt her as a spy, and an intruder, and an indigent niece, and every thing most odious. By her other aunt, Susan was received with quiet kindness. Lady Bertram could not give her much time, or many words, but she felt her, as Fanny's sister, to have a claim at Mansfield, and was ready to kiss and like her; and Susan was more than satisfied, for she came perfectly aware, that nothing but ill humour was to be expected from Aunt Norris; and was so provided with happiness, so strong in that best of blessings, an escape from many certain evils, that she could have stood against a great deal more indifference than she met with from the others.

She was now left a good deal to herself, to get acquainted with the house and grounds as she could, and spent her days very happily in so doing, while those who might otherwise have attended to her, were shut up, or wholly occupied each with the person quite dependant on them, at this time, for every thing like comfort; Edmund trying to bury his own feelings in exertions for the relief of his brother's, and Fanny devoted to her aunt Bertram, returning to every former office, with more than former zeal, and thinking she could never do enough for one who seemed so much to want her.

To talk over the dreadful business with Fanny, talk and lament, was all Lady Bertram's consolation. To be listened to and borne with, and hear the voice of kindness and sympathy in return, was every thing that could be done for her. To be otherwise comforted was out of the question. The case admitted of no comfort. Lady Bertram did not think deeply, but, guided by Sir Thomas she thought justly on all important points; and she saw, therefore, in all its enormity, what had happened, and neither endeavoured herself, nor required Fanny to advise her, to think little of guilt and infamy.

Her affections were not acute, nor was her mind tenacious. After a time, Fanny found it not impossible to direct her thoughts to other subjects, and revive some interest in the usual occupations; but whenever Lady Bertram *was* fixed on the event, she could see it only in one light, as comprehending the loss of a daughter, and a disgrace never to be wiped off.

Fanny learnt from her, all the particulars which had yet transpired. Her aunt was no very methodical narrator; but with the help of some letters to and from Sir Thomas, and what she already knew herself, and could reasonably combine, she was soon able to understand quite as much as she wished of the circumstances attending the story.

Mrs. Rushworth had gone, for the Easter holidays, to Twickenham, with a family whom she had just grown intimate with—a family of lively, agreeable manners, and probably of morals and discretion to suit—for to *their* house Mr. Crawford had constant access at all times. His having been in the same neighbourhood, Fanny already knew. Mr. Rushworth had been gone, at this time, to Bath, to pass a few days with his mother, and bring her back to town, and Maria was with these friends without any restraint, without even Julia; for Julia had removed from Wimpole Street two or three weeks before, on a visit to some relations of Sir Thomas; a removal which her father and mother were now disposed to attribute to some view of convenience on Mr. Yates's account. Very soon after the Rushworths return to Wimpole Street, Sir Thomas had received a letter from an old and most particular friend in London, who hearing and witnessing a good deal to alarm him in that quarter, wrote to recommend

line 17: manners, and] **1814** manners and

Sir Thomas's coming to London himself, and using his influence with his daughter, to put an end to an intimacy which was already exposing her to unpleasant remarks, and evidently making Mr. Rushworth uneasy.

Sir Thomas was preparing to act upon this letter, without communicating its contents to any creature at Mansfield, when it was followed by another, sent express from the same friend, to break to him the almost desperate situation in which affairs then stood with the young people. Mrs. Rushworth had left her husband's house; Mr. Rushworth had been in great anger and distress to *him* (Mr. Harding), for his advice; Mr. Harding feared there had been *at least*, very flagrant indiscretion. The maid-servant of Mrs. Rushworth, senior, threatened alarmingly. He was doing all in his power to quiet every thing, with the hope of Mrs. Rushworth's return, but was so much counteracted in Wimpole Street by the influence of Mr. Rushworth's mother, that the worst consequences might be apprehended.

This dreadful communication could not be kept from the rest of the family. Sir Thomas set off; Edmund would go with him; and the others had been left in a state of wretchedness, inferior only to what followed the receipt of the next letters from London. Every thing was by that time public beyond a hope. The servant of Mrs. Rushworth, the mother, had exposure in her power, and, supported by her mistress, was not to be silenced. The two ladies, even in the short time they had been together, had disagreed; and the bitterness of the elder against her daughter-in-law might perhaps, arise almost as much from the personal disrespect with which she had herself been treated, as from sensibility for her son.

line 28: might perhaps, arise] **1814** might, perhaps, arise

However that might be, she was unmanageable. But had she been less obstinate, or of less weight with her son, who was always guided by the last speaker, by the person who could get hold of and shut him up, the case would still have been hopeless, for Mrs. Rushworth did not appear again, and there was every reason to conclude her to be concealed somewhere with Mr. Crawford, who had quitted his uncle's house, as for a journey, on the very day of her absenting herself.

Sir Thomas, however, remained yet a little longer in town, in the hope of discovering, and snatching her from farther vice, though all was lost on the side of character.[3]

His present state, Fanny could hardly bear to think of. There was but one of his children who was not at this time a source of misery to him. Tom's complaints had been greatly heightened by the shock of his sister's conduct, and his recovery so much thrown back by it, that even Lady Bertram had been struck by the difference, and all her alarms were regularly sent off to her husband; and Julia's elopement, the additional blow which had met him on his arrival in London, though its force had been deadened at the moment, must, she knew, be sorely felt. She saw that it was. His letters expressed how much he deplored it. Under any circumstances it would have been an unwelcome alliance, but to have it so clandestinely formed, and such a period chosen for its completion, placed Julia's feelings in a most unfavourable light, and severely aggravated the folly of her choice. He called it a bad thing, done in the worst manner, and at the worst time; and though Julia was yet as more pardonable than Maria as folly than vice, he could not but regard the step she had taken, as opening the worst probabilities of a conclusion hereafter, like her sister's. Such was his opinion of the set into which she had thrown herself.

Fanny felt for him most acutely. He could have no comfort but in Edmund. Every other child must be racking his heart. His displeasure against herself she trusted, reasoning differently from Mrs. Norris, would now be done away. *She* should be justified. Mr. Crawford would have fully acquitted her conduct in refusing him, but this, though most material to herself, would be poor consolation to Sir Thomas. Her uncle's displeasure was terrible to her; but what could her justification, or her gratitude and attachment do for him? His stay must be on Edmund alone.

She was mistaken, however, in supposing that Edmund gave his father no present pain. It was of a much less poignant nature than what the others excited; but Sir Thomas was considering his happiness as very deeply involved in the offence of his sister and friend, cut off by it as he must be from the woman, whom he had been pursuing with undoubted attachment, and strong probability of success; and who in every thing but this despicable brother, would have been so eligible a connection. He was aware of what Edmund must be suffering on his own behalf in addition to all the rest, when they were in town; he had seen or conjectured his feelings, and having reason to think that *one* interview with Miss Crawford had taken place, from which Edmund derived only increased distress, had been as anxious on that account as on others, to get him out of town, and had engaged him in taking Fanny home to her aunt, with a view to his relief and benefit, no less than theirs. Fanny was not in the secret of her uncle's feelings, Sir Thomas not in the secret of Miss Crawford's character. Had he been privy to her conversation with his son, he would not have wished her to belong to him, though her twenty thousand pounds had been forty.

line 13: than what] **1814** that what

That Edmund must be for ever divided from Miss Crawford, did not admit of a doubt with Fanny; and yet, till she knew that he felt the same, her own conviction was insufficient. She thought he did, but she wanted to be assured of it. If he would now speak to her with the unreserve which had sometimes been too much for her before, it would be most consoling; but *that* she found was not to be. She seldom saw him—never alone—he probably avoided being alone with her. What was to be inferred? That his judgment submitted to all his own peculiar and bitter share of this family affliction, but that it was too keenly felt to be a subject of the slightest communication. This must be his state. He yielded, but it was with agonies, which did not admit of speech. Long, long would it be ere Miss Crawford's name passed his lips again, or she could hope for a renewal of such confidential intercourse as had been.

It *was* long. They reached Mansfield on Thursday, and it was not till Sunday evening that Edmund began to talk to her on the subject. Sitting with her on Sunday evening—a wet Sunday evening—the very time of all others when if a friend is at hand the heart must be opened, and every thing told—no one else in the room, except his mother, who, after hearing an affecting sermon, had cried herself to sleep—it was impossible not to speak; and so, with the usual beginnings, hardly to be traced as to what came first, and the usual declaration that if she would listen to him for a few minutes, he should be very brief, and certainly never tax her kindness in the same way again—she need not fear a repetition—it would be a subject prohibited entirely—he entered upon the luxury of relating circumstances and sensations of the first

line 17: It *was* long.] **1814** It was long.

interest to himself, to one of whose affectionate sympathy he was quite convinced.

How Fanny listened, with what curiosity and concern, what pain and what delight, how the agitation of his voice was watched, and how carefully her own eyes were fixed on any object but himself, may be imagined. The opening was alarming. He had seen Miss Crawford. He had been invited to see her. He had received a note from Lady Stornaway[4] to beg him to call; and regarding it as what was meant to be the last, last interview of friendship, and investing her with all the feelings of shame and wretchedness which Crawford's sister ought to have known, he had gone to her in such a state of mind, so softened, so devoted, as made it for a few moments impossible to Fanny's fears, that it should be the last. But as he proceeded in his story, these fears were over. She had met him, he said, with a serious—certainly a serious—even an agitated air; but before he had been able to speak one intelligible sentence, she had introduced the subject in a manner which he owned had shocked him. "I heard you were in town," said she—"I wanted to see you. Let us talk over this sad business. What can equal the folly of our two relations?"—"I could not answer, but I believe my looks spoke. She felt reproved. Sometimes how quick to feel! With a graver look and voice she then added—'I do not mean to defend Henry at your sister's expence.' So she began—but how she went on, Fanny, is not fit—is hardly fit to be repeated to you. I cannot recall all her words. I would not dwell upon them if I could. Their substance was great anger at the *folly* of each. She reprobated her brother's folly in being drawn on by a woman whom he had never cared for, to do what must lose him the woman he adored; but still more the folly of—poor Maria, in sacrificing such a situation, plunging into such difficulties, under the idea of being really loved by a man who had long ago made his indifference clear. Guess what I must have felt. To hear the woman whom—no harsher name than folly given!—So voluntarily, so freely, so coolly to canvass it!—No reluctance, no horror, no feminine—shall I say? no modest loathings!—This is what the world does.[5] For where, Fanny, shall we find a woman whom nature had so richly endowed?—Spoilt, spoilt!—"

After a little reflection, he went on with a sort of desperate calmness—"I will tell you every thing, and then have done for ever. She saw it only as folly, and that folly stamped only by exposure. The want of common discretion, of caution—his going down to Richmond for the whole time of her being at Twickenham—her putting herself in the power of a servant;—it was the detection in short—Oh! Fanny, it was the detection, not the offence which she reprobated. It was the imprudence which had brought things to extremity, and obliged her brother to give up every dearer plan, in order to fly with her."

He stopt.—"And what," said Fanny, (believing herself required to speak), "what could you say?"

"Nothing, nothing to be understood. I was like a man stunned. She went on, began to talk of you;—yes, then she began to talk of you, regretting, as well she might, the loss of such a——. There she spoke very rationally. But she has always done justice to you. 'He has thrown away,' said she, 'such a woman as he will never see again. She would have fixed him,[6] she would have made him happy for ever.'—My dearest Fanny, I am giving you I hope more pleasure than pain by this retrospect of what might have been—but what

line 25: she has always] **1814** she always has

never can be now. You do not wish me to be silent?—if you do, give me but a look, a word, and I have done."

No look or word was given.

"Thank God!" said he. "We were all disposed to wonder—but it seems to have been the merciful appointment of Providence that the heart which knew no guile,[7] should not suffer. She spoke of you with high praise and warm affection; yet, even here, there was alloy, a dash of evil—for in the midst of it she could exclaim 'Why would not she have him? It is all her fault. Simple girl!—I shall never forgive her. Had she accepted him as she ought, they might now have been on the point of marriage, and Henry would have been too happy and too busy to want any other object. He would have taken no pains to be on terms with Mrs. Rushworth again. It would have all ended in a regular standing flirtation, in yearly meetings at Sotherton and Everingham.' Could you have believed it possible?—But the charm is broken. My eyes are opened."

"Cruel!" said Fanny—"quite cruel! At such a moment to give way to gaiety and to speak with lightness, and to you!—Absolute cruelty."

"Cruelty, do you call it?—We differ there. No, her's is not a cruel nature. I do not consider her as meaning to wound my feelings. The evil lies yet deeper; in her total ignorance, unsuspiciousness of there being such feelings, in a perversion of mind which made it natural to her to treat the subject as she did. She was speaking only, as she had been used to hear others speak, as she imagined every body else would speak. Her's are not faults of temper. She would not voluntarily

line 4: he. "We] **1814** he. We   //   line 8: here, there] **1814** here there   //
line 9: "Why, would [**1814** 'Why would   //   line 29: of temper.] **1814** of
emper.

give unnecessary pain to any one, and though I may deceive myself, I cannot but think that for me, for my feelings, she would—Her's are faults of principle, Fanny, of blunted delicacy and a corrupted, vitiated mind. Perhaps it is best for me—since it leaves me so little to regret.—Not so, however. Gladly would I submit to all the increased pain of losing her, rather than have to think of her as I do. I told her so."

"Did you?"

"Yes, when I left her I told her so."

"How long were you together?"

"Five and twenty minutes. Well, she went on to say, that what remained now to be done, was to bring about a marriage between them.[8] She spoke of it, Fanny, with a steadier voice than I can." He was obliged to pause more than once as he continued. "We must persuade Henry to marry her," said she, "and what with honour, and the certainty of having shut himself out for ever from Fanny, I do not despair of it. Fanny he must give up. I do not think that even *he* could now hope to succeed with one of her stamp, and therefore I hope we may find no insuperable difficulty. My influence, which is not small, shall all go that way; and, when once married, and properly supported by her own family, people of respectability as they are, she may recover her footing in society to a certain degree. In some circles, we know, she would never be admitted, but with good dinners, and large parties, there will always be those who will be glad of her acquaintance; and there is, undoubtedly, more liberality and candour on those points than formerly. What I advise is, that your father be quiet. Do not let him injure his own cause by interference. Persuade him to let things take their course. If by any officious exertions of his, she is induced to leave Henry's protection,

line 5: regret.—Not] **1814** regret. Not

there will be much less chance of his marrying her, than if she remain with him. I know how he is likely to be influenced. Let Sir Thomas trust to his honour and compassion, and it may all end well; but if he get his daughter away, it will be destroying the chief hold."

After repeating this, Edmund was so much affected, that Fanny, watching him with silent, but most tender concern, was almost sorry that the subject had been entered on at all. It was long before he could speak again. At last, "Now, Fanny," said he, "I shall soon have done. I have told you the substance of all that she said. As soon as I could speak, I replied that I had not supposed it possible, coming in such a state of mind into that house, as I had done, that any thing could occur to make me suffer more, but that she had been inflicting deeper wounds in almost every sentence. That, though I had, in the course of our acquaintance, been often sensible of some difference in our opinions, on points too, of some moment, it had not entered my imagination to conceive the difference could be such as she had now proved it. That the manner in which she treated the dreadful crime committed by her brother and my sister—(with whom lay the greater seduction I pretended not to say)—but the manner in which she spoke of the crime itself, giving it every reproach but the right, considering its ill consequences only as they were to be braved or overborne by a defiance of decency and impudence in wrong; and, last of all, and above all, recommending to us a compliance, a compromise, an acquiescence, in the continuance of the sin, on the chance of a marriage which, thinking as I now thought of her brother, should rather be prevented than sought—all this together most grievously convinced me that I had never understood her before, and that, as far as

line 17: too, of] **1814** too of // line 26: above, all [**1814** above all, related to mind, it had been the creature of my own imagination, not Miss Crawford, that I had been too apt to dwell on for many months past. That, perhaps it was best for me; I had less to regret in sacrificing a friendship—feelings—hopes which must, at any rate, have been torn from me now. And yet, that I must and would confess, that, could I have restored her to what she had appeared to me before, I would infinitely prefer any increase of the pain of parting, for the sake of carrying with me the right of tenderness and esteem. This is what I said—the purport of it—but, as you may imagine, not spoken so collectedly or methodically as I have repeated it to you. She was astonished, exceedingly astonished—more than astonished. I saw her change countenance. She turned extremely red. I imagined I saw a mixture of many feelings— a great, though short struggle—half a wish of yielding to truths, half a sense of shame—but habit, habit carried it. She would have laughed if she could. It was a sort of laugh, as she answered, 'A pretty good lecture upon my word. Was it part of your last sermon? At this rate, you will soon reform every body at Mansfield and Thornton Lacey; and when I hear of you next, it may be as a celebrated preacher in some great society of Methodists,⁹ or as a missionary into foreign parts.' She tried to speak carelessly; but she was not so careless as she wanted to appear. I only said in reply, that from my heart I wished her well, and earnestly hoped that she might soon learn to think more justly, and not owe the most valuable knowledge we could any of us acquire—the knowledge of ourselves and of our duty—to the lessons of affliction, and immediately left the room. I had gone a few steps, Fanny, when I heard the door open behind me. 'Mr. Bertram,' said she. I looked back. 'Mr. Bertram,' said she, with a smile—but it was a smile ill-suited to the conversation that had passed, a saucy playful smile, seeming to invite, in order to subdue me; at least, it appeared so to me. I resisted; it was the impulse of the moment to resist, and still walked on. I have since— sometimes—for a moment—regretted that I did not go back; but I know I was right; and such has been the end of our acquaintance! And what an acquaintance has it been! How have I been deceived! Equally in brother and sister deceived! I thank you for your patience, Fanny. This has been the greatest relief, and now we will have done."

And such was Fanny's dependance on his words, that for five minutes she thought they *had* done. Then, however, it all came on again, or something very like it, and nothing less than Lady Bertram's rousing thoroughly up, could really close such a conversation. Till that happened, they continued to talk of Miss Crawford alone, and how she had attached him, and how delightful nature had made her, and how excellent she would have been, had she fallen into good hands earlier. Fanny, now at liberty to speak openly, felt more than justified in adding to his knowledge of her real character, by some hint of what share his brother's state of health might be supposed to have in her wish for a complete reconciliation. This was not an agreeable intimation. Nature resisted it for a while. It would have been a vast deal pleasanter to have had her more disinterested in her attachment; but his vanity was not of a strength to fight long against reason. He submitted to believe, that Tom's illness had influenced her; only reserving for himself this consoling thought, that considering the many counteractions of opposing habits, she had certainly been *more* attached to him than could have been expected, and for his sake been more near doing right. Fanny thought

line 1: subdue me;] **1814** subdue, me;   //   line 22: while. It] **1814** while It   //   line 29: *more* attached] **1814** more attached

exactly the same; and they were also quite agreed in their opinion of the lasting effect, the indelible impression, which such a disappointment must make on his mind. Time would undoubtedly abate somewhat of his sufferings, but still it was a sort of thing which he never could get entirely the better of; and as to his ever meeting with any other woman who could—it was too impossible to be named but with indignation. Fanny's friendship was all that he had to cling to.

Chapter 17

LET other pens[1] dwell on guilt and misery. I quit such odious subjects as soon as I can, impatient to restore every body, not greatly in fault themselves, to tolerable comfort, and to have done with all the rest.

My Fanny indeed at this very time, I have the satisfaction of knowing, must have been happy in spite of every thing. She must have been a happy creature in spite of all that she felt or thought she felt, for the distress of those around her. She had sources of delight that must force their way. She was returned to Mansfield Park, she was useful, she was beloved; she was safe from Mr. Crawford, and when Sir Thomas came back she had every proof that could be given in his then melancholy state of spirits, of his perfect approbation and increased regard; and happy as all this must make her, she would still have been happy without any of it, for Edmund was no longer the dupe of Miss Crawford.

It is true, that Edmund was very far from happy himself. He was suffering from disappointment and regret, grieving over what was, and wishing for what could never be. She knew it was so, and was sorry; but it was with a sorrow so founded on satisfaction, so tending to ease, and so much in harmony with every dearest sensation, that there are few who might not have been glad to exchange their greatest gaiety for it.

Sir Thomas, poor Sir Thomas, a parent, and conscious of errors in his own conduct as a parent, was the longest to suffer.

He felt that he ought not to have allowed the marriage, that his daughter's sentiments had been sufficiently known to him to render him culpable in authorising it, that in so doing he had sacrificed the right to the expedient, and been governed by motives of selfishness and worldly wisdom. These were reflections that required some time to soften; but time will do almost every thing, and though little comfort arose on Mrs. Rushworth's side for the misery she had occasioned, comfort was to be found greater than he had supposed, in his other children. Julia's match became a less desperate business than he had considered it at first. She was humble and wishing to be forgiven, and Mr. Yates, desirous of being really received into the family, was disposed to look up to him and be guided. He was not very solid; but there was a hope of his becoming less trifling—of his being at least tolerably domestic and quiet; and, at any rate, there was comfort in finding his estate rather more, and his debts much less, than he had feared, and in being consulted and treated as the friend best worth attending to. There was comfort also in Tom, who gradually regained his health, without regaining the thoughtlessness and selfishness of his previous habits. He was the better for ever for his illness. He had suffered, and he had learnt to think, two advantages that he had never known before; and the self-reproach arising from the deplorable event in Wimpole Street, to which he felt himself accessary by all the dangerous intimacy of his unjustifiable theatre, made an impression on his mind which, at the age of six-and-twenty, with no want of sense, or good companions, was durable in its happy effects. He became what he ought to be, useful to his father, steady and quiet, and not living merely for himself.

line 13: him and be] **1814** him to be   //   line 16: and, at] **1814** and at   //
line 20: health, without] **1814** health without

Here was comfort indeed! and quite as soon as Sir Thomas could place dependence on such sources of good, Edmund was contributing to his father's ease by improvement in the only point in which *he* had given him pain before—improvement in his spirits. After wandering about and sitting under trees with Fanny all the summer evenings, he had so well talked his mind into submission, as to be very tolerably cheerful again.

These were the circumstances and the hopes which gradually brought their alleviation to Sir Thomas, deadening his sense of what was lost, and in part reconciling him to himself; though the anguish arising from the conviction of his own errors in the education of his daughters, was never to be entirely done away.

Too late he became aware how unfavourable to the character of any young people, must be the totally opposite treatment which Maria and Julia had been always experiencing at home, where the excessive indulgence and flattery of their aunt had been continually contrasted with his own severity. He saw how ill he had judged, in expecting to counteract what was wrong in Mrs. Norris, by its reverse in himself, clearly saw that he had but increased the evil, by teaching them to repress their spirits in his presence, as to make their real disposition unknown to him, and sending them for all their indulgences to a person who had been able to attach them only by the blindness of her affection, and the excess of her praise.

Here had been grievous mismanagement; but, bad as it was, he gradually grew to feel that it had not been the most direful mistake in his plan of education. Something must have been wanting *within*,[2] or time would have worn away much

line 28: but, bad] **1814** but bad

of its ill effect. He feared that principle, active principle,[3] had been wanting, that they had never been properly taught to govern their inclinations and tempers, by that sense of duty which can alone suffice. They had been instructed theoretically in their religion, but never required to bring it into daily practice. To be distinguished for elegance and accomplishments—the authorised object of their youth—could have had no useful influence that way, no moral effect on the mind. He had meant them to be good, but his cares had been directed to the understanding and manners, not the disposition; and of the necessity of self-denial and humility, he feared they had never heard from any lips that could profit them.

Bitterly did he deplore a deficiency which now he could scarcely comprehend to have been possible. Wretchedly did he feel, that with all the cost and care of an anxious and expensive education, he had brought up his daughters, without their understanding their first duties, or his being acquainted with their character and temper.

The high spirit and strong passions of Mrs. Rushworth especially, were made known to him only in their sad result. She was not to be prevailed on to leave Mr. Crawford. She hoped to marry him, and they continued together till she was obliged to be convinced that such hope was vain, and till the disappointment and wretchedness arising from the conviction, rendered her temper so bad, and her feelings for him so like hatred, as to make them for a while each other's punishment, and then induce a voluntary separation.

line 16: anxious and] **1814** anxious an   //   line 17: daughters, without] **1814** daughters without

She had lived with him to be reproached as the ruin of all his happiness in Fanny, and carried away no better consolation in leaving him, than that she *had* divided them. What can exceed the misery of such a mind in such a situation?

Mr. Rushworth had no difficulty in procuring a divorce;[4] and so ended a marriage contracted under such circumstances as to make any better end, the effect of good luck, not to be reckoned on. She had despised him, and loved another—and he had been very much aware that it was so. The indignities of stupidity, and the disappointments of selfish passion, can excite little pity. His punishment followed his conduct, as did a deeper punishment, the deeper guilt of his wife. *He* was released from the engagement to be mortified and unhappy, till some other pretty girl could attract him into matrimony again, and he might set forward on a second, and it is to be hoped, more prosperous trial of the state—if duped, to be duped at least with good humour and good luck; while *she* must withdraw with infinitely stronger feelings to a retirement and reproach, which could allow no second spring of hope or character.[5]

Where she could be placed, became a subject of most melancholy and momentous consultation. Mrs. Norris, whose attachment seemed to augment with the demerits of her niece, would have had her received at home, and countenanced by them all. Sir Thomas would not hear of it, and Mrs. Norris's anger against Fanny was so much the greater, from considering *her* residence there as the motive. She persisted in placing his scruples to *her* account, though Sir Thomas very solemnly assured her, that had there been no young woman in question, had there been no young person of

line 4: situation. [**1814** situation?

either sex belonging to him, to be endangered by the society, or hurt by the character of Mrs. Rushworth, he would never have offered so great an insult to the neighbourhood, as to expect it to notice her. As a daughter—he hoped a penitent one—she should be protected by him, and secured in every comfort, and supported by every encouragement to do right, which their relative situations admitted; but farther than *that*, he would not go. Maria had destroyed her own character, and he would not by a vain attempt to restore what never could be restored, be affording his sanction to vice, or in seeking to lessen its disgrace, be anywise accessary to introducing such misery in another man's family, as he had known himself.

It ended in Mrs. Norris's resolving to quit Mansfield, and devote herself to her unfortunate Maria, and in an establishment being formed for them in another country[6]—remote and private, where, shut up together with little society, on one side no affection, on the other, no judgment, it may be reasonably supposed that their tempers became their mutual punishment.

Mrs. Norris's removal from Mansfield was the great supplementary comfort of Sir Thomas's life. His opinion of her had been sinking from the day of his return from Antigua; in every transaction together from that period, in their daily intercourse, in business, or in chat, she had been regularly losing ground in his esteem, and convincing him that either time had done her much disservice, or that he had considerably over-rated her sense, and wonderfully borne with her manners before. He had felt her as an hourly evil, which was so much the worse, as there seemed no chance of its ceasing but with life; she seemed a part of himself, that must be borne for ever. To be relieved from her, therefore, was so great a felicity, that had she not left bitter remembrances behind her, there might have been danger of his learning almost to approve the evil which produced such a good.

She was regretted by no one at Mansfield. She had never been able to attach even those she loved best, and since Mrs. Rushworth's elopement, her temper had been in a state of such irritation, as to make her every where tormenting. Not even Fanny had tears for aunt Norris—not even when she was gone for ever.

That Julia escaped better than Maria was owing, in some measure, to a favourable difference of disposition and circumstance, but in a greater to her having been less the darling of that very aunt, less flattered, and less spoilt. Her beauty and acquirements had held but a second place. She had been always used to think herself a little inferior to Maria. Her temper was naturally the easiest of the two; her feelings, though quick, were more controulable; and education had not given her so very hurtful a degree of self-consequence.

She had submitted the best to the disappointment in Henry Crawford. After the first bitterness of the conviction of being slighted was over, she had been tolerably soon in a fair way of not thinking of him again; and when the acquaintance was renewed in town, and Mr. Rushworth's house became Crawford's object, she had had the merit of withdrawing herself from it, and of chusing that time to pay a visit to her other friends, in order to secure herself from being again too much attracted. This had been her motive in going to her cousins. Mr. Yates's convenience had had nothing to do with it. She had been allowing his attentions some time, but with very little idea of ever accepting him; and, had not her sister's conduct burst forth as it did, and her increased

line 9: Maria was] **1814** Maria, was   //   line 15: two; her] **1814** two, her
//   line 16: controulable; and] **1814** controulable, and

dread of her father and of home, on that event—imagining its certain consequence to herself would be greater severity and restraint—made her hastily resolve on avoiding such immediate horrors at all risks, it is probable that Mr. Yates would never have succeeded. She had not eloped with any worse feelings than those of selfish alarm. It had appeared to her the only thing to be done. Maria's guilt had induced Julia's folly.

Henry Crawford, ruined by early independence and bad domestic example, indulged in the freaks of a cold-blooded vanity a little too long. Once it had, by an opening undesigned and unmerited, led him into the way of happiness. Could he have been satisfied with the conquest of one amiable woman's affections, could he have found sufficient exultation in overcoming the reluctance, in working himself into the esteem and tenderness of Fanny Price, there would have been every probability of success and felicity for him. His affection had already done something. Her influence over him had already given him some influence over her. Would he have deserved more, there can be no doubt that more would have been obtained; especially when that marriage had taken place, which would have given him the assistance of her conscience in subduing her first inclination, and brought them very often together. Would he have persevered, and uprightly, Fanny must have been his reward—and a reward very voluntarily bestowed—within a reasonable period from Edmund's marrying Mary.

Had he done as he intended, and as he knew he ought, by going down to Everingham after his return from Portsmouth, he might have been deciding his own happy destiny. But he was pressed to stay for Mrs. Fraser's party; his staying

line 1: father] **1814** Father   //   line 18: him had] **1814** him, had was made of flattering consequence, and he was to meet Mrs. Rushworth there. Curiosity and vanity were both engaged, and the temptation of immediate pleasure was too strong for a mind unused to make any sacrifice to right; he resolved to defer his Norfolk journey, resolved that writing should answer the purpose of it, or that its purpose was unimportant—and staid. He saw Mrs. Rushworth, was received by her with a coldness which ought to have been repulsive, and have established apparent indifference between them for ever; but he was mortified, he could not bear to be thrown off by the woman whose smiles had been so wholly at his command; he must exert himself to subdue so proud a display of resentment; it was anger on Fanny's account; he must get the better of it, and make Mrs. Rushworth Maria Bertram again in her treatment of himself.

In this spirit he began the attack; and by animated perseverance had soon re-established the sort of familiar intercourse— of gallantry—of flirtation which bounded his views, but in triumphing over the discretion, which, though beginning in anger, might have saved them both, he had put himself in the power of feelings on her side, more strong than he had supposed.—She loved him; there was no withdrawing attentions, avowedly dear to her. He was entangled by his own vanity, with as little excuse of love as possible, and without the smallest inconstancy of mind towards her cousin.—To keep Fanny and the Bertrams from a knowledge of what was passing became his first object. Secrecy could not have been more desirable for Mrs. Rushworth's credit than he felt it for his own.—When he returned from Richmond, he would have been glad to see Mrs. Rushworth no more.—All that

line 14: Mrs. Rushworth Maria] **1814** Mrs. Rushworth. Maria   //   line 27: passing became] **1814** passing, became   //   line 28: credit than] **1814** credit, than

followed was the result of her imprudence; and he went off with her at last, because he could not help it, regretting Fanny, even at the moment, but regretting her infinitely more, when all the bustle of the intrigue was over, and a very few months had taught him, by the force of contrast, to place a yet higher value on the sweetness of her temper, the purity of her mind, and the excellence of her principles.

That punishment, the public punishment of disgrace, should in a just measure attend *his* share of the offence, is, we know, not one of the barriers,[7] which society gives to virtue. In this world, the penalty is less equal than could be wished; but without presuming to look forward to a juster appointment hereafter, we may fairly consider a man of sense like Henry Crawford, to be providing for himself no small portion of vexation and regret—vexation that must rise sometimes to self-reproach, and regret to wretchedness—in having so requited hospitality, so injured family peace, so forfeited his best, most estimable and endeared acquaintance, and so lost the woman whom he had rationally, as well as passionately loved.

After what had passed to wound and alienate the two families, the continuance of the Bertrams and Grants in such close neighbourhood would have been most distressing; but the absence of the latter, for some months purposely lengthened, ended very fortunately in the necessity, or at least the practicability of a permanent removal. Dr. Grant, through an interest on which he had almost ceased to form hopes, succeeded to a stall in Westminster,[8] which, as affording an occasion for leaving Mansfield, an excuse for residence in London, and an increase of income to answer the expenses

line 6: mind, and the] **1814** mind, the   //   line 13: sense like] **1814** sense, like   //   line 23: neighbourhood would] **1814** neighbourhood, would

of the change, was highly acceptable to those who went, and those who staid.

Mrs. Grant, with a temper to love and be loved, must have gone with some regret, from the scenes and people she had been used to; but the same happiness of disposition must in any place and any society, secure her a great deal to enjoy, and she had again a home to offer Mary; and Mary had had enough of her own friends, enough of vanity, ambition, love, and disappointment in the course of the last half year, to be in need of the true kindness of her sister's heart, and the rational tranquillity of her ways.—They lived together; and when Dr. Grant had brought on apoplexy and death, by three great institutionary dinners in one week, they still lived together; for Mary, though perfectly resolved against ever attaching herself to a younger brother again, was long in finding among the dashing representatives,[9] or idle heir apparents, who were at the command of her beauty, and her 20,000*l.* any one who could satisfy the better taste she had acquired at Mansfield, whose character and manners could authorise a hope of the domestic happiness she had there learnt to estimate,[10] or put Edmund Bertram sufficiently out of her head.

Edmund had greatly the advantage of her in this respect. He had not to wait and wish with vacant affections for an object worthy to succeed her in them. Scarcely had he done regretting Mary Crawford, and observing to Fanny how impossible it was that he should ever meet with such another woman, before it began to strike him whether a very different kind of woman might not do just as well—or a great deal better; whether Fanny herself were not growing as dear, as

line 5: to; but] **1814** to, but // line 11: together; and] **1814** together;—and important to him in all her smiles, and all her ways, as Mary Crawford had ever been; and whether it might not be a possible, an hopeful undertaking to persuade her that her warm and sisterly regard for him would be foundation enough for wedded love.

I purposely abstain from dates on this occasion, that every one may be at liberty to fix their own, aware that the cure of unconquerable passions, and the transfer of unchanging attachments, must vary much as to time in different people.— I only intreat every body to believe that exactly at the time when it was quite natural that it should be so, and not a week earlier, Edmund did cease to care about Miss Crawford, and became as anxious to marry Fanny, as Fanny herself could desire.

With such a regard for her, indeed, as his had long been, a regard founded on the most endearing claims of innocence and helplessness, and completed by every recommendation of growing worth, what could be more natural than the change? Loving, guiding, protecting her, as he had been doing ever since her being ten years old, her mind in so great a degree formed by his care, and her comfort depending on his kindness, an object to him of such close and peculiar interest, dearer by all his own importance with her than any one else at Mansfield, what was there now to add, but that he should learn to prefer soft light eyes to sparkling dark ones.—And being always with her, and always talking confidentially, and his feelings exactly in that favourable state which a recent disappointment gives, those soft light eyes could not be very long in obtaining the pre-eminence.

Having once set out, and felt that he had done so, on this road to happiness, there was nothing on the side of prudence to stop him or make his progress slow; no doubts of her deserving, no fears from opposition of taste, no need of drawing new hopes of happiness from dissimilarity of temper. Her mind, disposition, opinions, and habits wanted no half concealment, no self deception on the present, no reliance on future improvement.[11] Even in the midst of his late infatuation, he had acknowledged Fanny's mental superiority. What must be his sense of it now, therefore? She was of course only too good for him; but as nobody minds having what is too good for them, he was very steadily earnest in the pursuit of the blessing, and it was not possible that encouragement from her should be long wanting. Timid, anxious, doubting as she was, it was still impossible that such tenderness as hers should not, at times, hold out the strongest hope of success, though it remained for a later period to tell him the whole delightful and astonishing truth. His happiness in knowing himself to have been so long the beloved of such a heart, must have been great enough to warrant any strength of language in which he could clothe it to her or to himself; it must have been a delightful happiness! But there was happiness elsewhere which no description can reach. Let no one presume to give the feelings of a young woman on receiving the assurance of that affection of which she has scarcely allowed herself to entertain a hope.

Their own inclinations ascertained, there were no difficulties behind, no drawback of poverty or parent. It was a match which Sir Thomas's wishes had even forestalled. Sick of ambitious and mercenary connections, prizing more and more the sterling good of principle and temper, and chiefly anxious to bind by the strongest securities all that remained

line 4: reliance future[**1814** reliance on future   //   line 8: as nobody] **1814** a nobody   //   line 8: is too good] **1814** is to good   //
line 12: hers should] **1814** her's, should   //   line 18: clothe] **1814** cloathe

to him of domestic felicity, he had pondered with genuine satisfaction on the more than possibility of the two young friends finding their mutual consolation in each other for all that had occurred of disappointment to either; and the joyful consent which met Edmund's application, the high sense of having realised a great acquisition in the promise of Fanny for a daughter, formed just such a contrast with his early opinion on the subject when the poor little girl's coming had been first agitated, as time is for ever producing between the plans and decisions of mortals, for their own instruction, and their neighbour's entertainment.

Fanny was indeed the daughter that he wanted. His charitable kindness had been rearing a prime comfort for himself. His liberality had a rich repayment, and the general goodness of his intentions by her, deserved it. He might have made her childhood happier; but it had been an error of judgment only which had given him the appearance of harshness, and deprived him of her early love; and now, on really knowing each other, their mutual attachment became very strong. After settling her at Thornton Lacey with every kind attention to her comfort, the object of almost every day was to see her there, or to get her away from it.

Selfishly dear as she had long been to Lady Bertram, she could not be parted with willingly by *her*. No happiness of son or niece could make her wish the marriage. But it was possible to part with her, because Susan remained to supply her place.—Susan became the stationary niece—delighted to be so!—and equally well adapted for it by a readiness of mind, and an inclination for usefulness, as Fanny had been by sweetness of temper, and strong feelings of gratitude. Susan could never be spared. First as a comfort to Fanny, then as

line 6: realised] **1814** realized   //   line 25: niece could] **1814** niece, could

an auxiliary, and last as her substitute, she was established at Mansfield, with every appearance of equal permanency. Her more fearless disposition and happier nerves made every thing easy to her there.—With quickness in understanding the tempers of those she had to deal with, and no natural timidity to restrain any consequent wishes, she was soon welcome, and useful to all; and after Fanny's removal, succeeded so naturally to her influence over the hourly comfort of her aunt, as gradually to become, perhaps, the most beloved of the two.—In *her* usefulness, in Fanny's excellence, in William's continued good conduct, and rising fame, and in the general well-doing and success of the other members of the family, all assisting to advance each other, and doing credit to his countenance and aid, Sir Thomas saw repeated, and for ever repeated reason to rejoice in what he had done for them all, and acknowledge the advantages of early hardship and discipline, and the consciousness of being born to struggle and endure.

With so much true merit and true love, and no want of fortune or friends, the happiness of the married cousins must appear as secure as earthly happiness can be.—Equally formed for domestic life, and attached to country pleasures, their home was the home of affection and comfort; and to complete the picture of good, the acquisition of Mansfield living by the death of Dr. Grant, occurred just after they had been married long enough to begin to want an increase of income, and feel their distance from the paternal abode an inconvenience.

On that event they removed to Mansfield, and the parsonage there, which under each of its two former owners, Fanny

line 4: understanding the] **1814** understanding, the   //   line 10: *her* usefulness,] **1814** her usefulness,

had never been able to approach but with some painful sensation of restraint or alarm, soon grew as dear to her heart, and as thoroughly perfect in her eyes, as every thing else, within the view and patronage[12] of Mansfield Park, had long been.

FINIS

line 4: Park, had] **1814** Park had

LOVERS' VOWS

Elizabeth Inchbald (1753–1821), actress, novelist, playwright and critic, has been described as the foremost English female dramatist. In a period when women playwrights began to consolidate their precarious position in the profession, Inchbald achieved conspicuous artistic and professional success. Between 1780 and 1805 she wrote twenty-one plays, nearly all comedies; ten of these were skilful adaptations from contemporary French or German works. She moved in London literary and bohemian circles, associating with the Kembles and William Godwin among others.

In 1780, after eight years acting on provincial stages, Inchbald joined Thomas Harris' company at Covent Garden, continuing to perform there and at other London theatres until her earnings from writing permitted her retirement from acting in 1789. Her novel *A Simple Story* appeared in 1791. The later part of her literary career involved overseeing and writing biographical and critical prefaces for *The British Theatre*, a 25-volume collection of English plays published by Longman, making Inchbald the first woman professional drama critic in England.

Lovers' Vows, freely adapted by Inchbald from August F. F. von Kotzebue's sentimental melodrama *Das Kind der Liebe* (1790), opened at the Theatre Royal, Covent Garden on 11 October 1798 and was performed there for forty-two nights over that season, a success instantly replicated at the other legitimate London playhouses and in the chief provincial theatres. Well received in public performance, the play soon became favourite material for private or amateur representation. Excerpts from *Lovers' Vows* were published in magazines, often with illustrations: see for example *European Magazine*, 37 (April 1800), p. 302; *Universal Magazine*, 103 (December 1798), pp. 418–22; *Lady's Magazine*, 30 (February 1799), pp. 53–5. The whole play was printed in twelve inexpensive editions by the end of 1799, and in 1805 it was anthologised with other of Inchbald's plays. It continued a staple of the English dramatic repertoire until well into the nineteenth century.

Robust critical debate over the moral and political tendencies of *Lovers' Vows* accompanied its unqualified commercial success. Of particular concern, for reviewers who condemned the play, was its depiction of the lower-class characters, the Cottagers and Anhalt, as more pious and upright than the aristocrats Count Cassel and Baron Wildenhaim, both of whom are seducers of poor young women, Cassel unapologetically. Some thought it insufficiently shocked by Frederick's banditry; still others were disturbed by the final lifting of Agatha's pall of wretchedness. '[H]er restoration to happiness, notwithstanding her repentance, forms too much of an apology for error . . . on the stage, a seduced female should never be suffered to appear but as an object of terror', the *Porcupine and Anti-Gallican Monitor* declared.[1] The theatrical correspondent for the *Times* argued differently: 'the sentiments are pure and edifying, and the moral instruction which they convey is of the most important kind'.[2] Defenders and

[1] Unsigned review, *Porcupine and Anti-Gallican Monitor*, 7 (September 1801); quoted in William Reitzel, '*Mansfield Park* and *Lovers' Vows*', *Review of English Studies*, 9 (1933), pp. 451–6, p. 453.

[2] Unsigned review, *Times* (12 October 1798); quoted in Colin Pedley, '"Terrific and Unprincipled Compositions": The Reception of *Lovers' Vows* and *Mansfield Park*', *Philological Quarterly*, 74, 3 (Summer 1995), pp. 297–316, p. 305.

detractors alike attributed the play's 'irresistible fascination' to its 'resistless controul over the feelings of the audience': 'we are absolutely forced to take part in the respective interests, and enter into the motives and the "cue for passion," with which the characters are supposed to be animated'.[3] The *Times* ascribes the general excellence of effect to 'the skill of the Poet', while Inchbald herself includes 'the exertions of every performer engaged in the play'[4] among the factors involved in its success. The *Morning Chronicle* apparently thought some performances almost too interesting, if somewhat off-key: 'her coquetry is so playful that even her errors please us' wrote the reviewer of the actress playing Amelia.[5]

Inchbald's adaptation modifies the more incendiary aspects of Kotzebue's play, as she says in her Preface, in conformity with 'the English, rather than the German taste' (p. 559); her play is lighter, more amusing and shorter than his. Two other adaptations of *Das Kind der Liebe* were in circulation during the 1790s, neither enjoying anything approaching the prominence of Inchbald's version. Nevertheless, *Lovers' Vows*' detractors, tactically perhaps, wrote of it as essentially an 'anglicised German'[6] import, and a work authored by Kotzebue, whose plays were then enjoying a great vogue in England. (Of nineteen plays in Thompson's 1800 collection *German Plays*, ten were by Kotzebue, with only one from Goethe.) Inchbald's Preface makes clear the pains she took to 'alter' or adapt the play to English taste; her Remarks

---

[3] *Times* (13 October 1798); quoted in Pedley, '"Terrific and Unprincipled Compositions"', p. 304.

[4] Elizabeth Inchbald, Preface to *Lovers' Vows*, p. 560.

[5] *Morning Chronicle* (12 October 1798), quoted in Pedley, '"Terrific and Unprincipled Compositions"', p. 307.

[6] *Porcupine and Anti-Gallican Monitor* (7 September 1801), quoted in Reitzel, '*Mansfield Park*', p. 453.

on its republication in 1805 defend its morality and artistic integrity. Exciting Continental dramas did not please all English audiences. The *Anti-Jacobin Review* thought they were expressly designed for 'corrupting the public taste and national morality of Englishmen'.[7]

Austen attended and apparently enjoyed several performances of Kotzebue adaptations: she saw *The Bee-Hive* in 1813. She may have seen an amateur performance of *Lovers' Vows* some years before the composition of *Mansfield Park*. A series of letters, written to Cassandra from London in March 1814, jokingly alludes to a very slight acquaintance (a relation of the Evangelical Tilson family with whom Austen was on friendly terms) as 'Frederick': 'We met only General Chowne today, who has not much to say for himself – I was ready to laugh at the remembrance of Frederick and such a different Frederick as we chose to fancy him to the real Christopher!'[8] This is the letter in which Henry Austen's 'approbation' of *Mansfield Park* is recorded. 'In view of the very heavy weather Jane Austen is often said to have made of the theatricals in *Mansfield Park*', notes Margaret Kirkham, 'it is striking that what is recalled in the references to "Frederick" is, quite emphatically, laughter.'[9]

Harris, the manager of Covent Garden Theatre, suggested Inchbald might adapt the Kotzebue play; John Taylor, who wrote the Prologue, assisted her with the Butler's verses. The reference in the Baron's speech in Act 2, scene 2, just before Anhalt's entrance, to 'one German woman, who

[7] *Anti-Jacobin Review*, 5 (1800), quoted in Pedley, ' "Terrific and Unprincipled Compositions" ', p. 302.

[8] Letter 9 March 1814 *Letters*, p. 262.

[9] Margaret Kirkham, 'The Theatricals in "Mansfield Park" and "Frederick" in "Lovers' Vows" ', *Notes and Queries*, 220 (September 1975), pp. 388–90, p. 388.

possesses every virtue that ornaments the whole sex' is a compliment to George III's consort, Queen Charlotte. As in *Mansfield Park*, 'comfortable' in Act 3, scene 2, here used of food, means 'sustaining', and 'nice' – 'severely nice' (Act 4, scene 2) – fastidious. The dollar was the unit of German currency at the time.

Laura Carroll

LOVERS' VOWS;

A PLAY,

IN FIVE ACTS;

ALTERED FROM THE GERMAN OF KOTZEBUE

By Mrs. INCHBALD.

AS PERFORMED AT THE

THEATRE ROYAL, COVENT GARDEN.

PRINTED UNDER THE AUTHORITY OF THE MANAGERS

FROM THE PROMPT BOOK.

———————

LONDON:

PRINTED FOR LONGMAN, HURST, REES, AND ORME,
PATERNOSTER-ROW.

PREFACE ON THE FIRST PUBLICATION
OF *LOVERS' VOWS*

It would appear like affectation to offer an apology for any scenes or passages omitted or added, in this play, different from the original: its reception has given me confidence to suppose what I have done is right; for Kotzebue's "Child of Love," in Germany, was never more attractive, than "Lovers' Vows" has been in England.

I could trouble my reader with many pages to disclose the motives, which induced me to alter, with the exception of a few common-place sentences only, the characters of Count Cassel, Amelia, and Verdun the Butler—I could explain why the part of the Count, as in the original, would have inevitably condemned the whole play—I could inform my reader why I have pourtrayed the Baron, in many particulars, different from the German author, and carefully prepared the audience for the grand effect of the last scene in the fourth act, by totally changing his conduct towards his son, as a robber—why I gave sentences of a humourous kind to the parts of the two Cottagers—why I was compelled, on many occasions, to compress the substance of a speech of three or four pages, into one of three or four lines—and why, in no one instance, I would suffer my respect for Kotzebue to interfere with my profound respect for the judgment of a British audience. But I flatter myself such a vindication is not requisite to the enlightened reader, who, I trust, on comparing this drama with the original, will, at once, see all my motives—and the dull admirer of mere verbal translation, it would be vain to endeavour to inspire with taste by instruction.

Wholly unacquainted with the German language, a literal translation of the "Child of Love" was given to me by the manager of Covent Garden Theatre, to be adapted, as my opinion should direct, for his stage. This translation, tedious and vapid, as most literal translations are, had the peculiar disadvantage of having been put into our language by a German—of course, it came to me in broken English. It was no slight misfortune, to have an example of bad grammar, false metaphors and similes, with all the usual errors of imperfect diction, placed before a female writer. But if, disdaining the construction of sentences,—the precise decorum of the cold grammarian,—she has caught the spirit of her author,—if, in every altered scene,—still adhering to the nice propriety of his meaning, and still keeping in view his great catastrophe,—she has agitated her audience with all the various passions he depicted, the rigid criticism of the closet will be but a slender abatement of the pleasure resulting from the sanction of an applauding theatre.

It has not been one of the least gratifications I have received from the success of this play, that the original German, from which it is taken, was printed in the year 1791; and yet, that, during all the period which has intervened, no person of talents or literary knowledge (though there are in this country many of that description, who profess to search for German dramas,) has thought it worth employment to make a translation of the work. I can only account for such an apparent neglect of Kotzebue's "Child of Love," by the consideration of its being in the original discordant with an English stage, and the difficulty of making it otherwise—a difficulty, which once appeared so formidable, that I thought I must have declined it, even after I had proceeded some length in the undertaking.

Independently of objections to the character of the Count, the dangerous insignificance of the Butler, in the original, embarrassed me much. I found, if he was retained in the *Dramatis Personæ*, something more must be supplied than the author had assigned him: I suggested the verses I have introduced; but not being blessed with the Butler's happy art of rhyming, I am indebted for them, except the seventh and eleventh stanzas in the first of his poetic stories, to the author of the prologue.

The part of Amelia has been a very particular object of my solicitude and alteration: the same situations which the author gave her, remain, but almost all the dialogue of the character I have changed: the forward and unequivocal manner, in which she announces her affection to her lover, in the original, would have been revolting to an English audience: the passion of love, represented on the stage, is certain to be either insipid or hateful, unless it creates smiles or tears: Amelia's love, by Kotzebue, is indelicately blunt, and yet, void of mirth or sadness: I have endeavoured to attach the attention and sympathy of the audience, by whimsical insinuations, rather than coarse abruptness: she is still the same woman, I conceive, whom the author drew, with the self-same sentiments, but with manners conforming to the English, rather than the German taste; and if the favour in which this character is held by the audience, together with every sentence and incident, which I have presumed to introduce in the play, may be offered as the criterion of my skill, I am sufficiently rewarded for the task I have performed.

In stating the foregoing circumstances relating to this production, I hope not to be suspected of arrogating to my own exertions only, the popularity which has attended "The Child of Love," under the title of "Lovers' Vows:"—the exertions of every performer engaged in the play deservedly claim a share in its success; and I most sincerely thank them for the high importance of their aid.

REMARKS

Plays, founded on German dramas, have long been a subject both of ridicule and of serious animadversion. Ridicule is a jocund slanderer; and who does not love to be merry? but the detraction, that is dull, is inexcusable calumny.

The grand moral of this play is—to set forth the miserable consequences which arise from the neglect, and to enforce the watchful care, of illegitimate offspring; and surely, as the pulpit has not had eloquence to eradicate the crime of seduction, the stage may be allowed an humble endeavour to prevent its most fatal effects.

But there are some pious declaimers against theatrical exhibitions, so zealous to do good,—they grudge the poor dramatist his share in the virtuous concern.

Not furnished with one plea throughout four acts of "Lovers' Vows" for accusation, those critics arraign its catastrophe, and say,—"the wicked should be punished."—They forget there is a punishment called *conscience*, which, though it seldom troubles the defamer's peace, may weigh heavy on the fallen female and her libertine seducer.

But as a probationary prelude to the supposed happiness of the frail personages of this drama, the author has plunged the offender, Agatha, in bitterest poverty and woe; which she receives as a contrite penitent, atoning for her sins. The Baron Wildenhaim, living in power and splendour, is still more rigorously visited by remorse: and, in the reproaches uttered by his outcast son, (become, by the father's criminal disregard of his necessities, a culprit subject to death by the law,) the Baron's guilt has sure exemplary chastisement. But yet, after all the varied anguish of his mind, should tranquillity promise, at length, to crown his future days, where is the immorality? If holy books teach, that the wicked too often prosper, why are plays to be withheld from inculcating the self-same doctrine? Not that a worldly man would class it amongst the prosperous events of life, to be (like the Baron) compelled to marry his cast-off mistress, after twenty years absence.

It may not here be wholly useless to observe—that, in the scene in the fourth act, just mentioned, between the Baron and his son—the actor, who plays Frederick, too frequently forms his notion of the passion he is to pourtray, through the interview, from the following lines, at the end of one of his speeches:

"And, when he dies, a funeral sermon will praise his great benevolence, his christian charities."

The sarcasm here to be expressed, should be evinced in no one sentence else. Where, in a preceding speech, he says, the Baron is—"a man, kind, generous, beloved by his tenants:"— he certainly means *this* to be his character. Frederick is not ironical, except by accident. Irony and sarcasm do not appertain to youth: open, plain, downright habits, are the endearing qualities of the young. Moreover, a son, urged by cruel injuries, may upbraid his father even to rage, and the audience will yet feel interest for them both; but if he contemn or deride him, all respect is lost, both for the one and the other.

The passions which take possession of this young soldier's heart, when admitted to the presence of the Baron, knowing him to be his father, are various; but scorn is not amongst the number. Awe gives the first sensation, and is subdued by pride: filial tenderness would next force its way, and is overwhelmed by anger. These passions strive in his breast, till grief for his mother's wrongs, and his own ignominious state, burst all restraint—and as fury drives him to the point of distraction, he changes his accents to a tone of irony, in the lines just quoted.

"Oh! there be actors I have seen, and heard others praise, who, (not to speak it profanely,) have"—scornfully sneered at their father through this whole scene, and yet, been highly applauded.

While it is the fashion to see German plays, both the German and the English author will patiently bear the displeasure of a small party of critics, as the absolute conditions on which they enjoy popularity. Nor, till the historian is forbid to tell, how tyrants have success in vanquishing nations; or the artist be compelled to paint the beauteous courtezan with hideous features, as the emblem of her mind, shall the free dramatist be untrue to his science; which, like theirs, is to follow nature through all her rightful course. Deception, beyond the result of genuine imitative art, he will disclaim, and say with Shakspeare to the self-approving zealot:

> "Virtue itself turns vice, being misapplied,
> And vice sometime's by action dignified."

PERSONS REPRESENTED.

BARON WILDENHAIM	*Mr. Murray.*
COUNT CASSEL	*Mr. Knight.*
ANHALT	*Mr. H. Johnston.*
FREDERICK	*Mr. Pope.*
VERDUN, the Butler	*Mr. Munden.*
LANDLORD	*Mr. Thompson.*
COTTAGER	*Mr. Davenport.*
FARMER	*Mr. Rees.*
COUNTRYMAN	*Mr. Dyke.*
AGATHA FRIBURG	*Mrs. Johnson.*
AMELIA WILDENHAIM	*Mrs. H. Johnston.*
COTTAGER'S WIFE	*Mrs. Davenport.*
COUNTRY GIRL	*Miss Leserve.*

Huntsmen, Servants, &c.

SCENE—Germany.

LOVERS' VOWS.

ACT THE FIRST.

SCENE I.

A high road, a town at a distance.—A small inn on one side the road.—A cottage on the other.

The LANDLORD *of the inn leads* AGATHA *by the hand out of his house.*

Land. No, no! no room for you any longer—It is the fair to-day in the next village; as great a fair as any in the German dominions. The country people with their wives and children take up every corner we have.

Agatha. You will turn a poor sick woman out of doors, who has spent her last farthing in your house?

Land. For that very reason; because she *has* spent her last farthing.

Agatha. I can work.

Land. You can hardly move your hands.

Agatha. My strength will come again.

Land. Then *you* may come again.

Agatha. What am I to do? where shall I go?

Land. It is fine weather—you may go any where.

Agatha. Who will give me a morsel of bread to satisfy my hunger?

Land. Sick people eat but little.

Agatha. Hard, unfeeling man, have pity.

Land. When times are hard, pity is too expensive for a poor man. Ask alms of the different people that go by.

Agatha. Beg! I would rather starve.

Land. You may beg, and starve too. What a fine lady you are! Many an honest woman has been obliged to beg. Why should not you? [AGATHA *sits down upon a large stone under a tree.*] For instance, here comes somebody; and I will teach you how to begin. [*A* COUNTRYMAN, *with working tools, crosses the road.*] Good day, neighbour Nicholas.

Countr. Good day.   [*Stops.*

Land. Won't you give a trifle to this poor woman? [COUNTRYMAN *takes no notice, but walks off.*] That would not do—the poor man has nothing himself but what he gets by hard labour. Here comes a rich farmer; perhaps he will give you something.

Enter FARMER.

Land. Good morning to you, sir. Under yon tree sits a poor woman in distress, who is in need of your charity.

Far. Is she not ashamed of herself? Why don't she work?

Land. She has had a fever. If you would but pay for one dinner—

Far. The harvest has been but indifferent, and my cattle and sheep have suffered by a distemper.   [*Exit.*

Land. My fat smiling face was not made for begging: you'll have more luck with your thin, sour one—so, I'll leave you to yourself.   [*Exit.*

[AGATHA *rises, and comes forward.*

Agatha. Oh Providence! thou hast till this hour protected me, and hast given me fortitude not to despair. Receive my humble thanks, and restore me to health, for the sake of my poor son, the innocent cause of my sufferings, and yet my only comfort. [*Kneeling.*] Oh, grant, that I may see him once more! See him improved in strength of mind and body; and that by thy gracious mercy he may never be visited with afflictions great as mine. [*After a pause.*] Protect his father too, merciful Providence, and pardon his crime of

perjury to me! Here, in the face of Heaven (supposing my
end approaching, and that I can but a few days longer
struggle with want and sorrow,) here, I solemnly forgive my
seducer for all the ills, the accumulated evils, which his
allurements, his deceit and cruelty, have for twenty years
past drawn upon me.

Enter a COUNTRY GIRL, *with a basket.*

Agatha. [*Near fainting.*] My dear child, if you could spare
me a trifle—
Girl. I have not a farthing in the world—But I am
going to market to sell my eggs, and as I come back I'll
give you three-pence—And I'll be back as soon as ever I
can.   [*Exit.*
Agatha. There was a time, when I was as happy
as this country girl, and as willing to assist the poor in
distress.   [*Retires to the tree, and sits down.*

Enter FREDERICK—*He is dressed in a German soldier's
uniform, has a knapsack on his shoulders, appears in high spirits,
and stops at the door of the inn.*

Fred. Halt! Stand at ease! It is a very hot day—A draught
of good wine will not be amiss. But first let me consult my
purse. [*Takes out a couple of pieces of money, which he turns
about in his hand.*] This will do for a breakfast—the other
remains for my dinner; and in the evening I shall be at
home. [*Calls out.*] Ha! Halloo! Landlord! [*Takes notice of*
AGATHA, *who is leaning against the tree.*] Who is that? A
poor sick woman! She don't beg; but her appearance makes
me think she is in want. Must one always wait to give till
one is asked? Shall I go without my breakfast now, or lose
my dinner? The first I think is best. Ay, I don't want a

breakfast, for dinner-time will soon be here. To do good satisfies both hunger and thirst. [*Going towards her with the money in his hand.*] Take this, good woman.

> [*She stretches her hand for the gift, looks stedfastly at him, and cries out with astonishment and joy.*

Agatha. Frederick!

Fred. Mother! [*With amazement and grief.*] Mother! For God's sake what is this! How is this! And why do I find my mother thus? Speak!

Agatha. I cannot speak, dear son! [*Rising, and embracing him.*] My dear Frederick! The joy is too great—I was not prepared—

Fred. Dear mother, compose yourself: [*Leans her head against his breast.*] now then, be comforted. How she trembles! She is fainting.

Agatha. I am so weak, and my head so giddy—I had nothing to eat all yesterday.

Fred. Good heavens! Here is my little money, take it all! Oh mother! mother! [*Runs to the inn.*] Landlord! Landlord! [*Knocking violently at the door.*]

Land. What is the matter?

Fred. A bottle of wine—quick, quick!

Land. [*Surprised.*] A bottle of wine! For who?

Fred. For me. Why do you ask? Why don't you make haste?

Land. Well, well, Mr. Soldier: but can you pay for it?

Fred. Here is money—make haste, or I'll break every window in your house.

Land. Patience! Patience! [*Goes off.*

Fred. [*To* AGATHA.] You were hungry yesterday, when I sat down to a comfortable dinner. You were hungry, when I partook of a good supper. Oh! Why is so much bitter mixed with the joy of my return?

568

Agatha. Be patient, my dear Frederick. Since I see you, I am well. But I *have been* very ill: so ill, that I despaired of ever beholding you again.

Fred. Ill, and I was not with you? I will, now, never leave you more. Look, mother, how tall and strong I am grown. These arms can now afford you support. They can, and shall, procure you subsistence.

LANDLORD, *coming out of the house with a small pitcher.*

Land. Here is wine—a most delicious nectar. [*Aside.*] It is only Rhenish; but it will pass for the best old Hock.

Fred. [*Impatiently snatching the pitcher.*] Give it me.

Land. No, no—the money first. One shilling and two-pence, if you please.   [FRED. *gives him money.*

Fred. This is all I have.—Here, here, mother.

          [*While she drinks,* LANDLORD *counts the money.*

Land. Three halfpence too short! However, one must be charitable.   [*Exit* LANDLORD.

Agatha. I thank you, my dear Frederick—Wine revives me—Wine from the hand of my son gives me almost a new life.

Fred. Don't speak too much, mother—Take your time.

Agatha. Tell me, dear child, how you have passed the five years, since you left me.

Fred. Both good and bad, mother. To-day plenty—to-morrow not so much—And sometimes nothing at all.

Agatha. You have not written to me this long while.

Fred. Dear mother, consider the great distance I was from you!—And then, in the time of war, how often letters miscarry.—Besides——

Agatha. No matter, now I see you. But have you obtained your discharge?

Fred. Oh, no, mother—I have leave of absence only for two months; and that for a particular reason. But I will not quit you so soon, now I find you are in want of my assistance.

Agatha. No, no, Frederick; your visit will make me so well, that I shall in a very short time recover strength to work again; and you must return to your regiment, when your furlough is expired. But you told me leave of absence was granted you for a particular reason.—What reason?

Fred. When I left you, five years ago, you gave me every thing you could afford, and all you thought would be necessary for me. But one trifle you forgot, which was, the certificate of my birth from the church-book. You know in this country there is nothing to be done without it. At the time of parting from you, I little thought it could be of that consequence to me, which I have since found it would have been. Once I became tired of a soldier's life, and in the hope I should obtain my discharge, offered myself to a master to learn a profession; but his question was, "Where is your certificate from the church-book of the parish, in which you were born?" It vexed me that I had not it to produce, for my comrades laughed at my disappointment. My captain behaved kinder, for he gave me leave to come home to fetch it—and you see, mother, here I am.

[*During this speech*, AGATHA *is confused and agitated.*]

Agatha. So you are come for the purpose of fetching your certificate from the church-book.

Fred. Yes, mother.

Agatha. Oh! oh!

Fred. What is the matter? [*She bursts into tears.*] For Heaven's sake, mother, tell me what's the matter?

Agatha. You have no certificate.

Fred. No!

Agatha. No.—The laws of Germany excluded you from being registered at your birth—for—you are a natural son.

Fred. [*Starts*]—[*After a pause.*] So!—And who is my father?

Agatha. Oh, Frederick, your wild looks are daggers to my heart. Another time.

Fred. [*Endeavouring to conceal his emotion.*] No, no—I am still your son—and you are still my mother. Only tell me, who is my father?

Agatha. When we parted, five years ago, you were too young to be intrusted with a secret of so much importance.—But the time is come, when I can, in confidence, open my heart, and unload that burthen, with which it has been long oppressed. And yet, to reveal my errors to my child, and sue for his mild judgment on my conduct—

Fred. You have nothing to sue for; only explain this mystery.

Agatha. I will. I will. But—my tongue is locked with remorse and shame. You must not look at me.

Fred. Not look at you! Cursed be that son, who could find his mother guilty, although the world should call her so.

Agatha. Then listen to me, and take notice of that village, [*Pointing.*] of that castle, and of that church. In that village I was born—In that church I was baptized. My parents were poor, but reputable farmers.—The lady of that castle and estate requested them to let me live with her, and she would provide for me through life. They resigned me; and, at the age of fourteen, I went to my patroness. She took pleasure to instruct me in all kind of female literature and accomplishments, and three happy years had passed, under her protection, when her only son, who was an officer in the Saxon service, obtained permission to come home. I had never seen him before—he was a handsome young man—in my eyes a prodigy; for he talked of love, and promised me marriage. He was the first man, who had ever spoke to me on such a subject.—His flattery made me vain, and his repeated vows——Don't look at me, dear Frederick!—I can say no more. [FREDERICK, *with his eyes cast down, takes her hand, and puts it to his heart.*] Oh! oh! my son! I was intoxicated by the fervent caresses of a young, inexperienced, capricious man, and did not recover from the delirium till it was too late.

Fred. [*After a pause.*] Go on.—Let me know more of my father.

Agatha. When the time drew near that I could no longer conceal my guilt and shame, my seducer prevailed on me not to expose him to the resentment of his mother. He renewed his former promises of marriage at her death;—on which relying, I gave him my word to be secret—and I have to this hour buried his name deep in my heart.

Fred. Proceed, proceed! give me full information——I will have courage to hear it all.   [*Greatly agitated.*]

Agatha. His leave of absence expired, he returned to his regiment, depending on my promise, and well assured of my esteem. As soon as my situation became known, I was questioned, and received many severe reproaches: but I refused to confess who was my undoer; and for that obstinacy was turned from the castle.—I went to my parents; but their door was shut against me. My mother, indeed, wept as she bade me quit her sight for ever; but my father wished,—that increased affliction might befal me.

Fred. [*Weeping.*] Be quick with your narrative, or you'll break my heart.

Agatha. I now sought protection from the old clergyman of the parish. He received me with compassion. On my knees I begged forgiveness for the scandal I had caused to his parishioners; promised amendment; and he said he did not doubt me. Through his recommendation I went to town; and, hid in humble lodgings, procured the means of subsistence by teaching to the neighbouring children what I had learnt under the tuition of my benefactress.—To instruct you, my Frederick, was my care and my delight; and, in return for your filial love, I would not thwart your wishes, when they led to a soldier's life: but I saw you go from me with an aching heart. Soon after, my health declined, I was compelled to give up my employment, and, by degrees, became the object you now see me. But, let me add, before I close my calamitous story, that—when I left the good old clergyman, taking along with me his kind advice and his blessing, I left him with a firm determination to fulfil the vow I had made of repentance and amendment. I *have* fulfilled it—and now, Frederick, you may look at me again.   [*He embraces her.*

Fred. But my father all this time? [*Mournfully.*] I apprehend he died.

Agatha. No—he married.

Fred. Married!

Agatha. A woman of virtue——of noble birth and immense fortune. Yet, [*Weeps.*] I had written to him many times; had described your infant innocence and wants; had glanced obliquely at former promises——

Fred. [*Rapidly.*] No answer to these letters?

Agatha. Not a word.—But in the time of war, you know, letters miscarry.

Fred. Nor did he ever return to this estate?

Agatha. No—since the death of his mother this castle has only been inhabited by servants—for he settled as far off as Alsace, upon the estate of his wife.

Fred. I will carry you in my arms to Alsace. No—why should I ever know my father, if he is a villain! My heart is satisfied with a mother.—No—I will not go to him. I will not disturb his peace—I leave that task to his conscience. What say you, mother, can't we do without him? [*Struggling between his tears and his pride.*] We don't want him. I will write directly to my captain. Let the consequence be what it will, leave you again I cannot. Should I be able to get my discharge, I will work all day at the plough, and all the night with my pen. It will do, mother, it will do! Heaven's goodness will assist me—it will prosper the endeavours of a dutiful son for the sake of a helpless mother.

Agatha. [*Presses him to her breast.*] Where could be found such another son?

Fred. But tell me my father's name, that I may know how to shun him.

Agatha. Baron Wildenhaim.

Fred. Baron Wildenhaim! I shall never forget it.—Oh! you are near fainting. Your eyes are cast down. What's the matter? Speak, mother!

Agatha. Nothing particular.—Only fatigued with talking, I wish to take a little rest.

Fred. I did not consider, that we have been all this time in the open road. [*Goes to the inn, and knocks at the door.*] Here, Landlord!

LANDLORD *re-enters.*

Land. Well, what is the matter now?

Fred. Make haste, and get a bed ready for this good
woman.

Land. [*With a sneer.*] A bed for this good woman! Ha! ha!
ha! She slept last night in that pent-house; so she may
to-night.   [*Exit, shutting the door.*

Fred. You are an infamous—[*Goes back to his mother.*] Oh!
my poor mother—[*Runs to the cottage at a little distance, and
knocks.*] Ha! halloo! Who is there?

Enter COTTAGER.

Cot. Good day, young soldier.—What is it you want?

Fred. Good friend, look at that poor woman. She is
perishing in the public road! It is my mother.—Will you
give her a small corner in your hut? I beg for mercy's
sake—Heaven will reward you.

Cot. Can't you speak quietly? I understand you very well.
[*Calls at the door of the hut.*] Wife, shake up our bed—here's
a poor sick woman wants it.

Enter WIFE.

Why could not you say all this in fewer words? Why such a
long preamble? Why for mercy's sake, and Heaven's reward;
Why talk about reward for such trifles as these? Come, let
us lead her in; and welcome she shall be to a bed, as good as
I can give her; and to our homely fare.

Fred. Ten thousand thanks, and blessings on you!

Wife. Thanks and blessings! here's a piece of work indeed
about nothing! Good sick lady, lean on my shoulder. [*To*
FREDERICK.] Thanks and reward, indeed! Do you think

575

husband and I have lived to these years, and don't know our duty? Lean on my shoulder.   [*Exeunt into the cottage.*

ACT THE SECOND.

SCENE I.
A room in the Cottage.

AGATHA, COTTAGER, *his* WIFE, *and* FREDERICK *discovered*—AGATHA *reclining upon a wooden bench.* FREDERICK *leaning over her.*

Fred. Good people, have you nothing to give her? Nothing that's nourishing?

Wife. Run, husband, run, and fetch a bottle of wine from the landlord of the inn.

Fred. No, no—his wine is as bad as his heart: she has drank some of it, which I am afraid has turned to poison.

Cot. Suppose, wife, you look for a new laid egg?

Wife. Or a drop of brandy, husband—that mostly cures me.

Fred. Do you hear, mother—will you, mother? [AGATHA *makes a sign with her hand as if she could not take any thing.*] She will not. Is there no doctor in this neighbourhood?

Wife. At the end of the village there lives a horse doctor. I have never heard of any other.

Fred. What shall I do? She is dying. My mother is dying—Pray for her, good people!

Agatha. Make yourself easy, dear Frederick, I am well, only weak—Some wholesome nourishment—

Fred. Yes, mother, directly—directly. [*Aside.*] Oh! where shall I—no money—not a farthing left.

Wife. Oh, dear me! Had you not paid the rent yesterday, husband—

Cot. I then should know what to do. But as I hope for mercy, I have not a penny in my house.

Fred. Then I must—[*Apart, coming forward.*]—Yes, I will go, and beg.—But should I be refused—I will then—I leave my mother in your care, good people—Do all you can for her, I beseech you! I shall soon be with you again. [*Goes off in haste and confusion.*]

Cot. If he should go to our parson, I am sure he would give him something.

[AGATHA *having revived by degrees during the scene, rises.*]

Agatha. Is that good old man still living, who was minister here some time ago?

Wife. No—It pleased Providence to take that worthy man to Heaven two years ago. We have lost in him both a friend and a father. We shall never get such another.

Cot. Wife, wife, our present rector is likewise a very good man.

Wife. Yes! But he is so very young.

Cot. Our late parson was young once.

Wife. [*To* AGATHA.] This young man being tutor in our Baron's family, he is very much beloved by them all; and so the Baron gave him this living in consequence.

Cot. And well he deserved it, for his pious instructions to our young lady; who is, in consequence, good, and friendly to every body.

Agatha. What young lady do you mean?

Cot. Our Baron's daughter.

Agatha. Is she here?

Wife. Dear me! Don't you know that? I thought every body had known that. It is almost five weeks since the Baron and all his family arrived at the castle.

Agatha. Baron Wildenhaim?

Wife. Yes, Baron Wildenhaim.

Agatha. And his lady?

Cot. His lady died in France, many miles from hence, and her death, I suppose, was the cause of his coming to this estate– For the Baron has not been here till within these five weeks ever since he was married. We regretted his absence much, and his arrival has caused great joy.

Wife. [*Addressing her discourse to* AGATHA.] By all accounts the Baroness was very haughty, and very whimsical.

Cot. Wife, wife, never speak ill of the dead. Say what you please against the living, but not a word against the dead.

Wife. And yet, husband, I believe the dead care the least what is said against them.—And so, if you please, I'll tell my story. The late Baroness was, they say, haughty and proud; and they do say, the Baron was not so happy as he might have been;—but he, bless him, our good Baron is still the same as when a boy. Soon after madam had closed her eyes, he left France, and came to Wildenhaim, his native country.

Cot. Many times has he joined in our village dances. Afterwards, when he became an officer, he was rather wild, as most young men are.

Wife. Yes, I remember when he fell in love with poor Agatha, Friburg's daughter: what a piece of work that was—It did not do him much credit. That was a wicked thing.

Cot. Have done—no more of this—It is not well to stir up old grievances.

Wife. Why you said I might speak ill of the living. 'Tis very hard indeed, if one must not speak ill of one's neighbours, dead, or alive.

Cot. Who knows whether he was the father of Agatha's child? She never said he was.

Wife. Nobody but him—that I am sure—I would lay a wager—no, no, husband, you must not take his part—it is very wicked! Who knows what is now become of that poor creature? She has not been heard of this many a year. May be she is starving for hunger. Her father might have lived longer too, if that misfortune had not happened.

[AGATHA *faints.*

Cot. See here! Help! She is fainting—take hold.

Wife. Oh, poor woman!

Cot. Let us take her into the next room.

Wife. Oh, poor woman! – I am afraid she will not live. Come cheer up, cheer up. You are with those who feel for you. [*They lead her off.*]

SCENE 2.

An apartment in the Castle.

*A table spread for breakfast—Several Servants in livery disposing the equipage—*BARON WILDENHAIM *enters, attended by a* GENTLEMAN *in waiting.*

Baron. Has not Count Cassel left his chamber yet?

Gent. No, my lord, he has but now rung for his valet.

Baron. The whole castle smells of his perfumery. Go, call my daughter hither. [*Exit* GENTLEMAN.] And am I after all to have an ape for a son-in-law? No, I shall not be in a hurry—I love my daughter too well. We must be better acquainted before I give her to him. I shall not sacrifice my Amelia to the will of others, as I myself was sacrificed. The poor girl might, in thoughtlessness, say yes, and afterwards be miserable. What a pity she is not a boy! The name of Wildenhaim will die with me. My fine estates, my good peasants, all will fall into the hands of strangers. Oh! why was not Amelia a boy?

  Enter AMELIA—[*She kisses the* BARON'S *hand.*]

Amelia. Good morning, dear my lord.

Baron. Good morning, Amelia. Have you slept well?

Amelia. Oh! yes, papa. I always sleep well.

Baron. Not a little restless last night?

Amelia. No.

Baron. Amelia, you know you have a father, who loves you, and I believe you know you have a suitor who is come to ask permission to love you. Tell me candidly how you like Count Cassel.

Amelia. Very well.

Baron. Do not you blush, when I talk of him?

Amelia. No.

Baron. No:—I am sorry for that. [*Aside.*]—Have you dreamt of him?

Amelia. No.

Baron. Have you not dreamt at all to-night?

Amelia. Oh yes—I have dreamt of our Chaplain, Mr. Anhalt.

Baron. Ah ha! As if he stood before you and the Count to ask for the ring.

Amelia. No: not that—I dreamt we were all still in France, and he, my tutor, just going to take his leave of us for ever.—I 'woke with the fright, and found my eyes full of tears.

Baron. Pshaw! I want to know if you can love the Count. You saw him at the last ball we were at in France: when he capered round you; when he danced minuets; when he——. But I cannot say what his conversation was.

Amelia. Nor I either—I do not remember a syllable of it.

Baron. No? Then I do not think you like him.

Amelia. I believe not.

Baron. But I think proper to acquaint you, he is rich, and of great consequence: rich, and of great consequence; do you hear?

Amelia. Yes, dear papa. But my tutor has always told me, that birth and fortune are inconsiderable things, and cannot give happiness.

Baron. There he is right—But if it happens, that birth and fortune are joined with sense and virtue——

Amelia. But is it so with Count Cassel?

Baron. Hem! Hem! [*Aside.*] I will ask you a few questions on this subject; but be sure to answer me honestly—Speak the truth.

Amelia. I never told an untruth in my life.

Baron. Nor ever *conceal* the truth from me, I command you.

Amelia. [*Earnestly.*] Indeed, my lord, I never will.

Baron. I take you at your word—And now reply to me truly—Do you like to hear the Count spoken of?

Amelia. Good, or bad?

Baron. Good. Good.

Amelia. Oh yes; I like to hear good of every body.

Baron. But do not you feel a little fluttered, when he is talked of?

Amelia. No.   [*Shaking her head.*

Baron. Are not you a little embarrassed?

Amelia. No.

Baron. Don't you wish sometimes to speak to him, and have not the courage to begin?

Amelia. No.

Baron. Do not you wish to take his part, when his companions laugh at him?

Amelia. No—I love to laugh at him myself.

Baron. Provoking! [*Aside.*] Are not you afraid of him, when he comes near you?

Amelia. No, not at all.—Oh, yes—once.

[*Recollecting herself.*

Baron. Ah! Now it comes!

Amelia. Once at a ball he trod on my foot; and I was so afraid he should tread on me again.

Baron. You put me out of patience. Hear me, Amelia! [*Stops short, and speaks softer.*] To see you happy is my wish. But matrimony, without concord, is like a duetto badly performed; for that reason, nature, the great composer of all harmony, has ordained, that, when bodies are allied, hearts should be in perfect unison. However, I will send Mr. Anhalt to you——

Amelia. [*Much pleased.*] Do, papa.

Baron. He shall explain to you my sentiments. [*Rings.*] A clergyman can do this better than——

Enter Servant.

Go directly to Mr. Anhalt, tell him I shall be glad to see him for a quarter of an hour, if he is not engaged.

[*Exit* Servant.

Amelia. [*Calls after him.*] Wish him a good morning from me.

Baron. [*Looking at his watch.*] The Count is a tedious time dressing.—Have you breakfasted, Amelia?

Amelia. No, papa.   [*They sit down to breakfast.*

Baron. How is the weather? Have you walked this morning?

Amelia. Oh, yes—I was in the garden at five o'clock; it is very fine.

Baron. Then I'll go out shooting. I do not know in what other way to amuse my guest.

Enter COUNT CASSEL.

Count. Ah, my dear Colonel! Miss Wildenhaim, I kiss your hand.

Baron. Good morning! good morning! though it is late in the day, Count. In the country we should rise earlier.   [AMELIA *offers the* COUNT *a cup of tea.*

Count. It is Hebe herself, or Venus, or——

Amelia. Ha! ha! ha! Who can help laughing at his nonsense?

Baron. [*Rather angry.*] Neither Venus, nor Hebe; but Amelia Wildenhaim, if you please.

Count. [*Sitting down to breakfast.*] You are beautiful, Miss Wildenhaim.—Upon my honour, I think so. I have travelled, and seen much of the world, and yet I can positively admire you.

Amelia. I am sorry I have not seen the world.

Count. Wherefore?

Amelia. Because I might then, perhaps, admire you.

Count. True;—for I am an epitome of the world. In my travels I learnt delicacy in Italy—hauteur, in Spain—in France, enterprize—in Russia, prudence—in England, sincerity—in Scotland, frugality—and in the wilds of America, I learnt love.

Amelia. Is there any country where love is taught?

Count. In all barbarous countries. But the whole system is exploded in places that are civilized.

Amelia. And what is substituted in its stead?

Count. Intrigue.

Amelia. What a poor, uncomfortable substitute!

Count. There are other things—Song, dance, the opera, and war.   [*Since the entrance of the* COUNT, *the* BARON
                    has removed to a table at a little distance.

Baron. What are you talking of there?

Count. Of war, Colonel.

Baron. [*Rising.*] Ay, we like to talk on what we don't understand.

Count. [*Rising.*] Therefore, to a lady, I always speak of politics; and to her father, on love.

Baron. I believe, Count, notwithstanding your sneer, I am still as much of a proficient in that art as yourself.

Count. I do not doubt it, my dear Colonel, for you are a soldier: and, since the days of Alexander, whoever conquers men, is certain to overcome women.

Baron. An achievement to animate a poltron.

Count. And, I verily believe, gains more recruits than the king's pay.

Baron. Now we are on the subject of arms, should you like to go out a shooting with me for an hour before dinner?

Count. Bravo, Colonel! A charming thought! This will give me an opportunity to use my elegant gun: the butt is inlaid with mother-of-pearl. You cannot find better work, or better taste.—Even my coat of arms is engraved.

Baron. But can you shoot?

Count. That I have never tried—except, with my eyes, at a fine woman.

Baron. I am not particular what game I pursue.—I have an old gun; it does not look fine; but I can always bring down my bird.

Enter SERVANT.

Serv. Mr. Anhalt begs leave——

Baron. Tell him to come in.—I shall be ready in a moment. [*Exit* SERVANT.

Count. Who is Mr. Anhalt?

Amelia. Oh, a very good man. [*With warmth.*

Count. A good man! In Italy, that means a religious man; in France, it means a cheerful man; in Spain, it means a wise man; and in England, it means a rich man.—Which good man of all these is Mr. Anhalt?

Amelia. A good man in every country, except England.

Count. And give me the English good man, before that of any other nation.

Baron. And of what nation would you prefer your good woman to be, Count?

Count. Of Germany.   [*Bowing to* AMELIA.

Amelia. In compliment to me?

Count. In justice to my own judgment.

Baron. Certainly. For have we not an instance of one German woman, who possesses every virtue that ornaments the whole sex; whether as a woman of illustrious rank, or in the more exalted character of a wife, and a mother?

Enter MR. ANHALT.

Anhalt. I come by your command, Baron——

Baron. Quick, Count.—Get your elegant gun.—I pass your apartments, and will soon call for you.

Count. I fly.—Beautiful Amelia, it is a sacrifice I make to your father, that I leave for a few hours his amiable daughter.   [*Exit.*

Baron. My dear Amelia, I think it scarcely necessary to speak to Mr. Anhalt, or that he should speak to you, on the subject of the Count; but as he is here, leave us alone.

Amelia. [*As she retires.*] Good morning, Mr. Anhalt.—I hope you are very well.   [*Exit.*

Baron. I'll tell you in a few words, why I sent for you. Count Cassel is here, and wishes to marry my daughter.

Anhalt. [*Much concerned.*] Really!

Baron. He is—he—in a word, I don't like him.

Anhalt. [*With emotion.*] And Miss Wildenhaim——

Baron. I shall not command, neither persuade her to the marriage—I know too well the fatal influence of parents on such a subject. Objections to be sure, if they could be removed—But when you find a man's head without brains, and his bosom without a heart, these are important articles to supply. Young as you are, Anhalt, I know no one so able to restore, or to bestow, those blessings on his fellow creatures, as you. [ANHALT *bows.*] The Count wants a little of my daughter's simplicity and sensibility.—Take him under your care while he is here, and make him something like yourself.—You have succeeded to my wish in the education of my daughter.—Form the Count after your own manner.—I shall then have what I have sighed for all my life—a son.

Anhalt. With your permission, Baron, I will ask one question. What remains to interest you in favour of a man, whose head and heart are good for nothing?

Baron. Birth and fortune. Yet, if I thought my daughter absolutely disliked him, or that she loved another, I would not thwart a first affection;—no, for the world, I would not. [*Sighing.*] But that her affections are already bestowed, is not probable.

Anhalt. Are you of opinion, that she will never fall in love?

Baron. Oh! no. I am of opinion, no woman ever arrived at the age of twenty without that misfortune.—But this is another subject.—Go to Amelia—explain to her the duties of a wife, and of a mother.—If she comprehends them, as she ought, then ask her, if she thinks she could fulfil those duties, as the wife of Count Cassel.

Anhalt. I will.—But—I—Miss Wildenhaim—[*Confused.*] I—I shall—I—I shall obey your commands.

Baron. Do so. [*Gives a deep sigh.*] Ah! so far this weight is removed; but there lies still a heavier next my heart.—You understand me.—How is it, Mr. Anhalt? Have you not yet been able to make any discoveries on that unfortunate subject?

Anhalt. I have taken infinite pains; but in vain. No such person is to be found.

Baron. Believe me, this burthen presses on my thoughts so much, that many nights I go without sleep. A man is sometimes tempted to commit such depravity when young.—Oh, Anhalt! had I, in my youth, had you for a tutor;—but I had no instructor but my passions; no governor but my own will.   [*Exit.*

Anhalt. This commission of the Baron's, in respect to his daughter, I am—[*Looks about.*]—If I should meet her now, I cannot—I must recover myself first, and then prepare.—A walk in the fields, and a fervent prayer—After these, I trust, I shall return, as a man, whose views are solely placed on a future world; all hopes in this, with fortitude resigned.

[*Exit.*

ACT THE THIRD.

SCENE I.

An open Field.

FREDERICK *alone, with a few pieces of money, which he turns about in his hands.*

Fred. To return with this trifle, for which I have stooped to beg! return to see my mother dying! I would rather fly to the world's end. [*Looking at the money.*] What can I buy with this? It is hardly enough to pay for the nails, that will

587

be wanted for her coffin. My great anxiety will drive me to distraction. However, let the consequence of our affliction be what it may, all will fall upon my father's head; and may he pant for Heaven's forgiveness, as my poor mother——[*At a distance is heard the firing of a gun, then the cry of halloo, halloo*—GAMEKEEPERS *and* SPORTSMEN *run across the stage—he looks about.*] Here they come—a nobleman, I suppose, or a man of fortune. Yes, yes—and I will once more beg for my mother.—May Heaven send relief!

> Enter the BARON, *followed slowly by the* COUNT.
> *The* BARON *stops.*

Baron. Quick, quick, Count! Aye, aye, that was a blunder, indeed. Don't you see the dogs? There they run—they have lost the scent.   [*Exit* BARON, *looking after the dogs.*
Count. So much the better, Colonel, for I must take a little breath.   [*He leans on his gun*—FREDERICK *goes up to him with great modesty.*
Fred. Gentleman, I beg you will bestow from your superfluous wants something to relieve the pain, and nourish the weak frame, of an expiring woman.

> *The* BARON *re-enters.*

Count. What police is here! that a nobleman's amusements should be interrupted by the attack of vagrants.
Fred. [*To the* BARON.] Have pity, noble sir, and relieve the distress of an unfortunate son, who supplicates for his dying mother.
Baron. [*Taking out his purse.*] I think, young soldier, it would be better if you were with your regiment on duty, instead of begging.

Fred. I would with all my heart: but at this present moment my sorrows are too great.—[BARON *gives something.*] I entreat your pardon. What you have been so good as to give me, is not enough.

Baron. [*Surprised.*] Not enough!

Fred. No, it is not enough.

Count. The most singular beggar I ever met in all my travels.

Fred. If you have a charitable heart, give me one dollar.

Baron. This is the first time I was ever dictated by a beggar what to give him.

Fred. With one dollar you will save a distracted man.

Baron. I don't choose to give any more. Count, go on.

[*Exit* COUNT—*as the* BARON *follows,* FREDERICK *seizes him by the breast, and draws his sword.*]

Fred. Your purse, or your life.

Baron. [*Calling.*] Here! here! seize and secure him.

[*Some of the* GAMEKEEPERS *run on, lay hold of* FREDERICK, *and disarm him.*]

Fred. What have I done!

Baron. Take him to the castle, and confine him in one of the towers. I shall follow you immediately.

Fred. One favour I have to beg, one favour only.—I know that I am guilty, and am ready to receive the punishment, my crime deserves. But I have a mother, who is expiring for want—pity her, if you cannot pity me—bestow on her relief. If you will send to yonder hut, you will find that I do not impose on you a falsehood. For her it was I drew my sword—for her I am ready to die.

Baron. Take him away, and imprison him where I told you.

Fred. [*As he is forced off.*] Woe to that man, to whom I owe my birth.   [*Exit.*

Baron. [*Calls another* KEEPER.] Here, Frank, run directly to yonder hamlet, inquire in the first, second, and third, cottage for a poor sick woman—and if you really find such a person, give her this purse.   [*Exit* GAMEKEEPER.

Baron. A most extraordinary event!—and what a well-looking youth! something in his countenance and address, which struck me inconceivably!—If it is true, that he begged for his mother—But if he did——for the attempt upon my life, he must die. Vice is never half so dangerous, as when it assumes the garb of morality.   [*Exit.*

SCENE 2.

A room in the Castle.

AMELIA *alone.*

Amelia. Why am I so uneasy; so peevish; who has offended me? I did not mean to come into this room. In the garden I intended to go. [*Going, turns back.*] No, I will not—yes, I will—just go, and look if my auriculas are still in blossom; and if the apple-tree is grown, which Mr. Anhalt planted.—I feel very low-spirited—something must be the matter.—Why do I cry?—Am I not well?

Enter MR. ANHALT.

Ah! good morning, my dear sir—Mr. Anhalt, I meant to say—I beg pardon.

Anhalt. Never mind, Miss Wildenhaim—I don't dislike to hear you call me as you did.

Amelia. In earnest!

Anhalt. Really. You have been crying. May I know the reason? The loss of your mother, still?—

Amelia. No—I have left off crying for her.

Anhalt. I beg pardon if I have come at an improper hour; but I wait upon you by the commands of your father.

Amelia. You are welcome at all hours. My father has more than once told me, that he, who forms my mind, I should always consider as my greatest benefactor. [*Looking down.*] And my heart tells me the same.

Anhalt. I think myself amply rewarded by the good opinion you have of me.

Amelia. When I remember what trouble I have sometimes given you, I cannot be too grateful.

Anhalt. [*To himself*] Oh! Heavens! [*To* AMELIA.] I—I come from your father with a commission.—If you please, we will sit down [*He places chairs, and they sit*] Count Cassel is arrived.

Amelia. Yes I know.

Anhalt. And do you know for what reason?

Amelia. He wishes to marry me.

Anhalt. Does he? [*Hastily.*] But, believe me, the Baron will not persuade you—No, I am sure he will not.

Amelia. I know that.

Anhalt. He wishes, that I should ascertain whether you have an inclination——

Amelia. For the Count, or for matrimony, do you mean?

Anhalt. For matrimony.

Amelia. All things, that I don't know, and don't understand, are quite indifferent to me.

Anhalt. For that very reason I am sent to you to explain the good and the bad, of which matrimony is composed.

Amelia. Then I beg first to be acquainted with the good.

Anhalt. When two sympathetic hearts meet in the marriage state, matrimony may be called a happy life.

When such a wedded pair find thorns in their path, each will be eager, for the sake of the other, to tear them from the root. Where they have to mount hills, or wind a labyrinth, the most experienced will lead the way, and be a guide to his companion. Patience and love will accompany them in their journey, while melancholy and discord they leave far behind.—Hand in hand they pass on from morning till evening, through their summer's day, till the night of age draws on, and the sleep of death overtakes the one. The other, weeping and mourning, yet looks forward to the bright region, where he shall meet his still surviving partner, among trees and flowers, which themselves have planted, in the fields of eternal verdure.

Amelia. You may tell my father—I'll marry.   [*Rises.*

Anhalt. [*Rising.*] This picture is pleasing; but I must beg you not to forget, that there is another on the same subject.—When convenience, and fair appearance joined to folly and ill humour, forge the fetters of matrimony, they gall with their weight the married pair. Discontented with each other—at variance in opinions—their mutual aversion increases with the years they live together. They contend most, where they should most unite; torment, where they should most soothe. In this rugged way, choked with the weeds of suspicion, jealousy, anger, and hatred, they take their daily journey, till one of these also sleep in death. The other then lifts up his dejected head, and calls out in acclamations of joy—Oh, liberty! dear liberty!

Amelia. I will not marry.

Anhalt. You mean to say, you will not fall in love.

Amelia. Oh no! [*Ashamed.*] I am in love.

Anhalt. Are in love! [*Starting.*] And with the Count?

Amelia. I wish I was.

Anhalt. Why so?

Amelia. Because *he* would, perhaps, love me again.

Anhalt. [*Warmly.*] Who is there that would not?

Amelia. Would you?

Anhalt. I—I—me—I—I am out of the question.

Amelia. No; you are the very person to whom I have put the question.

Anhalt. What do you mean?

Amelia. I am glad you don't understand me. I was afraid I had spoken too plain.   [*In confusion.*

Anhalt. Understand you!—As to that—I am not dull.

Amelia. I know you are not—And as you have for a long time instructed me, why should not I now begin to teach you?

Anhalt. Teach me what?

Amelia. Whatever I know, and you don't.

Anhalt. There are some things, I had rather never know.

Amelia. So you may remember I said, when you began to teach me mathematics. I said, I had rather not know it—But now I have learnt it, it gives me a great deal of pleasure—and [*Hesitating.*] perhaps, who can tell, but that I might teach something as pleasant to you, as resolving a problem is to me.

Anhalt. Woman herself is a problem.

Amelia. And I'll teach you to make her out.

Anhalt. You teach?

Amelia. Why not? None but a woman can teach the science of herself: and though I own I am very young, a young woman may be as agreeable for a tutoress as an old one.—I am sure I always learnt faster from you than from the old clergyman, who taught me before you came.

Anhalt. This is nothing to the subject!

Amelia. What is the subject?

Anhalt. ———Love.

Amelia. [*Going up to him.*] Come, then, teach it me—teach it me as you taught me geography, languages, and other important things.

Anhalt. [*Turning from her.*] Pshaw!

Amelia. Ah! you won't—You know you have already taught me that, and you won't begin again.

Anhalt. You misconstrue—you misconceive every thing, I say or do. The subject I came to you upon was marriage.

Amelia. A very proper subject for the man, who has taught me love, and I accept the proposal.   [*Courtesying*.

Anhalt. Again you misconceive and confound me.

Amelia. Ay, I see how it is—You have no inclination to experience with me "the good part of matrimony:" I am not the female, with whom you would like to go "hand in hand up hills, and through labyrinths"—with whom you would like to "root up thorns; and with whom you would delight to plant lilies and roses." No, you had rather call out, "Oh, liberty! dear liberty!"

Anhalt. Why do you force from me, what it is villanous to own?—I love you more than life—Oh, Amelia! had we lived in those golden times, which the poets picture, no one but you——But, as the world is changed, your birth and fortune make our union impossible—To preserve the character, and, more, the feelings of an honest man, I would not marry you without the consent of your father—And could I, dare I, propose it to him?

Amelia. He has commanded me never to conceal or disguise the truth. I will propose it to him. The subject of the Count will force me to speak plainly, and this will be the most proper time, while he can compare the merit of you both.

Anhalt. I conjure you not to think of exposing yourself and me to his resentment.

Amelia. It is my father's will that I should marry—It is my father's wish to see me happy—If, then, you love me as you say, I will marry; and will be happy—but only with you.—I will tell him this.—At first he will start; then grow angry; then be in a passion—In his passion he will call me "undutiful:" but he will soon recollect himself, and resume his usual smiles, saying, "Well, well, if he love you, and you love him, in the name of Heaven, let it be."—Then I shall hug him round the neck, kiss his hands, run away from him, and fly to you; it will soon be known, that I am your bride, the whole village will come to wish me joy, and Heaven's blessing will follow.

Enter VERDUN, *the Butler.*

Amelia. [*Discontented.*] Ah! is it you?

Butler. Without vanity, I have taken the liberty to enter this apartment, the moment the good news reached my ears.

Amelia. What news?

Butler. Pardon an old servant, your father's old butler, gracious lady, who has had the honour to carry the Baron in his arms—and afterwards with humble submission to receive many a box o'the ear from you—if he thinks it his duty to make his congratulations with due reverence on this happy day, and to join with the muses in harmonious tunes on the lyre.

Amelia. Oh! my good butler, I am not in a humour to listen to the muses, and your lyre.

Butler. There has never been a birth-day, nor wedding-day, nor christening-day, celebrated in your family, in which I have not joined with the muses in full chorus.—

In forty-six years, three hundred and ninety-seven congratulations on different occasions have dropped from my pen. To-day, the three hundred and ninety-eighth is coming forth;—for Heaven has protected our noble master, who has been in great danger.

Amelia. Danger! My father in danger! What do you mean?

Butler. One of the gamekeepers has returned to inform the whole castle of a base and knavish trick, of which the world will talk, and my poetry hand down to posterity.

Amelia. What, what is all this?

Butler. The Baron, my lord and master, in company with the strange Count, had not been gone a mile beyond the lawn, when one of them——

Amelia. What happened? Speak, for Heaven's sake!

Butler. My verse shall tell you.

Amelia. No, no; tell us in prose.

Anhalt. Yes, in prose.

Butler. Ah, you have neither of you ever been in love, or you would prefer poetry to prose. But excuse [*Pulls out a paper.*] the haste in which it was written. I heard the news in the fields—always have paper and a pencil about me, and composed the whole forty lines crossing the meadows and the park in my way home. [*Reads.*]

> *Oh Muse, ascend the forked mount,*
> *And lofty strains prepare,*
> *About a Baron and a Count,*
> *Who went to hunt the hare.*
>
> *The hare she ran with utmost speed,*
> *And sad and anxious looks,*
> *Because the furious hounds indeed*
> *Were near to her, gadzooks.*

At length the Count and Baron bold
    Their footsteps homeward bended;
For why, because, as you were told,
    The hunting it was ended.

Before them strait a youth appears,
    Who made a piteous pother,
And told a tale with many tears,
    About his dying mother.

The youth was in severe distress,
    And seem'd as he had spent all,
He look'd a soldier by his dress,
    For that was regimental.

The Baron's heart was full of ruth,
    And from his eye fell brine o!
And soon he gave the mournful youth
    A little ready rino.

He gave a shilling, as I live,
    Which sure, was mighty well;
But to some people if you give
    An inch—they'll take an ell.

The youth then drew his martial knife,
    And seiz'd the Baron's collar,
He swore he'd have the Baron's life,
    Or else another dollar.

Then did the Baron, in a fume,
    Soon raise a mighty din,
Whereon came butler, huntsman, groom,
    And eke the whipper-in.

Maugre this young man's warlike coat,
    They bore him off to prison;
And held so strongly by his throat,
    And almost stopp'd his whizzen.

Soon may a neckcloth, call'd a rope,
  Of robbing cure this elf;
If so, I'll write, without a trope,
  His dying speech myself.
And had the Baron chanc'd to die,
  Oh! grief to all the nation,
I must have made an elegy,
  And not this fine narration.

MORAL.
Henceforth let those who all have spent,
  And would by begging live,
Take warning here, and be content
  With what folks chuse to give.

Amelia. Your muse, Mr. Butler, is in a very inventive
humour this morning.

Anhalt. And your tale too improbable even for fiction.

Butler. Improbable! It's a real fact.

Amelia. What, a robber in our grounds at noon-day? Very
likely indeed!

Butler. I don't say it was likely—I only say it is true.

Anhalt. No, no, Mr. Verdun, we find no fault with your
poetry; but don't attempt to impose it upon us for truth.

Amelia. Poets are allowed to speak falsehood, and we
forgive yours.

Butler. I won't be forgiven, for I speak truth—and here
the robber comes, in custody, to prove my words. [*Goes off,
repeating*] "I'll write his dying speech myself."

Amelia. Look! as I live, so he does—They come nearer;
he's a young man, and has something interesting in his
figure. An honest countenance, with grief and sorrow in his
face. No, he is no robber—I pity him! Oh! look how the
keepers drag him unmercifully into the tower—Now
they lock it—Oh! how that poor, unfortunate man must
feel!

Anhalt. [*Aside.*] Hardly worse than I do.

Enter the BARON.

Amelia. [*Runs up to him.*] A thousand congratulations, my dear papa.

Baron. For Heaven's sake, spare your congratulations. The old butler, in coming up stairs, has already overwhelmed me with them.

Anhalt. Then, it is true, my lord? I could hardly believe the old man.

Amelia. And the young prisoner, with all his honest looks, is a robber?

Baron. He is; but I verily believe for the first and last time. A most extraordinary event, Mr. Anhalt. This young man begged; then drew his sword upon me; but he trembled so, when he seized me by the breast, a child might have overpowered him. I almost wish he had made his escape—this adventure may cost him his life, and I might have preserved it with one dollar: but now, to save him would set a bad example.

Amelia. Oh no! my lord, have pity on him! Plead for him, Mr. Anhalt.

Baron. Amelia, have you had any conversation with Mr. Anhalt?

Amelia. Yes, my lord.

Baron. Respecting matrimony?

Amelia. Yes; and I have told him——

Anhalt. [*Very hastily.*] According to your commands, Baron——

Amelia. But he has conjured me——

Anhalt. I have endeavoured, my lord, to find out——

Amelia. Yet, I am sure, dear papa, your affection for me——

Anhalt. You wish to say something to me in your closet, my lord?

Baron. What the devil is all this conversation? You will not let one another speak—I don't understand either of you.

Amelia. Dear father, have you not promised you will not thwart my affections when I marry, but suffer me to follow their dictates?

Baron. Certainly.

Amelia. Do you hear, Mr. Anhalt?

Anhalt. I beg pardon—I have a person who is waiting for me—I am obliged to retire.   [*Exit in confusion.*

Baron. [*Calls after him.*] I shall expect you in my closet. I am going there immediately.

                       [*Retiring towards the opposite door.*

Amelia. Pray, my lord, stop a few minutes longer: I have something of great importance to say to you.

Baron. Something of importance! to plead for the young man, I suppose! But that's a subject I must not listen to.

                                                        [*Exit.*

Amelia. I wish to plead for two young men—For one, that he may be let out of prison: for the other, that he may be made a prisoner for life. [*Looks out.*] The tower is still locked. How dismal it must be to be shut up in such a place! and perhaps—[*Calls.*] Butler! Butler! come this way. I wish to speak to you. This young soldier has risked his life for his mother, and that accounts for the interest I take in his misfortunes.

Enter the BUTLER.

Pray, have you carried any thing to the prisoner to eat?

Butler. Yes.

Amelia. What was it?

Butler. Some fine black bread; and water as clear as crystal.

Amelia. Are you not ashamed! Even my father pities him. Go directly down to the kitchen, and desire the cook to give you something good and comfortable; and then go into the cellar for a bottle of wine.

Butler. Good and comfortable indeed!

Amelia. And carry both to the tower.

Butler. I am willing at any time dear lady, to obey your orders; but, on this occasion, the prisoner's food must remain bread and water—It is the Baron's particular command.

Amelia. Ah! My father was in the height of passion, when he gave it.

Butler. Whatsoever his passion might be, it is the duty of a true and honest dependent to obey his lord's mandates. I will not suffer a servant in this house, nor will I, myself, give the young man any thing except bread and water— But I'll tell you what I'll do—I'll read my verses to him.

Amelia. Give me the key of the cellar—I'll go myself.

Butler. [*Gives the key.*] And there's my verses—[*Taking them from his pocket.*] carry them with you, they may comfort him as much as the wine. [*She throws them down.*]

[*Exit* AMELIA.

Butler. [*In amazement.*] Not take them! Refuse to take them!—[*He lifts them from the floor with the utmost respect*]—

"I must have made an elegy,
And not this fine narration."

[*Exit.*

ACT THE FOURTH.

SCENE I.

A Prison in one of the Towers of the Castle.

FREDERICK *alone.*

Fred. How a few moments destroy the happiness of a man! When I, this morning, set out from my inn, and saw the sun rise, I sung with joy.—Flattered with the hope of seeing my mother, I formed a scheme how I would lovingly surprise her. But, farewell all pleasant prospects—I return to my native country, and the first object I behold, is my dying parent; my first lodging, a prison; and my next walk will perhaps be—oh, merciful Providence! have I deserved all this?

> *Enter* AMELIA, *with a small basket covered with a napkin.—She speaks to some one without.*

Amelia. Wait there, Francis, I shall soon be back.

Fred. [*Hearing the door open, and turning round.*] Who's there?

Amelia. You must be both hungry and thirsty, I fear.

Fred. Oh, no! neither.

Amelia. Here's a bottle of wine, and something to eat. [*Places the basket on the table.*] I have often heard my father say, that wine is quite a cordial to the heart.

Fred. A thousand thanks, dear stranger. Ah! could I prevail on you to have it sent to my mother, who is upon her death-bed, under the roof of an honest peasant, called Hubert! Take it hence, my kind benefactress, and save my mother.

Amelia. But first assure me, that you did not intend to murder my father.

Fred. Your father! Heaven forbid.—I meant but to preserve her life, who gave me mine.—Murder your father! No, no—I hope not.

Amelia. And I thought not—or, if you had murdered any one, you had better have killed the Count; nobody would have missed him.

Fred. Who, may I inquire, were those gentlemen, whom I hoped to frighten into charity?

Amelia. Ay, if you only intended to frighten them, the Count was the very person for your purpose. But you caught hold of the other gentleman.—And could you hope to intimidate Baron Wildenhaim?

Fred. Baron Wildenhaim?—Almighty powers!

Amelia. What's the matter?

Fred. The man to whose breast I held my sword—

[*Trembling.*

Amelia. Was Baron Wildenhaim—the owner of this estate—my father!

Fred. [*With the greatest emotion.*] My father!

Amelia. Good Heaven, how he looks! I am afraid he's mad. Here! Francis, Francis. [*Exit, calling.*

Fred. [*All agitation.*] My father! Eternal Judge! thou dost not slumber! The man, against whom I drew my sword this day, was my father! One moment longer, and provoked, I might have been the murderer of my father!

[*Sinks down on a chair.*

Enter MR. ANHALT.

Welcome, sir! By your dress you are of the church, and consequently a messenger of comfort. You are most welcome, sir.

Anhalt. I wish to bring comfort, and avoid upbraidings; for your own conscience will reproach you more than the voice of a preacher. From the sensibility of your countenance, together with a language and address superior to the vulgar, it appears, young man, you have had an education, which should have preserved you from a state like this.

Fred. My education I owe to my mother. Filial love, in return, has plunged me into the state you see. A civil magistrate will condemn according to the law—A priest, in judgment, is not to consider the act itself, but the impulse, which led to the act.

Anhalt. I shall judge with all the lenity my religion dictates: and you are the prisoner of a nobleman, who compassionates you for the affection which you bear towards your mother; for he has sent to the village where you directed him, and has found the account you have relating to her true.—With this impression in your favour, it is my advice, that you endeavour to see and supplicate the Baron for your release from prison, and all the peril of his justice.

Fred. [*Starting.*] I—I see the Baron! I!—I supplicate for my deliverance.—Will you favour me with his name?—Is it not Baron——

Anhalt. Baron Wildenhaim.

Fred. Baron Wildenhaim! He lived formerly in Alsace?

Anhalt. The same.—About a year after the death of his wife, he left Alsace; and arrived here a few weeks ago to take possession of this his paternal estate.

Fred. So! his wife is dead;—and that generous young lady, who came to my prison just now, is his daughter?

Anhalt. Miss Wildenhaim, his daughter.

Fred. And that young gentleman, I saw with him this morning, is his son?

Anhalt. He has no son.

Fred. [*Hastily.*] Oh, yes, he has—[*Recollecting himself.*]—I mean him that was out shooting to-day.

Anhalt. He is not his son.

Fred. [*To himself.*] Thank Heaven!

Anhalt. He is only a visitor.

Fred. I thank you for this information; and if you will undertake to procure me a private interview with Baron Wildenhaim——

Anhalt. Why private? However, I will venture to take you for a short time from this place, and introduce you; depending on your innocence, or your repentance—on his conviction in your favour, or his mercy towards your guilt. Follow me.   [*Exit.*

Fred. [*Following.*] I have beheld an affectionate parent in deep adversity.—Why should I tremble thus?—Why doubt my fortitude, in the presence of an unnatural parent in prosperity?   [*Exit.*

SCENE II.

A Room in the Castle.

Enter BARON WILDENHAIM *and* AMELIA.

Baron. I hope you judge more favourably of Count Cassel's understanding, since the private interview you have had with him. Confess to me the exact effect of the long conference between you.

Amelia. To make me hate him.

Baron. What has he done?

Amelia. Oh! told me of such barbarous deeds he has committed.

Baron. What deeds?

Amelia. Made vows of love to so many women, that, on his marriage with me, a hundred female hearts will at least be broken.

Baron. Pshaw! do you believe him?

Amelia. Suppose I do not; is it to his honour that I believe he tells a falsehood?

Baron. He is mistaken merely.

Amelia. Indeed, my lord, in one respect I am sure he speaks truth. For our old butler told my waiting-maid of a poor young creature who has been deceived, undone; and she, and her whole family, involved in shame and sorrow by his perfidy.

Baron. Are you sure the butler said this?

Amelia. See him, and ask him. He knows the whole story, indeed he does; the names of the persons, and every circumstance.

Baron. Desire he may be sent to me.

Amelia. [*Goes to the door and calls.*] Order old Verdun to come to the Baron directly.

Baron. I know tale-bearers are apt to be erroneous. I'll hear from himself the account you speak of.

Amelia. I believe it is in verse.

Baron. [*Angry.*] In verse!

Amelia. But, then, indeed it's true.

Enter BUTLER

Amelia. Verdun, pray have you not some true poetry?

Butler. All my poetry is true—and so far, better than some people's prose.

Baron. But I want prose on this occasion, and command you to give me nothing else. [BUTLER *bows.*] Have you heard of an engagement which Count Cassel is under to any other woman than my daughter?

Butler. I am to tell your honour in prose?

Baron. Certainly. [BUTLER *appears uneasy and loath to speak.*] Amelia, he does not like to divulge what he knows in presence of a third person—leave the room.

[*Exit* AMELIA.

Butler. No, no—that did not cause my reluctance to speak.

Baron. What then?

Butler. Your not allowing me to speak in verse—for here is the poetic poem.   [*Holding up a paper.*

Baron. How dare you pretend to contend with my will? Tell me in plain language all you know on the subject I have named.

Butler. Well then, my lord, if you must have the account in quiet prose, thus it was—Phœbus, one morning, rose in the east, and having handed in the long-expected day, he called up his brother Hymen——

Baron. Have done with your rhapsody.

Butler. Ay; I knew you'd like it best in verse—

> *There liv'd a lady in this land,*
>   *Whose charms the heart made tingle;*
> *At church she had not given her hand,*
>   *And therefore still was single.*

Baron. Keep to prose.

Butler. I will, my lord; but I have repeated it so often in verse, I scarce know how.—Count Cassel, influenced by the designs of Cupid in his very worst humour,

> *"Count Cassel woo'd this maid so rare,*
>   *And in her eye found grace;*
> *And if his purpose was not fair,"*

Baron. No verse.

Butler. "*It probably was base.*"

I beg your pardon, my lord; but the verse will intrude, in spite of my efforts to forget it. 'Tis as difficult for me at times to forget, as 'tis for other men at times to remember. But in plain truth, my lord, the Count was treacherous, cruel, forsworn.

Baron. I am astonished!

Butler. And would be more so if you would listen to the whole poem. [*Most earnestly.*] Pray, my lord, listen to it.

Baron. You know the family? All the parties?

Butler. I will bring the father of the damsel to prove the veracity of my muse. His name is Baden—poor old man!

> *"The sire consents to bless the pair,*
> *And names the nuptial day,*
> *When, lo! the bridegroom was not there,*
> *Because he was away."*

Baron. But tell me—Had the father his daughter's innocence to deplore?

Butler. Ah! my lord, ah! and you *must* hear that part in rhyme. Loss of innocence never sounds well except in verse.

> *"For, ah! the very night before,*
> *No prudent guard upon her,*
> *The Count he gave her oaths a score,*
> *And took in change her honour.*

MORAL.

> *Then you, who now lead single lives,*
> *From this sad tale beware;*
> *And do not act as you were wives,*
> *Before you really are."*

Enter COUNT CASSEL.

Baron. [*To the* BUTLER.] Leave the room instantly.

Count. Yes, good Mr. family poet, leave the room, and take your doggerels with you.

Butler. Don't affront my poem, your honour; for I am indebted to you for the plot.

> *"The Count he gave her oaths a score,*
> *And took in change her honour."*   [Exit BUTLER.

Baron. Count, you see me agitated.

Count. What can be the cause?

Baron. I'll not keep you in doubt a moment. You are accused, sir, of being engaged to another woman, while you offer marriage to my child.

Count. To only *one* other woman?

Baron. What do you mean?

Count. My meaning is, that when a man is young and rich, has travelled, and is no personal object of disapprobation,—to have made vows but to one woman is an absolute slight upon the rest of the sex.

Baron. Without evasion, sir, do you know the name of Baden? Was there ever a promise of marriage made by you to his daughter? Answer me plainly: or must I take a journey to inquire of the father?

Count. No—he can tell you no more than, I dare say, you already know; and which I shall not contradict.

Baron. Amazing insensibility! And can you hold your head erect, while you acknowledge perfidy?

Count. My dear Baron,—if every man, who deserves to have a charge such as this brought against him, was not permitted to look up—it is a doubt whom we might not meet crawling on all fours.

> [*He accidentally taps the* BARON'S *shoulder.*

Baron. [*Starts—recollects himself—then in a faultering voice.*] Yet—nevertheless—the act is so atrocious—

Count. But nothing new.

Baron. [*Faintly.*] Yes—I hope—I hope it is new.

Count. What, did you never meet with such a thing before?

Baron. [*Agitated.*] If I have—I pronounced the man, who so offended—a villain.

Count. You are singularly scrupulous. I question if the man thought himself so.

Baron. Yes he did.

Count. How do you know?

Baron. [*Hesitating.*] I have heard him say so.

Count. But he ate, drank, and slept, I suppose?

Baron. [*Confused.*] Perhaps he did.

Count. And was merry with his friends; and his friends as fond of him as ever?

Baron. Perhaps [*Confused.*]—perhaps they were.

Count. And perhaps he now and then took upon him to lecture young men for their gallantries?

Baron. Perhaps he did.

Count. Why, then, after all, Baron, your villain is a mighty good, prudent, honest fellow; and I have no objection to your giving me that name.

Baron. But do you not think of some atonement to the unfortunate girl?

Count. Did *your* villain atone?

Baron. No: when his reason was matured, he wished to make some recompense, but his endeavours were too late.

Count. I will follow his example, and wait till my reason is matured, before I think myself competent to determine what to do.

Baron. And till that time I defer your marriage with my daughter.

Count. Would you delay her happiness so long? Why, my dear Baron, considering the fashionable life I lead, it may be these ten years before my judgment arrives to its necessary standard.

Baron. I have the head-ache, Count—These tidings have discomposed, disordered me—I beg your absence for a few minutes.

Count. I obey—And let me assure you, my lord, that, although, from the extreme delicacy of your honour, you have ever through life shuddered at seduction; yet, there are constitutions, and there are circumstances, in which it can be palliated.

Baron. Never.   [*Violently.*

Count. Not in a grave, serious, reflecting man such as *you*, I grant. But in a gay, lively, inconsiderate, flimsy, frivolous coxcomb, such as myself, it is excusable: for me to keep my word to a woman, would be deceit: 'tis not expected of me. It is in my character to break oaths in love; as it is in your nature, my lord, never to have spoken any thing but wisdom and truth.   [*Exit.*

Baron. Could I have thought a creature so insignificant as that, had power to excite sensations such as I feel at present! I am, indeed, worse than he is, as much as the crimes of a man exceed those of an idiot.

Enter AMELIA.

Amelia. I heard the Count leave you, my lord, and so I am come to inquire——

Baron. [*Sitting down, and trying to compose himself.*] You are not to marry Count Cassel—And now, mention his name to me no more.

Amelia I won't—indeed I won't—for I hate his name.—But thank you, my dear father, for this good news. [*Draws a chair, and sits on the opposite side of the table, on which he leans.—After a pause.*] And who am I to marry?

Baron. [*His head on his hand*] I can't tell.

[AMELIA *appears to have something on her mind which she wishes to disclose.*]

Amelia. I never liked the Count.

Baron. No more did I.

Amelia. [*After a pause.*] I think love comes just as it pleases, without being asked.

Baron. [*In deep thought.*] It does so.

Amelia. [*After another pause.*] And there are instances, where, perhaps, the object of love makes the passion meritorious.

Baron. To be sure there are.

Amelia. For example; my affection for Mr. Anhalt as my tutor.

Baron. Right.

Amelia. [*After another pause.*] I should like to marry.

[*Sighing.*

Baron. So you shall. [*A pause.*] It is proper for every body to marry.

Amelia. Why, then, does not Mr. Anhalt marry?

Baron. You must ask him that question yourself.

Amelia. I have.

Baron. And what did he say?

Amelia. Will you give me leave to tell you what he said?

Baron. Certainly.

Amelia. And what I said to him?

Baron. Certainly.

Amelia. And won't you be angry?

Baron. Undoubtedly not.

Amelia. Why, then—you know you commanded me never to disguise or conceal the truth.

Baron. I did so.

Amelia. Why, then he said——

Baron. What did he say?

Amelia. He said—he would not marry me without your consent for the world.

Baron. [*Starting from his chair.*] And pray, how came this the subject of your conversation?

Amelia. [*Rising.*] *I* brought it up.

Baron. And what did you say?

Amelia. I said, that birth and fortune were such old-fashioned things to me, I cared nothing about either: and that I had once heard my father declare he should consult my happiness in marrying me, beyond any other consideration.

Baron. I will once more repeat to you my sentiments. It is the custom in this country for the children of nobility to marry only with their equals; but as my daughter's content is more dear to me than an ancient custom, I would bestow you on the first man I thought calculated to make you happy; by this I do not mean to say, that I should not be severely nice in the character of the man to whom I gave you; and Mr. Anhalt, from his obligations to me, and his high sense of honour, thinks too nobly——

Amelia. Would it not be noble to make the daughter of his benefactor happy?

Baron. But when that daughter is a child, and thinks like a child——

Amelia. No, indeed, papa, I begin to think very like a woman. Ask *him* if I don't.

Baron. Ask him! You feel gratitude for the instructions you have received from him, and you fancy it love.

Amelia. Are there two gratitudes?

Baron. What do you mean?

Amelia. Because I feel gratitude to you; but that is very unlike the gratitude I feel towards him.

Baron. Indeed!

Amelia. Yes; and then he feels another gratitude towards me. What's that?

Baron. Has he told you so?

Amelia. Yes.

Baron. That was not right of him.

Amelia. Oh! if you did but know how I surprised him!

Baron. Surprised him!

Amelia. He came to me by your command, to examine my heart respecting Count Cassel. I told him, that I would never marry the Count.

Baron. But him?

Amelia. Yes, him.

Baron. Very fine indeed! And what was his answer?

Amelia. He talked of my rank in life; of my aunts and cousins; of my grandfather, and great grandmother; of his duty to you; and endeavoured to persuade me to think no more of him.

Baron. He acted honestly.

Amelia. But not politely.

Baron. No matter.

Amelia. Dear father! I shall never be able to love another—Never be happy with any one else.

[*Throwing herself on her knees.*

Baron. Rise, I insist.

As she rises, enter ANHALT.

Anhalt. My lord, forgive me! I have ventured, on the
privilege of my office, as a minister of holy charity, to bring
the poor soldier, whom your justice has arrested, into the
adjoining room; and I presume to entreat you will admit
him to your presence, and hear his apology, or his
supplication.

Baron. Anhalt, you have done wrong. I pity the unhappy
boy; but you know I cannot, must not, forgive him.

Anhalt. I beseech you then, my lord, to tell him so
yourself. From your lips he may receive his doom with
resignation.

Amelia. Oh father! See him and take pity on him; his
sorrows have made him frantic.

Baron. Leave the room, Amelia, I command you. [*On her
attempting to speak, he raises his voice.*] Instantly.—

[*Exit* AMELIA.

Anhalt. He asked a private audience: perhaps he has some
confession to make that may relieve his mind, and may be
requisite for you to hear.

Baron. Well, bring him in,—and do you wait in the
adjoining room, till our conference is over. I must then, sir,
have a conference with you.

Anhalt. I shall obey your commands. [*He goes to the door,
and re-enters with* FREDERICK. ANHALT *then retires at
the same door.*]

Baron. [*Haughtily to* FREDERICK.] I know, young man,
you plead your mother's wants in excuse for an act of
desperation: but powerful as this plea might be in palliation
of a fault, it cannot extenuate a crime like yours.

Fred. I have a plea for my conduct even more powerful
than a mother's wants.

Baron. What's that?

Fred. My father's cruelty.

Baron. You have a father then?

Fred. I have, and a rich one—Nay, one that's reputed virtuous, and honourable. A great man, possessing estates and patronage in abundance; much esteemed at court, and beloved by his tenants; kind, benevolent, honest, generous—

Baron. And with all those great qualities, abandons you?

Fred. He does, with all the qualities I mention.

Baron. Your father may do right; a dissipated, desperate youth, whom kindness cannot draw from vicious habits, severity may.

Fred. You are mistaken—My father does not discard me for my vices—He does not know me—has never seen me—He abandoned me, even before I was born.

Baron. What do you say?

Fred. The tears of my mother are all that I inherit from my father. Never has he protected or supported me—never protected her.

Baron. Why don't you apply to his relations?

Fred. They disown me, too—I am, they say, related to no one—All the world disclaim me, except my mother—and there again, I have to thank my father.

Baron. How so?

Fred. Because I am an illegitimate son.—My seduced mother has brought me up in patient misery. Industry enabled her to give me an education; but the days of my youth commenced with hardships, sorrow, and danger.—My companions lived happy around me, and had a pleasing prospect in their view, while bread and water only were my food, and no hopes joined to sweeten it. But my father felt not that!

Baron. [*To himself.*] He touches my heart.

Fred. After five years' absence from my mother, I returned this very day, and found her dying in the streets for want—Not even a hut to shelter her, or a pallet of straw—But my father feels not that! He lives in a palace, sleeps on the softest down, enjoys all the luxuries of the great; and, when he dies, a funeral sermon will praise his great benevolence, his christian charities.

Baron. [*Greatly agitated.*] What is your father's name?

Fred. —He took advantage of an innocent young woman, gained her affection by flattery and false promises; gave life to an unfortunate being,—who was on the point of murdering his father.

Baron. [*Shuddering.*] Who is he?

Fred. Baron Wildenhaim.

[*The* BARON'S *emotion expresses the sense of amazement, guilt, shame, and horror.*]

Fred. In this house did you rob my mother of her honour; and in this house I am a sacrifice for the crime. I am your prisoner—I will not be free—I am a robber—I give myself up.—You shall deliver me into the hands of justice—You shall accompany me to the spot of public execution. You shall hear in vain the chaplain's consolation and injunctions. You shall find how I, in despair, will, to the last moment, call for retribution on my father.

Baron. Stop! Be pacified—

Fred. —And when you turn your head from my extended corse, you will behold my weeping mother.—Need I paint how her eyes will greet you?

Baron. Desist—barbarian, savage, stop!

Enter ANHALT, *alarmed.*

Anhalt. What do I hear? What is this?—Young man, I hope you have not made a second attempt?

Fred. Yes; I have done what it was your place to do. I have made a sinner tremble.   [*Points to the* BARON, *and exit.*

Anhalt. What can this mean?—I do not comprehend—

Baron. He is my son!—He is my son!—Go, Anhalt,—advise me—help me—Go to the poor woman, his mother—He can show you the way—make haste—speed to protect her——

Anhalt. But what am I to——

Baron. Go.—Your heart will tell you how to act.

[*Exit* ANHALT.

[BARON *distractedly.*] Who am I? What am I? Mad—raving—no—I have a son—A son! The bravest—I will—I must—oh! [*With tenderness.*] Why have I not embraced him yet? [*Increasing his voice.*] why not pressed him to my heart? Ah! see—[*Looking after him.*]—He flies from the castle—Who's there? Where are my attendants?

Enter two SERVANTS.

Follow him—bring the prisoner back.—But observe my command—treat him with respect—treat him as my son—and your master.   [*Exeunt.*

ACT THE FIFTH.

SCENE I.

Inside of the Cottage.

AGATHA, COTTAGER, *and his* WIFE, *discovered.*

Agatha. Pray look and see if he is coming.

Cot. It is of no use. I have been in the road; have looked up and down; but neither see nor hear any thing of him.

Wife. Have a little patience.

Agatha. I wish you would step out once more—I think he cannot be far off.

Cot. I will; I will go.   [*Exit.*

Wife. If your son knew what Heaven had sent you, he would be here very soon.

Agatha. I feel so anxious——

Wife. But why? I should think a purse of gold, such as you have received, would make any body easy.

Agatha. Where can he be so long? He has been gone four hours. Some ill must have befallen him.

Wife. It is still broad day-light—don't think of any danger.—This evening we must all be merry. I'll prepare the supper. What a good gentleman our Baron must be! I am sorry I ever spoke a word against him.

Agatha. How did he know I was here?

Wife. Heaven only can tell. The servant that brought the money was very secret.

Agatha. [*To herself.*] I am astonished! I wonder! Oh! surely he has been informed—Why else should he have sent so much money?

Re-enter COTTAGER.

Agatha. Well!—not yet!

Cot. I might look till I am blind for him—but I saw our new Rector coming along the road; he calls in sometimes. May be, he will this evening.

Wife. He is a very good gentleman; pays great attention to his parishioners; and where he can assist the poor, he is always ready.

Enter MR. ANHALT.

Anhalt. Good evening, friends.

Both. Thank you, reverend sir.

> [*They both run to fetch a chair.*

Anhalt. I thank you, good people—I see you have a
stranger here.

Cot. Yes, your reverence; it is a poor sick woman, whom I
took in doors.

Anhalt. You will be rewarded for it. [*To* AGATHA.] May
I beg leave to ask your name?

Agatha. Ah! If we were alone——

Anhalt. Good neighbours, will you leave us alone
for a few minutes? I have something to say to this poor
woman.

Cot. Wife, do you hear? Come along with me.

> [*Exeunt* COTTAGER *and his* WIFE.

Anhalt. Now——

Agatha. Before I tell who I am, what I am, and what I
was——I must beg to ask——Are you of this country?

Anhalt. No—I was born in Alsace.

Agatha. Did you know the late rector personally, whom
you have succeeded?

Anhalt. No.

Agatha. Then you are not acquainted with my
narrative?

Anhalt. Should I find you to be the person whom I have
long been in search of, your history is not altogether
unknown to me.

Agatha. "That you have been in search of!" Who gave you
such a commission?

Anhalt. A man, who, if it so prove, is much concerned for
your misfortunes.

Agatha. How? Oh, sir! tell me quickly—Whom do you
think to find in me?

Anhalt. Agatha Friburg.

Agatha. Yes, I am that unfortunate woman; and the man, who pretends to take concern in my misfortunes, is——Baron Wildenhaim——he who betrayed me, abandoned me and my child, and killed my parents. He would now repair our sufferings with this purse of gold. [*Takes out the purse.*] Whatever may be your errand, sir, whether to humble, or to protect me, it is alike indifferent. I therefore request you to take this money to him, who sent it. Tell him, my honour has never been saleable. Tell him, destitute as I am, even indigence will not tempt me to accept charity from my seducer. He despised my heart—I despise his gold.—He has trampled on me.—I trample on his representative.   [*Throws the purse on the ground.*

Anhalt. Be patient—I give you my word, that when the Baron sent this present to an unfortunate woman, for whom her son had supplicated, he did not know that woman was Agatha.

Agatha. My son? what of my son!

Anhalt. Do not be alarmed—The Baron met with an affectionate son, who begged for his sick mother, and it affected him.

Agatha. Begged of the Baron! of his father!

Anhalt. Yes; but they did not know each other; and the mother received the present on the son's account.

Agatha. Did not know each other? Where is my son?

Anhalt. At the castle.

Agatha. And still unknown?

Anhalt. Now he is known—an explanation has taken place; and I am sent here by the Baron, not to a stranger, but to Agatha Friburg—not with gold! his commission was——"do what your heart directs you."

Agatha. How is my Frederick? How did the Baron receive him?

Anhalt. I left him just in the moment the discovery was made. By this time your son is, perhaps, in the arms of his father.

Agatha. Oh! is it possible, that a man, who has been near eighteen years deaf to the voice of nature, should change so suddenly?

Anhalt. I do not mean to justify the Baron. But—he has loved you—and fear of his noble kindred alone caused his breach of faith to you.

Agatha. But to desert me wholly, and wed another—

Anhalt. War called him away—Wounded in the field, he was taken to the adjacent seat of a nobleman, whose only daughter by anxious attention to his recovery, won his gratitude; and, influenced by the advice of his worldly friends, he married. But no sooner was I received into the family, and admitted to his confidence, than he related to me your story; and at times would exclaim in anguish—"The proud imperious Baroness avenges the wrongs of my deserted Agatha." Again, when he presented me this living, and I left France to take possession of it, his last words, before we parted, were—"The moment you arrive at Wildenhaim, make all inquiries to find out my poor Agatha." Every letter I afterwards received from him contained "Still, still, no tidings of my Agatha." And fate ordained it should be so till this fortunate day.

Agatha. What you have said has made my heart overflow—where will this end?

Anhalt. I know not yet the Baron's intentions: but your sufferings demand immediate remedy; and one way only is left—Come with me to the castle. Do not start— you shall be concealed in my apartments, till you are called for.

Agatha. I go to the Baron's;—No.

Anhalt. Go for the sake of your son—reflect, that his fortunes may depend upon your presence.

Agatha. And he is the only branch on which my hope still blossoms: the rest are withered.—I will forget my wrongs as a woman, if the Baron will atone to the mother—he shall have the woman's pardon, if he will merit the mother's thanks—[*After a struggle.*]—I *will* go to the castle—for the sake of my Frederick, go even to his father. But where are my good host and hostess, that I may take leave, and thank them for their kindness?

Anhalt. [*Taking up the purse which* AGATHA *had thrown down.*] Here, good friend! Good woman!

Enter the COTTAGER *and his* WIFE.

Wife. Yes, yes, here am I.

Anhalt. Good people, I will take your guest with me. You have acted an honest part, and therefore receive this reward for your trouble. [*He offers the purse to the* COTTAGER, *who puts it by, and turns away.*]

Anhalt. [*To the* WIFE.] Do *you* take it.

Wife. I always obey my pastor. [*Taking it.*]

Agatha. Good bye. [*Shaking hands with the* COTTAGERS.] For your hospitality to me, may ye enjoy continued happiness!

Cot. Fare you well—fare you well.

Wife. If you find friends and get health, we won't trouble you to call on us again: but if you should fall sick or be in poverty, we shall take it very unkind if we don't see you.   [*Exeunt* AGATHA *and* ANHALT *on one side,*
                   COTTAGER *and his* WIFE *on the other.*

SCENE 2.

A Room in the Castle.

BARON *sitting upon a sofa.*—FREDERICK *standing
near him, with one hand pressed between his—the*
BARON *rises.*

Baron. Been in battle too!—I am glad to hear it. You have
known hard services, but now they are over, and joy and
happiness will succeed.—The reproach of your birth shall
be removed, for I will acknowledge you my son, and heir to
my estate.

Fred. And my mother——

Baron. She shall live in peace and affluence. Do you think
I would leave your mother unprovided, unprotected? No!
About a mile from this castle I have an estate called
Weldendorf—there she shall live, and call her own whatever
it produces. There she shall reign, and be sole mistress of
the little paradise. There her past sufferings shall be
changed to peace and tranquillity. On a summer's morning,
we, my son, will ride to visit her; pass a day, a week with
her; and in this social intercourse time will glide pleasantly.

Fred. And, pray, my lord, under what name is my mother
to live then?

Baron. [*Confused.*] How?

Fred. In what capacity?—As your domestic—or as——

Baron. That we will settle afterwards.

Fred. Will you allow me, sir, to leave the room a little
while, that you may have leisure to consider *now*?

Baron. I do not know how to explain myself in respect to
your mother, more than I have done already.

Fred. My fate, whatever it may be, shall never part me
from her's. My lord, it must be Frederick of Wildenhaim,

and Agatha of Wildenhaim—or Agatha Friburg, and
Frederick Friburg. This is my firm resolution, upon which I
call Heaven to witness.   [*Exit.*

Baron. Young man! Frederick!—[*Calling after him.*]
Hasty indeed! would make conditions with his father. No,
no, that must not be. I just now thought how well I had
arranged my plans—had relieved my heart of every burden,
when, a second time, he throws a mountain upon it. Stop,
friend conscience, why do you take his part?—For near
twenty years thus you have used me, and been my
torture.

Enter MR. ANHALT.

Ah! Anhalt, I am glad you are come. My conscience and
myself are at variance.

Anhalt. Your conscience is in the right.

Baron. You don't know yet what the quarrel is.

Anhalt. Conscience is always right—because it never
speaks unless it *is* so.

Baron. Ay, a man of your order can more easily attend to
its whispers, than an old warrior. The sound of cannon has
made him hard of hearing.—I have found my son again,
Mr. Anhalt, a fine, brave young man—I mean to make him
my heir—Am I in the right?

Anhalt. Perfectly.

Baron. And his mother shall live in happiness—My
estate, Weldendorf, shall be her's—I'll give it to her, and she
shall make it her residence. Don't I do right?

Anhalt. No.

Baron. [*Surprised.*] No? And what else should I do?

Anhalt. [*Forcibly.*] Marry her.

Baron. [*Starting.*] I marry her!

Anhalt. Baron Wildenhaim is a man, who will not act inconsistently—As this is my opinion, I expect your reasons, if you do not.

Baron. Would you have me marry a beggar?

Anhalt. [*After a pause.*] Is that your only objection?

Baron. [*Confused.*] I have more—many more.

Anhalt. May I entreat to know them likewise?

Baron. My birth!

Anhalt. Go on.

Baron. My relations would despise me.

Anhalt. Go on.

Baron. [*In anger.*] 'Sdeath! are not these reasons enough?—I know no other.

Anhalt. Now, then, it is my turn to state mine for the advice I have given you. But first I presume to ask a few questions.—Did Agatha, through artful insinuation, gain your affection? or did she give you cause to suppose her inconstant?

Baron. Neither—but for me, she had been always virtuous and good.

Anhalt. Did it cost you trouble and earnest entreaty to make her otherwise?

Baron. [*Angrily.*] Yes.

Anhalt. You pledged your honour?

Baron. [*Confused.*] Yes.

Anhalt. Called God to witness?

Baron. [*More confused.*] Yes.

Anhalt. The witness you called at that time was the Being, who sees you now. What you gave in pledge was your honour, which you must redeem. Therefore, thank Heaven that it is in your power to redeem it. By marrying Agatha the ransom's paid and she brings a dower greater

than any princess can bestow—peace to your conscience. If
you then esteem the value of this portion, you will not
hesitate a moment to exclaim,—Friends, wish me joy, I will
marry Agatha.

[BARON, *in great agitation, walks backwards and forwards,*
then takes ANHALT *by the hand.*

Baron. "Friend, wish me joy—I will *marry* Agatha."

Anhalt. I do wish you joy.

Baron. Where is she?

Anhalt. In the castle—In my apartments here—I
conducted her through the garden, to avoid curiosity.

Baron. Well, then, this is the wedding-day. This very
evening you shall give us your blessing.

Anhalt. Not so soon, not so private. The whole village
was witness of Agatha's shame—the whole village must be
witness of Agatha's re-established honour. Do you consent
to this?

Baron. I do.

Anhalt. Now the quarrel is decided. Now is your
conscience quiet?

Baron. As quiet as an infant's. I only wish the first
interview was over.

Anhalt. Compose yourself. Agatha's heart is to be your
judge.

Enter AMELIA.

Baron. Amelia, you have a brother.

Amelia. I have just heard so, my lord; and rejoice to find
the news confirmed by you.

Baron. I know, my dear Amelia, I can repay you for the
loss of Count Cassel; but what return can I make to you for
the loss of half your fortune?

Amelia. My brother's love will be ample recompense.

Baron. I will reward you better. Mr. Anhalt; the battle I have just fought, I owe to myself: the victory I gained, I owe to you. A man of your principles, at once a teacher and an example of virtue, exalts his rank in life to a level with the noblest family—and I shall be proud to receive you as my son.

Anhalt. [*Falling on his knees, and taking the* BARON'S *hand.*] My lord, you overwhelm me with confusion, as well as with joy.

Baron. My obligations to you are infinite—Amelia shall pay the debt.   [*Gives her to him.*

Amelia. Oh, my dear father! [*Embracing the* BARON.] what blessings you have bestowed on me in one day. [*To* ANHALT.] I will be your scholar still, and use more diligence than ever to please my master.

Anhalt. His present happiness admits of no addition.

Baron. Nor does mine—And there is yet another task to perform that will require more fortitude, more courage, than this had done! A trial that—[*Bursts into tears.*]—I cannot prevent them—Let me—let me—A few minutes will bring me to myself—Where is Agatha?

Anhalt. I will go, and fetch her.

                              [*Exit* ANHALT *at an upper entrance.*

Baron. Stop! Let me first recover a little. [*Walks up and down, sighing bitterly—looks at the door through which* ANHALT *left the room.*] That door she will come from—That was once the dressing-room of my mother—From that door I have seen her come many times—have been delighted with her lovely smiles—How shall I now behold her altered looks! Frederick must be my mediator.—Where is he?—Where is my son?—Now I am

ready—my heart is prepared to receive her—Haste! haste!
Bring her in.

[*He looks stedfastly at the door*—ANHALT *leads in*
AGATHA—*The* BARON *runs and clasps her in his
arms*—*Supported by him, she sinks on a chair which* AMELIA
places in the middle of the stage—*The* BARON *kneels by her
side, holding her hand.*]

Baron. Agatha, Agatha, do you know this voice?

Agatha. Wildenhaim.

Baron. Can you forgive me?

Agatha. Forgive you!   [*Embracing him.*

Enter FREDERICK.

Fred. [*As he enters.*] I hear the voice of my mother!—Ha!
Mother! Father!

[FREDERICK *throws himself on his knees by the other side
of his mother*—*She clasps him in her arms.*—AMELIA *is
placed by the side of her father attentively viewing*
AGATHA.—ANHALT *stands on the side of* FREDERICK
with his hands gratefully raised to Heaven.——*The curtain
slowly drops.*

CORRECTIONS AND EMENDATIONS TO
1816 TEXT

The differences between the first (1814) edition and the second (1816) edition of *Mansfield Park* are shown on the relevant page of the text of the novel. The corrections and emendations that have been made to the copy text of the 1816 edition are listed below.

	1816	corrected to
Volume I		
p. 11 line 6	else.	else."
p. 11 line 18	daughter	daughters
p. 34 line 29	friend.	friend."
p. 41 line 23	anny	Fanny
p. 65 line 3	weather.	weather."
p. 86 line 14	Edmund,	Edmund,"
p. 86 line 15	it	"it
p. 90 line 4	Miss Grant	Mrs. Grant
p. 92 line 30	her	his
p. 115 line 1	"After	After
p. 116 line 25	"Fanny	Fanny
p. 131 line 28	"What	What
p. 156 line 1	The storm	To storm
p. 158 line 22	heart.	heart."
p. 163 line 28	"Maria	Maria
p. 200 line 31	since; he	since he
p. 202 line 2	an usual	unusual

Volume II

p. 213 line 30	Wildenheim	Wildenhaim
p. 238 line 8	is would	it would
p. 268 line 9	most	must
p. 269 line 4	shall.	shall."
p. 285 line 13	"Yes	Yes
p. 294 line 14	couse	course
p. 301 line 18	Crawfurd	Crawford
p. 303 line 10	come	came
p. 320 line 7	exclamation	exclamation
p. 322 line 24	ater	later
p. 337 line 23	—I could	"—I could
p. 341 line 5	ther proper	their proper
p. 351 line 22	M. C.	M. C."
p. 353 line 5	must	most

Volume III

p. 362 line 4	long.	long."
p. 367 line 31	imagine	imagines
p. 371 line 22	yoursel	yourself
p. 375 line 3	it is me	it it is me
p. 395 line 2	'I should	"I should
p. 413 line 2	migh	might
p. 413 line 3	th mselves	themselves
p. 416 line 9	aud	and
p. 424 line 28	appearence	appearance
p. 443 line 20	journey"	journey."
p. 455 line 14	my	"my
p. 459 line 26	own.	own,
p. 475 line 14	tha	that
p. 477 line 17	house;"	house;
p. 484 line 9	expectations.	expectation.
p. 492 line 2	settled?"	settled?
p. 495 line 10	neglec	neglect
p. 499 line 30	"it was	it was
p. 509 line 2	What's	"What's
p. 513 line 2	&c.	&c."

p. 518 line 0	XIV	16
p. 527 line 9	"Why	'Why
p. 529 line 26	above, all	above all,
p. 530 line 28	duty to	duty—to
p. 530 line 28	affliction—and	affliction, and
p. 537 line 4	situation.	situation?
p. 545 line 5	future	on future

Commentary on the text

It is likely, as suggested in the Introduction, that many of the variations between 1814 and 1816 are due to the earlier edition being closer to the author's original fair copy. It is also reasonable to argue that many of these would be errors that Austen would wish to see corrected, and which were corrected in the 1816 text. These traces of the authorial presence would include spellings such as 'teize', the frequent capitalisation of such words as 'Uncle', 'Clergyman' and 'Navy or Army' (especially notable in vol. 1, ch. 11), which, on the evidence of her letters and other documents, reflect Jane Austen's MS habits. (Parsonage, however, is sometimes given a capital in 1816, and not in 1814: vol. 2, ch. 2.) They might also include capitalisations after a comma ('Oh, cousin, If': vol. 1, ch. 3), (mis)spellings such as 'tête à téte' or 'Lovers Vows' ('Lover's vows' in vol. 2, ch. 3), the failure to register a subjunctive (as soon as the business 'was arranged' in 1814, but 'were arranged' in 1816 (vol. 2, ch. 8)), and contractions of verbs ('whisk'd': vol. 2, ch. 1). Many parenthetical phrases beginning with a dash are not completed with a dash in 1814.

The numerous missed or inconsistent quotation marks in 1814, or double quotation marks within a speech when single are needed, must have been vexing to the author: these are usually but not infallibly corrected in 1816. This edition uses capitalisation much more sparingly, corrects misspellings, and removes traces of contractions. Exclamation marks are supplied in 1816 where the expression definitely calls for them: '"Not at all!"—cried Miss Crawford with alacrity' (vol. 2, ch. 11). Generally speaking, too, 1816 supplies commas around interpolated or adverbial phrases. In vol. 2, ch. 8, and throughout volume 3, however, some commas present in 1814 are deleted, so that the text reads, for example, 'Every thing where she now was was in full contrast' (vol. 3, ch. 8). Colons, often substituted for semi-colons in the 1816 text of volume 1, occur quite often in volume 2 of 1814. This may suggest either that the printer of this volume (Roworth) is here following house style, or alternatively that he is reflecting the fair copy more accurately than the notably careless printer (Sidney) of volumes 1 and 3.

Spelling is not regularised in the 1816 text, and nor is hyphenation. Within the same speech we have 'school-room' and 'dining room' (vol. 1, ch. 18). In vol. 2, ch. 13, for the only time, 'east-room' occurs. On the other hand, Mrs Norris' allowing 'a spare room for a friend, of which she made a very particular point;—the spare-rooms at the parsonage had never been wanted' (vol. 1, ch. 3) is a careful distinction common to both editions. Italicising of French words and phrases is erratic in 1816: thus we find 'eclaircissment' (vol. 3, ch. 5) but *etourderie* (vol. 3, ch. 15). In vol. 2, ch. 6, 'tout ensemble' is not italicised and nor is 'tête-à-tête', but we find '*tête-à-tête*' in vol. 1, ch. 4.

Apart from italics, briefly discussed in the Introduction, the most interesting aspect of the text is the use of the dash. In her letters, and in the surviving manuscripts of 'Sanditon' and *Persuasion*, Jane Austen characteristically follows the end of one sentence with a dash before the next. In this 1816 text, dashes between sentences frequently occur in dialogue or conversation, and in letters, such as Mary's in vol. 3, ch. 9. But for the most part they have been removed. The remains of the original punctuation may be discerned, however, for example in the second and third paragraphs of vol. 1, ch. 18, and occasionally in other spots of the authorial narrative. Sometimes a dash substitutes for a full stop at the end of a sentence. When Maria's anguish on Crawford's desertion is recorded – '—The hand which had so pressed her's to his heart!— The hand . . .' (vol. 2, ch. 2) – the insertion of a dash after the exclamation mark may well be the author's restoration of an expressive effect lost in the 1814 text. In both editions double-length dashes are also used, especially in volume 3, to indicate interrupted speech or thought, as when Fanny starts to resent her reception at Portsmouth: 'she had not such a welcome as——she checked herself' (vol. 3, ch. 7). These probably reproduce features of the author's original manuscript, but are not consistently applied.

The punctuation of 1816 arguably produces a more incisive text, as well as generating effects absent in 1814. Fanny waits 'in the hall, in the lobby, on the stairs for' William in 1814; in 1816 the addition of the (strictly speaking unnecessary) comma – 'in the hall, in the lobby, on the stairs, for' – makes the sentence dramatic (vol. 2, ch. 6). Their 'unchecked, equal, fearless' conversation is another moment that the additional comma of 1816 seems to intensify (vol. 2, ch. 6). Henry's insistence on 'Constancy. I am not afraid of the word' (vol. 3, ch. 3) seems weaker when 1816 substitutes a comma for the full stop, but this may be an intentional effect. 'Her poor mother now, did not look so very unworthy of being Lady Bertram's sister' (vol. 3, ch. 11) is one of several occasions when the punctuation of 1814 seems more responsive to natural emphasis than that in 1816, when the comma is removed. There is no way of knowing which and how many of these changes were authorial. The deletion of a punctuation mark in the novel's first sentence in 1816 certainly makes a change of emphasis, just as does the addition of one in its last.

ABBREVIATIONS

Brewster   John Brewster MA, *Practical Reflections on the Ordination Services for Deacons and Priests . . . for the use of Candidates for Orders* (London: Rivingtons, 1817).

Clarkson   Thomas Clarkson MA, *The History of the . . . Abolition of the African Slave-Trade by the British Parliament* (2 vols., London, 1808, reprinted 1968).

Cœlebs   Hannah More, *Cœlebs in Search of a Wife*, 12th edn. (London: Cadell and Davies, 1809).

E   *Emma*

FR   Deirdre Le Faye (ed.), *Jane Austen: A Family Record*, 2nd edn (Cambridge: Cambridge University Press, 2004).

J   *Juvenilia*

JA   Jane Austen

Johnson   Samuel Johnson LLD, *A Dictionary of the English Language*, 6th edn (1785).

L   *Jane Austen's Letters*, 3rd edn, ed. Deirdre Le Faye (Oxford: Oxford University Press, 1995).

Letters from England   Robert Southey, *Letters from England* (London, 1809).

Life   G. B. Hill and L. F. Powell (eds.), *Boswell's Life of Johnson* (6 vols., Oxford: Clarendon Press, 1934–50).

LS   *Lady Susan*

MP   *Mansfield Park*

NA   *Northanger Abbey*

Navy   Brian Southam, *Jane Austen and the Navy* (London: Hambledon and London, 2000).

Our Village	Mary Russell Mitford, *Our Village: Sketches of Rural Character and Scenery* (5 vols., London: G. and W. B. Whittaker, 1824–32).
P	*Persuasion*
P&P	*Pride and Prejudice*
S	*Sanditon*
S&S	*Sense and Sensibility*
Sutherland	Kathryn Sutherland (ed.), *Mansfield Park* (London: Penguin, 1996).
The Task	*The Task: A Poem in Six Books*, in *Poems*, by William Cowper of the Inner Temple, Esq., 4th edn (London, 1788).
W	*The Watsons*

EXPLANATORY NOTES

A note on notes

Words whose meaning has changed are not discussed if their meaning is clarified by their context. When the young Fanny's 'increased sobs' tell Edmund where 'the grievance lay' (vol. 1, ch. 2), for example, it is apparent that she has no complaint, but only a particular sadness. ('Grievance' in its more modern sense is used later in that chapter.) There, too, Fanny has a 'quick apprehension as well as good sense' when we might rather say a quick comprehension. The 'soft monotony' of Lady Bertram's voice is another example: we might say monotone, but modern readers readily make the substitution. There are intermediate cases, as for example when Lady Bertram is said to 'spend her days sitting nicely dressed on a sofa', where the strict meaning of nicely – neatly – already overlaps with the more generalised modern usage criticised by Henry Tilney in *Northanger Abbey*. 'Nice' and 'view' (to give two examples) are only noticed when the modern meaning is made plausible by the context, but is misleading.

VOLUME I, CHAPTER 1

1 **Miss Maria Ward of Huntingdon:** Huntingdon, a small county town, is in the adjacent county to Northamptonshire in the Midlands of England, about thirty miles or forty-eight kilometres from Northampton itself. The address of 'Miss Maria Ward of Huntingdon' is carefully distinguished from that of 'Sir Thomas Bertram, of Mansfield Park, in the county of Northampton', the

name of whose property implies large acreage, with consequent seclusion and separation from the working populace.

2 **a baronet's lady**: a baronet held an hereditary title, which passed to his son or heir, unlike men individually knighted for services to the crown. Baronets were not noblemen, and Sir Thomas would sit in the House of Commons, not the upper house, the House of Lords, and would naturally associate with the gentry rather than the aristocracy. The phrase 'her uncle, the lawyer, himself' succinctly suggests both the social status of the Ward family (not upper gentry, with family in the professions) and that this uncle did the conveyancing of the formal articles that would be signed before the marriage. Miss Maria Ward would bring a 'portion', a sum of money – in this case £7,000 – settled on her by her father, which would pass over to her husband on the marriage. In this professional view (and if her personal attractions are left out of the account) she has no 'equitable claim', since the calibration of social status with the size of this portion was precise, and openly canvassed. Maria is the second Ward sister; it is likely that each would have the same sum settled on them.

3 **the living of Mansfield**: a living is, literally, a livelihood as a clergyman of the Church of England, more than five thousand of which were in the gift of private landowners like Sir Thomas. Such an appointment assured the incumbent of a rent-free residence and an income in the form of tithes, payable by the residents of the parish, and profits from the farming of land ('glebe') belonging to the church.

4 **Lieutenant of Marines**: the Royal Marines were a body of armed men employed to carry out policing duties on board ship and on shore in the large naval dockyards at Portsmouth, on the south coast of England, the key port in the Napoleonic wars (1803–15). To qualify for a commission in the Royal Navy, a man had to have served at least six years at sea, but commissions in the Marines could be obtained by very young men with little or no sea-going experience. They were regarded as inferior, socially and professionally, to the naval officers.

5 **connections**: people, usually of higher social status, related by marriage, to whom one might look for patronage or advice.

6 **interest**: the power to obtain places or appointments through the exercise of political clout. Stronger, more quantifiable and more legitimate than the modern 'influence', interest is a form of cultural capital: 'Nelson was fortunate in possessing good interest at the time when it could be most serviceable to him: his promotion had been almost as rapid as it could be.' Robert Southey, *Life of Nelson* (London, 1813), p. 18.

7 **from principle**: 'principle' will be used frequently in the novel as a collective noun for what are sometimes specified as a range of 'principles'. The 'general wish of doing right', which appears to define 'principle' here, is as indefinite as the term itself, but would summon up the idea of sincere adherence to Christian precepts, and the desire to subdue one's own interest and passions, in conformity with 'the will of God'.

8 **no interest could reach**: not Sir Thomas' interest alone, since a career in the Marines afforded virtually no chance of promotion beyond the lower ranks. After 1755 the Marines lost senior ranks, were put under the command of naval captains, and might rise 'in regular rotation only'. 'From 1809 to the peace in 1814, no general promotion took place in the Marines, nor at the latter period were all the vacancies of officers *killed in action* filled up' (Paul Harris Nicolas, *Historical Record of the Royal Marine Forces* (2 vols., London, 1845), vol. 1, p. xvii). A petition from Officers of the Marines to the Admiralty in March 1808 complained that 'although consisting of upwards of 30,000 men, [the Marine service] alone of all his Majesty's forces is destitute of a superior staff, and consequently both of that respectability which it confers, and those remunerations which are bestowed upon the line, [the regular army] the royal artillery and the royal engineers' (Nicolas, *Historical Record*, vol. 1, p. 375).

9 **active service**: actually manning a vessel involved in the naval war against France and its allies.

10 **the friends she had so carelessly sacrificed**: 'friends' here means both family and, more broadly, people of higher social and financial status, able to advance one's fortunes. Later in the chapter, when Sir Thomas hopes that his daughters and Fanny Price will be 'very good friends', the more modern meaning, people who share common interests and mutual regard, is

invoked. Samuel Johnson packs both meanings into one line in his poem 'On the death of Dr Robert Levet' (1782) when he calls this kindly man 'Of ev'ry friendless name, the friend' (line 8).

11 **lying-in**: the period of sequestration and bed-rest which accompanied the birth of a child.

12 **to the East**: Sir Thomas owns an estate in the West Indies, from which region most of Europe's supply of sugar came. The wealth derived from trade in this commodity formed a significant part of the income of many English gentry families, as is suggested in Mrs Smith's case in *P* (vol. 2, ch. 12), though there is little evidence that the West Indian estate is the primary source of the Bertram fortunes. Woolwich is an important dockyard of the Royal Navy, which housed the Royal Arsenal, where a boy might be employed, and the Royal Military Academy, where he might be trained. When she mentions 'the East', Mrs Price is rather desperately asking whether Sir Thomas' interest extends to securing her son a position with the East India Company, which administered India and had a monopoly on trade between England, India and beyond.

13 **professions**: assurances of future aid.

14 **benevolence of the action**: 'Upon the whole, . . . nothing can bestow more merit on any human creature than the sentiment of benevolence in an eminent degree.' David Hume, *An Enquiry Concerning the Principles of Morals*, ed. Tom L. Beauchamp (1751; London: Oxford University Press, 1998), p. 82, para. 22 of section 2 'On benevolence'. Partly as a result of the influence of Hume and other moral philosophers, benevolence has a great deal of cultural credibility in this period. Aligned with charity, benevolence betokened distinct moral value and sensibility in those who professed to feel or exercise it.

15 **cousins in love, &c**: courtship and marriage between first cousins was common enough, and need not have aroused anxiety on that ground alone. It had been legal in England since Henry VIII's reforms (1533–40). Frances Burney's play *Edwy and Elgiva* (performed at Drury Lane in 1795) treats cousin marriage sympathetically, as against papal attempts to disallow the union. In JA's own family, both her brothers James and Henry

Austen courted Eliza de Feuillide, daughter of JA's father's sister Philadelphia (Austen) Hancock, and Henry eventually married her. Mrs Austen's cousin Henry Leigh had also married his cousin, Mary Leigh. There was a first-cousin marriage in the next Austen generation, between Fanny Palmer Austen (1812–82) and Francis William Austen (1809–58). In English novels of the period, cousin marriage is often treated as romantic and gratifying, because of what it implies about familial affection. See also the opening of JA's early 'Frederic and Elfrida': 'The Uncle of Elfrida was the Father of Frederic; in other words, they were first cousins by the Father's side. Being both born in one day & both brought up in one school, it was not wonderful that they should look on each other with something more than bare politeness. They loved with mutual sincerity.'

16 **my mite**: 'And there came a certain poor widow, and she threw in two mites, which make a farthing. And [Jesus] called unto him his disciples, and saith unto them, Verily I say unto you, That this poor widow hath cast more in, than all they which have cast into the treasury: For all they did cast in of their abundance; but she of her want did cast in all that she had, even all her living' (Mark, ch. 12, vs. 42–4).

17 **creditable establishment**: if the niece were introduced 'into the world' (the social circles of the county gentry, who composed the 'society of this country') she would readily find a husband who would be able to support her financially. If such an 'establishment' does not materialise, Sir Thomas would need to settle upon her a sum of money large enough to generate a secure income – 'the provision of a gentlewoman'.

18 **morally**: an intensifying adverb meaning 'virtually', or according to all reason and probability.

19 **so benevolent a scheme**: Mrs Norris proposes that Fanny, ten years old, travel from Portsmouth to London, a journey of some 72 miles or 115 kilometres, taking about 10 hours, in the 'coach', or public transport, under the care of a stranger; in London she is to stay with Nanny, also a stranger, with Nanny's cousin, a tradesman or artisan, before travelling the further 70 or so miles to Mansfield.

20 **her views**: her plans.

21 **come to us**: the conjunction of a question mark with 'said', as again at the opening of vol. 2, ch. 5, ' "But why should Mrs Grant ask Fanny?" said Lady Bertram', is common in the novel.

22 **pug**: a miniature bulldog, the mastiff associated, patriotically, with John Bull, which became fashionable at the end of the eighteenth century.

CHAPTER 2

1 **regaled in**: literally, feasted upon, took delight in.

2 **awful**: frightening.

3 **their address**: their self-presentation and elocution, or manner of speaking to others.

4 **moderation in all things**: from the Latin 'est modus in rebus', a familiar saying, used later also by Sir Thomas.

5 **peculiar**: particular.

6 **your uncle will frank it**: as a member of Parliament, Sir Thomas is entitled to send letters through the post free, provided he addresses them in his own hand and adds his signature.

7 **orthography**: Edmund's penknife is, literally, the pocket knife used to sharpen the end of the quill pen when it became blunt; orthography is the 'science' of spelling.

8 **half a guinea under the seal**: half a guinea is a small thin gold coin, just under an inch or exactly 2 centimetres across, which could be hidden under the wax seal that Sir Thomas would use to close the sheets of the letter. The practice of sending money under the seal was not uncommon. Austin Dobson's edition of *Mansfield Park* (London, 1897) cites the *Life of Macaulay* (London, 1876) by his nephew, G. O. Trevelyan: 'Macaulay wrote to me at Harrow [school] pretty constantly . . . sealing his letters with an amorphous mass of red wax, which, in defiance of post-office regulations, not infrequently concealed a piece of gold' (p. xv). A half guinea, worth 10s. 6d, would be a considerable sum to a young man like William Price.

9 **read, work, and write**: Fanny can sew or do (needle) work, meaning she can make and repair clothes. Her education has been that of a lower-class young woman.

10 **cannot put the map of Europe together**: maps broken into pieces, resembling jig-saw puzzles, were often used to teach children

geography, as in Hannah More's *Cœlebs*, where 'a fourth child had spread a dissected map on the carpet, and had pulled down her eldest sister . . . to show her Copenhagen' (ch. 13).

11 **the Isle of Wight**: the island off the south coast of England visible across the Solent estuary from Portsmouth, Fanny's home.

12 **Metals, Semi-Metals, Planets, and distinguished philosophers**: textbooks, such as Richmal Mangnall's *Historical and Miscellaneous Questions for the Use of Young People*, promoted rote learning. The tenth edition of 1813 contains 'Abstracts of Biography', 'The Planetary System', etc, though not lists of metals, for pupils to learn by heart. The numerous editions of Oliver Goldsmith's *History of England* (originally published London, 1764) prepared for schoolroom use included chronological tables of the Kings of England. Severus, both King and Emperor (193–211 A.D.), is positioned 'low' on such a table, 'From the invasion of Julius Caesar, to the departure of the Romans'. Educationalists like Maria Edgeworth (*Practical Education* (London, 1798) severely criticised the unreflecting absorption of facts.

13 **genius and emulation**: genius is mental power, but the whole phrase sounds second-hand.

14 **accomplished**: 'elegant . . . used commonly of acquired qualifications [such as skill in drawing or music] without including moral excellence', (Johnson, sense 2).

15 **acquirements**: if 'self-knowledge, generosity and humility' are 'acquirements', as the narrator suggests, they are not innate, as pre- or proto-Romantic theories might assume.

16 **on a sofa**: Cowper writes of 'the soft recumbency of outstretched limbs' made possible by the invention of the sofa, which was a long seat made comfortable by being stuffed, usually with horsehair (*The Task*, book 1, 'The Sofa', line 82). The sofa might have supports at both ends, but more usually one, at an incline from the main seat. A lady would sit or lie along the sofa, her upper body supported by the raised end. Thus, later, in vol. 2, ch. 1, Fanny can be screened 'behind her aunt's end of the sofa'.

17 **Eton**: one of the great 'public' (i.e. private) schools: visited by George III, it was Tory in tone and affiliation, as was Oxford.

The Universities of Oxford and Cambridge were the training ground for clergy of the Church of England: their terms, being shorter than school terms, would allow Edmund to be at home more.

18 **daily portion of History**: probably from Goldsmith's *History of England in a Series of Letters from a Nobleman to his Son* (2 vols., London, 1764) or his expanded *History of England, from Earliest Times to the Death of George II* (4 vols., London, 1771).

CHAPTER 3

1 **a different disposal of the next presentation**: the Bertrams own two 'family-livings' – positions as clergy which can support family members. Instead of keeping the Mansfield living, which would form part of Edmund's income, Sir Thomas must raise capital by disposing of it, at an agreed sum, for the lifetime of a new incumbent.

2 **to procure him better preferment**: it may be possible, by the exercise of political influence (such as friendship with a bishop, who held the key to appointments), to advance Edmund's status in the church, and thus obtain for him a higher income.

3 **his West India Estate**: JA does not yet specify the site of Sir Thomas' estate, and this passage, with its allusion to 'some recent losses', is couched in generalised language appropriate to the figure. The reference is made plausible by common knowledge that soil exhaustion and competition from other producers had reduced profits on these estates. There is, for example, a review in the *Quarterly Review* (August and November 1809) of 'The Radical Cause of the Present Distresses of the West India Planters etc' by William Spence.

4 **tack on my patterns**: patterns for appliqué, embroidery or patchwork would be 'tacked' onto the cloth with loose temporary stitching.

5 **considering . . . six hundred a year**: though the 1816 text does make sense, the 1814 reading is more probably correct. Later there is a parallel use by Mr Rushworth when he speaks of Crawford as 'gentleman-like, considering' (vol. 2, ch. 1). Six hundred pounds was a very comfortable income for a single gentlewoman: the income of the Dashwood sisters and their mother in *S&S* is £500

a year. Though it was earlier, Samuel Johnson supported a house-hold of five indigent people in London on a pension of £300 a year.

6 **the Antigua estate . . . poor returns**: Antigua is one of the islands in the Caribbean collectively known as the West Indies, ceded to Britain in 1667. There, as in the rest of the West Indies, 'the English barbarians that cultivate the southern islands of America', in Samuel Johnson's phrase, used slave labour imported from West Africa (Introduction to *The World Displayed*, in Johnson, *Works* (12 vols., London, 1820), vol. 2, p. 218). Slaves laboured mainly on sugar plantations, which supplied England and Europe with this commodity. Antigua was sometimes singled out by opponents of slavery, such as Wilberforce, as modelling the ameliorated future that should follow abolition. Speaking on the Parliamentary motion to abolish the slave trade in May 1791, he claimed that on Antigua, in contrast to others in the group, religious instruction by Methodists and Moravians had brought about 'the happiest effects', such as 'increased habits of regularity and industry' (Clarkson, vol. 2, p. 228). This resulted in less mortality, so that Antigua, as Lord Holland reiterated in the final debate of the campaign in 1806, had been able to export rather than import slaves (Clarkson, vol. 2, p. 552). These arguments are less humanitarian than hard-headed and economic, but suggest, since Austen had very probably read Clarkson (*L*, p. 198; note 4, p. 410), that the choice of Antigua as the site of the Bertram property was not random. It was the one island on which Sir Thomas, a Christian gentleman, might own estates with less compromise to his principles. The exceptional status of Antigua is perhaps signalled by the fact that JA's father was the trustee of an estate on Antigua, owned by his erstwhile pupil James Langford Nibbs. Profits from sugar production declined in the later eighteenth century, and by 1807 planters were producing at a loss. The preceding passage, which shows that despite Mrs Norris' difficulty in making 'ends meet' she actually has an ample income, throws some doubt on her ascription to Sir Thomas of 'straitened' 'means'.

7 **squadron**: a group of ships, forming a division of the fleet, sailing together.

CHAPTER 4

1 **after a favourable voyage**: the voyage across the Atlantic ocean from England to the West Indies in a sailing ship might take between four weeks and two months, depending on the weather. In this case the wind has been favourable, or conducive to fast sailing and speedy arrival. Ships returning from the West Indies would typically make a faster passage than on their journey out, owing to the transatlantic current then known as the 'Florida stream', and now as the Gulf Stream.

2 **participate them**: share them. Participate is used here as a transitive verb.

3 **overlook**: to keep a jealous eye on.

4 **a post of such honourable representation**: Mrs Norris is deputising for Lady Bertram, the young ladies' mother, and thus represents the family, and its social status.

5 **embarrassments**: perplexities or hesitations due to shyness or timidity.

6 **finest places in the country**: a place is a mansion, or country house, including its surroundings. The implication of the term is that grandeur in house and grounds expresses social and political eminence. 'In the country' means in the neighbouring area, or within reasonable visiting distance.

7 **in town**: in the fashionable parts of London, west of the city proper, and centring on Mayfair. A house in town allowed one to take part in the London 'season', with its receptions, balls and other social activities of the leisured classes.

8 **ten miles of indifferent road**: ten miles or sixteen kilometres is a long way for horses to travel, and might well take two hours. The roads are 'indifferent' because, as is clear later, they are untarred, rough and narrow country lanes.

9 **difficult**: here meaning discriminating or, possibly, hard to please.

10 **twelve thousand a year**: Mr Rushworth is certainly one of the wealthier members of the gentry, possibly better off even than Mr Darcy in *P&P*, a novel apparently set at an earlier period. Darcy has £10,000 a year, though wartime inflation would have brought their incomes closer together.

11 **in the same county, and the same interest**: an 'interest' is a political alliance, akin to, but broader than, the modern 'lobby', concerned

to conserve or advance the fortunes of a specific social group. Here the interest is probably that of the Tory landed gentry, as distinct from the great Whig magnates of the capital, or the commercial and mercantile interests of the East India Company, or the slave-traders.

12 **twenty thousand pounds**: invested in government funds, which returned 5 per cent per annum, this would produce an annual income of £1,000. Miss Crawford can thus expect to marry a rich man, who would provide her, for example, with the house in town to which Maria Bertram also looks forward.

13 **preciseness or rusticity**: preciseness is old-fashioned formality of manners – 'exactness, rigid nicety' (Johnson); together with rusticity (the 'qualities of one that lives in the country; simplicity; artlessness') this suggests that Mary has feared that her sister's manners would lack elegance or polish.

14 **air and countenance**: the deportment, demeanour and confidence of a gentleman.

15 **the address of a Frenchwoman**: the capacity to manipulate others through charm, supposed to be typical of French manners, and contrasted with English straightforwardness. An English character in Maria Edgeworth's *Manœuvring* (1812), ch. 14, disclaims 'all that paltry system of artifice, which is sometimes called address' (Maria Edgeworth, *Tales and Novels* (London: Baldwin and Craddock, 1832), vol. 7). In the same author's *Ormond* (1817) the hero, visiting France, is introduced to his childhood sweetheart, now become Madame de Connal, 'improved in coquetry by Parisian practice and power' (ch. 28). In her salon, 'all were received with ease, respect, vivacity, or sentiment, as the occasion required . . . Regaining always, imperceptibly, the most advantageous situation and attitude for herself'. Later occurs the phrase 'all the innocence of a Frenchwoman – if that term be intelligible' (ch. 27).

16 **Heaven's *last* best gift**: after the creation of animals and birds, God formed Eve out of Adam's side so that he would not be alone in Paradise (Genesis ch. 2, vs. 18–23). This is recalled in book 5 of John Milton's *Paradise Lost* (1667) when Adam wakes to find Eve still asleep beside him. He '[Hung] over her enamour'd' and

649

> Her hand soft touching, whisper'd thus: 'Awake,
> My fairest, my espous'd, my latest found,
> Heav'n's last best gift, my ever new delight,
> Awake; the morning shines . . .'
>> (*Paradise Lost with the life of the author,*
>> *to which is prefaced the celebrated critique by Sam.*
>> *Johnson* (London, 1799), book 5, lines 17–20,
>> pp. 129–30.)

The relation of Adam and Eve was widely influential as a model of marriage in which the woman was the gratefully subservient and the man the dominant, and providing, partner. In context, 'last' means 'final, culminating'.

CHAPTER 5

1 **Hill Street**: in Mayfair, the most fashionable part of London; runs westwards from Berkeley Square: most of the rather grand houses there were built shortly after the west side of the Square was completed in 1745. In Charlotte Smith's *Emmeline* (London, 1788) the lodgings of the 'gay and fashionable' lieutenant-colonel Fitz-Edward are in Hill-street; in Scott's *Waverley* (1814; 3 vols., Edinburgh, 1816) the house of the ambitious and unscrupulous politician Sir Richard Waverley is in 'Hill Street, Berkeley-square' (vol. 3, p. 183): the address probably signals fast living and scandal.

2 **manœuvring business**: meaning to scheme, or to manage the attainment of a goal by trick and artifice; the verb 'to manœuvre', originally French, is new to the language at this time, as is pointed out in Maria Edgeworth's *Manœuvring* (1812; in Edgeworth, *Tales and Novels*, vol. 7). Mrs Beaumont, always 'assuming an appearance contrary to her real feelings' (p. 185) is an adept in 'domestic diplomacy' (p. 209), whose wiles and stratagems are devoted to obtaining advantageous marriages for her children. 'I remember her manœuvring to gain a husband and then manœuvring to manage him, which she did with triumphant address', says a character in the first chapter.

3 **admiration**: attraction towards a person, including especially their physical features.

4 **reversion**: 'the state of being to be possessed after the death of the present possessor' (Johnson): Tom has already the legal right to the estate.

5 **any collection of engravings of gentlemen's seats**: such as [William Angus] *The Seats of the Nobility and Gentry. In a collection of the most interesting and picturesque views, engraved by W. A. With descriptions of each view* (London, 1779–86); or William Watts (engraver), *Picturesque Views of the Principal Seats of the Nobility and Gentry, in England and Wales. By the most eminent British artists. With a description of each seat* (London, 1786–8).

6 **the horse he had to run at the B—— races**: Tom evidently owns, and would bet on, the horse, for which he would hire a jockey at the racecourse for the occasion. Most towns would have a racecourse: within reasonable distance of Northampton are Banbury, Bedford and Buckingham.

7 **Pray, is she out, or is she not**: young women of the genteel classes were usually introduced into 'society' by a ball held in their honour at the age of eighteen or so. This marked their entry into adult company and their potential marriageability. The young ladies of a family would usually 'come out' in turn, so as to allow each of them the best chance of finding a husband: Lady Catherine in *P&P* asks Elizabeth Bennet if any of her 'younger sisters' are 'out', and is astonished to hear that 'the younger ones [are] out before the elder are married!' (vol. 2, ch. 6).

8 **close bonnet**: a bonnet with a broad rim, shading the face, and tied beneath the chin, suggesting modesty.

9 **quizzing**: making fun of.

10 **Baker Street**: runs north-south on the western edge of Mayfair, with many fine houses constructed after the Building Act of 1774, which regulated materials and appearance.

11 **stared me out of countenance**: abashed me by her own impudence.

12 **Albion place**: a recently built (1795) and fashionable square in Ramsgate, Kent, a resort on the south coast of England.

CHAPTER 6

1 **near the bottom end of the table**: seating at the dining table appears to follow roughly the order of social status. Rushworth, as the guest, and Lady Bertram, as the hostess, sit at the 'top'

end. Maria is placed next to her fiancé; Edmund is next to her. Mary, taking 'her chosen place', is opposite Edmund. Fanny, next to Edmund, is presumably at the bottom, in the position of least prestige.

2 **grounds laid out by an improver**: a term used to describe a landscape designer or, to use the eighteenth-century term, 'artist', employed to redesign an estate in conformity with later eighteenth-century and proto-Romantic taste. Humphry Repton (1752–1818), the most famous landscape artist of the time, who designed well over two hundred gardens, mostly in the south and east of England, calls himself a 'professional Improver' in *Fragments on the Theory and Practice of Landscape Gardening* (London, 1816), p. 193.

3 **the approach**: the staging of the 'approach' – so that the house was at first hidden, and then revealed as part of a picturesque view – was an essential part of Repton's designs. In the Red Book, his prospectus for work at Antony House, Cornwall, Repton wrote: 'Few parts of modern gardening have been so much mistaken as the management of approaches, there is no branch of the art on which I have so often had occasion to deliver my opinion' (Edward Malins, *The Red Books of Humphry Repton* (London: Basilisk Press, 1976), f. 11.

4 **improvement**: Rushworth means in effect, 'modernisation', or bringing up to date. Improvement was a fashionable term of the day, with a wide range of possible applications: 'this execrable improvement, as every novelty is called in England' (*Letters from England*, letter 5).

5 **Mr. Repton**: a rare, though not unique, use of a historical person in JA's novels. Humphry Repton had been called in by Mrs Austen's cousin, the Rev. Thomas Leigh, to alter the property at Adlestrop, Gloucester in 1799. When JA and her mother visited Adlestrop in 1806, Repton's 'improvements', which involved merging the rectory garden with the estate, so as to give the effect of the house standing in a park, had been carried out. During their visit, Thomas Leigh inherited the much larger estate of Stoneleigh Abbey in Warwickshire; the Austens accompanied him when he visited his new property, which Mrs Austen described in a letter (*FR*, pp. 156–7). Leigh again employed Repton, who set out his

concept for Stoneleigh in a Red Book (1809) of commentary and designs.

6 **five guineas a day**: a guinea was worth £1. 1s. In a letter to Pole Carew, the owner of Antony House, Repton encloses his account for work done in October and November 1792. His eight visits 'with frequent conversations on the spot' total £42, apart from £21 for expenses on the road, so this information is correct. Despite inflation, Repton's fees stabilised at this amount. Guineas were the usual form in which professional fees were expressed, a 'gentleman's fee', intimating that the odd shilling made no difference to either side; a tradesman, on the other hand, would calculate his bill to the last penny.

7 **a moor park**: apricots were difficult to grow in England until Sir William Temple (1628–99) cultivated a standard tree later called the Moor Park after his estate in Hertfordshire, famous for its fruit. In 1760, Lord Anson, Admiral of the Fleet, then owner of Moor Park, introduced a new improved apricot strain, which is what would be meant here. Moor Park fruit are large and paler in colour than many other apricots.

8 **dilapidations**: responsibility for maintaining a parsonage was the clergyman's, not the church's, and if a house were allowed to fall into disrepair, his successor could claim compensation from his predecessor or executors for making good these 'dilapidations'. This often led to bitter disputes.

9 **shrubbery**: the shrubbery evolved in the mid-eighteenth century from the earlier garden feature of the wilderness, and would include deciduous as well as exotic evergreen species, such as bays. Seats would be provided in the shade 'for the comfort of the ladies'.

10 **a good seven hundred**: the fictional 'Compton', with its 100 acres, corresponds to Adlestrop; 'Sotherton', with 700, to Stoneleigh Abbey, which, too, has 'water-meadows' ('meadows washed by a stream', *E*, vol. 3, ch. 6) on the borders of the river Avon.

11 **the avenue at Sotherton down**: for landscape artists from 'Capability' Brown (1716–83) onwards, the view from and towards the house across greensward was a prime concern. In order to provide this uninterrupted 'prospect', many trees were often removed. In *Observations on the Theory and Practice of Landscape Gardening*

(1803) Repton, commenting on Sufton Court, declares 'improvement may be effected by the axe rather than by the spade' and illustrates this by a watercolour showing the effect of breaking up a formal row of trees in front of the drawing room to improve the prospect. 'Having the avenue down', as Rushworth crassly assumes, is another matter. 'The greatest objection to an avenue is, that . . . it often acts as a curtain drawn across the most interesting scenery: it is in undrawing this curtain in proper places that the utility of what has been called breaking an avenue consists' (*An Inquiry into the Changes of Taste in Landscape Gardening*, in *The Landscape Gardening and Landscape Architecture of the late H. Repton*, ed. J. C. Loudon (London, 1840), p. 336. Repton also declares that the 'man of taste' would not destroy an avenue of oaks 'for his hand is not guided by the levelling principles or sudden innovation of modern fashion'. The avenue, stretching out over a large tract of land, is a potent expression of private ownership and control; that at Sotherton, being 'of oak entirely', also signifies English patriotism since oaks provided timber for shipping. 'India may boast her plants', asserts Alexander Pope in *Windsor Forest* (1713), but 'by our oaks the precious loads are born, / And realms commanded which those trees adorn' (lines 29, 31–2). No such avenue appears on Repton's plan of Stoneleigh.

12 **an avenue! . . . Cowper:** Fanny is remembering lines from Cowper's *The Task* (1785).

> Ye fallen avenues! once more I mourn
> Your fate unmerited, once more rejoice
> That yet a remnant of your race survives.
> How airy and how light the graceful arch,
> Yet awful as the consecrated roof
> Re-echoing pious anthems!
> ('The Sofa', lines 338–430, book 1
> of *The Task*)

The poet mourns the fallen avenues 'once more' because he has earlier in the poem lamented 'the obsolete prolixity of shade' (line 265) of 'chestnuts ranged in corresponding lines' (line 263). The context of Fanny's citation links the older man-made landscape with religious feeling, since Cowper's lines allude to the widespread notion that the arching roofs of Gothic cathedrals imitate the effect of an avenue of tall trees meeting together. Cowper's feeling for the local landscape is intimately connected with his sense of God's sustaining presence in the world.

13 **I collect**: I gather, or understand.

14 **Elizabeth's time**: the reign of Elizabeth I (1558–1603). The confidence and prosperity of the period, and the rise of many trading families into gentility, led to the building of large houses.

15 **a stream . . . a good deal of**: Repton's improvements often involved the damming and widening of a stream in front of the house, as at Pemberley (where 'a stream of some natural importance was swelled into a greater' *P&P*, vol. 3, ch. 1). Repton made the stream at Stoneleigh Abbey into a lake.

16 **the admiral . . . at Twickenham**: 'The village of Twickenham is agreeably seated on the margin of the Thames, at a distance of rather more than ten miles from London . . . Nature and art unite to render the scenery attractive; and at various points of the Middlesex shore we find mansions admirable for elegance of construction' (*The Gleaner* (1823)). Increasing in fashion as a rural retreat from the city, 'unpretending little places' like 'Solus Lodge' (1810), the house of J. M. W. Turner, were built in the early nineteenth century.

17 **my harp**: the figure of the Bard having become important, the harp became a fashionable instrument in this period. By 1810 Sebastien Erard had patented the double-action harp. A new mechanism meant that the instrument could be played in any key by the simple expedient of fixing the pedals in the requisite notes in a box at the base of the harp, making it rather easier to give a competent performance on the harp than on the piano. Mary's harp will be similar to one made for Lady Clive of Powys Castle in 1802, one of the 4,000 harps Erard made in the first decades of the century. It stands 66.5 inches or 169 cm high, and is 34.5 inches or 87.5 cm wide. Weighing approximately 20–5 lb or 9–11 kg such a harp could readily be lifted by one man into a cart or barouche.

18 **Dr. Grant's bailiff**: since much of Dr Grant's income comes from farming, like Sir Thomas Bertram he employs a bailiff to oversee the farm work.

19 **the true London maxim**: 'We who have long lived amidst the conveniences of a town immensely populous, have scarce an idea of a place where desire cannot be gratified by money.' Samuel Johnson, *Adventurer*, 67 (26 June 1753). *Romæ omnia venalia* [everything is for sale in Rome] was a common tag.

20 **embarrassed**: here, perplexed.

21 **barouche**: a fashionable, sporty conveyance (as in *E*, vol. 2, ch. 14), a barouche was a four-wheeled carriage, seating four, with a half hood at the back which could be raised or lowered depending on the weather.

22 **in the King's service of course**: in the Royal Navy, not the merchant fleet: Mary's assumption underlines the point that service in the Royal Navy might be the route to wealth and fame, even for a relatively poor, or unconnected, young man.

23 **situation . . . profession**: as in the current 'situations vacant' column, 'situation' means a position within a firm or government agency, usually implying the possibility of promotion; 'foreign stations' is ports abroad in which his ship would dock, to be repaired and reloaded with supplies, in stays often lasting several weeks.

24 **Admirals**: the fleet was divided into three divisions or grades – in ascending order, the Blue, White and Red. Ships in each division flew an ensign or flag of the appropriate colour. Each of these three divisions was commanded by a Rear Admiral, a Vice-Admiral and a full Admiral, in ascending order of status and salary. The most prestigious position, obtained by seniority, not meritorious service, was Admiral of the Fleet. The Post Captain was the highest rank in the Royal Navy below that of Rear Admiral, except that for special duty a Captain might be given the rank of Commodore and would then rank above all other Captains.

25 **bickerings and jealousies**: Admirals and Captains often went to law over shares in prize-money: one historian writes of their 'endless disputes and lawsuits'. Michael Lewis, *A Social History of the Navy, 1793–1815* (London: Allen and Unwin, 1960), p. 322.

26 ***Rears* and *Vices***: the 'pun' (singular) is on 'vices', though both words are italicised. Mary has already spoken of the Admirals' 'jealousies', and by implication of their greed, and now moves on to hint at what the narrative has earlier described as her adulterous uncle's 'vicious conduct' (vol. 1, ch. 4). Later readers, less innocent

than Edmund and Fanny, put the two words together and take the reference to be to sodomy in the Navy, though the context is heterosexual. JA might have heard of the practice through her naval brothers, Frank and Charles, but it is inconceivable, given the proprieties of the period, that, consciously, she would introduce such a subject into her text (see, for example, her remark on the 'indelicacies' that disgrace de Genlis' *Alphonsine* (*L*, p. 114)). Mary's verbally teasing style is intended to seduce the imagination of her listeners, but Fanny and Edmund appear less shocked by the pun itself than by Mary's public disparagement of her uncle in front of comparative strangers. Nevertheless, the text here – and later, in the cleft between what Edmund feels and how he responds – deposits the suggestion that Mary's imagination flirts with forbidden topics. She may be speaking only what she has heard others speak, as Edmund is to avow later; or, more interestingly and disturbingly, the possibility of her own 'corruption' (Fanny's term: vol. 3, ch. 13) is already here intimated. A parallel instance is Mary's question in vol. 1, ch. 15: 'What gentleman among you am I to have the pleasure of making love to?', also followed by a brief silence interpretable in different ways.

27 **such timber**: as at Donwell Abbey in *E* (vol. 3, ch. 6), timber refers to established trees, which represent latent wealth on an estate, since they can be cut down and converted into income when their wood is sold for the construction of ships, houses, etc.

28 **Westminster**: like Eton, a great 'public' school; Crawford, like Mr Wickham in *P&P*, is educated at Cambridge, whereas Edmund, as JA's father and her brothers James and Henry had been, is an undergraduate at Oxford.

CHAPTER 7

1 **the harp arrived**: the harp became popular in part because in playing it a lady was able to display her upper body and arms. Austen would have read in Scott's *Marmion* (1808) of the seductive Lady Heron:

> Dame Heron rises with a smile
> Upon the harp to play.
> Fair was her rounded arm, as o'er
> The strings her fingers flew;

> And as she touched, and tuned them all,
> Ever her bosom's rise and fall
> Was plainer given to view.
> (Walter Scott, *Marmion, a tale of*
> *Flodden Field*, illustrated with engavings
> (London, 1809), canto 5, line 11)

2 **as elegant as herself:** Erard's harps were beautifully decorated in a 'Grecian' style with gold figures of classical graces at the foot.

3 **tambour frame:** a circular frame formed of one hoop fitting into another, across which cloth is stretched to facilitate needlework.

4 **her own remarks to him:** not Mary's witticisms, but what she, Fanny, has remarked upon or noticed as Mary's 'faults'.

5 **essay:** experiment or attempt.

6 **demesnes...in Dr. Grant's meadow:** demesnes is the land adjoining and belonging to the parsonage (and not to Mansfield) which Dr Grant, as the incumbent, farms. Mansfield, a 'modern-built house' (vol. 1, ch. 5), is situated on rising ground, unlike for example Donwell Abbey, which is 'low and sheltered' (*E*, vol. 3, ch. 6).

7 **what the eye could not reach:** compare Cowper's line in *The Task*, 'I gazed, myself creating what I saw' (book 6, line 290), recalled also by Mr Knightley in *E* (vol. 3, ch. 5).

8 **Mansfield common:** Mansfield is a village, where the 'common', or land held in common by the community, would be used for the grazing of cattle or sheep by poorer parishioners. Northamptonshire was the county ultimately most affected by the enclosure of common lands, but by the date of the novel this may not have proceeded as rapidly as elsewhere.

9 **the poor-basket:** the sewing basket in which materials, like the cheap and hardwearing Indian cotton, calico, are kept for making clothes for the parish poor; although considered a duty of ladies in the genteel classes, only Fanny, not Maria or Julia, is seen doing this (needle) 'work'.

10 **the alcove:** the flower garden and alcove, or summer house, suggest that Mansfield, a 'modern-built house' (vol. 1, ch. 5), also has modern surroundings. As the park and its expanse grew in

importance in the course of the eighteenth century, the garden, and especially the flower garden close to the house, was increasingly viewed as a female space: 'I should recommend Miss Elliot to be on her guard with respect to her flower-garden' (Sir Walter in *P*, vol. 1, ch. 3).

11 **aromatic vinegar**: a traditional wine vinegar flavoured with a herb such as tarragon or basil, used as a stimulant.

12 **your aunt wished to have them**: full-blown roses would be gathered, dried and later made into pot-pourri, as an air freshener.

13 **John Groom**: whereas Mrs Jefferies, an employer, is given her correct name, Mrs Norris calls the servant by the generic name of his job or profession. This was not an uncommon practice: Sam Weller in *Pickwick Papers* (London, 1836–7) is called 'Boots'.

14 **a quarter of a mile**: Mansfield Park and the parsonage are 'scarcely half a mile apart'; Mrs Norris' house is situated in the village, beyond the parsonage. The true distance is probably three-quarters of a mile or about a kilometre.

15 **knocked up**: exhausted.

16 **Madeira**: a sweet fortified white wine produced on the Portuguese island of Madeira in the Atlantic. It obtained a distinctive flavour from being stored in the hull of a ship during the long voyage to England, and became a fashionable pick-me-up or restorative.

CHAPTER 8

1 **a barouche**: in a barouche two couples sat facing each other: on the 'box' up front, there was room for the driver and a companion. A chaise was a carriage in which all passengers, who would sit in a row of three ('box'd up'), faced the horses; it might have a folding hood. A post-chaise refers disparagingly to the carriages used commercially to convey the mails, which would not have a hood. Both chaise and post-chaise would be driven by the family's coachman: later in the novel it appears that there would be four horses, with a driver in charge of each pair. Julia is exaggerating the inconvenience of the family conveyance in her desire to have a seat next to Henry.

2 **his cousin**: both editions read 'her cousin': since three females are each referred to in this long sentence the compositors were understandably confused.

3 **country**: here meaning countryside.

4 **capital freehold mansion and ancient manorial residence of the family**: the house is not leased, as for instance Netherfield is by Bingley in *P&P*, but is held freely, that is, wholly owned by Rushworth, who may do with it what he pleases. 'Mansion' and 'manorial' emphasise not so much the size or splendour of the house as its status as the head or 'capital' residence of a landed proprietor, and the fact that it has been in the same family for generations.

5 **all its rights of Court-Leet and Court-Baron**: originally a manor was land granted by the King for service to the crown. The grant also delegated to the proprietor, or Baron, rights of jurisdiction over those to whom he would in turn sell or lease the land; in other words he had authority not only to divide the land, and set rents, but also to act as judge, as for example in disputes. A court-leet (leet meaning law) is an assembly of the residents of the district or manor, held usually in the presence of the chief proprietor, to carry out these functions; the right of a court-Baron is to call an assembly of the freehold tenants of the manor. Known as the 'liberties' of the manor, these rights would remain in force, even if the proprietor changed. By this time, though, they were long since ceded to the county courts, and these are archaic terms. In *P&P*, 'the liberty of a manor' which Bingley acquires as tenant of Netherfield means no more than the right to hunt and shoot over its grounds (vol. 1, ch. 4).

6 **made it**: the road has been tarred and sealed, unlike the rest of the route from Mansfield. Improvement of the roads was associated with Thomas Telford (1757–1834) and John MacAdam (1750–1836). 'The Macadamised roads . . . have so abridged . . . distance in this fair island, that what used to be a journey is now a drive' (*Our Village*, vol. 4, p. 288).

7 **alms-houses**: with the dissolution of the monasteries, which had sheltered the poor and infirm, aristocratic and wealthy families took over this role, and built cottages, often in a row, as works of charity in which indigent and unfortunate parishioners might live

for little or no rent. They would usually be endowed with a sum for maintenance. Johnson quotes Pope: 'Behold yon almshouse, neat, but void of state, / Where age and want sit smiling at the gate.'

8 **lodge gates**: eighteenth-century country houses usually had large and ornamental gateways, which fronted the drive to the house: next to them would be a house where lodged the gatekeeper in charge.

CHAPTER 9

1 **collation**: Johnson defines collation as 'a repast: a treat less than a feast' (definition 3). The meal usually consisted of cold meats and delicacies.

2 **his curricle**: a light two-wheeled carriage. Since a curricle only carries two people, and is drawn by two horses abreast, it is an expensive way of getting about.

3 **the chaise**: the family carriage. Mr Rushworth proposes taking his curricle, which would seat himself and Crawford. If the Rushworth family vehicle is taken out also, it will be driven by the family coachman, and Crawford will not ride in it, hence the sisters' sulkiness.

4 **shewing the house**: touring of 'great houses' by the genteel classes grew in popularity during the last decades of the eighteenth century. Servants, most commonly the housekeeper, would show the visitors round. 'A well-drest elderly housekeeper, a most distinct articulator, shewed us the house', writes Boswell of a visit to Kedleston Hall, Derby in 1777 (*Life*, vol. 3, p. 161). The fictional Mrs Reynolds shows Elizabeth Bennet and the Gardiners around Pemberley (*P&P*, vol. 3, ch. 1).

5 **solid mahogany . . . gilding and carving**: mahogany was imported from the tropical American colonies and Cuba from the early eighteenth century and came into fashion gradually between 1725 and 1750. William Kent (1685–1748), the Palladian architect, specialised in rich interiors, with coffered ceilings and marble columns, but the mention of carving suggests late seventeenth-century taste, as exemplified in the work of Grinling Gibbons.

6 **regal visits and loyal efforts**: like much else, this suggests that Sotherton is based on Stoneleigh Abbey, Warwickshire.

Mrs Cassandra Austen, JA's mother, was a member of the Leigh family, whose fidelity to the Stuarts earned them the title of the 'loyal Leighs'. 'A strong attachment to the Stuarts pervaded this family' (J. N. Brewer's *Beauties of England and Wales . . . Warwickshire* (London, 1814), p. 44). Charles I had sheltered at Stoneleigh after the gates of Coventry were shut against him in 1642; in 1745, their loyalty to the cause undiminished, the Leighs were prepared to receive the Young Pretender at Stoneleigh. 'Regal visits' though, might also suggest one of the many great houses visited by Elizabeth I (1558–1603) on a royal 'progress': the implication is that the house has more than one glorious association.

7 **iron palisades**: a fence of iron stakes.

8 **window tax**: essentially a property tax, first imposed in 1696. The basis of assessment was altered a number of times in the eighteenth century, and increased on several occasions during the Napoleonic wars. The highest point of taxation was reached in 1808, when a house with forty to forty-four windows would be taxed at £28.17s.6d annually. After forty-four, the scale of taxation rose steeply in five-window increments. Many Elizabethan houses, such as Hardwick Hall ('more glass than wall') in Derbyshire, have large numbers of windows. JA's mother remarked on the '45 windows in front' – meaning the eighteenth-century west front – of the 'vast house' of Stoneleigh (*FR*, p. 157).

9 **mere, spacious, oblong room**: the anomaly of a 'mere, spacious, oblong room' in a house 'built in Elizabeth's time' (with no mention of later additions), the family gallery above, as well as the reference to the large number of windows, is explained if Stoneleigh is in JA's mind. Stoneleigh is an amalgam of buildings constructed from the remains of a Cistercian monastery and a massive early eighteenth-century West Wing, which houses the chapel.

10 **awful . . . No banners, cousin . . . sleeps below**: awful here means awe-inspiring. Fanny's quotation is from the description of Melrose Abbey in canto 2 of Walter Scott's romantic poem *The Lay of the Last Minstrel* (1805), his first great success. William of Deloraine, sent by the Ladye of Branksome 'to win the treasure of the tomb', wakes the Monk of St Mary's and together by moonlight they enter the Abbey.

ix
By a steel-clenched postern door,
    They enter'd now the chancel tall;
The darken'd roof rose high aloof
    On pillars lofty and light and small:
. . .

x
Full many a scutcheon and banner, riven,
Shook to the cold night-wind of heaven,
    Around the screened altar's pale;
And there the dying lamps did burn,
Before thy low and lonely urn
. . .

xii
They sate them down on a marble stone
(A Scottish monarch slept below);
Thus spoke the Monk, in solemn tone
. . .

(*The Lay of the Last Minstrel*,
10th edn (1809), p. 51)

The ruins of Melrose, according to Scott's note 21 in J. L.
Robertson (ed.), *The Poetical Works of Walter Scott* (Oxford:
Frowde, 1906), p. 62, 'afford the finest specimen of Gothic architecture and Gothic sculpture which Scotland can boast'. Fanny's
imagination will have been 'prepared' also by settings in many
novels of the time, like the deserted chapel in Charlotte Smith's
The Old Manor House (1793), by which Scott's may have been
influenced: 'the old banners which hung over her head, wav-
ing and rustling with the current of air, seemed to repeat the
whispers of some terrific and invisible being, foretelling woe and
destruction; while the same wind by which these fragments were
agitated hummed sullenly among the helmets and gauntlets, trophies of the prowess of former Sir Orlandos and Sir Hildebrands,
which were suspended from the pillars of the chapel'. *The Old
Manor House* (vol. I, ch. 10). The 'atchievements' Edmund refers
to are shield-shaped monuments decorated with a coat of arms,
granted in reward for a patriotic or noble achievement.

11 **James the Second's time**: the reign of the last Stuart king lasted three years, from 1685 to 1688, and led to the 'Glorious' or 'Bloodless' revolution – the installation of James' daughter Mary and her husband William of Orange on the throne of England, usually understood as marking Parliamentary power as definitive over the monarchy. The reference to the last Stuart king once more underlines the royalist affiliations of the Rushworth family. (At Stoneleigh, the Leighs worshipped in their private chapel in order to avoid joining in prayers for the House of Hanover at the parish church.)

12 **wainscot**: used for panelling, wainscot was oak, a native wood, which blackens with time; mahogany, imported and expensive, becomes richer in colour with age. Mrs Rushworth may be wrong about the date of the chapel's being 'fitted up', or JA misdates the vogue for mahogany: the point is that the chapel, anomalously, is the site of conspicuous display.

13 **purple cloth**: this signals more clearly what the fabric was not, than what it was. The colour purple conveyed a richness, associated with royalty, that the cloth, not being silk, damask or velvet, did not actually have.

14 **domestic chaplain**: as Mrs Rushworth's speech implies, keeping a domestic chaplain in a great house was more common before the eighteenth century than during it – another sign of the archaic, even moribund, practices of Sotherton. The chaplain, besides officiating at family prayers in a private chapel, was often the friend or confidant of the lady of the house and tutor to her children.

15 **such a household should be**: Johnson's first definition of 'family' is 'Those who live in the same house, household.' Fanny thinks of the 'family' in this older fashion, as including the servants. 'At nine in the morning we meet and say our prayers in the handsome Chapel', Mrs Austen noted during their visit to Stoneleigh in August 1806. Park Honan, *Jane Austen: Her Life*, revised edn (London: Orion, 1997), p. 226.

16 **Mrs. Eleanors and Mrs. Bridgets**: Mary is using the older form for an unmarried woman, a contraction of 'mistress'. In the third chapter of *Tom Jones* (1749) for instance, Squire Allworthy's elderly 'maiden' servant is called 'Mrs Deborah'. Mary refers to

young ladies but she mischievously titles them in the archaic manner as well as emphasising their 'starched' clothes – suggestive of ruffs and cuffs – in contrast to the lighter muslins and cottons of Regency fashion. 'Starched' also implies assumed or artificial propriety, as when JA teases Cassandra with 'I know your starched Notions (4 February 1813; *L*, p. 203).

17 **parsons**: Mary's term 'parsons' has betrayed that her conception of 'society' is in fact fashionable London 'Society'. The Evangelical Hannah More had written that 'The ladies of *ton* [fashion] have certain watch-words which may be detected as indicative' of a spirit she describes as 'that cold compound of irony, irreligion, selfishness and sneer': 'The clergy are spoken of under the contemptuous appellation of *The Parsons*'. *Strictures on the Modern System of Female Education* (London, 1799), ch. 1.

18 **serious subjects**: the unwitty Edmund's reply depends upon a distinction between 'serious', meaning straightforward or unplayful, and 'serious' subjects, usually meaning religious matters, a not uncommon turn of phrase, as when Sir Charles Grandison tells his cousin Everard that he will be allowed to join the conversation 'when you can be serious on serious subjects'. Samuel Richardson, *The History of Sir Charles Grandison*, 7th edn (7 vols., London: Strahan, 1781), vol. 2, letter 2.

19 **closet**: 'a small room of privacy and retirement' (Johnson sense 1), usually off the bedroom, and used for reading, private conversation and prayers.

20 **what chapel prayers are**: 'Service is performed in the chapels twice every day, at seven in the morning and at five in the afternoon' (*Letters from England*, letter 32). Times were different at different colleges, but the early morning service was compulsory, and aroused much resentment. Thomas de Quincey, who was at Oxford between 1803 and 1807, writes of 'the persecution of the chapel bell, sounding its unwelcome summons to six o'clock matins'. *Confessions of an English Opium Eater, and Other Essays* (London, 1901), p. 82.

21 **proper license**: ordinarily, marriages were validated by a preliminary calling of the banns in a parish church: 'The priest reads a list of all the persons in the parish who are about to be married. This is done three successive Sundays, that if any person should

be acquainted with any existing impediment to the marriage, he may declare it in time. The better classes avoid this publicity by obtaining a licence at easy expense. Those of high rank choose to be married at their own houses, a licence for which can be obtained from only the primate [the Archbishop of Canterbury]' (*Letters from England*, letter 19). Thus 'proper' does not mean regular, but a licence proper to this situation – which would be expensive.

22 **ordained**: to become a minister of the church of England, or 'in orders', a young man had normally first to undergo a ceremony, conducted by a bishop, in which he became a deacon. In theory, he was to be 'learned in the Latin tongue, and sufficiently instructed in holy scripture' and had to be at least twenty-three years of age (Edmund is twenty-four) (Brewster, p. xv). After a year serving as a deacon, he would be admitted as a minister.

23 **probably at Christmas**: strictly speaking, ordination could only take place on the four periods of fasting and prayer marking each season of the year, known as the Ember days, but this could be relaxed into 'some other Sunday or holiday' (Brewster, p. xv). The winter Ember days would in 1808 be 14, 15 and 16 December.

24 **the cloth**: the clergy; more literally, a man in the clothing – the vestments, cassock and surplice – of a clergyman.

25 **dine at five**: fashionably late to take the main meal of the day.

26 **pleasure-grounds**: 'Pleasure-ground, may be said to comprehend all ornamental compartments, or divisions of ground and plantation, surrounding a noble site, consisting of lawns, plantations of trees and shrubs, flower compartments, walks, pieces of water, &c, whether situated wholly within the space generally considered as the Pleasure-garden, or extended over the ha-ha's to the adjacent fields, parks, paddocks, or other outgrounds.' T. Mawe and J. Abercrombie, *The Universal Gardener and Botanist* (London, 1778), no pagination. Sotherton's pleasure grounds (on the south side of the house, where it is 'insufferably hot') include a bowling green and a 'pheasantry' (where birds are reared for the table rather than for gentlemen to shoot), both facilities more commonly associated with the seventeenth- than the eighteenth-century house.

27 **I see walls of great promise:** Henry looks forward to trans-
forming Sotherton into a modern estate. 'I congratulate you on
the fall of the wall and the opening prospect', wrote Nelson to
Emma Hamilton in 1805 concerning the estate at Merton. Terry
Coleman, *Nelson: The Man and the Legend* (London: Bloomsbury,
2001), p. 317. The layout of the 'pleasure-grounds' and the 'park'
beyond at Sotherton is typical of the geometric garden designs
of the late seventeenth and the first half of the eighteenth century. Earlier great houses were often surrounded with brick or
stone walls, secluding gardens, including kitchen gardens and
recreation areas, from the surrounding countryside, and providing a sheltered microclimate. 'Capability' Brown and the school
of landscape designers who followed him favoured an uninterrupted prospect to and from the house across parkland, and often
swept them away. (Humphry Repton's Red Book for Stoneleigh
Abbey includes 'before' and 'after' watercolours demonstrating
the improved aspect from the west front with walls removed).
Fashion and aesthetics now dominated the requirements of hor-
ticulture, as the house standing isolated in its park became a
symbol of conspicuous wealth. Maria's remark that 'those cottages are really a disgrace' (vol. 1 ch. 8) suggests too how the new
aesthetic of landscaping divorced the great landowner from the
local community (with the village church also reduced here to an
'annoyance').

28 **wilderness:** not a naturally occurring feature, but a planted
wood of fast-growing introduced softwoods such as the larch.
The geography of Sotherton is not entirely clear, in contrast
to the narratological signposting, in which the iron palisades
and gates are mentioned five times before the action focuses on
them.

29 **that principle of right:** this passage comes very close to
Evangelically-inspired rhetoric: 'natural benevolence . . . may produce . . . acts deserving of praise; but one principle alone can lead
to virtuous exertions persevering and unremitting', Mary Brunton
declared in *Self-Control* (1810; Edinburgh, 1811), ch. 15.

30 **beech cut down:** the beech trees have been layered, or in other
words, branches have been partially cut and interwoven with other
branches: in the cuts new shoots grow and are progressively woven

again, so that the whole forms a hedge. 'About two acres' is about 0.8 of a hectare.

31 **the ton**: the fashion.

32 **the office**: the position or public role of a clergyman, as distinguished from his personal character. 'It is the interest of the people that their ministers should be good . . . It is the more necessary, as, the common people especially, either do not, or will not, distinguish between the character and the office . . . But as a bad man may occupy an holy office, the twenty-sixth Article of Religion pronounces that, *the unworthiness of ministers hindereth not the effects of the Sacraments*' (Brewster, p. 13: Brewster's italics).

33 **Blair's to his own**: Hugh Blair's *Sermons* (5 vols. London: Cadell and Davies, 1777–1801) were described by Boswell as 'one of the most successful theological books that has ever appeared' (*Life*, vol. 3, p. 97). Though Blair was a Presbyterian not an Anglican, his sermons were praised by Johnson as 'excellently written both as to doctrine and language' (*Life*, vol. 3, p. 104), and were frequently reprinted: Boswell notes that copies were 'offered second-hand for a few pence' (*Life*, vol. 3, p. 167). It was common in this period for clergymen to read a printed sermon in preference to writing their own each Sunday. Addison, in *The Spectator*, 107 (1711), had advised the country clergy to preach the published sermons of famous divines, 'instead of wasting their spirits in laborious compositions of their own', advice criticised in More's *Cœlebs* in a discussion that overlaps with this in *Mansfield Park* at several points (ch. 27). Cowper (*The Task*, book 2, lines 410–11) also criticises the fashionable preacher who, 'reading what they never wrote', delivers printed sermons. Mary's preference for Blair, a famous stylist, is picked up later in Henry's comments on preaching.

34 **for the length of a street**: the custom of undergraduates walking arm in arm at Oxford continued into the twentieth century.

35 **a furlong in length**: an eighth of a mile (approximately 200 metres).

36 **within compass**: within the range of possibility.

37 **looking over a ha-ha into the park**: a ha-ha is a wide trench, cut to prevent cattle and sheep from crossing into the pleasure grounds, and allowing a view across parkland uninterrupted by fencing:

often, as here, there was a path running along it. Invented by the royal gardener Charles Bridgeman, it is thus another sign of the loyalist affiliations of the house. Like all the landscaping features mentioned in this sequence, the ha-ha readily carries symbolic or metaphoric meaning: 'We never have a large lawn of agreeable life. It is cut to pieces with sunk fences, ha-has, even where it is smoothest.' *Boswell for the Defence*, ed. W. K. Wimsatt Jr. and F. A. Pottle (Melbourne: Heinemann, 1960), p. 226 (25 June 1774).

38 **this morning**: it is now about 3 p.m.: the 'morning' extended for the whole period up to the time of dining.

CHAPTER 10

1 **a knoll**: a small hill or prominence, possibly a man-made feature. Prodigious feats of earth-moving were performed in order to provide vantage points from which the gentry might view the expanse of their estates.

2 **man of the world**: the phrase 'man of the world' is ambivalent in meaning. Maria uses it much as the narrator does in vol. 1, ch. 7, where Edmund is thought by Mary not to be 'a man of the world', or in other words not a frequenter of sophisticated society, but Henry's slight change to '*the* man of the world' gives it a different ring. Probably given circulation by Henry Mackenzie's novel *The Man of the World* (London, 1777), the phrase is there specifically attached to the 'votary of voluptuousness' (vol. 1, p. 187) Sir Thomas Sindall, who 'though he was not subject to the internal principles of honour or morality, . . . was man of the world enough to know their value in the estimation of others' (vol. 1, p. 317). There was also a successful comedy with the same title by Charles Macklin (c. 1785). The phrase is further debased when it is ironically reiterated, in, for example, Mary Hays' *The Victim of Prejudice* (London, 1799). The 'man of the world' in Hays's novel is one corrupted by the vices of London, whose memory of the past is indeed short-lived, since he forgets his childhood sweetheart, with fatal consequences for her. Thus the partially approbationary phrase signifies not much more than libertinism in some contexts, an equivocal quality that the dialogue turns on and Henry exploits.

3 **I cannot get out, as the starling said:** Maria remembers a well-known passage from Laurence Sterne's *A Sentimental Journey Through France and Italy* (London, 1768) in the chapter called 'The Passport, The Hotel at Paris'. Sterne's narrator, Yorick, has come to Paris during wartime without the necessary passport; the probable consequence, if he is caught, is imprisonment in the Bastille. He tries to persuade himself that captivity would be no more inconvenient than confinement with the gout:

> the Bastile is not an evil to be despised. – But strip it of its towers, – fill up the foss, – unbarricade the doors, – call it simply a confinement, and suppose 'tis some tyrant of a distemper . . .
>
> I was interrupted in the hey-day of this soliloquy, with a voice which I took to be of a child, which complained 'it could not get out' . . .
>
> In my return back through the passage, I heard the same words repeated twice over; and looking up, I saw it was a starling hung in a little cage.—'I can't get out,—I can't get out,' said the starling.

Yorick tries to free the bird, which is still repeating its cries. 'In one moment they overthrew all my systematic reasonings upon the Bastile; and I heavily walk'd up stairs, unsaying every word I had said in going down them. Disguise thyself as thou wilt, still, Slavery, said I,—still thou art a bitter draught! . . . 'Tis thou, thrice sweet and gracious goddess, addressing myself to *Liberty*, whom all in public or in private worship'. Sterne brings together the sentimentalist doctrine of the primacy of feeling, of the 'affections', over 'systematic reasonings' and the association of these with the valorisation of (British) 'Liberty' over the despotic culture of France. At this point, the symbolic form of the garden, which has already loaded into 'the vista closed by iron gates' meanings which suggest archaic authority and confinement, coalesces with the quotation to give Maria's cry an intense resonance. 'As she spoke, and it was with expression' suggests an unequivocal utterance unknown to men of the world; but, like the bird, Maria is speaking what she does not understand. Her sudden quotation is all the more startling in light of the current Evangelical view that *A Sentimental Journey* was a 'corrupt' work (*Cœlebs*, ch. 29). The passage appears in the popular compilation *Elegant Extracts*, compiled by Vicesimus

Knox (4th edn, London, 1794), book 4: 'Narratives, Dialogues, etc', item 144.

4 **here, with my assistance**: Henry is probably holding back part of the hedge brambles that adjoins the gate to make a gap through which Maria can step.

5 **posting away**: 'posting', with fresh horses at each stage or post of the journey, was the fastest mode of travel.

6 **scrambled across the fence**: fence is a general word for boundary, but here means hedge. Maria can earlier pass 'round the edge of the gate' because the boundary in this place is not iron railings or a wooden fence, which would come up to the iron gate, but a hedge of hawthorn or privet, perhaps, leaving gaps, and that is why Fanny fears she will tear her gown. Julia's 'scrambling' means that she performs a bodily manoeuvre that was forbidden Maria in the presence of a gentleman.

7 **five foot nine**: or 175 cm. The point of this is that gentlemen were normally several inches taller than men of lower social standing. The mean height of working-class men recruited into the army or the Royal Marines in 1800 was between 64 and 66 inches (5 ft 4 or 5 ft 6) or 162–7 cm. In 1810, recruits to the London Marine Society were on average 5 inches or 13 cm shorter than the upper-class recruits to the officer training college at Sandhurst. See R. Floud, K. Wachter and A. Gregory, *Height, Health and History: Nutritional Status in the United Kingdom, 1750–1980* (Cambridge: Cambridge University Press, 1990), graphs on pp. 136, 140, 197.

8 **ague . . . charm**: Johnson defines ague as 'an intermitting fever, with cold fits succeeded by hot'. The charm Mrs Norris promises is probably a written one; hung around the neck, such charms invoked Christ's shaking on the cross to claim, in the language of one of them, that 'wosoever beleveth in me and wereth these wordes shall never have the ague nor fever'. But the term might also refer to herbal medicines, gathered at propitious times of the year. Mrs Norris practises old-fashioned, and at this date irresponsible, folk doctoring.

9 **heath**: the common name for species of *Erica*: presumably this is a cultivar.

10 **Quarterly Reviews**: the *Quarterly Review*, which published articles on affairs of state as well as reportage about life in foreign parts

and reviews of new publications, was founded by John Murray in 1809, as a Tory or conservative riposte to the Whig or reforming *Edinburgh Review*, founded in 1802. By 1812 its circulation had reached over 9,000 copies. The mention confirms the Tory politics of the Rushworths and Bertrams.

11 **second table**: the table in the steward's or housekeeper's room for the upper domestics, such as the butler, who would eat meals similar to the first, or master's, table in the dining room. That Mrs Norris even asked the question of Mrs Whitaker suggests that the practice of serving wine was not unheard of. Retrogressive tyranny and pettiness towards underlings in her eyes is the preservation of old-fashioned values.

12 **white gowns**: servants generally wore dark clothes, which is why, when he is later urging Fanny to take the part of 'Cottager's wife', Tom says 'You must get a brown gown' (vol. 1, ch. 15). White dress is a sign of gentility: in Charlotte Smith's *Emmeline, or The Orphan of the Castle* (1788), for instance, the gentility of the poor Mrs Stafford is assured on first meeting by her wearing a 'long white muslin morning gown' (vol. 2, ch. 11). The recent affordability of white cotton, the result of the transformation in textile technology, allowed housemaids to dress 'above' their station: the insurrectionary potential of this is spotted by Mrs Whitaker.

13 **spunging**: more commonly spelt 'sponging': appropriating from others in a parasitical manner, as a sponge absorbs liquid.

CHAPTER 11

1 **packet**: a boat plying between two ports (here Liverpool and St John's, Antigua) for the monthly conveyance of mail, as well as goods and passengers.

2 **friend**: supporter, or ally: though it refers to her father, the word here conveys the sense that the marriage has a political dimension.

3 **a competence**: enough money to live comfortably.

4 **preferment**: a position in the church which confers social and financial advantages. In this instance Edmund means that, after a provisional period as deacon, he will be 'preferred' over others to the family living.

5 **curate**: 'a clergyman hired to perform the duties of another' (Johnson): notoriously poorly paid, curates were often employed by clergymen to do the everyday work of the parish for them, such as visiting the sick.

6 **the chaplain of the Antwerp**: chaplains, in short supply, were usually to be found only on a large ship, or man of war, of seventy-four guns and above. The invented name associates William's ship with Britain's safety and security, since the capture of Antwerp, an important naval base in the Austrian Netherlands, was a consistent tenet of British foreign policy during the Napoleonic wars. Between July and September 1809 the English Navy attacked, but failed to capture, Antwerp, with the loss of some four thousand lives.

7 **green goose**: at four or five months old, possibly too young, lean and tough for eating at this date (August). Usually geese were hatched in spring, and fattened and eaten at seven or eight months old, during the Michaelmas festivities later in the year. But since Parson Woodforde ate a 'green Goose and peas' on 10 June 1784, as part of a 'very genteel Dinner', it appears that the problem here is not with the youth or greenness of the goose but with its cooking. James Woodforde, *The Diary of a Country Parson, 1785–1802*, ed. John Beresford (Oxford: Oxford University Press, 1949), p. 227.

8 **whose amiableness depends on his own sermons**: the ironic turn in Mary's rebuke to Fanny resembles Portia's to Nerissa in *The Merchant of Venice*: 'It is a good divine that follows his own instructions' (Act 1, scene 2, line 14).

9 **glee**: a song for three or more voices, in which each voice takes a different part.

10 **tread**: JA's first readers might have recalled Milton's 'L'Allegro', in which the poet addresses the 'Nymph', who has 'wanton Wiles/ Nods and Becks, and wreathèd Smiles' (lines 27–8):

> Come and trip it as you go,
> On the light fantastic toe;
> (lines 33–4)

Mrs Elton (mis)quotes another familiar tag from the poem in *E* (vol. 2, ch. 18).

11 **the sublimity of Nature**: this passage echoes many such scenes in the novels of Ann Radcliffe, as for example in *The Romance of the Forest* (1791):

> The mountains, darkened by twilight, assumed a sublimer aspect . . . Clara and Adeline loved to pass the evenings in this hall, where they had acquired the first rudiments of astronomy, and from which they had a wide view of the heavens. La Luc pointed out to them the planets and the fixed stars, explained their laws, and from thence taking occasion to mingle moral with scientific instruction, would often ascend towards that *great first Cause*, whose nature soars beyond the grasp of human comprehension.
>
> (Ann Radcliffe, The Romance of the Forest,
vol. 3, ch. 18)

The association of the night sky, seen from a window, with romantic melancholy (usually complemented by music), is a recurrent motif in Radcliffe's novels; here, it is ironised, since the music's 'harmony' is in effect in competition with the Romantic 'sublime'. Fanny does not read the night sky as evidence of its divine author, as is usual in works of the period: rather, the emphasis on the 'soothing', 'tranquillizing' quality of the scene implies her own psychological need. The exclamation 'Here's harmony' refers antiphonally back to Edmund's glance after Mary: 'There goes good humour'.

12 **enthusiasm**: enthusiasm was earlier seen as akin to insanity; however, as the eighteenth century goes on it gradually acquires a more approbationary sense, implying the capacity for strong and idealistic feeling. But reservations still remain, as when the heroine of Mary Hays' *Memoirs of Emma Courtney* (London, 1796) reads Rousseau's *Heloise*: 'Ah, with what transport, with what enthusiasm, did I peruse this dangerous, enchanting work!' (ch. 8). Edmund's praise of Fanny marks a further shift towards the Romantic register of the term, but at the opening of vol. 2, ch. 11, Fanny's 'tender enthusiasm' is treated ironically.

13 **Arcturus . . . Cassiopeia**: Arcturus is the brightest star in the constellation Boötes or The Waggoner, situated at the tail of the

Great Bear or Ursa Major; Cassiopeia is another constellation in the northern sky, neither of which set because they are so close to the pole. Remarking on Fanny's 'self-consciously worn learning' here, Sutherland appropriately quotes the passage in Austen's early letter where she makes fun of 'hard names for the stars' (9 Jan. 1799: Sutherland, p. 400).

CHAPTER 12

1 **September . . . gamekeeper**: the first of September is the beginning of the northern game-shooting season.
2 **Weymouth**: In 1789 George III put the royal stamp of approval on the idea of sea bathing when he recuperated his health at Weymouth, on the south coast of England. From then on Weymouth became a fashionable resort of the aristocracy and gentry.
3 **Everingham . . . September**: the emphasis is on his 'shooting', but with the end of summer, and the holiday month of August, he might also be expected to take up the business affairs of the estate and hold a harvest festival entertainment for his tenants.
4 **their qualification . . . poachers**: the right to hunt game (hares, partridges, pheasants, etc) was restricted to those with the legal qualification of a freehold worth at least £1,000 a year, or a leasehold of at least £150 per annum. Poaching, or the taking of game by stealth, was very common, since it was one way for the poor to survive. A poacher, if caught alone, could be fined £5 or jailed for three months; if in concert with others, much severer penalties applied.
5 **candidly**: impartially, with fairness.
6 **the common forms**: as is clear from the context, custom dictated that dancers changed partners after dancing a set of two dances. Mrs Rushworth thinks that Maria and Rushworth should have been allowed to keep dancing together. At this point in the action, two sets have been danced (the 'four dances' during which Fanny has been happy) and the third is in progress. Maria and Rushworth have danced the first set together, and are now, after changing partners for the second as decorum required, dancing the third. JA leaves it to be surmised that Crawford was Maria's partner for the second.

7 **the couple above**: in country dances there is a top and bottom of the row of dancers; each couple gradually moves down the row from the top to the bottom with the steps of the dance. Maria and Rushworth are second in the line from Julia and Crawford, who may be at the top.

8 **business . . . America**: during the first decade of the nineteenth century there were continual tensions over American trade with Europe. As neutral traders in wartime, Americans reaped inflated profits, but both the British and French enacted orders restricting neutral shipping. British ships attacked American vessels, causing passionate outrage in the States, and leading to the Embargo Act of December 1807, which was intended to punish Britain and France, but instead crippled the American economy. President Jefferson was forced to repeal this in March 1808, and substituted a Non-Intercourse Act, which proved even harder to enforce. His successor, Madison, replaced this in 1810 with a measure which in effect played off one belligerent against the other. Napoleon responded with a pledge of repeal; when nothing was heard from London, ships and goods from Britain were excluded from the States. From this point on Anglo-American relations deteriorated, not helped by a Native American uprising on the north-western frontier, allegedly incited by British officials. A declaration of war against Britain was made in June 1812, Americans learning too late that Britain had already revoked its oppressive regulations. Tom is improvising, but his remark would have seemed plausible to contemporary readers. At a family dinner party attended by Joseph Farington in January 1809, for example, among other politics, 'America & the Embargo was spoken of': evidently this was the sort of topic middle-class men talked about among themselves. *The Diary of Joseph Farington* (17 vols., New Haven and London: Yale University Press, 1982), vol. 9, ed. Kathryn Cave, p. 3387.

9 **a rubber**: the best of three games of Whist, which is the popular card game they are playing. Whist requires four players playing in pairs against each other, which is why Tom is being sought to make up the numbers.

10 **half-crowns**: there were four crowns to a pound in the imperial system; a half-crown was a coin worth an eighth of a pound, or

2s.6d. The mention of half-crowns – in the period of the novel, not a small sum – as well as half-guineas, indicates the scope of the party's financial horizons. By contrast, the stakes at Mr Woodhouse's card-parties are sixpences (*E*, vol. 1, ch. 3).

CHAPTER 13

1 **The Honourable**: the title given to the younger sons of peers.
2 **tolerable independence**: Yates has a sufficient, though not a large, income of his own – he doesn't need to wait for the death of a rich relative.
3 **private theatricals at Ecclesford**: as the reference to 'a long paragraph' in a newspaper suggests, amateur performances of plays in specially built or makeshift theatres in country houses were rarely wholly private events, and might involve the co-option of professional actors, and the calling in of neighbouring families to fill out parts.
4 **Lovers' Vows**: Elizabeth Inchbald's adaptation of August von Kotzebue's *Das Kind der Liebe* [The Child of Love] (1790) was first performed at Covent Garden in 1798. It was well received from the first, with forty-two performances in the 1798–9 season, and was staged at the Theatre Royal in Bath at least seventeen times during JA's residence there between 1801 and 1806. It was frequently revived in amateur performances. On 7 January 1808, for example, an item in the *Morning Post* reports that officers returning from Sicily attended 'the theatre at Nuthurst Lodge, where *Lovers' Vows* was performed and gave general satisfaction'. JA assumes some knowledge of this play on the part of her readers, but does not rely upon it for their understanding of the references. The lavish sprinkling of aristocratic titles in Yates's speech makes clear his claim to be socially a cut above the family of a baronet.
5 **dowager**: a widow who holds property or a title.
6 **after-piece**: a typical evening's programme in the eighteenth- and early nineteenth-century theatre would include a five-act play, followed by a farcical afterpiece. These were often pantomimes, with, as Edmund later contemptuously observes, many scene changes, made by flats 'shifted' in grooves, dances, and farcical 'tricks'. They were popular, since they could be enjoyed by the late-comers to

677

the theatre, admitted at half-price. The *Morning Post* of 23 May 1808 announces Kemble in *King Lear*, 'with *Harlequin and Mother Goose*'.

7 **my Grandmother**: *My Grandmother* was by Prince Hoare (1793–4): 'the Much-Admired Musical Entertainment', as advertised on a play-bill for the Theatre Royal, Bath in February 1795. A farcical afterpiece, it proved so popular that it often became the main entertainment.

8 **the jointure**: property or a financial sum held jointly by husband and wife, which would provide an annuity for the wife should her husband predecease her. The assumption is that, following the death of the dowager, the money would revert to her descendants. If the grandmother were Lady Ravenshaw's mother, the sum would presumably be left to her, and hence become her husband's property.

9 **our manager**: the manager of a London theatre would be its owner; he might well be the chief actor himself. Tom is flattering Yates with the implied comparison to actor-managers such as David Garrick who retired as actor-manager of Drury Lane in 1776.

10 **the riot of his gratifications**: defining 'riot' as 'wild and loose festivity', Johnson quotes Shakespeare's *Henry IV Part 2* on Prince Hal (Act 4, scene 3, lines 62–4): 'his headstrong riot hath no curb . . . When means and lavish manners meet together'. The phrase is one of several suggestions that Henry is a licentious 'man of the world'.

11 **from Shylock or Richard III**: both villainous starring parts, very popular in the eighteenth-century theatre: Shylock in Shakespeare's *The Merchant of Venice*, Richard III in his history play of the same name.

12 **cut capers**: leap and frolic about.

13 **green baize for a curtain**: baize is a coarse woollen material. 'The color most closely associated with the eighteenth-century stage was green. A custom of great antiquity was that the front, or proscenium curtain should be of this color . . . If a latecomer saw any other kind of curtain or one of any other color he would know that he had come into the theatre at the end of an act'. Introduction to *The London Stage 1660–1800*, ed.

C. B. Hogan (Carbondale: Southern Illinois University Press, 1965), p. xlvi. There were other, painted curtains behind the proscenium curtain, which was made of the baize that was also used to upholster the benches of the pit and on the floor of the stage. Baize was also used to line drawers, as a protective cloth for polished furniture, etc.

14 **a side wing or two . . . scenes to be let down**: side wings are pieces of scenery which give an illusion of depth to the stage space; flats are sections of scenery which are assembled to form a set. These and the idea of 'scenes' (or painted backdrops) to be 'let down' suggest how very expensive Yates' 'nothing more' would be.

15 **a German play**: Edmund implies that German plays are morally dubious, a view often taken by English commentators, as in Wordsworth's Preface to *Lyrical Ballads* (1802): 'The invaluable works of our elder writers . . . are driven into neglect by frantic novels, sickly and stupid German Tragedies'. The *Quarterly Review* 1809 review of '*Amelie Mansfield* par Madam Cottin' concludes 'We lament . . . that there should be a wish in Britain for importing, from the schools of France and Germany, those novels and dramas which tend at once to corrupt the taste and deprave the national character.' *Quarterly Review*, 1:2 (May 1809), p. 315. Kotzebue was the leading figure. His *Menschenhass und Reue* was adapted by Benjamin Thompson as *The Stranger* (1798). A sentimental drama about a sinful but repentant woman and the misanthropic husband from whom she fled with another man years before, it deals sympathetically, like *Lovers' Vows*, with errant female sexuality: in one an adulteress, in the other an unmarried mother, go unpunished by society. Mrs Siddons starred in the play's 26-night run in 1798. Sheridan's version of Kotzebue's conquistador drama *Pizarro* played for twenty-five nights in 1799 with Siddons as Elvira.

16 **horn-pipe . . . a song between the acts**: songs and dances were inserted between the acts of plays in the eighteenth-century theatre: a 'Hornpipe in Wooden Shoes' was, for instance, once performed between the acts of *Hamlet*. Many of the songs, which increased in popularity during the wars with France, were patriotic and on nautical or military themes, like the most popular, 'Rule Britannia' composed by Thomas Arne, 1740. Commenting

on the London theatre in a letter of 25 September 1813, JA remarks 'the Clandestine Marriage was the most respectable of the performances, the rest were Sing-song & trumpery' (*L*, p. 230).

17 **bred to the trade**: 'Garrick's trade was to represent passion, not to feel it', Reynolds makes Samuel Johnson say ('Two Dialogues by Joshua Reynolds', in *Johnsonian Miscellanies*, ed. G. B. Hill (2 Vols., Oxford, 1897), vol. 1, p. 248). The shifting status of the actor in the eighteenth century is reflected in Johnson's saying that Garrick had 'advanced the dignity of his profession' (*Life*, vol. 3, p. 263). George Crabbe specifically defines the 'labour' of professional actors: 'To bear each other's spirit, pride and spite / To hide in rant the heart-ache of the night . . . This is laborious' (*The Borough* (London, 1810), letter 12, lines 89–96). Acting was not considered a proper occupation for ladies: R. B. Sheridan, the playwright, for example, wrote to Thomas Linley to persuade him not to allow his daughter on the stage: 'What is the *modesty* of any Woman whose trade it is eternally to represent all the different modifications of Love before a mix'd Assembly of Rakes, Whores, Lords and Blackguards in succession!' (letter of 1775, in *The Letters of Richard Brinsley Sheridan*, ed. Cecil Price (3 vols., Oxford: Clarendon Press, 1966), vol. 3, p. 297).

18 **billiard-room**: during the later eighteenth century country house plans begin to show separate rooms for different functions – a breakfast-room, a billiard-room, etc. Mansfield is one such 'modern-built' house. In *S&S*, Mr Palmer grumbles at Sir John Middleton's not having a billiard-room at Barton Park: 'How few people know what comfort is!' (vol. 1, ch. 20).

19 **doors . . . communicating with each other**: there are two doors, each of which leads to Sir Thomas' 'room' (not his bedroom, but his study, as the reference to the book-case indicates). One of them is blocked by the book-case, which when removed would allow the actors to go off stage at one door, and make their entrances through the other, an arrangement that duplicates one common in the eighteenth-century theatre.

20 **green-room**: a room for actors and actresses when waiting to appear on the stage, usually in the eighteenth-century theatre lined with green baize.

21 **objections**: moralists such as Thomas Gisborne – 'pious disclaimers against theatrical exhibitions' in the words of Inchbald's 'Remarks' on *Lovers' Vows* – condemned the stage and acting, and especially 'the custom of acting plays in private theatres', which is 'liable to this objection among others; that it is almost certain to prove, in its effects, injurious to the female performers'. Thomas Gisborne, 'The Subject of Amusements Continued', in his *An Enquiry into the Duties of the Female Sex*, 2nd edn (London, 1797), ch. 9.

22 **in some degree of constant danger**: crossing the Atlantic – which in a sailing ship might take four to six weeks – in time of war, Sir Thomas' ship would be open to attacks from the French Navy and privateers. There was also the danger of tropical disease, which, for instance, killed Cassandra Austen's fiancé Tom Fowle in the West Indies in 1797.

23 **Julius Cæsar . . . to be'd and not to be'd**: Mark Antony's speech before uncovering Caesar's body, beginning 'If you have tears, prepare to shed them now' in Shakespeare's *Julius Caesar*, Act 4, scene 2; Hamlet's soliloquy, *Hamlet*, Act 3, scene 1. Some editors emend to '*to be'd or not to be'd*', with the whole phrase in italics.

24 **Norval**: from the second act of the Sophoclean blank-verse tragedy *Douglas* by John Home (1757). Norval, a young stranger who has saved the life of Lord Randolph in battle, tells his story. Though brought up in obscure poverty, he has become a valiant warrior:

> My name is Norval: on the Grampian hills
> My father feeds his flocks: a frugal swain,
> Whose constant cares were to increase his store,
> And keep his only son, myself, at home.
> For I had heard of battles, and I long'd
> To follow to the field some warlike Lord:
>> (*Douglas; a Tragedy by Mr Home . . . with*
>> *remarks by Mrs Inchbald* (London: Longman,
>> Hurst, 1810), lines 44–9)

Like many others in the play, this speech celebrates the natural valour of noble 'blood': appropriate educational material for a baronet's sons. Norval is in fact the long-lost son of Lady

Randolph, the play's tragic heroine. This recognition scene was so popular and well known that it was parodied in Sheridan's *The Critic* (1779) where Puff declares: 'There, you see, relationship, like murder, will out' (Act 3, scene 1).

25 **quite as great an interest**: interest in the sense of material investment or claim. Tom is probably in fact already the legal owner of the house, since this was the arrangement most propertied families came to in order to ensure continuity of the estate.

26 **my sister's piano forte**: the sisters play duets (vol. 1, ch. 1), but it is quite possible that the piano was bought for Maria, the more spoilt of the two. Most editors emend to 'sisters' piano forte'.

27 **a whole twenty pounds**: not such a small sum. Frances Burney's *Cecilia* shows the heroine dispensing charity to a carpenter's wife: 'A hard working family, like mine, Madame', says Mrs Hill, 'with the help of twenty pounds will go on for a long while quite in paradise.' *Cecilia, or, Memoirs of an Heiress* (1782), vol. 1, book 1, ch. 9. In 1800 the butler at Englefield House in Berkshire received a salary of £20 per annum.

28 **altogether by the ears**: at variance, at war with each other, a phrase deriving from dogs fighting.

29 **his representation**: the legal overtones of the word (one 'represents' a case or a client) suggest the seriousness with which Edmund puts arguments against play-acting before his sisters.

30 **hands . . . under strappers**: a hand is a helper; a strapper attends to and grooms horses, so under strapper must mean a junior or ancillary helper.

31 **Duenna . . . Confidante**: both stock theatrical roles. A duenna (the title of a musical play by Sheridan, 1775) is an older woman who acts as chaperone to young ladies; a confidante ('a person trusted with private affairs, commonly with affairs of love' – Johnson) is a role which allows the heroine to deliver information to the audience, under the guise of confiding in her friend.

32 **the mind of genius**: a spirited, lively mind, often in the period contrasted, to its disadvantage, with the mind of 'taste'. Describing a woman of 'taste' Hannah More writes that 'She has rather a playful gaiety than a pointed wit . . . she may rather be said to be a nice judge of the genius of others, than to be a genius herself' (*Cœlebs*, ch. 14).

CHAPTER 14

1 **Douglas . . . Heir at Law:** Like *Hamlet*, *Macbeth*, *Othello* and the other Shakespeare plays already mentioned by Henry Crawford, *Richard III* and *The Merchant of Venice*, these are standards of the late eighteenth-century theatrical repertoire. The popularity of Home's *Douglas* is clear in Tom Bertram's earlier mention of it in the same breath as *Hamlet*; the discovery there by a grieving mother of a long-lost son, a standard eighteenth-century theatrical trope, is repeated in *Lovers' Vows*. Edward Moore's sentimental tragedy *The Gamester* (1753) was also widely performed. Later the roles of Lady Randolph in *Douglas* and Mrs Beverley in *The Gamester* provided opportunities for the great Sarah Siddons (1755–1831), with whose acting Austen was familiar (see her letter of 30 November 1814; *L*, p. 287). Sheridan's comedies, *The Rivals* (1775), performed at Steventon in July 1794, and *The School for Scandal* (1777), in which Jane Austen probably took the part of Mrs Candour in a reading or staging at Manydown Park in 1808, were also popular. *Wheel of Fortune* (1791) is a comedy by Richard Cumberland, and *Heir at Law*, also a comedy, is by George Colman the younger.

2 **nice:** fastidious, or particular. See Henry Tilney's pronouncements on the usage of this word in *NA*: 'Originally perhaps it was applied only to express neatness, propriety, delicacy, or refinement:— people were nice in their dress, in their sentiments, or their choice. But now every commendation on every subject is comprised in that one word' (vol. 1, ch. 14). William Price later uses the word correctly ('You and Miss Crawford have made me too nice'; 'your nice ways and orderliness' (vol. 3, ch. 4; vol. 3, ch. 6)) but compare Mrs Norris on Sotherton: 'I would have everything done in the best style, and made as nice as possible' (vol. 1, ch. 6).

3 **Lord Duberley or Dr Pangloss:** Lord Duberly (sic) is a vulgar provincial tradesman who has come into the title and a country estate of £15,000 a year on the presumed death of the true heir overseas. The play is set in London, where Dr Pangloss, as Duberly says, is 'the man as learns me to talk English' (Act 1, scene 1). Pangloss can hardly make a speech without including a learned quotation, but he abandons whatever dignity a scholar may possess when Lady Duberly and her son, Dick, bribe him by

each promising to double his annuity. Although there is many a sentimental tear in the rest of the play, needless to say there are no 'fine tragic parts'. The name Pangloss is taken from the tutor in Voltaire's *Candide* (1759): the name became a by-word for a hypocritical pedant in the early nineteenth century.

4 **every rant**: 'rant' has already been used several times (Henry: 'I feel . . . as if I could rant and storm', 'let us have no ranting tragedies'). Ranting – to declaim in a bombastic manner – is associated with the early eighteenth-century theatre, where 'Declamation roar'd while Passion slept' (Johnson, 'Prologue, spoken by Mr Garrick at the Opening of the Theatre in Drury Lane, 1747' line 33), and particularly with the actor Colley Cibber. 'The stage, at this period, was in a low condition . . . in tragedy, declamation roared in a most unnatural strain; rant was passion; whining was grief; vociferation was terror, and drawling accents were the voice of love'. This rhetorical approach to acting was challenged by David Garrick's offering a more subdued performance: 'He banished ranting, bombast and grimace; and restored nature, ease, simplicity, and genuine humour'. Arthur Murphy, *Life of Garrick* (2 vols., London, 1802), vol. 1, pp. 17, 45. But rant enjoyed a revival when the new Covent Garden (1792) and Drury Lane (1794) theatres were built: these were huge barns, and actors again began to raise their voices above a natural pitch and use exaggerated gestures. Yates wants to imitate in a small private theatre the acting he has seen on the London stage.

5 **short parley of compliment**: 'parley' is 'much used in war for a meeting of enemies to talk' (Johnson). The phrase thus suggests the mutual flattery of men.

6 **an Agatha**: the part of the tragic or sentimental heroine, originally played by Sarah Siddons. Agatha opens the play: she is begging for food, having been long reduced to poverty and misery by the desertion of her 'seducer', Baron Wildenhaim. Within minutes she sees and recognises Frederick, the soldier who is her illegitimate son.

CHAPTER 15

1 **hardly doubting a contradiction**: *Lovers' Vows* was notoriously the object of attack by conservative moralists: Edmund's reaction

suggests JA's reliance here on her reader's previous knowledge of this and of the play.

2 **deal board**: a plank of cheap timber, usually sawn from a fir or pine log, and used for framing. Mrs Norris mimics Dick's uneducated speech, implying that his excuse is a lie.

3 **lubberly**: 'lazy and bulky' (Johnson).

4 **making love to**: to 'make love to' is to address the other person in a seductive or flirtatious manner.

5 **puzzle them**: distract or inhibit them.

6 **creepmouse**: this seems to be a word coined for the occasion. Johnson defines 'creephole' as 'a hole into which any animal may creep to escape danger'. Later, in ch. 18, it is a pleasure for Fanny 'to creep into the theatre'.

7 **requisition**: not just a request, closer to a formal demand for service.

8 **his picture drawn before he went to sea again**: the word 'drawn' is also used of the 'small miniature painting' of Captain Benwick promised to Fanny Harville (*P*, vol. 2, ch. 11). Mary is probably suggesting not a miniature, which would be slow and costly to produce, but a 'cabinet' portrait sketch, executed in crayon, pencil and watercolour wash on vellum or paper. The capital 'S' in the next phrase has been retained, though strict grammar requires this sentence to run on.

9 **Stoke**: a common English place name. In Northamptonshire are Stoke Albany, Stoke Bruerne and Stoke Doyle.

CHAPTER 16

1 **meet**: suitable.

2 **commanding a shilling**: the phrase is not meant literally since books were expensive, and would cost much more than a few shillings each. Presumably Sir Thomas makes Fanny an allowance.

3 **harmonized by distance**: by its very length and the elaboration of subordinate clauses the previous sentence structure has represented Fanny's pained retrieval of past occasions. Leading to a temporary depletion of attention on the reader's part, its summation, 'and the whole was now so blended together', offers the syntactical equivalent of a viewer stepping back, so that a visible scene goes out of focus. JA could have read in Thomas Campbell's 1799 poem *The Pleasures of Hope* that

'Tis distance lends enchantment to the view,
And robes the mountain in its azure hue.
Thus, with delight, we linger to survey
The promis'd joys of life's unmeasur'd way;
Thus, from afar, each dim discover'd scene
More pleasing seems than all the past hath been;
(Thomas Campbell, *The Pleasures of Hope,
with other poems*, (Edinburgh, 1810),
pp. 3–4, part 1, lines 7–12)

4 **of Julia's work**: covered by a piece of tapestry embroidered by Julia.
5 **Cumberland**: transparencies are a substitute for stained glass, produced by painting in special pigments and indian ink on paper,
and then touching in the brightest parts with spirits of turpen-
tine and varnish to increase their vitreosity. Rudolph Ackermann
issued the second edition of his pamphlet *Instructions for Painting Transparencies* in 1802. At his Repository of the Arts, 101
Strand, London, he also sold the 'artificial flower paper' and 'fancy
gold paper' which provided the Bertram sisters with other holiday
entertainment in ch. 1. Transparencies worked best with dramatic
subjects. 'None is so admirably adapted', writes Ackermann, as
'the gloomy gothic ruin, whose antique towers and pointed tur-
rets finely contrast their dark battlements with a pale, yet brilliant
moon.' Tintern Abbey was well known from Gilpin's *Observations
on the River Wye . . . relative Chiefly to Picturesque Beauty; Made
in the Summer of the Year 1770* (1782; 5th edn, London, 1800), in
which it is described as 'a very enchanting piece of ruin' (p. 50),
and illustrated in two plates (facing pp. 47, 49). Gilpin's next book,
*Observations, relative Chiefly to Picturesque Beauty, Made in the Year
1772, On Several Parts of England; Particularly the Mountains, and
Lakes of Cumberland and Westmoreland* (2 vols., London, 1786) also
included plates. The 'cave in Italy' might be copied from a mez-
zotint or engraving of one of Joseph Wright of Derby's numerous
paintings of such night scenes, like *Grotto in the Gulf of Salerno,
Moonlight*, c.1780.
6 **complaisance**: obligation: she ought to desire to please them.
7 **netting-boxes**: netting is crochet work out of which small objects
like purses were made; the box would contain the crochet hooks
and yarn.

8 **concentrating our folly**: Johnson defines 'concentration' as 'to drive into a narrow compass'.

9 **How does Lord Macartney go on**: Lord Macartney was sent by the East India Company to the Imperial court of China in Peking in 1792 to lay the foundations for British trade with China. The embassy required great diplomatic skill, and much of the suspense of his Journal (referred to in Edmund's question 'How does Lord Macartney go on?') lies in Macartney's negotiation of the elaborate labyrinth of protocols surrounding the Emperor, on which the success of the expedition would depend. The 'Journal of an Embassy to the Emperor of China' was published in John Barrow, *Some Account of the Public Life and a Selection from the Unpublished Writings of the Earl of Macartney* (1807), in two large volumes ('your great book'). George Crabbe's *Tales in Verse* was published in 1812, though his earlier volumes, such as *The Borough* (1810), include tales; Samuel Johnson's 103 *Idler* essays, originally contributed to a weekly journal, the *Universal Chronicle*, in 1758–9, were collected and frequently reprinted. Crabbe and Johnson were notable anti-romantic writers whose Christianity was expressed in comic severity and moral intensity; Barrow's volumes record the events of a life devoted to the military and commercial interests of the emerging British Empire.

CHAPTER 17

1 **action and emphasis**: in the final scene of the play, Anhalt persuades Baron Wildenhaim to make complete restitution to Agatha, whom Anhalt forces him to admit he seduced, by marrying her. The Baron's conscience is finally quieted.

2 **too much admiration**: a polite way of referring to sexual attraction: 'don't let yourself get too involved'.

3 **in the way of doing any thing yet**: in other words, he has not found a nobleman or great landowner who has a parliamentary seat in his patronage, which he can offer to a relative or friend. Before the Reform Act of 1832, there were many such 'pocket boroughs'. Other seats in parliament were held by representatives of 'rotten boroughs', depopulated towns with very few voters, who might readily be persuaded to vote for the candidate supported by the patron. Mrs Grant's assumption that Sir Thomas can put

Rushworth 'in the way' of a parliamentary seat suggests that the baronet has established connections and that Rushworth, without the leverage that direct descendants of an ancient family would have acquired, has not.

4 **in imitation of Pope**: Isaac Hawkins Browne, *A Pipe of Tobacco: in Imitation of Six Several Authors* (1736). The poem appears in Robert Dodsley's *Collection of Poems. By Several Hands* (3 vols., 1748), vol. 2. This is Imitation 5, pp. 281–2:

> Blest leaf! Whose aromatic gales dispense
> To Templars modesty, to Parsons sense
> . . .
> By thee protected, and thy sister, beer,
> Poets rejoice, nor think the bailiff near.
> Nor less the critic owns thy genial aid,
> While supperless he plies the piddling trade.

This is an 'imitation', not a parody: no specific passage of Alexander Pope's poetry is focused on.

5 **before the articles were signed**: marriage was a financial as well as a social transaction. The prospective wife would bring a 'portion' to her husband, which would become part of his estate on marriage. In turn, the prospective husband was required to settle money on a wife so that she would have a suitable maintenance in the event of his death. These and other arrangements, undertaken before the ceremony, required the services of lawyers and the signing of legal documents or 'articles' by the parties.

6 **half-a-crown**: a trivial sum in the scale of the Bertram finances. Integrity here means intentness of purpose.

CHAPTER 18

1 **from town**: as elsewhere, from London, and thus a considerable additional expense.

2 **eclat**: showiness, fame; here, especially publicity.

3 **the first scene between her and Mr. Crawford**: in Act 1 of the play, Frederick offers money to the starving Agatha and they recognise each other as mother and son. She 'rising and embracing him',

he 'leans her head against his breast'. The scene continues with Agatha's revelation that Frederick is 'a natural son'.

4 **some speeches for Maria**: particularly perhaps the one in which Agatha, remembering her seduction, speaks of being 'intoxicated by the fervent caresses' of the young Baron, not recovering from 'the delirium till it was too late'.

5 **catchword**: either the last word in an actor's speech, which is the cue for the next speaker to take ('catch') his or her breath before replying with the immediacy that is necessary for a natural effect, or, the key word of the speech which would enable the actor to recall the whole.

6 **executive part**: the active, working part, as opposed to the supervisory role Mrs Norris fancies she has taken.

7 **festoons**: when the proscenium curtain rose to announce the beginning of the play in the London theatres, it was pulled up in the form of three or four shallow festoons, and not pulled all the way out of sight.

8 **a scene between them**: in Act 3, scene 2, Amelia obliquely confesses her love for her tutor, Anhalt, who has been sent to persuade her into accepting Count Cassel's proposal. Anhalt describes an unhappy and a happy marriage. After much provocative teasing from Amelia, Anhalt passionately confesses that he loves her 'more than life'.

9 **against the evening . . . not in the way**: as an insurance against poor performance in the evening; not about, not around.

10 **bring forward . . . stage**: a detail which suggests JA's knowledge of actual performance practice. The stage direction reads: 'He places chairs and they sit.' In the theatre the chairs would be placed on the forestage, just beyond the proscenium curtain.

11 **when they were trying not to embrace**: during a scene of high emotion in which the distressed Agatha relates her story, Frederick, moved and appalled, commiserates with her.

12 **the ladies moved . . . followed them**: after dinner the ladies would remove to the drawing room, leaving the gentlemen to relax with port and tobacco. On this occasion they cut short these ceremonies.

13 **absolutely necessary**: Cottager's wife is important in Act 2, where she supplies essential information about the Baron and his unhappy marriage.

14 **unusual noise**: both 1814 and 1816 texts print 'an usual', but 'unusual' would be correct. This is the sort of error that might easily pass without notice in the printing house, since texts were read very quickly aloud for collation.

VOLUME II, CHAPTER 1

1 **pressing her hand to his heart**: in Act 1, scene 1 of *Lovers' Vows*, Agatha tells Frederick the story of her seduction by the Baron: 'His flattery made me vain, and his repeated vows – don't look at me, dear Frederick! I can say no more. [Frederick with his eyes cast down, takes her hand, and puts it to his heart.] Oh! Oh! my son! I was intoxicated by the fervent caresses of a young, inexperienced, capricious man, and did not recover from the delirium till it was too late.'

2 **development**: that which is to be revealed; revelation.

3 **family confidence**: trust, intimacy and privacy within the family circle.

4 **quick**: animated.

5 **Antigua . . . Liverpool**: Liverpool is a large port on the north-west coast of England, from which many vessels departed to, and arrived from, the West Indies. It had been notorious as a port from which many slave-ships sailed.

6 **carpet work**: possibly tapestry: compare 'the faded footstool of Julia's work' (vol. 1 ch. 16).

7 **a lengthened absence**: Sir Thomas has in fact been absent more than two years.

8 **French privateer**: acknowledging their inability to defeat the Royal Navy, Great Britain's enemies during the Napoleonic wars resorted increasingly to a strategy of attack on Britain's commercial shipping, which traded around the globe. Privateers, 'licenced pirates' or commerce-raiders, were merchant vessels with a government commission to attack British ships. Since America was allied with France, British shipping on the Atlantic routes was harassed by American as well as French privateers, adding to the perils of Sir Thomas' passage from Antigua to Liverpool.

9 **since October began**: it must be now approaching mid-October, well into the game-shooting season.

10 **Mansfield Wood . . . brace**: pheasants make their nests low in woodland; a copse is a small wood or group of trees; a brace is a couple, or pair.

11 **the very best start**: a 'start' is a technical feature of eighteenth-century acting, much admired and watched for by audiences. One of the most famous 'starts' on the eighteenth-century stage was Hamlet's when he first sees his father's ghost. The illustrations of this moment in nineteenth-century reprints of the novel allude to Garrick's famous performance of this scene in *Hamlet*. The Baron's scenes with Frederick in *Lovers' Vows* give plenty of scope for starts: the stage directions include 'greatly agitated', 'shuddering' and 'the Baron's emotion expresses the sense of amazement, guilt, shame and horror' (Act 4, scene 2).

12 **the house**: the playhouse, Tom's 'Theatre'.

13 **his own character**: since he has a public role as baronet and member of parliament, Sir Thomas is required to preserve an appearance of cordiality and politeness with social equals and superiors, and as a member of the gentry he would be especially careful with the aristocratic Mr Yates.

14 **bewildered**: made to feel his own house is unfamiliar territory.

15 **the ceiling . . . room**: stucco is a fine plaster used for the making of decorative cornices and mouldings. The ceiling of the room might well also feature a decorative design in plasterwork. Making the billiard room into 'the Theatre' will have included the erection of a proscenium arch and the installation of flats, which might well have damaged these features.

16 **the infection**: Tom copies the rhetoric of Thomas Gisborne and other conservative moralists. Though the metaphor does not appear in the passage of Gisborne's *Enquiry into the Duties of the Female Sex* on the dangers of 'acting plays in private theatres' (pp. 173–5), it is used in the same chapter to condemn both time-wasting ('the malady . . . among the mental disorders most difficult to cure') and watering places, where 'the contagion' of thoughtlessness counteracts the healthy effect of the waters (pp. 209, 205). Metaphors of disease, common in Johnson, are also reiterated in other moralists, such as Hannah More: 'Too

many religious people fancy that the infectious air of the world is confined to the ball-room or the play-house' (*Cœlebs*, ch. 49).

17 **knelt . . . uncle**: an histrionic moment which may imply the influence of *Lovers' Vows* on Fanny's susceptible imagination, a brief excursion into the rhetoric of sensibility. In Act 4, scene 2, for instance, Amelia begs her father to be allowed to marry Anhalt: '"Dear father! I shall never be able to love another – Never be happy with any one else." [Throwing herself on her knees.]'

18 **we bespeak your indulgence**: a common phrase in the theatre, used in Prologues and Epilogues.

CHAPTER 2

1 **too much indeed for many words**: Sir Thomas is pained to realise how little the thought of his journey's perils has interfered with his family's amusements.

2 **shaken hands with Edmund**: a detail which briefly suggests the seriousness of the potential rupture. Sir Thomas forgives Edmund for in effect betraying his trust.

3 **cured him at last**: rheumatism, then as now, is not so readily 'cured'. Miss Lucilla Stanley, the heroine of *Cœlebs*, also takes care of a servant's rheumatism. 'I can never be grateful enough to God and my benefactors', he declares (ch. 30).

4 **upon the leaders**: managing the reins of the two leading horses in the team of four.

5 **steward . . . bailiff . . . plantations**: the steward is responsible for the general running of the estate, the bailiff for its finances. The estate has plantations of new timber, from which in the future income will derive, as distinguished from its woods, which are largely ornamental features.

6 **unbound copy**: most books, and certainly play scripts, were sold unbound, to be given a personal and expensive binding by their owner. There may also have been bound copies, which presumably were not burned.

7 **eclaircissement**: 'explanation: the act of clearing up an affair by verbal expostulation' (Johnson): the French word decorates Maria's wishes with a touch of irony.

8 **Bath**: in the south-west of England, originally a Roman settlement on the site of a medicinal spring, developed into the

principal resort city of the gentry in the latter part of the eighteenth century: Lady Russell, in *P*, spends 'some part of every winter there' (vol. 1, ch. 2); the Bath 'season' ran from October to May. Sir Thomas has returned in mid October.

9 **Banbury**: travelling south-west, Banbury is a town and staging post between Northampton and Oxford. Depending on the route, it would be about thirty or forty miles (fifty or sixty-five kilometres) from Mansfield.

10 **motionless and passive now**: not merely motionless in the sense of still, but in the older sense meaning without the desires or impulses of a living body.

11 **the admirer**: 'in common speech, a lover' (Johnson): 'lover' in the earlier sense of someone who is attracted by, and is seeking to be attractive to, another person.

CHAPTER 3

1 **so much countenance**: a special use of the common term: 'I have seen women as striking, but I never saw one so interesting. Her beauty is countenance: it is the stamp of mind intelligibly printed on the face' (*Cœlebs*, ch. 14).

2 **admiration**: here appreciation of a person's physical attributes or beauty.

3 **the slave-trade**: the British slave trade was abolished in 1807, through the efforts of Thomas Clarkson, William Wilberforce and others, largely of Evangelical persuasion, after twenty years of parliamentary activity. It is implied, since Edmund suggests that 'It would have pleased your uncle to be inquired of further', that Sir Thomas, perhaps himself influenced by the Evangelicals, has a clear conscience with regard to this traffic, which had been regarded with abhorrence by the liberal and educated classes who made up Austen's readership for many years, but which dragged on for some time after abolition. Slavery still continued on the sugar plantations on Antigua (as elsewhere in the West Indies), though perhaps in an ameliorated form there, and the question of what contribution it made to the Bertram family's fortunes is not addressed in the novel.

4 **repulsive**: uninviting, unattractive (not as strong as the modern meaning).

5 **talents to value his powers**: as an intelligent woman she will be able to appreciate Sir Thomas' capable authority.

6 **Tunbridge or Cheltenham**: Tunbridge Wells (in Kent) and Cheltenham (in Gloucestershire) are both some distance from the capital, but as fashionable spa towns would not qualify as country. Tunbridge was less fashionable than Cheltenham, whose fortunes were in the ascendent after a visit by the royal family in 1788.

7 **the embarrassing evils of a rupture**: an engagement was a contract between two families as well as between two individuals, and breaking it off might have legal implications. The parties here being a very rich man and the daughter of an MP, the evils would also include loss of 'character' or public esteem, possible newspaper publicity, and incitement to malicious gossip.

8 **all the comfort . . . self-revenge**: a compressed and telling phrase. Acting proudly and as if Henry were nothing to her, Maria will sustain herself ('comfort' in one of its older implications) by acts which, as she knows, will in effect destroy her prospects for future happiness. JA's coinage here inaugurates a passage of free indirect speech in which the influence of the Shakespearean tragic soliloquy may be detected. Johnson illustrates the combination of 'self' with other words including many from Shakespeare ('self-wrong', 'self-subdued', 'self-neglecting', 'self-harming' etc). Later in the novel, more common conjunctions like 'self-deceit', 'self-inquiry' and 'self-distrust' are used (vol. 2, ch. 4; vol. 2, ch. 6).

9 **the world**: fashionable society and its activities: 'See how the World its Veterans rewards! / A Youth of Frolicks, an old Age of Cards' (Alexander Pope, *Moral Essays*, Epistle 2: 'To a Lady. Of the Characters of Women', lines 243–4). As in Pope, the word here also carries a religious meaning.

10 **the principals**: the parties to a legal contract.

11 **salts in her hand**: 'smelling salts', 'sal volatile' or salt of ammonia, ammonium carbonate, in solution; the vapours were inhaled as a restorative in fainting fits.

12 **Brighton**: a resort town on the south coast of England, associated at this time with the group around the Prince Regent, and thus with fast living and expense.

CHAPTER 4

1 **improvement**: Mrs Grant fancies that Fanny's manners and knowledge will benefit from conversation with Mary, a person of more sophistication and wider acquaintance.

2 **idea**: 'mental image' (Johnson). 'Idea' is the Lockean term for the form in which understanding or information presents itself to consciousness: 'Whatsoever is the Object of the Understanding when a Man thinks', in John Locke, *Essay concerning Human Understanding* (1690), book 1, ch. 1.

3 **nothing but a rough hedgerow**: in Austen's native Hampshire, 'a hedgerow does not mean a thin formal line of quickset [planted thorns, for example], but an irregular border of copse-wood and timber, often wide enough to contain within it a winding footpath'. J. E. Austen-Leigh, *A Memoir of Jane Austen*, ed. R. W. Chapman (Oxford: Clarendon Press, 1926), p. 21. It is not clear that this is what is meant here however, nor how a line of rough hedgerow is converted into a walk.

4 **faculty…memory**: Fanny's reflections are reminiscent of Johnson's essays on memory in the *Rambler* and the *Idler* (nos. 44, 72 and 74). In *Rambler*, 41 (7 August 1750), for example, Johnson celebrates that 'faculty of remembrance [which] may be said to place us in the class of moral agents'. Fanny's description of the volatility of memory – 'sometimes so retentive, so serviceable, so obedient—at others so bewildered and so weak—and at others again, so tyrannic' – recapitulates the characteristic Johnsonian sense of the mind's dynamic qualities and reflects his insistence that mental life is often beyond our control: 'no man will be found in whose mind airy notions do not sometimes tyrannize' (Samuel Johnson, *Rasselas, Prince of Abissinia*, in *Works* (12 vols., London, 1820), vol. 3 ch. 43).

5 **speakingly**: strikingly.

6 **country parson**: the derogatory term partly accounts for Fanny's turning the conversation.

7 **evergreens**: being primarily exotics, evergreens were still regarded as too tender to mix with the resilient deciduous 'tribe'. Most, such as bays, had been introduced from milder climates and had been originally grown in greenhouses and only subsequently tested as hardy out of doors. Gardeners remained over-protective of

evergreens. They were often separated from deciduous plants for aesthetic reasons.

8 **the variety**: the novelty or exception.

9 **rhapsodizing**: both speaking in a loose, disconnected way, and exaggeratedly ecstatic in manner. Like 'enthusiasm' which Edmund has earlier used of Fanny's talk (vol. 1, ch. 11) 'rhapsody' is shifting at this time away from the derogatory and into the more Romantic register.

10 **the famous Doge at the court of Lewis XIV**: the anecdote is in Voltaire, from whom Johnson, who would be JA's immediate source, took it. 'You remember the Doge of Genoa who being asked what struck him most at the French Court, answered "Myself". I can not think many things here more likely to affect the fancy than to see Johnson ending his Sixty fourth year in the wilderness of the Hebrides'; letter to Hester Thrale, 30 September 1773, in Mrs Hester Lynch Piozzi's *Letters to and from the late Samuel Johnson* (2 vols., London, 1788), vol. 1, p. 158, a book which JA quotes from in a letter of 9 December 1808. The original anecdote is in Voltaire's *Siècle de Louis XIV*: 'Ce doge était un homme de beaucoup d' esprit. Tout le monde sait que le marquis de Seignelai lui ayant demandé ce qu'il trouvait de plus singulier à Versailles, il répondit: *C'est de m'y voir.*' ('This doge was a very witty man. Everyone knows that when the Marquis de Seignelai asked him what he found most remarkable at Versailles, he replied "To see myself there."') Voltaire, *Oeuvres complètes* (Paris, 1878), vol. 14, p. 291.

11 **nobleness . . . Edmund**: the name has conservative and royalist associations. Fanny may have in mind such figures as Edmund I (921–46), King of the English (from 939), and Edmund II (Edmund Ironside) (c. 980–1016). Another relevant figure is Sir Edmund Verney (1590–1642), Charles I's standard bearer, whose loyalty to his King at the battle of Edgehill was often commemorated – a link with Fanny's feelings about Sotherton Court. Also pertinent are Edmund Spenser, whose *Faerie Queene* (1590, 1596) relates the adventures of knights, and Edmund Burke, who had notably celebrated what Fanny calls 'the spirit of chivalry and warm affections' in *Reflections on the Revolution in France* (1790). Clara Reeve's *The Old English Baron, a Gothic story* (1778), set in

the fifteenth century, features the pious and handsome Edmund Twyford who, like Fanny, begins as a poor ward in the household of a baronet; as events turn out, he is in fact its heir, and marries his cousin. The names of Edmund and William are linked together in one of the young Jane Austen's entries in her father's parish register: 'Edmund Arthur William Mortimer, of Liverpool'. 'Nobleness' is a quality ('the nobleness of life/ Is to do thus': *Antony and Cleopatra*, Act 1, scene 1, lines 38–9), as distinct from 'nobility', a rank.

12 **commend me to the nurseryman and the poulterer**: 'commend me' here means 'bring me to their kindly notice', meant ironically: but since nurserymen and poulterers, who would take care of Mrs Grant's worries for her, would only be found in a large town or city, Mary's meaning is more like 'I can't do without the amenities of a city'.

13 **the deanery of Westminster or St. Paul's**: the dean was the head of a chapter in a cathedral church. Dean of either of these two most important churches in London would be a highly desirable appointment.

14 **the myrtle and turkey part of it**: myrtle is 'a fragrant tree sacred to Venus' (Johnson), thus an emblem of love. Both myrtle and turkey suggest festivity and luxury.

15 **to eat his mutton**: a facetious masculine expression meaning to dine with, later used also by Mr Price.

CHAPTER 5

1 **first invitation**: 'she dined at the parsonage, with the rest of you' says Mary in vol. 1, ch. 5. That was evidently a general invitation, also including Lady Bertram; Fanny would have been included as her attendant. On this occasion, her cousins being absent, there is a particularity in just Fanny's being asked which makes this a special distinction.

2 **agreeable day**: we should call it the evening, but this customarily began only after dinner.

3 **lowest and last**: a phrase which originates probably in Matthew, ch. 19, v. 30: 'But many that are first shall be last; and the last shall be first'. In Mrs Norris's mouth it has lost its biblical association or meaning.

4 **taking place of her**: Fanny, as the female guest, would normally lead the way into the dining room, but Mrs Norris reminds her that in rank she is generally inferior, and thus should follow Mary. There were strict rules of etiquette governing who went in and came out first, as exemplified in Elizabeth Elliot's 'walking immediately after Lady Russell out of all the drawing-rooms and dining-rooms in the country' (*P*, vol. 1, ch. 1).

5 **twenty minutes after four**: evidently the Grants are dining late, probably at five. Fanny would have had to walk in the dark, or at least the dusk, 'at this time of the year', in November.

6 **gallantry**: courteous or polite conversation of a gentleman with a woman, especially conversation designed to flatter and persuade.

7 **the equinox**: the equinox is one of the two periods of the year when day and night are of equal length, and here means 22 or 23 September, when Sir Thomas was on his homeward voyage across the Atlantic. The equinox is traditionally associated with unusual weather and often strong winds; the mad astronomer in Johnson's *Rasselas* (1759) seeks to, but cannot, govern the 'equinoctial tempests' (ch. 41).

8 **instructions about the living**: a living involved, besides running a parish, farming the glebe land, and collecting tithes. Negotiating with parishioners as to the amount of the tithe due to him would often take up a large part of a clergyman's time.

9 **make ducks and drakes with**: to squander money, have a few flings with – the reference is to the game of skimming stones across the surface of a pond or pool.

10 **of course he will still live at home**: Henry assumes that Edmund will be an absentee clergyman: he expresses what at this date is a scandalously relaxed view of the duties of a parish priest.

11 **menus plaisirs**: small pleasures, little luxuries; pocket money.

12 **tablets and a pencil**: tablets were two small, flat, thin pieces of wood or ivory, hinged together, on which brief notes would be inscribed by a graphite pencil, or other sharp writing instrument, and later erased.

CHAPTER 6

1 **his hunters**: the price of a good hunter was between £75 and £150. A horse cost about £20 a year to stable in the country.

2 **the bread of idleness**: from the characterisation of 'a virtuous woman' in Proverbs ch. 31, vs. 26–7. 'She looketh well to the ways of her household, and eateth not the bread of idleness'; a familiar biblical phrase.

3 **her tout ensemble**: her whole appearance.

4 **Is she queer—Is she prudish**: is she odd or strange – an eccentric? Johnson defines a 'prude' as 'a woman over nice and scupulous, and with a false affectation'; to be prudish is, paradoxically, to make a display of one's modesty.

5 **plunge her deep**: Mary is quoting from the first verse of a song in Robert Burns' *The Scots Musical Museum*

> Talk not of love, it gives me pain,
> For Love has been my foe;
> He bound me with an iron chain,
> And plunged me deep in woe.
>
> (2 vols., Aldershot, 1788,
> vol. 2, p. 194)

The lines were composed by Burns' friend 'Clarinda': he tells her that 'the latter half of the first verse would have been worthy of Sappho'. Robert Burns, *Letters to Clarinda* (London: Sisley's, n.d.), p. vi. Songs by Burns were popular: in *P&P*, Miss Bingley plays (and apparently sings) 'a lively Scotch air' (vol. 1, ch. 10).

6 **read about them**: in More's *Cœlebs*, Lucilla, 'a girl of eighteen, refuse[s] a young nobleman of clear estate, and neither disagreeable in person or manner, on the single avowed ground of his loose principles' (ch. 31). But the rebuke is more pointedly directed towards Mary Brunton's *Self-Control* (1810). Laura Montreville is eighteen when the handsome and charming Colonel Hargrave attempts to seduce her. This 'pious Christian' heroine, whose 'enthusiastic mind' has 'imbibed the stories of self-devoting patriots and martyrs' (ch. 1), spurns him (though she apparently cares for him) and remains 'unconquerable' through many trials during the next two years. (JA remarks in a letter of 11 October 1813 that she is 'looking over Self Control again, & my opinion is confirmed of its' being an excellently-meant, elegantly-written Work, without anything of Nature or Probability in it' (*L*, p. 234)). Both novels

were highly successful: hence the pointedness of 'or one should not read about them'.

7 **in Spithead**: Spithead 'is the sea-road [or channel] between the Isle of Wight and the continent of Hampshire, and which, from Cowes to St Helens, is near twenty miles in length, and in some places, three miles broad. This road is capable of receiving with ease, more than a thousand sail of shipping.' *The History of Portsmouth: Containing its Origin, Progressive Improvements, and Present State of its Public Buildings* (Portsmouth, 1809), p. 50. Ships would anchor at Spithead, and the officers transfer to shore in small boats.

8 **the Mediterranean**: as an island nation, Great Britain was vulnerable to attack by sea. Much of the effort of the Royal Navy during the Napoleonic wars, therefore, was devoted to blockading enemy fleets in their ports in the Mediterranean sea.

9 **earliest naval intelligence**: probably the *Morning Post*, or the weekly *London Gazette*.

10 **only a midshipman**: leave was a private arrangement between the Captain and his officers. Because William is 'only' a midshipman, a rank filled with many men waiting to be promoted, but not yet an officer, it is not necessary for him to find a substitute.

11 **complacency**: pleasure mixed with gratification.

12 **that queer fashion**: William's word 'trim' is a joke, both a nautical term meaning the look of a ship, especially a ship fully rigged and ready to sail, and the 'trimming' of Fanny's hair. The fashion was for the hair to be held in bands round the head, 'dressed in a new style', writes the *Literary and Fashionable Magazine* for March 1808, 'ornamented with a pearl crown placed over the right eye' (p. 183), or 'dressed à la Grec, ornamented with a pink flower, fastened with silver' (*The Lady's Magazine* (August 1809), p. 369). Fanny has no jewellery of this kind: most likely she is wearing her hair held back, perhaps trimmed with a real or artificial flower, 'which were never more general, indeed so much that a fashionable female, in her own parterre, might be mistaken for the presiding goddess', *La Belle Assemblée*, 7 (July–Dec. 1809), p. 42.

13 **the Commissioner's, at Gibraltar**: Gibraltar, a British territory, is at the southern tip of Spain. After 1807, it became an important victualling station where vessels would replenish their supplies

and water, but not a key naval base. There was a small garrison, and in the later eighteenth century dwellings for officers were built, including The Mount, a modest detached house bought by the Navy Board in 1799 for the newly appointed commissioner, a captain in charge of the station.

14 **terrific**: 'dreadful; causing terror' (Johnson). There is little of the modern implication of spectacle.

15 **moral taste**: not an uncommon phrase, though nowhere else used by JA. See, for instance, *Our Village* (p. 289): 'our farmer, by no means wanting in moral taste, was charmed with her cheerfulness, her good humour, and the total absence of vanity and selfishness'.

16 **in the Mediterranean again**: the sentence's construction suggests an allusion to the chase of Nelson across the Atlantic and back (May–July 1805), easily within William's 'course of seven years' if the time in the novel is December 1808. Early in 1805, Napoleon conceived a plan to decoy the British fleet to the West Indies whilst the combined French and Spanish fleets invaded England. Vice-Admiral Nelson, in command of the Mediterranean fleet, failed to prevent a French squadron, under Villeneuve, from escaping from Toulon, and after some delay set off in pursuit across the ocean to Barbados and Antigua. But the French had already set sail back to France, and were never less than a hundred miles north of the English on the return voyage. Frank Austen's ship, the *Canopus*, with Rear-Admiral Louis on board, had been in this English squadron.

17 **on shore by the favour of his Captain**: strictly speaking, midshipmen were crew, and therefore would be confined to the ship when in port, but by this time most midshipmen were 'young gentlemen', like Price, aspiring to be officers, and therefore might be treated as such.

18 **every body else was attentive**: this passage is reminiscent of a similar domestic vignette in *Cœlebs* which ends 'Nay, once I remember, when I was with much agitation hurrying through the gazette of the battle of Trafalgar, whilst I pronounced, almost agonized, the last memorable words of the immortal Nelson, I heard one lady whisper to another that she had broken her needle' (ch. 22).

19 **proofs of mind**: mental resources (in parallel with 'bodily' endurance).

CHAPTER 7

1 **a round game**: in a round game of cards each player is out for him- or herself, in competition with the other players.

2 **Speculation**: 'This is a noisy round game, . . . the highest trump in each deal, wins the pool . . . the cards are not to be looked at, except in this manner, – the eldest hand [the person on the dealer's left hand] shews the uppermost card, which, if a trump, the company may speculate on or bid for; the highest bidder buying and paying for it, provided the price offered is approved of by the seller . . . To play this game well, little more is requisite than recollecting what superior cards of that particular suit have appeared in the preceding deals and calculating the probability of the trump offered proving the highest in the deal then undetermined.' *Hoyle's Games*, revised and corrected by Charles Jones (London, 1808), pp. 154– 5. Essentially it is a matter of putting a value on and bidding for cards.

3 **Whist**: 'This game, which requires great attention, is played by four persons, who cut for partners . . . No intimations of any kind during the play of the cards between partners are to be admitted' (*Hoyle's Games*, p. 1).

4 **which will amuse me most?**: Speculation is a gambling game, whist a game of strategy. Speculation was often played with and by children. Instructions and tactics for playing the game of whist occupy the first seventy pages in *Hoyle's Games*, 1808 edition.

5 **downy field**: downs are treeless undulating hills, characteristic of the south and south-east of England.

6 **farm-yard must be moved**: the discussion here, as in vol. 1, ch. 6, turns on the importance of the 'approach'. To display a house to advantage, improvements often involved the removal or dis- guise of features such as farm-yards, barns or labourers' cottages. 'Since the beauty of pleasure ground, and the profit of a farm, are incompatible, it is the business of taste and prudence so to disguise the latter and limit the former, that park scenery may be obtained without much waste or extravagance . . . In a park, the fences cannot be too few, the trees too majestic, or the views too unconfined. In a farm, small enclosures are often necessary'.

Humphry Repton, *Observations on the Theory and Practice of Landscape Gardening* (1803), in John C. Loudon, *The Landscape Gardening and Landscape Architecture of the Late Humphry Repton Esq.* (London, 1840). Meadows 'laid together', as Crawford proposes, would mean the removal of hedges or fences to give uninterrupted views.

7 **the house must be turned**: Thomas Leigh, Mrs Austen's cousin, had made changes similar to those that Crawford envisages for Thornton Lacey at Adlestrop, Gloucestershire, between 1797 and 1803 ('work for five summers at least'). These improvements, under Repton's supervision, involved moving the entrance to the rectory, and merging its garden with surrounding parkland. The garden at what was now the back of the house was made to slope towards a new artificial lake.

8 **the air of a gentleman's residence**: 'it would be a reflection on the good taste of the country to suppose that the habitation of the gentleman ought not to be distinguished from that of the farmer, as well as in the character of the place as by the size of the house'. Repton, *Observations*, in Loudon, *Landscape Gardening*, pp. 178–9.

9 **solid**: the change from 'solid walled' in the 1814 edition is interesting. 'Solid' is more idiomatic and more comprehensive, but JA first specified the thickness of the walls of a gentleman's residence, in contrast to the 'thinness of the walls' of Fanny's Portsmouth home (vol. 3, ch. 7).

10 **bids a dozen**: the unit of 'speculation' was not real money but 'fish' or counters, bearing arbitrary values.

11 **a place**: a mansion, or country house, including its surroundings: the implication of the term is that grandeur expresses social and political eminence.

12 **the odd trick**: 'in whist, the thirteenth trick, after each side has won six' (OED). A trick is the cards played or taken in one round of the game.

13 **Beachey Head**: a promontory about fifteen miles, or twenty-seven kilometres, east of Brighton on the south coast of England: William is remembering the coast as seen from a vessel at sea.

14 **scrubby**: as scrub is low growth, insignificant or under-developed vegetation, a scrubby midshipman is stunted in his professional career.

15 **private secretary to the first Lord**: the first Lord of the Admiralty, who would have the power to promote William. His private secretary would be personally appointed and have great influence.

16 **homestall**: literally homestead; but Crawford uses the word with reference to himself and his horses, so the meaning is a property that will conveniently accommodate both, the horses needing 'stalls'. As with 'under strappers' (vol. 1, ch. 13) and making 'a small hole in Fanny Price's heart' (vol. 2, ch. 6), Crawford's language is coloured by sporting terms. He later refers to a suitable house as a 'small hunting-box' in vol. 3, ch. 10.

17 **residence**: this touches on an important debate within the church in the early nineteenth century. Many Anglican ministers held two or more livings, but only visited them infrequently, riding over to a distant parish, like Henry Tilney in *NA*, once in a while. With the influence of the Evangelical movement in the Anglican church such infrequent attendance to the needs of a parish was felt to be dereliction of duty on the part of the clergy, and residency in the parish came to be required. Sir Thomas Bertram's next speech articulates this position. If a minister, of a higher social class, proved himself 'by constant attention' a 'friend' to his parishioners, the inroads on the established church's influence made by Methodists, who were often working class themselves, might be checked.

18 **Assembly night**: Thursday: 'With respect to Portsmouth itself, the Assemblies . . . held every Thursday fortnight, are a most charming resort for the gay, the elegant, and the distinguished, of both sexes' (*The History of Portsmouth*, p. 74). The Crown Inn was on the High Street, and could not be far from William's home. William Farington R. N. attended such an Assembly at the time of the Derby races in August 1808, and reported 'much company, but a much greater proportion of men than of women . . . dancing till one o'Clock when a supper is set out for everybody – the price of admittance to Gentlemen 7 shillings' (*The Diary of Joseph Farington*, vol. 9, p. 3337). The fact that

Farington's nephew was freely admitted underlines the non-exclusive character of these balls, which provided opportunities for rising tradesmen and professionals to mingle with the local gentry.

19 **a commission**: an appointment to a position of Lieutenant on a vessel, given by the Board of Admiralty, and verified by a signed document. After a minimum of six years at sea, a midshipman might be examined by the Navy Board, who would require certificates from the captains he had served under, and who would inquire into his seamanship. If passed, he would be qualified to apply for a commission as a lieutenant on a specified ship, but these were not easy to come by, and could usually only be obtained by 'interest' – i.e. the intervention and influence of family or friends with connections in the Navy office or government. Many men who passed the examination were never commissioned; but once made an officer, the prospect of promotion up the ladder of naval ranking to Admiral was open. 'A lieutenant in his majesty's navy is as good a gentleman as any in England', declares a seaman in Maria Edgeworth's *Manœuvring* (1812; in Edgeworth, *Tales and Novels*, vol. 7, p. 24). This is the 'consequence' referred to in Fanny's speech a little later. Hence the key importance conveyed by the verb 'made', which means here something stronger than 'promoted'.

20 **hand-organ was in the street**: hand- (or 'barrel-') organs were operated by a hand-cranked rotating barrel. The barrel was studded with pins which let air, driven by a bellows, into pipes. They weighed about 40 lb or 18 kilograms and were able to play about ten tunes. Hired by the day by itinerants or buskers, they were a popular form of street entertainment in London and other urban centres during the nineteenth century.

CHAPTER 8

1 **pretty amber cross . . . from Sicily**: amber is a yellow or orange resin, used for jewellery and ornaments. Charles Austen, then a lieutenant of the *Endymion*, had in 1801 bought gold chains and topaz crosses for his sisters out of his share of prize money from the capture of a French vessel, the *Scipio*, in the Mediterranean

off the coast of Spain (Letter of 27 May 1801; *L*, p. 91; J. H. and E. C. Hubback, *Jane Austen's Sailor Brothers* (London: John Lane, 1946), p. 91). Amber, being cheaper than topaz, a gemstone, implies William's more limited resources, since as a midshipman he would earn about a quarter of the pay of a lieutenant and his prize money would also be much less. The island of Sicily was Britain's nodal naval base in the Mediterranean.

2 **Peterborough**: Peterborough is a cathedral city, about thirty-five miles or fifty-six kilometres north-east of Northampton; Edmund will be ordained in the cathedral by the bishop.

3 **the wife . . . duties**: among other questions the bishop would put to the candidate in the ordination service is whether he is 'truly called' to the ministry of the Church of England. The ordination service would require the candidate 'to frame and fashion' the life of his family, as well as of himself. In his *Practical Reflections on the Ordination Services* John Brewster enjoins the candidate to 'remember then [his] solemn promise to fashion my own life and the lives of my family with all diligence, according to the doctrine of Christ' (Brewster, pp. 137, 99).

4 **coze**: from the French *causer*, to chat, and cosy, meaning sheltered and warm: a friendly chat.

5 **through all the heads**: 'heads' in the sense of headings in a pamphlet or newspaper: she covered all the points that might be raised.

6 **a family remembrancer**: something that calls to mind the family as well as the individual who has made the gift.

7 **a prettier consciousness**: Johnson's second definition of consciousness is 'internal sense of guilt, or innocence'.

8 **complaisant**: obliging, accommodating.

CHAPTER 9

1 **the niceness**: here, the delicacy and elegance.

2 **must not suppose it not wanted**: amid all the 'nots' hereabouts, both editions perhaps insert an unnecessary one here. This should probably read 'She must suppose it not wanted'. Edmund is arguing against Fanny. The rest of the sentence after the semi-colon does not really make sense unless, in the first phrase, he is reiterating his earlier claim that Mary would be mortified by the rejection of her gift.

3 **all the heroism of principle**: 'To conquer a well-founded affection, a justifiable attachment . . . requires the powerful principle
of Christian piety. And what cannot that effect?' writes Hannah
More in *Cœlebs* (Ch. 18) of a character who displays the 'triumph
of religion' that Fanny strives for.

4 **fondest biographer**: the most likely allusion is to James Boswell,
who writes on the first page of his *Life of Johnson*: 'I have spared
no pains in obtaining materials concerning him, from every quarter where I could discover that they were to be found.' Boswell
also relates, such was his 'enthusiasm', that, coming across two
manuscript volumes of Johnson's autobiography, he had read a
great deal of them, and 'felt half an inclination to commit theft. It
had come into my mind to carry off those two volumes, and never
see him [Johnson] more' (*Life*, vol. 4, p. 406).

5 **accustomary late dinner-hour**: the later one dined, the higher one's
social standing. Early dinner hours were partly at least a matter of
economy, saving candles and coal in the winter, so dining late
was a sign of 'elegance' and income: it was especially common in
London. The Prices dine early, at about 3 o'clock (vol. 3 ch. 11).

6 **travelling post**: by hired coach or carriage, with fresh horses at
each staging post of the journey – the fastest and most expensive
mode of transport.

7 **dispatches**: an officer returning to England with the official dispatches reporting a great victory at sea would be honoured with
promotion or a commendation, or perhaps be rewarded financially
as the representative of the victorious Fleet. William's comparison
also turns on the speed with which such a messenger would travel.

8 **go up by the mail**: the regular public stage-coach service which
carried the mail: though London is south of Northampton, 'going
up' to London is still the idiom used.

9 **trade of coming out**: the italics suggest a reference to a received
idea: 'What can be more indelicate than a girl's *coming out* in the
fashionable world? Which, in other words, is to bring to market a
marriageable miss'. Mary Wollstonecraft, *Vindication of the Rights
of Woman* (1792), in Wollstonecraft, *Political Writings*, ed. Janet
Todd (London: Pickering, 1993), p. 266. Not only radicals took
this view: Hannah More published a pamphlet on 'The White
Slave Trade, hints towards forming a bill for the Abolition of the

White Female Slave Trade, in the Cities of London and West-minster', in 1805: 'A multitude of fine fresh young slaves are annu-ally imported at the age of seventeen or eighteen: or, according to the phrase of the despot, [Society] *they come out.' The Weekly Entertainer or Agreeable and Instructive Repository*, 45 (12 August 1805).

10 **snipe shooting**: snipe are 'game' birds which inhabit low marshy places and are shot at from a distance.

11 **evil . . . she speaks it**: the about-to-be-ordained Edmund uses a biblical phrase: 'the unrighteous' are said to 'speak evil of the things that they understand not' (2 Peter, ch. 2, vs. 12–15). The promise which the ordinand makes to fashion the life of his family according to the doctrines of Christ 'is very comprehensive, and not only enjoins an abstinence from vice and crime, but from levity and folly. Every *appearance of evil*, whether designed or not, should be avoided; for that mode of conduct which leads your good to be evil-spoken of degenerates into a foul offence' (Brewster, p. 99).

CHAPTER 10

1 **It was but to think**: she had only to think.

2 **à la mortal, finely chequered**: in the style of mortals, common to humanity; 'finely chequered' means a mixture of happy and anxious feelings, as a cloth might be woven in checks of white and black.

3 **secured against the dancing began**: an elision – secured (as an insurance) against the time when the dancing began.

4 **the top of the room**: as on the more informal occasion (vol. 1, ch. 12), this is a country dance, in which dancers stand opposite each other, in a row with a top and a bottom. Fanny 'placed above so many elegant young women', and Crawford, move in turn down the line of dancers, making their 'progress down the dance' referred to a little later.

5 **murmuring**: complaint or protest, a biblical usage. The Israelites 'murmur against' Moses in Exodus, ch. 16, v. 4 and ch. 17, v. 3; Jesus rebukes the Jews for murmuring at him in John, ch. 6, vs. 41–3, etc.

6 **one moment and no more**: from Walter Scott, *The Lay of the Last Minstrel* (1805), Canto 1, vs. 19 and 20:

xix

The Ladye sought the lofty hall,
　Where many a bold retainer lay,
And, with jocund din, among them all,
　Her son pursued his infant play
. . .

xx

The Ladye forgot her purpose high,
　One moment and no more;
One moment gaz'd with a mother's eye,
　As she paused at the arched door:
Then from amid the armed train,
She called to her William of Deloraine.

The Ladye 'was a woman of masculine spirit', fierce, vengeful, and thought to be possessed of supernatural powers (Scott's note 9). This determined woman's attention is only briefly arrested by her son's gambols because she knows that the time has come for her knight to retrieve 'the treasure of the tomb' buried in the ruins of Melrose Abbey. A moment of memorable psychological insight in Scott's poem, the allusion suggests how Fanny shapes her understanding of her own life through literary associations. She has already quoted lines from the poem in the chapel at Sotherton (vol. 1, ch. 9). Walter Scott, *The Lay of the Last Minstrel, A Poem*, 12th edn (London, 1811), p. 29.

7 **soup and negus**: balls always included a supper, and the supper invariably included soup, as the need to prepare 'white soup' for the Netherfield ball in *P&P* indicates. Negus is another nourishing and warming drink, a mixture of lemon, spices, calves-foot jelly, wine and boiling water.

CHAPTER II

1 **con amore**: from the heart, literally 'with love'.
2 **second breakfast**: since the young men are to set off at half past nine, it can be assumed that a second meal is made ready for the ladies an hour or so later. The usual breakfast hour would be late in a house such as Mansfield Park: in *P&P* Elizabeth has breakfast, talks with her parents and walks three miles across fields before she

arrives at Netherfield whilst everyone is in the breakfast parlour (vol. 1, ch. 7).

3 **cribbage**: a card game, usually for two players, supposed to have been invented by Sir John Suckling (1609–42) and played by Charles II in exile. Players take turns to deal; each player then discards two cards, placed down on the table 'in crib'. Each player's aim is to retain 'in hand' cards which form scoring combinations according to the rules of the game. If a player can add a card without exceeding thirty-one they must do so: the player of the last card scores one point, or two points for making the total thirty-one exactly. The score is kept by moving pegs or match-sticks in holes on a board.

4 **the present quiet week**: Edmund left for Peterborough on 23 December; Fanny meets Mary and Mrs Grant on Christmas Eve. Christmas was not celebrated with the festivity it later acquired in the Victorian period, but in *E*, Mr Elton remarks on the 'Christmas weather' (vol. 1, ch. 13) of the Westons' dinner party, and Emma is unable to go to church on Christmas morning (vol. 1, ch. 16). Here it passes without a mention, though in the next chapter Mary suggests that Edmund's staying longer at the Owens' might be for 'Christmas gaieties'.

5 **the last winter of his belonging to us**: possibly Edmund will not take up residence at Thornton Lacey until after his year of probation as a deacon.

CHAPTER 12

1 **the sweep**: the curved carriage drive leading to the housefront.

2 **views**: plans.

3 **how the pleasing plague had stolen on him**: from 'The Je ne scai Quoi, A Song' by William Whitehead (1715–85), in Dodsley's *Collection of Poems*, vol. 2, p. 260:

> I
> Yes, I'm in love, I feel it now,
>   And Caelia has undone me;
> And yet I'll swear I can't tell how
>   The pleasing plague stole on me . . .

III
'Tis not her air, for sure in that
   There's nothing more than common;
And all her sense is only chat
   Like any other woman.
IV
Her voice, her touch might give th'alarm –
   'Twas both perhaps or neither;
In short, 'twas that provoking charm
   Of Caelia all together.

Caelia's 'charm', like Fanny's for Henry, is displayed against a background of misogyny.

4 **well principled and religious**: the only explicit use of the term 'religious' to describe Fanny, whose Christian convictions are rather assumed than brought out. The apparently general term 'religious' in 1814, influenced by Evangelical propaganda, would suggest not a merely nominal Christian, but one who inwardly and sincerely attempts to live by the gospel. Henry, not being used to 'serious reflection' – here 'serious' means religious or pious, and 'reflection' examination of one's own conscience – is without the mental vocabulary to do her justice. But 'well principled', as with the earlier 'the worth of good principles', leaves the reader to acknowledge what such 'principles' are, and the narrator's use of the modifier 'well' implies that she does not wish to make too much of this, and that Fanny is not to be considered a strictly Evangelical heroine.

5 **such a creature**: generally 'creature' means any person, but here is closer to Johnson's sense 6, 'a word of petty tenderness'.

6 **Stanwix Lodge**: Stanwick (sic) is north-east of Northampton.

7 **confusion**: embarrassment or blushing.

8 **inmate**: as guest of the Grants. An inmate is a temporary resident, in contrast to one who dwells.

CHAPTER 13

1 **commission as second Lieutenant of H. M. sloop Thrush**: a sloop is a ship of between ten and eighteen guns; the *Thrush* is a fictional name for a larger sloop, which would carry two lieutenants. 'Friend', here as later in Henry's speech, means, in effect, one who will act advantageously on one's behalf. As a lieutenant, Price will

earn just over £100 a year, about a fortieth of Crawford's annual income. But he is now an officer, the vital first step on the ladder of promotion.

2 **two shawls, Fanny**: since the fashionable muslin dresses were thin and flimsy, India shawls, made of wool from Kashmir, were much sought after. There are two advertisements in the *Morning Post* for 18 August 1808, for example:

EAST INDIA GOODS – WANTED – a variety of shawls and shawl handkerchiefs, and other curious articles of East India Produce, apply to . . .

INDIA SHAWLS – Ladies or Gentlemen having INDIA SHAWLS to DISPOSE OF may immediately receive the full value in cash . . .

VOLUME III, CHAPTER I

1 **presently**: Johnson's definition is 'immediately; soon after': the commas suggest that there is a brief pause.

2 **for her cousin's sake**: many editors amend to 'cousins' sake', looking forward to the reference to both sisters in the following sentence.

3 **that independence of spirit**: 'that' suggests how, in his anger, Sir Thomas has recourse to the rhetoric of conservative or anti-Jacobin educational theorists, such as Thomas Gisborne, *Duties of the Female Sex* (London, 1796) and Hannah More, *Strictures on the Modern System of Female Education* (London, 1799) who, influenced by Burke, attributed the increased independence or 'insubordination' of children within the family to revolutionary French ideas.

4 **on the gravel**: on the gravel paths, which would have been cleared of snow by the gardeners.

5 **right reason**: a Lockean conception, denoting the capacity of the properly disposed Christian to attain decisions that are both rationally correct and in conformity with Christian principle. Locke argues that there is consonance between biblical precepts and human rationality.

CHAPTER 2

1 **how always known no principle**: this passage, identical in both the 1814 and 1816 editions, was thought by R. W. Chapman

to be 'certainly corrupt' (*Mansfield Park*, ed. Chapman (Oxford: Oxford University Press, 1923), p. 548): some editors emend. Sutherland argues that it is 'a matter of compression', and does not need amendment. 'To read the passage aright we must listen to the *rhythms* of Fanny's inner monologue' (Sutherland, p. 408). There are parallels for this kind of compression in Shakespeare, and especially in Milton, as for example in this passage describing Satan's assumption of 'saintly show':

> Deep malice to conceal, couch'd with revenge;
> Yet not enough had practis'd to deceive
> Uriel once warned;
>
> (*Paradise Lost*, book 4, lines 123–5)

which means: 'Yet [*he – Satan*] had not enough practised to deceive/ Uriel once [*he*] Uriel [*had been*] warned.' If Austen's compression runs on similar lines, 'how always known no principle' becomes: 'How [*she had*] always known [*he had*] no principle'. The sentence still remains however a rendering of feeling rather than a grammatically correct statement.

2 **sober sadness**: full seriousness – sober means earnest here, not temperate. Mary uses the same phrase in vol. 3, ch. 5.

3 **Romantic delicacy**: romantic is defined by Johnson as 'resembling the tales of romances: wild'. 'Romantic' in this sense means extraordinary, far-fetched, being over-scrupulous and unrealistic, but JA's use here is interestingly on the cusp of the more modern use of the word, which conveys some approval of idealism.

4 **pug has a litter**: 'pug' was previously male (see e.g. vol. 1 ch. 7), but perhaps this is a new dog, bearing the same generic name. Fanny, married to 'a man of such good estate' as Crawford, will be able to afford the tax paid by owners: 'The puppy had grown into a dog, and of this the old man had forgotten to give notice to the tax-gatherer'. Maria Edgeworth, *Patronage* (4 vols., London, 1814), vol. 1, ch. 5.

CHAPTER 3

1 **purport**: design (Johnson) or intention.

2 **sped**: how well or ill he fared with her (past participle of the verb 'to speed' meaning to succeed in getting one's desire).

3 **those books**: a multi-volume edition of Shakespeare, possibly that by George Steevens, in ten volumes (1773), but evidently not Bowdler's *The Family Shakespeare* (4 vols., 1807) which among its twenty plays does not include *Henry VIII*.

4 **Cardinal Wolsey**: in *Henry VIII* (*c*. 1613). The play enjoyed a vogue in the later years of the eighteenth and earlier years of the nineteenth century, partly because of the acting of Sarah Siddons. In October 1783 Samuel Johnson asked Mrs Siddons 'which of Shakspeare's characters she was most pleased with. Upon her answering that she thought the character of Queen Catherine [sic] in *Henry the Eighth*, the most natural: – "I think so too, Madam, (said he;) and whenever you perform it, I will once more hobble out to the theatre myself."' (*Life*, vol. 4, p. 242). The play's many 'fine speeches' by male characters, together with the absence of bawdy passages, probably also contributed to its popularity and its choice by JA for Fanny's reading aloud. It is now believed that Shakespeare collaborated with John Fletcher in writing the play, but this was not suspected in Austen's time.

5 **half the books we open**: Shakespearean quotations appear, for instance, as epitaphs to many chapters of Radcliffe's novels; phrases from 'all-pervading Shakespeare' occur frequently in Burney ('to display the ensigns of death . . . To see the hand of scorn point at me': Elinor in *The Wanderer* (5 vols., London, 1814), vol. 1, ch. 8; vol. 2, ch. 38). Wollstonecraft, More and Scott, among others, frequently adapt Shakespearean phrases to their own purposes.

6 **every-day talent**: reading aloud in the family circle was common. When done well it was understood as a testimony, as Edmund makes explicit in the next chapter, to the speaker's 'warm heart and benevolent feelings'. Edward Waverley's qualities as the manly, but sympathetic hero are demonstrated when he entertains the company by reading Shakespeare: 'Romeo and Juliet was selected, and Edward read with taste, feeling, and spirit, several scenes from that play. All the company applauded with their hands, and many with their tears.' Sir Walter Scott, *Waverley; or, 'Tis Sixty Years Since*, 6th edn (1814; 3 vols., Edinburgh, 1816), vol. 3, pp. 90–1.

7 **The two young men . . . great entertainment**: the logistic terms 'secondary causes' and 'first cause' in this lengthy and complex

sentence contribute to its rendering of the formal debating style of Edmund and Crawford's exchange.

8 **a spirit of improvement abroad**: Edmund is pointing to the influence of the Evangelical movement on the practices of the Anglican church.

9 **through the service**: he has officiated as priest at a service (presumably at Lessingby, where the Owens live).

10 **seriousness on serious subjects**: the second occurrence of this phrase, used earlier by Edmund about Mary in the chapel at Sotherton (vol. 1, ch. 9). 'Serious subjects' are religious matters, and 'seriousness' here denotes inward commitment. William Law's *A Serious Call to a Devout and Holy Life* (London, 1728) was deeply influential on John Wesley and Samuel Johnson and, through them, on the Evangelical movement. 'Serious' also denoted the conscientious observance of religious duties which the Evangelicals had instigated. 'She never plays at cards; and upon the strength of this abstinence had very nearly passed for *serious*, till it was discovered that she could not abide a long sermon'. Mary Russell Mitford, *Our Village*, 'The Talking Lady', vol. 1 (1824), the articles were earlier published in 'respectable' publications such as the *Lady's Magazine*.

11 **our liturgy**: the order of service in the Church of England, read by the minister leading the congregation.

12 **eloquence of the pulpit**: Hugh Blair's chapter on 'Eloquence of the Pulpit' in his *Lectures on Rhetoric and Belles Lettres* offered advice on this topic, and heightened public awareness of sermon delivery. His emphasis contrasts with Henry's: 'It is of the utmost consequence that the Speaker firmly believe both the truth and the importance of those principles which he inculcates on others; and, not only that he believe them speculatively, but have a lively and serious feeling of them. This will always give an earnestness and strength, a fervour of piety to his exhortations, superior in its effects to all the arts of studied Eloquence' (1784), vol. 2.

13 **a constancy**: literally a permanent or perpetual condition, but here meaning a regular commitment.

14 **advertisements**: advertisements in nineteenth-century newspapers generally filled the first page. Edmund is scanning the front page of the *Morning Post*. On 8 January 1808, for example, there

are many advertisements for real estate, and ones that read: 'To Parents and Guardians – WANTED an APPRENTICE, by a Surgeon and Apothecary . . . in a principal Watering Place'; and 'Two Hunters – to be SOLD, at Fozards in Park Lane, well worth attention, being in condition for immediate work'.

15 **you have given the name such reality of sweetness**: 'sweetness' suggests an Elizabethan or Shakespearean usage and perhaps Henry's words are intended to convey a memory of Juliet's well-known lines in *Romeo and Juliet*: 'What's in a name? That which we call a rose / By any other name would smell as sweet' (Act 2, scene 1, lines 85–6) though Juliet's lines concern not the identity of name and person but rather the randomness of their association.

16 **tea-board, urn, and cake-bearers**: this is the evening in the drawing-room, when a light meal was taken. The tea-board is a tray on wheels brought in by the butler, Baddely (whose name is spelt Baddeley in vol. 3, ch. 1). 'The mistress sits at the head of the board, and opposite to her the boiling water smokes and sings in an urn of Etruscan shape' (*Letters from England*, letter 15). The urn might supply both tea- and coffee-pots. In contrast, the 'tea-things' (vol. 3, ch. 7) at Portsmouth are unspecified.

CHAPTER 4

1 **serious subjects**: Edmund's next speech contrasts 'serious' thinking with '*feelings*', recapitulating a debate long continued in the church between latitudinarians, who, influenced by Shaftesbury, believed mankind to be endowed with natural affection and instinctive benevolence, and the main Anglican tradition, which contended, in Samuel Johnson's words, that 'man's chief merit consists in *resisting* the impulses of his nature', or in Hannah More's, that 'contagion follows wherever there is a human heart left to its natural impulse' (*Cœlebs*, ch. 49), and thus that 'principle(s)' were necessary to ensure goodness or good conduct. The implication, here as with the earlier description of 'the really good feelings by which [Mary] was almost purely governed' (vol. 1, ch. 15), is that 'good feelings' alone cannot be relied upon, a point that Johnson made repeatedly.

CHAPTER 5

1 **two long speeches**: the beginning of the first (*Lovers' Vows*, Act 3, scene 2) is quoted. It paints an idyllic 'picture' of a couple devoted to each other, who together surmount the challenges of their marital 'journey'. Anhalt's next speech is about marriage contracted from 'convenience and fair appearance joined to folly and ill-humour' in which the partners are fettered together. When one dies, the other 'calls out in acclamations of joy – Oh, liberty! dear liberty!' To this Amelia replies, 'I will not marry'. Though commonplace in expression and imagery, there are connections between these speeches and Maria's cry before the iron gate at Sotherton.

2 **in sober sadness**: in earnest, in full seriousness. The same phrase has been used of Fanny's thoughts about Henry in vol. 3, ch. 2.

3 **melancholy . . . last**: one of the touches that suggest Fanny's affinity with the heroines of the novel of sentiment. 'I wandered over the scenes of my past pleasures, and recalled to my remembrance, with a sad and tender luxury, a thousand little incidents, that derived all their importance from the impossibility of their renewal. I gazed on every object *for the last time*. – What is there in these words that awakens our fanaticism?' Mary Hays, *Memoirs of Emma Courtney* (2 vols., London, 1796), vol. 1, ch. 11. See also Johnson's final *Idler* (April 5, 1760): 'there are few things not purely evil, of which we can say, without some emotion of uneasiness, *this is the last*.'

4 **quite the hero of an old romance**: the chivalric romances, such as those satirised in *Don Quixote* (Part 1, 1605; Part 2, 1615), in which the knight was utterly dedicated to his mistress, proclaimed her as the motive of his endeavours, and served her through thick and thin.

5 **exigeant**: demanding, exacting: hard to please: a French expression.

6 **the Blues**: the Royal Regiment of Horse Guards, stationed in London, so called because of the dark blue of their uniform jackets. They were an élite regiment, and a commission in the Blues was expensive.

7 **allowed himself in gallantries**: permitted himself flirtatious behaviour.

8 **token of friendship had passed**: the narrative leaves it to be supposed that Henry takes, and possibly kisses, Fanny's hand.

CHAPTER 6

1 **led astray and . . . fancying itself light**: there is a strong biblical colouring to the language in which Fanny formulates her condemnation of Mary here: 'Then spake Jesus again unto them, saying, I am the light of the world: he that followeth me shall not walk in darkness, but shall have the light of life' (John, ch. 8, v. 12). The notion of a person 'led astray' also recalls the biblical use, as for example the diatribe in 2 Peter, ch. 2, vs. 12–15, against those who 'speak evil of the things they understand not', 'which have forsaken the right way, and are gone astray'.

2 **describe his uniform**: as a lieutenant, Price would have both a full-dress, worn for formal occasions, and an 'undress' (or 'frock') uniform for everyday wear, which is probably what is indicated here. A lieutenant's undress uniform had nine buttons at the lapels, and narrow white trim at the cuff, but none of the gold lace worn by senior ranks. Cocked hats were usually worn with both uniforms. The uniform for lieutenants prescribed by Admiralty order in 1787 remained unchanged until 1813, when epaulettes were introduced. Price would not have been entitled to wear any full-dress uniform as a midshipman, and his undress uniform would have been much plainer.

3 **every comfort**: opposed to the 'pain' Mary causes her, the 'pain' that has grown out of the separation from her birth family, Fanny imagines not merely ease, but assistance or support and spiritual sustenance: in Johnson's *Dictionary* 'comfort' is defined as meaning 'consolation, support under calamity or danger'. This older meaning is still discernible in William's exclamation a few moments later 'How right and comfortable it will all be!'

4 **cruise**: Johnson defines 'cruise' as 'a voyage in search of plunder'; in this instance the purpose of the cruise would be to locate, attack and take enemy ships.

5 **improvements in the dock-yard**: the vast Portsmouth dockyards, 'a depôt of naval stores, truly calculated to impress every visitor with an idea of the power and grandeur of the first maritime nation in the world'. They included a mast house, a rope house, for the making of cables, itself 'nearly a quarter of a mile long', enormous forges, including the anchor forge, and 'the block manufactory, where machinery of the most ingenious invention, saws, chips

and shapes the block, drives the hole in the centre, even polishes the iron and brass work'. Anon., *Journal of a Tour to the Western Counties of England Performed in the Summer of 1807* (London: Richard Phillips, 1809), p. 12. The forty-five great Block Mills were built in 1802–6; they would be among the 'improvements' William indicates.

6 **nice**: neat and tidy.

7 **notes for the purpose**: in 1797 Bank of England notes were made legal tender to any amount. 'Notes of one and two pounds were then issued, and these have almost superceded guineas [the gold coin worth £1.1s]' (*Letters from England* (1809), letter 22).

8 **the vicissitudes of the human mind**: the Johnsonian phrasing underlines the slight absurdity of this girl of eighteen's thinking she might have seen everything.

CHAPTER 7

1 **prize money**: the value of a captured vessel and its cargo was distributed to the crew of the ship that had captured her, in a graduated scale from the captain downwards.

2 **all for love**: the phrase is familiar as the title of John Dryden's (1678) version of *Antony and Cleopatra*, *All for Love, or The World Well Lost*, but 'all for' here has a different meaning: William is idealistic about love, committed to the notion that love on both sides is essential to marriage.

3 **Oxford . . . Newbury**: William and Fanny travel on a more or less direct route south from Northampton to Portsmouth, bypassing London. They travel about fifty miles or eighty kilometres to Oxford, and complete the first day's long journey twenty miles further south at Newbury. From there it would be about fifty miles to Portsmouth. They arrive some time after half past four in the February afternoon, when the light is 'beginning to fail'. In 1794, the composer Joseph Haydn left London at five in the morning and arrived in Portsmouth at eight o'clock in the evening, after travelling the seventy-two miles in fifteen hours. This was in July. Fanny and William are travelling to Portsmouth in the depths of winter. *Collected Correspondence and London Notebooks of Joseph Haydn*, ed. H. C. Robbins Landon (London: Barrie and Rockliff, 1959), p. 292.

4 **the environs of Portsmouth . . . the Drawbridge**: Portsmouth, the headquarters of the British Navy, and its largest and most important base, was a guarded and fortified garrison town, protected by bastions and ramparts. The 'new buildings' outside the fortifications, which prevented any expansion, would be at Half Way Houses, later Landport, and Nelson Square. Passing the 'Drawbridge' (or the Landport gate) over the moat, Fanny and William enter the 'town', or the old town, contained within the fortifications. Landport Gate, the barrier nearest the town, led into the north end of the High Street, from which several narrow lanes, including Highbury Lane, run. Portsmouth had paved streets by this time: 'rattled' is the sound of the carriage wheels on cobblestones.

5 **trollopy-looking**: slovenly or sluttish-looking.

6 **gone out of harbour**: sailed out of Portsmouth harbour, to anchor at Spithead, to join the other ships in the squadron and wait for orders to sail.

7 **dish of tea**: when tea was first imported from China, Chinese porcelain bowls were also imported. Later in the eighteenth century, cups with handles became standard. Mrs Price's phrase is the survival in the vernacular of an earlier expression.

8 **dress a steak**: to dress is 'to prepare victuals for the table' (Johnson's sense 10).

9 **starved with cold**: colloquial phrase, meaning 'almost frozen with cold', commoner in the north of England.

10 **portmanteau . . . band-box**: a portmanteau is 'a chest or bag in which clothes are carried' (Johnson), usually by a traveller, and here probably a large bag, easier to stow away on board ship. Fanny's trunk, containing her clothes, has been carried upstairs: her bandbox would contain her bonnet, as does Lydia's in *P&P* (vol. 2, ch. 14).

11 **the doctor**: the ship's surgeon, 'Mr' Campbell, William Price's friend. From 1808 surgeons ranked with lieutenants; they were carried on even the smallest of sloops. The title 'doctor' properly belongs only to the fleet or squadron physician: Price uses the loose vernacular term for a medical man.

12 **Turner's . . . mess**: William Turner, a naval supplier and agent, listed in Portsmouth High Street in 1811. 'Your mess':

William Price's private equipment, such as eating vessels, utensils, knives etc, and probably including food. In 1795 Dr George Pinckard described the scene in Portsmouth prior to the departure of a fleet, when 'suddenly all was converted into extreme hurry and activity'. In 'all the confusion of a general scramble' for supplies, men would be seen in the streets 'bending under heavy bundles of clothes, wet from the wash; others loaded with camp-stools, deal boxes, sea-coffers, pewter utensils', as well as shoulders of mutton, sides of beef, etc. George Pinckard, *Notes on the West Indies: Written during the Expedition of . . . Sir R. Abercrombie* (3 vols., London, 1806), vol. 1, pp. 79, 82.

13 **Elephant**: like the *Canopus*, the *Endymion* and the *Cleopatra*, the *Elephant*, which took part in the Battle of Copenhagen in 1801, is the name of an actual vessel. JA's brother Frank was captain of the *Elephant* when she wrote to ask whether he would mind her mentioning it, '& two or three of your old Ships', in a letter of 6 July 1813 (*L*, p. 217). Frank served on the *Canopus* in 1805–6; Charles, her younger brother, served as midshipman and later lieutenant on the *Endymion*, and took command of the *Cleopatra*, in September 1810. The *Canopus* was a vessel of eighty guns, once the French ship *Franklin* captured at the Battle of the Nile in August 1798; the *Elephant* was of seventy-four guns, the *Cleopatra* had thirty-two guns and the *Endymion*, of forty guns, was a frigate.

14 **I wish you may**: a cruise to the westward would mean across the Atlantic, in search of French vessels which, if captured, would mean prize money. A letter from Nelson to Earl Moira of March 1805 reads '[a] frigate would have been better calculated to have given Capt. Austin [sic] a fortune out of the Medn. than coming under my command, where nothing is to be got except the French fleet should put to sea' (*Navy*, p. 90). Joining a fleet to the east, William's ship, like Francis Austen's, could not expect to go cruising for prizes.

15 **the Texel**: the most westerly of the West Friesian Islands, eastwards from Portsmouth. The Texel Channel, between it and the Dutch mainland, was the main outlet for the Dutch (enemy) naval base at Amsterdam. Hence it was a key site for British naval blockades.

16 **slipped her moorings**: left the fixed anchorage in the harbour. The
   Thrush would not, strictly speaking, be 'under weigh' (moving
   off, having weighed, or lifted, the anchor) as the 1814 text has
   it, since within the harbour she would have been moored to a
   permanent mooring buoy.

17 **the platform**: the Platform, which is a fort-like building at
   the bottom of the High Street, surmounted with trophies
   of French cannon at this time, would provide an unimpeded
   view of the ship as it sailed south to Spithead. Portsmouth
   Point (in the 1814 edition) is at the end of Broad Street, a
   promontory from which many of the boats serving the ships
   in the harbour departed. Looking north, this would command a good view of the vessel in the harbour, but since the
   Thrush is sailing southwards it would be hidden by intervening
   buildings.

18 **an eight-and-twenty**: a frigate with twenty-eight guns. The
   Thrush was a sloop, differently rigged, and with fewer guns.
   The name of the vessel is reminiscent of Francis Austen's ship
   the *Lark*, which carried sixteen guns. Other ships were called
   Kingfisher, *Eagle*, *Redwing*, etc.

19 **eastward of the sheer hulk**: in 1814 JA located the position of
   the *Thrush* by using the seaman's terms 'just astern' and 'larboard'
   (meaning 'port' or left hand, the side on which a ship is loaded).
   But a ship did not take her position from a ship to one side of her,
   but from the ships ahead and astern. A hulk is a disused vessel,
   used for storage, or as a floating dockyard for maintenance, and,
   since convicts were used as labour in the dockyards, hulks were
   also used as prison ships. Southam describes the sheer hulk as
   'equipped with "sheers" for the removal and fitting of masts and
   spars' (*Navy*, p. 210).

20 **talked to**: the reading of 1814 and 1816 is possible, meaning
   that Fanny both 'nursed' the child (looked after him whilst
   a toddler) and, during that time, chattered to him about his
   love for her. But this is rather strained, since the context suggests Fanny's typical wish for continuity; she wants to renew
   the past tie with this brother who once loved her best. R. W.
   Chapman's emendation of 'talk to him' would therefore also make
   sense.

21 **an Indiaman**: a merchant vessel of large tonnage belonging to the East India Company or its Dutch equivalent, and engaging in trade with India.

22 **boatswain**: boatswains were in charge of the ship's rigging and sail management. Responsible also for keeping order and discipline on board, they did much of their work by yelling, but they also used whistles to call the crew. Sam's 'pipe' is his (unbroken) boy's voice.

23 **the sally-port**: the gap in the sea wall fortifications through which officers and crew 'sallied forth' in men-of-war boats to join their vessels, moored further off in the harbour or in Spithead. William has already mentioned that 'there is a boat ashore', in which he 'had better go off at once'. The sally-port, at the end of the High Street, could not be far from the Prices' house.

24 **when her year was up**: it was customary for domestic servants to be employed by the year (and paid quarterly). Hire agreements were usually verbal, and had no binding force, so that in practice domestic servants, town dwellers in particular, could and did change their situation much more often.

CHAPTER 8

1 **the ramparts . . . dock-yard**: Portsmouth was surrounded by defensive ramparts, which were celebrated for their views; the dockyard, north of the High Street, was the chief shipyard of the British Navy, where visitors could watch vessels being repaired and constructed. 'As a walk, [the ramparts] possesses considerable claims to public partiality. By its encircling the town, in a circumference of about a mile and a quarter [two kilometres], all the inhabitants have the same easy means of enjoying its beauties and accommodations. At all avenues, easy ascents invite the passenger to participate of the healthy exercise the terrace affords by the freshness of the air, either blowing from the sea on one side, or Portsdown on the other.' 'Besides its vast extent of premises [the dockyard] contains four great docks, capable of receiving each two capital ships at a time . . . the Dock-yard being esteemed the largest in the known world, is a subject of such curiosity as to render it the envy and admiration of every country'. *The History of Portsmouth*, pp. 10, 40.

2 **the navy-list**: probably *Steel's Original and Correct List of the Royal Navy*, published monthly, at 6d, with up-to-date listings of serving and retired officers, ships in commission, etc.

3 **Motherbank**: the stretch of shallow water, to the west of Spithead, where ships would anchor when the weather was unsuitable for sailing.

4 **confidence**: capacity to confide in, intimacy.

5 **the instinct of nature**: the 'natural affection' made much of by Shaftesbury and the sentimentalists: JA is again recording the limitations of feeling as a source of moral capacity.

6 **celebrated judgment**: the chapter concludes with an allusion to the Princess Pekuah's conclusion to her investigation into the happiness of domestic life in chapter 26 of Samuel Johnson's *Rasselas*, first published in 1759: 'Marriage has many pains, but celibacy has no pleasures'. The Princess's 'remarks upon private life' are delivered in a taut unsparing prose akin to JA's analysis of the Price family dynamics. 'In families, where there is or is not poverty, there is commonly discord . . . Parents and children seldom act in concert: each child endeavours to appropriate the esteem or fondness of the parents, and the parents, with yet less temptation, betray each other to their children; thus some place their confidence in the father and some in the mother, and, by degrees, the house is filled with artifices and feuds.' 'Many other evils infest private life', Pekuah furthermore declares, and goes on to relate them. *Rasselas* was widely reprinted in the decades after 1780; different publishers produced editions each year from 1809 to 1812. This condensed summarising chapter, largely without dialogue, reproduces Johnson's mode.

CHAPTER 9

1 **passionées**: ardent, impassioned: a French expression.

2 **Wimpole Street**: a principal street running north to south in Marylebone, north of Mayfair, in London's most fashionable and expensive district. Streets in what was originally the Cavendish-Harley estate, developed in the eighteenth century, took their names from the noble families who built there; the shorter Mansfield Street runs parallel.

3 **some old woman . . . to be converted**: Evangelicals regularly spoke
of high church or orthodox Christians who had become Evangelical as having been 'converted': 'the illumination or conversion of
a minister who had been walking in darkness'. *Christian Observer*
(November 1816). JA disliked the sermons of her cousin, the Revd
Edward Cooper, 'fuller of Regeneration & Conversion than ever'
(September 1816: *L*, p. 322).

4 **pelisses**: a pelisse is a long mantle of silk, velvet or other material,
which reaches to the ankles, usually has sleeves, and is worn over
the dress.

5 **circulating library**: first established in 1726, private circulating
libraries had by the later years of the eighteenth century been
set up in all major cities and towns, and even in some smaller
towns. To borrow books one became a subscriber, and differing
rates, which would vary from 3s a quarter to more than a guinea,
entitled one to borrow one or more volumes, usually not complete
works, at a time. This was a far more economical way for the
gentry to obtain reading matter than purchasing books, since even
novels might be published at the price of 18s for three volumes,
and the purchaser would normally have the additional expense of
providing a binding – advantages which were made much of in the
proprietors' advertising. Though novels made a high proportion of
their stock, sometimes as much as 40 per cent, the biography and
poetry which Fanny reads, as well as history and religious literature,
was also to be found on their shelves. Many of the libraries also
stocked trinkets and other supplies and became popular meeting
places for the gentry, as is, for example, Mrs Whitby's Circulating
Library in *Sanditon* (ch. 6).

6 **the postman's knock**: postmen identified themselves by two knocks
at a door; normally letters that were not franked had to be paid
for by the recipient, until the introduction of prepaid postage by
stamps in 1840.

CHAPTER 10

1 **port-admiral . . . Dock-yard**: the port-Admiral commanded all
seamen and ships in the harbour 'in commission' or engaged in the
war effort. His house was on the High Street. The Commissioner,

whose house was in the dockyard, was in charge of the large labour force – at this time over two thousand men – employed in the building and repairing of ships, the manufacture of anchors and ropes, etc.

2 **Crown**: one of three large inns on the High Street, the Crown was where the Portsmouth Assemblies were held, and was patronised by naval officers.

3 **that season of the year**: it is now early March, early spring.

4 **a sad place**: this euphemistic, half-jocular phrase hides the real meaning, that Portsmouth is an ugly and dangerous town. Full of sailors on leave or awaiting ships, marines awaiting a posting, workmen and convicts at the dockyards, visitors and tourists, Portsmouth was notorious for its prostitutes and rowdiness. 'The riotous, drunken, and immoral scenes of this place, perhaps, exceed all others', wrote Pinckard of the town in 1795. George Pinckard, *Notes on the West Indies: Written during the Expedition of . . . Sir R. Abercrombie* (3 vols., London, 1806), vol. 1, p. 37. JA's first readers would understand how limited would be Fanny's opportunities for leaving the house during the week, and that she would certainly be suffering from lack of exercise and confinement indoors. Mary Crawford employs the same evasive idiom when in vol. 3, ch. 16 she describes the elopement as 'this sad business'. Much earlier, the infant Samuel Johnson was told by his mother of 'a *sad* place, called Hell'. Johnson, 'Annals', in *Johnsonian Miscellanies*, ed. G. B. Hill (2 vols., Oxford: Clarendon Press, 1897), vol. 1, p. 135.

5 **whose appearance . . . Saturday**: perhaps Price has been drinking with old friends or mates who have Saturday afternoon off work.

6 **three deckers now in commission**: one of the largest sea-going vessels, a man of war of the first or second rate with 3 gun decks, upwards of 90 guns, and a crew of 900 men (Nelson's 'Victory' was a three-decker). *The Gentleman's Magazine* reported in November 1811 that 'There are at present in commission 746 ships of war, of which 159 are of the line, 20 from 50 to 44 guns, 169 frigates, 140 sloops of war, 6 fire ships, 153 armed brigs, 36 cutters, and 70 gun vessels and luggers, besides which there are in ordinary, repairing for service and building, several ships, which make the total amount, 1024, of which 261 are of the line' (p. 480).

7 **vessel in the stocks**: a ship in the course of construction or being repaired.

8 **this unusual time of year**: in other words, Henry would usually be in London during the winter 'season' when masquerades, grand dinners, parties and balls were held. Mrs Rushworth has given her opening party at this time.

9 **his agent**: like Mr Shepherd, Sir Walter Elliot's 'agent' in *P* (vol. 1, ch. 1), Crawford's agent (later, 'Maddison') is probably a lawyer (*P*, vol. 1, ch. 2), who is in confidential charge of the estate's finances and here apparently also active in arranging tenancies.

10 **small hunting-box**: a house for himself, with accommodation for his hunters, like the 'homestall' earlier.

11 **luxury and epicurism**: the pursuit of sensual gratification, especially, in this context, in matters of food and drink.

CHAPTER II

1 **the Garrison chapel**: the Garrison chapel is near the sea and the Grand Parade, and served the officers and men of Portsmouth Garrison. A medieval building, built in 1212 as a hospice, it was later, after the dissolution of the monasteries, used as a garrison and later as the residence for the military governor of Portsmouth. Outside the church's south door a flight of stone steps leads up to the walk along the ramparts and views of the harbour, with 'the island', the Isle of Wight, beyond.

2 **salutary**: healthy: 'wholesome; healthful; safe; advantageous; contributing to health or safety' (Johnson).

3 **to displace me**:

> Divided, I'm a Gentleman
> In public Deeds and Powers
> United, I'm a Man who oft
> That Gentleman devours.

This is a riddle on 'agent' attributed to 'Jane': David Selwyn (ed.), *Jane Austen: Collected Poems and Verse of the Austen family* (Manchester: Carcanet, 1996), p. 18. Another version substitutes 'Monster' for 'Man' in line 3. 'Simple' in this speech means 'foolish'.

4 **a better guide in ourselves**: a common way of referring to the conscience or, in more Evangelical terms, inner light.

5 **puddings . . . hashes**: a pudding would be a meat dish, either mixed with flour, or covered with a soft crust, cooked by steaming or boiling; a hash is a dish of previously cooked meat, cut up and served with gravy or sauce.

6 **biscuits and buns**: biscuits are crisp, dry breads made in thin, flat cakes, either sweet or savoury (as in 'ship's biscuit'); buns are small soft loaves, often sweet.

CHAPTER 12

1 **a fine girl of fifteen**: Susan is 'a well-grown fine girl of fourteen' (vol. 3, ch. 7).

2 **my great mind**: 'great' as in the expression 'great with child', full or burdened with material.

3 **no distinction of dress now-a-days**: 'The clergy here are as little distinguished from the laity in their dress as in their lives; they are confined to black, indeed, but with no distinction of make, and black is a fashionable colour' (*Letters from England*, letter 20).

4 **St. George's, Hanover-Square**: the fashionable church in May-fair. On coming to power in 1710, the Tories passed an Act commissioning 'fifty new churches' in the city. St George's is one of these, completed for the Commissioners in 1724 by John James. The building has a grand Corinthian portico, and was a favourite venue for society weddings. The 'inside' is undistinguished, making it likely that Mary is teasing Fanny about the possibility of such a wedding.

5 **staggered**: this is 'to hesitate . . . to become less confident or determined' (Johnson, sense 3), as, for example, 'my suspicions were staggered . . . . my doubts were fast giving ground'. Mary Brunton, *Discipline*, 3rd edn (Edinburgh, 1815), ch. 9.

6 **every chapter of history**: as the later term 'morals' implies, Fanny and Susan are reading 'moral essays', possibly Johnson's, though many other volumes imitative of his like Henry Mackenzie's *The Mirror* (Edinburgh, 1779–80), referred to in *NA* (vol. 2, ch. 15), were available, and such essays were reprinted in the *Elegant Extracts*. Oliver Goldsmith published two histories, *An History of England, in a Series of Letters from a Nobleman to his Son* (2 vols., 1764) and a *History of England* (4 vols., 1771). It is probably the latter, in its abridged form of 1774 that Fanny and Susan

are reading, since this was widely known and frequently reprinted. JA owned and annotated a copy of Goldsmith's *History* in four volumes, which is parodied in her 'The History of England from the reign of Henry the 4th to the Death of Charles I' (1791).

CHAPTER 13

1 **leading her astray for years:** Sutherland (p. 431) supplies quotation marks around this phrase, which is akin to the others Fanny is reading aloud to herself from Edmund's letter. His phrase contains a distant echo of the General Confession in the Anglican liturgy: 'we have erred and strayed from Thy ways'.

2 **early in her marriage . . . keeping correspondents:** 'early in her marriage', when the Bertrams had 'a house in town', Lady Bertram was able to send letters, franked by her husband, a member of parliament, which would involve no cost to the recipient, and so had got into the habit (see vol. 1 ch. 2).

3 **by express:** a relay of messengers on horseback has brought the news from Newmarket, which is east of Northampton and Cambridge, and might well be fifty miles or eighty kilometres from Mansfield Park.

4 **Newmarket:** the horse-racing course. Since racing was unregulated at this time, it is just possible that Tom was taking part in a race: the 'fall' is from a horse.

5 **his physician:** a licensed physician, a member of the Royal College of Physicians, who has graduated from either the English or the Scottish universities; not an ordinary surgeon-apothecary. But JA is probably giving the local Newmarket doctor an honorific title.

6 **a keener solicitude:** this refers obliquely to Fanny's fear that if Tom dies, he will, in Samuel Johnson's words, be 'sent to Hell, Sir, and punished everlastingly' (*Life*, vol. 4, p. 299) or not go to heaven. Compare the narrator's remark in the final chapter about a 'juster appointment hereafter' for Henry Crawford.

7 **cant:** 'a whining pretension to goodness', Johnson's sense 3.

CHAPTER 14

1 **hectic:** 'At present by this term is meant slow, but long continued, fevers, which induce, and impair the strength . . . Intemperate drinkers, and those who indulge in excesses of any kind, are

very subject to it'. Bartholomew Parr M. D., *The London Medical Dictionary, Including under Distinct Heads Every Branch of Medicine* (3 vols., London, 1809), vol. 1, p. 734. Hectic is usually thought of as a fever itself. Here it may refer to the flushed cheeks (the 'hectic red,/Pestilent-stricken' of Shelley's 'Ode to the West Wind' (1819)) and hot dry skin of the tubercular patient; but the phrase 'to seize the frame' makes it more likely that this is a polite reference to vomiting and the spitting of blood. Pneumonia is another possibility: Tom has been put to bed, attended only by servants, and the prolonged immobility might well be supposed to lead to pneumonia.

2 **his lungs**: they fear tuberculosis of the lungs, otherwise known as consumption. This was widely believed to be an inherited disease, and therefore the fact that 'the family were not consumptive', as mentioned two paragraphs later, is a hopeful sign. In *E*, the fuss that is made over Jane Fairfax's health is partly due to the fact that her mother has died of consumption (vol. 2, ch. 2).

3 **Easter ... late this year**: the timetable of the novel has been following the calendar of 1808–9 closely, but Easter was not particularly late in 1809 (2 April). It was however late in 1811 and 1812 (at the end of April), when Austen was writing, or possibly rewriting, the novel.

4 **a state of penance**: Fanny has been at Portsmouth during Lent, the period of forty days between Ash Wednesday and Easter, which Christians keep as a time of abstinence and penitence, in commemoration of Christ's fasting in the wilderness before the crucifixion. Fanny has little to be penitent for, though she has been near to starving, so the reference is clearly theological.

5 **wants her home**: from William Cowper's 'Tirocinium : or, A Review of Schools' (1785). The lines Fanny remembers are addressed to a father who sends his son away to school:

> Why hire a lodging in a house unknown,
> For one whose tend'rest thoughts all hover round your own?
> This second weaning, needless as it is,
> How does it lacerate both your heart and his!
> Th' indented stick that loses day by day
> Notch after notch, 'till all are smooth'd away,

Bears witness long ere his dismission come,
With what intense desire he wants his home.

(lines 551–62, in *Poems*,
by William Cowper, 4th edn (2 vols.,
London, 1788), vol. 2)

The boy returns from boarding school to find, as Fanny does, that his home has become strange to him, and that he is 'least familiar where he should be most' (line 573). The Latin word of Cowper's title, meaning a soldier's first service on campaign, adopted into English, means a young person's first experience of training, their initiation in a discipline. 'Tirocinium' was published in the same volume as *The Task* (1785), which Fanny recalls earlier, when the avenue at Sotherton is mentioned (vol. 1, ch. 6).

6 **regale**: 'an entertainment, a treat' (Johnson): close to the 'indulgence' described earlier.

7 **warmest divisions of her aunt's garden**: this part of the park, set aside as a garden, was partly, at least, walled, to provide protection against wind and frost. Gardens like this, such as Lady Buckinghamshire's Garden at Blickling (Norfolk), were often named after the owner's wife.

8 **plantations . . . woods**: woods are distinct from plantations of timber, which the reference implies are saplings; 'glory' suggests that 'his woods', the more decorative parts of the estate, are full of long-established trees.

9 **bad air, bad smells**: before the sanitary discoveries and reforms of the mid-nineteenth century, diseases such as cholera and typhoid were thought to be caused by 'miasma', or the inhalation of bad air arising, for example, from burial grounds. Fanny is probably thinking mostly of domestic smells, but – even in a city near the sea – cess-pits and poor drainage would be malodorous. A visitor in 1807 described the town of Portsmouth as 'low, and aguish; the streets uncleanly, and in many places wretched'. Anon., *Journal of a Tour to the Western Counties of England Performed in the Summer of 1807* (London: Richard Phillips, 1809), p. 11.

10 **cut off in the flower of his days**: a biblical echo: 'And the man of thine, whom I shall not cut off from mine altar, shall be to consume thine eyes, and to grieve thine heart: and all the increase

of thine house shall die in the flower of their age' (1 Samuel, ch. 2, v. 33).

11 **Twickenham . . . near Bedford Square**: Twickenham was close by Richmond, also on the Thames, where Admiral Crawford has his 'cottage'. Bedford Square, built in the last quarter of the eighteenth century, is not in the most fashionable district of London, but probably a house on the eastern edge of Mayfair is indicated.

12 **queer fancies . . . Richmond**: in the communities of Twickenham and Richmond, away from the city, more informal manners than usual were the norm; artists, actors and musicians, as well as gentry and aristocrats, could mingle freely, and drop in to each other's homes and gardens without formal invitation. This relaxed style, combined with the fact that 'Mrs. R. has been spending the Easter . . . at Twickenham', is behind the inference that Fanny might have 'queer fancies' (or in other words guess that Henry has been seeing Maria).

CHAPTER 15

1 **etourderie**: this French word means a thoughtless action or careless mistake.

2 **no candle was now wanted**: it is early May, and the time is about half past four or five in the afternoon.

3 **rope's end**: 'To stop its unravelling, the end of a rope was bound up tightly with twine, a heavy and painful instrument of punishment' (*Navy*, p. 296, note). Blows with this instrument were an unofficial and immediate mode of discipline on board ship, whereas flogging – a term Price uses loosely – was a ceremonial punishment, inflicted by officers before the assembled crew. Marines were responsible for keeping order among the crew, so Price is enjoying the idea of taking the punishment of these miscreants into his own hands.

4 **the newspaper**: reports of elopements were quite frequently published under the heading 'Fashionable World' in the *Morning Post*. JA imitates the initials given in them, the obvious clues provided by addresses, and the archly suggestive language. On 23 April 1808, for example, 'A young lady of the name of K– of Pulteney-street, Bath, being smitten with the war-like

appearance of Captain C–ke of the Marines . . . and the little rogue Cupid having penetrated his heart also' marries without the knowledge of her parents. On 20 July 1808, 'Lady E B', previously living 'in a state of connubial felicity', is reported as eloping with 'Mr H–y, a Gentleman, (an *intimate* friend of the Lady's mother)', and being waylaid at the 'Keys' in Chandos Street. See JA's letter of 21–2 June 1808, 'This is a sad story about Mrs Powlett. I should not have suspected her of such a thing . . . A hint of it, with Initials, was in yesterday's Courier' (*L*, p. 131). Other newspapers, such as the *Morning Chronicle*, also published items about 'fashionable faux pas' (*Chronicle*, 3 Jan. 1809).

5 **fracas**: originally from the Italian *fracassare*, to make an uproar, but received into English as a row, a showdown, or disturbance.

6 **the lists of hymen**: Hymen is the Graeco-Roman god of marriage: this is a journalistic phrase meaning that Maria has not long been married.

7 **Whose views might it not effect**: whose plans or prospects might it not bring to pass or facilitate? The usual emendation, 'affect' for 'effect' (the reading of both editions), is persuasive, but 'effect' gives a tenable meaning.

8 **his meaning**: one implication is that Sir Thomas now sees Fanny's rejection of Henry in a different light, and wishes to solicit her forgiveness.

9 **early, by the mail**: mail coaches travelled at speeds of up to eight miles (thirteen kilometres) an hour: 'the rate of fare is considerably higher than in other stages; but preference is given to these, because they go faster, no unnecessary delays are permitted, and the traveller who goes in them can calculate his time accurately' (*Letters from England*, letter 37). The mail coach from London to Portsmouth would travel overnight.

10 **cordial**: a stimulant, or restorative.

11 **employment . . . relieving sorrow**: 'The safe and general antidote against sorrow is employment', Johnson, *Rambler* 47.

12 **less than visited their agitated spirits**: in other words, neither Fanny, out of perturbation, nor Susan, out of happiness, slept that night much more than Edmund, who was travelling in the mail coach from London.

13 **barriers of Portsmouth**: 'Portsmouth, with all its gates, ditches, bastions, batteries, and other works': William Gilpin, *Observations on the Coasts of Hampshire, Sussex and Kent in 1774* (London: Cadell and Davies, 1804), p. 17. As a key strategic port, the city was defended by the Landport Gate over the moat and two further drawbridges beyond the town.

14 **catching his eye, revived an affectionate smile**: the earlier reading of 'received' is certainly plausible, but 'revived' is interesting, since this use of 'catching' is unusual for the period. It would usually convey the way objects or people are brought to one's attention, as in 'his uniform caught my eye'; here the phrasing endows Fanny with agency. In the next chapter, similarly, Fanny tries to 'revive' Lady Bertram's 'interest in the usual occupations'.

15 **to Oxford**: from Portsmouth to Oxford, travelling northwards would be about 70 miles or 112 kilometres, an exhausting journey of at least 10 hours by coach.

16 **finger glasses**: glasses holding water, in which one would rinse one's fingers after dessert, handling fruit, etc.

17 **falling on her neck**: an idiom with telling biblical associations: 'But when he was yet a good way off, his father saw him, and had compassion, and ran, and fell on his neck, and kissed him' (Luke, ch. 15, v. 20: the parable of the prodigal son). The phrase is also used in the Old Testament to describe the reunion of Joseph with his father after many years during which he had believed his son was dead: 'Joseph . . . went up to meet his father . . . and he fell on his neck, and wept on his neck a good while' (Genesis, ch. 46, v. 29).

CHAPTER 16

1 **the dæmon of the piece**: a colloquial phrase, presumably from the theatre, meaning the agent of misfortune, or the agent of the devil. Dæmon is the Latin spelling of demon, an evil spirit.

2 **repulsive**: 'driving off' (Johnson), 'tending to repel by . . . coldness of manner' (OED).

3 **character**: public reputation.

4 **a note from Lady Stornaway**: etiquette would forbid an unengaged woman, such as Mary, writing directly to Edmund herself.

5 **the world**: here meaning both the 'world' of fashionable London society, and 'the world' in the religious sense, meaning a concern for material as opposed to spiritual values. The word recalls Maria and Henry's banter about the 'man of the world' in the pleasure grounds at Sotherton.

6 **fixed him**: steadied him, but with the implication, present in Mary's earlier use of the near-slang term ('then, Fanny, the glory of fixing one who has been shot at by so many': vol. 3, ch. 5), of capture.

7 **the heart which knew no guile**: Edmund's idiom alludes to, or paraphrases, Psalm 32, v. 2: 'Blessed is the man unto whom the Lord imputeth not iniquity, and in whose spirit there is no guile.'

8 **to bring about a marriage between them**: since an Act of divorce annulled or dissolved a marriage, both partners were free to remarry.

9 **celebrated . . . Methodists**: Mary derides what she perceives as the Evangelical tendency in Edmund's reproaches. Though both were revivalist movements within the Church of England, the Evangelicals addressed themselves to the upper classes of society in their project to reform English culture, and avoided what they saw as the Methodists' mistake, of appealing to the illiterate and powerless. Often preaching in the open air, the Methodists reached those from whom the orthodox clergy, having a University education, had become increasingly distant. Their sermons made powerful appeals to their unlettered congregations: 'they address themselves to the conscience, and the imagination, and all the mainsprings of the human mind. The corruption of the will, the necessity of redemption, and the all-sufficiency of grace, are the powerful themes on which they harangue. They do not seek to establish the truth of Christianity . . . the doctrine they preach is that of a perpetual revelation vouchsafed to all who seek it'. 'Evangelical Sects', *Quarterly Review* (November 1810), p. 489. The Society of Methodists broke away from the Anglican church in 1795. The movement flourished in the American colonies and other 'foreign parts' (such as Antigua). Mary is thus mocking both Edmund's religious fervour and his descent into a lower class.

CHAPTER 17

1 **Let other pens**: the introduction of the author as narrator is a not uncommon metatextual gesture, as in *NA* (vol. 2, ch. 14) 'A heroine returning . . . is an event on which the pen of the contriver may well delight to dwell'. It is self-confessedly a near-cliché, as the similarity to Lady Bertram's epistolary opening 'I take up my pen to communicate' (vol. 3, ch. 13) indicates. Like the shift into the indeterminate or subjunctive tense of 'must' in the next paragraph, frequently employed in this chapter, the introduction of the authorial first person here indicates the termination or abdication of the 'realist' premise that the events related come directly to the reader without mediation, and acknowledges the materiality of writing.

2 **something must have been wanting within**: Evangelical Christians always insisted on the importance of inner conviction: More writes of 'that inward principle of genuine piety' (*Cœlebs*, vol. 2, ch. 33). 'Principle' and inwardness are commonly linked, as when she distinguishes true Christians, for whom love of God is 'the spring of active duty', from those who 'had adopted religion as a form, and not as a principle . . . It was conformity to custom, and not the persuasion of the heart' (vol. 2, ch. 34).

3 **principle, active principle**: what follows is a summation, intensification and explication of a term, introduced in the novel's first paragraph, which has been reiteratively deployed in different contexts. Sir Thomas' inner rhetoric here can be paralleled in the work of Evangelicals. The 'christian religion', writes More, 'is an active, vital, influential principle, operating on the heart, restraining the desires, affecting the general conduct, and as much regulating our commerce with the world, our business, pleasures and enjoyments, our conversations, designs and actions, as our behaviour in public worship, or even in private devotions'. Hannah More, *An Estimate of the Religion of the Fashionable World* (London, 1791), p. 204. The slight differences in the account of 'principle' here are as notable, however. JA avoids such phrases as 'operating on the heart', and the reference to '*that* sense of duty which can alone suffice' is a quite oblique invocation of what in Evangelical writings would be plainly termed duty to God, rather than to man.

4 **no difficulty in procuring a divorce**: a wife's adultery would provide grounds for divorce, but the procedure could take years, and was so

costly that it was only available to wealthy men. Legal action began in the civil court, continued to the ecclesiastical court, and finally ended in the House of Lords, which when petitioned, might pass a parliamentary Act of divorce. In 1798 the House had resolved that divorce petitions should be supported by a decree of divorce already granted by an ecclesiastical court, an archaic institution whose procedures were very slow and expensive. In addition, the Lords required the petitioner to have attempted to obtain compensation from the seducer, in a civil 'criminal conversation' trial for damages, to ensure that there was no collusion. The Lords examined each case afresh, and the parties were liable to cross-examination. Each Bill had three readings, and witnesses whose testimony supported the petitioner's allegations of adultery had to be present at the second reading. The procedure was public and the exposure of private affairs shaming. The published Act, of which there were less than three a year at this period, specifically declared the marriage to be dissolved.

5 **no second spring of hope or character**: since the Act of divorce declared the marriage to be dissolved, both parties were theoretically free to marry again, as Mary assumes earlier. Evangelical morality however sought increasingly to make divorce a more shameful experience and attempts were made in 1771, 1779 and in the 1800 Adultery Bill to legislate 'no marriage' clauses forbidding the divorced wife to marry the co-respondent. Crawford, her 'seducer', has in any case declined to marry Maria: the narrator assumes that her public shame, or loss of 'character', is so great that future marriage to another gentleman is impossible.

6 **an establishment . . . in another country**: a house and servants are found for them in a different county or part of the country, outside London. Maria would have been allowed some financial support from Rushworth in the Act of divorce.

7 **barriers**: fortifications or re-enforcements.

8 **stall in Westminster**: 'the seat of a dignified clergyman in the choir' (of a cathedral or minster church) (Johnson); hence the occupant of such a seat, such as a canon, to which status Dr Grant has been promoted at Westminster Abbey in London.

9 **representatives**: probably members of parliament, the elected 'representatives' of towns and counties ('A man might represent the

county with such an estate' (vol. 1, ch. 17)), or, possibly, diplomats, known as 'representatives of majesty'.

10 **to estimate:** to have esteem for.

11 **no reliance future improvement:** the sense requires 'on' before 'future', which is omitted in the text of 1816. But both editions may be faulty and perhaps the passage should read 'no half concealment, no self deception in the present, no reliance on future improvement'. If the author struck out the first 'on' in the text of the 1814 edition, where the two 'on's appear on the same line, intending to replace the word by 'in', this might have confused the 1816 compositor, working fast to complete the volume.

12 **the view and patronage:** 'view' here means prospect; 'patronage' is used for the first time in the novel since Sir Thomas resolved in its first chapter to be 'the real and consistent patron' of Fanny Price.